Anne Perry lives in Portmahomack, Scotland, and is also the author of the well-loved series featuring Thoma███████████████████████████████ently been adapte█████████████████████████████ acclaimed Willia██████ KT-431-006 ████████steries are available from Headline.

Praise for Anne Perry:

'Give her a good murder and a shameful social evil, and Anne Perry can write a Victorian mystery that would make Dickens' eyes pop out' *New York Times Book Review*

'A complex plot supported by superb storytelling' *Scotland on Sunday*

'Her Victorian England pulsates with life and is peopled with wonderfully memorable characters' Faye Kellerman

The Twisted Root

Anne Perry

HEADLINE

First published in 1999
by HEADLINE BOOK PUBLISHING

First published in paperback in 2000
by HEADLINE BOOK PUBLISHING

10 9 8 7 6 5 4 3 2

ISBN 0 7472 6323 X

Printed and bound in Great Britain by
Clays Ltd, St Ives plc

Typeset by CBS, Martlesham Heath, Ipswich, Suffolk

HEADLINE BOOK PUBLISHING
A division of the Hodder Headline Group
338 Euston Road
London NW1 3BH

www.headline.co.uk
www.hodderheadline.com

To June Anderson,
for her unfailing friendship

Chapter One

❧

The young man stood in the doorway, his face pale, his fingers clenched on his hat, twisting it round and round.

'Mr William Monk, agent of inquiry?' he asked.

'Yes,' Monk acknowledged, rising to his feet. 'Come in, sir.'

'Lucius Stourbridge.' The visitor held out his hand, coming further into the room. He did not even glance at the two comfortable armchairs, nor the bowl of flowers pleasantly scenting the air. These had been Hester's idea. Monk had been perfectly happy with the sparse and serviceable appearance the rooms had presented before.

'How can I help you, Mr Stourbridge?' Monk asked, indicating one of the chairs.

Lucius Stourbridge sat on the edge of it, looking uncomfortably as if he did so more because he had been instructed to than from any desire. He stared at Monk intently, his eyes filled with misery.

'I am betrothed, Mr Monk,' he began. 'My future wife is the most charming, generous and noble-minded person you could wish to meet.' He glanced down, then up at Monk again quickly. The ghost of a smile crossed his face. 'I am aware that my opinion is prejudiced, and I must sound naïve, but you will find that others also regard her most highly, and my parents have a sincere affection for her.'

'I don't doubt you, Mr Stourbridge,' Monk assured him, but he was uncomfortable with what he believed this young man would ask of him. Even when he most urgently needed work he only reluctantly accepted matrimonial cases. But having just returned from an extravagant three-week honeymoon in the Highlands of Scotland, this was rapidly becoming one of those needy times. He had an agreement with his friend and patron, Lady Callandra Daviot, that in return for informing her of his most interesting cases, and – where she wished – including her in the day-to-day investigation, she would replenish his funds at least sufficiently for his survival. But he had no desire or intention that he should avail himself of that arrangement any longer.

'What is it that troubles you, Mr Stourbridge?' he asked.

Lucius looked utterly wretched. 'Miriam – Mrs Gardiner – has disappeared.'

Monk was puzzled. 'Mrs Gardiner?'

Lucius shook himself impatiently. 'Mrs Gardiner is a widow. She is . . .' He hesitated, a mixture of irritation and embarrassment in his face. 'She is a few years older than I. It is of no consequence.'

If a young woman fled her betrothal it was a purely private matter. If there was no crime involved, and no reason to suppose illness, then whether she returned or not was her own decision. Monk would not ordinarily have involved himself. However, his own happiness was so sharp he felt an uncharacteristic sympathy for this anguished young man so obviously at his wits' end.

He could never before remember having felt that the world was so supremely right. Of course, this was summer 1860, and he had no memory, except in flashes, of anything at all before the coaching accident in 1856, from which he had woken in hospital with a mind completely blank. Even so, it was beyond his ability to imagine anything so complete as the wellbeing that filled him now.

After Hester had accepted his proposal of marriage he had been alternately elated, and then beset by misgivings that such a step would destroy for ever the unique trust they had built between them. Perhaps they could not satisfactorily be anything more than friends, colleagues in the fierce pursuit of justice. He had spent many bleak nights awake, cold with the fear of losing something which seemed more and more precious with every additional thought of no longer possessing it.

But in the event, every fear had vanished like a shadow before the rising sun over the great sweeping hills they had walked together. Even though he had discovered in her all the warmth and passion he could have wished, she was still as perfectly willing and capable of quarrelling with him as always, of being perverse, of laughing at him, and of making silly mistakes herself. Not a great deal had changed, except that now there was a physical intimacy of a sweetness he could not have dreamed, and it was the deeper for having been so long in the discovery.

So he did not dismiss Lucius Stourbridge as his better judgement might dictate.

'Perhaps you had better tell me precisely what happened,' Monk said gently.

Lucius took a gulp of air. 'Yes.' Deliberately he steadied himself. 'Yes, of course. Naturally. I'm sorry, I seem to be a little incoherent. This has all struck me . . . very hard. I don't know what to think.'

So much was quite apparent, and Monk with difficulty

3

forbore from saying so. He was not naturally tolerant. 'If you would begin by telling me when you last saw Miss – Mrs – Gardiner, that would be a place from which to proceed,' he suggested.

'Of course,' Lucius agreed. 'We live in Cleveland Square, in Bayswater, not far from Kensington Gardens. We were having a small party in celebration of our forthcoming marriage. It was a beautiful day and we were playing a game of croquet, when quite suddenly, and for no apparent reason, Miriam – Mrs Gardiner – became extremely distraught and rushed from the garden. I did not see her go, or I would have gone after her – to find out if she were ill, or if I could help . . .'

'Is she often ill?' Monk asked curiously. Genuine invalids were one thing, but women subject to fits of the vapours were creatures with whom he had no patience at all. And if he were to help this unfortunate young man, he must know as much of the truth as possible.

'No,' Lucius said sharply. 'She is of excellent health and most equable and sensible temperament.'

Monk found himself flushing very slightly. If anyone had suggested Hester were the fainting sort he would have pointed out with asperity that she indisputably had more stomach for a fight, or a disaster, than most. As a nurse on the battlefields of the Crimea she had proved that more than true. But there was no need to apologise to Lucius Stourbridge. It was a necessary question.

'Who saw her leave?' he asked calmly.

'My uncle, Aiden Campbell, who was staying with us at the time – indeed he still is. And I believe my mother also, and one or two of the servants and other guests.'

'And was she ill?'

'I don't know! That is the point, Mr Monk! No one has seen her since. And that is three days ago!'

4

'And those people who did see her,' Monk said patiently, 'what did they tell you? Surely she cannot simply have walked out of the garden into the street alone, without money or luggage, and disappeared?'

'Oh . . . no,' Lucius corrected himself. 'The coachman, James Treadwell, is missing also, and, of course, one of the coaches.'

'So it would appear that Treadwell took her somewhere,' Monk concluded. 'Since she left the croquet match of her own will, presumably she asked him to take her. What do you know of Treadwell?'

Lucius shrugged slightly, but his face was, if anything, even paler. 'He has been with the family for three or four years. I believe he is perfectly satisfactory. He is related to the cook – a nephew or something. You don't think he could have . . . harmed her?'

Monk had no idea, but there was no purpose in causing unnecessary distress. The young man was in a desperate enough state as it was.

'I think it far more likely he merely took her wherever she wished to go,' he replied, and then realised his answer made no sense. If that were the case he would have returned within hours. 'But it does seem as if he may have taken your carriage for his own purposes.' Other, far darker, thoughts came to his mind, but it was too soon to speak of them yet. There were many other simpler answers of everyday private tragedy which were more likely, the most probable being that Miriam Gardiner had simply changed her mind about the marriage, but had lacked the courage to face young Lucius Stourbridge and tell him so.

Lucius leaned forward. 'But I fear for Miriam's safety, Mr Monk. If she is safe, why has she not contacted me?' His throat was so tight his words were half-strangled. 'I have done

5

everything I can think of. I have spoken with every one of my friends she might have gone to. I have searched my mind for anything I could have said or done to cause her to mistrust me, and I can think of nothing. We were so close, Mr Monk. I am as certain of that as of anything on earth. We were not only in love, but we were the best of friends. I could speak to her of anything, and she seemed to understand, indeed to share my views and tastes in a way which made her at once the most exciting and yet the most comfortable person to be with.' He coloured faintly. 'Perhaps that sounds absurd to you . . .'

'No,' Monk said quickly, too quickly. He had spoken it from the heart, and he was not accustomed to revealing so much of himself, certainly not to a prospective client in a case he did not really want, and which he even now believed impossible of a happy solution.

Lucius Stourbridge was gazing at him intently, his wide, brown eyes deeply troubled.

'No,' Monk repeated with less emphasis. 'I am sure it is possible to feel such an affinity with someone.' He hurried on, away from emotion to facts. 'Perhaps you would tell me something of your family, and the circumstances of your meeting Mrs Gardiner.'

'Yes, yes, of course.' Lucius seemed relieved to have something definite to do. 'My father is Major Harry Stourbridge. He is now retired from the army, but he served with great distinction in Africa, and particularly in Egypt. He spent much time there early in his career. In fact he was there when I was born.' A faint smile touched his face. 'I should like to go there some day myself. I have listened to him speak of it with the greatest pleasure.' He dismissed it ruefully.

'Our family comes from Yorkshire – the West Riding. That is where our land is. All entailed, of course, but most substantial. We go there occasionally, but my mother prefers to spend the season in town. I dare say most people do, especially women—'

'Do you have brothers or sisters?' Monk interrupted.

'No. Regrettably, I am an only child.'

Monk did not remark that Lucius would thus inherit this very considerable property, but it was evident in the young man's face that he too had taken the point and his lips tightened, a faint flush marking his cheeks.

'My family has no objections to my marriage,' he said with a slight edge of defensiveness. He sat perfectly still in the chair, looking straight at Monk, his eyes unblinking. 'My father and I are close. He is happy for my happiness, and indeed he is fond of Miriam, Mrs Gardiner, himself. He sees no fault in her character or her reputation. The fact that she has little dowry and no property to bring to the marriage is immaterial. I shall have more than sufficient for our needs, and physical possessions are of no importance to me, compared with the prospect of spending my life in the companionship of a woman of courage, virtue and good humour, and whom I love more than anyone else on earth.' His voice cracked a little on the last few words, and the effort it cost him to keep his composure was apparent.

Monk felt the other man's distress with a reality far greater than he could have imagined even a few weeks ago. In spite of his intention to concentrate entirely upon Lucius Stourbridge's situation, his mind recreated pictures of himself and Hester walking side by side along a quiet beach in the late evening sunlight, the colour blazing across the northern sky, shadowing the hills purple in the distance and filling the air with radiance. They had not needed to speak to each other, knowing wordlessly that they saw the same beauty and felt the same desire to keep it, and the knowledge that it was impossible. And yet the fact that they had shared it gave the moment a kind of immortality.

And there had been other times: laughter shared at the antics of a dog with a paper bag in the wind; the pleasure of a really good sandwich of fresh bread and cheese after a long walk; the climb to the top of a hill; the gasp of wonder at the view, and the relief at not having to go any further.

If Lucius had had any such happiness in his life, and lost it for no reason he could understand, no wonder he was at his wits' end to find the answer. However ugly or shattering to his dreams the truth might be, he could not begin to heal until he knew it.

'Then I shall do all I can to discover what happened,' Monk said. 'And if she is willing to return to you—'

'Thank you!' Lucius said eagerly, his face brightening. 'Thank you, Mr Monk! Cost will be no consideration, I promise you. What may I do to assist you?'

'Tell me the story of your acquaintance, and all you know about Mrs Gardiner,' Monk replied with a sinking feeling.

'Of course.' Lucius' face softened; the strain eased out of it as if merely remembering their meeting were enough to fill him with happiness. 'I had called upon a friend of mine who lived in Hampstead, and I was walking back across the Heath. It was about this time of year, and quite beautiful. There were several people around, children playing, an elderly couple quite close to me, just smiling together in the sun.' He smiled to himself as he described it. 'There was a small boy rolling a hoop, and a puppy chasing a stick. I stopped and watched the dog. It was so full of life, bounding along with its tail wagging, and returning the stick, immensely pleased with itself. I found I was laughing at it. It was a little while before I realised it was a young woman who was throwing the stick. Once it landed almost at my feet, and I picked it up and threw it back again, just for the pleasure of watching. Of course she and I fell into conversation. It all happened so naturally. I asked her about the dog, and she told me it belonged to a friend of hers.'

His eyes were far away, memory sharp. 'One subject of conversation led to another, and before I realised it I had been talking with her for nearly an hour. I made it my business to return the following day, and she was there again.' He gave a very slight shrug of self-mockery. 'I don't suppose for a moment she thought it was chance, nor did I feel any inclination to pretend. There was never that between us. She seemed to perceive what I meant as naturally as if she had had the same thoughts and feelings herself. We laughed at the same things, or found them beautiful, or sad. I have never felt so totally at ease with anyone as I did with her.'

Monk tried to imagine it. It was certainly not as he had felt with Hester! Invigorated, tantalised, furious, amused, admiring, even awed, but not very often comfortable.

No – that was not entirely true. Now that he had at last acknowledged to himself that he loved her, and stopped trying to force her into the mould of the kind of woman he used to imagine he wanted, but accepted her as herself, he was comfortable more often than he was not.

And of course there had always been the times when they were engaged in the same cause, she had fought side by side with the courage and imagination, the compassion and tenacity that he had seen in no other woman – no other person. Then it was a kind of companionship which even Lucius Stourbridge could not guess at.

'And so your friendship progressed,' he summarised what must have followed. 'In time you invited her to meet your family, and they also found her most likeable.'

'Yes – indeed,' Lucius agreed. He was about to continue

but Monk interrupted him. He needed the information that might help in his efforts to find the missing woman, although he held little hope the outcome would prove happy for Lucius, or indeed for any of them. A woman would not flee from her prospective husband and his house, and remain gone for the space of several days, without sending word, unless there were a profound problem which she could see no way of solving.

'What do you know of Mrs Gardiner's first husband?' Monk asked.

'I believe he was somewhat older than she,' Lucius answered, 'a man in a moderate way of business, sufficient to leave her provided for, and with a good reputation, and no debts of money or of honour.' He said it firmly, willing Monk to believe him and accept the value of such things.

Monk read within this brief summary that the late Mr Gardiner was also of a very much more ordinary background than Lucius Stourbridge, with his inherited lands and wealth, and his father's outstanding military career. He would like to have known Miriam Gardiner's personal background, whether she spoke and comported herself like a lady, whether she had the confidence to face the Stourbridge family, or if she was secretly terrified of them. Was she afraid every time she spoke, of betraying some inadequacy in herself? Monk could imagine it only too easily. He had been the country boy from a Northumbrian fishing village, down in London trying to play the gentleman. Funny, he only remembered that now, thinking of Miriam Gardiner also trying to escape from an ordinary background and fit in with a different class of person without the effort showing. Every time she sat at the table had she also worried about using the wrong implement, or making a foolish observation, of being ignorant of current events, or of knowing no one? But he could not ask Lucius such things. If he were capable of seeing the answer, he would not now be staring at Monk so earnestly, his dark eyes full of hope.

'I think I had better begin by visiting your home, Mr Stourbridge,' Monk said aloud. 'I would like to see where the event happened which apparently distressed Mrs Gardiner so much, and with your family's permission, speak to them, and to your servants, and learn whatever they are able to tell me.'

'Of course!' Lucius shot to his feet. 'Thank you, Mr Monk. I am eternally grateful to you. I am sure if you can just find Miriam, and I could be certain that she is unhurt, then we shall overcome everything else.' Shadows filled his face again as he realised how strong was the possibility that she was not all right. He could think of no reason otherwise why she would not have sent him some message. 'When shall you be ready to depart?'

Monk felt rushed, and yet Lucius was right: the matter was urgent, in fact they might already be too late. If he were to attempt the job at all, it should be immediately. He could leave a note for Hester, explaining that he had accepted a case, and would return whenever he had made his first assessment of the situation. He could not tell her in person because she was at the hospital working with Callandra Daviot. Of course it was in a purely voluntary way. He had refused absolutely to allow her to help to support them by earning her own living. The subject was still one of contention between them. No doubt she would return to it sooner or later.

For the moment Monk had a case himself, and he must make ready to go with Lucius Stourbridge.

The Stourbridge house in Cleveland Square in Bayswater was handsome in the effortless way of property of those to whom money is not of concern. Its beauty was restrained

11

and it had obviously been designed in an earlier and simpler age. Monk found it greatly pleasing and would have paused to admire it longer had not Lucius strode ahead of him to the front door and opened it without waiting for a footman or maid.

'Come in,' he invited him, standing back and waving his hand as if to urge Monk to hurry.

Monk stepped inside, but was given no time to look around him at the hallway with its family portraits against the oak panelling. He was dimly aware of one picture dominating the others, of a horseman in the uniform of a hussar at the time of Waterloo. Presumably he was some earlier Stourbridge, also of military distinction.

Lucius was walking rapidly across the dark-tiled floor towards the furthest doorway. Monk followed after him, no more than glancing up at the finely plastered ceiling or the wide stairway.

Lucius knocked on the door and after the slightest hesitation, turned the handle and opened it. Only then did he look back at Monk. 'Please come in,' he urged. 'I am sure you will wish to meet my father, and perhaps compare with him all that I have told you.' He stood aside, his face furrowed with anxiety, his body stiff. 'Father, this is Mr William Monk. He has agreed to help us.'

Monk walked past him into the room beyond. He had a brief impression of comfortable, well-used furniture not there for effect, but for the pleasure of the occupant, before his attention was taken by the man who stood up from one of the dark leather armchairs and came towards him. He was slender, and of little more than average height, but there was a vigour and grace in him which made him commanding. He was of similar build to Lucius, but in no other way resembled him. He must have been in his fifties, but his fair hair was hardly touched with grey and his blue eyes were surrounded by fine lines, as if he had spent years narrowing them against brilliant light.

'How do you do, Mr Monk?' he said immediately, offering his hand. 'Harry Stourbridge. My son tells me you are a man who may be able to help us in our family misfortune. I am delighted you have agreed to try, and most grateful.'

'How do you do, Major Stourbridge?' Monk said with unaccustomed formality. He shook Stourbridge's hand and, looking at him a little more closely, saw the anxiety in his face that courtesy could not hide. There was no sign of relief that Miriam Gardiner had gone. He was deeply troubled by her disappearance also. 'I shall do my best,' Monk promised, painfully aware of how little that might be.

'Sit down.' Stourbridge indicated one of the other chairs. 'Luncheon will be in an hour. Will you join us?'

'Thank you,' Monk accepted. It would give him an opportunity to observe the family together and to form some opinion of their relationships, and perhaps how Miriam Gardiner might have fitted in as Lucius' wife. 'But before that, sir, I should like to speak more confidentially to you. There are a number of questions I need to ask.'

'Of course, of course,' Stourbridge agreed, not sitting but moving restlessly about the room, in and out of the broad splashes of sunlight coming through the windows. 'Lucius, perhaps if you were to call upon your mother . . .?' It was a polite and fairly meaningless suggestion, intended to offer the young man an excuse to leave.

Lucius hesitated, evidently finding it difficult to tear himself away from the only thing that mattered to him at the moment.

'She has missed you,' Stourbridge prompted. 'She will be pleased to hear that Mr Monk is willing to assist us.'

'Yes . . . yes, of course,' Lucius agreed, glancing at Monk

with the shadow of a smile, then going out and closing the door.

Harry Stourbridge turned to Monk, the sunlight bright on his face, catching the fine lines and showing more nakedly the tiredness around his eyes.

'Ask what you wish, Mr Monk. I will do anything I can to find Miriam, and if she is in any kind of difficulty, to offer her all the help I can. As you can see, my son cares for her profoundly. I can imagine no one else who will make him as happy.'

Monk found it impossible to doubt his sincerity, which placed upon himself an even greater emotional burden. Why had Miriam Gardiner fled their house, their family, without a word of explanation? Had it been one sudden event, or an accumulation of small things amounting to a whole too great for her? What could it be that she could not even offer these people who loved her some form of explanation?

And where was the coachman James Treadwell?

Stourbridge was staring at Monk, waiting for him. But Monk was uncertain where to begin. Harry Stourbridge was not what he had imagined and he found himself unexpectedly sensitive to his feelings.

'What do you know of Mrs Gardiner?' he asked, more brusquely than he had intended. Pity was of no use to Lucius or his father. Monk was here to address the problem, not wallow in emotions.

'You mean her family?' Stourbridge understood straight away what he was thinking. 'She never spoke of them. I imagine they were fairly ordinary. I believe they died when she was quite young. It was obviously a matter of sadness to her and none of us pursued the subject.'

'Someone will have cared for her while she was growing up,' Monk pressed him. He had no idea if it was relevant, but

14

there were so few obvious avenues to follow.

'Of course,' Stourbridge agreed, sitting down at last. 'She was taken in by a Mrs Anderson, who treated her with the greatest kindness. Indeed, she still visits her quite frequently. It was from Mrs Anderson's home that she met Mr Gardiner, when she was about seventeen, and married him two years later. He was considerably older than she.' He crossed his legs, watching Monk anxiously. 'I made enquiries myself, naturally. Lucius is my only son, and his happiness is of the greatest importance to me. But nothing I learned explains what has happened. Walter Gardiner was a quiet, modest man who married relatively late. He was nearly forty. But his reputation was excellent. He was rather shy, a trifle awkward in the company of women, and he worked extremely hard at his business – which incidentally was the selling of books. He made a modest success of it and left Miriam well provided for. By all accounts she was very happy with him. No one had an ill word to say of either of them.'

'Did they have children?' Monk asked curiously.

A shadow crossed Stourbridge's eyes. 'No. Unfortunately not. That is a blessing that does not come to every marriage.' He drew in his breath and let it out silently. 'My wife and I have only the one child.' There was sharp memory of pain in his face and Monk was very aware of it. It was a subject he himself had considered little. He had no title or estates to leave, and he felt in no way incomplete without a family. But then Hester was not an ordinary woman. He had married her with no thought of the comfort of domestic life. She was not the one he would have chosen if he had! The thought made him smile unconsciously. One could not tell what the future might bring. He had already surprised himself by changing as radically as he had. Perhaps in a few years he would think of children. Now he was honest enough to know that he would resent such other demands on Hester's time and emotion.

Stourbridge was waiting for his attention.

'She is somewhat older than your son,' Monk put in as tactfully as he could. 'Exactly how much older is she?'

A flash of amusement crossed Stourbridge's face.

'Nine years,' he replied. 'If you are going to ask if she could give him an heir, the answer is that I do not know. Of course we would like it if Lucius were to have a son, but it is not our main concern. There is no guarantee of such a thing, Mr Monk, whomever one marries, and Miriam was never made to believe it was.'

Monk did not argue, but he would judge for himself whether Mrs Stourbridge shared her husband's feelings. So far his questions had elicited nothing in which he could see any reason for Miriam Gardiner to have fled. He wished he had a clearer picture of her in his mind. Seen through the eyes of Lucius and Harry Stourbridge she was the ideal woman. Their image gave her no flesh and blood, and certainly no passions. Had they seen anything of the real woman beneath the surface they so much admired? Was it any use asking Harry Stourbridge anything further, except bare facts?

'Was this her first visit to this house?' he said suddenly.

Stourbridge looked slightly surprised.

'No, not at all. She had been here half a dozen times. If you are thinking we did not make her welcome, or that she felt overwhelmed or less than comfortable with the idea of living among us, you are mistaken, Mr Monk.'

'Would she have lived here, in this house?' Monk asked, envisioning a score of reasons why she might have found the prospect unendurable. Having been mistress of her own home, no matter how ordinary compared with this house, so close to Kensington Gardens, she might find the sheer loss of privacy insupportable. Hester would have! He could not imagine her spending the best part of her life under someone else's roof. When she had nursed privately, as she had since returning from the Crimea, she had always known that any position was temporary, and whatever its difficulties, it would reach an end. And she had a measure of privacy, and of autonomy in that the care of the patient was in her charge.

A whole new concept of imprisonment opened up to him.

Harry Stourbridge was smiling.

'No, Mr Monk. I have properties in Yorkshire, and Lucius is very fond of life in the north. Miriam had visited there some months ago – I confess when the weather was a good deal less clement – but she was charmed by the area and was looking forward to moving there and being mistress of her own household.'

So fear of losing a certain freedom was not what had driven Miriam Gardiner away. Monk tried again. 'Was there anything different about this visit, Major Stourbridge?'

'Not that I am aware, except that it was a trifle more celebratory.' His face pinched with sadness and his voice dropped. 'They were to be married in four weeks. They desired a quiet wedding, a family affair. Miriam did not wish large crowds or great expense. She thought it both unseemly and unnecessary. She loved Lucius very deeply, of that I have no doubt whatever.' He looked bemused. 'I don't know what has happened, Mr Monk, but she did not leave because she ceased to love him, or to know how profoundly he loves her.'

It was pointless to argue. The conviction in Stourbridge was complete. It was going to be uniquely painful if facts proved him to be mistaken, and Monk were to find himself in the position of having to tell him so. He should never have accepted this case. He could not imagine any happy solution.

'Tell me something of your coachman, James Treadwell,' he asked instead.

Stourbridge's fair brows rose. 'Treadwell? Yes, I see what you mean. A perfectly adequate coachman. Good driver, knows horses, but I admit he is not a man for whom I have any natural liking.' He rested his elbows on the arms of his chair and made a steeple with his fingers. 'I knew men like him in the army. They can sit a horse like a centaur, wield a sword, ride over any terrain, but one cannot rely on them. Always put themselves first, not the regiment. Don't stand their ground when the battle's against them.'

'But you kept him on?'

Stourbridge shrugged slightly. 'You don't put a man out because you think you know his type. Could be wrong. I wouldn't have had him as a valet, but a coachman is a very different thing. Besides, he's a nephew of my cook, and she's a good woman. She's been with the family nearly thirty years. Started as a scullery maid when my own mother was still alive.'

Monk understood. Like everything else, it was so easily appreciated, so very normal. It left him little more to ask, except for an account of the day itself on which Miriam Gardiner had fled.

'I can give you a guest list, if you wish,' Stourbridge offered. 'But it included no one Miriam had not met before, indeed no one who was not a friend. Believe me, Mr Monk, we have all searched our minds trying to think of anything that could have happened to cause her such distress, and we can think of nothing whatever. No one is aware of any quarrel, even any unfortunate or tactless remark!' Instinctively he glanced out of the window, then back at Monk again. 'Miriam was standing alone. The rest of us were either playing croquet, or watching, when quite suddenly she gasped, turned as white as paper, stood frozen for a moment, then turned and stumbled away, almost falling, and ran towards the house.' His voice cracked. 'None of us has seen her since!'

Monk leaned forward. 'You saw this?'

'No, not personally. I would have gone after her if I had.' Stourbridge looked wretched, as if he blamed himself. 'But it was described to me by several others, and always in those terms. Miriam was standing alone. No one spoke to her or in any other way approached her.' He frowned, his eyes puzzled. 'I have considered every possibility that common sense suggests, Mr Monk. We have called you because we can think of nothing further.'

Monk rose to his feet. 'I shall do all I can, sir,' he said with misgiving. When Lucius Stourbridge had first explained his case Monk had thought it an impossible one; now he was even more convinced. Whatever had happened to Miriam Gardiner had arisen from her own emotions and her future family would probably never know what it was that had so suddenly precipitated her into flight. But even if they were to learn, it would bring no happiness to them. Monk began to feel an anger against this young woman who had gone so thoughtlessly far along the path which a little consideration would have told her she could not complete. She had hurt deeply at least two decent and honourable people, probably more.

Stourbridge stood also. 'Who would you like to speak with next, Mr Monk?'

'Mrs Stourbridge, if you please,' Monk replied without hesitation. He knew from experience of Hester that women observed each other in ways men did not; they read expressions, understood what was left unsaid.

'Of course.' Stourbridge led the way out into the hall. 'She will be in her sitting room at this hour.'

Monk followed him up the wide, curving staircase and this time had an opportunity to look more closely at the magnificently plastered ceiling and the carving on the newel post at the top of the banister.

Stourbridge crossed the landing. A long window looked over the smooth lawn and Monk caught a glimpse of croquet hoops still set up. The garden looked peaceful in the sun, a place of quiet happiness, family games, and afternoon tea in the summer. Trees sheltered azaleas beyond, their last flowers dropping in a blaze of colour on to the dark earth beneath.

Stourbridge knocked on the third door along and, at a murmur from inside, opened it, ushering Monk in.

'My dear, this is Mr Monk,' he introduced him. 'He has promised to assist us in finding Miriam.'

Mrs Stourbridge was sitting on a large chintz-covered chair, a scrapbook of poetry and photographs spread open on the cherry-wood table beside her where she had apparently laid it when interrupted. Her resemblance to her son was clear even at a glance. She had the same dark eyes and slender line of cheek and throat. Her hair grew from her brow in the same broad sweep. If Lucius had indeed come to see her as his father had suggested, he had not remained long. She looked at Monk with concern. 'How do you do?' she said gravely. 'Please come in. Tell me how I can help my son.'

Monk accepted and sat in the chair opposite her. It was more comfortable than its straight back would have suggested, and the bright, warm room would, in any other circumstances, have been restful. Now he was searching his mind for questions to ask this woman which could help him to understand what had driven Miriam Gardiner to such extraordinary flight.

Stourbridge excused himself and left them.

Mrs Stourbridge looked at Monk steadily, waiting. There

was no time or occasion for skirting around the edges of meaning.

'Would you please describe Mrs Gardiner for me?' Monk asked. He wanted a picture in his mind, not only to imagine her himself, but to know how Mrs Stourbridge saw her.

She appeared surprised. 'Where will you look, Mr Monk? We have no idea where she could have gone. Obviously we have already tried her home, and she has not returned there. Her housemaid had not heard from her since she left to come here.'

'I would like a woman's view of her,' he explained. 'Rather less romantic, and perhaps more accurate than any I have heard so far.'

'Oh. I see. Yes, of course.' She leaned back. She was slender, probably in her mid-forties, and there was a natural elegance in the way she held her hands and the sweep of her huge skirts over the chair. Looking at her intelligent face, Monk thought her observation of Miriam Gardiner would be clear and unsentimental, perhaps the first that might offer some genuine insight into her character.

'She is of average height,' Mrs Stourbridge began, measuring her words. 'Perhaps a trifle plumper than would be the choice for a young woman. I dare say my son had already told you she was at least nine years older than he?'

'At least?' he questioned. 'You mean she admitted to nine, but you personally think it might be more?'

She shrugged delicately without answering. 'She has excellent hair, fair and thick and with a becoming natural wave,' she continued. 'Blue eyes, quite good complexion and teeth. Altogether a generous face indicating good nature and at least averagely good health. She dressed becomingly, but without extravagance. I should imagine well within a moderate income.'

'She sounds a paragon of virtue, Mrs Stourbridge,' Monk remarked a little drily. 'I do not yet see a woman of flesh and blood, indeed a real woman at all, merely a recital of admirable qualities.'

Her eyebrows rose sharply. She stared at him with chill, then as he stared back, gradually she relaxed.

'I see,' she conceded. 'Of course. You asked me what she looked like. She was most pleasing. Her character was also agreeable, but she was not incapable of independent thought. You are asking me if she had faults? Of course. She was stubborn at times. She had some strange and unsuitable views on certain social issues. She was over familiar with the servants, which caused difficulties now and then. I think she had much to learn in the running of a house of the size and standard my son would have required.' She kept her eyes steadily on Monk's. 'Very possibly she would not have been our first choice of wife for him. There are many more suitable young women of our acquaintance, but we were not unhappy with her, Mr Monk, nor could she have imagined that we were.'

'Might she not have given him an heir?' It was an intrusive and intimate question, and a subject upon which emotions were often deep. Women had been abandoned because of it throughout history.

Mrs Stourbridge looked a little pale, but her hands did not tighten in her lap.

'Of course it is what anyone would wish, but if you accept a person, then you must do so wholeheartedly. It is not something she could help. If I thought she would have deliberately denied him, then I would blame her for it, but one thing I am perfectly sure of, and that is that she loved him. I do not know where she has gone, or why, Mr Monk. I would give a great deal for you to be able to find her and

22

bring her back to us, unharmed and as gentle and loving as she was before.'

Monk could not doubt her. The emotion in her voice betrayed a depth of distress he could feel, in spite of the fact that they had met only moments before and that he knew nothing of her beyond the little that was obvious to see.

'I will do all I can, Mrs Stourbridge,' he promised. 'I believe you did not see her leave the croquet party?'

'No. I was speaking to Mrs Washburne and my attention was engaged. She is not an easy woman.'

'Was Mrs Gardiner apprehensive before the party?'

'Not at all. She was extremely happy.' There was no shadow in her face.

'Did she know all the guests?'

'Yes. She and I made up the list together.'

'Did anyone come who was uninvited? Perhaps a companion to one of the invited guests?'

'No.'

'Was there any disagreement or unpleasantness, any unwished for attention?'

'No.' She shook her head slightly but her eyes did not leave his. 'It was a most enjoyable day. The weather was perfect. No one spoiled the occasion by inappropriate behaviour. I have questioned all the servants, and no one saw or heard anything except the usual trivial talk. The worst that anyone knew of was a disagreement between Mr Wall and the Reverend Mr Dabney over a croquet shot being rather poor sportsmanship. It did not concern Miriam.'

'She didn't play?'

Mrs Stourbridge smiled very slightly, but there was no criticism in it.

'No. She said she preferred to watch. I think actually she never learned, and did not like to admit it.'

He changed the subject. 'The coachman, Treadwell. He has not reappeared and I am told no one knows what happened to him either.'

Her face darkened. 'That is true. Not entirely a satisfactory young man. We employed him because he is the nephew of the cook, who is a most loyal and excellent woman. We cannot choose our relatives.'

'And of course your coach is still missing too?'

'Indeed.'

'I shall ask your groom for a description of it, and of Treadwell.' That was a more hopeful line to pursue. 'Was there a maid who particularly looked after Mrs Gardiner while she stayed here?'

'Yes, Amelia. If you wish to speak with her I shall send for her.'

'Thank you. And your cook as well. She may know something of Treadwell.'

There was a knock on the door and it opened before she had time to answer. The man who came in was tall and broad-shouldered, a trifle thick about the waist. His features were strong and the family resemblance was marked.

'This is my brother, Mr Monk,' Mrs Stourbridge said.

'You must be the agent of inquiry Lucius fetched in.' The man looked at Monk with gravity and there was a note of sadness in his voice that could almost have been despair. 'Aiden Campbell,' he introduced himself, offering his hand. 'I am afraid you are unlikely to have any success,' he continued, glancing at his sister in half apology, then back to Monk. 'Mrs Gardiner left of her own free will. In the little we know of the circumstances, that seems unarguable. Possibly she was experiencing severe doubts about her marriage which up to that moment she had managed to conceal. We may never know what suddenly caused her to realise her feelings.'

He frowned at Monk. 'I am not convinced that seeking her will not lead to further unhappiness.' He took a deep breath. 'We none of us desire that. Please be very careful what you do, Mr Monk. You may be led, in sincerity, to make discoveries we might be better not knowing. I hope you understand me?'

Monk understood very well. He shared the view. He wished now he had been wise enough to follow his original judgement and refuse the case when Lucius had first asked him.

'I am aware of the possibilities, Mr Campbell,' he answered quietly. 'I share your opinion that I may not be able to find Mrs Gardiner, and that if I do, she still might wish to stand by her decision. However, I have given my word to Mr Stourbridge that I would look for her, and I will do so.' Then sensing the sharpness in Campbell's face, he added: 'I have informed him of my opinion as to the chances of success, and I shall continue to be honest with him as to my progress, or lack of it.'

Campbell remained silent, pushing his hands into his pockets and staring at the floor.

'Aiden,' his sister said gently, 'I know you believe that she will not return, and that only more disillusion and unhappiness will follow from seeking her, but neither Harry nor Lucius will accept that. They both feel compelled to do all they can to find out where she is, if she is unhurt, and why she left – Harry almost certainly for Lucius' sake, of course, but he is nonetheless resolved. I believe we should help them rather than make them feel isolated and as if we do not understand.'

He raised his eyes and looked at her steadily. 'Of course.' He smiled, but the effort behind it was apparent to Monk. 'Of course, Verona. You are perfectly right. It is something which must run its course. How can I assist you, Mr Monk? Let me take you to the stables and enquire after James

Treadwell. He may be at the heart of this.'

Monk accepted, thanking Mrs Stourbridge and excusing himself. He followed Campbell down the stairs and out of the side door to the mews. The light was bright as he stepped outside. The smell of hay, horse sweat and the sharp sting of manure were strong in the closed heat of the yard. He heard a horse whinnying and stamping its feet on the stones.

A ginger-haired boy with a brush in one hand looked up at him with curiosity.

'Answer Mr Monk's questions, Billy,' Campbell instructed. 'He's come to help Major Stourbridge find Treadwell and the missing carriage.'

'Yer in't never goin' ter see them again, I reckon,' Billy replied, pulling his mouth into a grimace of disgust. 'Carriage like that's worth a fair bit.'

'You think he sold it and went off?' Monk asked.

Billy regarded him with contempt. 'Course I do! Wot else? 'E lit outta 'ere like 'e were on fire! Nobody never told 'im ter! 'E never came back! If 'e din't flog it, why in't 'e 'ere?'

'Perhaps he met with an accident?' Monk suggested.

'That don't answer why 'e went in the first place.' Billy stared at him defiantly. 'Less 'e's dead, 'e should 'a told us wot 'appened, shouldn't 'e?'

'Unless he's too badly hurt,' Monk continued the argument.

Billy's eyes narrowed. 'You a friend of 'is, then?'

'I've never met him. I wanted your opinion, which obviously was not very high.'

Billy hesitated. 'Well – can't say as I like 'im,' he hedged. 'On the other 'and, can't say as I know anythink bad abaht 'im neither. Just that he's gorn, like – which is bad enough.'

'And Mrs Gardiner?' Monk asked.

Billy let his breath out in a sigh. 'She were a real nice lady, she were. If 'e done anythink to 'er, I 'ope as 'e's dead – an' 'orrible dead at that.'

'Do you not think she went with him willingly?'

Billy glanced at Campbell, then at Monk, his face registering his incredulity. 'Wot'd a lady like 'er be wantin' with a shifty article like 'im? 'Ceptin' 'e drive 'er abaht now an' then, as wot is 'is job!'

'Did she think he was a shifty article?'

Billy thought for a moment. 'Well, p'haps she din't. A bit too nice for 'er own good, she were. Innocent, like, if yer know wot I mean?'

'Mrs Gardiner was a trifle too familiar with the servants, Mr Monk,' Campbell clarified. 'She may well have been unable to judge his character. I dare say no one told her Treadwell was employed largely because he was a relative to the cook, who is highly regarded.' He smiled, biting his lip. 'Good cooks are a blessing no household discards lightly, and she has been loyal to the family since before my sister's time.' He looked around the stable towards the empty space where the carriage should have been. 'The fact remains, Treadwell is gone, and so is a very valuable coach and pair, and all the harness.'

'Has it been reported to the police?' Monk asked.

Campbell pushed his hands into his pockets, swaying a little on the back of his feet. 'Not yet. Frankly, Mr Monk, I think it unlikely my brother-in-law will do that. He makes a great show, for Lucius' sake, of believing that Mrs Gardiner had not met some accident, or crisis, and all will be explained satisfactorily. I am afraid I gravely doubt it. I can think of no such circumstance which would satisfy the facts as we know them.' He started to walk away from the stable across the yard and towards the garden, out of earshot of Billy, and whoever else might be in the vicinity. Monk followed, and they were on the gravel path surrounding the lawn before Campbell continued.

'I very much fear that the answer may prove to be simply that Mrs Gardiner, who was very charming and attractive in her manner, but nonetheless not of Lucius' background, realised that after the first flame of romance wore off, she would never make him happy, or fit into his life. Rather than face explanations which would be distressing, and knowing that both Lucius, and Major Stourbridge, as a matter of honour, would try to change her mind, she took the matter out of their hands, and simply fled.'

He looked sideways at Monk, a slightly rueful sadness in his face. 'It is an action not entirely without honour. In her own way, she has behaved the best. There is no doubt she is in love with Lucius. It was plain for anyone to see that they doted upon each other. They seemed to have an unusual communion of thought and taste, even of humour. But she is older than he, already a widow, and from a very – ordinary – background. This way it remains a grand romance. The memory of it will never be soured by a fading into the mundane realities. Think very carefully, Mr Monk, before you precipitate a tragedy.'

Monk stood in the late morning sun in this peaceful garden, full of birdsong, where perhaps such a selfless decision had been made. It seemed the most likely answer. A decision like that might be hysterical, perhaps, but then Miriam Gardiner was a woman giving up her most precious dream. Possibly she had not even written to Lucius in case such a letter inadvertently revealed her whereabouts.

'I have already told Major Stourbridge that if I find Mrs Gardiner I would not attempt to persuade her to return against her will,' he answered. 'Or report back to him anything beyond what she wished me to. That would not necessarily include her whereabouts.'

Campbell did not reply immediately. Eventually he looked up, regarding Monk carefully, as if making some judgement which mattered to him deeply.

'I trust you will behave with discretion, and keep in mind that you are dealing with the deepest emotions, and men of a very high sense of honour.'

'I will,' Monk replied, wishing again Lucius Stourbridge had chosen some other person of whom to ask assistance, or that he himself had had the sense to follow his judgement, not his sentimentality, in accepting. Marriage seemed already to have robbed him of his wits!

'I imagine they will be serving luncheon,' Campbell looked towards the house. 'I assume you are staying?'

'I still have to speak to the servants,' Monk answered grimly, walking across the gravel. 'Even if I learn nothing.'

Chapter Two

❧

Hester shifted from foot to foot impatiently as she stood in the waiting room in the North London Hospital. The sun was hot and the closed air claustrophobic. She thought with longing of the green expanse of Hampstead Heath only a few hundred yards away. But she was here with a purpose. There was a massive amount to do and, as always, too little time. Too many people were ill, confused by the medical system, if you could call it by so flattering a word, and frightened of authority.

Her desire was to improve the quality of nursing from the manual labour it was at present in the vast majority of cases, to a skilled and respected profession. Since Florence Nightingale's fame had spread after the Crimean War, the public in general regarded her as a heroine. She was second in popularity only to the Queen! But the popular vision of her was a sentimental image of a young woman wandering around hospital with a lamp in her hand, mopping fevered brows and whispering words of comfort, rather than the reality Hester knew. She had nursed with her and experienced the despair, the unnecessary deaths brought on by disease and incompetence rather than the injuries of battle. She also knew

Florence Nightingale's true heroism, the strength of her will to fight for better conditions, for the use of common sense in sanitation and efficiency in administration. Above all she fought to make nursing an acceptable profession which would attract decent women, and treat them with respect. Old-fashioned ideas must be got rid of, up-to-date methods must be used, and skills rewarded.

Now that Hester no longer needed to work to support herself, she could also devote her time to this end. She had made it plain to Monk from the outset that she would never agree to sit at home and sew a fine seam and gossip with other women who had too little to do. He had offered no disagreement, knowing it was a condition of acceptance.

They had had certain differences, and would no doubt have more. She smiled now in the sun as she thought of them. It was not easy for either of them to make all the changes necessary to adapt to married life. Deeply as she loved him, sharing a bedroom – let alone a bed – with another person was a loss of privacy she found not as easy to overcome as she had imagined. She was not especially modest – nursing life had made that impossible – but she still revelled in the independence of having the window open or closed as she wished, of putting the light out when she chose, and having as many or as few blankets over her as she liked. On too many nights in the Crimea she had worked until she was exhausted, and beyond. Too often she had lain hunched up, shaking with cold, muscles too knotted up to sleep. Roused in the morning when she was still almost drunken with tiredness.

But to have the warmth, the gentleness of someone beside her whom she knew without question loved her, was greater than all the tiny things. They were only pinpricks. She knew he felt them too. She had seen in his face the quick smothering of a flash of temper, and then decisions reversed when he realised he was being inconsiderate, thinking only of himself. He was used to both privacy and independence also.

But he had less to forfeit than she. They were living in his rooms in Fitzroy Street. It made excellent sense, of course. She had had only sufficient lodgings to house her belongings and to sleep in between the cases she had taken after being dismissed from hospital service for insubordination, and gone into private nursing. He was developing a good practice as an agent of inquiry for private cases, now that he was dismissed from the police force – also for insubordination!

For him to have moved would have been unwise. People knew where to find him. The house was well situated and the landlady had been delighted to allow them an extra room to make into a kitchen, and to give up having to cook and clean for Monk, a duty she had done only from necessity before, realising he would probably starve if she didn't. She was very pleased to have both the additional rent, and more time to devote to her increasingly demanding husband, and whatever other pursuits she enjoyed beyond Fitzroy Street.

So Hester was, with some difficulty, learning to become domestic, and trying to do it with a modicum of grace.

Her real passion was still to reform nursing. Lady Callandra Daviot shared her feelings, which was why Hester was standing here now waiting for her to come and recount the success or failure of their latest attempt.

She heard the door opening and swung around. Callandra came in, her hair sticking out in tufts as if she had run her fingers through it, her face set tight and hard with anger. There was no need to ask if she had succeeded.

Callandra had dignity, courage and good humour, but not even her dearest friend would have said she was graceful. In spite of the best efforts of her maid, her clothes looked as if she paid no regard to them, merely picking up what first came to her hand. Today it was a green skirt and a blue blouse. It was warm enough inside the hospital that whatever jacket she had chosen, she was not wearing it now.

'The man is a complete idiot!' she said furiously. 'How can anyone see to diagnose what ails a person for any of a hundred diseases, and still be blind as a bat to the facts before his face?'

'I don't know,' Hester admitted. 'But it happens frequently.'

The door was still wide open behind Callandra. She turned on her heel and marched out again, leaving Hester to follow after her.

'How many hours are there in a day?' Callandra demanded over her shoulder.

'Twenty-four,' Hester replied as they reached the end of the passage and went through the now empty operating theatre with its table in the centre, benches for equipment, and the railed-off gallery on three sides from which pupils and other interested parties could observe.

'Exactly,' Callandra agreed. 'And how much of that time can a surgeon be expected to care for his patient personally? One hour, if the patient is important – less if he is not! Who cares for him the rest of the time?' She opened the further door into the wide passageway that ran the length of the entire ground floor.

'The Resident Medical Officer—' Hester began.

'Apothecary!' Callandra said dismissively, waving her hand in the air.

Hester closed the door behind them. 'They prefer to call them resident medical officers now,' she remarked. 'And the dressers and nurses. I know your point. If we do not train dressers and nurses, and pay them properly, everyone else's efforts are largely wasted. The most brilliant of surgeons is still dependent upon the care we give his patients after he has treated them.'

'I know that!' Callandra hesitated, deciding whether to go right towards the casualty room, or left past the post-mortem room to the eye department, and the secretary's office and the boardroom. 'You know that!' She decided to go left. 'Dr Beck knows that!' She spoke his name quite formally, as if they had not been friends for years, and not cared for each other far more than either dared say. 'But Mr Ordway is very well satisfied with things as they are! If it were up to him we'd still be wearing fig leaves and eating our food raw.'

'Figs, presumably,' Hester said drily. 'Or apples?'

Callandra shot her a sharp look. 'Figs,' she retorted with absolute certainty. 'He'd never have had the courage to take the apple!'

'Then we'd have not been wearing the fig leaves either, heaven preserve us!' Hester pointed out, hiding her smile.

'Marriage has made you decidedly immodest!' Callandra snapped, but there was satisfaction in her voice. She had long wished Hester's happiness, and had once or twice alluded to fears that she might become too wasp-tongued to allow herself the chance.

They reached the end of the corridor and Callandra turned right towards the boardroom. She hesitated in her step so slightly that had Hester not felt the trepidation herself, she might not have noticed it at all.

Callandra knocked on the door.

'Come in!' the voice inside commanded.

Callandra pushed it open and went inside, Hester on her heels.

The man sitting at the large table was stocky of build, his hair receding from a broad brow, his features strong and stubborn. His was not a handsome face, but it had a certain distinction. He was extremely well dressed in a suit of pinstriped cloth which must have been very warm on this midsummer day. His white collar was high and stiff. A gold watch chain was draped across his broad chest.

The expression on his face tightened when he beheld Callandra. It positively flinched when he saw Hester behind her.

'Lady Callandra . . .' He half rose from his seat, as a gesture towards courtesy. She was not a nurse or an employee, however much of a thorn in his side she might be. 'What can I do for you?' He nodded at Hester. 'Miss Latterly.'

'Mrs Monk,' Callandra corrected him with satisfaction.

His face flushed slightly and he gave a perfunctory nod towards Hester in mute apology. His hand brushed the papers in front of him, indicating how busy he was, and that only politeness prevented him from pointing out the fact that they were interrupting him.

'Mr Thorpe,' Callandra began purposefully, 'I have just spoken again with Mr Ordway, to no avail. Nothing I can say seems to make him aware of the necessity for improving the conditions—'

'Lady Callandra,' he cut across her wearily, his voice hard-edged. 'We have already discussed this matter a number of times. As Chairman of the governors of this hospital, I have a great many considerations to keep in mind when I make my decisions, and cost has to be high among them. I thought I had adequately explained that to you, but I perceive that my efforts were in vain—' He drew breath to continue, but this time Callandra in her turn interrupted.

'I understood you perfectly, Mr Thorpe. I do not agree. All the money in the world is wasted if it is spent on operating upon a patient who is not adequately cared for afterwards.'

'Lady Callandra,' he sighed heavily, his patience

exceedingly thin. His hands moved noisily over the papers, rustling them together, 'Our success rate in this hospital is as good as most others, if not rather better. If you were as experienced in medicine as I am, you would realise that it is regrettably usual for a great number of patients to die after surgery. It is something that cannot be avoided. All the skill in the world cannot—'

Hester could endure it no longer.

'We are not talking about skill, Mr Thorpe,' she said firmly. 'All that is required to ease at least some of the distress is common sense! Experience has shown that—'

Thorpe closed his eyes in exasperation. 'Not Miss Nightingale again, Miss . . . Mrs Monk.' He jerked his hand sharply, scattering the papers over the desk-top. 'I have had enough letters from that woman to paper my walls! She has not the faintest idea of the realities of life in England! She thinks because she did a fine work in utterly different circumstances in a different country, that she can come home again and reorganise the entire medical establishment according to her own ideas! She has delusions both as to the extent of her knowledge and the degree of her own importance.'

'It's not about personal importance, Mr Thorpe,' Hester replied, staring straight at him. 'Or about who gets the praise – at least it shouldn't be. It is about whether a patient recovers or dies. That is what we are here for.'

'That is what I am here for, madam!' he said grimly. 'What you are here for I have no idea. Your friends would no doubt say it is from a devotion to the welfare of your fellow human beings in their suffering. Your detractors might take the view that it is to fill your otherwise empty time, and to give yourself a feeling of importance you would not have in the merely domestic setting of running your own household.'

Hester was furious. She knew perfectly well that losing her temper would also lose her the argument; and it was just possible that Thorpe knew that also. Personally she did not think he had the wit. Either way she had no intention of catering to him.

'There are always people willing to detract with a spiteful remark,' she answered with as good a smile as she could manage. 'It is largely made from ignorance and meanness of spirit. I am sure you have more sense than to pay attention to them. I am here because I have some practical experience in nursing people after severe injury, whether caused by battle or surgery, and as a consequence have learned some methods that work rather better than those currently practised here at home.'

'You imagine so,' Thorpe looked at her icily. His light brown eyes were large, but a trifle deep set. His lashes would have been the envy of many a woman.

Hester raised her brows very high. 'Is it not better that the patient lives than that he dies?'

Thorpe half rose in his chair, his face pink. 'Do not be flippant with me, madam! I would remind you that you have no medical training whatsoever. You are unlearned and totally ignorant and, as a woman, unsuited to the rigours of medical science. Just because you have been of use abroad to soldiers in the extremity of their injuries while fighting for Queen and country, do not imitate the unfortunate Miss Nightingale in imagining that you have some sort of role to teach the rest of us how we should behave!'

Hester was quite well aware of Florence Nightingale's nature, far more so than Fermin Thorpe, who knew her only through her voluminous correspondence to everyone even remotely concerned with hospital administration. Hester knew Miss Nightingale's courage, her capacity for work and her spirit which fired the labour and sacrifice; and also her inexhaustible nagging and obsession with detail, her high-handed manner, and the overwrought emotions which drained her almost to the point of collapse. She would certainly outlast Fermin Thorpe and his like, by sheer attrition, if nothing else.

Experience of the Crimea, of its hardships and its rare victories, above all of its spirit, calmed the retort that came to Hester's tongue.

'I am sure Miss Nightingale believes she is sharing the reward of experiences you have been unable to have for yourself,' she said with curdling sweetness. 'Having remained here in England. She has not realised that her efforts are not welcome.'

Thorpe flushed scarlet. 'I'm sure she means well,' he replied in a tone he presumably intended to be placating, although it was through his teeth. 'She simply does not realise that what was true in Sebastopol is not necessarily true in London.'

Hester took a deep breath. 'Having been in both places, she may imagine that as far as the healing of injury is concerned, it is exactly the same. I suffer from that illusion myself.'

Thorpe's lips narrowed to a knife-thin line.

'I have made my decision, madam. The women who work in this establishment are quite adequate to our needs, and they are rewarded in accordance with their skills and their diligence. We will use our very limited financial resources to pay for that which best serves the patients' needs – namely skilled surgeons and physicians who are trained, qualified and experienced. Your assistance in keeping good order in the hospital, in offering encouragement and some advice on their moral welfare, is much appreciated. Indeed,' he added meaningfully, 'it would be greatly missed were you no longer to come. I am sure the other hospital governors will agree with me wholeheartedly. Good day.'

There was nothing to do but reply as civilly as possible, and retreat.

'I suppose that man has a redeeming virtue, but so far I have failed to find it,' Callandra said as soon as they were outside in the corridor, and beyond being overheard.

'He's punctual,' Hester said drily. 'He's clean,' she went on after a minute's additional thought.

They walked hastily back towards the surgeons' rooms, passing an elderly nurse, her shoulders stooping with the weight of the buckets she carried in each hand. Her face was puffy, her eyes red-rimmed. 'And sober,' Hester added.

'Those are not virtues,' Callandra said bitterly. 'They are accidents of breeding and circumstance. He has the opportunity to be clean, and no temptation to be inebriated, except with his own importance. And that is of sufficient potency that after it alcohol would be redundant.'

They passed the apothecary's room. Callandra hesitated as if to say something, then apparently changed her mind and hurried on.

Kristian Beck came out of the operating theatre, but he had his coat on and his shirt cuffs were clean, so apparently he had not been performing surgery. His face lit when he saw Callandra; then he perceived her expression.

'Nothing?' he said, more in answer than a question. He was of barely average height. His hair was receding a little above his temples, but his mouth had a remarkable passion and sensitivity to it, and his voice had a timbre of great beauty. Hester was aware that his friendship with Callandra was more profound than merely the trust of people who have the same compassion and the same anger, and the will to fight for the same goals. How personal it was she had not asked. Kristian was married, though she had never heard him speak of his

40

wife. Now he was regarding Callandra earnestly, listening to her recount the burden of their conversation with Thorpe. He looked tired. Hester knew he had almost certainly been at the hospital all night, seeing some patient through a crisis, and snatching a few hours' sleep as he could. There were shadows around his eyes and his skin had very little colour.

'He won't even listen,' Callandra said. She had been weary the moment before, and angry with Thorpe and with herself. Now suddenly her voice was gentler and she made the effort to hide her sense of hopelessness. 'I am not at all sure I approached him in the best way . . .'

Kristian smiled. 'I imagine not,' he said with mild irony, full of ruefulness and affection. 'Mr Thorpe has not been blessed with a sense of humour. He has nothing with which to soften the blows of reality.'

'It was my fault,' Hester said quietly. 'I am afraid I was sarcastic. He provokes the worst in me – and I let him. We shall have to try again from a different angle. I cannot think of one yet.' She looked at Kristian and forced herself to smile. 'He actually suggested that we should busy ourselves with discipline in the hospital, and being of comfort to the patients!' She gritted her teeth. 'Perhaps I should go and say something uplifting?' Her intention was to leave Kristian and Callandra alone for one of the few moments they had together, even if they were only to discuss the supply of bandages or domestic details of nurses' boarding allowances, and who should be permitted to leave the premises to purchase food.

Callandra did not look at her. They knew each other too well for the necessity of words, and it was far too delicate a matter. Perhaps she was also self-conscious. So much was known, and so little said.

Kristian's mouth curled in acknowledgement of the absurdity of it. Hospital discipline was a shambles where the nurses were concerned, and yet rigidly enforced upon the patients. Anyone who misbehaved, used obscene or blasphemous language, fraternised with patients of the opposite sex, or generally conducted themselves in an unseemly fashion, could be deprived of food for one meal, or more. Drunkenness was punished without fail, with the loss of privileges, and, if persisted in, with dismissal, and gaming incurred discharge altogether, regardless of whether the person in question was healed or not.

Drunkenness for nurses was a different matter. Part of their wages was paid in porter, and they were largely the type of person of whom no better was expected. What other sort of woman scrubs, sweeps, stokes fires, and carries slops? And who but a maniac would allow such women to assist in the skilled science of medicine?

Hester marched off, actually to the apothecary's store, leaving Callandra alone in the corridor with Kristian.

'Have you heard from Miss Nightingale?' Kristian asked, turning to walk slowly back towards the surgeons' area of rooms.

'It is very difficult,' Callandra replied, trying to choose her words with care. Like Hester, she knew the reality behind the popular image of the heroine of the Crimea. There was no sentimentality there, no murmured words of peace and devotion. She was as much a fighter as any of the soldiers, and a better tactician than most, certainly than the grossly incompetent generals who had led them into the slaughter. She was also erratic, emotional, hypochondriac, and of inexhaustible passion and courage, a highly uncomfortable creature of contradictions. Callandra was not always sure that Hester appreciated quite what a difficult woman Miss Nightingale was. Her loyalty sometimes blinded her. But that was Hester's nature, and they had both been more than glad of it in the past.

Kristian glanced at her questioningly. He knew little of the realities of the Crimea. He was from Prague, in the Austrian principality of Bohemia. One could still hear the slight accent in his speech, perfect as his English was. He used few idioms, although after this many years he understood them easily enough. But he was dedicated entirely to his own profession in its immediacy. The patients he was treating now were his whole thought and aim: the woman with the badly broken leg, the old man with the growth on his jaw, the boy with a shoulder broken by the kick of a horse – he was afraid the wound would become gangrenous – the old man with kidney stones, an agonising complaint.

Thank God for the marvellous new ability to anaesthetise patients for the duration of surgery. It meant speed was no longer the most important thing. One could afford to take minutes to perform an operation, not seconds. One could use care, even consider alternatives, think and look instead of being so hideously conscious of pain that ending it quickly was always at the front of the mind, driving the hands regardless.

'Oh, she's perfectly right!' Callandra explained, referring back to Florence Nightingale again. 'Everything she commands should be done, and some of it would cost nothing at all, except a change of mind.'

'For some, the most expensive thing of all,' Kristian replied, the smile rueful and on his lips, not in his eyes. 'I think Mr Thorpe is one of them. I fear he will break before he will bend.'

She sensed a new difficulty he had yet to mention. 'What makes you believe that?' she asked.

Even walking as slowly as they were, they had reached the

end of the corridor and the door to the surgeons' rooms. He
opened it and stood back for her as two medical students,
deep in conversation, passed by them to the front door. They
nodded to him in deference, barely glancing at her.

She went into the waiting room and he came after her.
There were already half a dozen patients. He smiled at them,
then went across to his consulting room and she followed.
When they were inside he answered her.

'Any suggestion he accepts is going to have to come from
someone he regards as an equal,' he replied with a slight shrug.

Kristian Beck was in every way, intellectually and morally,
Thorpe's superior, but it would be pointless for her to say so,
and embarrassing. It would be far too personal. It would
betray her own feelings, which had never been spoken between
them. There was trust, a deep and passionate understanding
of values, of commitment to what was good. She would never
have a truer friend in these things, not even Hester. But what
was personal, intimate, was a different matter. She knew her
own emotions. She loved him more than she had loved anyone,
even her husband when he had been alive. Certainly she had
cared for her husband. It had been a good marriage, and
youth and nature had lent it fire in the beginning, and mutual
interest and kindness had kept it companionable. But for
Kristian Beck she felt a hunger of the spirit which was new to
her, a fluttering inside, both a fear and a certainty, which
were constantly disturbing.

She had no idea if his feelings for her were more than the
deepest friendship, the warmth and trust that came from the
knowledge of a person's character in times of hardship. They
had seen each other exhausted in mind and body, drained
almost beyond bearing when they had fought the typhus
outbreak in the hospital in Limehouse. A part of their inner
strength had been laid bare by the horror of it, the endless

days and nights that had melted into one another, sorrow over the deaths they had struggled so hard to prevent, the supreme victory when someone had survived. And of course there was the danger of infection. They were not immune to it themselves. Enid Ravensbrook was terrible proof of that! Callandra hoped profoundly that she had found some form of happiness now. The whole experience had been one that could not be shared by anybody who had not been there.

Kristian was waiting for her to make some response, standing in the sun, which made splashes of brightness through the long windows on to the worn, wooden floor. Time was short, as it always seemed to be between them. There were people waiting – frightened, ill people, dependent upon their help. But they were also dependent upon being adequately nursed after surgery. Their survival might hang on such simple things as the circulation of air around the ward, the cleanliness of bandages, the concentration and sobriety of the nurse who watched over them. The depth of her knowledge and the fact that someone listened to what she reported might be the difference between recovery or death.

'I wish he wasn't such a fool!' Callandra said with sudden anger. 'It doesn't matter a jot who you are, all that matters is if you are right! What is he so afraid of?'

'Change,' Kristian said quietly. 'Loss of power, not being able to understand.' He did not move as another man might have, looking at the papers on his desk, tidying this or that, checking on instruments set out ready to use. He had a quality of stillness. She thought again with a hollow loneliness how little she knew of him outside hospital walls. She knew roughly where he lived, but not exactly. She knew of his wife, although he had seldom spoken of her. Why not? It would have been so natural. One could not help but think of those one loved.

A sudden coldness gripped her. Was it because he knew how she felt, and did not wish to hurt her? The colour must be burning up her face even as she stood here!

Or was it an unhappiness in him, a pain he did not wish to touch, far less to share? And did she even want to know?

Would she want him to say aloud that he loved her? It could break for ever the ease of friendship they had now. And what would take its place? A love that was forever held in check by the existence of his wife? And would she want him to betray that? She knew, without even having to waste time on the thought, that such a thing would destroy the man she believed he was.

No words could be sweeter than to hear him say he loved her. And none could be more dangerous, more threatening to the sweetness of what they now had.

Was she being a coward, leaving him alone when he most needed to share, to be understood? Or being discreet, when he most needed her silence?

Or was friendship all he wanted? He had a wife; perhaps all he needed here, in this separate life from the personal, was an ally.

'There are still medicines missing,' she said, changing the subject radically.

He drew in his breath. 'Have you told Thorpe?'

'No!' It was the last thing she intended to do. 'No,' she repeated more calmly. 'It's almost certainly one of the nurses taking them. I'd rather find out who myself, and put a stop to it before he ever has to know.'

Kristian frowned. 'What sort of medicines?'

'All sorts, but particularly morphine, quinine, laudanum, Dutch liquid and several mercurial preparations.'

He looked down, his face troubled. 'It sounds as if she's selling them. Dutch liquid is one of the best local anaesthetics

46

I know. No one could be addicted to all those, or need them for herself.' He moved towards the door. 'I've got to start seeing patients. I'll never get through them all. Have you any idea who it is?'

'No,' she said unhappily. It was the truth. She had thought about it hard, but she barely knew the names of all the women who fetched and carried and went about the drudgery of keeping the hospital clean and warm, the linen washed and ironed and the bandages rolled, let alone their personal lives or their characters. All her attention had been on trying to improve their conditions collectively.

'Have you asked Hester?' he said.

Her hand was on the door knob.

'I don't think she knows either,' she replied.

His face relaxed very slightly in a smile, humour, not happiness. 'She's rather a good detective, though,' he pointed out.

Callandra had not needed to tell Hester that medicines were missing; she had already been unhappily aware of it. However, it was not to the forefront of her mind as she left Callandra and Kristian and went to the physicians' patients' waiting room. She resented bitterly Fermin Thorpe's admonition to her to go and offer comfort to the troubled and more guidance to the nurses, although both were tasks she fully believed in and intended to carry out. It was their limitations she objected to, not their nature.

She passed one of the nurses, a comfortable woman of almost fifty, pleasant-faced, grey-brown hair always falling out of its pins, a little like Callandra's. Had their backgrounds not been so different the resemblance might have been more apparent. This woman could barely read or write – not much more than her name and a few familiar words of her trade –

but she was intelligent and quick to learn a new task, and Hester had frequently seen her actually tending to patients when she knew there were no doctors anywhere near. She seemed to have an aptitude for it, an instinctive understanding of how to ease distress, lower a fever, or whether someone should eat or not. Her name was Cleo something.

She lowered her eyes now as Hester passed her, not to attract attention. Hester was sorry. She would have liked to encourage her, even with a glance.

There were some patients in the waiting room already, five women and two men. All but one of them were elderly, their eyes watchful in unfamiliar surroundings, afraid of what would happen to them, of what they could be told was wrong, of the pain of treatment, and of the cost. Their clothes were worn thin. Here and there a clean shirt showed under a faded coat.

Some of their treatment was free, but there was still food to pay for while they were here, and then after they left there was medicine as well, if the cure was not complete.

She chose the most wretched-looking of the patients and went over to him.

He peered up at her, his eyes full of fear. Her bearing suggested authority to him, and he thought he was about to be chastised, although he had no idea what for.

'What's your name?' she enquired with a smile.

He gulped. ''Arry Jackson, ma'am.'

'Is this your first time here, Mr Jackson?' Hester spoke quietly, so only those closest to him would overhear.

'Yes, ma'am,' he mumbled, looking away. 'I wouldn't 'a come, but our Lil said as I 'ad ter. Always fussin', she is. She's a real good girl. Said as they'd find the money some'ow.' He lifted his head, defiantly now. 'An' she will, ma'am. Yer won't be done short, wotever!'

'I'm sure,' she agreed softly. 'But it wasn't money I was concerned about.'

A spasm of pain shot through him and for a moment he gasped for breath. She did not need Mr Thorpe's medical training to see the ravages of disease in the old man's gaunt body. He almost certainly had tuberculosis and probably pleurisy as well, by the way he held his hand over his chest. He looked considerably over sixty, but he might not actually have been more than fifty. There would be little the physician could do for him. He needed rest, food, clean air and someone to care for him. Morphine would help the pain, and sherry in water was an excellent restorative. They were probably all impossibly expensive for him. His clothes and, even more, his manner spoke of extreme poverty.

He looked at her with disbelief.

She made up her mind. 'I'll speak to Dr Warner and see if you shouldn't stay here a few days . . .' She stopped at the alarm in his face. 'Rest is what you need.'

'I got a bed!' he protested.

'Of course. But you need quiet, and someone who has time to look after you.'

His eyes widened. 'Not one o' them nurses!' The thought obviously filled him with dread.

She struggled for an argument to persuade him, but all that came to her lips were lies, and she knew it. Many of the nurses meant kindly enough, but they were ignorant and often hard-pressed by poverty and unhappiness themselves.

'I'll be here,' she said instead. She had placed herself in a position where she had to say something.

'Wot are yer, then?' His curiosity got the better of his awe.

'I'm a nurse,' she answered rashly, and with a touch of pride. 'I was out in the Crimea.'

He looked at her with amazement. The word was still magic.

'Was yer?' His eyes filled with hope, and she felt guilty for how simply she'd done it, and with so little consideration of what she could fulfil. If only they could persuade Thorpe to see how much it mattered that all nurses should inspire this trust, not in miracles, but in competence, gentleness and sobriety.

But how could they, when they were given no training, and it was so blatantly apparent that the doctors had little but contempt for them? The anger inside her was rock hard. Unconsciously her body clenched.

Harry Jackson was still staring at her. She must talk to him, reassure him. No one could heal his illness. Like half of the people in this room, he was long past that kind of help, but she could comfort his fear, and for a time at least alleviate his pain.

The physician came to the door. He looked frustrated and tired in a clean frock coat and trousers that were a little wrinkled at the knees. He also knew, even as he called the first patient, that he could do little that was of real help.

Hester moved to another patient and talked with him, listening to his tales of family, home, the difficulties of trying to make ends meet when you were too sick to work, let alone to pay for medicine.

A nurse walked through the room carrying an empty pail, its metal handle clinking against the rings that held it. The woman was stout, dark, about forty. She did not look to either side of her as she passed the waiting people. She hiccuped as she went out of the far door. She was in a world of her own, exhausted by hard, physical labour, lifting, bending, carrying, scrubbing. Mealtimes, and more importantly drink times, would be the highlight of her day. Then she could share the odd joke with the other women, and the brief euphoria of alcohol which shut out reality.

It was all a long way from the dream of the sweet-faced woman with the lamp in her hand who would murmur words of hope and miraculously save the dying.

And that too was a long way from the passionate, tireless, short-tempered, vulnerable woman who sat in her house passing out orders, pleas and advice – almost all of it good – and being stoically ignored by men like Fermin Thorpe.

It was six o'clock before the last patient had been seen. Hester had managed to persuade the physician to admit Harry Jackson for a few days, and she savoured that small victory. She was consequently smiling as she tidied the waiting room.

The door opened and she was pleased to see Callandra, who now looked even more dishevelled than usual. Her skirt was crumpled, her blouse open at the neck in the heat, and she had obviously been working because her sleeves were rolled up, and stained with splashes of water and blood. Her hair was coming out of its pins in all directions. It needed taking down, brushing, and doing again.

Absent-mindedly Callandra pulled out a pin, caught up a bunch of hair and replaced it all, making the whole effect worse.

She closed the door and glanced around to make sure the room was empty and all other doors closed also.

'He's gone,' Hester assured her.

Callandra rubbed the back of her hand across her brow.

'There's more medicine gone today,' she said wearily. 'I checked it this morning, and again now. It's not a lot, but I'm quite sure.'

Hester should not have been surprised, but she felt a cold grip close tighter inside her. It was systematic. Someone was taking medicines every day or two, and had been doing so for

51

a long time, perhaps months, possibly even years. A certain amount of error or theft was expected, but not of this order.

'Does Mr Thorpe know yet?' she asked quietly.

'Not about this,' Callandra replied. 'It's getting worse.'

For a wild moment Hester actually entertained the idea that the theft could be used to pressure Fermin Thorpe into seeing the necessity for training and paying better nurses. Then she realised such a move would only end in a full-scale investigation, possibly involving the police, and all the present nurses, innocent and guilty alike, suffering, possibly even being dismissed. In all probability not one would be able to prove her honesty, still less her sobriety. The whole hospital would grind to a standstill and no good would be achieved at all.

'He's going to find out soon,' Callandra interrupted her thoughts. 'They'll have to be replaced.'

'Have we any idea who it is?' Hester struggled for something tangible to pursue. 'We've got twenty-eight women here, doing one thing or another. All of them are hard up, very few of them can read or write more than a few words, some not that much. Half of them live in, the other half come and go at all hours. The apothecary's rooms are locked,' she pointed out. 'Are they stealing the keys? Or do you suppose they can pick the lock?'

'Pick the lock,' Callandra said without hesitation. 'Or sneak in and out when he's got his back turned. He's as careful as he can be.'

'But he knows there are losses?'

'Oh, yes. He doesn't like Thorpe any more than we do. Well, not much. He'll not report it till he has to. He knows what chaos that would cause. But he can't carry on hiding it much longer.'

There was a knock on the door. Callandra opened it and Cleo stood there, a look of polite enquiry on her face. 'Yer 'ungry, love?' she said cheerfully. 'There's a nice bit o' cold beef an' pickle goin' if yer fancy it? An' fresh bread. A glass o' porter?'

Hester had not realised it, but at the mention of food she was aware of how long it had been since she'd last eaten, or sat down comfortably, without the need to find words to say to frightened, inarticulate old men and women in order to take their minds from their troubles, powerless as she was to give any real help.

'Yes,' she accepted quickly. 'Please.'

Cleo jerked her hand to the right. 'Along there, love, same as usual.' She withdrew and they heard the feet clattering away on the hard floor.

They went together up to the staff room and sat at one of the plain wood tables. All around them other women were eating with relish and the porter glasses were lifted even more often than the forks. There was a little cheerful conversation in between mouthfuls, or during. Callandra and Hester overheard many snatches.

'. . . dead 'e were, in a week, poor devil. But wot can yer 'spect, eh? 'Ad no choice but ter cut 'im open. Went bad, it did. Seen it comin'.'

'Yeah. Well, 'appens, don' it? 'Ere, 'ave another glass o' porter.'

'Fanks. I'm that tired I need summink ter keep me eyes open. I gorn an' popped that 'at, like yer told me. Got one and tenpence fer it. Bastard. I'd 'a thought 'e' a given me two bob. Still, it'll do the rent, like.'

'Your Edie still alive, is she?'

'Poor ol' sod, yeah. Coughin' 'er 'eart up, she is. Forty-six, goin' on ninety.'

'Yer gonner get 'er up 'ere, then, ter see the doc?'

'Not likely! 'Oo's gonner pay fer it? I can't, an' Lizzie in't got nuffink. Fred's mean as muck. Makin' shillin's, 'e is, at the fish market most days, but drinks more'n 'alf of it.'

'Tell me! My Bert's the same. Still, knocked seven bells outa Joe Pake t'other day and got 'isself locked up fer a while. Good riddance, I say. Yer got any more o' that pickle? I'm that 'ungry. Ta.'

Hester had heard a hundred conversations like it – the small details of life for the women who were entrusted with the care of frightened and ignorant people after the surgeon's knife had done its best to remove the cause of their pain, and the long road to recovery lay ahead of them.

'Perhaps if I got figures together?' Hester said, as much to herself as to Callandra. 'I could prove to Thorpe the practical results of having women with some degree of training! I know it would cost more, as he would be the first to point out, but money's only the excuse, I'm sure of that.' She was reaching for reasons, arguments, the weakness in his armour. 'If he thought he would get the credit . . . if his hospital were to have a greater success rate than any other . . .'

Callandra looked up from her bread and pickle. 'I've tried that.' A heavy bunch of hair fell out of its pins and she poked it back, leaving the ends sticking out. 'I thought I'd catch his vanity. Nothing he'd like better than to outdo Dr Gilman at Guy's. But he hasn't the courage to try anything he isn't sure of. If he spent money, and there were no immediate results, soon enough . . .' She left the rest unsaid. They had been round and round these arguments, or ones like them, so many times. It was all a matter of convincing him of something he did not want to know.

'I suppose it's back to writing more letters,' Hester said wearily, taking another slice of bread.

Callandra nodded, her mouth full. She swallowed. 'How's William?'

'Bored,' Hester said with a smile. 'Longing for a case to stretch his wits.'

When Hester arrived home at Fitzroy Street it was a little after seven o'clock that evening. Monk was already returned and waiting for her. There were faint lines of tiredness in his face, but nothing disguised his pleasure in seeing her. She still found it extraordinary; it brought a strange quickening of the heart and tightness in the stomach to remember that she belonged here now, in his rooms, that when night came she would not stand up and say goodbye, uncertain when she would see him again. There was no more pretending between them, no more defence of their separateness. They might go to the bedroom one at a time, but underlying everything was the certainty that they would both be there together, all night, and waken together in the morning. She did not even realise she was smiling as she thought of it, only the warmth was always in her mind, like sunshine on a landscape, lighting everything.

She kissed him now when he rose to greet her, feeling his arms close around her. The gentleness of his touch perhaps surprised him more than her.

'What's for dinner?' was the first thing he said after he let her go.

It had not crossed her mind that she would need to cook for him. She had eaten at the hospital as a matter of habit. The food was there. She had been thinking of the missing medicines and Thorpe's stubbornness.

There was food in their small kitchen, of course, but it would require preparing and cooking. Even so, it would not take more than three-quarters of an hour at most. She could not bear the thought of eating again so soon but she could not possibly tell him! To have forgotten about him was inexcusable!

She turned away, thinking frantically. 'There's cold mutton. Would you like it with vegetables? And there's cake.'

'Yes,' he agreed without enthusiasm. Had he expected her to be a good cook? Surely he knew her better than that? Did he imagine marriage was somehow going to transform her magically into a housekeeping sort of woman? Perhaps he did.

All she wanted to do was sit down and take her boots off! Tonight was her own fault, but the spectre of years of nights like this was appalling, coming home from whatever she had been doing, been fighting for – or against – and having to start thinking of shopping for food, bargaining with tradesmen, making lists of everything she needed, peeling, chopping, boiling, baking, clearing away! And then laundry, ironing, sweeping! She swallowed hard, emotions fighting each other inside her. She loved him, liked him, at times loathed him, admired him, despised him . . . a hundred things, but always she was tied to him by bonds so strong they crowded out everything else.

'What did you do today?' she asked. What was racing through her head was the possibility of acquiring a servant, a woman to come in and do the basic chores she herself was so ill-equipped to handle. How much would it cost? Could they afford it? She had sworn she was not going to go back to nursing in other people's houses, as she had done until their marriage. Her smile widened as she remembered the day.

Automatically she washed her hands, filled the pan with cold water and set it on the small stove to boil, then reached for potatoes, carrots, onions and cabbage.

The wedding day had been typical of late spring, glittering sunshine gold on wet pavements, the scent of lilacs in the air, the sound of birdsong and the jingle of harnesses, horses' hoofs on the cobbles, church bells. Excitement had fluttered in her chest so fiercely she could hardly breathe. Inside the church was cool. A flurry of wind had blown her skirt around her.

She could see the rows of pews now in her mind's eye, the floor leading to the altar worn uneven by thousands of feet down the centuries. The stained glass of the windows shone like jewels thrown up against the sun. She had no idea what the pictures were. All she had seen after that had been Monk's stiff shoulders and his dark head, then his face as he could not resist turning towards her.

He was leaning against the door lintel talking to her now, and she had not heard what he had said.

'I'm sorry,' she apologised. 'I was thinking about the dinner. What did you say?' Why had she not told him what she was really thinking? Too sentimental. It would embarrass him.

'Lucius Stourbridge,' he repeated very clearly. 'His bride-to-be left the party in the middle of a croquet game and has not been seen since. That was three days ago.'

She stopped scraping the carrots and turned to look at him.

'Left how? Didn't anybody go after her?'

'They thought at first she'd been taken ill.' He told her the story as he had heard it.

Hester tried to imagine herself in Miriam Gardiner's place. What could have been in her mind as she ran from the garden? Why? It was easy enough to think of a moment's panic at the thought of the change in her life she was committing herself to and things that would be irrevocable once she had walked down the aisle of the church, and made her vows before God – and the congregation. But you overcame such things. You came back with an apology, and made some excuse about feeling faint.

Or if you really had changed your mind, you said so, perhaps with hideous embarrassment, guilt, fear. But you did not simply disappear.

'What is it?' he asked, looking at her face. 'Have you thought of something?'

She remembered the carrots and started working again, although the longer it took to prepare the more chance there was she could force herself to eat again. Her fingers moved more slowly.

'I suppose there wasn't someone else?' she asked. The pan was coming to the boil, little bubbles beginning to rise from the bottom and burst. She should hurry with the potatoes, and put on a second pan for the cabbage. If she chopped it fiercely it would not take long.

He said nothing for a few moments. 'I suppose it's the only answer,' he concluded. 'Treadwell must be involved somehow, or why didn't he come back?'

'He saw his chance to steal the coach, and he just took it,' she suggested, putting the potatoes and carrots into the pan, a little salt in it, then the lid on. 'William?'

'What?'

How should she approach this without either inviting him to tell her to give up working at the hospital on one hand, or on the other, implying that she expected a higher standard of living than he was able to offer her?

'Are you going to take the case?'

'I already told you that! I wish I hadn't, but I gave my word.'

'Why do you regret it?' She kept her eyes on the knife, her fingers and the cabbage.

'Because there's nothing I could find out that would bring

anything but tragedy to them,' he replied a little tartly.

She did not speak for a few minutes, busying herself with getting out the mutton first and carving slices off it and then replacing it in the pantry. She found the last of the pickles – she should have purchased more – and set the table.

'Do you think . . .' she began.

He was watching her as if seeing her performing those domestic duties gave him pleasure. Was it her, or simply the warmth of belonging, particularly after the unique isolation of his years without memory, the comforts of the past which for him did not exist, except in shadows, and fear of what he would find?

'Do I think what?' he asked. 'Your pan is boiling!'

'Thank you.' She eased the lid a little. It was time to put the cabbage in as well.

'Hester!'

'Yes?'

'You used to be the most straightforward woman I ever knew, now you are tacking and jibbing like—'

She pushed past him. 'Please don't stand in the doorway. I can't move around you.'

He stepped aside. 'What do you think made Miriam Gardiner change her mind so suddenly?'

Fear, she thought. Sudden overwhelming knowledge of what promises she was making. Her life, her fortunes for good or ill, her name, her obedience, perhaps most of all her body, would belong to someone else. Maybe in that moment as she had stood in the sunlight in the garden, it had all been too much. For ever! Till death do us part. You have to love someone very much indeed, overwhelmingly . . . you have to trust them in a deep, fierce and certain way that lies even closer to the heart than thought, in order to do that.

'William, do you think we could afford to have a woman

in during the day, to cook for us, and purchase food and so on? So that we could spend together the time we have, and be sure of a proper meal?' She did not look at him. She stood with body tight, waiting for his response. The words were said.

There was silence except for the bubbling of the water and the jiggling of the pan lid. She moved it a little further off and the steam plumed out.

She wished she knew what he was thinking. Money? Or principle? Would someone else be an intrusion? Hardly. Everyone had servants. Money. They had already discussed that. He had accepted Callandra's help earlier on as a matter of necessity. Now it was different. He would never permit anyone else to support his wife. They had battled over her independence already. She had won. It was an unspoken condition of happiness. It was the only thing in which he had been prepared to give ground. It was probably the surest gauge of his love for her. The memory of it filled her with warmth.

'It's not important,' she said impulsively. 'I . . .' Then she did not know what else to say without spoiling it. Over-explanation always did.

'There's no room for anyone to live in,' he said thoughtfully. 'She would have to come every day.'

Hester found herself smiling, a little skip of pleasure inside her. 'Oh, of course. Perhaps just afternoons.'

'Is that sufficient?' He was generous now, possibly even rash. One never knew what cases he would have in the future.

'Oh certainly,' she agreed. She took a skewer and tested the potatoes. Not ready yet. 'Could she have discovered something about Lucius that made the thought of marrying him intolerable?' she asked. 'Or about his family, perhaps?'

'Not that instant,' he answered. 'No one was standing anywhere near her, far less speaking to her. It was just a garden croquet match, full of social chatter, very open, quite public. She couldn't have surprised him with another woman, if that's what you are thinking. And there was certainly no quarrel. Nor was it a question of being overwhelmed or feeling a stranger. She had been there many times before, and already knew everyone present. She helped compile the guest list.'

Hester said nothing.

'I want your thoughts,' he prompted. 'You are a woman. Do you understand her?'

Should she tell him the truth? Would he be hurt? She had learned that he was far more vulnerable than his hard exterior showed. He had courage, anger, wit. He was not easily wounded; he felt too fiercely and too completely for others to sway him. He knew what he believed. It was part of what drew her to him, and infuriated her, sometimes even frightened her.

But since they had been married she had learned the tenderness underneath. It was seldom in his words, but it was in his touch, the way his fingers moved over her body as if even in moments of greatest passion, he never forgot her heart and her spirit inside the flesh. She was never less than herself to him. For that, she would always love him, hold back no portion of herself in fear or reserve.

But she could not have known that before. Miriam Gardiner could not know that. She turned round to face him.

'We don't know what her first marriage was like, not truly,' she said, meeting his eyes. 'Not when the doors were closed, and they were alone together. Perhaps there were things in that which made her suddenly afraid of committing herself irrevocably again.'

His grey eyes searched hers. She saw the question in them, the flicker of uncertainty.

'You cannot know beforehand how well or ill it will be,'

she said very quietly. 'One can be hurt.' She did not say, or repulsed, exhausted, feel used or soiled, but she knew he understood it. 'Perhaps they knew each other very little in that regard,' she said aloud. Then in case he should imagine she had the slightest doubt or fear herself, she put her arms around his neck and brushed her fingers gently over his ears and into his hair, and kissed his mouth.

His response spoiled the dinner and sealed his determination to begin looking for a woman to take over domestic duties from now on.

Chapter Three

❧

Monk left home early the following morning. It was long before he felt like it, but if he were to have any success in helping Lucius Stourbridge, he must find out what had happened to James Treadwell and the carriage. From that he would have a far better chance of tracing some clue or indication where Miriam had gone, perhaps even why. He surprised himself how much he dreaded the answer.

It was now four days since her disappearance, and getting more difficult to follow her path with each hour that passed. He took a hansom to Bayswater and began by seeking the local tradesmen who would have been around at the hour of the afternoon when Miriam fled.

He was lucky almost immediately to find a gardener who had seen the carriage and knew both the livery and the horses, a distinctive bay and a brown, ill-matched for colour but perfect for height and pace.

'Aye,' he said, nodding vigorously, a trowel in his hand. 'Aye, it passed me going at a fair lick. Din't see who were in it, mind. Wondered at the time. Knew as they 'ad a party on. Seed all the carriages comin'. Thought as someone were took ill, mebe. That wot 'appened?'

'We don't know,' Monk replied. He would not tell anyone the Stourbridge tragedy, but it would be public knowledge soon enough, unless he managed not only to find Miriam, but to persuade her to return as well, and he held no real hope of that. 'Did you see which way they went?'

The gardener looked puzzled.

'The coachman seems to have stolen the coach and horses,' Monk explained.

The gardener's eyes widened. 'Arrr,' he sighed, shaking his head. 'Never heard that. What a thing. What's the world coming to?' He lifted his hand, trowel extended. 'Went round that corner there, I never seed 'im after that. Road goes north. If 'e'd wanted to go to town, 'e'd 'a gone t'other way. Less traffic. Weren't nobody after 'im. Got clean away, I s'pose.'

Monk agreed, thanked him, and followed the way the man had indicated, walking smartly to see if he could find the next sighting.

He had to cast around several times and walked miles in the dusty heat, but eventually, footsore and exhausted, he got as far as Hampstead Heath, and then the trail petered out. By this time it was dusk and he was more than ready to find a hansom and go home. The idea held more charm than it had a month or two ago, when it would have been merely a matter of taking his boots off his aching feet and waiting for his landlady to bring his supper. Now the hansom could not move rapidly enough for him, and he sat upright watching the streets and traffic pass.

In the morning he went early to the Hampstead police station. When he had been a policeman himself he could have demanded assistance as a matter of course. Now he had to ask for favours. It was a hard difference to stomach. Perhaps he had not always used authority well. That was a conclusion he had been forced to reach when his loss of memory had shown him snatches of his life through the eyes of others. It was unpleasant, and unexpectedly wounding, to discover how many people had been afraid of him, partly of his superior skills, but far too often of his cutting tongue. Anything he was given today would be a courtesy. He was a member of the public, no more.

Except, of course, if he had had occasion to come here in the past, and they remembered him with unkindness. That thought made him hesitate in his step as he turned the corner of the street for the last hundred yards to the station doors. He had no idea whether they would know him or not. He felt the same stab of anxiety, guilt and anticipation that he had ever since the accident and his realisation of the kind of man he had been, and still was, very often. Something in him had softened, but the hard tongue was still there, the sharp wit, the anger at stupidity, laziness, cowardice, above all at hypocrisy.

He took a deep breath and went up the steps and in through the door.

The duty sergeant looked up, pleased to see someone to break his morning. He hated writing ledgers, though it was better than idleness – just.

''Mornin', sir. Lovely day, in't it? Wot can I do for you?'

'Good morning, Sergeant,' Monk replied, searching the man's pleasant face for recognition, and feeling a tentative hope that it was not there. He had already decided how he was going to approach the subject. 'I am looking into a matter for a friend who is young, and at present too distressed to take it up himself.'

'I'm sorry, sir. What matter would that be? Robbery, is it?' the sergeant enquired helpfully, leaning forward a little over the counter.

'Yes,' Monk agreed with a rueful smile and a slight shrug.

'But not what you might expect. Rather more to it than that – something of a mystery.' He lowered his voice. 'And I fear a possible tragedy as well, although I am hoping that it is not so.'

The sergeant was intrigued. This promised to occupy his whole day, maybe longer.

'Oh yes, sir. What, exactly, was stolen?'

'A coach and horses,' Monk answered. 'Good pair to drive, a bay and a brown, very well matched for height and pace. And the coach was excellent too.'

The sergeant looked puzzled. 'You sure as it's stole, sir? Not mebbe a member o' the family got a bit irresponsible, like, and took it out? Young men will race, sir, bad as it is – an' dangerous too.'

'Quite sure,' Monk nodded. 'I am afraid it was five days ago now and it is still missing. Not only that, but the driver who took it has not come back, and neither has the young lady who was betrothed to my friend. Naturally we fear some harm has befallen her, or she would have contacted a member of the family.'

The sergeant's face was full of foreboding. 'Oh dear. That don't sound good, sir, I must say.'

Monk wondered if he was thinking that Miriam had run off with Treadwell. It was not impossible. Monk would have formed a better judgement on that if he had seen either of them, but from the description he had of Treadwell from the other Stourbridge servants, he did not seem a man likely to have attracted a charming and gentle widow who had the prospect of marrying into an excellent family, and to a man with whom, by all accounts, she was deeply in love.

'No it doesn't,' he said aloud. 'I have traced the carriage as far as the edge of Hampstead Heath, but then I lost it. If it has been seen anywhere around this area, it would help me greatly to know it.'

'Course,' the sergeant agreed, nodding. 'We got a good 'ospital 'ere. Mebbe she was took ill sudden, like. They'd 'a taken 'er in. Very charitable, they are. Or mebbe she 'ad a sudden breakdown in 'er mind, like young women can 'ave, sometimes.'

'I shall certainly enquire at the hospital,' Monk agreed, although the sergeant had to be speaking about the hospital where Hester was, and he had already asked her if there had been any such young woman either seen or admitted. In either case, unless she were unconscious, why had she not made some effort to contact the Stourbridge family? 'But I must also look further for the coach,' he went on. 'That may lead me to where she is. And in truth, the theft of the coach is the only aspect of the matter which breaches the law.'

'Course,' the sergeant said sagely. 'Course. Sergeant Robb is very busy at the moment. Got a murder, 'e 'as. Poor feller beaten over the 'ead and left on the path outside some woman's 'ouse. But 'e in't gorn out yet today. I know that for a fact. An' I'm sure as 'e'll spare yer a few minutes, like.'

'Thank you very much,' Monk accepted. 'I shan't hold him up for long.'

'You wait there, sir, an' I'll tell 'im as yer 'ere.' And the sergeant lumbered dutifully out of sight. He returned, followed by a slender young man with a good-humoured face, and dark, intelligent eyes. He looked harassed, and it was obvious he was sparing Monk time only to be civil and because the desk sergeant had committed him to it. Little of his mind was on the subject.

'Good morning, sir,' he said pleasantly. 'Sergeant Trebbins says you are acting on behalf of a friend who has had a coach stolen, seemingly by his fiancée. I am afraid if they have chosen to . . . elope . . . it is probably ill-advised, and certainly less than honourable, but it is not a crime. The matter of stealing a coach and pair, of course, we can look into, if you have reason to believe they came this way.'

'I do. I have followed the sightings of the coach as far as the edge of the Heath.'

'Was that yesterday, sir?'

'No. I'm afraid it was five days ago.' Monk felt foolish as he said it, and he was ready for disinterest and even contempt in the young man's eyes. Instead he saw his whole body stiffen and heard a sharp intake of breath.

'Could you describe the driver of this coach, sir, and the coach itself? Possibly the horses, even?'

Monk's pulse quickened. 'You've seen them?' Then instantly he regretted the unprofessionalism of such a betrayal of emotion. But it was too late to withdraw it. Comment would only make it more obvious.

Robb's face was guarded. 'I don't know, sir. Could you describe them for me?' He could not keep the edge from his voice, the sharpness of needing to know.

Monk told him every detail of the coach: the colour, style, dimensions, maker's name. He said that the horses were a brown and a bay, no white markings, fifteen hands, and fifteen one respectively, and seven and nine years old.

Robb looked very grave. 'And the driver?' he said softly.

The knot tightened in Monk's stomach. 'Average height, brown hair, blue eyes, muscular build. At the time he was last seen he was wearing livery.' He knew even before he had finished speaking that Robb knew much about it, and none of it was good.

Robb pressed his lips together hard a moment before speaking.

'I'm sorry, sir, but I think I may have found your coach and horses . . . and your driver. I don't know anything about the young lady. Would you come inside with me, sir?'

The desk sergeant's face fell as he realised he was going to be excluded from the rest of the story.

Monk remembered to thank him, something he would not have done even a short while ago. The man nodded, but it did not dissipate his disappointment.

Robb led Monk to a tiny office piled with papers. Monk felt a jolt of familiarity, as if he had been carried back in time to the early days of his own career. He still did not know how long ago that was.

Robb took a pile of books off the guest chair and dropped them on the floor. There was no room on the already precariously piled table.

'Sit down, sir,' he offered. He had not yet asked Monk's name. He sat in the other chair. He was a young man in whom good manners were so schooled they came without thought.

'William Monk,' Monk introduced himself, and was idiotically relieved to see no sign of recognition in the other man's face. The name meant nothing to him.

'I'm sorry, Mr Monk,' Robb apologised. 'But I am investigating a murder at the moment, of a man who answers fairly well to the description you have just given me. What is worse, I'm afraid, is that about half a mile away we found a coach and two horses which are almost certainly the ones you are missing. The coach is exactly as you say, and the horses are a brown and a bay, well-matched, about fifteen hands or so.' He tightened his lips again. 'And the dead man was dressed in livery.'

Monk swallowed. 'When did you find him?'

'Five days ago,' Robb replied, meeting Monk's eyes gravely. 'I'm sorry.'

'And he was murdered? You are sure?'

'Yes. The police surgeon can't see any way he could have come by his injuries by accident. If he'd fallen off the box his clothes would show it. You can't land on the road hard enough for injuries like that and leave no mark on the shoulders and back of your coat, no threads torn or pulled, no stains of mud or manure. Even though the streets are pretty dry now, there's always something. Even his breeches would have been scuffed differently if he'd rolled.'

'Differently?' Monk said quickly. 'What do you mean? In what way were they scuffed?'

'All on the knees, as if he'd crawled quite a distance some time before he died.'

'Trying to escape?' Monk asked.

Robb chewed his lip. 'Don't know. It wasn't a fight. He was only struck the one blow.'

Monk was startled. 'One blow killed him? Then he crawled before he was struck? Why?'

'Not necessarily,' Robb shook his head again. 'Doctor says he bled inside his head. Could have been alive for quite a while, and crawled a distance, knowing he was hurt, but not how bad, nor that he was dying.'

'Then could he have fallen forward and caught himself one severe blow on an angle of the box? Or even been down, and kicked by one of the horses?'

'Doctor said he was struck from behind,' Robb swung his arms out to his right, and brought them sideways and forwards hard, 'like that . . . when he was standing up. Caught him on the side of the head. Not a lot of blood – but lethal.'

'Couldn't have been a kick?' Monk clung on to the last hope.

'No. Indentation was nothing like a horse's hoof. A long, rounded object like a crowbar or pole. Wasn't a corner of the box either.'

'I see.' Monk took a deep breath. 'Have you any idea who

it was that killed him? Or why?' He added the last as an afterthought.

'Not yet,' Robb admitted. He looked totally puzzled and Monk had an impression that he was finding it overwhelming. Already the fear of failure loomed in his sight. 'He was hardly worth robbing. The only thing of value he had was the coach and horses, and the murderer or murderers didn't take them.'

'A personal enemy,' Monk concluded. The thought troubled him even more, for reasons Robb could not know. Where was Miriam Gardiner? Had she been there at the time of the murder? If so, she was either a witness, or an accomplice – or else she too was dead. If she had not been there, then where had Treadwell left her, and why? At her will, or not?

How much should he tell Robb? If he were to serve Miriam's interests, perhaps nothing at all – not yet, anyway.

'May I see the body?' he asked.

'Of course.' Robb rose to his feet. Identification might help. At the least it would make him feel as if he were achieving something. He would know who his victim was.

Monk thanked him and followed as he led him out of his tiny office, back down the stairs and into the street where there was a stir of air in the hot day, even if it smelled of horses and household smoke and dry gutters. The morgue was close enough to walk to, and Robb strode out, leading the way. He jammed his hands in his pockets and stared downwards, not speaking. It was not possible to know his thoughts. Monk judged him to be still in his late twenties. Perhaps he had not seen many deaths. This could be his first murder. He would be overawed by it, afraid of failure, disturbed by the immediacy of violence which was suddenly and uniquely his responsibility to deal with, an injustice he must resolve.

Monk walked beside him, keeping pace for pace, but he

did not interrupt the silence. Carriages passed them, moving swiftly, harnesses bright in the sun, horses' hoofs loud. The breeze was very light, only whispering through the leaves of the trees at the end of the street by the Heath. The smell of the air over the stretch of grass was clean and sweet. Somebody was playing a barrel organ.

The morgue was a handsome building, as if the architect had intended it as some kind of memorial to the dead, however temporarily there.

Robb tensed his shoulders and increased his pace, as if determined not to show any distaste for it or hesitation in his duty. Monk followed him up the steps and in through the door. The familiar odour caught in his throat. Every morgue he remembered smelled like this, cloyingly sweet with an underlying sourness, leaving a taste at the back of the mouth. No amount of scrubbing in the world removed the knowledge of death.

The attendant came out and asked politely if he could help them. He spoke with a slight lisp, and peered at Robb for a moment before he recognised him.

'You'll be for your coachman again,' he said with a shake of his head. 'Can't tell you any more.'

They followed him into a tiled room, which echoed their footsteps. It held a dampness from running water, and the sting of disinfectant. Beyond was the icehouse where it was necessary to keep the bodies they could not bury within a day or two. It had been five days since this particular one had been found.

'No need to bring him out,' Robb said abruptly. 'We'll see him in there. It's just that this gentleman might be able to tell us who he is.'

The icehouse was extremely cold. The chill of it made them gasp involuntarily, but neither complained. Monk was glad of it. He had known less efficient morgues than this.

He lifted the sheet. The body was that of a well-fed man in his thirties. He was muscular, especially in the upper torso and across his shoulders. His skin was very white until it came to his hands and neck and face, which were darkened by sun and wind. He had brownish hair, sharp features, blemished by a huge bruise covering his right temple, as if someone who hated him had struck him extremely hard, just once.

Monk looked at the body carefully for several minutes. There were fresh bruises and breaks on the skin on his knees, and the palms of his hands, but apart from those Monk could find no other marks, except one old scar on the leg, long since healed over, and a number of minor cuts and scrapes on the man's hands, some as old as the scar on the leg. It was what Monk would expect from a man who worked with horses and drove a coach for his living.

He studied the face last, but with the eyes closed and the animation gone in death, it was hard to make any judgement of what he had looked like beyond the mere physical facts. His features were strong, a trifle sharp, his lips narrow, his brow wide. Intelligence and charm could have made him attractive; ill-temper or a streak of greed or cruelty could equally have made him ugly. So much lay in the expression which was now gone.

Was this James Treadwell? Only someone from the Stourbridge household could tell him beyond doubt.

'Do you want to see the clothes?' Robb asked, watching his face.

'Please.'

But they told him no more than Robb himself had. There was only one likely conclusion; the man had been standing upright when someone had hit him a powerful blow which had sent him forward on to his knees, possibly even stunned him senseless for a while. The knees of his breeches were stained and torn, as if he had crawled a considerable distance. It was difficult to be certain of anything about the person who had delivered the blow. The weapon had not been found, but it must have been long, heavy and rounded, and swung with great force.

'Could a woman have done that, do you think?' Monk asked, then immediately wished he had not. He should not look for Robb to offer him the comfort that it could not have been Miriam. Why should she do such a thing? She could be a victim too. They simply had not found her yet!

But if she were alive, where was she? If she were free to come forward, and were innocent, surely she would have?

And why had she left the Stourbridge house in the first place?

'May I see the coat?' he requested, before Robb could answer.

'Of course,' the sergeant replied. He did not answer as to whether he thought a woman could have dealt the blow. It was a foolish question and Monk knew it. A strong woman, angry or frightened enough, with a heavy object to hand, could certainly have hit a man sufficiently hard to kill him, especially with a blow as accurate as this one.

They left the morgue and went out into the sun again, walking briskly along the pavement. Robb seemed to be in a hurry, glancing once or twice at his watch. It was apparently more than a simple desire to be away from the presence of death which urged him on.

Monk would have freed him from the necessity of showing him the carriage and horses if he felt he could overlook them, but they were the deciding factor whether to bring Harry or Lucius Stourbridge all the way to Hampstead, and distress them with identifying the body, which would certainly cause them additional anguish.

Robb was going at such a pace he stepped out into the street almost under the wheels of a hansom and Monk had to grasp him by the arm to stop him.

Robb flushed and apologised.

'Have you an appointment?' Monk enquired. 'This is only a courtesy you are doing me. I can wait.'

'The horses are in a stable about a mile away,' Robb answered, watching the traffic for a break so they could cross. 'It's not exactly an appointment . . .' The subject seemed to embarrass him.

A coach and four went by, ladies inside looking out, a flash of pastels and lace. It was followed by a brewer's dray, drawn by shire horses with braided manes and feathered feet, their flanks gleaming. They tossed their heads as if they knew how beautiful they were.

Monk and Robb seized the chance to cross behind them. On the further side Robb drew in breath, looking straight ahead of him. 'My grandfather is ill. I drop in to see him every so often, just to help. He's getting a little . . .' His features tightened and still he did not look at Monk. Strictly speaking, he was taking police time to go home in the middle of the day.

Monk smiled grimly. He had no happy memories of the police hierarchy. He knew his juniors had been afraid of him, with just cause, which was painful to him now. His own superior was another matter. Runcorn was the only one he could recall, and between them there had been friendship once, long ago, but for years before his final quarrel which had led to Monk's dismissal, there had been nothing but rivalry and bitterness.

He felt his own body tighten, but he could not help it.

'We'd better go and see him,' he answered. 'I'll get a pie or a sandwich and eat it while you do whatever you have to do for him. I'll tell you what I know about Treadwell. If this is him, it'll help.'

Robb considered it only for a second before he accepted.

The old man and his grandson lived in two rooms in a house about five minutes' swift walk from the police station. Inside was shabby but clean, and Robb deliberately made no apology. What Monk thought did not matter to him. All his emotions and his attention were on the old man who sat hunched up in the one comfortable chair. His shoulders were wide but thin now, and bowed over as if his chest hurt when he breathed. His white hair was carefully combed and he was shaved, but his face had no colour and it cost him a great effort to put on a show of dignity necessary when his grandson had brought a stranger into his sanctuary.

'How do you do, sir?' Monk said gravely. 'Thank you for permitting me to eat my pie in your house while I speak with Sergeant Robb about the case we are working on. It is very civil of you.'

'Not at all,' the old man said huskily, obliged to clear his throat even for so few words. 'You are welcome.' He introduced himself as John Robb, then looked at Robb anxiously.

Monk sat down and busied himself with the pie he had bought from a barrow on the way, keeping his eyes on it so as not to appear to be aware of Robb helping the old man through to the privy and back again, washing his hands for him and heating some soup on the stove in the corner, which seemed to be burning even in the heat of midsummer, as if the old man felt cold all the time.

Monk began to talk, to mask the sounds of the old man's

struggle to breathe and his difficulty swallowing the soup and the slices of bread Robb had buttered for him and was giving to him a little at a time. He had already thought clearly how much he would say of Lucius' request. For the time being he would leave out references to Miriam. It was a great deal less than the truth. He would be deliberately misleading Robb, but until he knew more himself, to speak of her would have set Robb on her trail instantly, and that would not be in her interest – yet.

'Mr Lucius Stourbridge told me Treadwell had taken the coach, without permission, in the middle of the afternoon of the day it appears he was killed,' he began. He took another mouthful of the pie. It was good, full of meat and onions, and he was hungry. When he swallowed it he went on. 'He lives with his parents in Bayswater.'

'Is it his coach, or theirs?' Robb asked, offering his grandfather another slice of bread, and waiting anxiously while the old man had a fit of coughing, spitting up blood-streaked phlegm into a handkerchief. Robb automatically passed him a clean one, and a cup of water, which the old man sipped without speaking.

It was a good question and to answer it Monk was forced to be devious.

'A family vehicle, not the best one.' That was true if not the whole truth.

'Why you and not the police?' Robb asked.

Monk was prepared for that. 'Because he hoped to recover it without the police being involved,' he said smoothly. 'Treadwell is the nephew of their cook, and Mr Stourbridge did not want any criminal proceedings. Of course, since the man is dead, if it is Treadwell, that will be inevitable now.'

Robb was very carefully measuring powder from a twist of paper, making certain he used no more than a third, and then re-wrapping what was left and replacing it on the cabinet shelf. He returned to the table and mixed water into the dose he had prepared, then held the glass to the old man's lips.

Monk glanced at the shelf where the paper had been replaced, and noticed several other containers: a glass jar with dried leaves, presumably for an infusion, a vial of syrup of some sort, and two jars with more paper twists of powder. So much medicine would cost a considerable amount. He recalled noticing Robb's frayed cuffs, carefully darned, the worn heels of his boots, an overstitched tear in the elbow of his jacket. He was taken by surprise with how hard compassion gripped him for the difficulty of it, for the pain, and then a surge of joy for the love which inspired it. He found himself smiling.

Robb was wiping the old man's face gently. He then turned to his own meal of bread and soup, which was now rapidly getting cold. 'Do you know anything else about this Treadwell?' he asked, beginning to eat quickly. Perhaps he was hungry; more probably he was aware of the amount of time he had been away from police business.

'Apparently not entirely satisfactory,' Monk replied, remembering what Harry Stourbridge had told him. 'Only kept on because he is the cook's nephew. Many families will go to considerable lengths to keep a really good cook, and especially if they entertain.' He smiled slightly as he said it.

Robb glanced at him quickly. 'And a scandal wouldn't help. I understand. But if this is your man, I'm afraid it can't be avoided.' He frowned. 'Doesn't throw any light on who killed him, though, does it? What was he doing here? Why didn't whoever killed him take the coach? It's a good one, and the horses are beauties.'

'No idea,' Monk admitted. 'Every new fact only makes it harder to understand.'

Robb nodded, then turned back to his grandfather. He made sure the old man was comfortable and could reach everything he would need before Robb could come home again, then he touched him gently, smiled, and took his leave.

The old man said nothing, but his gratitude was in his face. He seemed better now he had had his meal, and whatever medicine it was.

They walked the three-quarters of a mile or so to the stable where the horses and the carriage were being housed. Robb explained to the groom in charge who Monk was.

Monk needed only to glance at the carriage to remove any doubt in his own mind that it was the Stourbridges'. He examined it to see if there were any marks on it, or anything left inside which might tell him of its last journey, but there was nothing. It was a very well-kept, cleaned, polished and oiled family coach. It had slight marks of wear and was about ten years old. The manufacturer was the one whose name Harry Stourbridge had given him. The description answered exactly.

The horses were also precisely as described.

'Where exactly were they found?' Monk asked again.

'Cannon Hall Road,' Robb replied. 'It's yours, isn't it?' That was barely a question. He knew the answer from Monk's face.

'And the body?'

'On the path to number five, Green Man Hill. It's a row of small houses close on to the Heath.'

'And of course you've asked them about it.' That too was a statement, not a question.

Robb shrugged. 'Of course. No one is saying anything.'

Monk was not surprised. Whether they did or not few people admitted to knowing anything about a murder.

'I'll need the body identifying formally,' Robb said. 'And I'll have to speak to Major Stourbridge, of course. Ask him all I can about Treadwell.' He did not even bother to add 'if it is him'.

'I'll go to Cleveland Square and bring someone,' Monk offered. He wanted to be the one to tell Harry and Lucius, and preferably to do it without Robb present. He could not avoid his being there when they identified the body.

'Thank you,' Robb accepted. 'I'll be at the morgue at four.'

Monk took a hansom back to Bayswater, and when the footman admitted him, asked if he could speak to Major Harry Stourbridge. He would prefer, if possible, to tell him about Treadwell without Lucius having to know until it was necessary. Perhaps, beside dashing the young man's hopes about Miriam's probable safety, it was also cowardice. He did not want to be the one to tell him.

He was shown into the withdrawing room with French doors wide open on to the sunlit lawn. Harry Stourbridge was standing just inside, but Monk could see the figure of his wife in the garden beyond, her pale dress outlined against the vivid colours of a herbaceous border.

'You have news, Mr Monk?' Stourbridge said almost before the footman had closed the door from the hall. He looked anxious. His face was drawn and there were dark smudges under his eyes as if he had slept little. It would be cruel to stretch out the suspense. It was hard enough to have to kill the hope struggling in him as it was.

'I am sorry, it is not good,' Monk said bluntly. He saw Harry Stourbridge's body stiffen and the last, faint touch of colour drain from his skin. 'I believe I have found your coach and horses,' he continued. 'And the body of a man I am almost certain is Treadwell. There is no sign whatever of Mrs Gardiner.'

'No sign of Miriam?' Stourbridge looked confused. He swallowed painfully. 'Where was this, Mr Monk? Do you know what happened to Treadwell, if it is he?'

'Hampstead, just off the Heath. I'm very sorry, it seems Treadwell was murdered.'

Stourbridge's eyes widened. 'Robbery?'

'Perhaps, but if so, what for? He wouldn't be carrying money, would he? Have you missed anything from the house?'

'No! No, of course not, or I should have told you. But why else would anyone attack and kill the poor man?'

'We don't know . . .'

'We?'

'The police at Hampstead. I traced the carriage that far, then went to ask them,' Monk explained. 'A young sergeant called Robb. He told me he was working on a murder and I realised from his description that the victim could be Treadwell. Also the carriage and horses were found half a mile away, quite undamaged. I have looked at them, and from what you told me, they appear to be yours. I am afraid you will need to send someone to identify them – and the body – to be certain.'

'Of course,' Stourbridge agreed. 'I will come myself.' He took a step forward across the bright, sunlit carpet. 'But you have no idea about Miriam?'

'Not yet. I'm sorry.'

Verona was walking towards them across the grass, her curiosity too powerful to allow her to remain apart.

Stourbridge squared his shoulders as she came in through the door.

'What is it?' she asked him, only glancing at Monk. 'You know something.' That was a conclusion, not a question. 'Is it Miriam?'

Monk searched her expression for the slightest trace of

relief, or false surprise, and saw none.

'Not yet,' Stourbridge answered before Monk could. 'But it appears Mr Monk may have found Treadwell . . .'

'May?' She picked up the inference instantly, looking from her husband to Monk. 'You did not approach him, speak with him? Why? What has happened?'

'He has met with misfortune,' Stourbridge evaded. 'I am about to accompany Mr Monk to see what else may be learned. I shall tell you, of course, when I return.' There was finality in his voice, sufficient to tell her it was useless pressing any further questions now.

Monk's relief at not having to tell Lucius what he had discovered was short-lived. They were crossing the hall towards the front door when Lucius came down the stairs, his face pale, eyes wide.

'What have you found?' he demanded, fear sharp in his voice. 'Is it Miriam? Where is she? What has happened to her?'

Stourbridge turned and put up his hands as if to take Lucius by the shoulders to steady him, but Lucius stepped back. His throat was too tight to allow him to speak and he gulped air.

'I don't know anything about Mrs Gardiner,' Monk said quickly. 'But I may have found Treadwell. I need someone to identify him before I can be certain.'

Stourbridge put his hand on Lucius' arm. 'There was nothing to indicate that Miriam was with him,' he said gently. 'We don't know what happened, or why. Stay here. I will do what is necessary. But be discreet. Until we are sure, there is no purpose in distressing Cook.'

Lucius recalled with an effort that he was not the only one to be affected, even bereaved. He looked at Monk. 'Treadwell is dead?'

'I think it is Treadwell,' Monk replied. 'But he was found alone, and the coach is empty and undamaged.'

A fraction of the colour returned to Lucius' cheeks. 'I'm coming with you.'

'There is no need . . .' Stourbridge began, then seeing the determination in his son, and perhaps realising it was easier to do something than simply to wait, he did not protest any further.

It was a miserable journey from Bayswater back to Hampstead. They took their own carriage, driven now by the groom, and rode for the most part in silence, Lucius sitting upright with his back to the way they were going, his eyes wide and dark, consumed in his own fears. Stourbridge sat next to Monk, staring ahead, but oblivious of the streets and the houses they were passing. Once or twice he made as if to say something, then changed his mind.

Monk concentrated on determining what he would tell Robb if the body proved to be Treadwell, and he had no real doubt that it was. It was also impossible to argue whether or not it was murder. The body, whosoever it was, had not come by such an injury by any mischance. To conceal such information as Treadwell's flight with Miriam Gardiner, and the fact that she had gone without explanation, and was still missing, would now be a crime. Also concealment would suggest that they had some fear that she was implicated. Nothing they said afterwards would be believed, unless it carried proof.

Not that either Harry or Lucius Stourbridge would be remotely likely to hide the truth. They were both far too passionately involved to conceal anything at all. Their first question to Robb would be regarding what he knew about Miriam. They were so convinced of her entire innocence of any wrongdoing beyond a breach of good manners, they would only think of how she might be implicated when it was too late.

How would Monk then explain to Robb his own silence about a passenger in the carriage? He had not so far even mentioned her.

They jolted to a stop as traffic ahead of them thickened and jammed the streets. All around drivers shouted impatiently. Horses stamped and whinnied, jingling harnesses.

Lucius sat rigid, still unspeaking.

Stourbridge clenched and unclenched his hands.

They moved forward again at last.

Monk would tell Robb as little as possible. All they knew for certain was that Miriam had left at the same moment as Treadwell. How far they had gone together was another matter. Should he warn Stourbridge and Lucius to say no more about Miriam than they had to?

He looked at their tense faces, each staring into space, consumed in their fears, and decided that any advice would only be overridden by emotion and probably do more harm than good. If they remembered it to begin with, then forgot, it would give the impression of dishonesty.

He kept silent.

They reached the morgue at ten minutes past four. Robb was already there, pacing restlessly up and down, but he made no comment on the time as they alighted. They were all too eager to complete the business for which they had come to do more than acknowledge each other with the briefest courtesies, and then follow Robb inside.

The morgue attendant drew the sheet back from the body, showing only the head.

Lucius drew in his breath sharply and seemed to sway a little on his feet.

Stourbridge let out a soft sigh. He was a soldier and he

must have seen death many times before, and usually of men he had known to a greater or lesser extent, but this was a man of his own household, and murder was different from war. War was not an individual evil. Soldiers expected to kill and be killed. Frequently they even respected their enemies. There was no hatred involved. The violence was huge and impersonal. It did not make the pain less, or the death or the bereavement less final, but death in war was mischance. This was different, a close, intended and covert evil, meant for this man alone.

'Is it your coachman, sir?' Robb asked, but he could not help being aware that the question was unnecessary. The recognition was in both father and son's faces.

'Yes, it is,' Stourbridge said gently. 'This is James Treadwell. Where did you find him?'

The morgue attendant drew back the sheet to cover the face.

'In the street, sir,' Robb replied, leading them away from the table and back towards the door. 'On the path to one of a row of houses on Green Man Hill, about half a mile or so from here.' Robb was sympathetic, but the detective in him was paramount. 'Are you aware of his knowing anyone in this area?'

'What?' Stourbridge looked up. 'Oh . . . no, I don't think so. He is a nephew of our cook. I can ask her. I have no idea where he went on his days off.'

'Was it one of his days off when he disappeared, sir?'

'No . . .'

'Did he have your permission to use your coach, sir?'

Stourbridge hesitated a moment before replying. He looked across at Lucius, then away again.

'No, he did not. I am afraid the circumstances of his leaving the house are somewhat mysterious, and not understood by any of us, Sergeant. We know when he left, but nothing more than that.'

'You knew he had taken your coach,' Robb pointed out, 'but you did not report it to the police. It is a very handsome coach, sir, and exceptionally well-matched horses. Worth a considerable amount.'

'Major Stourbridge has already mentioned that Treadwell was related to his cook,' Monk interrupted, 'who is a long-standing servant of the family. He wished to avoid scandal, if possible. He hoped Treadwell would come to his senses and return . . . even with a reasonable explanation.'

Lucius could bear it no longer. 'My fiancée was with him!' he burst out. 'Mrs Miriam Gardiner. It was to find her that we employed Mr Monk's services. Treadwell is beyond our help, poor soul, but where is Miriam? We should be turning all our skill and attention to searching for her! She may be hurt . . . in danger . . .' His voice was rising out of control as his imagination tortured him.

Robb looked startled for a moment, then his jaw hardened. He did not even glance at Monk. 'Do I understand Mrs Gardiner left your house in the carriage, with Treadwell driving?' he demanded.

'We believe so,' Stourbridge answered before Lucius could speak. 'No one saw them go.' He seemed to have appreciated something of the situation in spite of Monk's silence. 'But we have not heard from her since, nor do we know what has happened to her. We are at our wits' end with worry.'

'We must look for her!' Lucius cut across them. 'Treadwell is dead and Miriam may be in danger! At the very least she must be in fear and distress! You must deploy every man you can to search for her!'

Robb stood still for a moment, surprise taking the words from him. Then slowly he turned to Monk, his eyes narrow and hard. 'You omitted to mention that a young woman was a passenger in the carriage when Treadwell was murdered, and she has since disappeared! Why is that, Mr Monk?'

Monk had foreseen the question, though there was no excuse that was satisfactory, and Robb would know that as well as he did.

'Mrs Gardiner left with Treadwell,' he replied with as honest a bearing as he could, 'but we have no idea when she left him . . .'

Lucius was staring at him, his eyes wide and horrified.

'Sophistry!' Robb snapped.

'Reality!' Monk returned with equal harshness. 'This was five days ago. If anything happened to Mrs Gardiner we are far too late to affect it now, except by careful thought and consideration before we act.' He was acutely conscious of Lucius and of Harry Stourbridge. Their emotions filled the air. 'If she met with violence as well, she would have been found long before now.' He did not glance at either of them but kept his eyes level on Robb. 'If she was kidnapped then a ransom will be asked for, and it has not so far. If she witnessed the murder, then she may well have run away, for her own safety, and we must be careful how we look for her, in case we bring upon her the very harm she fears.' He drew in his breath. 'And until Major Stourbridge identified the body as that of Treadwell, we did not know that the business was anything more than a domestic misunderstanding between Mr Stourbridge and Mrs Gardiner.'

Lucius stood appalled.

Stourbridge looked from one to the other of them. 'We know now,' he said grimly. 'The question is, what are we to do next?'

'Discover all the facts that we can,' Monk answered him. 'And then deduce what we can from them.'

Robb bit his lip, his face pale. He turned to Lucius. 'You have no idea why Mrs Gardiner left your home?'

'No, none at all,' Lucius said quickly. 'There was no quarrel, no incident at all which sparked it.' He explained the occasion and the suddenness of her departure.

'She left with Treadwell?'

'She left in the carriage,' Stourbridge corrected him. 'She could hardly have driven it herself.'

A flash of irritation crossed Robb's face, and disappeared, as if he had remembered their distress. 'Had Mrs Gardiner any previous acquaintance with Treadwell, perhaps through the cook?'

'No,' Lucius said instantly. 'She had met no one in the house before I first took her there.'

'Where did you meet Mrs Gardiner?'

'On Hampstead Heath! Why? It is natural enough that Treadwell should bring her back here. She lives in Lyndhurst Road.'

Robb pursed his lips. 'That is about three-quarters of a mile from where the carriage was found, and rather more from where Treadwell's body was. I assume you have already been to her home to see if she is there?'

'Of course! No one there has seen her since she left to come to Bayswater,' Lucius answered. 'It is the first place we looked. Please, tell us what you know of Treadwell's death, I beg you!'

They were outside in the street again now. Lucius stood breathing deeply, as if trying to clear his lungs of the choking air of the morgue with its close smell of death. Even so, he did not take his eyes from Robb's face.

'We know nothing except that he was murdered,' Robb replied. 'We did not even know his name until you gave it to us, although from his clothes we assumed his occupation.'

'Was there nothing found in the carriage?' Stourbridge asked with a frown. 'No marks or stains to indicate where it had been? What about the horses? Are they hurt?'

'No, they were lost, confused, aware that something was wrong. There was nothing to indicate they had bolted. The harness was not broken. The reins were still tied to the bar, as if the driver had stopped, then climbed down rather than fallen. The carriage itself has no scratches or marks but those of ordinary use.'

Stourbridge turned questioningly to Monk.

'There is nothing further you can do here now,' Monk assured him. 'Thank you for coming to identify Treadwell. Perhaps you had better return home and inform your family, and of course the cook. She is bound to be distressed. As soon as I learn anything more, I will tell you.'

Lucius stood still. 'The answer must be here!' he insisted desperately, loath to leave without something further accomplished.

Stourbridge touched his elbow. 'Perhaps, but Mr Monk will find it more easily if we do not hamper him.'

Lucius did not move.

'Come,' Stourbridge said gently. 'We shall only make it more difficult.'

Reluctantly, still half-disbelieving, Lucius bade goodbye and permitted himself to be led away.

'You realise I shall have to find this woman?' Robb shoved his hands deep in his pockets, staring grimly at Monk. He looked guarded, careful, his shoulders hunched a little. 'At best she may be witness to the murder, at worst a victim herself.'

It was unarguable. Monk said nothing.

'As she may be guilty herself,' Robb went on. 'That blow could have been struck by a woman, if she were frightened enough, or angry enough. Perhaps you will now be frank and tell me what you know of this Mrs Gardiner. Since Mr Stourbridge seems to have hired you to find her, presumably you know a great deal more than you have so far told me!'

There was no evading it now, and perhaps it was the only way to help Lucius Stourbridge. Whatever the truth was, one day he would have to face at least part of it. Some details might be kept from him, but not the essence. If Miriam Gardiner were involved in the murder of Treadwell, it would be public knowledge sooner or later. Monk could not protect Lucius from that, even if she were no more than a witness. And unless Treadwell had set her down somewhere before he reached the Heath, that seemed an unavoidable conclusion. It was plain in Robb's face now as he looked grimly at Monk, ignoring the traffic passing by and the people on foot having to walk round them.

Monk told Robb the outline of his interview with Lucius Stourbridge and his visit to Bayswater. He gave no more detail than was necessary to be honest, and none of his own impressions, except that he had believed what he had been told so far.

Robb looked thoughtful, biting his lips. 'And no one gave you any idea why Mrs Gardiner should have run off in this way?'

'No.'

'Where did Treadwell serve before Bayswater? Where was he born?'

Monk felt himself flush with annoyance. They were obvious questions, and he had not thought to ask them. It was a stupid oversight. He had concentrated on Miriam, thinking of Treadwell only as someone to drive the coach for her. It was instinctive to try to defend himself, but there was nothing to say which would not make his omission look worse.

'I don't know.' The words were hollow, an open failure. Robb was tactful. He even seemed faintly relieved.

'And about her?' he asked.

This time Monk could answer, and did as fully as he knew. Robb thought for several moments before he spoke again.

'So a relationship between Mrs Gardiner and this coachman is unlikely, but it is not impossible. It seems she turned to him to take her away from the Stourbridge house, at least.' He looked at Monk nervously. 'And you still have no idea why?'

'None.'

Robb grunted. 'I cannot stop you looking for her also, of course, and perhaps finding her before I do. But if she is involved in this crime, even as a witness, and you assist her, I shall charge you!' His young face was set, his lips tight.

'Of course,' Monk agreed. 'I would in your place.' That was unquestionably true. He had a suspicion from what he had learned of himself and the past that Robb was being gentler with him than he had been with others. He smiled bleakly. 'Thank you for your civility. I expect we'll meet again. Good day.'

Monk arrived home at Fitzroy Street a little after seven and found dinner ready and Hester waiting for him. It was extremely satisfying. The house was clean and smelled faintly of lavender and polish. There were fresh flowers on the table, a white cloth with blue cross-stitch pattern on it, set out with crockery and silverware. Hester served cold game pie with crisp pastry and hot vegetables, then an egg custard with nutmeg grated over the top, and lastly cheese and crusty bread. There were even a few early strawberries to finish. He sat back with a feeling of immense wellbeing to watch Hester clear away the dishes, and was pleased to see her return some twenty-five minutes later ready to sit down and talk with him for the rest of the evening. He wanted to tell her about Treadwell, and about Robb and his grandfather.

'Did you find the coach yet?' she asked.

He leaned back in the chair, crossing his legs.

'Yes. And I found Treadwell also.' He saw her eyes widen, then the knowledge came into her face that there was far more to what he said. She understood the tragedy before he put it into words. She did not ask him, but waited.

'I went to the local police station to see if they had seen the coach. The sergeant was occupied with a murder case, but he spared me a few minutes . . .' He knew she would leap to the conclusion before he told her.

'Treadwell!' She swallowed. 'Not Miriam too?' Her voice was strained with expectation of pain.

'No,' he said quickly. 'There's no sign of her at all. I would not have had to mention her, except that I brought Major Stourbridge to identify Treadwell, and Lucius insisted on coming as well. Of course they had to ask Robb about her.'

'Robb is the sergeant?'

'Yes.' He described him for her, trying to bring to life in words both the gentleness he had seen in the young man, and the determination, and a little of the edge of his nervousness, his need to succeed.

He saw in her face that he had caught her interest. She had understood that there was far more he had not yet told her.

'How was Treadwell killed?' she asked.

'With a blow over the head with something hard and heavy.'

'Did he fight?'

'No. It was as if he were taken by surprise.'

'Where was he found?' She was leaning forward now, her attention wholly absorbed.

'On the path of a small house in Green Man Hill, just off the Heath.'

'That's close to the hospital,' she said quietly. 'One or two of our part-time nurses live around there.'

'I doubt he was going to see a nurse!' he said drily, but it brought to mind his visit with Robb to the old man, and the poverty in which they lived. Robb's return home would be so different from his own, no wife with a fine meal ready and a quiet evening in the last of the sun. He would find a sick old man who needed caring for, washing, feeding, cleaning often, and who was always either in distress, or close to it.

'What?' she said softly, as if reading his thoughts, or at least his emotions.

He told her about his lunchtime visit, his feelings pouring through his words in a kind of release. He had not realised how much it had cost to contain it within himself, until now that he could share it with her with the certainty that she understood. He could sense her response as surely as if she had answered every sentence, although she did not interrupt at all. Only when he was finished did she speak.

'I'll go and see him. Perhaps the hospital can—'

He did not allow her to complete the words. 'No you won't!' He did not even know why he said it, except that he did not want Robb to think he had interfered, implying that he was not looking after the old man adequately. For someone else to go in unasked would be an intrusion.

Hester stiffened; the whole angle of her body changed. 'I beg your pardon?' Her voice was cool.

Now was the time to make sure she understood him and that it was plain between them where the bounds of authority lay.

'You are not to interfere,' he stated clearly. He did not explain why. His reasons were good, but that was not the point. If he explained now, she would require it every time. 'It would be inappropriate.'

'Why?' she asked, her eyes bright and challenging.

He had not intended to allow the exchange to become an argument. This was precisely what he had meant to avoid.

'I am not going to discuss it,' he replied. 'I've told you, that is sufficient.' He rose to his feet to signal the end of the matter. Worse than being offended, Robb might feel some implied pressure because he was using police time to go home and attend to the old man.

Hester rose also. Her voice was low and very precise, each word spoken carefully. 'Are you telling me whether I may or may not do what I believe to be right, William?'

'You may do anything that is right,' he said with a tiny smile of relief, because she had offered him a route of escape. 'Always. This is not right.'

'You mean I may do what you believe to be right?' she challenged.

'You may,' he agreed. 'You do not have to. The choice is yours.' And with that he went out into the office, leaving her in the middle of the floor, furious. It was not what he wanted at all, but it was a victory that mattered. There were any number of reasons why he must be master in his own home, for the happiness of both of them. When her temper cooled, she would appreciate that.

He sat in the room alone for over an hour, but she did not join him. At first he missed her, then he became irritated. She was childish. She could not expect to have her own way in everything.

But she always had! He remembered with considerable disquiet how she had governed her own life in the past, how wilful she had been. Even the hospital authorities could not tolerate her – and did not! She was opinionated in everything, and not loath to express these opinions, even at the least opportune moments, and with a wit which made it even more offensive to some. He had laughed when he had not been on the receiving end. It was less funny when he was.

Not that his own tongue was not equally sharp, and every bit as well-informed. That was one of the reasons she could accept marriage to him, because he was more than her equal – well, occasionally.

But she must not be allowed to sulk. That was unacceptable. He stood up and went to find her. This could not continue.

She was sitting at the table writing. She looked up when he came in.

'Ah, good,' she said with a smile. 'You've come to tell me more about it. I thought you would. The kettle is on. Would you like a cup of tea? And there is cake as well.'

He thought of the night to come, and lying beside her warm, slender body, either rigid and turned away from him, or gentle and willing in his arms. More than that, deeper in his soul, he thought of all that they had shared that mattered above any petty battle of wills or convention of behaviour. The issue could wait until another time. There would certainly be other battles, dozens of them, perhaps hundreds.

'Yes,' he agreed, sitting down on the other chair. 'Tea would be nice, thank you. And cake.'

Obediently, with a little smile, she rose to make it.

Chapter Four

‹❦›

In the morning Monk left home to continue his search for Miriam Gardiner, only now there was the added difficulty that he must do so without at the same time leading Robb to her. He did not underestimate Robb's intelligence. He had already had the chastening experience of being out-thought in conversation, and the memory still stung.

Horses were intelligent animals, and very much creatures of habit. If Treadwell had driven them to Hampstead before then, they were likely to have returned to the same place.

Accordingly, the still, summer morning at seven o'clock found Monk standing in the sun in Lyndhurst Road, studying its tidy house fronts with their neat gardens and whitened steps.

He knew Miriam's address from Lucius Stourbridge. Naturally it was the first place he had enquired, but all his questions had elicited only blank ignorance and then growing alarm. That might still be where Robb would begin.

Monk stood with the lazy sun warming his shoulders and the early morning sounds of kitchen doors opening and closing, the occasional whack of a broom handle beating a carpet. Errand boys' feet were loud on the cobbles, as was the uneven step of one of them carrying a heavy bucket of coal. The only thought occupying Monk's mind was where had Miriam been when James Treadwell was murdered. Had she been present? If she had, had anyone else, or had she killed him herself? The surgeon had said it seemed a single, extremely heavy blow, but not impossible to have been inflicted by a woman, given the right weapon. And he had not died straight away, but crawled from wherever it had happened, presumably looking for help. Neither Robb nor the police surgeon had offered any suggestion as to where the crime had taken place, but it could not have been far away.

Had Miriam struck him once, and then fled? Had she taken the coach, driving it herself? If so, why had she abandoned it in the street so close by?

Perhaps she had panicked and simply run, as the blind, instinctive thing to do. Possibly she was unused to horses and did not know how to drive.

Or had there been a third person there? Had Miriam witnessed the murder and fled, perhaps for her own survival? Or had she not been there at all?

He would learn nothing standing in the sun while the world woke up and busied itself around him. He walked forward and up the step to the nearest door. He knocked on it and the maid answered, looking startled and ready to tell any errant tradesman where his appropriate entrance was, and not to be so impertinent as to come to the front. Then she saw Monk's face, and her eyes travelled down his smart jacket to his polished boots, and she changed her mind.

'Yes, sir?' she said curiously, absent-mindedly pushing her hand through her hair to tidy it out of her eyes. 'Master's not up yet, I'm afraid.' Then she realised that was a little too revealing. 'I mean 'e in't 'ad 'is breakfast yet.'

Monk made himself smile at the girl. 'I'm sure you can help me without disturbing the household. I'm afraid I am lost. I don't know the area very well. I am looking for a Mrs Miriam Gardiner. I believe she lives somewhere near here.' He knew perfectly well that she lived about five houses along, but he wanted to learn all he could from someone who almost certainly would have noticed her, and heard all the below-stairs gossip. If indeed there were some relationship between her and Treadwell, then they might have been less guarded here, away from Cleveland Square.

'Mrs Gardiner? Oh yeah,' she said cheerfully. She came further out on to the step and swung around, pointing. 'Four doors up that way she lives. Or mebbe it's five, number eight. Just along there, any'ow. Yer can't miss it.'

'Would you know if she is at home now?' he asked without moving.

'Cor luv yer, no I wouldn't. I int't seen 'er fer a week ner more. I 'eard as she were gettin' married again, an' good for 'er, I says.'

'Would that be an elderly gentleman who lives about a mile from here?' Monk assumed an ingenuous air.

'Dunno, I'm sure,' the girl replied. 'Shouldn't 'a thought so, though. Comes in a right smart carriage, 'e does. Matched pair like nobody's business. Step fer step they goes, like they was machines.'

'Same colour?' Monk asked with interest.

'Colour don't matter,' she replied with ill-concealed impatience. 'Size an' pace is wot makes 'em ride well.'

'Know something about horses?' he observed.

'Me pa were a coachman,' she said. 'None better, if I says so as shouldn't.'

He smiled at her, quite genuinely. Something in her pride in her father pleased him. It was simple and without self-consciousness. 'Seen them about quite often, I suppose? Was that coachman much good?'

'Fair,' she replied with careful judgement. 'Not near as good as me pa. Too 'eavy 'anded.'

'Have you seen him lately? I'd like a word with him.' He thought he had better give some reason for all the questions.

'I in't seen 'im fer a few days now.' She shook her head as if it puzzled her. 'But 'e's around 'ere often enough. I seen 'im in the High Street. I recognise them 'orses. Goin' towards the 'Eath.'

'You mean not to Mrs Gardiner's house?' he said with surprise. 'To a public house, perhaps?'

'In't none up that way,' she replied. ''E must 'a know'd someone.'

'Thank you! Thank you very much.' He stepped back. 'Good day.'

She stood on the path smiling as he walked away, then went back into the house to continue with her far less interesting duties.

Monk was speaking to a gardener busy pulling weeds when he saw Sergeant Robb turn the corner of the street and come towards him, frowning, deep in thought. His hands were in his pockets and from the concentration in his face he was mulling over something that caused him concern.

It was as well for Monk that he was, otherwise Robb would almost certainly have recognised him, and that was something he did not wish. Robb had to be searching for Miriam just as diligently as he was. Monk must find her first, even if only to give her time to prepare what she would say.

He thanked the gardener, turned on his heel and strode away as fast as he could without drawing undue attention to himself. He went down the first side street he came to.

Robb did not pass him. Damn! He must have stopped to

speak to the same gardener. It was the obvious thing to do. Then the man would also tell him of seeing the carriage drive by regularly over the last year or more. And Robb would ask who it was that had just been talking to him, and the gardener would say that he had given him the same information. Even if he had not recognised the well-cut jacket and the square set of his shoulders, Robb would know it was Monk. Who else would it be?

What had James Treadwell been doing here other than collecting and returning Miriam to her home after visiting Lucius Stourbridge? Had he relatives here? Was there a woman, or more than one? Or some form of business? Had it anything to do with Miriam, or not?

A vehicle like that would be remembered by anyone who knew horses. This was not an area with many stables or mews where they could be kept out of sight. Most people here used public transport – hansoms, or even omnibuses. Short journeys would be made on foot.

Monk spent the next three hours combing the neighbourhood, asking boot-boys, errand boys, and a scullery maid about the houses. He stopped a man delivering coal for kitchen fires kept burning to cook, even on this hot summer day, his face black, sweat trickling through the coal dust that caked his skin.

Twice more he only narrowly avoided running into Robb. He spoke to a boy selling newspapers and a man with a tray of ham sandwiches, from whom he purchased what was going to have to serve him for a late luncheon. Most of them were happy to admit they knew Miriam Gardiner, at least by sight, and smiled when they said it, as if the memory were pleasant.

But they knew that Treadwell had been murdered, and none of them wished to be associated with that, however loosely. Yes, they had seen him in the past, but no, not lately, certainly not on the night he had met his death. They gazed back at Monk with blank eyes and complete denial. He could only hope Robb met with the same.

The only thing left to do was move closer to where the body had been found, and try again. It was a matter of searching for the kind of person who was in a position to observe the comings and goings, and who might feel free to speak of them without involving themselves in something which could only be unpleasant. Servants caught gossiping were invariably in trouble. The advantage Monk had over Robb was that he was not police. It also held disadvantages. He could only persuade, he could oblige nothing.

He walked slowly along the pavement in the sun. It was a pleasant neighbourhood, with rows of small, respectable houses. Inside, the front parlours would be neat and stuffy, seldom used, filled with paintings and samplers with God-fearing messages on them, possibly a picture of the family posed self-consciously in their Sunday best. Life would be conducted mostly in the kitchen and bedrooms. Prayers would be said every morning and night. The generations would be listed in the family Bible, that was probably opened once a week. Sunday morning would be very sober indeed, although Saturday night perhaps a little tipsy, for the men anyway.

He tried to think what Treadwell would do when he came here. Did he meet friends, perhaps a woman? Why not? He would certainly be very foolish to form a friendship with a woman in the Stourbridge house, or become close enough for others to be made aware of it. Backstairs gossip had ruined more than a few men in service.

Had he come to buy, or to pay something, or to settle or collect an old debt? Or had it been simply to escape his daily life of obedience to someone else? Here, for an hour or two, he would have been his own master.

Monk crossed the street, still strolling gently because he had reached no decision. A young woman passed him. She was wearing the starched uniform and simple dress of a nursemaid and she had a little girl by the hand. Every now and again the child took a little skip, the ribbon in her hair bobbing, and the young woman smiled at her. Far away in the distance, probably on the Heath, a barrel organ played.

If Treadwell had come here he would not have left the carriage and horses standing unattended. Even if he had merely stopped for a drink, he would have had to leave them in some suitable place, such as an ostler's yard.

There was a shop across the road ahead of Monk. He was not more than a quarter of a mile from Miriam Gardiner's house. This would be an excellent place to start. He increased his pace. Now he had a specific purpose.

He opened the door and a bell clanked rustily somewhere inside. An elderly gentleman appeared from behind a curtain and looked at Monk hopefully.

'Yes, sir. Lovely day, in't it? What can I get for you, sir? Tea, candles, half a pound of mint humbugs perhaps?' He waved a hand at the general clutter around him which apparently held all these things and more. 'Or a penny postcard? Ball of string, maybe you need, or sealing wax?'

'Ball of string and sealing wax sounds very useful,' Monk agreed. 'And the humbugs would be excellent on such a warm day. Thank you.'

The man nodded several times, satisfied, and began to find the articles named.

'Mrs Gardiner said you would have almost anything I might want,' Monk remarked, watching the man carefully.

'Oh, did she?' the shopkeeper replied without looking up. 'Now there's a nice lady, if you like! Happy to see her marry again, and that's not a lie. Widowed too young, she was. Oh!

There's the sealing wax.' He held it up triumphantly. 'It's a nice colour, that is. Not too orange. Don't like it to be too orange. Red's better.'

'I suppose you've known her a long time,' Monk remarked casually, nodding back in approval of the shade of the wax.

'Bless you, only since she first came here as a girl, and that's not a lie,' the man agreed. 'Poor little thing!'

Monk stiffened. What should he say to encourage more confidences without showing his own ignorance or curiosity?

The man found the string and came up from his bending with a ball in each hand.

'There you are, sir!' he said triumphantly, his face shining. 'Which would you prefer? This is good string for parcels and the like, and the other's softer, better for tying up plants. Don't cut into the stems, you see?'

'I'll take both,' Monk answered, his mind racing. 'And two sticks of the sealing wax. As you say, it's a good colour.'

'Good! Good! And the mint humbugs. Never forget the mint humbugs!' He laid the string on the counter and disappeared below it again, presumably searching for more sealing wax. Monk hoped it was not the humbugs down in the dusty recesses.

'I hadn't realised she was so young when it happened,' Monk observed, hoping he sounded more casual than he felt.

'Bless you, no more than twelve or thirteen, and that's not a lie,' the man answered from his hands and knees, where he was searching in the cupboards under the counter. He pulled out a huge box full of envelopes and linen paper. 'Poor little creature. Terrible small she was. Not a soul in the world, so it seemed. Not then. But of course our Cleo took her in.' He pulled out another box of assorted papers. Monk did not care in the slightest about the sealing wax, but he did not want to interrupt the flow. 'Good woman, Cleo Anderson. Heart of gold, whatever anybody says,' the man continued vehemently.

'Please don't go to trouble,' Monk was abashed by the work he was causing, and he had what he wanted. 'I don't need more wax, I merely liked the colour.'

'Mustn't be beaten,' the shopkeeper mumbled from the depth of the cupboard. 'That's what they said at Trafalgar – and Waterloo, no doubt. Can't have a customer leaving dissatisfied.'

'I suppose you know Mr Treadwell also?' Monk tried the last question.

'Not as I recall. Ah! Here it is! I knew I had some more somewhere. Half a box of it.' He backed out and stood up, his shoulders covered in dust, a lidless cardboard box in one hand. He beamed at Monk. 'Here you are, sir. How much would you like?'

'Three sticks, thank you,' Monk replied, wondering what on earth he could use it for. 'Is there a good ostler's yard near here?'

The man leaned over the counter and pointed leftwards, waving his arm. 'About half a mile up that way, and one street over. Can't miss it. Up towards Mrs Anderson's, it is. But you'd know that, knowing Mrs Gardiner an' all. That'll be tenpence ha'penny altogether, sir, if you please. Oh . . . an' here are the humbugs. That'll be another tuppence, if you please.'

Monk took them, thanked him and paid, then set out towards the ostler's yard feeling pleased with himself at what he had discovered, although the details of Miriam's youth were of value only in as much as they either explained her extraordinary behaviour, or indicated where she was now.

The ostler's yard was precisely where the shopkeeper had pointed.

'Yes,' an old man said, sucking on a straw. He was

bow-legged and smelled of the stable yard, horse sweat, hay and leather. ''E come 'ere often. Right 'andsome pair they was. Perfick match, pace fer pace.'

'Good with horses, was he?' Monk enquired casually.

'Not as I'd say "good",' the ostler qualified. ' "Fair", more like it.' He looked at Monk through narrowed eyes, waiting for him to explain himself.

Monk made a grimace of disgust. 'Not what he told me. That's why I thought I'd check.'

'Don't make no matter now.' The ostler spat out the straw. 'Dead, poor swine. Not that I'd much time fer 'im. Saucy bastard, 'e were. Always full o' lip. But I wouldn't wish that on 'im. Yer not from round 'ere, or yer'd o' know'd 'e were dead. Murdered, 'e were. On Mrs Anderson's footpath, practically, an' 'er a good woman, an' all. Looked after my Annie, she did, summink wonderful.' He shook his head. 'Nuffink weren't too much trouble for 'er.'

Monk seized the chance. 'A very fine woman,' he agreed. 'Took in Mrs Gardiner too, I believe, when she was just a child.'

The ostler selected himself another straw and put it in his mouth. 'Oh yeah. Found her wandering around out of 'er wits, they did. Babblin' like a lunatic an' scarce knew 'er own name, poor thing. It were Cleo Anderson wot took 'er in an' cleaned 'er up and raised 'er like she was 'er own. Shame that no-good braggart got 'isself killed on her doorstep. That kind o' trouble nobody needs.'

'Can't prevent accident,' Monk said sententiously, but his mind was wondering what could have happened to the young Miriam to cause her such agony of mind. He could imagine it only too vividly, remembering his own fear after the accident, the horrors that lay within himself. Had she experienced something like that? Did she also not know who she was?

Was that what terrified her and drove her away from Lucius Stourbridge, who loved her so much?

The ostler spat out his straw. 'Weren't no haccident!' he said derisively. 'Like I told yer, 'e were murdered! 'It over the 'ead, 'e were.'

'He left his horses here quite often,' Monk observed, recalling himself to the present.

'I told you that too, didn't I? Course 'e did. Best place fer miles, this is. In't nuthin' abaht 'orses I don't know as is worth known'.' He waited for Monk to challenge him.

Monk smiled and glanced at the nearest animal. 'I can see that,' he said appreciatively. 'It shows. And your judgement of Treadwell is probably much what I'd concluded myself. An arrogant piece of work.'

The ostler looked satisfied. He nodded. 'That's wot I told that policeman wot come round 'ere askin'. Treadwell weren't much good, I told 'im. Yer can learn a lot abaht a man by the way 'e 'andles an 'orse, if yer know wot ter look fer. You know, yer a bit pleased wif yerself, an' all!'

Monk smiled ruefully. He knew it was true.

The ostler grinned back, pleased there was no offence.

Monk thanked him and left, digesting the information he had gained, not only about Treadwell being here, but about Miriam's strange early life, and the coincidence of Treadwell being murdered on the doorstep of the woman who had found her and had taken her in twenty or so years ago. And of course Robb had had the same idea. Monk knew he must be extremely careful he did not inadvertently lead the policeman right to Miriam.

Out in the street again, he walked slowly. He did not put his hands in his pockets. It would pull his suit out of shape. He was too vain for that. Why was he so fearful of leading Robb to Miriam? The answer was painful. Because he was afraid she was involved in Treadwell's death, even if indirectly. She was hiding from Lucius, but she was hiding from the police as well. Why? What was Treadwell to her, beyond the driver of Stourbridge's carriage? What did he know – or suspect?

It was time he went to see Cleo Anderson. He did not want to run into Robb, so he approached cautiously, aware that he was a conspicuous figure, with his straight, square shoulders and slightly arrogant walk.

He was already in Green Man Hill when he saw Robb crossing the street ahead of him and he stopped abruptly, bending his head and raising his hands as if to light a cigar, then he turned his back, making a gesture as if to shelter a match from the wind. Without looking up, in spite of the intense temptation, he strolled away again and around the first corner he came to.

He stopped, and to his annoyance, found he was shaking. It was absurd. What had it come to when he was scuttling around street corners to keep from being recognised by the police? And a sergeant at that! A short handful of years ago sergeants all over London knew his name and snapped to attention when they heard it. People cared what he thought of them; they wanted to please him and dreaded his contempt, earned or not.

How much had changed!

He felt himself ridiculous, standing here on the footpath pretending to light an imaginary cigar, so Robb would not see his face. And yet the man he had been then, in hindsight gave him little pleasure. Robb would have feared him, possibly respected his skills, but that fear was based in the power he had had, and his will to use it, and to exercise the sharp edge of his tongue.

He was still impatient, at times sarcastic. He still despised cowardice, hypocrisy, laziness and took no trouble to conceal it. But he equally despised a bully and felt a sharp stab of pain to think that he might once have been one.

If Robb had gone to see Cleo Anderson, either with regard to Miriam, or simply because Treadwell had been found on her pathway, then there was no point waiting here for him to leave. It might be an hour or two. Better to go and buy himself a decent supper, then return in the early evening when Robb would have gone back home, probably to minister to his grandfather.

He ate well, then filled in a little more of the waiting time asking further questions about Miriam. He pretended he had a sister who was recently married and was considering moving into the area. He learned more than he expected, and Miriam's name cropped up in connection with a botanical society, the friends of a missionary group in Africa, a circle who met every other Friday to discuss works of literature they had enjoyed, and the rota of duties at the nearest church. He should have thought of the church. He kicked himself for such an obvious omission. He would repair that tomorrow.

Altogether, by the time he stood on Cleo Anderson's doorstep in the early evening sunlight, the shadows so long across the street that they nearly engulfed his feet, he was feeling, as the ostler had remarked, pleased with himself.

Considering that Cleo Anderson had already sacrificed a great deal of her evening answering the questions of Sergeant Robb, she opened the door to Monk with remarkable courtesy. It occurred to him that she may have believed him to be a patient. After all, caring for the sick was her profession.

It took her only a moment to see that he was a stranger, and unlikely to belong to the immediate neighbourhood. Nevertheless she did not dismiss him summarily, though her eyes narrowed a trifle.

'Yes, love, what can I do for you?' she asked, keeping her

weight where she could slam the door if he tried to force his way.

He stood well back deliberately.

'Good evening, Mrs Anderson,' he replied. He decided in that moment not to lie to her. 'My name is William Monk. Mr Lucius Stourbridge has employed me to find Miriam Gardiner. As you may be aware, she has disappeared from his house where she was a guest, and he is frantic with concern for her.' He stopped, seeing the anxiety in her face, her rapid breathing and a stiffening of her body. But then considering Treadwell's corpse had been found on her path, she could hardly fail to fear for Miriam, unless she already knew that she was safe, not only from physical harm, but from suspicion also. Patently, she did not have any such comfort.

'Can you help me?' he said quietly.

For a moment she stood still, making up her mind, then she stepped back, pulling the door wider. 'You'd better come in,' she invited him reluctantly.

He followed her into a hallway hardly large enough to accommodate the three doors that led from it. She opened the furthest one into a clean and surprisingly light room with comfortable chairs by the fireplace. A row of cupboards lined one wall, all the doors closed and with brass-bound keyholes. None of the keys was present.

'Mr Stourbridge sent you?' she asked uncertainly. The thought seemed to offer her no comfort. She was still as tense, her hands held tightly, half hidden by her skirts.

He had walked miles and his feet were burning, but to sit unasked would be rushing her, and ill-mannered. 'He is terrified some harm may have come to her,' he answered. 'Especially in light of what happened to the coachman, Treadwell.'

In spite of all her effort of control, Cleo Anderson drew in her breath sharply. 'I don't know where she is!' Then she steadied herself, deliberately waiting a moment or two. 'I haven't seen her since she left to go and stay in Bayswater. She told me all about that, o' course.' She looked at him levelly.

He had the strong feeling that she was lying, but he did not know to what extent, nor why. There was fear in her face, but nothing he recognised as guilt. He tried the gentlest approach he could think of.

'Mr Stourbridge cares for her profoundly. He would act only in her best interest and for her welfare.'

Her voice was suddenly thick with emotion, and she choked back tears. 'I know that.' She took a shaky breath. 'He's a very fine young gentleman.' She blinked several times. 'But that doesn't alter nothin'. God knows.' She seemed about to add something else, then changed her mind and remained silent.

'You were the one who found Miriam the first time, weren't you,' he said gently, with respect rather than as a question.

She hesitated. 'Yes, but that was years back. She was just a child. Twelve or thirteen, she was.' A look of pain and defiance crossed her face. 'Bin in an accident. Dunno what 'appened to 'er. 'Ysterical . . . in a state like you never seen. Nobody around to claim 'er or care for 'er. I took 'er in. Course I did, poor little thing.' Her eyes did not move from Monk's. 'Nobody ever asked for 'er nor come lookin'. I expected someone every day, then it were weeks, an' months, an' nobody came. So I just took care of 'er like she were mine.'

Again the memory returned to Monk of lying in the narrow bed and staring at the ceiling, his first crippling thought was that he was in the workhouse. Then as he had looked around at the rows of other cots, he had realised it was daylight, and they were all occupied. That would never happen in a workhouse! It must be a hospital. And he could recall nothing! Not even his name. Nothing had ever come back, except snatches here and there, fears and dreams, pieces to be grasped after, emotions caught, more often lost. Could it be like that for Miriam Gardiner? Or Miriam whoever she was? Did she know? Or was Cleo Anderson all the life she had, all the identity?

Perhaps she caught something in his eyes, an understanding. Some of the defiance eased from her. 'She were scared 'alf out of 'er wits, poor little thing,' she went on. 'Didn't remember what happened at all.'

Cleo Anderson had taken her in and raised her until she had made a respectable and apparently happy marriage to a local man of honourable reputation. Then she had been widowed, with sufficient means to live quite contentedly . . . until she had met Lucius Stourbridge out walking in the sun on Hampstead Heath.

But it was what had happened one week ago that mattered, and where she was now.

'Did you know James Treadwell?' Monk asked her.

Her answer was immediate, without a moment's thought. 'No.'

It was too quick. But he did not want to challenge her. He must leave her room to change her mind without having to defend herself.

'So you were all the family Miriam had, after the accident.' He allowed his very real admiration to fill his voice.

The tenderness in her eyes, in her mouth, was undeniable. If she had permitted herself, at that moment she would have wept. But she was a strong woman, and well used to all manner of tragedy.

'That's true,' she agreed quietly. 'And she was the nearest thing to a child I ever had too. And nobody could want better.'

'So you must have been happy when she married a good man like Mr Gardiner,' he concluded.

'O' course. An' 'e were a good man! Bit older than Miriam, but loved 'er, 'e did. An' she were proper fond o' 'im.'

'It must have been very pleasant for you to have had her living so close.'

She smiled. 'O' course. But I don' mind where she lives if she's 'appy. An' she loved Mr Lucius like nothin' I ever seen. 'Er 'ole face lit up when she jus' spoke 'is name.' This time the tears spilled down her cheeks and it was beyond her power to control them.

'What happened, Mrs Anderson?' Monk said, almost in a whisper.

'I dunno.'

He had not really expected anything else. This was a woman protecting the only child she had nurtured and loved.

'But you must have seen Treadwell, even in the distance, when Miriam came back to visit you while she was staying in Bayswater,' he insisted.

She hesitated only a moment. 'I seen a coachman, but that's all.'

That might be true. Perhaps Treadwell had crawled here because he had heard Miriam say Cleo was a nurse. It was conceivable it was no more than that. But was it likely?

Who had killed Treadwell . . . and why? Why here?

'What did you tell Sergeant Robb?' he asked.

She relaxed a fraction. Her shoulders eased under the dark fabric of her dress, a plain, almost uniform dress such as he had seen Hester wear on duty. He was surprised at the stab of familiarity it gave inside him.

'Same as I'm tellin' you,' she answered. 'I 'aven't seen Miriam since she went off to stay with Mr Lucius an' 'is family. I don't know where she is now, an' I've no idea what happened to the coachman, or 'ow 'e got killed, nor why – except I've known Miriam since she were a girl, an' I've never known 'er lose 'er temper nor lash out at anyone, an' I'd stake my life on that.'

Monk believed her, at least for the last part. He accepted that she thought Miriam innocent. He very much doubted that she had no idea where Miriam was. If all were well with Miriam she would unquestionably not have fled from the Stourbridge house as she had, nor have remained out of touch with Lucius. If she were in trouble, whatever its nature, surely she would have turned to Cleo Anderson, the person who had rescued her, cared for her and loved her since that first time?

'I hope you won't have to do anything so extreme,' he said gravely, then bade her good night without asking anything further. He knew she would not answer, at least not with the truth.

He bought a sandwich from a pedlar about a block away, making conversation with him as he ate it. Then he took an omnibus back towards Fitzroy Street, and was glad to sit down, cramped and lurching as the vehicle was.

He let his thoughts wander. Where could Miriam go? She was frightened. She trusted no one, except perhaps Cleo. Certainly she did not trust Lucius Stourbridge. She would not want to be in unfamiliar territory, yet she would have to avoid those who were known to be her friends.

A fat woman next to him was perspiring freely. She mopped her face with a large handkerchief. A small boy blew a penny whistle piercingly, and his mother told him off, to no effect. An elderly man in a bowler hat sucked air through a gap in his teeth. Monk glared at the boy with the whistle, and he stopped in mid-blow. The man with the gap tooth smiled in relief.

Miriam would go to someone she could trust, someone

Cleo could trust, perhaps, who owed her a favour for past kindness. Cleo was a nurse. If she were even remotely like Hester, she could count on the trust of a good many people, and the unquestioning discretion also. That was where to begin, with those Cleo Anderson had nursed. He sat back and relaxed, keeping his eye on the child, in case he thought to blow his whistle again.

The day was already warm and still by five minutes before nine, when Monk began the next day. The rag-and-bone man's voice was echoed as he drove slowly away from the Heath towards the south. The dew was still deep in the shade of the larger trees, but the open grass was dusty.

Monk did not bother to pursue those patients with large families, and naturally those whose illness had ended in death. He learned of all manner of misfortune, and of kindness. Cleo Anderson's reputation was high. Few had a harsh word to say of her. Miriam also had earned a share of approval. It seemed often enough she had been willing to help in the duties of care, especially after she had been widowed and no longer had her time filled with the wellbeing of Mr Gardiner.

Monk followed every trail that seemed likely to lead to where Miriam might be now. By late morning he had crossed Sergeant Robb's path twice, and was wondering if Robb were equally aware of him. Surely he must be, by deduction even if he had not actually seen him?

A little after midday he came around the corner of Prince Arthur Road and stopped abruptly. Ten yards ahead of him Robb was glancing at his watch anxiously, and in reading the time he looked reluctantly, once, at a house on the further side, then biting his lip, set off at a very rapid pace the opposite way.

For a moment Monk was confused, then he realised Robb

was going in the direction of his home. His grandfather would have been alone since early in the morning, almost helpless, certainly needing food and in this warm weather above all, fresh water to drink, and assistance with his personal needs. Robb would never forget that, whatever the urgencies or the requirements of his job.

Monk was moved with an acute pity for him, and also for the sick old man sitting alone day after day, dependent on a young man desperate to do his job and torn between two duties.

But Monk's first duty was towards Miriam Gardiner, because that was what Lucius Stourbridge had hired him for, and what he had given his word to do. Robb had far more resources than he had, in information given to the police, his own local knowledge, and in his power to command co-operation. They wished the same thing, to find Miriam Gardiner; Monk because it was his final goal, Robb to learn from her what she knew of Treadwell's murder, perhaps even to charge her with complicity in it. It was imperative Monk found her first.

He sauntered slowly over towards the house Robb had eyed, and had then left with such reluctance. He had no idea who lived here or what Robb had hoped to find, but there was no time to investigate more carefully. This was his only chance to gain the advantage. He knocked on the door and stepped back, waiting for it to be answered.

The maid who peered out at him could not have been more than fourteen or fifteen years old, but she was determined to make a good impression.

'Yes, sir?'

He smiled at her. 'Good afternoon.' Time was short. 'Mrs Gardiner asked me if I could carry a message to your mistress, if she is in.' He wished he had some way of knowing the family name. It would have sounded more convincing.

For a moment the girl looked blank, but she wished to be helpful. 'Are yer sure yer got the right 'ouse, sir? There's no one but old Mr 'Ornchurch 'ere.'

'Oh.' He was confounded. What had Robb wanted with old Mr Hornchurch?

Her face brightened. 'Mebbe she meant the 'ousekeeper, Mrs Whitbread, as comes in every day an' cooks an' does fer Mr 'Ornchurch. She was took bad the winter before last, an' it were Mrs Gardiner wot looked after 'er.'

He could feel the sweat of relief prickle on his skin. He swallowed before he could catch his breath. 'Yes. Of course. That's what I should have said. Perhaps it would be more convenient if I were to speak to Mrs Whitbread at her home? Can you tell me how to get there from here?' The people Miriam would turn to would be the ones she had helped in their time of need?

The girl looked dubious. 'Mebbe. I'll ask 'er. She don' like nobody callin' on 'er at 'ome. Reckon as when yer orff, yer wanna be private, like.'

'Of course,' he agreed, still standing well back from the step. 'I'm sure you could simply give her the message, if you would be so kind?'

'I'm sure I could do that,' she agreed, obviously relieved.

He pulled out a piece of paper from his pocket, and a pencil, and wrote, 'Tell Sergeant Robb nothing about Miriam', then folded it twice, turning the ends in, and gave it to the girl. 'Be sure to give it to her straight away,' he warned. 'And if the police come here, be very careful what you say.'

Her eyes widened. 'I will,' she promised. 'Never say nothin' to the rozzers, that's wot me father tol' me. That's the best. Known nothin', seen nothin', 'eard nothin', me.'

'Very wise,' he nodded, smiling at her again. 'Thank you,'

and he stepped back and turned to leave.

He would wait until Mrs Whitbread finished her duties, and then follow her. He had real hope that she might lead him to Miriam. For the meantime, he would find something to eat, and stay well out of Robb's way when he returned to see Mrs Whitbread himself.

He sauntered quite casually along the pavement next to a small space of open grass, and bought a beef and onion sandwich from a stall. It was fresh and he ate it with considerable enjoyment. He bought a second and enjoyed that as well. He wondered how Robb had traced Mrs Whitbread. That was a good piece of detection. It commanded his respect and he gave it willingly.

He must stay within sight of Mr Hornchurch's house so he could see when the housekeeper left, but not so close that Robb, when returning, would observe him.

He expected Robb to come back the way he had seen him leave, so he was jolted by considerable surprise when he heard Robb's voice behind him, and swung around to see him only a yard away, his face grim, his mouth pulled tight.

'Waiting for me, Inspector Monk?' he said coldly.

Monk felt as if he had been slapped. In one sentence Robb had shown that he had learned Monk's history in the police and his reputation both for skill and for ruthlessness. It was there in his face now as he stood in sunlight dappled by the trees, his eyes guarded, challenging. Monk could see the anger in him, and something else which he thought might be fear.

Was there any point in lying? He did not want to make an enemy of Robb, for practical reasons as well as emotional ones, in fact he could not afford to. The first concern was Miriam. Her freedom might depend upon this, even her life. And he had no idea whether she was guilty of anything or not. She might have killed Treadwell! On the other hand she might be in danger herself, terrified and running. He knew no more of the truth now than he had when Lucius Stourbridge had walked into his rooms a few days ago.

He altered his weight to stand a little more casually. He raised his eyebrows. 'Actually I'd really been hoping to avoid you,' he said truthfully.

Robb's mouth curled downward. 'You thought I'd come back the way I left? I would have, if I hadn't seen you, and I admit, that was only chance. But I know this area better than you do. I have the advantage. I wondered if you'd follow me. It would seem the obvious thing to do, if you had no ideas yourself.' There was a contempt in his voice that stung. 'Why did you wait here for me? I suppose you already knew I would be going to my grandfather.'

Monk was startled, and surprised to find himself also hurt. He had not earned that from Robb. Certainly he was trying to beat him to Miriam, but that was what Lucius Stourbridge had hired him for. Robb would not have expected him to do less.

'Of course I knew where you were going,' he answered, keeping his voice level and almost expressionless. 'But the reason I didn't go after you was because I wasn't following you in the first place. Does it surprise you so much that my investigations should bring me to the same place as yours?'

'No,' Robb said instantly. 'You have a wide reputation, Inspector Monk.' He did not elaborate as to its nature, but the expression in his eyes told it well, leaving Monk no room to hope or to delude himself.

Memories of Runcorn flooded back, of his anger always there, thinly suppressed under his veneer of self-control, the fear showing through, the expectation that somehow, whatever he did, Monk would get the better of him, undermine his authority, find the answer first, make him look foolish or inept.

119

It had become so deep over the years it was no longer a conscious thought but an instinct, like wincing before you are struck.

After the accident Monk had heard fragments about himself here and there and pieced them together, learned things he had wished were not true. The cruel thing was that in the last year or so, surely they no longer were? His tongue was still quick, certainly. He was intolerant. He did not suffer fools – gladly or otherwise! But he was not unjust! Robb was judging him on the past.

'Apparently,' he said aloud, his voice cold. He also knew his reputation for skill. 'Then you should not be surprised that I came to the same conclusion you did and found the same people without having to trail behind you!'

Robb dug his hands into his pockets and his shoulders hunched forward, his body tightening. There was contempt and dislike in his face, but also the awareness of a superior enemy, and a sadness that it should be so, a disappointment.

'You have an advantage over me, Mr Monk. You know my one vulnerability. You must do about it whatever you think fit, but I will not be blackmailed into stepping aside from pursuing whoever murdered James Treadwell – whether it is Mrs Gardiner or not.' He looked at Monk unblinkingly, his brown eyes steady.

Monk felt suddenly sick. Surely he had never been a person who would descend to blackmailing a young man because he took time off his professional duty to attend to the far deeper duty of love towards an old man who was sick and alone, and utterly dependent upon him? He could not believe he had ever been like that – not to pursue any thief or killer; there were other ways – and certainly not to climb another step up the ladder of preferment!

He found his mouth dry and words difficult to form. What

did he want to say? He would not plead, it would be both demeaning and useless.

'What you tell your superiors is your own business,' he replied icily, 'if you tell them anything at all. Personally, I never had such a regard for them that I thought it necessary to explain myself. My work spoke for me.' He sounded arrogant and he knew it. But what he said was true. He had never explained himself to Runcorn, nor ever intended to.

He saw the flash of recognition in Robb's face, and belief.

'And you'll find plenty of sins I've committed,' he went on, his voice biting. 'But you'll not find anyone who knew me stoop to blackmail. You'll not find anyone who damned well thought I needed to!'

Slowly Robb's shoulders relaxed. He still regarded Monk carefully, but the hostility faded from his eyes as the fear loosened its grip on him. He licked his lips. 'I'm sorry – perhaps I underestimated your ability.' That was as far as he would go towards an apology.

It was not ability Monk cared about, it was honour, but there was no point pursuing that now. This was all he was going to get. The question was how to remain within sight of the house so he could follow Mrs Whitbread when she left, and yet at the same time elude Robb so he did not follow them both. And of course that only mattered if the maid at the door did not give Robb the same information she had given to Monk, albeit unwittingly. That might depend on Mrs Whitbread's quickness of thought, and he had no idea what that would be.

He looked at Robb a moment longer, then smiled steadily, bade him farewell, and turned and walked away, in the opposite direction from the house. He would have to circle around and come back, extremely carefully.

* * *

Mrs Whitbread left at a quarter to five. Robb was nowhere to be seen. As Monk followed her at a discreet distance, he felt his weariness suddenly vanish, his senses become keen and a lift of hope inside him.

They had not gone far, perhaps a mile and a quarter, before Mrs Whitbread, a thin, spare woman with a gentle face, turned in at a small house on Kemplay Road, and opened the front door with a key.

Monk waited a few moments, looking both ways and seeing no one, then he crossed and went to the door. He knocked.

After a minute or two it was opened cautiously by Mrs Whitbread. 'Yes?'

He had given much consideration to what he was going to say. It was already apparent Miriam did not wish to be found either by the police or by Lucius Stourbridge. If she had trusted him in this matter she would have contacted him long ago. Either she was afraid he would betray her to the police, or she wanted to protect him.

'Good evening, Mrs Whitbread,' Monk said firmly. 'I have an urgent message from Mrs Anderson – for Miriam. I need to see her immediately.' Cleo Anderson was the one name both women might trust.

She hesitated only a moment, then pulled the door wider.

'You'd better come in,' she said quickly. 'You never know who's watching. I had the rozzers round where I work just today.'

He stepped inside and she closed the door. 'I know. It was I who inadvertently sent them to you. You didn't tell them anything?'

'Course not,' she replied, giving him a withering look. 'Wouldn't trust them an inch. Can't afford to.'

He said nothing, but followed her down the passage and round the corner into the kitchen. Standing at the stove, facing them, eyes wide, was the woman he had come to find. He knew immediately it was Miriam Gardiner. She was just as Lucius had described, barely average height, softly rounded figure, a beautifully proportioned, gentle face but with an underlying strength. At first glance she might have seemed a sweet-natured woman, given to obedience and pleasing those she loved, but there was an innate dignity to her that spoke of something far deeper than mere agreeableness, something untouchable by anything except love. Even in those few moments Monk understood why Lucius Stourbridge was prepared to spend so much heartache searching for her, regardless of the truth of James Treadwell's death.

'Mrs Gardiner,' he said quietly, 'I am not from the police. But nor am I from Mrs Anderson. I lied about that because I feared you would leave before I could speak to you if you knew I came from Lucius Stourbridge.'

She froze, oblivious of the pots on the stove steaming till their lids rattled in the silence that filled the room. Her terror was almost palpable in the air.

Monk was aware of Mrs Whitbread beside him. He saw the fury in her eyes, her body stiff, lips drawn into a thin line. He was grateful the skillet was on the far wall beyond her reach, or he believed she might well have struck him with it.

'I haven't come to try to take you back to Bayswater,' he said quietly, facing Miriam. 'Or the police. If you would prefer that I did not tell Mr Stourbridge where you are, then I will not. I shall simply tell him that you are alive and unhurt. He is desperate with fear for you, and that will offer him some comfort, although hardly an explanation.'

Miriam stared back, her face almost white, an anguish in it that made him feel guilty for what he was doing, and frightened for what he might discover.

'He does not know what to believe,' Monk continued softly,

'except that you could and would do no intentional evil.'

She drew in her breath and her eyes spilled over with tears. She wiped them away impatiently, but it was a moment before she could control herself enough to speak.

'I cannot come back.' It was a statement of absolute. There was no hope in her voice, no possibility of change.

'I can try to keep the police from you,' he replied, as if it were the answer to what she had said. 'But I may not succeed. They are not far behind me.'

Mrs Whitbread walked around him and went over to the stove, taking the pans off it before they boiled over. She looked across at Monk with bitter dislike.

Miriam stepped out of her way, further into the middle of the room.

'What happened?' Monk asked as gently as he could.

She coughed a little, clearing her throat. Her voice was husky. 'Is Cleo – Mrs Anderson – all right?'

'Yes.' There was no purpose in pointing out Cleo Anderson's danger if Robb felt she was concealing information or even that it was not coincidence that had taken Treadwell to her front path.

Miriam seemed to relax a little. A faint tinge of colour returned to her cheeks.

'Where did you last see Treadwell?' he asked.

Her lips tightened and she shook her head a tiny fraction, not so much a denial to him as to herself.

He kept his voice low, patient, as devoid of threat as he could.

'You'll have to answer sometime, if not to me, then to the police. He was murdered, beaten over the head . . .' He stopped. She had turned so ashen-pale he feared she was going to faint. He lunged forward and caught her by the arms, steadying her, pushing her sideways and backwards into the kitchen chair, for a moment supporting her weight until she sank into it.

'Get out!' Mrs Whitbread commanded furiously. 'You get out of here!' She reached for the skillet to use on him.

He stood his ground, but wary of her. 'Put the kettle on,' he ordered. 'Sending me away isn't going to answer this. When the police come, and they will, they'll not come in friendship as I do. All they will want will be evidence, and justice – or what they believe to be justice.'

Miriam closed her eyes. It was all she could do to breathe slowly in and out, or to keep consciousness.

Mrs Whitbread, reluctantly, turned and filled the kettle, putting it on the hob. She eyed Monk guardedly before she took out cups, teapot, and the round tin caddy. Then she went to the larder for milk, her heels tapping on the stone floor.

Monk sat down opposite Miriam.

'What happened?' he asked. 'Where was Treadwell when you last saw him? Was he alive?'

'Yes . . .' she whispered, opening her eyes, but they were filled with horror so deep the words gave him no comfort at all.

'Were you there when he was killed?'

She shook her head, barely an inch.

'Do you know who killed him, or why?'

She said nothing.

Mrs Whitbread came back with a jug of milk in her hand. She glared at Monk, but she did not interrupt. She crossed the floor and tipped a little boiling water into the teapot to warm it.

'Who killed Treadwell?' Monk repeated. 'And why?'

Miriam stared at him. 'I can't tell you,' she whispered. 'I can't tell you anything. I can't come with you. Please go away.

I can't help – there's nothing – nothing I can do.'

There was such a terrible, hopeless pain in her voice the argument died on his lips.

The kettle started to shrill. Mrs Whitbread lifted it off the stove and turned to Monk.

'Go now,' she said levelly, her eyes hard. 'There's nothing for you here. Tell Lucius Stourbridge whatever you have to, but go. If you come back, Miriam won't be here. There's plenty others who'll hide her. If Mr Stourbridge is the friend he says he is, he'll leave well alone. You can see yourself out.' She still held the kettle, steam pouring out of its spout. It wasn't exactly a threat, but Monk did not misunderstand the determination in her.

He rose to his feet, took a last glance at Miriam, then went to the door. Then he remembered Robb, and changed his mind. The back kitchen door probably led to an area for coal or coke, and then an alleyway.

'I'll tell Mr Stourbridge you are alive and well,' he said softly. 'No more than that. But the police won't be far behind me, I know that for certain. I've been dodging them for the last two days.'

Mrs Whitbread understood his thought. She nodded. 'Go left,' she ordered. 'You'll come to the street again. Watch for the ash cans.'

'Was that all she said?' Hester was incredulous when he recounted to her what had happened. They were in the comfortable room where he received clients, and which also served as sitting room. The windows were open to the warm evening air drifting in. There was a rustle of leaves from a tree close by, and in the distance the occasional clip of hoofs from the traffic on the street.

'Yes,' he answered, looking across at her. She was not

sewing, as other women might have been. She did needlework only as necessity demanded. She was concentrating entirely upon what he was saying, her back straight, her shoulders square, her eyes intent upon his face. For all the confusion and tragedy he was aware of, it could not stifle the deep well of satisfaction within him that underlay everything else. She infuriated him at times, they still disagreed over countless things. He could have listed her faults using the fingers of both hands. And yet as long as she was there, he would never be alone, and nothing was beyond bearing.

'What was she like?' she asked.

He was startled. 'Like?'

'Yes,' she said impatiently. 'She didn't give you any explanations! She didn't tell you why she left Kensington? You did ask her, I suppose?'

He had not asked. By that point he already knew she would not tell him.

'You didn't!' Hester's voice rose an octave.

'She refused to tell me anything,' he said clearly. 'Except that she was not there when Treadwell was killed. I don't think she even knew he was dead. When I told her that, she was so horrified she was almost incapable of speech. She all but fainted.'

'So she knows something about it!' Hester said instantly.

That was an unwarranted leap of deduction, and yet he had made exactly the same one. He looked across at her and smiled bleakly.

'So you have learned no new facts,' she said.

'There's the fact that Mrs Whitbread was prepared to fight to defend her, and risk the police coming after her instead,' he pointed out. 'And the fact that almost certainly Robb will find her, sooner or later.' He did not want to tell her about Robb's opinion of him. It was painful, a dark thing he preferred she did not know.

'So what was she like?' she asked again.

He did not make any evasions, or comments on the obscurity of feminine logic.

'I've never seen anyone more afraid,' he said honestly. 'Or more anguished. But I don't believe she will tell me – or anyone else – what happened, or why she is running. Certainly she won't tell Lucius Stourbridge.'

'What are you going to do?' Her voice was little more than a whisper, and her eyes were full of pity.

He realised he had already made his decision.

'I will tell Stourbridge that I found her, and she is alive and well, and that she says she had no part in Treadwell's death, but I will not tell him where she is. I dare say she will not be there by the time I report to him anyway. I warned her that Robb was close behind me.' He did not need to add the risk he took in so doing. Hester knew it.

'Poor woman,' she said softly. 'Poor woman.'

Chapter Five

❧

It was the sixth day of Monk's inquiry into Miriam Gardiner's flight. Hester had gone to sleep thinking about her. She wondered what tragedy had drawn her to such an act that she could not speak of it, even to the man she was to marry.

But it was not that which woke her, shaking and so tense her head throbbed with a stiff, sharp pain. She had an overwhelming sense of fear, of something terrible happening which she was helpless to prevent, and inadequate to deal with. It was not a small thing, or personal to herself, but of all-consuming proportions.

Beside her Monk was asleep, his face relaxed and completely at peace in the clear, early light. He was as oblivious of her as if they had been in separate rooms, different worlds.

It was not the first time she had woken with this feeling of helplessness and exhaustion, and yet she could not remember what she had been dreaming, either now, or before.

She wanted to waken Monk, talk to him, hear him say it was all of no importance, unreal, belonging to the world of sleep. But that would be selfish. He expected more strength from her. He would be disappointed, and she could not bear that. She lay staring at the ceiling, feeling utterly alone, because it was how she had woken, and she could not cast it away. There was something she longed to escape from, and she knew that was impossible. It was everywhere around her.

The light through the chink in the curtains was broadening across the floor. In another hour or so it would be time to get up and face the day. Fill your mind with that, she resolved. It was always better to be busy. There were battles worth fighting, there always were. She would speak to Fermin Thorpe again. The man was impossible to reason with because he was afraid of change, afraid of losing control, and so becoming less important.

It would probably mean more of the interminable letters, few of which ever received a useful answer. How could anyone write so many words which, when disentangled from their dependent clauses and qualifying additions, actually had no meaning left?

Florence Nightingale was confined to her home, some said even to her bed, and spent nearly all her time in writing letters.

Of course hers were highly effective. In the four years since the end of the war she had changed an enormous number of things, particularly to do with the architecture of hospitals. First, naturally, her attention had been upon military hospitals, but she had won that victory, in spite of a change of government and losing her principal ally. Now she was bending her formidable will towards civilian hospitals and, just as Hester was, to the training of nurses. But it was a battle against stubborn and entrenched interests who held great power. Fermin Thorpe was merely one of many, a typical example of senior medical men throughout the country.

And poor Florence's health had declined ever since her

return. Hester found that hard to accept, even to imagine. In Scutari she had seemed inexhaustible – the last sort of woman on earth to succumb to fainting and palpitations, unexplained fevers and general aches and weaknesses. And yet apparently that was now the case! Several times her life had been despaired of. Her family was no longer permitted to visit her in case the emotion of the occasion should prove too much for her. Devoted friends and admirers gave up their own pursuits to look after her until the end should come, and make her last few months on earth as pleasant as possible.

Time and again this had happened. And lately, if anything, she seemed to be recovered and bursting with new and vigorous ideas. She had proposed a school for training nurses, and was systematically attacking the opposition. It was said nothing delighted her as much as a set of statistics which could be used to prove a point about clean water and good ventilation being necessary to the recovery of a patient.

Hester smiled to herself as she remembered Florence in the hot Turkish sun, determinedly ordering an army sergeant to bring his figures on the dead of the past week, their date of admittance to the hospital and the nature of their injuries and cause of death. The poor man had been so exhausted he had not even argued with her. One pointless task was much like another to him; only his pity for his fellows and his sense of decency had made him reluctant to obey. Florence had tried to explain to him, her pale face alight, eyes brilliant, that she could learn invaluable information from such things. Deductions could be made, lessons learned, mistakes addressed and perhaps corrected. People were dying who did not need to; distress was caused which could have been avoided.

The army, like Fermin Thorpe, did not listen. That was

the helplessness which overwhelmed her – injury, disease and death all around, too few of them to care for the sick, ignorance defeating so much of even the little they could have done.

What an insane, monstrous waste! What a mockery of all that was good and happy and beautiful in life!

And here she was, lying warm and supremely comfortable in bed, with Monk asleep beside her. The future stretched out in front of her with as bright a promise as the day already shining, just beyond the curtain. It would be whatever she made of it. Unless she allowed the past to darken it, old memories to cripple her and make her useless.

She still wanted to waken Monk, and talk to him – no, that was not true, what she wanted was that he should talk to her. She wanted to hear his voice, hear the assurance in it, the will to fight, and win.

She would like to get up and do something to take her mind from thinking, but she would disturb him if she did, and that would be the same thing as having deliberately woken him. So she lay still and stared at the patterns of sunlight on the ceiling, until eventually she went back to sleep again.

When she woke the second time it was to find Monk shaking her gently. She felt as if she had climbed up from the bottom of a well, and her head still hurt.

She smiled back at him, and forced herself to be cheerful. If he noticed any artificiality about it, he did not say so. Perhaps he was thinking of Miriam Gardiner already, and still worrying about what he could do to help her, and what he would say to Lucius Stourbridge.

It was mid-morning as Hester was coming down the main corridor that she encountered Fermin Thorpe.

'Oh, good morning, Miss – Mrs Monk,' he said, coming

to a halt so that it was obvious he wished to speak with her.
'How are you today?' He continued immediately so that she
should not interrupt him by replying. 'With regard to your
desire that women should be trained in order to nurse, I have
obtained a copy of Mr J. F. South's book, published three
years ago, which I am sure will be of interest to you, and
enlightenment on the subject.' He smiled at her, meeting her
eyes very directly.

They were passed by a medical student whom he ignored,
an indication of the gravity of his intent.

'You may not be familiar with who he is, so I shall tell you,
so you may correctly judge the importance of his opinion
and give it more weight.' He straightened his shoulders slightly
and lifted his chin. 'He is Senior Consulting Surgeon at St
Thomas's Hospital, and more than that, he is President of
the College of Surgeons, and Hunterian Orator.' He gave the
words careful emphasis so she should not miss any part of
their importance. 'I quote for you, Miss – Mrs Monk, he is –'
his voice became very distinct – ' "not at all disposed to allow
that the nursing establishments of our hospitals are inefficient
or that they are likely to be improved by any special Institution
for Training". As he further points out, even sisters in charge
of wards do, and can, only learn by experience.' He smiled at
her with increasing confidence. 'Nurses themselves are
subordinates, in the position of housemaids, and need only
the simplest of instructions.'

Two nurses passed them, faces flushed with exertion,
sleeves hitched up.

Hester opened her mouth to protest, but he continued,
raising his voice very slightly to override her. 'I am
perfectly aware of Miss Nightingale's Fund for training
young women,' he said loudly. 'But I must inform you,
madam, that only three surgeons and two physicians are

to be found among its supporters. That, surely, is an unfailing mark of the regard in which it is held by professional men who are the most highly qualified and experienced in the country. Now, Mrs Monk,' he pronounced her name with satisfaction at having remembered it, 'I trust you will turn your considerable energies towards the true welfare of both the nurses here, and the patients, and attend to their cleanliness, their sobriety and their obedience to do what they are commanded, both punctually and exactly. Good day.' And without waiting for her reply, which he seemingly took for granted in the affirmative, he strode away purposefully towards the operating theatre, satisfied he had dealt with the subject finally.

Hester was too furious to speak for the first few moments, then when she could have, no words seemed adequate to express her disgust. She marched in the opposite direction towards the physicians' waiting room.

There she found Cleo talking to an old man who was obviously frightened and doing his best to conceal it. He had several open ulcers on both his legs which must have been acutely painful, and looked as if they had been there for some time. He smiled at Cleo but his hands were clenched till his knuckles were white and he sat rigidly upright.

'Yer need 'em dressed reg'lar,' Cleo said gently. 'Gotta keep 'em clean, or they'll never 'eal up. I'll do it for yer, if yer come 'ere an' ask fer me.'

'I can't come 'ere every day,' he answered, his voice polite but with absolute certainty. 'In't possible, miss.'

'In't it, now?' She regarded him thoughtfully, looking down at the worn boots and threadbare jacket. 'Well, I s'pose I'll 'ave ter come ter you, then. Far, is it?'

'An' why would you be doing that?' he asked dubiously.

''Cos them sores in't goin' ter get no better otherwise,' she replied tartly.

'I in't askin' no favours,' he bristled. 'I don't want no nurse woman comin' into my 'ouse! Wot'll the neighbours think o' me?'

Cleo winced. 'That yer damn lucky at yer age to be pullin' a nice-lookin' woman like me!' she snapped back at him.

He smiled in spite of himself. 'But yer can't come all the same.'

She looked down at him patiently. 'Call yerself a soldier, an' can't take orders from someone as knows better'n you do – and don't make no mistake, I'm yer sergeant when it comes ter them sores.'

He drew in his breath, then let it out again without answering.

'Well?' Cleo demanded. 'Yer goin' ter tell me where yer live, or waste me time 'avin' ter find out?'

'Church Row,' he said reluctantly.

'And I'm goin' ter walk up an' down the 'ole lot askin' for yer, am I?' Cleo said with raised eyebrows.

'Number twenty-one.'

'Good! Like drawin' teeth, it is!'

He was not sure whether she was joking or not. He smiled uncertainly.

She smiled back at him, then saw Hester and came over to her, trying to look as if she were not out of composure.

'I in't goin' ter do it in 'ospital time,' she said in a whisper. 'Poor old soul fought at Waterloo, 'e did, an' look at the state of 'im.' Her expression darkened and she forgot the appropriate deference to a social superior. Anger filled her eyes. 'All for soldiers, we was, when we thought them French was gonna invade us an' we could lose. Now forty-five years on we forgotten all about 'ow fit we was, an' 'oo wants ter care for some old man wi' sores all over 'is legs oo's got no money, an' talks about wars we don' know nothin' about?'

Hester thought vividly of the men she had known in Scutari and Sebastopol, and the surgeons' tents after that chaotic charge at Balaclava. They had been so young, and in such terrible pain. It was their ashen faces that had filled her dreams last night. She could see them sharp in her mind's eye. Those that had survived would be old men in forty years' time. Would people remember them then? Or would a new generation be accustomed to peace, and resentful and bored by old soldiers who carried the scars and the pain of old wars?

'See that he's cared for,' Hester said quietly. 'That's what matters. Do it whenever you wish.'

Cleo stared back at her, eyes widening a little; uncertain for a moment whether to believe her. They barely knew each other. Here they had one purpose, but they went home to different worlds.

'Those debts cannot ever be understood,' Hester answered her. 'Let alone paid.'

Cleo stood still.

'I was at Scutari,' Hester explained.

'Oh . . .' It was just a single word, less than a word, but there was understanding in it, and profound respect. She nodded a little and went to the next patient.

Hester left the room again. She was in the mood now to see that moral standards were observed and that every nurse was clean, neat, punctual and sober.

As she went back along the corridor she was passed by a nurse just arriving, her shawl still on.

'You're late!' Hester said tartly. 'Don't do it again!'

The woman was startled. 'No, ma'am,' she said obediently, and hurried on, head down, pulling off the shawl as she went.

Just outside the apothecary's room Hester passed a young

medical student, unshaven and his jacket flapping open.

'You are untidy, sir!' she said with equal tartness. 'How do you expect your patients to have confidence in you when you look as if you had slept in your clothes and come in with the first post? If you aspire to be a gentleman, then you had better look like one!'

He was so startled he did not reply to her, but stood motionless as she swept past him and on to the surgeons' waiting rooms.

She spent the morning attempting to comfort and hearten the men and women awaiting care. She had not forgotten Florence Nightingale's stricture that the mental pain of a patient could be at least equal to the physical, and it was a good nurse's task to dispel doubt and lift spirits wherever possible. A cheerful countenance was invaluable, as was pleasant conversation and a willingness to listen with sympathy and optimism.

By the end of the morning she sat down at the staff dining-room table with gratitude for an hour's respite. Within fifteen minutes Callandra joined her. For once her hair was safely secured within its pins and her skirt and well-tailored jacket matched each other. Only her expression spoiled the effect. She looked deeply unhappy.

'What is it?' Hester asked as soon as Callandra had made herself reasonably comfortable in the hard-backed chair but not yet begun her slice of veal pie, which seemed to hold little interest for her.

'There is more medicine gone,' Callandra said so quietly she was barely audible. 'There is no possible doubt. I hate to think of anyone systematically stealing the amounts we are dealing with, but there can be no other explanation.' Her face tightened, her lips in a thin line. 'Just think what Thorpe will make of it, apart from anything else!'

'I've already had words with him this morning,' Hester replied, ignoring her own plate of cold mutton and new potatoes. 'He was quoting Mr South at me. I didn't even have a chance to reply to him – not that I had anything to say. Now I want to ask him if we couldn't make some sort of particular provision for the men who fought for us in the past and who are now old and ill.'

Callandra frowned. 'What sort of provision?'

'I don't know.' Hester grimaced. 'I suppose this is not a fortunate time to suggest we provide their medicine and bandages from the hospital budget?'

'We already do,' Callandra said with surprise.

'Only if they come here,' Hester pointed out. 'Some of them can't come every day. They are too old or ill, or lame, to use an omnibus. And a hansom costs far too much, even if they could climb into one of them.'

'Who could give them medicines at home?' Callandra asked, curiosity and the beginning of understanding in her eyes.

'Us,' Hester replied instantly. 'It wouldn't need a doctor, only a nurse with experience and confidence – someone trained!'

'And trustworthy,' Callandra added purposefully.

Hester sighed. The spectre of the stolen medicines would not leave. They could not keep the knowledge of it from Fermin Thorpe much longer. It was ugly, dishonest, an abuse of every kind of trust, both of the establishment of the hospital and of the other nurses, who would all be branded with the same stigma of thieving. It was also a breach of honour towards the patients for whom they were intended.

'It's a circular argument, isn't it?' she said with a thread of despair. 'Until we get trained women who are dedicated to an honourable calling and treated with respect and properly rewarded, we won't be able to stop this sort of thing happening all the time. And as long as it does, people, especially those like Thorpe – and that seems to be most of the medical establishment – will treat nurses as the worst class of housemaid.'

Callandra pulled her mouth into a grimace of disgust. 'I don't know any housemaid that wouldn't take that as an insult – possibly even give notice – if you compared her with a nurse.'

'Which is a complete summary of what we are fighting!' Hester replied, taking half a potato and a nice piece of cold mutton.

'The Nightingale School is just about to open.' Callandra made a visible effort to look more hopeful. 'But I believe they had great trouble finding suitable applicants. A very high moral standard is required, and total dedication, of course. The rules are almost as strict as a nunnery.'

'They don't call them "sisters" for nothing,' Hester answered with a flash of humour.

But there were other issues pressing on her mind. She had thought again of Sergeant Robb's grandfather sitting alone, unable to care for himself, dependent upon Robb to take time from his work. It must be a burden of fear and obligation to him.

And how many other old men were there, ill and poor now, who were victims of wars the young did not remember? And old women too, perhaps widows of men who had not come home, or those who were unmarried because the men who would have been their husbands were dead?

She leaned a little over the table. 'Would it not be possible to create a body of some sort who could visit those people . . . at least see to the more obvious troubles, advise when a doctor was needed . . .'

The look on Callandra's face stopped her. 'You are

dreaming, my dear,' she said gently. 'We have not even achieved proper nurses for the poor law infirmaries attached to the workhouses, and you want to have nurses to visit the poor in their homes? You are fifty years before your time. But it's a good dream.'

'What about some form of infirmary especially for men who have lost their health fighting our wars?' Hester persisted. 'Isn't that something at least honour demands, if nothing else?'

'If honour got all it demanded this would be a very different world.' Callandra ate the last of her pie. 'Perhaps enlightened self-interest might have a greater chance of success.'

'How?' Hester asked instantly.

Callandra looked at her. 'The best nursing reforms so far have been within army hospitals, due almost entirely to Miss Nightingale's work.' She was thinking as she spoke, her brow furrowed. 'New buildings have been designed with cleaner water, better ventilation and far less crowded wards . . .'

'I know.' Hester disregarded her plate, waiting for the suggestion which would link the two.

'I am sure Mr Thorpe would like to be thought of as enlightened . . .' Callandra continued.

Hester grimaced but did not interrupt again.

'. . . without taking any real risks,' Callandra concluded. 'A poor law infirmary for old soldiers would seem a good compromise.'

'Of course it would!' Hester agreed. 'Except that it would have to be called something else. A good many soldiers would rather die than be seen as accepting parish charity. And they shouldn't have to! We owe them that much at least.' She pushed her chair back and stood up. 'But I shall be very tactful when I speak to Mr Thorpe.'

'Hester!' Callandra called after her urgently, but Hester

was already at the door, and if she heard her she showed no sign of it. A moment later Callandra was staring at the empty room.

'Impossible,' Thorpe said without hesitation. 'Quite out of the question. There are workhouses to care for the indigent—'

'I'm not talking about indigent, Mr Thorpe.' Hester kept her voice level, but it required effort. 'I am thinking of men who obtained their injuries or damage to their health fighting in the Peninsula War, or at great battles like Quatre-Bras or Waterloo . . .'

He frowned. 'Quatre-Bras? What are you talking about?' he asked impatiently.

'It was immediately before Waterloo,' she explained, knowing she sounded patronising. 'It was not a matter of fighting to extend the Empire then, we were fighting to save ourselves from invasion and becoming a subject people—'

'I do not require a history lesson, Mrs Monk,' he said irritably. 'They did their duty, as we all do. I am sure that for a young woman, there is a certain glamour attached to the uniform, and one makes heroes of them—'

'No one makes a hero of someone else, Mr Thorpe,' she corrected him. 'I am concerned with the injured and ill who need our help, and I believe have a right to expect it. I am sure that as a patriot and a Christian, you will agree with that.'

A variety of emotions flickered across his face, conflicting with each other, but he would not deny her assessment of him, even if he suspected it contained a powerful element of sarcasm.

'Of course,' he agreed reluctantly. 'I shall take it under advisement. I am sure it is something we would all wish to do, if it should prove possible.' His face set in a mask of finality.

He would no longer argue with her, he would simply lie. Certainly he would consider it – indefinitely.

She knew she was beaten, at least in this skirmish. As many times as she came to him he would smile, agree with her, and say he was exploring avenues of possibility. And she would never prove him wrong. She had an overwhelming insight into the obstruction faced by Florence Nightingale, and why she had taken to her bed with exhaustion, fever, difficulties of the digestion, and such a fire of the mind as to consume the strength of her body.

Hester smiled back at Fermin Thorpe. 'I am sure you will succeed,' she lied as well. 'A man who is skilled enough to run a hospital the size of this one so very well, will be able to exert the right influence and put forward all the moral and social arguments to persuade others of the rightness of such a cause. If you could not, then you would hardly be the man for Hampstead . . . would you?' She would not have dared say such a thing were she dependent upon his good will for earning a roof over her head – but she was not! She was a married woman with a husband to provide for her. She was here as a lady volunteer – like Callandra – not a paid worker. It was a wonderful feeling, almost euphoric. She was free to battle him unhampered . . . as she most certainly would.

The flush in his cheeks deepened. 'I am glad you appreciate my position, Mrs Monk,' he said with tight jaw. 'I have not always been so certain that you were fully mindful that I do indeed run this hospital.'

'I am sorry for that,' she answered. 'One has but to look around one to see the standard of efficiency.'

He blinked, aware of the double meaning implied. His tone was infinitely condescending. 'I am sure you are a good-hearted woman, but I fear your lack of understanding of finance hampers your judgement as to what is possible. For instance, the cost of medicines is far greater than you probably appreciate, and we are unfortunate in suffering a considerable degree of pilfering from morally unworthy staff.' He opened his eyes very wide. 'If you were to direct your attentions towards the honesty and sobriety of the nurses here, we would lose far less, and consequently then have more to give to the sick who rely upon us. Turn your energies towards that, Mrs Monk, and you will do the greatest service. Honesty! That will save the sick from their diseases, and the morally destitute from the wages of sin, both spiritual and temporal.' He smiled. He was well satisfied with that.

Hester made a tactical retreat, before he could further pursue the question of missing medicines.

She had already made up her mind to call upon John Robb to see if there was anything she could do to help him. She could not forget Monk's description of his distress, and that was at least one thing she could accomplish regardless of Fermin Thorpe's power.

It was a fine summer afternoon, and not a long walk to the street where Monk had said Robb lived. She did not know the number, but only one enquiry was necessary to discover the answer.

The houses were all clean and shabby, some with whited steps, others merely well swept. She debated whether to knock or not. From what Monk had said, the old man could not rise to answer, and yet to walk in unannounced was a terrible intrusion into the privacy of a man too ill to defend even his own small space.

She settled for standing in the doorway and calling out his name. She waited a few moments in silence, then called again.

'Who is it?' The voice was a deep, soft rumble.

'My name is Hester . . . Monk.' She had so very nearly said 'Latterly'. She was not used to it yet. 'My husband called on you the other day.' She must not make him feel pitied, a suitable case for charity. It would be so easy to do with a careless phrase. 'He spoke of you so well, I wished to call upon you myself.'

'Your husband? I don't remember . . .' He started to cough and it became worse so quickly that she abandoned politeness, pushed the door open and went in.

The room was small and cluttered with furniture, but it was clean and as tidy as possible when it was occupied all the time and the necessities of life had to be kept available.

She went straight over to the sink and found a cup, filled it with water from the ewer standing on the bench, and took it over to him, holding it to his lips. There was little else she could do for him. His body shuddered as he gasped for breath and she could hear the rattling of phlegm in his chest, but it was too deep for him to bring up.

After a minute or two it subsided, more rapidly than she had expected, and he took the water from her gratefully, sipping it and letting it slide down his throat. He handed her back the cup.

'Sorry, miss,' he said huskily. 'Touch o' the bronchitis. Silly this time o' the year.'

'It can happen any time, if you are subject to it,' she answered, smiling at him. 'Sometimes in the summer it's worse. Harder to get rid of.'

'You're surely right,' he agreed, nodding slightly. He was still pale and his cheeks a little flushed. She guessed he probably had a low fever.

'What can I do for you, miss? If you' re looking for my grandson, he isn't here. He's a policeman, and he's at work. Very good he is too. A sergeant.' His pride was obvious, but far more than that, a kind of shining certainty that had nothing to do with the nature of his work, but the nature of the man.

'It was you I came to see,' she reminded him. She must find a reason he would accept. 'He said you were a sailor and had seen some great days – some of the most important battles in England's history.'

He looked at her sideways. 'An' what would a young lady like you want with stories of old battles what was over and won before you were even born?'

'If they were over and lost, I'd be speaking French,' she replied, meeting his eyes with a laugh.

'Well . . . I s'pose that's true. Still, you know that without coming all the way here to see me!' He was faintly suspicious of her.

Hester immediately understood. Young women of educated speech and good manners did not casually call by on an old and ill sailor who, from the contents of the room, was having desperate trouble finding sufficient money merely to eat; let alone buy fuel for the winter, or clothes for when these wore out, which would not be long.

A portion of the truth was the best answer, perhaps not as irrelevant as it first seemed.

'I was an army nurse in the Crimea,' she told him. 'I know more about war than you may think. I don't imagine I've seen as many battles as you have, but I've seen my share, and closer than I'd wish. I've certainly been part of what happens afterwards.' Suddenly she was speaking with urgency, and the absolute and fiercely relevant truth. 'And there is no one I know with whom I can discuss it, or bring back the miseries that still come into my dreams. No one expects it in a woman. They think it all better forgotten . . . easier. But it isn't always . . .'

He stared at her, his eyes wide. They were clear, pale blue. They had probably been darker when he was young.

'Well, now . . . did you really? And you such a slip of a thing!' He regarded her rather too slender body and square, thin shoulders, but with admiration, not disapproval. 'We found at sea, sometimes the wiry ones outlasted the great big ones like a side o' beef. I reckon strength, when it comes to it, is all a matter o' spirit.'

'You're quite right,' she agreed. 'Would you like a hot drink now? I can easily make one if you would. It might ease your chest a little.' Then, in case he thought she was patronising him: 'I should like very much to talk with you, and I can't if you are taken with coughing again.'

He understood very well what she was doing, but she had softened the request sufficiently. 'You're a canny one,' he smiled at her, pointing to the stove. 'Kettle's over there, and tea in the tin. Little milk in the larder, maybe. Could be we're out, till Michael comes home again.'

'Doesn't matter,' she replied, standing up. 'It's all right without milk, if it isn't too strong.'

She was scalding the pot ready to make the tea when the door opened and she turned to see a young man standing just inside the room. He was of average height, slender, with very handsome dark eyes. At this moment he was obviously angry.

'Who are you?' he demanded, coming further in. 'And what are you doing?' He left the door open behind him, as if for her to leave the more easily.

'Hester Monk,' she replied, looking at him squarely. 'I called upon Mr Robb to visit with him. We have much in common, and he was kind enough to listen to me. In order that he might speak with more comfort, he permitted me to make a cup of tea.'

The young man looked at her with total disbelief. From the expression in his eyes one might have presumed he thought she was here to steal the meagre rations on the shelf behind her.

'What on earth could you have in common with my grandfather?' he said grimly.

'It's all right, Michael,' the old man intervened. 'I'd fairly like to watch her take you on. Reckon as she might have the best of you, with her tongue, anyroad. Crimean nurse, she is! Seen more battles than you have – like me. She don't mean no harm.'

Michael looked uncertainly at the old man, then back at Hester. She respected his protectiveness of his grandfather and hoped she would have done the same had she been in his place. And she was unquestionably an intruder. But old Robb should not be treated like a child, even if he was physically all but helpless. She must refrain from defending his judgement now, though the words were on the end of her tongue.

The old man looked at Hester, a glint in his eye. 'Wouldn't mind getting another cup, would you, miss?'

'Of course not,' Hester said demurely, lifting the last cup from its hook on the shelf that served as a dresser. She finished scalding the pot, put in a meagre portion of leaves, then poured on the boiling water, keeping her back to Michael. She heard the door close and his footsteps across the floor.

He came up behind her, his voice very low. 'Did Monk send you here?'

'No.' She was about to add that Monk did not 'send' her anywhere, but on reflection, that was not true. He had frequently sent her to various places to enquire into one thing or another. 'So far as I know, he has no idea I am here. I remembered what he said to me of Mr Robb, and I felt that I wished to visit him. I have no intention of taking anything that belongs to you, Sergeant Robb, or of doing your grandfather any harm, either by meddling, or by patronising him. Nor am I interested in your police concerns with Mrs Gardiner.'

He blushed painfully, but his eyes remained sharp and steady, and considerable animosity in them.

'You are direct to a fault, ma'am.'

She smiled suddenly. 'Yes – I know. Would you rather I beat around the bush a little more? I can go back and make ten minutes' obscure conversation of it if you wish? Well – perhaps five . . .'

'No, I would not!' In spite of himself his voice rose. 'I—'

Whatever else he had been about to say was cut short by the old man beginning to cough again. He had struggled forward half out of his chair, and he was in considerable distress, his face flushed and already beads of sweat on his lip and brow.

Michael swung around and rushed towards him, catching him in his arms and easing him back into the chair. For the moment Hester was completely forgotten.

The old man was fighting for breath, trying desperately to drag the air into his damaged lungs, his whole body racked with violent spasms. He brought up great gobbets of phlegm, dark yellow and spotted with blood.

Hester had already guessed how seriously ill he was, but this was agonising confirmation. She wished that there was something she could do, but at least until the coughing subsided he was beyond all assistance except the physical support Michael was giving him.

If they had been at the hospital she could have got him a tiny dose of morphine which would have calmed the wrenching lungs and given him the opportunity to rest. Sherry and water would have been good as a restorative. She looked around the shelves to see what there was, her mind racing to think of a way of giving him what he lacked, without hurting his pride. She knew perfectly well that anxiety could make ill, fear could destroy the passion to survive. Humiliation and the conviction that one was useless, a burden to those one loved, had precipitated the death of many a person who might well have recovered, had they perceived themselves as valuable.

She saw bread and cheese, three eggs, a carefully covered piece of cold beef, some raw vegetables and a slice of pie. It was not much to feed two men. Perhaps Michael Robb bought his lunch while on duty. On the other hand, he very possibly sacrificed much of his own welfare to care for his grandfather, but in such a way that the old man was unaware of it.

There was a closed cupboard and she hesitated, reluctant to intrude any further. Was there some way that she could get Kristian Beck to come and visit Mr Robb, and then prescribe morphine for him? He was too old and his illness too far progressed for treatment to accomplish anything beyond alleviating his distress, but surely that was a side of medicine which was just as important. Many things could not be cured. No nurse worth her calling abandoned such cases.

What was there she could find in the meantime? Even hot tea alone might soothe, as soon as he could master himself enough to drink it. Then she saw a small jar of clear honey.

She poured a cup for him, added the honey and sufficient cold water to make it drinkable, and carried it over, waiting for a moment's ease in his coughing. Then she stepped in front of Michael and held the cup to the old man's lips.

'Take a sip,' she told him. 'It will help.'

Fumblingly he obeyed, and perhaps the honey soothed the spasms of his throat, because his body eased and he began to relax, sipping again, and then again. It seemed as if for the moment at least, the attack was over.

She took the cup away and set it down, then went back to the sink and found a bowl that would serve for washing, poured the rest of the water from the kettle into it and automatically put more on to heat. She added a little cold, tested it with her hand, and with a cloth and a towel, returned to the old man's chair.

He was exhausted and very pale, but far calmer. The fact that he had been for a while unable to control himself was obviously an embarrassment to him.

Michael stood anxiously, aware of the emotions, angry and protective. This should have been private, and Hester was an intruder.

Hester wrung out the cloth in the hot water and gently bathed the old man's face, then his neck, then as he did not protest, unfastened his shirt and took it off, very aware of Michael's eyes on her. Wringing out the cloth every few moments, she bathed the old man's arms and body. All the time she did not speak, and neither did they.

Once Michael had ascertained what she was doing, and that his grandfather was eased by it rather than further discomforted, he went to find a clean shirt and returned carrying it. It was rough-dried, but it smelled fresh and was quite soft to the touch. Hester helped the old man into it, then took away the bowl of water and emptied it outside down the drain.

She came back into the room to find Robb smiling at her, the hectic colour fading from his cheeks, and Michael still guarded, but less aggressive.

'Thank you, miss,' Robb said a little anxiously. 'I'm real sorry to have put you out.'

'You didn't.' She smiled. 'I still hope in time we may talk, and you will tell me tales of things I've only imagined.'

'I can that,' he agreed with a return of enthusiasm.

'Another day,' Michael cut across. 'You're tired . . .'

'I'm all right,' Robb insisted. 'Don't you worry yourself, Michael. I told you, this lady here's one o' them Crimean

150

nurses, so I reckon she knows all she needs to about the sick. You go back to your watch, lad. I know there's important things only you can do.' He looked at him steadily, his voice getting stronger, a touch of old authority back again. 'Don't you be worrying.'

Michael hesitated. He looked at Hester, frowning a little, his lips drawn tight.

'I appreciate your kindness, Mrs Monk.' He hesitated, the battle within him clear in his face. 'And I'm sure my grandfather will enjoy your company.'

'And I his,' Hester replied. 'I shall look forward to coming by whenever I am able to. I am frequently at the hospital not far away. It is no journey at all.'

'Thank you.' He must be sensitive to what a relief it would be to the old man to have company and assistance he could look forward to, without the anxiety of knowing that he was keeping Michael from his job, and every minute spent here was in some essence a risk for him. But he was still angry beneath the gratitude, for all its sincerity.

'It is not a trouble,' Hester repeated.

Michael moved towards the door, indicating that she should go with him.

'Goodbye, Grandpa,' he said gently. 'I'll try not to be late.'

'Don't worry,' Robb assured him again. 'I'll be all right.' They were brave words, and he said them as if they could be true, although they all knew they might not be.

Just outside on the step Michael lowered his voice and fixed Hester with an intense stare.

'You're a good nurse, Mrs Monk, and I surely appreciate the way you look after him, better than I can. And you didn't make him feel like it's charity. You've got a way with you. I suppose that comes from being out at the war, and all that.'

'It also comes from liking him,' she replied honestly.

There was no indication in his eyes as to whether he believed her.

'But don't be thinking anything you do here will make a difference because it won't,' he went on levelly. 'I won't stop looking for Miriam Gardiner. And when I find her, which I will, if she's guilty of killing James Treadwell, I'll arrest her and charge her, whatever you do for my grandfather.' His face tightened even more, his voice a little hoarse. 'And whether you tell the police station or not.' He coloured slightly, 'And if that insults you, I'm sorry.'

'I'm used to being insulted, Sergeant Robb,' she replied, surprised at how much the suggestion hurt. 'But I admit, this is a totally new manner of saying my work is worthless, incompetent or generally of morally questionable nature.'

'I didn't mean—' he began, then bit the words back, the pink deepening in his cheeks.

'Yes you did,' she contradicted him, making the most of his embarrassment. 'But I suppose I can understand it. You must feel very vulnerable, coming away from your post to care for your grandfather. I swear to you that I have no motive for being here, except to offer him some care, according to my profession, and to talk with him over old memories I can share with no one who has not had the experiences from which they spring. You must believe me or not, as circumstances prove me.' And without waiting to see his response, she turned and went back in through the door, leaving it ajar behind her for the warm air to come in. She was only half aware of Michael's footsteps as he walked away.

Hester remained far longer than she had originally intended. To begin with she had talked comparatively little, answering a few questions about what life had been like for her in the hospital at Scutari, and even describing Florence

Nightingale. Robb was interested to hear about her, what she looked like, her demeanour, her voice, even her manner of dress. Such was her reputation that the smallest details held his attention. Hester was happy to answer, feeling memory so sharp she could almost smell the blood and vinegar again, and the sickening odour of gangrene and the other acrid stenches of disease. She could feel the summer heat and hear the buzzing of flies, as if the mild English sun coming in through the windows were the same, and it would be a Turkish street outside.

Halfway through the afternoon Mr Robb fell asleep, and she was able to stand up and tidy the kitchen space a little, ready to prepare him another cup of tea, should he want it. She would certainly welcome one herself, milk or no milk to go with it. She considered going out to purchase some, but decided not to. It would be a slight to his hospitality, a small and needless hurt. It was perfectly adequate without.

She tried the closed cupboard, to see if there were anything in it which might help him should he have another attack, any herbal leaves such as camomile to settle the stomach, or feverfew to help headache or even a little quinine to reduce temperatures. She was pleased to find all those things, and also a small packet suggesting morphine to her. A taste on a moistened finger confirmed it. This was quite a respectable medicine cabinet, too accurate to his needs to be collected by an amateur, or by chance, and too expensive to have been met out of a police sergeant's pay, except by the most desperate economies elsewhere.

She closed the cupboard silently and stood facing the room, her mind whirling. Morphine was one of the principal medicines missing from the hospital. She had assumed, as everyone else had, that it was taken for addicts who had been given it for pain, and now could not survive without it. But perhaps it was taken to heal the sick who could not come to the hospital, people like John Robb. Certainly it was theft, but she could not find it in herself to disapprove of it.

The question that burned in her mind was who had brought the medicines and did Michael Robb know? Was that, even in part, the cause of his concern at her being here?

She did not believe it. Intelligence told her it was possible, instinct denied it without consideration.

The old man himself, so peacefully asleep in the afternoon sun, undoubtedly must know who had brought them, but would he know they might be stolen? He might guess, but she thought it unlikely. She would not ask him. There was no decision to make. The question did not arise that she should pursue it. She sat down and waited patiently until he should awaken, then she would make him tea again, with a little more honey. It would be a good idea to bring him a further supply, to make up for what she had drunk herself.

He awoke greatly refreshed, and delighted to find her still there. He started to talk straight away, not even waiting while she served tea and brought it for them both.

'You asked about my sailing days,' he said cheerfully. 'Well o' course the greatest o' them was the battle, weren't it?' He looked at her expectantly, his eyes bright.

'The battle?' she asked, turning around to face him.

'C'mon, girl! There's only one battle for a sailor – only one battle for England – really for England, like!'

She smiled at him. 'Oh . . . you mean Trafalgar?'

'Course I mean Trafalgar! You're teasin' me, aren't you? You've gotta be.'

'You were at Trafalgar! Really?' She was impressed, and she allowed it to show in her voice and her eyes.

'Surely I was. Never forget that, if I live to be a hundred – which I won't. Great day that was . . . an' terrible too. I reckon there's bin none other like it, nor won't be again.'

She poured the water on to the tea. 'What ship were you on?'

'Why, *Victory*, o' course.' He said it with pride in his voice so sharp and clear that for a moment she could hear in it the young man he had been over half a century ago, when England had been on the brink of invasion by Napoleon's armies, and nothing stood between them and conquest, except the wooden walls of the British fleet, and the skill and bravado of Horatio Nelson and the men who sailed with him. She felt a stirring of the same pride in herself, a shiver of excitement and knowledge of the cost, because she too had seen battle and knew its reality as well as its dream.

She brought the tea over to him and offered him a cup. He took it, and his eyes met hers over the rim.

'I was there,' he said softly. 'I remember that morning like it were yesterday. First signal come in about six. That was on the nineteenth of October. Enemy had their tops'l yards hoisted. Least that's what we heard later. Then they were coming out o' port under sail. Half-past nine and bright light over the sea when we heard it on *Victory*.' He shook his head. 'All day we tacked and veered around towards Gibraltar, but we never saw 'em. Visibility was poor – you got to understand that. Weather gettin' worse all the time. Under close-reefed topsails, we were, an' too close to Cadiz.'

Hester nodded, sipping her tea, not interrupting.

'Admiral gave the signal to wear and come northwest, back to our first position. Next day, that was, you see?'

'Yes, I see. I know the battle was on the twenty-first.'

He nodded again, appreciation in his face. 'By dawn o' the twenty-first the Admiral had it exactly right. Twenty-one miles north by west o' Cape Trafalgar, we were, and to windward o' the enemy.' His eyes were smiling, shining blue, like the sea that historic day. 'I can smell the salt in the air,' he said softly, screwing up his face as if the glare of the water blinded him still. 'Ordered us into two columns and make full sail.'

She did not speak.

He was smiling, his tea forgotten. 'Made a notch on me gun, I did, like the man next to me. He was an Irishman, I remember. The Admiral came around all of us. He asked what we were doin'. The Irishman told him we were making a mark for another victory, like all the others, just in case he fell in the battle. Nelson laughed, an' said as he would make notches enough in the enemy's ships.

'About eleven in the morning the Admiral went below to pray, and wrote in his diary, as we learned afterwards. Then he came up to be with us all. That was when he had the signal run up.' He smiled and shook his head, as if some thought consumed him. 'He was going to say "Nelson confides", but Lieutenant Pascoe told him that "expects" was in the Popham code, an' he didn't have to spell it out letter by letter. So what he sent was "England expects that every man will do his duty."' He gave a little shrug, looking at her to make sure she knew how those words had become immortal. He saw it in her face, and was satisfied.

'I don't really know what happened in the lea column,' he went on, still looking at her, but his eyes already sea blue and far away, his inner vision filled with the great ships, sails billowing in the wind high up masts that scraped the sky, coming around to fire on the enemy, men at the ready, muscles taut, silent by their guns, the decks behind them painted red, not to show the blood when the slaughter began.

She could see in his eyes and the curve of his lips the memory of a sharper light than this English summer, the pitch of the deck as the ship hit the waves, the waiting, and then the roar and slam of cannon-fire, the smell of saltpetre, the sting of smoke in the eyes and nose.

'You can't imagine the noise,' he said so softly it was almost a whisper. 'Make them train engines they got now sound like silence. Gunner, I was, an' a good one. Nobody knows how many broadsides we fired that day. But it was about half-past one that the Admiral was hit. Pacing the quarterdeck, he was. With the Captain – Captain Hardy.' He screwed up his face. 'There was some idiots as says he was paradin' with a chest full o' medals. They haven't been in a sea battle! Anyway, when he was at sea he never dressed like that! Shabby, he was, wore an ordinary blue jacket, like anyone else. He wore sequin copies of his orders, but if you ever spent time at sea, you'd know they tarnish in a matter o' days.' He shook his head in denial again. 'And you couldn't hardly see anybody to make 'em out clear during a battle. Smoke everywhere. Could miss your own mother not a dozen feet from you!' He stopped for a few minutes to catch his breath.

Hester thought of offering him more tea, fresh and hot, but she could see that memory was more important, so she sat and waited.

He resumed his story, telling her of the knowledge of victory, and the crushing grief felt by the entire fleet when they knew Nelson was dead. Then of the other losses, the ships and the men gone, the wounded, the securing of the prizes, and then the storm which had arisen and caused even further devastation. He described it in simple, vivid words and his emotion was as sharp as if it had all happened weeks ago, not fifty-five years.

He told of putting Nelson's body in a cask of brandy to preserve it, so it could be buried in England, as he had wished.

'Just a little man, he was. Up to my chin, no more,' he said with a fierce sniff. 'Funny that. We won the greatest victory at sea ever – saved our country from invasion – an' we came

home with flags lowered, like we lost – because he were dead.'
He fell silent for some time.

Hester rose and boiled the kettle again, resetting the tray
and making a light supper for him with a piece of pie cut into
a thin slice, and fresh hot tea.

After he had eaten it with some pleasure, he told her of
Nelson's funeral and how all London had turned out to wish
him a last farewell.

'Buried in a special coffin, he was,' he added with pride.
'Plain an' simple, like death, or the sea. Made from wood
taken from the wreckage of the French flagship at the Battle
of the Nile. Pleased as punch when Hallowell gave it to him
way back, he was. Kept it all those years. Laid in the Painted
Hall in Greenwich Hospital. First mourners come on January
the fourth.' He smiled with supreme satisfaction. 'Prince o'
Wales hisself.'

He took a deep breath and let it out in a rasping cough,
but held up his hand to prevent her interrupting him. 'Laid
there four days. While all the world went by to pay their
respects. Then we took him up the river, on Wednesday
morning. The coffin was placed on one of the royal barges
made for King Charles the Second, an' all covered over in
black velvet, with black ostrich plumes, and went in a flotilla
up to London. Eleven other barges, there were, all the livery
companies with their banners flying. Never seen so much
gold and colour. Stiff wind that day, too. Fired the guns every
minute, all the way up to Whitehall Stairs.'

He stopped again, blinking hard, but he could not keep
the tears from spilling over and running down his cheeks.

'Next day we took him to St Paul's. Great procession, but
mostly army. Only navy there was us – from *Victory* herself.'
His voice cracked, but it was pride as well as grief. 'I was one
of them what carried our battle ensigns. We opened them up

now and again, so the crowd could see the shot holes in them. They all took their hats off as we passed. It made a sound like the noise of the sea.' He rubbed his hand across his cheek. 'There isn't anything I'd take this side o' heaven to trade places with any man alive who wasn't there.'

'I wouldn't understand it if you did,' she answered, smiling at him and unashamed to be weeping too.

He nodded slowly. 'You're a good girl. You know what it means, don't you!' That was a statement, not a question. He drew in his breath as if to thank her, then knew it was unnecessary, even inappropriate. It would have implied debt, and there was none.

Before she could say anything in answer the door opened and Michael Robb came in. Only then did she realise how long she had been there. It was early evening. The shadows of the sun were long across the floor and touched with a deeper colour. She felt a warmth of self-consciousness wash up her face. Automatically she stood up.

Michael's disapproval and alarm were too obvious to hide. He saw the tears on the old man's face and turned to glare at Hester.

'I had the best afternoon in years,' Robb said gently, looking up at his grandson. 'She kept me real company. We talked about all sorts o' things. I've got a kind o' peace inside me. Come, sit down and have a cup o' tea. You look like your feet hurt, boy, and you're mortal tired.'

Michael hesitated, confusion filling his face. He looked from one to the other of them, then finally accepted that his grandfather was telling the truth about his pleasure, and Hester really had given him a rare gift of companionship, unspoiled by duty or the seeking of recompense. A wide smile of relief lit his face, cutting through the weariness and showing for a moment the youth he wanted to be.

'Yes,' he agreed vehemently. 'Yes, I would.' He turned to Hester. 'Thank you, Mrs Monk.' His eyes shadowed. 'I'm sorry . . . I found Miriam Gardiner.'

Hester felt a sudden coldness inside. The sweetness of the moment before was gone.

'I had to arrest her for Treadwell's murder,' he finished, watching her to see her reaction.

'Why?' she protested. 'Why on earth would Miriam Gardiner murder the coachman? If she wanted to escape from Lucius Stourbridge, for whatever reason, all she had to do was have Treadwell leave her somewhere. He would never have known where she went after that!' She drew in her breath. 'And if she simply went somewhere near her home, Lucius would know more about that than Treadwell anyway.'

Michael looked as if the answer gave him no pleasure, barely even any satisfaction. He would probably dearly like to have taken off his boots which were no doubt tight and hot after the long day, but her presence prevented him. 'The most obvious reason is that Treadwell knew something about her which would have ruined her prospects of marriage into the Stourbridge family,' he answered. 'I dare say she loved young Mr Stourbridge, but whether she did or not, there's a great deal of money to it, more than she'll even have seen in her life.'

Hester wanted to protest that Miriam had no regard for the money, but she did not know if that were true. She had impressions, feelings, but barely any real knowledge.

She walked over to the kettle, refilled it from the ewer which was now almost empty, and set it on the stove again.

'I'm sorry,' Michael said wearily, sinking into the chair. 'It's too plain to ignore. The two of them left the Stourbridge house together. They came as far as Hampstead Heath. His body was found, and she ran away. Surely any innocent person

160

would have stayed, or at least come back and reported what had happened.'

She thought quickly. 'What if they were both attacked by someone else, and she was too afraid of them to tell anyone what happened?'

He looked at her doubtfully. 'So afraid that even when we arrested her, she still wouldn't say?' His voice denied his belief in it.

'Do you know this Miriam Gardiner, girl?' Mr Robb asked, looking at her sadly.

'No . . . no, I haven't met her.' She was surprised that that was true, since she felt so strongly about Mrs Gardiner's case. It defied sense. 'I . . . I just know a little about her . . . I suppose I put myself in her place . . . a little.'

'In her place?' Michael echoed. 'What would make you leave a man, beaten, dying, but still alive, and run away, never to come forward until the police hunted you down, and then give no explanation even when you were arrested for killing him?'

'I don't know,' she admitted reluctantly. 'I . . . can't think of anything . . . but that doesn't mean there couldn't be a reason.'

'She's protecting someone,' the old man said, shaking his head. 'Women'll do all sorts to protect someone they love. I'll lay you odds, girl, if she didn't kill him herself, she knows who did.'

Michael glanced at Hester. 'Could be she was having an affair with Treadwell,' he said, pursing his lips. 'Could be he tried to force her to keep it going, and she wanted to end it, because of Stourbridge.'

Hester did not argue any more. Reason was all on his side and she had nothing to marshal against it. She turned her attention to the kettle.

* * *

When she arrived home Monk was already there and she was startled to see that he had prepared cold game pie and vegetables for dinner, and it was set out on the table. She realised how late it was, and apologised with considerable feeling. She was also deeply grateful. She was hot and tired and her boots felt at least a size too tight.

'What is it?' he asked, seeing the droop in her shoulders and reading her too well to think it was only weariness.

'They've found Miriam,' she replied, looking up at him from where she had sat down to unlace her boots.

He stood still in the doorway, staring at her.

'They arrested her,' she finished quietly. 'Michael Robb thinks she killed Treadwell, either because he knew something about her which would have ended her chance of marrying Lucius, or because she was having an affair with him, and wanted to end it.'

His face was grave, the lines harder. 'How do you know that?'

She realised the necessity for explanation, a little late. 'I was visiting his father, because he is seriously ill, when Sergeant Robb came home.'

'And Robb just told you this?' His eyes were wide and steady.

'He knows I am your wife.'

'Oh.' He hesitated. 'And do you think Miriam killed Treadwell?' He was watching her, trying to read not only her words but her feelings. He looked strangely defeated, as if he had felt the same unreasoning hope that Miriam could be innocent.

It was very sweet not to be alone in her sense of disappointment, even disillusion.

She took her boots off and wriggled her feet, then stood

up and walked over to him. She smiled and kissed him lightly on the cheek. 'Thank you for the dinner.'

He grinned with satisfaction. 'Don't make a habit of it,' he said smugly.

She knew better than to reply. She walked a step behind him to the table.

Chapter Six

◦⟨❈⟩◦

Monk was unable to rid his mind of the thought of Miriam Gardiner's arrest. He slept deeply, but when he awoke the memory of her distress twisted his thoughts until he had no choice but to determine to see her.

In case there might be any difficulty with the prison authorities, he lied without compunction, meeting the gaoler's gaze with candour and saying he was her legal adviser, whom of course she was entitled to consult.

Monk found her sitting alone in a cell, her hands folded in her lap, her face pale but so composed as to be in a way frightening. There was no anger in her, no will to fight, no outrage at injustice. She seemed neither pleased nor displeased to see him, as if his presence made no difference with regard to anything that mattered.

The cell door clanged behind him and he heard the heavy bolt shoot home. The floor was perhaps five paces by five, black stone, the walls white-washed. A single high aperture was heavily glassed, letting in light but not colour. The sky beyond could have been blue or grey. The air was stuffy, smelling of decades, perhaps centuries of anger and despair.

'Mrs Gardiner . . .' Monk began. He had rehearsed what

to say to her, but now it seemed inadequate. Intelligence was needed, even brilliance, if he were to help her in this dreadful situation of confusion and pain, and yet all that seemed natural or remotely appropriate was emotion. 'I hoped Robb would not find you, but since he has, please allow me to do what I can to help.'

She looked at him blankly, her face almost expressionless. 'You cannot help, Mr Monk. I mean that as no reflection upon your abilities, simply that my situation does not allow it.'

He sat down facing her. 'What happened?' he asked urgently. 'Do you know who killed Treadwell?'

She kept her eyes averted, staring into some dark space that only she could see.

'Do you know?' he repeated more sharply.

'There is nothing I can tell you which will help, Mr Monk.' There was finality in her voice, no lift of hope, not even of argument. She had no will to fight.

'Did you kill him?' he demanded.

She lifted her head slowly, her eyes wide. Before she spoke, he knew what she was going to say.

'No.'

'Then who did?'

She looked away again.

His mind raced. The only reason for her silence must be to protect someone. Had she any conception of what it was going to cost her?

'Did Treadwell threaten you?' he asked.

'No.' But there was no surprise in her voice or in the profile of her face. Who was she protecting? Cleo Anderson, who had been almost a mother to her? Some lover from the past, or a relative of her first husband?

'Was he threatening someone else? Blackmailing you?'

Monk persisted. All sorts of arguments sprang to his lips about not being able to help her if she would not help herself, but they died unspoken because it was too painfully apparent she had no belief that help was possible. 'Was Treadwell blackmailing you about something in your life here in Hampstead?'

'No.' She lifted her head again, 'There was nothing to blackmail me about.' Tears filled her eyes. Emotion had broken through the ice of despair for a few moments, then it withered again. The stark cell with its wooden cot and straw mattress, the bare walls and stifling air were hardly real to her. Her world was within herself and her own pain. Surely she had not yet even imagined what would follow if she did not present some defence. Either she had some reason for attacking Treadwell, or else it was simply someone else who had killed him? The only other alternative was that she had not even been present, and had no idea what had happened. Then why did she not say so?

He looked at her hunched figure where she sat, half turned away from him, unresponsive.

'Miriam!' He put out his hand and touched her. Her body was rigid. 'Miriam! What happened? Why did you leave the Stourbridge house? Was it something to do with Treadwell?'

'No . . .' There was a driving core of emotion in her voice. 'No,' she repeated. 'It had nothing to do with Treadwell. He was merely good enough to drive me.'

'You simply asked him, and he agreed?' he said with surprise. 'Did he not require some reason?'

'Not reason. Recompense.'

'You paid him?'

'My locket. It doesn't matter.'

That she would part so easily with a personal item of jewellery was a measure of how desperate she had been. He wondered what had become of the locket. It was not with Treadwell's clothes. Had his murderer taken it?

'Where is it now?' he asked. 'Did you take it back?'

She frowned. 'Where is it? Isn't it with him . . . with his body?'

'No.'

She lifted her shoulders very slightly, less than a shrug. 'Then I don't know. But it doesn't matter. Don't waste your effort on it, Mr Monk. Maybe it will find its way to someone who will like it. I would rather it were not lost down some drain, but if it is, I can't help it now.'

'What should I put my effort into, Miriam?'

She did not answer for so long he was about to repeat himself when at last she spoke.

'Comfort Lucius . . .' Without warning her composure broke and she bent her head and covered her face, sobs shaking her body.

He longed to be able to help her. She was alone, vulnerable, facing trial and almost certainly one of the ugliest of deaths.

Impulse overcame judgement. He reached out and took hold of her arm.

'Words won't comfort him when you are in the dock, or when the judge puts on his cap and sentences you to hang! Tell me the truth while I can do something about it! Why did you leave the Stourbridge house? Or if you won't tell me that, at least tell me what happened in Hampstead. Who killed Treadwell? Where were you? Why did you run away? Who are you afraid of?'

It took her several moments to master herself again. She blew her nose, then still avoiding meeting his eyes, she answered in a low, choked voice.

'I can't tell you why I left, only that I had to. What happened in Hampstead is that Treadwell was attacked and murdered.

I think perhaps it was my fault, but I did not do it, that I swear. I never injured anyone with intent.' She looked at him, her eyes red-rimmed. 'Please tell Lucius that, Mr Monk. I never wilfully harmed anyone. I want him to believe that . . .' Her voice trailed off into a sob.

'He already believes that,' he said more gently. 'It is not Lucius you have to be concerned about. I doubt he will ever think ill of you. It is the rest of the world, especially Sergeant Robb, and then whatever jury he brings you before. And he will! Unless you give some better account. Did you see who killed Treadwell? At least answer me "yes", or "no".'

'Yes. But no one would believe me, even if I would say . . . and I will not.' She spoke with finality. There was no room to imagine she hoped to be dissuaded. She did not care what Monk thought and he knew it from everything about her, from the slump of the body to the lifelessness of her voice.

'Try me!' he urged desperately. 'Tell me the truth and let me decide whether I believe it or not! If you are innocent, then someone else is guilty, and he must be found! If he isn't, you will hang!'

'I know. Did you think I didn't understand that?'

He wondered fleetingly if she were of mental competence, if perhaps she were far more frail than Lucius had had any idea, but the thought lasted only moments.

'Will you see Lucius? Or Major Stourbridge?' he asked.

'No!' She pulled away from him sharply, for the first time real fear in her voice. 'No . . . I won't. If you have any desire to help me, then do not ask me again.'

'I won't,' he promised.

'You give me your word?' She stared at him, her eyes wide and intense.

'I do. But I warn you again that no one can help you until you tell the truth. If not to me, would you to a lawyer, someone

169

who is bound to keep in confidence whatever you say, regardless of what it is?'

A smile flickered over her face and vanished. 'It would make no difference whatever. It is the truth itself that wounds, Mr Monk, not what you may do with it. Thank you for coming. I am sure your intention was generous, but you cannot help. Please leave me to myself.' She turned away again, dismissing him.

He had no alternative but to accept. He stood up, hesitated a moment longer, without purpose, then called the gaoler to let him out.

Just outside the gates he encountered Michael Robb. He looked tired and it was obscurely pleasing to Monk that there was no air of triumph in him.

They stood facing each other on the hot, dusty footpath.

'You've been to see her,' Robb stated what was obvious.

'She won't tell you anything,' Monk said, not in answer but as a statement of fact. 'She won't speak to anyone. She won't even see Stourbridge.'

Robb looked him up and down from his neat cravat and the shoulders of the well-cut jacket to the tips of his polished boots. 'Do you know what happened?' he asked, raising his eyebrows.

'No,' Monk replied.

Robb put his hands in his pockets, deliberately casual, even sloppy by contrast. 'I shall find out,' he promised. 'No matter how long it takes me, I will know what happened to Treadwell – or enough to make a prosecution. There's something in his past, or hers, that made this happen.' He was watching Monk's face as he spoke, weighing his reaction, trying to read what he knew.

'You will have to,' Monk agreed wryly. 'All you have at the moment is suspicion – not enough to hang anyone on.'

Robb winced almost imperceptibly, just a stiffening of his body. It was an ugly word, an ugly reality. 'I will.' His voice was very soft. 'Treadwell may have been an evil man, for all I know deserving some kind of retribution, but the day we allow the man in the street to decide that for himself, without trial, without answering to anyone, then we lose the right to call ourselves civilised. Then law belongs to the quickest and the strongest, not to justice. We aren't a society any more.' He was self-conscious as he said it, daring Monk to laugh at him, but he was proud of it also.

Monk hoped he had never done anything in the past which made Robb imagine he would mock that decision. He would probably never know. A dray rumbled noisily past them.

'I won't stand in your way,' he answered levelly. 'None of us could afford private vengeance.' He smiled as he said it, wondering if Robb had any idea how true that was.

'She'd be better if she told us,' Robb frowned. 'Can't you persuade her of that? Otherwise I'll have to dig for it, go through all her life, all her friends, her first husband . . . everything.'

'That's one of the things about murder.' Monk nodded and lifted his shoulders very slightly. 'You have to learn more about everybody than you want to know, all the secrets that have nothing to do with the crime, as well as those that do. Innocent people are stripped of their masks of pretence, sometimes of decently covered mistakes they've long since mended. You have to know everything the victim ever did that could make someone take the last, terrible step of killing them, creep as close as their skin till you see every blemish and can read the hatred that destroyed them. Of course you'll know Treadwell . . . and you'll come to pity him, and probably hate him as well.'

People passed by and they ignored them.

'Have you solved a lot of murders?' Robb asked. It was not a challenge; there was respect and curiosity in his face.

'Yes,' Monk answered him. 'Some I understood, and might have done the same myself. Others were so cold-blooded, so consumed in self it frightened me that another human being I had talked with, stood beside, could have hidden that evil behind a face which looked at me like any other.'

Robb stared at him. For several seconds neither of them moved, oblivious of the noisy street around them.

'I think this is going to be one of the first,' the sergeant said at last. 'I wish it weren't. I wish I weren't going to find some private shame in Mrs Gardiner's life that Treadwell was blackmailing her about, threatening to ruin the happiness she'd found. But I have to look. And if I find it, I have to bring it to evidence.' That was a challenge.

Monk thought how young he was. And he wondered what evidence he himself had found – or lost, when he was that age. And, for that matter, what he would do now, if he were in Robb's place.

But he was not. He had no further interest in the case. His task was over, not very satisfactorily.

'Of course you do,' he answered. 'There are hundreds of judgements to make. You have to check which are yours, and which aren't. Good day, Sergeant Robb.'

Robb stood facing him in the sun. 'Good day, Mr Monk. It's been an interesting experience to meet you.' He looked as if he were about to add something more, then changed his mind, and went on past him towards the prison gate.

Monk had no duties in the case now. Even moral obligation took him no further. Miriam had refused to explain anything, either of her flight from Cleveland Square, or what had happened in Hampstead. There was nothing more he could do.

★ ★ ★

Monk sat at his desk writing letters, his mind only half on them, and was delighted when the doorbell rang. Only when he answered it, and saw Lucius Stourbridge, did his heart sink. Should he express some condolence for the situation? Lucius had hired him to find Miriam, and he had done so. The result had been catastrophic, even though it was none of his doing.

Lucius looked haggard, his eyes dark-ringed, his cheeks pale beneath his olive skin, giving him a sallow, almost grey appearance. He was a man walking through a nightmare.

'I know you have already done all that I asked of you, Mr Monk,' he began even before Monk could invite him inside. 'And that you endeavoured to help Mrs Gardiner, even concealing her whereabouts from the police, but they found her nevertheless, and arrested her . . .' The words were so hard for him to say, his voice cracked and he was obliged to clear his throat before he could continue, '. . . for the murder of Treadwell.' He swallowed. 'I know she cannot have done such a thing. Please, Mr Monk, at any cost at all, up to everything I have, please help me prove that!' He stood still on the front doorstep, his body rigid, hands clenched, eyes filled with his inner agony.

'It is not the cost, Mr Stourbridge,' Monk answered slowly, fighting his common sense and everything his intelligence told him. 'Please come in. It is a matter of what is possible. I have already spoken to her,' he continued as Lucius followed him into the sitting room. 'She will not tell me anything of what occurred. All she would say was that she did not kill Treadwell.'

'Of course she didn't,' Lucius protested, still standing. 'We must save her from . . .' He could not bear to use the word. 'We must defend her. I . . . I don't know how, or . . .' He trailed off. 'But I know your reputation, Mr Monk. If any

173

man in London can help, it is you.'

'If you know my reputation, then you know I will not conceal the truth if I find it,' Monk warned. 'Even if it is not what you wish to hear.'

Lucius lifted his chin. 'It may not be what I wish to hear, Mr Monk, but it will not be that Miriam killed Treadwell in any unlawful way. I believe it was someone else, but she dare not say so because she is afraid of him, either for herself, or for someone else.' His voice shook a little. 'But if she brought about his death herself, then it was either an accident, or she was defending herself from some threat which was too immediate and too gross to endure.'

Monk held very little hope of such a comfortable solution. If that were so, why had Miriam not simply said so? She would not be blamed for defending her virtue. More sharply in his mind was the image of Treadwell's head and his scarred knees, but no other injury at all. He had not been involved in a struggle with anyone. He had been hit one mighty blow which had caused him to bleed to death within his skull in a very short while. During that time he had crawled from wherever the attack had taken place, probably seeking help. He knew the area. Perhaps he even knew Cleo Anderson was a nurse and had tried to reach her. Had Miriam simply watched him crawl away, without any attempt to help? Why had she not at least reported the incident, if she were in any way justified? It was not the action of an honourable woman, the victim of an attack herself.

Further, and perhaps even more damning, what could she possibly have had to hand with which to inflict such a blow, and how had Treadwell, if he had been threatening her, had his back to her?

'Mr Stourbridge,' Monk said grimly. 'I have no idea whether I can find the truth of what happened. If you wish, I can try. But I hold far less hope than you do that it will be anything you can bear to believe. The facts so far do not indicate Mrs Gardiner's innocence.'

Lucius was very pale. 'Then find more facts, Mr Monk. By the time you have them all, they will prove her honour. I know her.' It was a blind statement of belief and his face allowed no argument, no appeal to a lesser thing like reason.

Monk would like to have asked him to wait and give himself time to consider all the consequences, but there was no time. Robb would be looking already. The Crown would prosecute as soon as it had sufficient evidence, whether it was the whole story or not. There was nothing on which to mount any defence.

'Are you quite sure?' he tried one more time, useless as he knew it.

'Yes,' Lucius replied instantly. 'I have twenty guineas here, and will give you more as you need it. Anything at all, just ask me.' He held out a soft leather pouch of coins, thrusting it at Monk.

Monk did not immediately take the money. 'The first thing will be your practical help. If Treadwell's death was not caused by Miriam, then it is either a chance attack, which I cannot believe, or it is to do with his own life and character. I will begin by learning all I can about that. It will also keep me from following Sergeant Robb's footsteps, and perhaps appearing to him to be obstructing his path. Additionally, if I do learn anything, I have a better chance of keeping the option of either telling him or not, as seems to our best advantage.'

'Yes . . . Yes,' Lucius agreed, obviously relieved to have some course of action at last. 'What can I do?' He gave a tiny shrug. 'I tried to think of what manner of man Treadwell was, and could answer nothing. I saw him almost every day. He's dead, killed by God knows whom, and I can't give an intelligent answer.'

'I didn't expect you to tell me from your observation,' Monk assured him. 'I would like to speak to the other servants, then discover what I can of Treadwell's life outside Bayswater. I would rather learn that before the police, if I can.'

'Of course! Of course,' Lucius agreed. 'Thank you, Mr Monk. I shall be forever in your debt. If there is anything—'

Monk stopped him. 'Please don't thank me until I have earned it. I may find nothing further, or worse still, what I do find may be something you would have been happier not to know.'

'I have to know,' Lucius said simply. 'Until tomorrow morning, Mr Monk . . .'

'Good day, Mr Stourbridge,' Monk replied, walking towards the door to open it for him.

Monk was in the house in Cleveland Square by ten o'clock the next morning, and with Lucius' help he questioned the servants, both indoor and outdoor, about James Treadwell. They were reluctant to speak of him at all, let alone to speak ill, but Monk read in their faces, and in the awkwardness of their phrases, that the coachman had not been greatly liked, but he had been respected because he did his job well.

A picture emerged of a man who gave little of himself, whose sense of humour was more founded in cruelty than goodwill, but who was sufficiently sensible of the hierarchy within the household not to overstep his place or wound too many feelings. He knew how to charm, and was occasionally generous when he won at gambling, which was not infrequently.

No maid reported any unwelcome attentions. Nothing had gone missing. He never blamed anyone else for his very few errors.

Monk searched Treadwell's rooms, which were still empty as no replacement for him had yet been employed. All his possessions were there as he had left them. It was neat, but there was a book open on the bedside table, on horse racing, a half-open box of matches beside the candle on the windowsill, and a smart waistcoat hung over the back of the upright chair. It was the room of a man who expected to return.

Monk examined the clothes and boots carefully. He was surprised how expensive they were – in some cases as good as his own. Treadwell certainly did not pay for them on a coachman's earnings. If it was from his gambling then he must spend a great deal of time at it, and be consistently successful. It seemed unpleasantly more and more likely that he had another source of income, a good deal more reliable.

Monk did enquire, without any hope, if perhaps the clothes were hand-me-downs from either Lucius or Harry Stourbridge. He was not surprised to learn that they were not. Such things went to servants of longer standing, and remained with them.

As far as Miriam Gardiner was concerned Monk learned nothing beyond what he had already been told: she was unused to servants, and therefore did not treat Treadwell with the distance that was appropriate, but that was equally true for all the other household staff. No one had observed anything different with regard to the coachman. Without exception they all spoke well of her and seemed confused and grieved by her current misfortune.

Monk spent the following day in Hampstead and Kentish Town as he had told Lucius he would. He walked miles, asked questions till his mouth was dry and his throat hoarse. He arrived home after nine o'clock, when it was still daylight but the heat of the afternoon was tempered by an evening breeze.

The first thing he wanted to do was to take his boots off and soak his burning feet, but Hester's presence stopped him. It was not an attractive thing to do and he was too conscious of her to indulge himself so. Instead, after accepting her welcome with great pleasure, he sat in the coolness of the office which doubled as a sitting room, a glass of cold lemonade at his elbow, his boots still firmly laced, and answered her questions.

'Expensive tastes, far more than Stourbridge paid him. At least three times as much.'

Hester frowned. 'Gambling?'

'Gamblers win and lose. He seems to have had his money pretty regularly. But more than that, he only had one day off a fortnight. Gambling to that extent needs time.'

She was watching him closely, her eyes anxious. Unexpectedly, she did not prompt him.

He was surprised. 'I considered a mistress with the means to give him expensive gifts,' he continued. 'But in going around the places where he spent his time off, he seems to have had money, and purchased the things himself. He enjoyed spending money. He wasn't especially discreet about it.'

'So you think it was come by honestly?' Her eyes widened.

'No . . . I think he was not afraid of anyone discovering the dishonesty in it,' he corrected. 'It wasn't stolen, but there are other dishonest means . . .'

'Available to a coachman? What?'

The answer was obvious. Why was she deliberately not saying it? He looked back at her, trying to fathom the emotion behind her eyes. He thought he saw reluctance and fear, but it was closed in. She was not going to share it with him.

He felt excluded. It was startlingly unpleasant, a sense of loneliness he had not experienced since the extraordinary night she had accepted his proposal of marriage. He was uncertain how to deal with it. Candour was too instinctive to him; the words were the only ones to his tongue.

'Blackmail,' he replied.

'Oh.' She looked at him so steadily he was now doubly sure she was concealing her thoughts, and that they were relevant to what they were discussing. Yet how could she know anything about Treadwell? She had been working at the hospital in Hampstead – hadn't she?

'It seems the obvious possibility,' he said, trying to keep his voice even. 'That, or theft, which he had little time for. He lived in at the Stourbridges', and they have nothing missing. He liked to live well on his time off, eat expensively, drink as much as he pleased, go out to music halls and pick up any woman that took his fancy.'

She did not look surprised, only sad – and if anything, more distressed.

'I see.'

'Do you?'

'No . . . I just meant, I suppose, that I follow your reasoning. It does look as if he might have been blackmailing someone . . .'

He could not bear the barrier. He broke it abruptly, aware that he might be hurt by the answer. 'What is wrong, Hester?'

'Wrong?' she parried uncharacteristically.

Was it a warning, or merely self-defence?

He met her eyes, trying to read them and seeing only anxiety.

'You have been arbitrary,' he said, 'officious, dogmatic, prudish – in the past – and frequently critical – but you have never been evasive, even when it might have been wiser and certainly more tactful to do so, and above all you have never lied.'

She blushed but she did not look away. 'I don't know who he was blackmailing, or even that he was, but I fear I might guess. It is something I have learned in the course of caring for the sick, therefore I cannot tell you. I'm sorry.' It was very plain in her face that indeed she was sorry, and equally plain that she would not change her position.

He hurt for her. He ached to be able to help. Being shut out was almost like a physical coldness. He must protect her from being damaged by it herself. That was a greater danger than she might understand.

'Hester – are you aware of any crime committed?'

'Not morally,' she answered instantly. 'Nothing has been done that would offend the sensibilities of any Christian person.'

'Except a policeman,' he concluded without hesitation.

Her eyes widened. 'Are you a policeman?'

'No . . .'

'That's what I thought. Not that it makes any difference. It would be dishonourable to tell you, even if you were. I can't.'

He said nothing. It was infuriating. She might hold the missing piece which would make sense of the confusion. She knew it also, and yet she would not tell him. She set her belief in trust, in her own concept of honour, before even her love for him. It was a hard thing, and beautiful, like clean light. It did not really hurt. He was quite sure he wanted it to be so. He was almost tempted to press her, to be absolutely certain she would not yield. But that would embarrass her. She might not understand his reason, or be quite sure he was not disappointed, or worse, childishly selfish.

'William?'

'Yes?'

'Do you know something anyway?'

'No. Why?'

'You are smiling.'

'Oh!' He was surprised. 'Am I? No, I don't know anything. I suppose I am just . . . happy . . .' He leaned forward and, much to her surprise, kissed her long and slowly, with increasing passion.

The following day was the tenth since Monk had first been approached by Lucius Stourbridge to find his fiancée. Now she was in prison charged with murder, and Monk had very little further idea what had happened the day of her flight. He had still less idea what had occasioned it, unless it was some threat of disclosure of a portion of her past which she believed would ruin either her, or someone she loved. And it seemed she would tell no one. Even trial and execution appeared preferable.

What secret could be so fearful?

He could not imagine any, even though, as he took a hansom to the Hampstead police station, his mind would not leave it alone.

He arrived still short of nine o'clock to be told that Sergeant Robb had been working until dark the previous evening and was not yet in. Monk thanked the desk sergeant and left, walking briskly in the sun towards Robb's home. He had no time to waste, even though he feared his discoveries, if he made them, would all be those he preferred not to know. Perhaps that was why he hurried. Good news could be savoured, bad should be bolted like evil-tasting medicine. The anticipation at least could be cut short, and hope was painful.

There was little he wanted to tell Robb, only his discoveries about Treadwell's extravagant spending habits. He had debated whether to mention the subject or not. It gave Miriam a powerful motive, if she were being blackmailed. But a man who would blackmail one person might blackmail others, therefore there would be other suspects. Perhaps one of them had lain in wait for him and Miriam had fled the scene, not because she was guilty, but because she could not prove her innocence.

It was a slender hope, and he did not believe it himself. What if there were an illegitimate child somewhere, Miriam and Treadwell's? Or simply that Treadwell knew of such a child by another man? That would be enough to ruin her marriage to Lucius Stourbridge.

But was any blackmail worth the rope?

Or had she simply panicked, and now believed all was lost? That was only too credible.

Monk could not alone pursue all the other possible victims Treadwell might have had. It required the numbers of the police, and their authority.

He reached Robb's home and knocked on the door. It was opened after several minutes by Robb himself, looking tired and harassed. He greeted Monk civilly, but with a further tightening of the tension inside him evident.

'What is it? Be as brief as you may, please. I am late and I have not yet given my grandfather his breakfast.'

Monk would like to have helped, but he had no skills that were of use. He felt the lack of them sharply.

'I have learned rather more about James Treadwell, and I thought I should share it with you. Let me tell you while you get breakfast,' Monk offered.

Robb accepted reluctantly.

Monk excused himself to the old man then, sitting down, recounted what he had discovered over the previous two days. As he did so, and Michael prepared bread and tea and assisted his grandfather, Monk's eyes wandered around the room. He noticed the cupboard door open and the small stack of medicines still well replenished and that there were eggs in a bowl on the table by the sink and a bottle of sherry on the floor. Michael did very well by his grandfather. It must cost him every halfpenny of his sergeant's wages. Monk knew what they were, and how far they went. It was little enough for two, when one of them needed constant care and expensive medicines.

Michael cleared away the plate and cup and washed them in the dish by the sink, his back to the room.

The old man looked at Monk. 'Good woman, your wife,' he said gently. 'Never makes it seem like a trouble. Comes here and listens to my tales with her eyes like stars. Seen the tears running down her cheeks when I told her about the death o' the Admiral, an' how we came home to England with the flags lowered after Trafalgar.'

'She loved hearing it,' Monk said sincerely. He could imagine Hester sitting in this chair, the vision so clear in her mind that the terror and the sorrow of it moved her to tears. She must have been here some considerable time to hear such a long account.

'Seen a good bit o' battle herself, she has,' the old man said with a smile. 'Told me about that. Calm and quiet as you like, but I could see in her eyes what she really felt. You can, you know. People who've really seen it don't talk that much. Just sometimes you need to, an' I could see it in her.'

Was that true? Hester needed to speak of her experiences in the Crimea, even now. She shared it with this old man she barely knew, rather than with him, or even Callandra. But then they had not seen war. They could not understand, and this man could. Most of the time horror was best forgotten. Occasionally it broke the surface of the mind and had to be faced. He knew that himself, with the ghosts of the past who were no more than shadows to him.

'She must have come several times,' he said aloud.

The old man nodded. 'Drops by every day, maybe just for half an hour or so, to see how I am. Not many people care about the old and the sick, if they're not their own.'

'No,' Monk agreed with a strangely sinking knowledge that that was true. It had not been said in self-pity but as a simple statement. He could imagine Hester's anger and her pity not just for John Robb, but for all the untold thousands he represented. When he spoke it was from instinct. 'Did she ask you about other sailors, and soldiers?'

'You mean old men like me? Yes she did. Didn't she tell you?'

'I'm afraid I wasn't paying as much attention as perhaps I should have been.'

Robb smiled and nodded. He too had not always listened to women. He understood.

'She would care,' Monk continued, hating himself for the thoughts of missing medicines and blackmail that were in his mind and he could not ignore. 'She's a good nurse. Puts her patients before herself, like a good soldier, duty first.'

'That's right,' the old man nodded, his eyes bright and soft. 'She's a real good woman. I seen a few good nurses. Come around now and again to see how you are.'

Monk was aware of what he was doing, but he had to do it.

'And bring medicines?'

'Of course,' Robb agreed. 'Can't go an' get 'em myself, and young Michael here wouldn't know what I needed, would he?'

He was unaware of anything wrong. He was speaking of kindness he had received. The darkness was all in Monk's mind.

Michael finished cleaning and tidying everything so he would have as little as possible to do if he managed to slip home in the middle of the day. He left a cup of water where the old man could reach it, and a further slice of bread, and checked once more that he was as comfortable as he could make him. Then he turned to Monk.

'I must go to the police station. I'll consider what you said. There could have been somebody else there when Treadwell was killed, but there's no evidence of it, or who it was. And why did Miriam Gardiner run? Why doesn't she tell us the truth now?'

Monk could think of several answers, but they were none of them convincing, nor did they disprove her guilt. The fear that was forming in his own mind he liked even less, but he could no longer evade it. He rose and took his leave of the old man, wishing him well, and feeling a hypocrite, then followed Michael Robb out into the sunny, noisy street.

A hundred yards along they parted, Robb to the left, Monk to the right towards the hospital. He was now almost convinced he knew the cause of Hester's anxiety, and why she could not share it with him. Medicines had been disappearing from the hospital. The authorities had assumed they were stolen either to feed the addiction of the thief, or else even more probably to sell. Hester had been to John Robb's house several times and must have observed the medicine cupboard. The old man had been quite candid that they were brought to him by a nurse. It was so easy from that to conclude that the thefts were not selfishly motivated; far from it. Someone was taking the medicines to treat the old and the sick who were too poor to purchase them for themselves.

John Robb had no idea. Apart from the guilt and the danger involved, his pride would never have allowed him to accept help at such a risk. He accepted it because he believed it was already paid for.

Hester had been very precise about the words she used in denying knowledge of a crime – 'not morally'. Legally it most certainly was.

The question was, could Treadwell have known?

Why not? He came to Hampstead on most of his days off. His body had been found on the path to the house of a nurse – Cleo Anderson. Monk remembered her vividly, her defence of Miriam and her denial of knowing where Miriam was after her flight from Cleveland Square. He hated having to pursue this, but the conclusion was inescapable. It was Cleo Anderson whom Treadwell had been blackmailing, and it was anything but chance that he had been found on her path. He had crawled there deliberately, knowing he was dying, and determined to the last to incriminate her and find both some kind of justice for himself, and revenge. His body would inevitably lead the police to her.

Perhaps, after all, Miriam had had nothing to do with the murder, but knowing why Cleo had stolen the medicines, and owing her a debt of gratitude for her kindness, she could not earn her own release at the cost of Cleo's implication. That would explain her silence! The debt was too great.

Monk found himself increasing his pace, dodging between pedestrians out strolling in the warm, mid-morning, pedlars offering sandwiches, toffee apples and peppermint drinks, and traders haggling over a good bargain. He barely saw them. The noise muted into an indistinguishable buzz. He wanted to get this over with.

He walked up the hospital steps and in at the wide front entrance. Almost immediately he was greeted by a young man in a waistcoat and rolled up shirtsleeves stained with blood.

'Good morning, sir!' he said briskly. 'Is it a physician or a surgeon you require? What can we do for you, sir?'

Monk felt a wave of panic and quashed it with a violent

effort. Thank God he had need of neither. The stoicism of those whose pain brought them here earned his overwhelming admiration.

'I am in good health, thank you, ' he said quickly. 'I should like to see Lady Callandra Daviot, if she is here.'

'I beg your pardon?' The young man looked nonplussed. It had obviously never occurred to him that anyone should wish to see a woman, any woman, rather than a qualified medical man.

'I should like to see Lady Callandra Daviot,' Monk repeated very distinctly. 'Or if she is not here, then Mrs Monk. Where may I wait?' He hated the place. The grey corridors smelled of vinegar and lye, and reminded him of another hospital, the one where he had awoken after the accident, not knowing who he was. The panic of that had long since receded, but it was too easily imagined again.

'Oh, try that way,' the young man waved airily in the general direction of the physicians' waiting rooms, then turned on his heel and continued the way he had been going.

Monk went to the waiting room where half a dozen people sat around, tense with apprehension, too ill or too anxious to speak to one another. Mercifully Callandra appeared after only a few moments.

'William! What are you doing here? I presume you wish to see Hester? I am afraid she is out. She has gone,' she hesitated, 'to see a patient.'

'Old and ill, and poor, I imagine,' he replied drily.

She knew him too well. She caught the edge of deeper meaning in his voice. 'What is it, William?' she demanded. Although he had naturally risen to his feet, and he was some eight inches taller than she, she still managed to make him feel as if he should respond promptly and truthfully.

'I believe you have been missing certain medicines from

the apothecary's rooms.' It was a statement.

'Hester never called you in on the matter?' She was amazed and openly disbelieving.

'No, of course not. Why? Have you solved the problem?'

'I don't think you need to concern yourself with it,' she answered severely. 'At least certainly not yet.'

'Why? Because it is a nurse who has taken them?' That was only half intended to be a challenge, but it sounded like one.

'We do not know who it is,' she replied. 'And since you agree that Hester did not ask you to investigate for us, why are we discussing the matter? You can have no interest in it.'

'You are wrong. Unfortunately I do have.' His voice dipped, the previous moment's confrontation suddenly changed to sorrow. 'I wish I could leave it alone. It is not the fact that you are missing them that concerns me, it is the question that whoever took them may have been blackmailed over the thefts, even though I believe she put them to the best possible use.'

'Blackmail!' Callandra stared at him in dismay.

'Yes . . . and murder. I'm sorry.'

She said nothing, but the gravity in her face showed her fear, and he felt that it also betrayed her guess as to what else lay beyond the thefts, to the steady draining away of supplies over months, perhaps years, to help those she perceived to be in need. It was a judgement no individual had the right to make, and yet if no one did, who would care and who would break the rules in order to show that they should be changed?

'Do you know who it is?' he asked.

She looked him straight in the eye. 'I have not the slightest idea,' she replied.

They both understood it was a lie, and that she would not change it. He did not really expect her to, nor would he have been pleased if she had.

'And neither has Hester!' she added firmly.

'No . . . I thought not,' he conceded with the ghost of a smile. 'But you can give me an estimate as to how much, and of which sorts.'

She hesitated.

'Surely you would prefer to do that yourself than for me to have to ask someone else?' he said without blinking.

She realised it was a threat, very barely disguised. He would carry it through, no matter how much he would dislike it.

'Yes,' she capitulated. 'Come with me and I will give you a list. It is only a guess, of course!'

'Of course,' he agreed.

Monk worked the rest of that day, and most of the following one, first with Callandra's list of medicines, then seeing who Cleo Anderson had visited and what illnesses afflicted them. He did not have to ask many questions among the sick and the poor. They were only too happy to speak well of a woman who seemed to have endless time and patience to care for their needs, and who so often brought them medicines the doctor had sent. No one questioned it, or doubted where she had obtained the quinine, the morphine, or the other powders and infusions she brought. They were simply grateful.

The more he learned, the more Monk hated what he was doing. Time and again he stopped short of asking the final question which could have produced proof. He wrote nothing down. He had nothing witnessed and took no evidence of anything with him.

By the afternoon of the second day he turned his attention to Cleo Anderson herself, her home, her expenses, what she purchased and where. It had never occurred to him that she might ask any return for either the care she gave or the medicines she provided. Even so, he was startled to find how very frugal her life was, considerably more so than he would have expected from her nurse's wages. Her clothes were hand-me-downs, often given her by grateful relatives of a patient who had died. Her food was of the simplest, again, often provided in the homes of those she visited: bread, oatmeal porridge, a little cheese and pickle. It seemed she frequently ate at the hospital and appeared glad of it.

The house was her own, a legacy from better times, but falling into disrepair and badly in need of reroofing.

No one knew her to drink or to gamble.

So where did her money go?

Monk had no doubt it went into the pocket of James Treadwell, at least so long as he had been alive. Since his death two weeks ago, Cleo Anderson had purchased a second-hand kitchen table and a new jug and bowl and two more towels, things she had not been known to do in several years.

Monk was in the street outside her house a little before half-past four when he saw Michael Robb coming towards him, walking slowly as if he were tired and his feet sore. He was hot and he looked deeply depressed. He stopped in front of Monk. 'Were you going to tell me?' he asked.

There was no need for explanation. Monk did not know whether he would have told him or not, but he was quite certain he hated the fact that Robb knew. Perhaps it was inevitable, and when he had wrestled with it and grieved over it he would have told him, but he was not ready to do that yet.

'I have no proof of anything,' he answered. That was uncharacteristically vague for him. Usually he faced a truth honestly, however bitter. This hurt more than he had foreseen.

'I have,' Robb said wearily. 'Enough to arrest her. Please don't stand in my way. At least we will release Miriam Gardiner. You can tell Mr Stourbridge. He'll be relieved . . .

not that he ever thought her guilty.'

'Yes . . .' Monk knew Lucius would be happy, but it would be short-lived, because Miriam had chosen to face trial herself rather than implicate Cleo Anderson. Her grief would be deep, and probably abiding.

On the way to the station, Robb explained that the police believed Miriam a material witness to the crime who had not offered them the truth, even when pressed. She was a woman apparently not guilty of murder, but quite plainly in a state close to hysteria, and not fit to be released except into the care of some responsible person who would look after her, and also be certain that she was present to appear in court on the witness stand as the law demanded. Lucius and his father were the obvious and willing candidates.

It was passionately against her will. She stood white-faced in the superintendent's office, turning from Robb to Monk as they entered the room.

'Please, Mr Monk, I will give any undertaking you like, pledge anything at all, but do not oblige me to go back to Cleveland Square! I will gladly work in the hospital day and night, if you will allow me to live there.'

The police station superintendent looked at her gravely, then at Robb.

'I think—' Robb began.

But the superintendent did not wish to hear his opinion. 'You are obviously distressed,' he said to Miriam, speaking slowly and very clearly. 'Mr Stourbridge is to be your husband. He is the best one to see that you are given the appropriate care, and to offer you comfort for the grief you naturally feel upon the arrest of a woman who showed you kindness in the past. You have suffered a great shock. You must rest quietly and restore your strength.'

Miriam swung around to gaze at Monk. Her eyes were

wild as if she longed to say something to him but the presence of others prevented her.

He could think of no excuse to speak to her alone. Major Stourbridge and Lucius were just beyond the door waiting to take her back to Cleveland Square. There was a constable on one side of her and the desk sergeant on the other. Their intention was to support her in case she felt faint, but in effect they closed her in as if she were under restraint.

There was nothing he could do. Helplessly he watched her escorted from the room. The door opened and Lucius Stourbridge stepped forward, his face filled with tenderness and joy. Behind him Harry Stourbridge smiled as if the end of a long nightmare were in sight.

Miriam tripped, staggered forward and had to be all but carried by the constable and the sergeant. She flinched as Lucius touched her.

Chapter Seven

Hester was home before Monk, and was looking forward to his arrival, but when he came in through the door and she saw his face, she knew instantly that something was very seriously wrong. He looked exhausted. His skin was pale and his dark hair limp and stuck to his brow in the heat.

Alarm welled up inside her. 'What is it?' she demanded urgently.

He stood in the middle of the floor. He lifted up his hand and touched her cheek very lightly. 'I know what it is you couldn't tell me . . . and why. I'm sorry I had to pursue it.'

She swallowed. 'It?'

'The stolen medicines,' he answered. 'Who took them and why, and where they went. It's a far more obvious cause for blackmail.'

She tried not to understand, pushing the realisation away from her. 'The medicines couldn't have anything to do with Miriam Gardiner.'

'Not directly, but one leads to the other.' His eyes did not waver and she knew that he was quite certain of what he said.

'What? What connection?' she asked. 'What's happened?'

There was no purpose in suggesting he sit down or rest in any fashion until he had told her, and neither of them pretended there was.

'Cleo Anderson stole the medicines to treat the old and the sick,' he answered her softly. 'Somehow Treadwell knew of it, and he was blackmailing her. Perhaps he followed Miriam. Maybe she unintentionally let something slip, and he pieced together the rest.'

'Do you know that?' She was confused, her mind whirling. 'If Treadwell was blackmailing Cleo Anderson, then why would Miriam kill him? To protect her? It doesn't explain why she left Cleveland Square suddenly. What about Lucius Stourbridge? Why didn't she go back to him and explain? Something . . .' she trailed off. None of it really made sense.

'Miriam didn't kill Treadwell,' Monk told her. 'The police have let her go. She was defending Cleo because of old loyalties, and probably because she believed in her cause as well.'

'That isn't enough,' Hester protested. 'Why did she leave Cleveland Square in the middle of the party? Why wouldn't she allow Lucius to know where she was?'

'I don't know,' he admitted. 'She was released into his care, and she looked as if she were going to an execution. She begged not to be, but they wouldn't listen to her.' A frown creased his face and there was pain etched more deeply than the weariness. 'For a moment I thought she was going to ask me to help her, but then she changed her mind. They all but carried her out.'

Hester heard the edge of pity in his voice. She felt it herself, and she was angered that the police authorities should consider Miriam needed to be released into anybody's care. She should have been permitted the dignity of going wherever she wished, and with whomever. She was no longer charged with anything.

But far more immediate, and closer to her own emotions, was her concern for Cleo Anderson.

'What are we to do to help her?' She took for granted that he would.

Monk was still standing in the middle of the room, hot, tired, dusty and with aching feet. Remarkably, he kept his temper.

'Nothing. It is a private matter between them now.'

'I mean Cleo!' she corrected. 'Miriam has other people to care for her. Anyway, she is not accused of a crime.'

'Yes she is: complicity in concealing Treadwell's murder. Even though she says she was not present and did not know he was dead. She is almost certainly a witness to the attack. The police want her to testify.'

She waved her hand impatiently. She did not know Miriam Gardiner, but she did know Cleo, and what she had done for old John Robb, and others like him.

'So she'll have to testify! It won't be pleasant, but she'll survive it. If she's worth anything at all, her first concern will be for Cleo, and ours must be too. What can we do? Where should we begin?'

His face tightened. 'There's nothing we can do,' he replied briefly, moving away from her and sitting down in one of the chairs. The way his body sank, the sudden release at the last moment, betrayed his utter weariness. 'I found Miriam Gardiner and she is returned to her family. I wish it were not Cleo Anderson who is guilty, but it is. The best I could do was stop short of finding any proof of it, but Robb will. He's a good policeman. And his father's involved.' He was angry with himself for his emotions, and it showed in his face and the sharp edge to his voice.

Hester stood in the centre of the floor, cool and fresh in a printed cotton dress with wide skirts and a small, white collar. It was pretty, and it all seemed terribly irrelevant. It was almost a sin to be comfortable and so happy when Cleo Anderson was in prison and facing . . . the long drop into darkness at the end of a rope!

'There must be something . . .' She knew she should not argue with him, especially now, when he was exhausted, and probably very nearly as distressed about this as she was. But her self-control did not extend to sitting patiently and waiting until a better time. 'I don't know what . . . but if we look . . . Maybe he threatened her. Perhaps there was some degree of self-defence.' She cast about wildly for a better thought. 'Maybe he tried to coerce her into committing some sort of crime. That could be justified . . .'

'So she committed murder instead?' he said sarcastically.

She blushed hotly. She wanted to swear at him, use some of the language she had heard in the barracks in Sebastapol, but it would be profoundly unladylike. She would despise herself afterwards, and more importantly, he would never look at her in the same way again. He would hear her words in his ears every time he looked at her face. Even in moments of tenderness, when she most fiercely desired his respect, the ugliness would intrude.

'All right, it wasn't a very good idea,' she conceded. 'But it isn't the only one!'

He looked up at her in some surprise, not for her words in themselves, but from the meekness of them.

She knew what was in his mind, and blushed the more hotly. This was ridiculous and most irritating.

'I wish I could help her,' he said gently. 'But I know of no way, and neither do you. Leave it alone, Hester. Don't meddle.'

She regarded him steadily, trying to judge how surely he

meant what he said. Was it advice, or a command?

There was no anger in his face, but neither was there any hint that he would change his mind. It was the first time he had forbidden her anything that mattered to her. She had never before found it other than slightly amusing that he should exercise a certain amount of authority, and she had been quite willing to indulge him. This was different. She could not abandon Cleo, even to please Monk. Or if it came to the worst, and it might, even to avoid a serious quarrel with him. To do so would make it impossible to live with herself. All happiness would be contaminated, and if for her, then for him also. How would she explain that to him? It was the first real difficulty between them, the first gulf which could not be bridged by laughter or a physical closeness.

She saw the shadow in his face. He understood, if not in detail, then at least the essence.

'Perhaps you could enquire,' he suggested cautiously. 'But you will have to be extremely careful, or you will make things worse. I don't imagine the hospital authorities will look on her kindly.'

It was retreat, made gracefully and so discreetly it was barely perceptible, but very definitely a retreat all the same. The rush of gratitude inside her was so fierce she felt dizzy. A darkness had been avoided. She wanted to throw her arms around him and hold him, feel the warmth and the strength of his body next to hers, the touch of his skin. She almost did, until intelligence warned her that it would be clumsy. It would draw attention to his retreat and that would be small gratitude for it. Instead she lowered her eyes.

'Oh, yes,' she said gravely. 'I shall have to be very careful indeed – should I make any enquiry. Actually at the moment I can't think of anything to ask. I shall merely listen and observe . . . for the time being.'

He smiled with the beginning of satisfaction. He was aware of her gratitude to him, and she knew he was. It was even a sense of obligation for the immense weight lifted, and he knew that also. She could either be annoyed or see the funny aspect of it. She chose the latter, and looked up at him, smiling too.

She prepared dinner: cold ham and vegetables, and hot apple pie with cream. Sitting at the table, and sharing it with considerable pleasure, she asked him a little more about Miriam and the Stourbridge family.

He obviously considered hard before answering, waiting several minutes, eating the last of his pie and accepting a second serving.

'All the facts I know seem to mean nothing,' he said at last. 'They have made Miriam more welcome than one might have foreseen, considering that she has little money or family connections and she is to marry their only son. Everything I can observe supports their assertion that they are fond of her and accept that she is the one woman who can make him happy. As to whether she will give him an heir or not, she is young enough.'

'But she did not have any children in her marriage to Mr Gardiner,' Hester pointed out. 'That would make the possibility less likely.'

'I am sure they have considered that.' He took more cream, pouring it liberally over the pie and eating it with unconcealed pleasure.

She watched with relief. She was still an unconfident pastry cook, and she had had no time even to look for a woman to come in during the day. It was something she really must attend to, and soon. A well-ordered domestic life was halfway not only to Monk's happiness, but her own. She did not wish to have to spend either time or emotional energy upon the details of living. She would make enquiries tomorrow – unless, of course, she was too busy with matters at the hospital, and with whatever might be done for Cleo Anderson. That was immeasurably more important, even if they ate sandwiches from a pedlar.

'Cleo Anderson!' Callandra said. 'Are you sure?' It was a protest against the truth rather than a real question. Hester was alone with Beck and Callandra for a few moments in the surgeons' waiting room.

Kristian stood a yard away from Callandra, but any careful observer would have seen the silent communication between them. There was never a meeting of eyes – almost the opposite; an awareness on a deeper level.

'I had no idea,' he said softly. 'What risks she was taking . . . all the time. How long have you known?' He was looking at Hester.

'I don't really know.' She was still being overcareful, as if Sergeant Robb were just beyond the door. 'At least . . . not with evidence.'

'Of course not,' Kristian said, twisting his lips a little. 'No one wishes to find evidence. You were quite right not to tell anyone of it. Poor woman.' His hands clenched more tightly by his sides. 'It is profoundly wrong that any person should have to take such risks to assist the poor and the sick.'

'It's monstrous!' Callandra agreed, without looking at him. 'But we must help! There has to be a way. What does William say?'

Hester had no intention of repeating the conversation, merely the conclusion, and that slightly altered. 'That we should be extremely careful in making any enquiries,' she replied.

'More than careful,' Kristian agreed. 'Thorpe would be delighted to brand all nurses as thieves—'

'He will do!' Callandra cut across him, her face pinched with unhappiness. 'He'll know soon enough. No doubt the police will be here to ask questions.'

'Is there anything we can conceal?' Hester looked from one to the other of them. She had no idea what good it would do; it was instinctive rather than rational. If they convicted Cleo Anderson of murdering Treadwell, a bottle or two of morphine one way or another was hardly going to make a difference. She knew the moment the words were out that it was foolish.

'What proof do they have that it was her?' Kristian asked more levelly. The first shock was wearing off. 'Possibly he was blackmailing her, but then he may have blackmailed others as well. She was hardly on an income to provide him with much.'

'Unless she gave him morphine,' Callandra said with quiet sadness. 'And he sold it. That would be worth a great deal more.'

Hester had not even thought of that. She did not believe Cleo would sell morphine herself, but she could understand the necessity, if Treadwell had been pressing her for money. But what had made the difference that suddenly, on that particular night, she had resorted to murder? Desperation . . . or simply opportunity?

Why was she accepting Cleo's guilt, even in her own mind?

'But what evidence?' Kristian repeated. 'Did anyone see her? Did she leave anything behind at the scene? Is there anything which excludes another person?'

'No . . . simply that his body was found on the path near her house, and he had crawled there from wherever he was attacked.' Hester could see the reasoning all too clearly. 'It was assumed at first that he had been trying to get help. Now they will be thinking it was no coincidence, but he was deliberately pointing towards her.'

Kristian frowned. 'You mean they met somewhere close by, she attacked him, left believing him dead, but still conscious, he crawled after her?'

Callandra's face pulled tight with distress.

'Why not?' Hester loathed saying it, but it was there in the air between them. 'He came to blackmail her, and she had reached the point of desperation – perhaps she had nothing more to pay him – and either she intended before she went, to kill him, or it happened on the spur of the moment.'

'And where was Miriam?' Callandra asked. Then her expression quickened. 'Or did he drop Miriam wherever she wished to be, and go back to Cleo Anderson? That would explain why Miriam did not know he was dead!'

Hester shook her head. 'Whatever the answer is, it does not help Cleo now.'

They looked at each other grimly, and none could think of anything hopeful to say.

Matters only seemed worse when, an hour or so later, Hester and Callandra were summoned to the office of an extremely angry Fermin Thorpe, and ordered by him to assist Sergeant Robb in his inquiries.

Robb stood uncomfortably to the side of Thorpe's desk, looking first at Thorpe himself, then at Callandra, lastly and unhappily at Hester.

'I'm sorry, ma'am,' he seemed to be addressing both of them. 'I'd rather not have had to place you in this position, but I need to know more about the medicines Mr Thorpe here says are missing from your apothecary's room.'

'I didn't know about it until this morning,' Thorpe said furiously, his face pink. 'It should have been reported to me at the very first instance. Somebody will answer for this!'

'I think first we had better see precisely what is provable, Mr Thorpe,' Callandra said coldly. 'It does not do to cast accusations around freely before one is certain of the facts. It is too easy to ruin a reputation, and too difficult to mend it again when one discovers mistakes have been made.' She stared at him defiantly, daring him to contradict her.

Thorpe was very conscious of his position as a governor of the hospital, and his innate general superiority. However he also had an acute social awareness, and Callandra had a title, albeit a courtesy one because of her late father's position. He decided upon caution, at least for the meantime.

'Of course, Lady Callandra. We do not yet know the entire situation.' He looked sideways at Robb. 'I assure you, Sergeant, I shall do all within my power to be of assistance. We must get the facts of the matter and put an end to all dishonesty. I shall assist you myself.'

It was what Hester had feared. It would be so much easier to make light of the losses, even to mislead Robb a little, if Thorpe were not there. She had no idea what the apothecary would do, where his loyalties lay, or how frightened he would be for his own position.

Thorpe hesitated, and Hester realised with a lurch of hope that he did not know enough about the medicines to conduct the search and inventory without assistance.

'Perhaps one of us might fetch Mr Phillips?' she offered. 'And perhaps come with you to make notes . . . for our own needs. After all, we shall have to attend to the matter and see that it doesn't happen again. We need to know the truth of it even more than Sergeant Robb does.'

Thorpe grasped the rescue. 'Indeed, Mrs Monk.' Suddenly he found he could remember her name without the usual difficulty.

She smiled at it, but did not remark. Before he could change his mind, she glanced at Callandra, then led the way out of the office and along the wide corridor towards the apothecary's room. She knew Callandra would fetch Mr Phillips, and possibly even have a discreet word with him as to the effects upon all of them of whatever he might say. Presumably he would not yet know of the charge against Cleo Anderson, far less the motive attributed to her.

She did not dare look at Sergeant Robb. He might too easily guess Callandra's intention. It was not a great leap of foresight.

They walked briskly, one behind the other, and she stopped at the apothecary's door. Naturally Thorpe had a key, as he had to all doors. He opened it and stepped in and they followed behind, crowding into the small space. It was lined with cupboards right up to the ceiling. Each had its brass-bound keyhole, even the drawers beneath the shelf.

'I am afraid I do not have the keys to these,' Thorpe said reluctantly. 'But as you may see, it is all kept with the utmost safety. I do not know what more we can do, except employ a second apothecary so that there is someone on duty at every moment. Obviously we may require medicines at night as well as during the day, and no one man can be available around the clock, however diligent.'

'Who has keys at night now?' Robb asked.

'When Mr Phillips leaves he passes them to me,' Thorpe replied with discomfort, 'and I give them to the senior doctor who will remain here at night.'

'From your wording I assume that is not always the same person,' Robb concluded.

'No. We do not operate during the night. Seldom does one of the surgeons remain. Dr Beck does, on occasion, if he has a particularly severe case. More often it will be a student doctor.' He seemed about to add something, then changed his mind. Perhaps he felt the whole hospital under accusation because one of its nurses had been given the opportunity to steal, which had resulted in murder. He would have liked to distance himself from it, and it was plain in his expression.

'Who gives the medicine during the night?' Robb asked.

Thorpe was further discomfited. 'The doctor on duty.'

'Not a nurse?' Robb looked surprised.

'Nurses are to keep patients clean and comfortable,' Thorpe said a trifle sharply. 'They do not have medical training or experience, and are not given responsibilities except to do exactly as they are told.' He did not look at Hester.

Robb digested that information thoughtfully and without comment. Before he could formulate any further questions the apothecary entered, closely followed by Callandra, who avoided Hester's eye.

'Ah!' Thorpe said with relief. 'Phillips. Sergeant Robb here believes that a considerable amount of medicine had gone missing from our supplies, stolen by one of our nurses, and that this fact has provided the motive and means for her to be blackmailed.' He cleared his throat. 'We need to ascertain if this is true, and if it is, precisely what amounts are involved, how it was taken, and by whom.' He had effectively laid the fault, if not the responsibility, at Phillips' door.

Phillips did not answer immediately. He was a heavy-set man, rather overweight, with wild dark hair and a beard severely in need of trimming. Hester had always found him most agreeable and to have a pleasing, if somewhat waspish sense of humour. She hoped he was not going to get the blame for this, and she would be painfully disappointed in him if it were too easy to pass it on to Cleo.

'Have you nothing to say, man?' Thorpe demanded impatiently.

'Not without thinking about it carefully,' Phillips replied.

'Sir,' he added. 'If there's medicine really missing, rather than just wastage or a miscount, or somebody's error in writing what they took, then it's a serious matter.'

'Of course it's a serious matter!' Thorpe snapped. 'There's blackmail and murder involved!'

'Murder?' Phillips said with a slight lift of surprise in his voice, but only slight. 'Over our medicines? There's been no theft that size. I know that for sure.'

'Over a period of time,' Thorpe corrected him. 'Or so the sergeant thinks.'

Phillips fished for his keys and brought out a large collection on a ring. First he opened one of the drawers and pulled out a ledger. 'How far back, sir?' he asked Robb politely.

'I don't know,' Robb replied. 'Try a year or so. That should be sufficient.'

'Don't rightly know how I can tell,' Phillips obligingly opened the ledger to the same month the previous year. He scanned the page, and the following one. 'Everything tallies here, an' there's no way we can know if it was what we had then in the cupboards. Doesn't look like anyone's altered it. Anyway, I'd know if they had, and I'd have told Mr Thorpe.'

Thorpe stepped closer and turned the pages of the ledger himself, examining from that date to the present. There were quite obviously no alterations made to the entries. It told them nothing. The checking in of medicines was all made in the one hand, the withdrawals in several different hands of varying degrees of elegance and literacy. There were a few misspellings.

Robb looked at them. 'Are these all doctors?' he asked.

'Of course,' Thorpe replied tartly. 'You don't imagine we give the keys to the nurses, do you? If the wretched woman has really stolen medicines from this hospital, then it will be sleight of hand while the doctor's back was turned, perhaps attending to a patient taken suddenly ill, or while he was otherwise distracted. It is a perfectly dastardly thing to do. I trust she will be punished to the fullest extent of the law, as a deterrent to any other person tempted to enrich themselves at the expense of those in their care!'

'Could just be wastage,' Phillips observed, his eyes wide, looking from Thorpe to Robb. 'Not easy to measure powders exact. Close enough, o' course, but over a couple o' dozen doses yer could be out a bit. Ever considered that, sir?'

'You couldn't blackmail anybody over that,' Robb replied, but his expression indicated that he said it with reluctance. 'There must be more. If there is nothing in the past that is provable now, would you check your present stocks exactly against what is in your books?'

'Of course.' Phillips had very little choice, nor, for that matter, had Robb.

They stood silently while Phillips went through his cupboards, weighing, measuring and counting, watched impatiently by Thorpe, anxiously by Callandra, and with unease by Robb.

Hester wondered if Robb had even a suspicion that his grandfather's suffering was treated by this very means, stolen not for gain but out of compassion, by Cleo Anderson whom he now sought to prove guilty of murdering Treadwell. She looked at his earnest face and saw pity in it, but no doubt, no tearing of loyalties . . . not yet.

Was Cleo guilty? If Treadwell were a blackmailer, was it possible she had believed him the lesser victim, rather than the patients she treated?

It was hard to believe, but it was not impossible.

'The quinine seems a bit short,' Phillips remarked, as if it were of no great moment. 'Could be bad measuring, I suppose. Or someone took a few doses in a crisis, an' forgot to make a note of it.'

'How far short?' Thorpe demanded, his face dark. 'Damn it, man, you can be more exact than that! What do you mean, "a bit"? You're an apothecary! You don't dose a patient with "a bit"!'

'About five hundred grains, sir,' Phillips answered very quietly.

Thorpe flushed deep pink. 'Good God! That's enough to dose a dozen men! This is very serious indeed. You'd better see what else is missing! Look at the morphine.'

Phillips obeyed. That measurement was even further short. Hester was not surprised. It was the obvious treatment for pain, as quinine was for fever. Cleo must have administered it, under supervision, often enough over the years to have an excellent idea of how much to give, and in what circumstances. Certainly Hester herself did.

Thorpe turned to Robb. 'I regret, Sergeant, but it seems you are perfectly correct. We are missing a substantial amount of medicine, and it is impossible any random thief could have taken it. It has to be one of our nurses.'

Hester drew breath to point out that it had only to be someone within the hospital staff over the last few years, but she knew that would be pointless. Thorpe would not entertain the idea of any of the doctors doing such a thing, and she had no desire to try to shift the blame on to Phillips.

Perhaps it was Cleo Anderson . . . in fact if Hester were honest, she had no doubt. It was the reason for it they had misunderstood, and she did not wish to draw their attention to that because it would make no difference whatever to the charge.

With Cleo in prison, who would now care for the old and ill that she had visited with medicines to give them respite from distress? Specifically, what of John Robb?

Callandra handed Robb the note she had made of the missing medicines and the amounts. He took it and put it in his pocket, thanking her. He looked at Phillips again.

'Over what period has this been missed, Mr Phillips?'

'Can't say, sir.' Phillips replied instantly. 'Haven't had occasion to check in that detail for some time. Could have been careless measuring, perhaps even someone spilled something.' His black eyes were bland, his voice reasonable. He turned to include Thorpe in his address. 'More likely careless noting down of what was given out proper, but in the heat of a bad night, or something of a crisis. Got to make an allowance. Medicine is an art, Mr Thorpe, not an exact science.'

'God damn it, man!' Thorpe exploded. 'Don't tell me how to conduct the practice of medicine in my own hospital!'

Phillips did not reply, nor did he seem particularly disturbed by Thorpe's anger, which had the effect of both heightening it, and confusing Thorpe into momentary silence. He had not expected an apothecary to be indifferent to him.

Phillips turned to Robb. 'If there is anything else I can do for you, Sergeant, I'm sure Mr Thorpe would want me to. Just tell me. And before you ask, I've got no suspicions of any o' the nurses . . . not in that way. Some o' them drink a spot too much porter on an empty stomach. But then I dare say half o' London does that from time to time. Specially as porter is included in the wages, like. You'll find me round an' about most any day except Sunday.' And without asking anything further he handed the keys to Thorpe and went out.

'Impertinent oaf!' Thorpe swore under his breath.

'But honest?' Robb asked.

Hester saw the abhorrence in Thorpe's face. He would dearly like to have paid Phillips out for his arrogance, and here was an ideal opportunity given him. On the other hand to admit he had employed an apothecary of whom he had doubts would be a confession of his own gross incompetence.

But just in case temptation should prove too powerful, Hester answered for him.

'Of course, Sergeant,' she said with a smile. 'Do you imagine Mr Thorpe would have permitted him to remain in such a responsible position if he were not trustworthy in every way? If a nurse is a little tipsy it is one thing. She may spill a pail of water or leave a floor unswept. If an apothecary is not above reproach people may die.'

'Quite!' Thorpe agreed hastily, with a venomous look at Hester, then with a considerable effort to alter his expression he turned to Robb. 'Please question anyone you wish to. I doubt you will find any proof that this wretched woman stole the quinine and morphine. If there were any, we should know of it ourselves. I presume you have her in custody?'

'Yes, sir, we have. Thank you, sir,' Robb bade them good day and left.

Hester glanced at Callandra, then excused herself also. She had other matters to attend to, and urgently.

Hester had no difficulty in obtaining permission to visit Cleo Anderson in her cell. She simply told the gaoler that she was an official from the hospital where Cleo worked, and it was necessary to learn certain medical information from her in order for treatments to continue in her absence.

It transpired that the gaoler knew Cleo – she had nursed his mother in her final illness – and he was only too pleased to repay the kindness in any way he could. Indeed he seemed embarrassed by the situation, and Hester could not guess from his manner whether he thought Cleo could be guilty or not. However, word had spread that the charge was that she had killed a blackmailer, and he had a very low regard for such people, possibly sufficiently low that he was not overly concerned by the death of one of them.

The cell door shut with the heavy, echoing sound of metal on metal, sending a shiver of memory through Hester, bringing back her own few hideous days in Edinburgh when she was where Cleo sat now, alone and facing trial, and perhaps death.

Cleo looked at her in surprise. Her face was pale and she had the bruised, staring look of someone deeply shocked, but she seemed composed, even resigned. Hester could not recall if she had felt like that. She believed she had always wanted to fight, that inside herself she was screaming out against the injustice. There was too much to live for not to struggle, always far too much.

But then she had not killed Mary Farraline.

Even if Cleo had killed Treadwell, if he had been blackmailing her over the medicines, it was a highly understandable action. Not excusable, perhaps, but surely any God worth worshipping would find more pity than blame for her?

Maybe she did not believe that? At least not now . . . at this moment, facing human justice.

'Can I help you?' Hester said aloud. 'Is there anything I can bring for you? Clothes, soap, a clean towel, rather better food? What about your own spoon? Or cup?'

Cleo smiled faintly. The very practicality of the suggestions contrasted with what she had expected. She had anticipated anger, blame, pity, curiosity. She looked puzzled.

'I've been in prison,' Hester explained. 'I hated the soap and the scratchy towels. It's a little thing. And I wanted my own spoon. I remember that.'

'But they let you go . . .' Cleo looked at her with anxiety so sharp it was close to breaking her composure. 'An' they let Miriam go? Is she all right?'

Hester sat in the chair, leaning forward a little. She liked Cleo more with each encounter. She could not watch her distress with any impartiality at all, or think of her fate with acceptance. 'Yes, they let her go.'

''Ome?' She was watching Hester intently.

'No . . . with Lucius and Major Stourbridge.' She searched Cleo's face for anything that would help her understand why Miriam had dreaded it. She saw nothing, no flicker of comprehension, however swiftly concealed.

'Was she all right?' Cleo repeated fearfully.

It seemed cruel to tell her the truth, but Hester did not know enough to judge which lies would do least harm.

'No,' she answered. 'I don't think so. Not from what my husband said. She would far rather have gone anywhere else at all – even remained in prison – but she was not given the choice. The police could not hold her because there was no charge any more, but it was obvious to everyone that she was deeply distressed, and since she is a witness to much of what happened, they have a certain authority over where she should go.'

Cleo said nothing. She stared down at her hands folded in her lap.

Hester watched her closely. 'Do you know why she ran away from Cleveland Square, and why she had to be all but dragged back there?'

Cleo looked up quickly. 'No – no, I don't. She wouldn't tell me.'

Hester believed her. The confusion and distress in her eyes were too real. 'Don't answer me whether you took the medicines or not,' she said quietly. 'I know you did, and I know what for.'

Cleo regarded her thoughtfully for several moments before she spoke. 'Wot's going to 'appen to them, miss? There's nobody to look after them. The ones with family are better off than those 'oo 'aven't, but even they can't afford wot they need, or they don't know wot it is. They get old, an' their children move on, leavin' 'em behind. The young don't care about Trafalgar an' Waterloo now. A few years an' they'll forget the Crimea too. Those soldiers are all the thing now, because they're young and 'andsome still. We get upset about a young man wi' no arms or no legs, or insides all ter pieces. But when they get old we can't be bothered. We say they're goin' to die soon anyway. Wot's the point in spendin' time an' money on 'em?'

There was no argument to make. Of course it was not true everywhere, but in too many instances it was.

'What about John Robb, sailor from the victory at Trafalgar?' Hester asked. 'Consumption, by the sound of him.'

Cleo's face tightened and she nodded. 'I don't think 'e 'as long. 'Is grandson does everythin' 'e can for 'im, but that isn't much. 'E can't give 'im any ease without the morphine.' She did not ask, but it was in her eyes, willing Hester to agree.

Hester knew what that would involve. She would have to give him the morphine herself. It would involve her in theft. But to refuse would compound the old man's suffering, and his sense of being abandoned. When he understood, he would also know that his suffering was of less importance to her than keeping herself from risk. Alleviating pain was all right, as long as the cost was small – a little time, even weariness, but not personal danger.

'Yes, of course.' The words were out of her mouth before she had time to weigh what she was committing herself to.

'Thank you,' Cleo said softly, a momentary gleam in her eyes, as if she had seen a light in enclosing darkness. 'And I would like the soap, and the spoon, if it is not too much trouble.'

'Of course.' She brushed them aside as already done. What she really wanted was to help with some defence, but what was there? She realised with bitterness that she was half convinced that Cleo had killed Treadwell. 'Have you got a lawyer to speak for you?'

'A lawyer? What can he say? It won't make no difference.' The tone of her voice was flat, as if she had suddenly been jerked back to the harshness of the present and her own reality, not John Robb's. There was a closed air about her, excluding Hester from her emotions till she felt rebuffed, an intruder. Was Cleo still somehow defending Miriam Gardiner? Or was she guilty, and believed she deserved to die?

'Did you kill Treadwell?' Hester said abruptly.

Cleo hesitated, was about to speak, then changed her mind and said nothing. Hester had the powerful impression that she had been going to deny it, but she would never know, and asking again would be useless. The mask was complete.

'Was he blackmailing you?' she asked instead.

Cleo sighed. 'Yeah, 'course 'e was. Do most things for money, that one.'

'I see.' There did not seem much else to say. Hester had resolved without question or doubt that she would do all she could to help Cleo, it was a matter of thinking what that would be. Already Oliver Rathbone's name was in her mind.

Cleo grasped her wrist, holding hard, startling her. 'Don't tell the sergeant!' she said fiercely. 'It can't change wot 'e does, an' . . .' she blinked, her face bruised with hurt, 'an' don't tell old Mr Robb why I'm not there. Tell 'im something else . . . anything. Perhaps by the time they try me, an' . . . well, 'e may not 'ave to know. 'E could be gone 'isself by then.'

'I'll tell him something else,' Hester promised. 'Probably that you've gone to look after a relative, or something.'

'Thank you.' Cleo's gratitude was so naked, Hester felt guilty. She was on the edge of saying that she intended to do far more, but she had no idea what it could be, and to raise hope she could not fulfil was thoughtlessly cruel.

'I'll come back with the soap,' she promised. 'And the spoon.' Then she went to the door and banged for the gaoler to let her out.

The next thing she did she expected to be the most difficult, and it was certainly the one of which she was most afraid. She felt guilty even as she walked up the steps and in through the hospital door. She returned the stare of two young medical students too directly, as if to deny their suspicion of her. Then she felt ridiculous, and was sure she was blushing. She had done nothing yet. She was no different from the person she had been yesterday, or this morning when she had been perfectly happy to confront Fermin Thorpe in his office and rack her brain to defend Cleo Anderson. Would Callandra in turn have to rack her brain tomorrow to defend her?

And yet she could not escape it. Quite apart from her fondness for John Robb, she had given Cleo the promise. She had tried to form a plan, but so much depended on opportunity. It was impractical to try stealing Phillips' keys, and unfair to him. Added to which, he really was extremely careful with them, and might be the more so now.

How long would she have to wait for a crisis of some sort to present a chance, the apothecary's room open and unattended, or Phillips there, but his back turned? She was suddenly furious with herself. She had been alone with Cleo, and not had the wits to ask her how she had accomplished it! She had just blithely promised to do the same, without the faintest idea how to go about it. It was very humbling to realise her own stupidity.

She stood in the middle of the passage and was still there when Kristian Beck reached her.

'Hester?' he said with concern. 'Are you all right?'

She recalled herself swiftly, and began speaking with the idea only half formed in her mind. 'I was wondering how Cleo Anderson managed to steal the morphine. Phillips is really very careful. I mean, how do you think it happened, in practical detail?'

He frowned. 'Does it matter?'

Why did he ask? Was he indifferent to the thefts? Was he so certain Cleo was guilty that the details did not matter? Or was it even conceivable that he had some sympathy with her?

'I don't want to prove it,' she answered steadily, meeting his eyes with complete candour. 'I would like above all things to disprove it, but failing that, at least to understand.'

'She is charged with murdering Treadwell,' he said softly. 'The jury cannot excuse that, whatever they privately feel. There is no provision or law for murdering blackmailers, or for stealing medicine, even if it is to treat the old and ill for whom there is no other help.' The lacerating edge in his voice betrayed his own feelings too clearly.

'I know that,' she said in little above a whisper. 'I should still like to know exactly how she did it.'

He stood in silence for several moments.

She waited. Part of her wanted to leave before it was too late. But escaping would be only physical. Morally and emotionally she was still trapped. And that was trivial compared with Cleo – or John Robb.

'What do you think she took?' Kristian asked at length.

She swallowed. 'Morphine, for an old man who has consumption. It won't cure him, but it gives him a little rest.'

'Very understandable,' he answered. 'I hope she gave him some sherry in water as well?'

'I believe so.'

'Good. I need a few things from the apothecary myself. I'll go and get the keys. You can help me, if you would.' And without waiting for her answer, he turned sharply and strode off.

He came back a few minutes later with the keys and opened the door. He went inside and left her to follow him. He started to unlock various cupboards and take out leaves for infusions, cordials and various powders. He passed several of them to Hester while he opened bottles and jars, then closed them again. When he had finished he ushered her out, relocked the door, took some of the medicines back from her, then thanked her, and left her standing in the corridor with a small bottle of cordial and a week's dosage of morphine, plus several small paper screws of quinine.

She put them quickly into her pockets and went back towards the front door and out of it. She felt as if dozens of eyes were boring holes in her back, but actually she passed only one nurse with a mop and bucket, and Fermin Thorpe himself, striding along with his face set, hardly recognising her.

John Robb was delighted to see Hester. He had had a bad night, but was a trifle better towards late afternoon, and the loneliness of sitting in his chair in the empty house, even with the sun slanting in through the windows, had made him melancholy. His face lit with a smile when he recognised her step and even before she entered the room he was tidying the little space around him and making ready for her.

'How are you?' he said the moment she came through the door.

'I'm very well,' she answered cheerfully. He must never

know about Cleo, if there was any way it could be prevented.

She could not warn Michael without explaining to him the reason, and that would place him in an impossible situation. He would then have either to benefit indirectly from the thefts, which he would find intolerable, or else have to testify against Cleo from his own knowledge. That would also be unbearable, for the old man's sake as well as his own. Such disillusion and sense of betrayal might be more than Mr Robb's old and frail body could take. And then Michael's guilt would be crippling.

'I'm very well indeed,' she repeated firmly. 'How are you? I hope you are well enough to share a cup of tea with me? I brought some you might like to try, and a few biscuits.' She smiled back at him. 'Of course it was all an excuse, so you will tell me more stories of your life at sea, and the places you have been to. You were going to describe the Indies for me. You said how brilliant the water was, like a cascade of jewels, and that you had seen fishes that could fly.'

'Oh, bless you, girl, I have an' all,' he agreed with a smile. 'An' more than that too. You put the kettle on an' I'll tell you all you want to know.'

'Of course.' She walked across the room and pulled the biscuits and tea out of the bag they were in, filled the kettle from the jug and set it on the stove, then with her back to him, took out the cordial bottle and placed it on the shelf, half behind a blue bag of sugar. Then she slipped the morphine out of her other pocket and set it underneath the two thin papers that were left from Cleo's last visit.

'Was it very hot in the Indies?' she asked.

'You wouldn't believe it, girl,' he replied. 'Felt as if the sea itself were on the boil, all simmerin' an' steamin'. The air were so thick it clogged up in your throat, like you could drink it.'

217

'I think you could drink it here too, when it gets cold enough!' she said with a laugh.

'Aye! An' I bin north too!' he said enthusiastically. 'Great walls of ice rising out o' the sea. You never seen anything like it, girl. Beautiful an' terrible, they was. An' they'd freeze your breath like a white fog in front of you.'

She turned and smiled at him, then began to make the tea. 'Mrs Anderson had to go away for a little while. Someone in her family ill, I think.' She scalded the pot, tipped out the water, then put the fresh leaves in and poured the rest of the water from the kettle. 'She asked me to come and see you. I think she knew I'd like that. I hope it's all right with you?'

He relaxed, looking at her with undisguised pleasure. 'Sure it's all right. Then you can tell me some o' the places you've bin. About them Turks an' the like. Although I'll miss Cleo. Good woman, she is. Nothin' ever too much trouble. An' I seen her so tired she were fit to drop. I hope as her family appreciates her.'

A lie was the only thing. 'I'm sure they will,' she said without a shadow in her voice. 'And I'll get a message to her that you're fine.'

'You do that, girl. An' tell her I was asking after her.'

'I will.' Suddenly she found it difficult to master herself. It was ridiculous to want to cry now! Nothing had changed. She sniffed hard and blew her nose, then set out the rest of the things for tea and opened the bag of biscuits. She had bought him the best she could find. They looked pretty on the plate. She was determined this should be a party.

Hester did not broach the subject with Monk until after they had eaten. They were sitting quietly watching the last of the light fade beyond the windows and wondering if it was time to light the gas, or if it would be pleasanter just to allow the dusk to fill the room.

Naturally she had no intention whatever of even mentioning John Robb, let alone telling Monk that she was taking over his care from Cleo. Apart from the way he would react to such information, the knowledge would compromise him. There was no need for both of them to tell lies.

'What can we do to help Cleo Anderson?' she said, in a sentence taking it for granted that there was no argument as to whether they would.

He lifted his head sharply.

She waited.

'Everything we've done so far has made it worse,' he said unhappily. 'The best service we can do the poor woman is to leave the case alone.'

'If we do that she may well be hanged!' Hester argued. 'And that would be very wrong. Treadwell was a blackmailer. She is guilty of a crime in law, maybe, but no sin. We have to do something. Humanity requires it.'

'I discover facts, Hester,' he said quietly. 'Everything I've found so far indicates that Cleo killed him. I may sympathise with her, in fact I do. God knows, in her situation I might have done the same.'

She could see memory of the past sharp in his face, and knew what he was thinking. She remembered Joscelin Grey also, and the apartment in Mecklenburgh Square, and how close Monk had come to murder then.

'But that would not excuse me in law,' he continued. 'Nor would it alter anything the judge or jury could do. If she did kill him, there may be some mitigation, but she will have to say what it is. Then I could look for proof of it, if there is any.'

She was hesitant to ask him about Oliver Rathbone. There was too much emotion involved, old friendship, old love, and perhaps pain. She did not know how much. She had not seen

Rathbone since her marriage, but she remembered with a vividness so sharp she could see the candlelight in her mind's eye, and smell the warmth of the inn dining room, the night Rathbone had so nearly asked her to marry him. He had stopped only because she had allowed him to know, obliquely, that she could not accept, not yet. And he had let the moment pass.

'It's not only what happened,' she began almost tentatively. 'It's the interpretation, the argument, if you like.'

Monk regarded her gravely before replying. There was no criticism in his face, but an acute sadness. 'Some plea of mitigation? Don't you think you are holding out a false hope to her?'

That could be true.

'But we must try . . . mustn't we? We can't just give in without a fight?'

'What do you want to do?'

She said what he expected. 'We could ask Oliver . . .' She took a breath. 'We could at least set it before him, for his opinion?' She made it a question.

She could see no change in his expression, no anger, no stiffening.

'Of course,' he agreed. 'But don't expect too much.'

She smiled. 'No . . . just to try.'

Hester woke in the dark, feeling the movement as Monk got out of bed. Downstairs there was a banging on the front door, not loud, just sharp and insistent, as of someone who would not give up.

Monk pulled his jacket on over his nightshirt and Hester sat up, watching him go out of the bedroom in bare feet. She heard the door open and a moment later close again.

She saw the reflection of the hall light on the landing ceiling as the gas was lit.

She could bear it no longer. She slipped out of bed and put on a robe. She met Monk coming up the stairs, a piece of paper in his hand. His face was bleak with shock, his eyes dark.

'What is it?' she said with a catch in her breath.

'Verona Stourbridge.' His voice shook a little. 'She's been murdered! Just the same way as Treadwell. A single, powerful blow to the head . . . with a croquet mallet.' His fist closed over the white paper. 'Robb asked me to go.'

Chapter Eight

It took Monk nearly a quarter of an hour to find a hansom, first striding down Fitzroy Street to the Tottenham Court Road, then walking south towards Oxford Street.

He had left Hester furious at being excluded, but it would be in every way inappropriate for him to have taken her. She could serve no purpose except to satisfy her own curiosity, and she would quite obviously be intrusive. She had not argued, just seethed inside because she felt helpless and as confused as he was.

It was a fine night. A thin film of cloud scudded over a bright moon. The air was warm, the pavements still holding the heat of the day. His footsteps were loud in the near silence. A carriage rumbled by out of Percy Street and crossed towards Bedford Square, the moonlight shining for a moment on gleaming doors and the horses' polished flanks. Whoever had murdered Verona Stourbridge, it had not been Cleo Anderson. She was safely locked up in Hampstead police station.

What could this new and terrible event have to do with the death of James Treadwell?

Monk could see pedestrians on the footpath at the corner of Oxford Street, two men and a woman, laughing.

He tried to picture Mrs Stourbridge on the one occasion he had met her. He could not bring back her features, or even the colour of her eyes, only the overriding impression he had had of a kind of vulnerability. Underneath the poised manner and the lovely clothes was a woman who was acquainted with fear. Or perhaps that was only hindsight, now that she was dead . . . murdered.

It had to be one of her own family, or a servant – or Miriam. But why would Miriam kill her, unless she truly were insane.

He turned the corner and walked along the edge of the footpath in Oxford Street, watching the road all the time for sight of a cab. He could recall Miriam only too easily, the wide eyes, the sweep of her hair, the strength in her mouth. She had behaved without any apparent reason, but he had never met anyone who had given him more of a sense of inner sanity, of a wholeness no outside force could destroy.

Maybe that was what madness was . . . something inside you which the reality of the world did not touch?

A hansom slowed down and he hailed it, giving the Stourbridge address in Cleveland Square. The driver grumbled about going so far, and Monk ignored him, climbing inside and sitting down, engulfed in silence and thought again.

He reached the Stourbridge house, paid the driver and went up the steps. It was after one o'clock in the morning. All the surrounding houses were in darkness but here the hall and at least four other rooms blazed with light between the edges of imperfectly drawn curtains. There was another carriage outside, waiting. Presumably it was the doctor's.

The butler answered the door the moment after Monk knocked, and invited him in with a voice rasping with tension. The man was white-faced and his body beneath his black suit was rigid and very slightly shaking. He must have been told to expect Monk, because without seeking any instruction he showed him into the withdrawing room.

Three minutes later Robb came in, closing the door behind him. He looked almost as if he had been bereaved himself. The sight of Monk seemed to cheer him a little.

'Thank you for coming,' he said simply. 'This . . . it's the last thing I expected. Why should anybody attack Mrs Stourbridge?' His voice rose with desperate incomprehension. He looked exhausted and there was a stiffness about him that Monk recognised as fear. This was not the sort of crime he understood or the kind of people he had ever dealt with before. He knew he was out of his depth.

'Begin with the facts,' Monk said calmly, more confidence in his manner than he felt. 'Tell me exactly what you know. Who called you? What time? What did they say?'

Robb looked slightly startled, as if he had expected to begin with the body and accounts of where everyone was.

'A little before midnight,' he began, steadying himself, but still standing. 'Maybe quarter to. A constable banged on my door to say there'd been a murder in Bayswater that was part of my case, and the local police said I should come straight away. They had a cab waiting. I was on my way in not more than five minutes.' He started moving about restlessly, looking at Monk, then away again. 'He told me it was Mrs Stourbridge, and as soon as I knew that, I sent the beat constable around to get you.' He shook his head. 'I don't understand it! It can't be Cleo Anderson this time.' He faced Monk. 'Was I wrong about Mrs Gardiner, and she's done this too? Why? It makes no sense!'

'If the local police were called,' Monk said thoughtfully, 'and then they sent for you, then the body must have been found about eleven o'clock. That's over two hours ago. Who found her and where was she?'

'Major Stourbridge found her,' Robb answered. 'She was in her bedroom. It was only chance that he went in to say something to her, after he'd said good night and all the family had retired. He said he'd forgotten to mention something about a cousin coming to visit and just wanted to remind her. Poor man went into the bedroom and saw her crumpled on the floor and blood on the carpet.'

'Did he move her?' Monk asked. It would have been a natural enough thing to do.

'He says he half picked her up.' Robb's voice tightened, as if his throat were too stiff to speak properly. 'Sort of cradled her in his arms. I suppose for a moment he half hoped she wasn't dead.' He swallowed. 'But it's a pretty terrible wound. Looks like one very hard blow. The croquet mallet's still there, lying on the floor beside her. At least, that's what they told me it was. I've never seen one before.'

Monk tried not to visualise it, and failed. His mind created the crumpled figure and the broken bone and the blood.

'He says he laid her back where she was,' Robb added miserably.

'What was she wearing?' Monk asked.

'Er . . .'

'A nightgown, or a dress?' Monk pressed.

Robb coloured faintly. 'A long, whitish sort of robe. I think it could be a nightgown.' He was transparently uncomfortable discussing such things. It belonged in the realms where he felt a trespasser.

'Where was she lying, exactly?' Monk asked. 'What do you think she was doing when she was struck? Was it from behind or in front?'

Robb thought for a moment. 'She was lying half on her side, about six feet away from the bed. Looked as if she had been talking to someone and turned away from them, and

226

they struck her from behind. At least that's what I would guess. It fits.'

'She had her back to them? You're sure?'

'If the Major didn't move her too much, yes. The wound is at the back on one side a bit. Couldn't hit someone like that from the front.' His eyes widened a little. 'So considering it was in her bedroom, she would hardly turn her back on anyone she was frightened of.' His lips pulled tight. 'Not that I ever held out hope it was a burglar. There's no sign of anyone forcing their way in. Nothing broken. Too early for burglars anyway. Nobody breaks into a house when half the household is still up and about. It was one of them, wasn't it?' That was less than half a question.

'Looks as if the local police worked that out,' Monk said drily. 'Not surprised they wanted to be rid of this. Have you asked where everyone in the house was yet?'

'Only Major Stourbridge. He seems to have a good command of himself, but he's as white as a ghost and looks pretty poorly to me. He said he was in bed. He'd dismissed his man for the night and was about to put out the light when he remembered this cousin who's coming. Seems Mrs Stourbridge wasn't very fond of him. He was wondering whether to write tomorrow morning and say it wasn't convenient.'

'What time was Mrs Stourbridge last seen alive?'

'I don't know. Her maid is hysterical and being looked after by the housekeeper and I haven't spoken with her yet.' He glanced around the spacious room where they were talking. Even in the dim light of one lamp there was a warmth to it. The glow reflected on silver frames and winked in the faceted crystal of a row of decanters. 'I'm not used to this kind of people having to do with violence,' he said miserably. 'Questioning them. It's more often a matter of burglary, and asking the servants about strangers being by, and not locking up properly.'

'This kind of thing doesn't happen very often in anybody's house,' Monk replied. 'But it's best to ask now, before they have time to forget, or talk to each other and think up any lies.'

'Only one of them's going to lie—' Robb began.

Monk snorted. 'People lie for all sorts of reasons, and about things they think have nothing to do with the case. You'd better see the maid, hysterics or not. You need to know what time Mrs Stourbridge was left alone and alive, or if she was expecting anyone. What she said, how she seemed, anything the woman can tell you.'

'Will you stay?'

'If you want.'

The maid was sent for, and came, supported by the butler and looking as if she might buckle at the knees any moment. Her eyes were red-rimmed and she kept dabbing her face with a handkerchief, which was now little more than a twisted rag.

She had been guided to one of the armchairs and the butler permitted to remain. Robb began his questions. He was very gentle with her, as if he himself were embarrassed.

'Yes, sir,' she gulped. 'Mrs Stourbridge went to bed about ten o'clock, or a little after. I laid out 'er clothes for tomorrow. A green an' white dress for the morning. She was going to visit a picture gallery.' Her eyes filled with tears.

'What time did you leave her?' Robb asked.

She sniffed fiercely, and made an attempt to dab her cheeks with the wet handkerchief. 'About quarter to eleven.'

'Was she already in bed?' Monk interrupted.

She looked at him with surprise.

'I'm sure you'll remember, if you think for a moment,' he

encouraged. 'It's rather important.'

'Is it?'

'Yes. It matters whether she was expecting someone to call on her, or not.'

'Oh. Yes. I see. No I don't. She wouldn't hardly expect a thief who'd break in an' kill her!'

'No one broke in, Pearl.'

'What are you saying?' She was aghast. Her hands tightened in her lap till the handkerchief tore.

Robb took charge of the situation again.

'We are saying it was someone already in the house who killed Mrs Stourbridge.'

'It . . . it never is!' she shook her head. 'No one 'ere would do such a thing! We in't murderers!' Now she was both frightened and affronted.

'Yes, it was,' Robb insisted. 'The local police and your own butler and footman have made a thorough search. No one broke in. Now tell me all you know of everyone's comings and goings from the time you left the dinner table until now.'

She replied dutifully, but nothing she had to say either incriminated anyone, or cleared them.

The maid assigned to Miriam was of no greater help. She had seen Miriam to her bed even earlier, and had no idea whether she had remained there or not. She had been excused and gone up to her own room in the attic. Mrs Gardiner was extremely easy to work for and she could not believe any ill of her, no matter what anyone said. People who couldn't speak well shouldn't speak at all!

Nor could any of the other servants swear to the movements of any of the family. However, the maids knew the time of each other's retiring. The cook, whose room was nearest the stairs down, was a light sleeper, and the second stair creaked. She was certain no one had passed after she had gone up at quarter to eleven.

At last Monk forced himself to go and look at the body. A local constable was on duty on the landing outside the door. He was tired and unhappy. He showed them in without looking past them.

Verona Stourbridge lay as if eased gently on to her back, halfway between the chest of drawers and the bed. It must have been where her husband had laid her when he realised he could do nothing more for her, and at last let her go. The carpet was soaked dark with blood about a foot away from her head. It was easy to see where she had originally fallen.

Her hands were limp and there was nothing in either of them. She was wearing a robe over her nightgown. It looked like silk, and when Monk bent to touch it he knew instantly that it was: soft, expensive and beautiful. He wondered if he would ever be able to buy Hester anything like that. This one would be thrown away after the case was closed. No one would ever want to wear it again.

He stood up and turned to Robb.

'Member of the family?' Robb said hoarsely.

'Yes,' Monk agreed.

'Why?' Robb was bewildered. 'Why would any of them kill her? Her husband, do you think? Or Lucius?' He took a deep breath. 'Or Miriam Gardiner? But why would she?'

'We'll look for the reason afterwards,' Monk answered. 'Let's go and speak to Major Stourbridge.'

Robb turned reluctantly and allowed Monk to lead the way.

Harry Stourbridge met them in the library. He was fully dressed in a dark suit. His fair hair was poking up in tufts and his eyes were sunken into the bones of his head as if the flesh no longer had life or firmness. He did not speak, but looked from Robb to Monk, and then back again.

'Please sit down, Major Stourbridge,' Robb said awkwardly. He did not know whether the man was a bereaved husband with whom he should sympathise, or a suspect who deserved his hostility and contempt.

Stourbridge obeyed. His legs seemed to fold under him and he hit the seat rather too hard.

Robb sat opposite him, and Monk took the third chair in the group.

In a low, husky voice Stourbridge retold the story of the forgotten message, of leaving his own room and going along the corridor, seeing and hearing no one else, of knocking on his wife's door and going in.

Monk stopped him. 'Was the light on, sir?'

'No . . . not the main light, just the bracket on the wall.' He turned to look at him with a lift of interest. 'Does that mean something? She sleeps with it like that. Doesn't like the dark. Just enough to see by, a glow, no more.'

'But enough if she were speaking with someone?' Monk persisted.

'Yes, I suppose so. If it were . . . someone she knew well. One would not receive . . .' He stopped, uncertainty filling his face again.

'We have already ascertained that it was not any of the servants,' Robb said quietly. 'That leaves only the family, and Mrs Gardiner.'

Stourbridge looked as if he had been struck again.

'That is not p-possible,' he stammered. 'No one would . . .' He stopped. He was a man experienced in war, the violence and pain of battle and the horror of its aftermath. There was little that could shock or astound him, but this had cut deep into his emotion in a way the honesty of battle never could. He turned to Monk.

There was nothing Monk could alter, but he could ease

the manner of dealing with it. Reality was a kind of healing, and the beginning of exerting some control over the chaos.

'We need to speak to everyone,' he said, looking at Stourbridge and meeting his eyes. 'Once we have eliminated the impossible, we will have a better idea of what happened.'

'What? Oh yes, I see. I don't think I can be of much help.' He seemed to focus a little more clearly. 'I believe Aiden retired quite early to his room. He had a number of letters to write. He has been away from his home for a while. Verona . . . Verona relied on him rather a lot. They have always been close. I . . .' He took a deep breath and mastered himself with difficulty. 'I was away a great deal during the early years of our marriage. Military duties.' He looked beyond Monk into some distance within his memory. 'A young army wife does not have an easy time. I was often posted to places where it was unsuitable for her to accompany me. No facilities for women, you see? We were fighting, moving about. She didn't lack courage, but she hadn't the physical strength. She,' he blinked fiercely, 'she lost several babies . . . early stages. Lucius was . . . long waited for. She was thirty-five. We had all but given up.' His voice cracked. 'She longed for a child so much.'

Monk was loath to interrupt him, even though he was wandering far from the point. Perhaps it was necessary to him to bring her back even if only in words, to try to make others see her as he had, who had known and loved her.

'When I was in Egypt and the Sudan,' he went on, 'which I was quite a lot, Aiden would be with her.'

'Mrs Gardiner . . . ?' Robb asked.

Stourbridge jerked up his head. 'No! No – I cannot believe it of her.'

Monk could not either, and yet the alternatives were little easier. Of course it was possible Stourbridge himself was lying, but then anyone might be.

'What time did she retire?' he asked. 'Perhaps you had better tell me the pattern of the whole evening, from sitting down to dinner.'

Again Stourbridge looked not at either of his listeners, but into the distance between them. 'Miriam did not dine with us. She said she felt unwell and would have a tray sent up to her room. I don't think she cared whether she ate or not, she did it to oblige us, and perhaps to avoid discussing the subject or causing Lucius to try to persuade her. In fact she would not speak to him except in company.'

'They had quarrelled?' Robb asked quickly.

'No.' He shook his head. 'That is the thing I do not understand. Nor does he. There has been no quarrel at all. She speaks to him in the gentlest manner, but will not explain why she left, nor what happened to Treadwell. And since the Anderson woman has been arrested, that question is no longer at issue.' He frowned, creasing up his face. 'She merely sits in her room and refuses to do or say anything beyond the barest civility.'

'She is deeply distressed over Mrs Anderson,' Monk interposed. 'She was in every sense except the literal, a mother to her, perhaps the only one she knows.'

Stourbridge looked down at the floor. 'I forgot. Of course she must be distressed beyond words. But I wish she would turn to us for comfort, and not grieve by herself. We are at our wits' end to know how to help her.'

'No one can help,' Monk replied. 'It must simply be borne. Please describe what happened during dinner, any conversation of importance, especially any differences of opinion, however trivial.'

Stourbridge looked up at him. 'That's just it, there were no differences. It was most agreeable. There was no shadow upon our lives except Miriam's silence.'

'What did you discuss?'

Robb was watching him, then looking at Monk.

Stourbridge shrugged very slightly, with no more than half a gesture.

'Egypt, as I recall. Verona came out there to see me once. It was marvellous. We saw such sights together. She loved it, even the heat, and the food she was unaccustomed to, and the strange ways of the native people.' He smiled. 'She kept a diary of it all, especially of the voyage back down the Nile. She allowed me to read some of it, when I came here again. She shared it with Lucius too. Had she been able to remain, he would have been born in Egypt. I think it was that knowledge which made him so keen to go there himself. It was almost as if he could remember it through her eyes.' He stopped abruptly, the colour rising in his cheeks. 'I'm sorry. I'm sure that is far more detail than you require. I just remembered . . . how close we were . . . it was all so . . . normal . . .'

'Is that all?' Monk pressed, seeking for something which could have precipitated the terrible violence he had seen. Egypt sounded such a harmless subject, something impersonal which any cultured family might have discussed pleasantly around the table.

'As far as I recall Aiden said something about the political news, but it was a mere observation on the Foreign Secretary, and his own feelings about the question of the unification of Germany. It was all . . .' he shook his head, '. . . of no importance. Verona retired to bed, Aiden to write letters. Lucius walked in the garden for a while. I don't know when he came in, but doubtless the footman would.'

They questioned him further but he could add nothing which explained the emotions that had exploded in the bedroom, nor any fact which implicated anyone, or precluded them.

Robb did not put words to his question, but it was clear in his face that he was struggling with the issue of whether Stourbridge himself could have killed his wife.

Monk was torn with the same indecision. He profoundly believed that he had not, but he was afraid it was his loyalty to a client, and his personal liking for the man which was forming his judgement. There was nothing he had seen or heard tonight which proved him innocent.

There was a knock on the door.

Robb rose and opened it.

Aiden Campbell came in. He was very pale and his hands shook a little. His eyes were unnaturally bright and his body stiff. He moved clumsily.

'Surely Harry didn't call you in to this?' he asked, looking at Monk with surprise.

'No. Sergeant Robb asked me to come, since I am already acquainted with some of the circumstances concerning the household,' Monk replied.

'Oh – I see. Well, I suppose that is sensible enough,' he conceded, coming a little further into the room. 'Anything that can be done to get this over as rapidly as possible. My family is suffering profoundly. First Mrs Gardiner's inexplicable behaviour, and now this – this tragedy to my poor sister. We hardly know which way to turn. Lucius is . . .'

He stopped. 'Worsnip tells me you have found no indication of intruders. Is that correct?'

'Yes, sir,' Robb answered. 'And I regret to say, all your household staff are also accounted for.'

'What?' Aiden turned to Monk.

'That is true, Mr Campbell,' Monk agreed. 'Whoever killed Mrs Stourbridge, it was one of her family. I'm sorry.'

'Or it was Mrs Gardiner,' Aiden said quickly. 'She is not family, Mr Monk, not yet, and I fear after the events of the last two weeks, it were better that she not become so. It was a pity that the police saw fit to release her into Lucius' custody. It would have been far better if she had gone back to her own people.'

'Mrs Anderson is the only one she has,' Monk pointed out. 'And she is presently in Hampstead gaol accused of murdering James Treadwell.'

'Then someone else should have been found!' Aiden protested. 'She lived in Hampstead for twenty years! She must have other friends.'

There was a moment's silence.

'I apologise,' Aiden said quietly, clenching his jaw and looking down. 'That was uncalled for. This has been a terrible night.' His voice broke. 'I was very close to my sister . . . all my life. Now my brother-in-law and my nephew are in the utmost distress, and there is nothing I can do to help them.' He lifted his head again. 'Except assist you to deal with this as rapidly as possible, and leave us to begin a decent mourning.'

Robb looked wretchedly uncomfortable. His rawness at murder showed clearly in his young face. Monk was also sharply aware that the sergeant could not afford to fail. He needed his job not only for himself but to provide for his grandfather. The shadows of weariness streaked his skin and it obviously cost him an effort to stand straight-backed.

'We will do everything we can to solve it as quickly as we can, sir,' he promised. 'But we must go according to the law, and we must be right in the end. Now, if you would like to recount the evening as you remember it, sir . . . ?'

'Of course. From what time?'

'How about when you all sat down to dinner?'

Aiden sank into the large chair opposite where Robb and Monk were standing, then they also sat. He told them largely what Harry Stourbridge had, varying only in a description here and there. He had been asleep when Harry Stourbridge had awakened him to tell him of the terrible thing that had happened. He fancied that his man, Gibbons, could substantiate most of it.

'Well?' Robb asked, when he had gone and closed the door behind him. 'Not much help, is it?'

'None at all,' Monk agreed. 'Can't see any reason why he should lie. According to Stourbridge he was on the best possible terms with his sister, and always had been.'

'I can't see any money in it,' Robb added disconsolately. 'If Mrs Stourbridge had had any of her own before her marriage, it would belong to her husband since then, and Lucius would inherit it when his father dies . . . along with the property and lands.'

Monk did not bother to answer. 'And if Mrs Stourbridge gave Campbell any financial gifts or support that would end at her death. No, I can't see any reason for him to be anything except exactly what he says. We'd better see Lucius.'

This was the interview Monk was dreading the most, perhaps because Lucius had been his original client, and so far he had brought the young man only tragedy, one appalling disaster after another. And now it could appear as if he suspected him of murder as well, or suspected Miriam, which Lucius might feel to be even worse. And yet what alternative was there? It was someone in the house, and not a servant. Not that he had seriously considered the servants.

When Lucius came he was haggard. His eyes were sunken with shock, staring fixedly from red-rimmed lids, and his dark complexion was bleached of all its natural warmth. He sat down as if he feared his legs might not support him. He did not speak, but waited for Monk, not regarding Robb except for a moment.

Monk had never flinched from duty, no matter how unpleasant. He tended, rather, to attack it more urgently the more daunting it was, as if anger at it could overcome whatever pain there might be.

'Can you tell us what happened this evening from the time you sat down to dinner, and anything before that if it was remarkable in any way?' he began.

'Yes.' Lucius' voice was a little higher than usual, as if his throat were so tight he could barely force the words through it. 'It was the most ordinary dinner imaginable. We talked of trivia, entirely impersonal. It was mostly about Egypt.' A ghost of dreadful humour crossed his face. 'My father was describing Karnak and the great hall there, how massive it is, beyond our imagining. We speculated a while on what happened to a whole lost civilisation capable of creating such beauty and power. Then he spoke of the Valley of the Kings. He described it for us. The depth of the ravines and how insignificant one feels standing on their floor staring up at a tiny slice of sky so vivid blue it seems to burn the eyes. He said it was a place to force one to think of God and eternity, whether one were disposed to or not. All those ancient pharaohs lying there in their huge sarcophagi with their treasures of the world around them – waiting out the millennia for some awakening to heaven, or hell. He knew a little of their beliefs. It was a strange, mystical conversation. My mother had been there to visit him, before I was born. She was so lonely in England without him.' His voice was so choked with tears he was obliged to stop.

Robb waited a few moments before he spoke. 'And there were no disagreements?' he asked at length.

Lucius swallowed. 'No, none. What is there to disagree about?'

'And Mrs Gardiner was not at the table?'

Lucius' face tightened. 'No. She was not well. She is terribly distressed about Mrs Anderson, who was in every way a mother to her for most of her life. How could she not be? I wish there were something we could do to help! Of course we will find the best lawyer to represent her, but it looks terribly as if she is guilty. I would do anything to protect Miriam from it, but what is there?' He looked back at Monk as if he still hoped he might think of something.

'You have already done all you can,' Monk agreed, 'unless Mrs Anderson herself can say something in mitigation, and so far she has refused to say anything at all. But tonight we have another issue to deal with, and that will not involve her.' He saw Lucius wince. 'Please continue. You were all together until your mother retired quite early?'

Lucius braced himself. 'Yes. No one wanted to move; there was no point in separating,' he said wearily. 'We talked a little of politics, I can't remember what. Something to do with Germany. No one was particularly interested. It was just something to say. I went for a walk in the garden. It was peaceful and I preferred to be alone. I . . . was thinking.' He did not need to explain what troubled him.

'Did you see anyone as you came in or went upstairs?' Monk asked him.

'Only the servants . . . and Miriam. I went to her room but she would not do more than bid me good night. I didn't see anyone else.'

'Did your man assist you to undress, or lay your clothes out for the next day?'

'No. I sent him to bed. I didn't need him, and I preferred to be alone.'

'I see. Did you hear anything after that? Any sound, movement, a cry, footsteps?'

'No. At least not that I recall.'

Monk thanked him. Lucius seemed about to ask something

further, then changed his mind and rose stiffly to his feet.

When he had gone Robb turned to Monk. They had learned nothing more. No one was implicated, neither were they excluded from suspicion. Robb ran his hand through his hair, his fingers closing so he pulled at it. 'One of them killed her! It couldn't have been an accident, and no one does that to themselves!'

'We had better see Miriam Gardiner,' Monk said grimly.

Robb shot him a look of helplessness and frustration, then rose and went to the door to send the maid for Miriam.

She looked a shadow of the woman she had been, even when Monk had found her frightened and hiding. Her body was skeletal, as if she had barely eaten since then. Her dress hung on her shoulders so the bones showed through the thin clothes and her bosom was scarcely rounded. Her skin had no colour at all and her beautiful hair was dressed with little attention. She looked as if she were a stranger to any kind of rest of mind or body.

She moved jerkily, and refused to be seated when Robb asked her. Her hands were clenched and shaking. She seemed not to blink but to stare fixedly as though her attention were only partly here.

Robb looked at Monk desperately, then as Monk said nothing, he began to question her.

She replied in a voice that was unnaturally calm that she knew nothing at all. She had taken dinner in her room and had not left it except to go to the bathroom. She had seen no one other than the servant who had ministered to her personal needs. She had no idea what had happened. She had never quarrelled with Mrs Stourbridge . . . or with anyone else. She refused to say anything further.

And no matter how either Robb or Monk pressed her, she did not yield a word. She walked away stiffly, swaying a little as if she might lose her balance.

'Did she do it?' Robb asked as soon as the door was closed.

'I have no idea,' Monk confessed. He hated the thought, but she appeared in a state of suppressed hysteria, almost as if she moved in a trance, a world of her own connected only here and there with reality. He judged that if there were one more pressure, however slight, she would lose control completely.

Was that what had happened? Had she, for some reason or other, gone to see Mrs Stourbridge in her bedroom, and something, however innocently or well meant, had precipitated an emotional descent into insanity? Had Verona Stourbridge made some remark about Cleo Anderson, suggesting Miriam leave the past and its griefs behind, and Miriam had reacted by releasing all the terror and violence inside her in one fearful blow?

But where had the croquet mallet come from? One did not keep such things in a bedroom! Whoever had killed Verona Stourbridge had brought it with them, and it could only be as a weapon.

The murder was premeditated. Monk said as much aloud.

'I know,' Robb admitted. 'I know. But she still seems the most likely one. We'll have to go further back than I thought. I'll start again with the servants. It's here, whatever it is, the reason, the jealousy or the fear, or the rage. It's in this house. It has to be.'

They worked all night, asking, probing, going back over detail after detail. They were so tired that the whole house seemed to be a maze going round and round itself, like a symbol of the confusion within. Monk's throat was dry and his eyes felt as if there were sand in them. The cook brought them a tray of tea at three o'clock in the morning, and another at quarter to five, this time with roast beef sandwiches.

They questioned Mrs Stourbridge's maid again. The woman looked exhausted and terrified, but she spoke quite coherently.

'I don't know nothing to her discredit, not really,' she said when Robb asked her about Miriam. 'She's always bin very civil, far as I know.'

Monk seized on the hesitation, reading the indecision in her face.

'You must be frank,' he said gravely. 'You owe Mrs Stourbridge that. What do you mean "not really"? What were you thinking about when you said that?

Still she was reluctant.

Monk looked at her grimly until she flushed and finally answered.

'Well . . . I was thinking of that time I brought back Mrs Stourbridge's clean petticoats, to hang them up, like, an' I found Mrs Gardiner sitting at Mrs Stourbridge's dressing table . . . and she had one of Mrs Stourbridge's necklaces on. She said as Mrs Stourbridge had said she could borrow it – but she never said nothing to me as anyone could. And . . . and Mrs Stourbridge's diary was lying open on her bed, an' that's a thing I've never seen before.'

'Did she explain that too?'

'No . . . I never asked.'

'I see.'

She looked wretched, and was glad to escape when they excused her.

It was half-past five. Robb stood facing the window and the brilliant sunlight as the first noises of awakening came in from the street. A horse and cart rolled by. Somewhere on the further side there were footsteps on the pavement. A door opened and closed. He turned back to the room. His face was pale and he looked exhausted and miserable.

'I've got to arrest her,' he said flatly. 'Seems she couldn't wait to get her hands on the pretty things . . . or to pry into Mrs Stourbridge's affairs. I wish that wasn't so. Money does strange things to some people.'

'She didn't have to hurt Verona Stourbridge to have that,' Monk pointed out. 'No one objected to the marriage.'

'Perhaps Mrs Stourbridge did,' Robb said, his back stiff, his head high. He was determined to stand up to Monk on the issue, because he believed it. It was a testing ground between them and he was going to prove his own authority. 'Perhaps Mrs Stourbridge knew whatever it was Treadwell knew, or even that Miriam killed him.'

Monk drew in his breath to argue, but each protest died on his lips. They were empty, and he knew it. No one else had any reason or motive to harm Verona Stourbridge, and there was no physical evidence to implicate any of them. Miriam was already deeply involved in the murder of James Treadwell. And, strangely enough, she had not defended herself in any coherent way. Any jury would find it easy enough to believe that she had set out deliberately to charm Lucius, a wealthy and naïve young man. He was handsome and intelligent enough, but not worldly-wise, and might be easily duped by a woman older than he and well practised in the ways of pleasing.

Then she had seen the luxury of the life she could expect, but through an unforeseeable misfortune, the coachman knew something of her past which was so ugly it would have spoiled her dream. He had blackmailed her.

Her mentor and accomplice, also blackmailed for theft by the same wretched coachman, either helped her kill him, or hid her afterwards, and obscured the evidence of the crime. Robb had no choice but to charge her.

The family was shattered. Harry stood white-faced,

stammering incoherent assurances that he would do all he could to help her. He looked as if he hardly knew what he was saying or doing. He kept turning to Lucius as if he would protect him, and then realised he was helpless to make any difference at all.

Monk had never felt more pity for any man, but he did not believe that even Oliver Rathbone could do anything to relieve this tragedy. The most compassionate thing would be to deal with it as quickly as possible. To prolong the suffering was pointless.

Miriam herself seemed the least surprised or distressed. She accepted the situation as if she had expected it, and made no protest or appeal for help. She did not even deny the charge. She thanked Harry Stourbridge for his behaviour towards her, then walked uprightly, now quite firmly, a step or two ahead of Robb out to the front door. She hesitated as if to speak to Lucius, then changed her mind.

At the doorway Monk looked back at the three men as they stood in the hall. Harry and Lucius were paralysed. Aiden Campbell put his arm around Lucius as if to support him.

It was after seven in the morning by the time Monk returned home. It was broad daylight and the streets were full of traffic, the hiss of wheels, the clatter of hoofs and people shouting to each other.

He went in at his own door and closed it behind him. All he wanted to do was wash the heat and grime off himself, then sink into bed and sleep all day.

He was barely across the room when Hester appeared, dressed in blue and white muslin and looking as if she had been up for hours.

'What happened?' she said instantly. 'You look terrible. The kettle is on. Would you like breakfast, or are you too tired?'

'Just tea,' he answered, following her into the kitchen and sitting down. His legs ached and his feet were hot and so tired they hurt. His head throbbed. He wanted somewhere cool and dark, and as quiet as possible.

She made the tea and poured it for him before asking any further, and then it was by a look, not words.

'She was struck once, with a croquet mallet,' Monk told her. 'There was enough evidence to prove it had to be one of the family . . . or Miriam Gardiner. There was no reason for any of the servants to do it.'

She sat across the small table from him, her face very solemn. 'And for her?' she asked.

'The obvious. Whatever Treadwell knew of her, Verona Stourbridge knew it as well . . . or else she deduced it from something Miriam said. I'm sorry. The best you can say of her is that she has lost her mind, the worst that she deliberately planned to marry Lucius and assure herself of wealth and social position for the rest of her life . . . and indirectly, of course, for Cleo Anderson as well. When Treadwell threatened that plan, either alone or with Cleo's help, she killed him. And then later when Verona threatened it, she killed her too. It makes a hideous sense.'

'But do you believe it?' Hester asked, searching his face.

'I don't know. Not easily. But logic forces me to accept it.' That was the truth, but he was reluctant to say it. When Miriam had denied it he had more than believed her, he had liked her, and felt compelled to go further than duty necessitated in order to defend her. But he was not governed by emotion. He must let reason be the last determiner.

Hester sat silent for several minutes, sipping her own tea.

'I don't believe Cleo Anderson was part of killing anyone for gain,' she said at last. 'I still think we should help her.'

'Do you?' He looked at her as closely as his weariness and

sense of disillusion would allow. He saw the bewilderment in her, the confusion of thought and feelings, and understood it precisely. 'Are you sure you are not looking for a spectacular trial to show people the plight of men like John Robb, old and ill and forgotten, now that the wars they fought are all won, and we are safe?'

She drew in her breath to deny it indignantly, then saw in his eyes that he was a step ahead of her.

'Well, I wouldn't mind if something were to draw people's attention to it,' she conceded. 'But I wasn't using Cleo. I believe she took the medicines to give to those who needed them, not for any profit for herself, and if she killed James Treadwell, at least in part he deserved it.'

'And when did it become all right for us to decide that someone deserved to die?'

She glared at him.

He smiled, and stood up slowly. It was an effort. He was even more tired than he had thought, and the few moments relaxing had made it worse.

'What are we going to do?' She stood up also, coming towards him almost as if she would block his way to the door. 'She hasn't any money. She can't afford a lawyer, never mind a good one! And now Miriam is charged as well, there is no one to help her. You can't expect Lucius Stourbridge to!'

He knew what she wanted: that they should go to Oliver Rathbone and try to persuade him to use his professional skill, free of charge, to plead for Cleo Anderson. Because of their past friendship – love would not be too strong a word at least on Rathbone's part – Hester would also probably rather that Monk asked him, so that it did not appear that she was abusing his affection.

Oliver Rathbone was the last person of whom Monk wanted to ask any favours, no matter on whose behalf. Was it guilt, because he had asked Hester to marry him before Rathbone had, knowing that Rathbone also loved her?

That was ridiculous! Rathbone had had his opportunity, and failed to take it . . . for whatever reason. Monk was not responsible.

Perhaps it was a certain guilt because he had seized a happiness that he knew Rathbone would have treasured, or in some ways would have been more worthy. There was too often a fear at the back of his mind that Rathbone could have made her happier, given her things Monk never could – not only material possessions and security, or social position, but emotional certainties. He would not have loved her more, but he might have been a better man to share her life with, an easier one, a man who would have caused her less fear or doubt, less anxiety. At the very least, she would have known his past. There were no ghosts, no black regions or forgotten holes.

She was waiting for an answer, her brow furrowed, her chin lifted a little because she knew he did not want to, even if she could not guess why.

He would not let Rathbone beat him.

'I think we should ask Rathbone's opinion,' he said slowly and quite distinctly. 'And if he is willing, his help. He'll take up a lost cause every now and again, if the issue is good enough. I'm sure we could persuade him this one is.' He smiled with a downward twist of his lips. 'And the appearance of Sir Oliver Rathbone in court to defend a nurse accused of theft and murder will ensure that the newspapers give it all the attention we could wish.'

She smiled very slowly, her body relaxing.

'Thank you, William. I knew you would say that.'

He had not known it, but if she thought so well of him he was certainly not going to argue.

'Now go to sleep,' she urged. 'I'll waken you in time to go to Vere Street and see Oliver before the end of the day.'

He grunted, too tired to argue that tomorrow would do, and climbed slowly up the stairs.

Monk hated presenting himself at Rathbone's chambers in Vere Street without an appointment, and fully expected to be turned away. If he were received, he was certain it would be because Hester was with him. He would rather she had not come, but he could understand her insistence. She wanted to be there not simply to add her own thoughts and words to the story and to try her own persuasion if Monk's should fail, but because she would feel cowardly if she sent Monk and did not go herself. It would seem as if she wanted a favour of Rathbone, but had not the courage to face him to ask it.

Therefore they stood in the outer office and explained to the clerk that they had no appointment, but they were well acquainted with Sir Oliver (which he knew), and had a matter of some urgency to lay before him. It was the end of the afternoon and the last client was presently in Sir Oliver's rooms with him. It was a fortunate time.

Some fifteen minutes passed by. Monk found it almost impossible to sit still. He glanced at Hester and read the misgiving in her face, and equally the determination. Cleo Anderson's life was worth a great deal more than a little embarrassment.

At twenty minutes past five the client left and Rathbone came to the door. He looked startled to see them. His eyes flew to Hester and there was a sudden warmth in them, and the faintest flush on his narrow cheeks. He forced himself to smile, but there was not the usual humour in it. He came forward.

'Hester! How nice to see you. You look extremely well.'

'We are sorry to intrude,' Hester replied with an equally uncertain smile. 'But we have a case that is so desperate we know of no one else who would have even a chance of success in it.'

Rathbone half turned to Monk. For the first time since the wedding their eyes met. Then Monk had been the bridegroom. Now he was the husband; the last barrier had been crossed, there was a new kind of intimacy from which Rathbone was for ever excluded. Rathbone's eyes were startlingly, magnificently dark in his fair face. Everything that had passed through Monk's mind he read in them. He held out his hand.

Monk shook it, feeling the strength and the coolness of Rathbone's grip.

'Then you had better come in and tell me,' Rathbone said calmly. His voice held no trace of emotion. He was supremely courteous. What effort of pride or dignity that had cost him Monk could only guess.

He and Hester followed into Rathbone's familiar office and sat down in the chairs away from the desk. It was a formal visit, but not yet an official one. The late sun poured in through the window, making bright patterns on the floor and shining on the gold lettering on the books in their mahogany case.

Rathbone leaned back and crossed his legs. As always he was immaculately dressed, but with an understated elegance, and the ease of someone who knows he does not have to try.

'What is this case?' he enquired, looking at each of them in turn.

Monk was determined to answer first, before Hester could speak and make it a dialogue between herself and Rathbone, with Monk merely an onlooker.

'A nurse, Cleo Anderson, has been stealing medicines from the North London Hospital where Hester is now assisting

Lady Callandra.' He had no need to explain that situation; Rathbone knew and admired Callandra. 'She doesn't want the medicines for herself, or to sell, but to give to the old and poor that she visits, who are in desperate need, many of them dying.'

'Laudable but illegal,' Rathbone said with a frown. His interest was already caught, and his concern.

'Precisely,' Monk agreed. 'Somehow a coachman named James Treadwell learned of her thefts and was blackmailing her. How he learned is immaterial. He comes from an area close by, and possibly he knew someone she was caring for. He was found dead on the path close to her doorway. She has been charged with his murder.'

'Physical evidence?' Rathbone said with pressed lips, his face already darker, brows drawn down.

'None, all on motive and opportunity. The weapon has not been found. But that is not all . . .'

Rathbone's eyes widened incredulously. 'There's more?'

'And worse,' Monk replied. 'Some twenty years ago Mrs Anderson found in acute distress a girl of about twelve or thirteen years old. She took her in and treated her as her own.' He saw Rathbone's guarded expression, and the further spark of interest in his eyes. 'Miriam grew up and married comfortably,' he continued. 'She was widowed, and then fell deeply in love with a young man, Stourbridge, of wealthy and respectable family, who more than returned her feelings. They became engaged to marry, with his parents' approval. Then one day, for no known reason, she fled, with the said coachman, back to Hampstead Heath.'

'The night of his death, I presume,' Rathbone said with a twisted smile.

'Just so,' Monk agreed. 'At first she was charged with his murder, and would say nothing of her flight, its reason, or what happened, except to deny that she killed him.'

'And she wasn't charged?' Rathbone was surprised.

'Yes, she was! Then when a far better motive was found for the nurse, Miriam Gardiner was released.'

'And the worse that you have to add?' Rathbone asked.

Monk's shoulders stiffened. 'Last night I had a message from the young policeman on the case – incidentally his grandfather is one of those for whom the nurse stole medicines in order to treat – to ask me to go to the Stourbridge family home in Cleveland Square where the mother of the young man engaged to Miriam had just been found murdered . . . in what seems to be exactly the same manner as the footman on Hampstead Heath.'

Rathbone shut his eyes and let out a long, slow breath. 'I hope that is now all?'

'Not quite,' Monk replied. 'They have arrested Miriam and charged her with the murder of Stourbridge's mother, and Miriam and Cleo as being accomplices in murder for gain. There is considerable money in the family, and lands.'

Rathbone opened his eyes and stared at Monk. 'Have you completed this tale to date?'

'Yes.'

Hester spoke for the first time, leaning forward a little, her voice urgent. 'Please help, Oliver. I know Miriam may be beyond anything anybody can do, except perhaps plead that she may be mad, but Cleo Anderson is a good woman. She took medicine to treat the old and ill who have barely enough money to survive. John Robb, the policeman's grandfather, fought at Trafalgar – on *Victory*! He, and men like him, don't deserve to be left to die in pain that we could alleviate! We asked everything of them when we were in danger! When we thought Napoleon was going to invade and conquer us, we expected them to fight and die for us, or to lose arms or legs or eyes . . .'

'I know!' Rathbone held up his slender hand. 'I know, my dear. You do not need to persuade me. And a jury might well be moved by such things, but a judge will not. He won't ask them to decide whether a blackmailer is of more or less value than a nurse, or an old soldier, simply did she kill him or not. And what about this other woman, the younger one? What possible reason or excuse did she have for murdering her prospective mother-in-law?'

'We don't know,' Hester said helplessly. 'She won't say anything.'

'Is she aware of her position, that if she is found guilty she will hang?'

'She knows the words,' Monk replied. 'Whether she comprehends their meaning or not I am uncertain. I was there when she was arrested, and she seemed numb, but she left with the police with more dignity than I have seen in anyone else I can recall.' He felt foolish as he said it. It was an emotional response, and he disliked having Rathbone see him in such a light. It made him vulnerable. He was about to add something to qualify it, defend himself, but Rathbone had turned to Hester and was not listening.

'Do you know this nurse?' he asked.

'Yes,' she said unhesitatingly. 'And I know John Robb. I have been to a few of the patients she visited. I can and will testify that the medicines were used for them, and no return of any kind was asked.'

Rathbone forbore from saying that that would be of no legal help. The sympathy of the jury would not alter her guilt and was unlikely to mitigate the sentence. Anyway, was hanging so very much worse than a lifetime spent in the Coldbath Fields, or some other prison like it? He stayed silent for several moments, considering the question, and neither

Monk nor Hester prompted him.

'I presume she has no money, this nurse?' Rathbone said at last. 'And the Stourbridge family are hardly likely to wish to defend her.'

Monk felt anger harsh inside him. So it was all a matter of payment!

'So she is unlikely to have anyone to represent her already,' Rathbone concluded. 'There will be no professional ethics to break if I were to go and visit her. I can at least offer my services, and then she may accept or decline them as she wishes.'

'And who is going to pay you?' Monk asked with a lift of his eyebrows.

Rathbone looked straight back at him. 'I have done sufficiently well lately that I can afford to do it without asking payment,' he replied levelly. 'I imagine she will have no means to pay you either.'

Monk felt an unaccustomed heat rise up his cheeks, but he knew the rebuke was fair. He had earned it.

'Thank you!' Hester said quickly, rising to her feet. 'Cleo Anderson is in Hampstead police station.'

Rathbone smiled with a dry twist of humour as if there were a highly subtle joke which was at least half against himself.

'Don't thank me,' he said softly. 'It sounds like a challenge which ought to be attempted, and I know no one else fool enough to try it!'

Chapter Nine

❧

Oliver Rathbone sat in his office after Monk and Hester had gone, aware that he had made an utterly impetuous decision, which was most unlike him. He was not a man who acted without consideration, which was part of the reason why he was probably the most brilliant barrister currently practising in London. It might also be why he had allowed Monk to ask Hester to marry him before he had asked her himself.

No, that was not entirely true. He had been on the verge of asking her, but she had very delicately allowed him to understand that she would not accept. It had been to save his feelings, and the awkwardness between them that would have followed.

But then if he were honest, the reason she would not accept him might easily have been her sense of his uncertainty. Monk would never have allowed his head to rule his heart. That was what Rathbone both admired in him, and despised. There was a dark element in Monk, something ungoverned.

And yet he had come with Hester to try to persuade Rathbone to take the hopeless case of defending a nurse certainly guilty of theft, and almost as certainly guilty of murder. That cannot have been easy for him. Rathbone leaned

255

back further in his chair and smiled a little as he remembered the look on Hester's face, the stiffness in her body. He could imagine her thoughts. Monk would have done it for Hester's sake, and he would know that Rathbone knew it also.

He was surprised how sharp the pain was on seeing Hester again, hearing the passion in her voice as she spoke of Cleo Anderson, and the old sailor John Robb. That was just like her, full of pity and anger and courage, bound on some hopeless cause, not listening to anyone who told her the impossibility of it.

And he had agreed to help, in fact more than advise, to undertake some kind of defence! He would be a fool to pretend it would be less than that. Now he had begun she would not allow him to stop – nor would he allow himself! He would never admit to Monk that he would quit a fight before he had either won it or lost. Monk would understand defeat, and forgive it and respect winner or loser alike. He had tasted bitterness too often himself not to understand. But he would not forgive surrender.

And Rathbone would always want to be all that Hester expected of him.

So now he was committed to a case he could not win, and probably could not even fight in any adequate manner. He should have been angry with himself, not analytical, and even in a faraway sense amused. He should have felt hopeless, but already his mind was beginning to explore possibilities, begin to think, to plan, to wonder about tactics.

Both women had been charged with conspiracy and murder. The penalty would unquestionably be death. Rathbone had a justifiably high opinion of his own abilities, but the obstacles in this seemed insuperable. It was extremely foolish to have such a will to win! In fact it was a classic example of a man allowing his emotions not merely to eliminate his judgement, but to sweep it away entirely.

He called his clerk in and enquired about his appointments for the next two days. There was nothing which could not be either postponed or dealt with by someone else. He duly requested that that be done, and left for his home, his mind absorbed in the issue of Cleo Anderson, Miriam Gardiner and the crimes with which they were charged.

In the morning Rathbone presented himself at Hampstead police station. He informed the desk sergeant that he was the barrister retained by Cleo Anderson's solicitor, and that he wished to speak with her without delay.

'Sir Oliver Rathbone?' the sergeant said with amazement, looking at the card Rathbone had given him.

Rathbone did not bother to reply.

The sergeant cleared his throat. 'Yes, sir. If you'll come this way, I'll take yer ter the cells . . . sir.' He was still shaking his head as he led the way through the narrow passage and down the steps, and finally to the iron door with its huge lock. The key squeaked in the lock as he turned it and swung the door open.

''Ere's yer lawyer ter see yer,' he said, the lift of disbelief in his voice.

Rathbone thanked him and waited until he had closed the door and gone.

Cleo Anderson was a handsome woman with fine eyes and strong, gentle features, but at the moment she was so weary and ravaged by grief that her skin looked grey and the lines of her face dragged downwards. She regarded Rathbone without comprehension, and – what worried him more – without interest.

'My name is Oliver Rathbone,' he introduced himself. 'I have come to see if I can be of assistance to you in your present difficulty. Anything you say to me is completely confidential, but you must tell me the truth, or I cannot be of any use.' He saw the beginning of denial in her face. He sat down on the one hard chair, opposite where she was sitting on the cot. 'I have been retained by Miss Hester Latterly.' Too late he realised he should have said 'Mrs Monk'. He felt the heat in his face as he was obliged to correct himself.

'She shouldn't have,' Cleo said sadly, her face pinched, emotion raw in her voice. 'She's a good woman, but she doesn't have money to spend on the likes o' you. I'm sorry for your trouble, but there's no job for you here.'

He was prepared for her answer.

'She told me that you took certain medicines from the hospital, and gave them to patients whom you knew were in need of them, but who were unable to pay.'

Cleo stared at him.

He had not expected a confession. 'If that were so, it would be theft, of course, and illegal,' he continued. 'But it would be an act which many people would admire, perhaps even wish that they had had the courage to perform themselves.'

'Maybe,' she agreed with a tiny smile. 'But it's still theft, like you said. Do you want me to admit it? Would it help Miriam if I did?'

'That was not my purpose in discussing it, Mrs Anderson.' He held her gaze steadily. 'But a person who would do such a thing obviously placed the welfare of other people before their own. As far as I can see it was an act, a series of acts, for which they expected no profit themselves, other than that of having done what they believed to be right, and of benefit to others for whose welfare they cared. Possibly they believed in a cause.'

She frowned. 'Why are you saying all this? You're talking about "ifs" and "maybes". What do you want?'

He smiled in spite of himself. 'That you should accept that occasionally people do things without expecting to be paid, because they care about the issues. Not only people like you – sometimes people like me, too.'

A flush of embarrassment spread up her cheeks and the line of her mouth softened. 'I'm sorry, Mr Rathbone, I didn't mean to insult you. But with the best will in the world, you can't clear me of thieving those medicines, unless you find a way to blame some other poor soul who's innocent – and if you did that, how would I go to my Maker in peace?'

'That's not how I work, Mrs Anderson.' He did not bother to correct her as to his title. It seemed remarkably unimportant now. 'If you took the medicines I have two options: either to plead mitigating circumstances and hope that they will judge you from the charity of your intent rather than the illegality of your act, or else to try to misdirect their attention from the theft altogether, and hope that they concentrate on other matters.'

'Other matters?' She shook her head. 'They're saying as I killed Treadwell because he was blackmailing me over the medicines. You can't misdirect anybody away from that!'

'And was he?'

She hesitated. Something inside her seemed to crumple. She took a deep breath and let it out in a sigh. 'Yes.'

He waited for her to say more, but she remained silent.

'How did he find out about the medicines?' he asked.

'I suppose it wasn't hard.' She stared ahead of her, a shadow of self-mockery in her expression. 'Lot o' people could have, if they'd wanted to think about it, and watch. I took stuff to about a score o' the old ones who were really in a bad way. I don't know why I talk about it in the past – they still are, an' here's me sittin' here useless!' She looked up at him. 'There's nothing you can do, Mr Rathbone. All the questions in the world aren't going to make any difference. I took the medicines and it'll be easy enough to prove. Treadwell worked it out. I don't know how.'

There was no argument to make. He heard footsteps along the corridor outside, but they continued on, and no one disturbed him and Cleo Anderson. He wondered briefly if the gaolers here sympathised with her; even were it possible that they might sooner have had the law turn a blind eye to her thefts. Maybe they had little time for a blackmailer.

It was academic, only a wish. The power was not in their hands. Maybe it was a thought each would have had individually, and never dared voice.

She was regarding him earnestly, her eyes anxious.

'Mr Rathbone – don't let them go talking to all the people I took medicines to. It's bad enough they won't get any help now. I don't want them to know they were part of a crime – even without they understood it.'

He wished there were some way he could prevent that from happening, but it would soon enough become common knowledge. The trial would be written up in all the newspapers, told and retold by the running patterers and in the gossip on every street corner. What should he tell her?

She was waiting, a flicker of hope in her face.

He regarded her almost as if he had not seen her before, not been speaking to her, forming judgements those last ten minutes. She had risked her own freedom, taken her own leap of moral decision in order to help the old and ill who could not help themselves. She had faced the most painful of realities, and dealt with it. She did not deserve the condescension of being lied to. She would know the truth eventually anyway.

'I can't stop them, Mrs Anderson,' he said gently, startled by the respect in his own voice. 'And they'll know anyway when it comes to trial. That is perhaps the only good thing about this whole affair. All London will hear of the plight of our old to whom we owe so much, and choose not to pay. We may even hope that a few will take up the fight to have things changed.'

She looked at him, hope and denial struggling in her face. She shook her head, pushing the thought away, and yet unable to let go completely.

'D'you think so?'

'It is worth fighting for.' He smiled very slightly. 'But my first battle is for you. How long have you been paying Treadwell, and how much?'

Her voice hardened and the pity vanished from her eyes. 'Five years – an' I paid him all I had, except a couple of shillings to live on.'

Rathbone felt a tightening around his heart.

'And he asked you for more the night of his death. How much?'

Her voice sank to a whisper. She hesitated a moment before answering at all. 'I never saw him the night he died. That's God's truth.'

He asked the question whose answer he did not want to hear, and possibly he would not believe.

'Do you know who did?'

She answered instantly, her voice hard. 'No, I don't! Miriam told me nothing, except it wasn't her. But she was in a terrible state, frightened half out of her mind, an' like the whole world had ended for her.' She leaned towards him, half put out her hand, then took it back, not because the emotion or the urgency was any less, simply that she dared not touch him. 'Never mind about me, Mr Rathbone. I took the medicines. You can't help me. But help Miriam, please! That's what I want! If you're my lawyer, like you said, you'll speak up for her. She never killed him. I know her – I raised her since she was thirteen. She's got a good heart an' she never deliberately hurt anyone, but somebody's hurt her so bad she's all but dead inside. Help her – please! I'd go to the rope happy if I knew she was all right . . .'

He met her eyes and felt his throat choke. He believed her. It was a wild statement. She might have no real conception of what it would be like when the moment came, when the judge put on his black cap, and later when she was alone in the end, walking the short corridor towards the trap in the floor, and the short drop. Then it would be too late. But he still believed her. She had seen much death. There could be little of loneliness or pain that she was not familiar with.

'Mrs Anderson, I am not sure there's anything I can do, but I promise I will not secure any leniency, or indeed any defence for you, at Miriam Gardiner's expense. And I will certainly do all I can to secure her acquittal, if she wishes it, and you do . . .'

'I do!' she said with fierce intensity. 'And if she argues with you – for me – tell her that is my wish. I've had a good life with lots of laughter in it, and done the things I wanted to. She's very young. It's your profession to convince people of things. You go and convince her of that, will you?'

'I can only work within the facts, but I will try,' he promised. 'Now if there is anything more of that night you can tell me, please do.'

'I don't know anything else of that night!' she protested. 'I wish I did, then maybe I could help either one of us!' she protested. 'I knew nothing until the police came because someone had reported finding a body on the pathway—'

'When was that, what time?' he interrupted her.

'About an hour after dark. I didn't look at the clock. I suppose Miriam must have left the party in late afternoon, and it would be close on dark by the time the carriage got as far as the Heath. I don't know where he was attacked, but I heard say he crawled from there to where they found him.'

'And when did you see Miriam Gardiner?'

'Next morning, early. About six, or something like that. She'd been out on the Heath all night and looked like the devil had been after her.'

'That she'd been in a fight?' he asked quickly. 'Were her clothes torn, dirty, stained with mud or grass?'

He saw something about her face close. She was afraid he was trying to implicate Miriam. 'No. Only like she'd been running, p'raps, or frightened.'

Was that a lie? He had no way of knowing. He recognised that she was not going to tell him any more. He rose to his feet. The fact that she had withdrawn her trust, at least as far as Miriam was concerned, did not alter his admiration for her, nor his intent to do all he could to find some way of helping.

'I shall go and speak with Mrs Gardiner,' he told her. 'Please do not discuss this with anyone else. I shall return when I have something to tell you, or if I need to ask you anything further. You have my word I shall take no steps without your permission.'

'Thank you,' she answered. 'I – I am grateful, Mr Rathbone. Will you tell Mrs Monk that too . . . and . . .'

'Yes?'

'No – nothing else.'

Rathbone banged on the door and the gaoler let him out. He walked away along the dim corridor with a fluttering fear inside him as to what else she might have been going to say to Hester. She was a woman prepared to go to any lengths, make any sacrifice for what she believed to be right, and to save those she loved. No wonder Hester was keen in her defence. In the same place she might so easily have done the same things! He could picture Hester with just this blind loyalty, sacrificing herself rather than deny the greater principle. Was that what Cleo had been going to say – some instruction or warning to Hester about the medicines? Was it a request, or was she already doing it even now?

He felt sick at the thought. His stomach knotted and sweat broke out on his skin. What could he do to help her, if she were caught? He could not even think clearly about Cleo Anderson, whom he had never seen before today.

Start with Miriam Gardiner, that was the only thing. Usually he would have told himself that the truth was his only ally, always to know the truth before he began. But in this case he was afraid there were truths he might prefer not to know – but he was uncertain which they were. He would have looked the other way, if only he were certain which way that was!

Rathbone was allowed in to see Miriam, but not as easily as he had been to Cleo Anderson. The atmosphere was different. Cleo was in police cells, a local woman known to the men – by repute if not personally – to be undoubtedly a good woman, one whose life they valued far more than that of any blackmailing outsider.

Miriam was in prison, accused of murdering her prospective mother-in-law, possibly because the unfortunate mother-in-law was aware of some scandal in her past which would have prevented the marriage. This was an altogether different matter.

Miriam was not at all as Rathbone had expected. It was not until he saw her that he realised he had pictured in his mind some rather brashly handsome, bold-eyed woman with accomplished charm, who would quickly try to win him to her cause. Instead he found a small woman with a fair, tired face full of inner quietness and a strength which startled him. She maintained a deep reserve, even after he had explained to her who he was and the exact circumstances and reason for his having come.

'It is good of you to take the time, Sir Oliver,' she said so softly he had to lean forward to catch her words. 'But I don't believe you can help me.' She did not meet his eyes, and he was aware that in a sense she had already dismissed him.

If he could not appeal to her mind, he would have to try her emotions. He sat down in the chair opposite her and crossed his legs, as if he intended to make himself comfortable.

'Have they told you that you and Mrs Anderson are to be charged together with conspiracy in the murders of Treadwell and Mrs Stourbridge?'

She stared at him, her eyes wide and dark grey. 'That's absurd! How can they possibly think Mrs Anderson had anything to do with Mrs Stourbridge's death? She was in their own prison at the time! You must be mistaken!'

'I am not mistaken.' He explained to her: 'They know all that. They are saying that they believe you and Mrs Anderson planned from the beginning that you should marry Lucius Stourbridge, thus gaining access to a very great deal of money, some now, far more later on Major Stourbridge's death, whenever that might be . . .'

'Why should he die?' she protested. 'He is quite young, not more than fifty, and in excellent health! He could have another thirty years, or more!'

He sighed. 'The mortality rate among those who seem to stand in the way of your plans is very high, Mrs Gardiner. They would not consider his age or his health to be matters which would deter you.'

She closed her eyes. 'That is hideous!'

Studying the lines of her face, of her mouth and the way it tightened, the sadness and the momentary surprise and anger in her, he could not believe she had even thought of Harry Stourbridge's death until this moment, and now that she did, the idea hurt her. But he could not afford to be gentle.

'That is what they are accusing you of – you and Mrs Anderson together. Unless you accuse each other, which neither of you has done, you will both either stand or fall.'

She looked up at him slowly, searching his eyes, his face, trying to read him.

'You mean I am to defend myself if I do not wish Cleo to suffer with me?'

'Yes, exactly that.'

'It is completely untrue. I . . . loved Lucius.' She swallowed, and he could almost feel the pain in her as if it had been in himself. 'I had no thought of anything but marrying him and being happy simply to be with him. Had he been a pauper it would have made not the slightest difference.'

He felt she was telling the truth, and yet why had she hesitated? Why had she spoken of her love for Lucius in the past? Was that because the love had died, or simply the hope?

'James Treadwell was blackmailing Mrs Anderson over the medicines she stole from the hospital to treat her patients. Was he blackmailing you also?'

Her head jerked up, her eyes wide. She seemed about to deny it vehemently, then instead she said nothing.

'Mrs Gardiner,' Rathbone said urgently, leaning forward towards her. 'If I am to help either of you then I must know as much of the truth as you do. I am bound to act in your interest, and believe me when I say that the outlook could not be worse for either of you than it already is. Whatever you tell me, it cannot harm you now, and it may help. In the end, when it comes to trial, I shall take your instructions, or at the very worst, if I cannot do that, then I shall decline the case. I cannot betray you! If I did so I should be disbarred and lose not only my reputation but my livelihood, both of which are of great value to me. Now – was James Treadwell blackmailing you or not?'

She seemed to reach some decision. 'No, he wasn't. He could not know anything which would harm me. Except, I suppose, a connection with Cleo and the medicines, but he never mentioned it. I had no idea he was blackmailing her. If I had I would had tried to do something about it.'

'What could you do?' He tried to keep the edge from his voice.

She gave a tiny, half-hearted shrug. 'I don't know. I suppose if I had told Lucius, or Major Stourbridge, they might have dismissed him, without references, and made certain it was very hard for him to find new employment.'

'Would that not have driven him to expose Mrs Anderson in retaliation?' he asked.

'Perhaps.' Then she stiffened and twisted around to stare at him, her face bleached with horror. 'You think I killed him to protect Cleo?'

'Did you?'

'No! I didn't kill him – for any reason!' The denial was passionate, ringing with anger and hurt. 'Neither did Cleo!'

'Then who did?'

Her expression closed again, shutting him out. She averted her eyes.

'Who are you protecting, if it isn't Mrs Anderson?' he asked very gently. 'Is it Lucius?'

She shivered, glanced up at him, then away again.

'Did Treadwell injure you in some way, and Lucius fought with him and it went further than he intended?'

'No!' She sounded as if the idea surprised her.

It had seemed to him so likely an answer he was disappointed that she denied it, and startled at himself for believing her for no better reason than the intonation of her voice and the angle and stiffness of her body.

'Do you know who killed him Mrs Gardiner?' he demanded with sudden force.

She said nothing. It was as good as an admission. He was frustrated almost beyond bearing. He had never felt more helpless, even though he had certainly dealt with many cases where people accused of fearful crimes had refused to tell him the truth, and had in the end proved to be innocent, morally if not legally. Nothing in his experience explained Miriam Gardiner's behaviour.

He refused to let it go. If anything he was even more determined to defend both Miriam and Cleo, not for Hester and certainly not to prove himself to Monk, but for the case itself, for these two extraordinary, devoted and blindly stubborn women, and perhaps because he would not rest until he knew the truth. And maybe also for the principle.

'Did Mrs Stourbridge know anything about Treadwell, or about Cleo Anderson?' he pursued.

Again she was surprised. 'No ... I can't imagine how she could! I didn't tell her, and I can hardly think that Treadwell would tell her himself! He was a ...' she stopped. She seemed to be torn by emotions which confused her, pulling her one way and then another: anger, pity, horror, despair.

Rathbone tried to read what she was feeling, even to imagine what was in her mind, and failed utterly. There were too many possibilities, and none of them made sense entirely.

'He was a man who did evil things,' she spoke quietly at last, as much to herself as to him. 'But he was not without virtue, and he is dead now, poor soul. I don't think Mrs Stourbridge knew anything about him except that he drove the carriage quite well, and of course that he was related to the cook.'

'Why was she killed?'

She winced. 'I don't know.' She did not look at him as she said it. Her voice was flat, the tone of it different.

He knew she was lying.

'Who killed her?'

'I don't know,' she repeated.

'Lucius?'

'No!' This time she turned to look at him, eyes dark and angry.

'Were you with him?'

She said nothing.

'You weren't. Then how do you know he did not?'

Again she said nothing.

'It was the same person who killed both people?'

She made a very slight movement. He took it for agreement.

'Has it anything to do with the stolen medicines?'

'No!' Suddenly she was completely frantic again. 'No, it has nothing to do with Cleo at all. Please, Sir Oliver, defend her.' Now she was pleading with him. 'She is the best person I have ever known. The only thing she has done against the law is to take medicines to treat the ill who cannot afford to buy them. She made nothing for herself out of it.' Her face was flushed. 'How can that be so wrong that she deserves to die for it? If we were the Christian people we pretend to be, she wouldn't have had to take them! We would care for our own old and sick. We would be grateful to those who fought to protect us when we needed it, and we'd be just as keen to protect them now! Please, don't let her suffer for this! It's nothing to do with her! She didn't kill Treadwell and she couldn't possibly have killed Mrs Stourbridge.' Her voice was tight with fear and strain, almost strangled in her throat. 'I'll say I killed them both, if it will free her, I swear it!'

He put his hand on her arm. 'No – it would only condemn you both. Say nothing. If you will not tell me the truth, at least do not lie to me. I will do anything I can for both of you. I accept that Mrs Anderson could not have killed Mrs Stourbridge, and I believe you that you did not kill Treadwell. If there is another answer I shall do everything in my power to find it.'

She shook her head fractionally. 'You can't,' she whispered. 'Just don't let them hang Cleo. She only took the medicines – that's all.'

Rathbone had a late luncheon at his club where he knew he would be left in complete solitude, should he wish it – and he did. Then he took a hansom out to the North London Hospital, intending to see Hester. He was not looking forward to it, and yet it was necessary to do so. He had not seen her alone since her marriage, but he had always known that this first meeting since then would be painful to him.

He sat in the cab as it clipped smartly through the streets, unaware of the other passing vehicles, even of where he was as it moved from one neighbourhood to another, as the scenery changed eventually from stone-façaded houses to the green stretch of the Heath.

He had altered his mind a dozen times as to what he would say to Hester, what manner he would adopt. Every decision was in one way or another unsatisfactory.

When he reached the hospital, paid the cabbie and alighted, he walked up the steps and met her without having had time to prepare himself. She was coming along the wide corridor at a brisk, purposeful walk, her head high. She was wearing a very plain blue dress with a small, white lace collar, almost like a kind of uniform. On anyone else it might have been a little forbidding, but it was how he always visualised her: as a nurse, determined about something, ready to start some battle or other. The familiarity of her appearance almost took his breath away. No amount of imagining this moment could stab like the reality. The sunlight in the corridor, the smell of vinegar, footsteps in the distance, all were printed indelibly in his mind.

'Oliver!' She was startled to see him, and pleased. He could detect none of the roar of emotion in her that he felt himself. But then he should not have expected it. She was happy. He wanted her to be. And part of him could not bear it.

He made himself smile. If he lost his dignity they would both hate it. 'I was hoping to see you. I trust I am not interrupting.'

'You have news of some sort?' She searched his face.

He must think only of the case. They had a common cause, one that mattered as fiercely as any they had ever fought. The lives of two women depended on it.

'Very little,' he replied, moving a step closer to her. He caught a warmth, a faint air of some perfume about her. He ached to move closer still. She was so different now, so much less vulnerable than before. And yet in so many ways she was exactly the same. The will to battle was there, the stubbornness, the unreason, the laughter he had never completely understood, the arbitrariness that exasperated and fascinated him.

There was a very faint flush on her cheeks, as if she guessed some part of his thoughts.

He looked away from her, avoiding her eyes, pretending to be thinking deeply of legal matters.

'I have been to see both Cleo Anderson and Miriam Gardiner. Both deny either conspiracy or murder, but Miriam at least is lying to me about the murders. She knows who committed them, but I believe her when she says it is not her. I have not met Lucius Stourbridge.'

She was startled. 'Do you believe he could be guilty of killing his own mother?'

'I don't think so, but it would seem to have been someone in the family, or else Miriam Gardiner,' he reasoned.

She looked up and down the corridor. 'Come into the waiting room here. There is no one needing it at the moment. We can speak more easily.' She opened the door and led him in.

He closed it, trying to force his emotions out of his consciousness. There were far more important issues between them.

'Major Stourbridge?' he asked. 'Or the brother, Aiden Campbell?'

She looked miserable. 'I don't know. I can't think of any reason why they would hurt either Mrs Stourbridge or Treadwell. But he was a blackmailer! If he would blackmail Cleo, then maybe he would others as well. William says he seemed to spend more money than he could have had from Cleo, so there will have been other victims.'

'Lucius?'

'Perhaps,' she said quietly. 'That would explain why Miriam is prepared to defend him, even at the price of being condemned for it herself.'

It was possible. It would explain Miriam's refusal to tell the truth. But he still found it hard to believe.

'I cannot think of anything we could argue which would convince a jury of that, especially in face of Miriam's denial,' he said, watching Hester. 'And she would not let me try. I have promised not to act against her wishes.'

A smile touched the corner of Hester's lips, and then

vanished. 'I would have assumed as much. I would like you to be able to defend Miriam, but I am more concerned with Cleo Anderson. I hope she did not kill Treadwell, but she cannot have killed Mrs Stourbridge. I am absolutely sure she would not have conspired for Miriam to marry Lucius, or anyone else, for money. That part of it is simply impossible.'

'Even to put to a good cause?' he asked gently.

'To put to any cause at all! It would be revolting to her. She loves Miriam. What kind of a woman would have her daughter marry for money? That's prostitution!'

'Hester, my dear! It is the commonest practice in civilisation! Or out of it, for that matter! Parents have sold their daughters in marriage and considered it doing all parties a service, since time immemorial – longer! Since pre-history.'

'Isn't that the same?' she said tartly.

'Actually, no. I believe "time immemorial" is in the middle of the twelfth century. It hardly matters.'

'No, it doesn't! Cleo would not sell her daughter, and she certainly would not conspire to murder someone who got in the way. If you knew her as I do, you wouldn't even have thought of it!'

He did not believe it either, but it was what a jury believed that mattered. He pointed that out to her.

'I know,' she said miserably, staring at the floor. 'But we've got to do something to help. I refuse to hide behind an intricacy of the law as if it excused one from fighting.'

He found himself smiling, but there was no laughter in it, no light at all, except irony. 'Murder is not an intricacy of the law, my dear.'

She looked at him with utter frankness, all the old friendship warm in her eyes, and suddenly he was short of breath. The final bit of denial of his emotions slipped away. He forced his mind back to the law, and Cleo Anderson.

'How much medicine is missing, and exactly what?'

She looked apologetic. 'We don't know, but it's a lot – a few grains a day I should think. I can't give you precise measurements and I wouldn't if I could. You would rather not know.'

'Perhaps you are right,' he admitted. 'I won't ask again. When the matter comes to court, who is likely to testify on the thefts?'

'Only Fermin Thorpe, willingly – or at least not willingly, but for the prosecution,' she amended. 'He's going to hate having to say that anything went missing from his hospital. He won't know whether to make light of it, and risk being thought to cover it up, or condemn it and be seen on the side of the law, all quivering with outrage at the iniquity of nurses. Either way, he'll be furious at being caught up in it at all.'

'Is he not likely to defend one of his staff?'

The look in her face was eloquent dismissal of any such prospect.

'I see,' he concluded. 'And the apothecary?'

'Phillips? He'll cover all he can – even to risking his own safety, but there's only so much he can do.'

'I see. I will speak with a few of the other nurses, if I may, and perhaps Mr Phillips. Then I shall go and see Sergeant Robb.'

It was early evening by the time Rathbone had made as thorough examination of the hospital routine as he wished to, and came to the regrettable conclusion that it required considerable forethought and some skill and nerve to steal medicines on a regular basis. The apothecary was very careful, in spite of his unkempt appearance and erratic sense of the absurd. Better opportunities occurred when a junior doctor was hurried, confused by a case he did not understand, or simply a little careless. Rathbone formed the opinion that in all probability Phillips was perfectly aware of what Cleo had been doing, and why, and had either deliberately connived at it, or at the very least turned a blind eye. Against all his training he found himself admiring the man for it, and quite intentionally ceased looking for evidence to support his theory.

It was consequently after seven o'clock by the time he went looking for Sergeant Robb, and was obliged to ask for his address at home in order to see him.

He found the house quite easily, but in spite of Michael Robb's courtesy, he felt an intruder. A glance told him he had interrupted the care of the old man who sat in the chair in the centre of the room, his white hair brushed back off his brow, his broad shoulders hunched forward over a hollow chest. His face was pale except for two spots of colour on his cheeks. The sight of him gave a passionate and human reality to the work Cleo Anderson was prepared to risk so much for. Rathbone was startled to find himself filled with anger at the situation, at his own helplessness to affect it, and at the world for not knowing and not caring. It was with difficulty he answered Michael Robb in a level voice.

'Good evening, Sergeant. I am sorry to intrude into your home, and at such an uncivil hour. If I could have found you at the police station I would have.'

'What can I do for you, Sir Oliver?' Michael asked. He was courteous but wary. Rathbone was of both a class and a profession he was unused to dealing with except in court, with the duty of their offices to prescribe the behaviour for both of them. For his part, Rathbone was acutely conscious of Robb's grandfather sitting tired and hungry, waiting to be assisted. But he was by nature, as well as occupation, a gentle-mannered man.

'I have undertaken to defend Mrs Anderson against the

charge of murder,' Rathbone replied with a faint, self-deprecating smile. He could not pretend to anyone he hoped for much success, and he did not wish Robb to think him a fool. 'The question of theft is another matter.'

'I'm sorry,' Michael said, and there was sincerity in his face as well as his voice. 'I took no pleasure in charging her. But I can't withdraw it.'

'I understand that. It provides the motive for the murder of Treadwell.'

'Are you talking about Cleo Anderson?' the old man interrupted, looking from one to the other of them.

Michael's face tightened and he shot Rathbone a look of reproach. 'Yes, Grandpapa.'

Rathbone had the strong impression that if Michael could have escaped with a lie about it he would have to protect the old man from knowledge which could only hurt. Had he any knowledge how much he also was compromised? Did he guess the debt he owed Cleo Anderson?

The old man looked at Rathbone. 'And you're going to defend her, young man?' He regarded him up and down from his beautifully made boots and tailored trousers to his coat and silk cravat. 'And what's an officer-type gentleman, with a title an' all, doing defending a woman like Mrs Anderson, who in't got two pence to rub together?' He cared about Cleo too much to be in awe of anyone. His faded eyes met Rathbone's without a flicker.

'I don't want payment, Mr Robb,' Rathbone answered. 'I undertook it as a favour to a friend, Mrs Monk. I believe you know her . . .' He saw the flash of recognition and of pleasure in the old man's face, and felt a warmth within himself. 'And I am continuing out of regard for Mrs Anderson herself, now that I have met her.'

Michael was looking at him with anxiety. Rathbone knew

what he feared, perhaps better than he did himself. He feared the same thing, and even more keenly. He did not have to look at the cabinet shelf in the far corner to be aware of the medicines that first Cleo had brought, and now he was terrified Hester would continue. There was no point in asking her not to, and he was in no position to forbid her – he doubted even Monk would succeed in that. Altogether it would be wiser not to try. It would provoke a quarrel and waste time and energy they all needed to address the problem rather than fight each other. The chances of success in dissuading Hester, in his opinion, did not exist.

He preferred, for legal reasons, as well as his own fast vanishing peace of mind, not to know what was in that cabinet, or how it got there.

Michael half-glanced at the cabinet, then averted his gaze. If the thought came to his mind, he forced it away. Just now he was too torn by his needs to allow himself to think it.

'So you're going to stand up an' speak for her?' the old man asked Rathbone.

'Yes, I am,' Rathbone replied.

John Robb screwed up his face. His voice was hoarse, whispering. 'What can you do for her, young man? Be honest with me.'

'I don't know,' Rathbone was candid. 'I believe she took the medicines. I don't believe she murdered Treadwell, even though he was blackmailing her. I think there is something of great importance that we have not imagined, and I am going to try to find out what it is.'

'That why you came to speak to Michael?'

'Yes.'

'Then you'd best get on with it. I can wait for me supper.' He turned to his grandson. 'You help this fellow. We can eat later.'

'Thank you,' Rathbone acknowledged the gesture. 'But I should feel more comfortable if you were to continue as you would have. I think I passed a pie seller on the corner about a hundred yards away. Would you allow me to fetch us one each, and then we can eat and discuss at the same time?'

Michael hesitated only a moment, glancing at the old man and seeing his flash of pleasure at the prospect, then he accepted.

Rathbone returned with the best three pies he could purchase, wrapped in newspaper and kept hot, and they ate together with mugs of tea. Michael was the police officer in charge and it was his duty to gather evidence and to present it in court. A few years earlier he would also have risked being sued for false arrest had the case failed, not as witness for the Crown, but in a personal capacity, and faced gaol himself could he not pay the fine. Even so he seemed as keen as his grandfather to find any mitigating evidence he could for Cleo Anderson.

Old John Robb was convinced that if she had killed Treadwell, then he had thoroughly deserved it, and if the law condemned her then the law was wrong, and should be overturned. His faith that Rathbone could do that was fuelled more by hope than realism.

Michael did not argue with him. His desire to protect the old man from more pain was so evident Rathbone was greatly moved by it.

Nevertheless when he left as dusk was falling, Rathbone had learned nothing that was of help to him. Everything simply confirmed what he already knew from Hester. He walked briskly along the footpath in the warm evening air, the smells of the day sharp around him: horse manure, dry grass and dust from the Heath, now and then the delicacy of meat and onions or the sharpness of peppermint from one pedlar or the other. There was the sound of a barrel organ playing a popular song in the distance, and children shouting.

He hailed the first hansom that passed him and gave the driver his address, then instantly changed his mind and directed him instead to his father's home in Primrose Hill.

It was almost dark when he arrived. He walked up the familiar path with a sense of anticipation, even though he had taken no steps to ensure that his father was home, let alone that it was convenient for him to call.

The sweetness of mown grass and deep shadow engulfed him, and a snare of honeysuckle so sharp it caught in his throat almost like a taste. As he walked around the house, and across the lawn to the French doors he saw that the study light was on. Henry Rathbone had not bothered to draw the curtains and Oliver could see him sitting in the armchair.

Henry was reading and did not hear the silent footsteps or notice the shadow. His legs were crossed and he was sucking on his pipe-stem, though as usual the pipe itself had gone out.

Oliver tapped on the glass.

Henry looked up, then, as he recognised his son, his lean face filled with pleasure and he beckoned him in.

Oliver felt the ease of familiarity wash over him like a warmth. Unreasonably some of his helplessness left him, although he had not even begun to explain the problem, let alone address it. He sat down in the big chair opposite his father's, leaning back comfortably.

For a few moments neither of them spoke. Henry continued to suck on his empty pipe. Outside in the darkness a night bird called and the branches of the honeysuckle, with its trumpet-shaped flowers, waved in the bright wind. A moth banged against the glass.

'I have a new case,' Oliver said at length. 'I can't possibly win it.'

Henry took his pipe out of his mouth. 'Then you must have had a good reason for taking it . . . or at least one that appeared good at the time.'

'I don't think it was a good one.' Oliver was pedantic, as his nature inclined. He had learned exactness from Henry and he never measured what he said to him. It was part of the basis of their friendship. 'It was compelling. They are not the same.'

Henry smiled. 'Not in the slightest,' he agreed.

'Monk asked me to,' Oliver added.

Henry nodded.

'There was a moral imperative!' Oliver said, justifying the choice. He did not want his father to think it was because of Monk, still less because of Hester.

'I see. Are you going to tell me what it is?'

'Of course.' Oliver moved and crossed his legs comfortably. He gave a succinct outline of the cases against both Cleo Anderson and Miriam Gardiner, then he waited while Henry sat deep in thought for several moments. Outside it was now completely dark except for the patch of luminous moonlight on the grass just short of the old apple tree at the end of the lawn.

'And you assume that this woman Cleo Anderson did not kill the coachman,' Henry said at last. 'Even in a manner for which there might be some mitigating circumstances – or possibly a struggle in which he died accidentally?'

Oliver thought for a moment before answering. The truth was that that was exactly what he had accepted. Cleo had said she was not present, and he had believed her. He still did.

'Yes. Yes, I am assuming that,' he agreed. 'She never denied taking the medicines. I have no proof of exactly how she did it, or any of the circumstances. I have deliberately avoided finding them.'

Henry made no comment. 'How is Monk involved?' he asked instead.

Rathbone explained.

'And Hester?' Henry asked, his voice gentle.

Oliver had not forgotten how fond his father was of Hester, nor his unspoken desire that Oliver should marry her. He sometimes feared Hester's regard for him was at least in part the affection she had for Henry, and the desire to belong to a family in which she could know the safety her own had not given her. Her father had shot himself after a financial disgrace visited upon him at the end of the Crimean War by an unscrupulous man who traded upon friendship and honour in order to cheat. Hester's mother had died shortly afterwards, largely of grief. Hester had spoken of it only once, unless she had done so more often to Henry, when Oliver was not there, perhaps needing to share the burden.

This was a topic of conversation he was dreading. He had deliberately avoided it as long as possible, even to the extent of not coming to Primrose Hill, but meeting his father in the City where private conversations were too liable to interruption. Now it could no longer be deferred.

'Hester seems very well,' he answered expressionlessly. At least he thought he had, but judging by Henry's face, perhaps he deluded himself. 'Of course she is deeply concerned for this nurse, both personally and in principle,' he added, feeling the warmth rush up his cheeks.

Henry nodded. 'I can imagine that she is consumed with her usual fire.' He did not say anything about Oliver's motives for accepting what seemed a hopeless case. He was the only person who induced Oliver to make explanations of himself where none had been asked for.

'It matters!' he said urgently, leaning forward a little. He looked at Henry, at his lean and slightly stooped form, his hair very grey, and imagined what he would feel if he had been a soldier or a sailor instead of a mathematician, if he were broken in body, bewildered and alone, unable to afford the care he needed, stripped of the dignity of old age, and left only with its helplessness. It was so painful it caught his breath. Now the battle was for John Robb, for Henry, for all those affected by injury and age, or who would be in time to come. 'It matters far more than any one person,' he said passionately. 'More than Cleo Anderson or even than Hester – or winning for its own sake. If we allow this injustice without doing all we can against it, what are we worth?'

Henry regarded him gravely, all the humour gone from his eyes. 'Very little,' he said quietly. 'But emotion will not win for you, Oliver. It is an excellent driving force, the best, and it will keep your courage high. Anger at injustice has righted more wrongs than most other things, and it is one of the great creative forces in a civilised society.' He shook his head. 'But in order not to replace one enemy with another, albeit innocently intended, you must use your intelligence. You told me that you are certain that both Mrs Anderson and Mrs Gardiner are lying to you. You cannot go into court without knowing at least what the lie is, and why they are telling it, at the risk of their own deaths. The reason must be a very powerful one indeed.'

'I know that,' Oliver agreed. 'And I have racked my brain to think what it could be.'

'Is it the same reason for each?'

'I don't even know that!'

Henry sat thoughtfully, elbows on the arms of his chair, fingers steepled together. 'I assume that you warned each of them that not only their own lives, but that of the other, rests upon the verdict. Therefore they each have a compelling reason for not telling you the truth. From what you say it seems possible that Mrs Anderson does not know it, but certainly Mrs Gardiner does. Why would a woman hang for a crime she did not commit?' He looked very steadily at Oliver. 'Only because the alternative to her is worse.'

'What could be worse than hanging?' Oliver asked.

'I don't know. That is what you must find out.'

'The hanging of someone you love . . .' Oliver said, as much to himself as to Henry.

'Is Lucius Stourbridge guilty?' Henry asked him.

'I don't know,' Oliver replied. 'I don't know why he could kill either Treadwell, or his own mother.'

'Treadwell is easier,' Henry said thoughtfully. 'The man may have threatened Mrs Gardiner, or threatened the marriage, either through Mrs Anderson, or in some other way. He was a blackmailer. Much is possible. It is far more difficult to think of any motive for Lucius to have killed his mother.'

'I've searched for one,' Oliver admitted. 'I've found nothing.'

'It would be extraordinary if the two murders were not connected,' Henry pursued, drawing his brows together. 'What elements do they have in common?'

'Treadwell himself, and Miriam Gardiner,' Oliver replied.

'And the unknown,' Henry added. 'One must always include the possibility of a factor we have not considered, perhaps something outside our knowledge entirely. From what you have told me so far, it seems this may be the case here. Proceed with logic, eliminate what is impossible, and then examine what is left, no matter how ugly it may be. I have a feeling, Oliver, that this may stretch your compassion to its limits, and require more of you than you had thought to give. I am sorry. I appreciate that this is not easy for you, especially considering Hester's involvement in it.'

'Her involvement makes no difference!' As soon as the words were on his lips he knew not only that they were untrue, but quite certainly that Henry knew it also, but it was difficult to withdraw them.

Henry shook his head so minutely it was barely a movement at all.

'It makes no difference to the issues,' Oliver amended. What he really meant, the aloneness, the knowledge of having held something precious and let it slip through his fingers because he would not commit his passions fully enough, the regret, were all there between them, unsaid. Henry knew him well enough that truth was not necessary, and lies were not only impossible, but damaging. Henry understood as well as he did that Hester made all the difference in the world to the way he felt about this case, to know he would continue to fight regardless of what he himself might lose in reputation, embarrassment or money.

Henry was smiling. Oliver knew in that moment that he approved. Much as he revered the law himself, and understood the dedication of a man to his chosen field, to his principles that superseded any individual, he also understood that to do all these things without caring was a kind of death to the heart. He would rather Oliver fought because he cared, and lost, then won with all the rewards, but without belief.

They sat in silence for another half-hour or so, then Oliver rose and took his leave. Henry strolled with him down the lawn in the darkness, heavy with the scent of wet grass, and looked at the moonlight reflected on the leaves in the orchard, then back up again towards the road.

It did not need to be said that tomorrow Oliver must begin

to prepare a sensible case to defend his clients, and look for whatever alternative was so hideous Miriam Gardiner would rather hang than have it revealed.

And if Oliver found it, where did his loyalty lie then? To Miriam, or to the truth?

But after they had parted and he walked towards the main thoroughfare he felt a strength restored inside him, a balance returned. He had faced certain lies and no longer allowed them to govern him.

Chapter Ten

❦

Five weeks later Cleo Anderson and Miriam Gardiner sat in the dock accused of conspiracy and murder. The courtroom was packed to suffocation, people sitting so close to one another that when they moved in discomfort the sound of fabrics rubbing together was audible. The shuffling and squeaking of boots was broken by a cough and the occasional gasp.

When the business of calling to order, reading the charge and pleadings had been accomplished, Robert Tobias opened for the prosecution. He was a man Rathbone had faced several times before and to whom he had lost as often as he had won. Tobias was of a fraction less than average height, slender in his youth, and now, at sixty, still supple and straight-backed. He had never been strictly handsome, but his intelligence and the power and beauty of his voice made him remarkable, and both intimidating and attractive. More than one society lady had begun by flirting with him for her own entertainment, and ended in caring more than she wished to, and eventually being hurt. He was a widower who intended to retain his freedom to do as he chose.

He smiled at Rathbone, and called his first witness, Sergeant Michael Robb.

Rathbone watched as Robb climbed the short steps to the witness stand and faced the court. He looked unhappy, and extraordinarily young. He must have been in his mid-twenties, but he had the scrubbed and brushed look of a child sent off to Sunday school, who would far rather be almost anywhere else.

Tobias sauntered out into the middle of the open space of the floor with the jury on one side, the witness ahead of him, and the judge to his right, high up against the wall in his magnificent seat, surrounded by panels of softly gleaming wood and padded red velvet.

'Sergeant Robb,' Tobias began politely, 'this whole case is very distressing. No decent man likes to imagine two women, especially when one is young and agreeable to look upon, and the other is entrusted with the care of the sick . . .' he lifted his hand very slightly towards the dock, '. . . would be capable of conspiring together to commit cold-blooded murder, for gain. Fortunately it is not your task, nor mine either, to determine if this is indeed what happened.' He turned with a graceful gesture to face the jury and gave a little bow in their direction. 'It is the awful duty of these twelve good men and true, and I do not envy them. Justice is a mighty weight! It takes a strong man, a brave man, an honest man to bear it.'

Rathbone was tempted to interrupt this piece of blatant flattery, but he knew Tobias would be only too happy if he did. He remained in his seat, nodding very slightly as if he agreed.

Tobias turned back to Robb. 'All we need from you is a simple, exact account of the facts you know. May we begin with the discovery of the body of James Treadwell?'

Robb stood to attention. Rathbone wondered if it were as apparent to the jury as it was to him how much Robb disliked his task. Would they imagine it was repugnance for the crime, or would they know, as he did, that it was a deeper knowledge of complex tragedy, right and wrong so inextricably mixed he could not single out one thread?

How did people judge? Instinct? Intelligence? Previous knowledge and experience? Emotion? How was evidence interpreted? How often he had seen two people describe a single chain of events, and draw utterly different conclusions from it.

Robb began by talking with bare, almost schoolboy simplicity, of having been called out to see the dead body of a man who had apparently died of a blow to the head.

'So you decided immediately that he was the victim of murder?' Tobias said with surprise and evident satisfaction. He barely glanced at Rathbone, as if he half expected to be interrupted, and took it as a sign of Rathbone's foreknowledge of defeat that he was not.

Robb breathed in deeply. 'From the kind of marks on his clothes, sir, I didn't think he'd fallen off a coach or carriage, or been struck by one that maybe didn't see him in the dark.'

'Very perceptive of you. You judged the matter of great seriousness right from the outset?'

'Death is always serious,' Robb answered.

'Of course. But murder has a gravity that accident does not. It is a dark and dreadful thing, a violation of our deepest moral order! Accident is tragic, but it is mischance. Murder is evil!'

Robb's face was pink. 'With respect, sir, I thought you said you and I were not here to judge, just to establish the facts. If you don't mind, sir, I'd prefer to stick to that.'

There was a murmur around the court.

Rathbone allowed himself to smile, indeed he could not help it.

Tobias controlled his temper with grace, but it cost him an effort. Rathbone could see it in the angle of his shoulders and the pull of the cloth in his expensive coat.

'I stand corrected,' he conceded. 'By all means let us have the bare facts. Will you describe this dead man that you found. Was he young or old? In good health or ill? Let us see him through your eyes, Sergeant Robb. Let us feel as you did when you stood on the pavement and stared down at this man so lately alive and full of hopes and dreams, and so violently torn from them.' He spread his arms wide in invitation. 'Take us with you!'

Robb stared at him glumly. Never once did he lift his glance towards the two women sitting in the dock, white-faced, motionless. Nor did he look beyond Tobias and Rathbone to search the audience for other faces familiar to him: Monk, Hester or Callandra Daviot.

'He was fairly ordinary, difficult to tell his height lying down. He had straight hair, strong hands, callused as if he'd held reins often enough—'

'Any signs of a fight?' Tobias interrupted. 'Any bruises or cuts as if he had tried to defend himself?'

'I saw none. Just the grazes on his hands from crawling.'

'I shall naturally ask the surgeon also, but thank you for your observation. Exactly where was this poor man, Sergeant?'

'On the pathway between number five and number six on Green Man Hill, near Hampstead Heath.'

'And which way was he facing?'

'Number five.'

'And is that where he was killed?'

'I don't think so. He looked to have crawled some distance.

His trouser knees were all torn and muddy, and his elbows in places.'

'How far? Can you tell?'

'No. At least forty or fifty yards, maybe more.'

'I see. What did you do then, Sergeant?'

Step by step Tobias drew from Robb the account of finding the carriage, the horses, and presuming they were connected with the dead man. Then he led him through Monk's arrival, seeking someone answering the dead man's description.

'How very interesting!' Tobias said with triumph. 'Presumably you took this Mr Monk to look at your corpse?'

'Yes, sir.'

'And did he identify him?'

'No, sir. He couldn't say. But he fetched two gentlemen from Bayswater who said he was James Treadwell, who had been their coachman.'

'And the names of these gentlemen?'

'Major Harry Stourbridge, and his son, Mr Lucius Stourbridge.'

There was a rustle of movement in the court as people's attention was caught. Several straightened in their seats. 'The same Lucius Stourbridge who is the son of Mrs Verona Stourbridge, and who was engaged to marry Mrs Miriam Gardiner?'

More movement in the gallery. Two women craned forward to stare at the dock.

'Yes, sir,' Robb answered.

'And when was Treadwell last seen alive, and by whom?'

Reluctantly Robb told of Miriam's flight from the garden party, Monk's duplicity on the matter, and how first Monk had tracked down Miriam, and then Robb had himself. There was nothing Rathbone could do to stop him.

'Most interesting,' Tobias said sagely. 'And did Mrs Gardiner give you a satisfactory account of her flight from Bayswater and any reason for this most strange behaviour?'

'No, sir.'

'Did she tell you who had killed Treadwell? I assume you did ask her?'

'I did, and no, she did not give me any answer, except to say she did not do it.'

'And did you believe her?'

Rathbone half rose to his feet.

The judge glanced at him.

Tobias smiled. 'Perhaps that could be better phrased. Sergeant Robb, did you subsequently arrest Mrs Gardiner for the murder of James Treadwell?'

'Yes, I did.'

Tobias raised his eyebrows. 'But you have not charged her with it!'

Robb's face was tight and miserable. 'She's charged with conspiracy . . .'

'That you should be sad about such a fearful tragedy is very proper, Sergeant,' Tobias observed, staring at him. 'But you seem more than that, you seem reluctant, as if you undertake your duty against your will. Why is that, Sergeant Robb?'

Rathbone's mind raced. Should he object that this was irrelevant, personal? He had intended to use Robb's high opinion of Cleo, his knowledge of her motives, as his only weapon in mitigation. Now Tobias had stolen it. He could hardly object now, and then raise it himself later. Even if he did so obliquely, Tobias himself would then object.

There was nothing he could do but sit quietly and try to keep his face from betraying him.

'Sergeant?' Tobias prompted.

Robb lifted his chin a little, glaring back. 'I am reluctant, sir. Mrs Anderson is well known in our community for going around visiting and helping the sick, especially them that's old and poor. Night and day, she did it, as well as working in the hospital. She couldn't have cared for them better if they'd been her own.'

'But you arrested her for murder!'

Robb clenched his jaw. 'I had to. We found evidence that Treadwell was blackmailing her—'

This time Rathbone did stand up. 'My lord . . .'

'Yes, yes,' the judge agreed, pursing his lips. 'Mr Tobias, you know better than this. If you have evidence, present it in the proper way.'

Tobias bowed, smiling. He had no cause to worry, and he knew it. He turned back to Robb in the witness stand.

'This high regard you have for Mrs Anderson, Sergeant, is it all upon local hearsay, or can you substantiate it from any knowledge of your own?'

'I have it from knowledge of my own,' Robb said wretchedly. 'She came regularly to see my grandfather, who lives with me.'

Tobias nodded slowly. He seemed to be weighing his words, judging what to say, and what to leave unsaid. Rathbone looked across at the faces of the jury. There was one man in particular, middle-aged, earnest, who was watching Tobias with what seemed to be understanding. He turned to Robb, and there was pity clear in his face.

Tobias did not ask if Cleo had brought medicines or not. It was not necessary; the jury had perceived it already. They would not want to see the sergeant embarrassed. Tobias was a superb judge of nature.

There was nothing Rathbone could do.

The day proceeded while Tobias drew out all the rest of

the evidence, piece by piece, from an unwilling Robb. He told how, at least in part by following Monk, he had learned of the missing medicines, of Cleo's own poverty and that she was being blackmailed by Treadwell. It provided her with a motive for murder that anyone could understand only too well. The jury sat sombre, shaking their heads, and there seemed as much pity in their faces as blame.

That would change when Miriam became involved, Rathbone knew it as well as he knew darkness followed sundown, but there was no protest or argument he could make. Tobias was precisely within all the rules, and had laid his plans perfectly. There was nothing for Rathbone to do but endure it, and hope.

The second day was no better. Robb finished his testimony and Rathbone was given the opportunity to question him, but there was nothing for him to ask. If he remained silent he would appear to have surrendered already, without even the semblance of a fight, as if he had no belief in his clients and no hope for them. And yet Tobias had touched on every aspect of Robb's knowledge of the case and there was nothing to challenge. Everything he had said was true, and not capable of kinder or more favourable interpretation. To have him repeat it would not only look ineffectual, it would reinforce it in the jury's minds. He rose to his feet.

'Thank you, my lord, but Mr Tobias has asked of Sergeant Robb everything that I would have. It would be self-indulgent of me to waste the court's time asking the sergeant to repeat it for me.' He sat down again.

Tobias smiled.

The judge nodded to him unhappily. He seemed to find the case distressing as if he would very much rather have had someone else here in his place, but he would see justice done. He had spent his life in this cause.

Tobias called the minister from the church in Hampstead, a genial man who looked uncomfortable in such surroundings, but gave his evidence with conviction. He had known Cleo Anderson for thirty years. He had no idea she had committed any crime whatsoever, and found this news difficult to comprehend. He apologised for expressing such bewilderment. However, human frailty was his field of experience.

Tobias sympathised with him. 'And how long have you known Miriam Gardiner?' he asked.

'Since she first came to Hampstead,' the vicar replied. Then under Tobias' gentle encouragement he told the story of Miriam's first appearance in acute distress, aged about thirteen years old, how Cleo had taken her in and cared for her while seeking her family. They had proved impossible to find and Miriam had remained with Cleo until her marriage to Mr Gardiner.

'A moment!' Tobias interrupted him. 'Could you describe Mr Gardiner for us, please? His age, his appearance, his social and financial standing.'

The vicar looked a trifle startled.

Rathbone was not. He knew exactly what Tobias was doing – establishing a pattern of Cleo and Miriam's loyalty to each other, of Miriam marrying a man with a prosperous business, and then sharing her good fortune with her original benefactress, who had become as a mother to her. He did it extremely well, painting a picture of the woman and child struggling in considerable hardship, their closeness to one another, the happiness of Miriam finding a worthy man, albeit older than herself, but gentle and apparently devoted to her.

It was not a great romance, but it was a good, stable

marriage and certainly all that a girl in Miriam's position might have hoped for. A love match with a man her own age and class would not have brought her much material status or security.

Tobias made his point well, and delicately. Again there was nothing whatever Rathbone could call in question.

Had Miriam shared her new good fortune with Cleo Anderson?

'Naturally,' the vicar replied. 'What loving daughter would not?'

'Just so,' Tobias agreed, and let the matter rest.

When the court was adjourned for the day Rathbone went immediately to see Miriam. She was alone in the police cells, her face drawn, her eyes dark. She did not ask him why he had not spoken, and her silence made it harder for him. He had no idea if she had even hoped for anything, or how much she understood. It was so easy when he was accustomed to the flow of a trial and its hidden meanings, to assume that others were as aware. He would like to have allowed her the mercy of remaining unaware how serious it was, but he could not afford to.

He drew in his breath to ask her the usual question, as to her feelings, offer some words of encouragement, true or not, but they would be empty and a waste of precious time and emotion, almost a greater division between them, if that were possible. Honesty, his honesty, was all they had.

'Mrs Gardiner, you must tell me the truth. I was silent today because I have no weapon to use against Tobias. He knows it, but if I make a show of fighting him, and lose, then the jury will know it as well. Now they think I am merely biding my time. But I am walking blindly. I don't know what he may know that I don't. Or what he may discover – which is worse.'

She turned half away from him. 'Nothing. There is nothing he can discover.'

'He can discover who killed James Treadwell!' he said sharply. The time for any consideration of feeling was past. The rope was already overshadowing not only her but Cleo also.

She turned slowly to look at him. 'I doubt that, Sir Oliver. They would not believe it, even if I were to tell them. And I won't. Believe me, it would cause far greater injury than it would ever heal. I have no proof, and all the evidence you have, as you have said, is against me.'

The cells were warm, even stuffy, but he felt chilled in spite of it.

'It is my task to make them believe it.' He feared even as he said it that she had closed her mind and was not listening to him. 'At least allow me to try?' he was sounding desperate. He could hear it in the stridency of his voice.

'I am sorry you don't believe me,' she said softly. 'But it is true that it would cause more pain than any good it would do. At least accept that I have thought long and very hard about it before I have made this decision. I do understand that I will hang. I have no delusion that some miracle is going to save me. And you have not lied to me or given me any false sense of comfort. For that I thank you.'

Her gratitude was like a rebuff, reminding him of how little he had actually done. He was going to be no more than a figurehead, barely fulfilling the requirements of the law that she be represented. The prosecution need not have called in Tobias, Rathbone thought. The merest junior could have presented this case and beaten him.

He found he was shaking, his hands clenched tight. 'It is not only you who will hang – Cleo Anderson will as well!'

Her voice choked. 'I know. But what can I do?' She looked at him, her eyes swimming with tears. 'I will testify that I was there, and it was not she who killed him, if you want. But who would believe me? They think we are conspirators anyway! They expect me to defend her. I can't prove she wasn't there, and I can't prove he wasn't blackmailing her, or that she didn't take the medicines. She did!'

What she said was true.

'Someone killed Treadwell.' He picked his words carefully, to hurt her enough to make her tell him at last.

'If it was not either you or Cleo, the only person I can think of that you would die to defend is Lucius Stourbridge.'

Her eyes widened and the last vestige of colour fled from her face. She was too horrified to respond.

'If you will hang for him,' he went on, 'that is your choice – but is he really worth Cleo Anderson's life as well? Does she deserve that from you?'

She swung around to face him, her eyes blazing, her lips drawn back in a snarl of such ferocity he was almost afraid of her, small as she was, and imprisoned in this police cell.

'Lucius had nothing to do with it! I am not defending Treadwell's murderer! If I could see him hang I would tie the rope with my own hands, and pull the trapdoor and watch him drop!' She took in a deep, gasping breath. 'I can't! God help me – there is nothing – nothing I can do! Now go away and leave me at least to solitude, if not to peace.'

Other questions beat in his mind, but his fury and his despair robbed him of the words. He longed to be able to help her, not anything to do with his own reputation, or his honour, but simply to ease the pain he could see, and even feel as he watched her. She was only a yard away from him, and yet an abyss existed between what she experienced, and what he understood. He had no idea at all how he could cross it. They could have been in separate countries. He did not even know what else he felt: anger, fear that she was guilty, fear that she was not, and he would fail her and she would be destroyed by the wheels of the law he was supposed to guide or pity, even a kind of admiration, because quite without reason, he believed there was something noble in her, something beautiful and strong.

He left, walking out of the cells blind to the heat of the late afternoon and the passers-by, the chatter of voices, wheels, hoofs, all the clamour of everyday living. He hailed a cab and gave the driver Monk's address in Fitzroy Street. He barely spared thought to how little he wanted to go into the house that Hester shared with Monk. It seemed secondary now, a wound to deal with at another time.

'I pleaded with her!' he said, pacing back and forth in the front room where Monk received clients. Monk was standing by the mantelpiece even though the fire was unlit, the evening being far too mild to require one. Hester was sitting upright on the edge of the big armchair, staring at him, her face furrowed in concentration. 'But she knows she will hang, and still refuses to tell me who killed Treadwell!' He threw his arms wide, almost banging against the high back of the other chair.

'Lucius Stourbridge,' Monk said unhappily. 'He is the only one she would hang for – apart from Cleo.'

'No it isn't,' Rathbone said quickly. 'I assumed that also. She denied it with fury – at me, not at whoever did kill Treadwell. She said she would willingly hang him herself, if she could, but no one would believe her, and she would not tell me any more.'

Monk stared at him in bewilderment. Rathbone wanted an answer above all things, at this moment, but it was a very small satisfaction to see Monk just as confused as he was.

They both looked at Hester.

'That leaves either Harry Stourbridge, or Aiden Campbell,' she said thoughtfully. 'I suppose Treadwell could have been blackmailing Harry Stourbridge. He had been in the house for several years. He drove the carriage. Maybe Major Stourbridge went somewhere, did something he would pay to hide?'

'What about the brother, Campbell?' Rathbone asked.

Monk shook his head. 'Unlikely. He lives in Wiltshire somewhere. Only came up for the engagement party. I did check, and as far as the other servants knew, he barely saw Treadwell. He had his own carriage and driver, and no one ever saw him go anywhere near the mews while he was staying there. And Treadwell never went to Wiltshire in his life, never went outside London, according to the Stourbridges' cook. And as for his killing Mrs Stourbridge, they were very close, everyone agreed on that, had been ever since they were children.'

'Even close siblings can quarrel,' Rathbone pointed out.

'Of course,' Monk agreed a touch sharply, staring down at the polished fender where his foot was resting. 'But no one with enough cold-blooded nerve to murder rather than pay blackmail, is going to kill the sister who is his only link with a fortune the size of the Stourbridges'. Now she is dead, he has no claim at all. He is not especially close to either Harry or Lucius. They are friendly enough, but they will not continue Verona's generosity.'

Another blind alley.

Hester bit her lip. 'Then we must find out if it was Major

Stourbridge. However unpleasant, if that is the truth, we should know it.'

'It would make sense,' Rathbone admitted, pushing his hands into his pockets, and taking them out again immediately. It was a habit he had been taught not to practise in boyhood because it looked casual, and pulled his clothes out of shape. He turned to Monk.

'Yes,' Monk agreed, not to the likelihood, but to accepting the task before Rathbone could ask him. 'I should have pursued it more tenaciously before. I didn't really look at the Stourbridges, either of them.'

'I don't know what you can find in a day or two,' Rathbone said wretchedly. 'I'm going in with nothing! I have no other reasonable suspect to offer the jury, only "person or persons unknown"! Nobody's going to believe that when Cleo and Miriam have perfect motives and every appearance of guilt.'

'They may be guilty,' Monk reminded him. 'Or one of them may, perhaps in conspiracy with someone else?'

'In the Stourbridge household?' Rathbone said with some sarcasm. 'That has to be Miriam. And why, for the love of heaven?'

'I don't know,' Monk said angrily. 'But there is obviously some critical feature about the whole story that we haven't found – even if it is only the reason both women would rather hang than tell the truth! We'd better damned well discover what it is!'

Hester looked from Monk to Rathbone. 'How long can you prolong the trial, Oliver?'

'We seem to spend our time asking him to sing songs while we scramble to find something vital!' Monk said bitterly. 'I'll start tomorrow morning as soon as it's light. But I don't even know where to look!'

'What can I do to help?' Hester asked, more to Rathbone than to Monk.

'I wish I knew,' he confessed. 'Cleo admits to taking the medicines. There is nothing we can do to mitigate that except show how she used them, and we already have all the witnesses we need for that. We have dozens of men and women to swear to her diligence, compassion, dedication, sobriety, and honesty in all respects except that of stealing medicines from the hospital. But that is the only thing he needs. We even have people who will swear she was chaste, modest and clean. It will achieve nothing. She was still paying Treadwell blackmail money, and he had all but bled her dry. The only decent meals she ate were those given her either at the hospital, or by the people she visited. She even dressed in cast-off clothes left her by the dead!'

Hester sat silently, steeped in misery.

'I must go home,' Rathbone said at last. 'Perhaps a good night of sleep will clear my mind sufficiently to think of something.' He bade them good night and left, acutely conscious of loneliness. He would lie by himself in his smooth linen sheets. Monk would lie with Hester in his arms. The moonlit autumn night held no magic for him.

Tobias was in expansive mood when he called his first witness the next day, but he was careful not to exaggerate his manner. He was too clever to alienate a jury by seeming to gloat over his triumph. Although Rathbone, sitting at his table, thought his care unnecessary. As things were going at present, and from all future prospect, Tobias could hardly lose, whatever he did.

Neither Hester nor Monk was in the court today, nor was Callandra Daviot. All of the Stourbridge family had yet to testify, and therefore were forbidden in, in case anything they heard should influence what they themselves would say.

Tobias' first witness was the Stourbridges' groom. He took great care to establish his exact position in the household and his so far blameless reputation. He left no avenue, however small, for Rathbone to call in question either his honesty or power of observation.

Rathbone was quite satisfied that he should do so. He had no useful argument to make and no desire to try to blacken the man's character. It was always a bad exercise in that it offended the jurors to malign a person who was no more than a witness and in no way involved in a crime. And it had the great advantage, indeed at the moment the only advantage, in that it took time.

All that he showed by it, unquestionably, was that Treadwell had on a number of occasions driven Miriam from Bayswater back to her home in Hampstead, or had collected her. He had also once or twice delivered messages or gifts from Lucius to her, in the early days of the courtship, before Lucius himself had done so. Undoubtedly Treadwell knew her home and had spent time in the area.

Next Tobias called the keeper of the local inn, The William Fourth, on the corner of the High Street and Church Lane, who swore that Treadwell had stopped there on more than a few occasions, had a pint of ale and played darts or dominoes, gambled a little and struck up casual conversation with the locals. Yes, he had seemed to ask a lot of questions. At the time the landlord had taken it for concern for his employer, who was courting a woman who lived in the area.

The landlord of The Flask, on the other side of the High Street said much the same, as did two locals from The Blind Boy, a short block further along. There Treadwell had asked more particularly abut Miriam Gardiner and Cleo Anderson.

Yes, he was free with his money, as if he knew there would be more where that had come from.

'What sort of questions did he ask?' Tobias enquired innocently.

'About Mrs Gardiner's general reputation,' he replied. 'Was she honest, sober, that kind of thing.'

'And chaste?' Tobias asked.

'Yes – that too.'

'Did you not think that impertinent of the coachman?'

'Yes – I did. When I caught him at it I told him in no uncertain terms that Mrs Gardiner was as good a woman as he'd be likely to find in all Hampstead – and a damn sight too good for the likes of him!' He glanced at the judge. 'Beggin' yer pardon, me lud.'

'Did he explain why he asked such questions?'

'Never saw him again,' the man said with satisfaction. He glanced up at the dock and gave both women a deliberate smile. Miriam attempted to return it, but it was a ghost on her ashen face. Cleo nodded to him very slightly, merely the acknowledgement courtesy demanded. It was a small gesture, but kindly meant.

'You would be glad to see Mrs Gardiner happily married again, after losing her first husband so young?' Tobias observed conversationally.

'I was glad, and that's the truth! So were everyone else as knew 'er.'

'Did you know the late Mr Gardiner well?'

'Knew 'im in passing, like. A very decent sort o' gent.'

'Indeed. But quite a lot older than his wife – his widow?'

The man's face darkened. 'What are you tryin' ter say?'

Tobias shrugged. 'What did James Treadwell try to say?'

'Nothing!' Now the man was plainly angry.

'You did not like him?' Tobias pressed.

'I did not!'

'No love for blackmailers?'

'No I 'aven't! Nor 'as any man fit ter walk an' breathe God's good air. Filth, they are.'

Tobias nodded. 'A feeling shared by many.' He glanced up at the dock, then back to the witness box.

Rathbone knew perfectly well what he was doing, but he was helpless to stop him.

'Of course,' Tobias smiled deprecatingly, 'Treadwell may have been asking his questions about Mrs Gardiner in loyal interest of his employer, Mr Stourbridge, in order to prevent him making an unfortunate marriage! Did that possibility occur to you? It may not have been for purposes of blackmail at all!'

Rathbone stood up at last. 'My Lord, the witness is not in a position to know why Treadwell asked questions, and his opinion is surely irrelevant. Unless Mr Tobias is implying he may have had some part in Treadwell's death?'

There was a sharp stir in the courtroom and one of the juror's jerked up his head.

'Quite,' the judge agreed. 'Mr Tobias, do not imperil your case by wandering too far afield. I am sure your point has already been taken. James Treadwell asked questions in the neighbourhood regarding Mrs Gardiner's character and reputation. Is that all you wish us to know?'

'For the moment, my lord.' Tobias thanked his witness and turned invitingly to Rathbone.

Again there was nothing for him to ask. The witness had already made it plain he admired Miriam and was partisan in her favour. As far as he was concerned, Treadwell had met with a fate he deserved. It would not help either Miriam or Cleo to hear him say so again.

'I have nothing to ask this witness,' he declined.

Tobias proceeded to call the Stourbridges' servants to tell
their accounts of the day of the party, and Miriam's still
unexplained departure with Treadwell. The parlour maid had
seen it all and told of it simply, and with obvious great
unhappiness.

At last Rathbone had something to ask.

'Miss Pembroke,' he said with a slight smile, moving into
the centre of the floor and looking up at her where she stood
high in the witness stand. 'You have told very clearly what
you saw. You must have had a view of Mrs Gardiner with no
one blocking your way.'

'Yes, sir, I did.'

'You said she seemed about to faint, as if she had suffered
a great shock, and then after she had recovered herself she
turned and ran, even fled, from the garden towards the stables.
Is that correct?'

'Yes, sir.'

The judge frowned.

Rathbone hurried on before he should be cautioned to
come to the point.

'Did anyone speak to her, pass her anything?'

'You mean a glass, sir? I didn't see no one.'

'No, I meant rather more like a message, something to
account for her shock, and from what you describe, even
terror.'

'No, sir, no one came that close to her. And I don't think
she had a glass.'

'You are not certain about the glass, but you are sure no
one spoke to her or passed her anything?'

'Yes, I am.'

'Have you any idea what caused her to run away?'

Tobias rose.

'No,' the judge said to him bluntly. 'Miss Pembroke is an

observant girl. She may very well know what happened. It has been my experience that servants frequently know a good deal more than some of us would believe, or wish to believe.' He turned to the witness stand. 'Do you know what caused Mrs Gardiner's flight, Miss Pembroke? If you do, this is the appropriate time and place to say so, whether it was a confidence or not.'

'No, sir, I don't know an' that's the truth. But I never seen anyone look as dreadful as she did that day. Like she'd seen the living dead she did.'

'Do you know where Treadwell was during the party?' Rathbone asked.

'In the stables, sir, same as always.'

'So Mrs Gardiner went to him – he did not come to her?'

'Must be.'

'Thank you. That is all I have to ask you.'

'But not all I have!' Tobias cut in quickly, striding forward from his table. 'You were on the lawn mixing with the guests in your capacity as parlour maid, were you not?'

'Yes, sir. I were carrying a tray of lemonade. Parkin had the champagne.'

'Is it easy to carry a tray loaded with glasses?'

'It's all right, when you're used to it. Gets heavy.'

'And you offered them to those guests whose glasses were empty?'

'Yes, sir.'

'So you were not watching Mrs Gardiner all the time?'

'No, sir.'

'Naturally. Could she have received some message, either in words or on paper, that you were unaware of?'

'I suppose she could.'

'Is it possible, Miss Pembroke, that this was the best time for her to catch Treadwell alone, and with no duties or responsibilities which would prevent him from driving her from Cleveland Square. Is it possible, Miss Pembroke, that she knew the working of the household sufficiently well that she was aware she would find Treadwell in the mews, with the carriage available, and had planned in advance to meet him there, and drive to a lonely place where she imagined they could do as they pleased together, unobserved, and where she intended – with the help of her foster mother – to get rid once and for all, of the man who was blackmailing them both?'

Rathbone shot to his feet, but the protest died on his lips.

Tobias shrugged. 'I only ask if it's possible!' he said reasonably. 'Miss Pembroke is an observant young woman. She may know!'

'I don't!' she protested. 'I don't know what happened, I swear!'

'Your loquacity seems to have ended in confusion,' the judge said acidly to Tobias. He turned to the jury. 'You will note that the question has gone unanswered, and draw your own conclusions. Sir Oliver, have you anything further to add?'

Rathbone hadn't but Tobias was unstoppable. His rich voice seemed to fill the court and there was hardly an eye which was not upon him. He called the lady's maid who had seen Miriam in Verona Stourbridge's room, and drew from her a highly damaging account of Miriam trying on the jewellery and apparently having read the diary.

'Do you know what is in the diary?' Tobias asked.

The girl's eyes widened in horror. 'No, sir, I do not!' Her tone carried bitter resentment that he should suggest such a thing.

'Of course not,' he agreed smoothly. 'One does not read another person's private writings. I wondered perhaps if Mrs

Stourbridge had confided in you. Ladies can become extremely close to their maids.'

She was considerably mollified. 'Well . . . well, I know she put in her feelings about things. She used to go back and read again some from years ago, when she was in Egypt. She did that just the day before she . . . died . . . poor lady.' She looked tearful, and Tobias gave her a moment or two to compose herself again before he continued – and to allow the jury to gather the full import of what had been said.

He then continued to elicit a picture of Miriam as gentle, charming, biddable, struggling to fit into a household with a great deal higher social status than she was accustomed to, and unquestionably a great deal more money. It was a portrait quite innocent and touching, until finally he turned to the jury.

'A lovely woman striving to better herself?' he said with a smile. 'For the sake of the man she loves – and met by chance out walking on Hampstead Heath.' His face darkened, his arms relaxed until his shoulders were almost slumped. 'Or a clever, greedy woman blessed with a pretty face, ensnaring a younger man, unworldly-wise, and doing everything she could, suppressing her own temper and will, to charm him into a marriage which would give her, and her foster mother, a life of wealth they could never have attained in their own station?'

He barely paused for breath, or to give Rathbone the chance to object. 'An innocent woman caught in a dreadful web of circumstances? Or a conniving woman overtaken by an equally cold-blooded and greedy coachman, who saw his chance to profit from her coming fortune, but had fatally miscalculated her ruthlessness – and thus met not with payment for his silence as to her past – perhaps their past

309

relationship with each other! Perhaps he was even the means of Mr Stourbridge and Miriam Gardiner meeting – far other than by chance? Instead he met with violent death in the darkness under the trees of Hampstead Heath.'

Rathbone raised his voice, cutting across Tobias scathingly, and without reference to the judge.

'Treadwell certainly seems to have been a villain, but neither you nor I have proved him a fool! Why in heaven's name would he threaten to expose Miriam Gardiner's past – which neither you nor I have found lacking in virtue of any kind – before she had married into the Stourbridge family?' He spread his hands as if in bewilderment. 'She had no money to pay him anything! Surely he would have waited until after the wedding – indeed done everything in his power to make sure it took place?' He became sarcastic. 'If, as you suggest, he even helped engineer the meeting between Mr Stourbridge and Mrs Gardiner, then it strains the bonds of credibility that he would sabotage his own work just as it was about to come to fruition.'

His point was valid, but it did not carry the emotional weight of Tobias's accusation. The damage was done. The jury's minds were filled with the image of a scheming and duplicitous woman manipulating a discarded lover into a position where she could strike him over the head and leave his murdered body on the Heath.

'Was it chance, or was it Treadwell's dying attempt to implicate his murderers that he used the last of his strength to crawl to the footpath outside Cleo Anderson's door?' Tobias demanded, his voice ringing with outrage and pity. 'Gentlemen, I leave it to you!'

The court adjourned with Miriam and Cleo all but convicted already.

* * *

Rathbone paced the floor of his rooms, resisting the temptation to call Monk and see if he had made any progress. So many times together they had faced cases that seemed impossible. He could list them all in his mind. But in this one he had no weapons at all, and he did not even know what he believed himself. He still was not prepared to accept that either Cleo or Miriam was guilty, let alone both. But there was very little else that made sense – except that Lucius or Henry Stourbridge was guilty instead. And if that were so, no wonder Miriam looked crushed beyond imagining any solution, or that even Rathbone could convince the court of the truth.

It all depended on Monk finding something. If he even knew where to look – and collect enough to prove it, if Rathbone could prolong the case more than another three days at the very outside. Two days seemed more likely.

He spent the evening thinking of tactics to give Monk more time, every trick of human nature or legal expertise. It was all profoundly unpromising.

Tobias called Harry Stourbridge as his first witness of the morning. He treated him with great deference and sympathy, not only for the loss of his wife, but the disillusion he had suffered in Miriam.

Many seats were empty in the court. The case had lost much of its interest for the public. They believed they knew the answer. It was common-or-garden greed, a pretty woman ambitious to improve herself by the age-old means of marrying well. It was no longer scandalous, simply sordid. It was a late summer day, the sun was shining, and there were better things to do than sit inside listening to what could be accurately predicted.

Harry Stourbridge looked ten years older than the age

Rathbone knew he was. He was a man walking in a nightmare to which he could see no end.

'I am sorry to force you to endure this,' Tobias said gently. 'I will keep it as brief as possible, and I am sure Sir Oliver will do the same. Please do not allow loyalty or compassion to direct your answers. This is a time and place when nothing but the truth will serve.'

Stourbridge said nothing. He stood like an officer in front of a court martial, stiffly to attention, facing forward, head high.

'We have already heard sufficient about the croquet party from which Mrs Gardiner fled. I shall not trouble you to repeat it. I turn your attention instead to the tragic death of Mrs Stourbridge. I need to ask you something about the relationship between your wife and Mrs Gardiner. Believe me, I would not do it if there were any way in which I could avoid it.'

Still Stourbridge made no reply.

It seemed to unnerve Tobias very slightly. Rathbone saw him shift his weight a little and straighten his jacket.

'How did Mrs Stourbridge regard Mrs Gardiner when your son first brought her to Cleveland Square?'

'She thought her a very pleasant young woman.'

'And when your son informed you of his intention to marry her?'

'We were both happy that he had found a woman whom he loved, and whom we believed to return his feelings wholeheartedly.'

Tobias pursed his lips. 'You did not regret the fact that she was markedly older than himself, and from a somewhat different social background? How did you imagine she would be regarded by your friends? How would she in time manage to be lady of your very considerable properties in Yorkshire?

Did those things not concern your wife?'

'Of course,' Stourbridge admitted. 'But when we had known Mrs Gardiner for a few weeks we were of the opinion that she would manage very well. She has a natural grace which would carry her through. And she and Lucius so obviously loved each other that that gave us much happiness.'

'And the question of grandchildren, an heir to the house and the lands which are, I believe entailed. Without an heir, they pass laterally to your brother, and to his heirs, is that not so?'

'It is.' He took a deep breath, hands still by his sides as if he were on parade. 'Any marriage may fail to provide an heir. One may only hope. I do not believe in governing the choice of wife for my son. I would rather he were happy than produced a dozen children with a woman he could not love, and share his heart as well as his bed.'

'And did Mrs Stourbridge feel the same?' Tobias asked. 'Many women care intensely about grandchildren. It is a deep need . . .' He left it hanging in the air, unfinished, for the jury to conclude for themselves.

'I do not believe my wife felt that way,' Stourbridge replied wretchedly. Rathbone gained the impression there was far more unsaid behind his words, but he was a private man, loathing this much exposure of his life. He would add nothing he was not forced to.

Step by step Tobias took him through Miriam's visits to Cleveland Square, her demeanour on each of them, her charm and her eagerness to learn. It was obvious to all that Harry Stourbridge had liked her without shadow of equivocation. He was shattered by her betrayal, not only for his son, but for himself. He seemed still unable to grasp it.

Throughout his evidence Rathbone glanced every now and

again up at the dock, and saw the pain in Miriam's face. She was a person enduring torture from which there was no escape. She had to sit still and abide it in silence.

Never once did he catch a member of the jury looking at either Miriam or Cleo. They were completely absorbed in Stourbridge's ordeal. As he studied them he saw in each both pity and respect. Once or twice there was even a sense of identity, as if they could put themselves in his place, and would have acted as he had, felt as he had. Rathbone wondered in passing if any of them were widowers themselves, or had sons who had fallen in love, or married less than fortunately. He could not choose jurors. They had to be householders of a certain wealth and standing, and, of course, men. It had never been possible he could have had people who would identify with Miriam or Cleo. So much for a jury of one's peers.

In the afternoon Tobias quietly and with dignity declined to call Lucius Stourbridge to the stand. It was an ordeal he did not need to inflict upon a young man already wounded almost beyond bearing.

The jury nodded in respect. They would not have forgiven it of him if he had. Rathbone would have done the same, and for the same reasons.

Tobias called the last witness, Aiden Campbell. His evidence was given quietly, with restraint and candour.

'Yes, she had great charm,' he said sadly. 'I believe everyone in the household liked her.'

'Including your sister, Mrs Stourbridge?'

The question remained unanswered.

Campbell looked very pale. His skin was bleached of colour and there were shadows like bruises under his eyes. He stood straight in the witness stand, but he was shaking very slightly and every now and again he had to stop and clear his throat.

It was apparent to everyone in the courtroom that he was a man labouring under profound emotion and close to losing control of himself.

Tobias apologised again and again for obliging him to relive experiences which had to be deeply distressing for him.

'I understand,' Campbell said, biting his lip. 'Justice requires that we follow this to its bitter end. I trust you will do it as speedily as you may.'

'Of course,' Tobias agreed. 'May we proceed to the days immediately prior to your sister's death?'

Campbell told them in as few words as possible, without raising his voice, of Miriam's last visit to Cleveland Square after her release from custody and from the charge of having murdered Treadwell. According to him, she was in a state of shock so deep she hardly came out of her room, and when she did she seemed almost to be in a trance. She was civil, but no more. She avoided Lucius as much as possible, not even allowing him to comfort her over her fearful distress on Cleo Anderson's account.

'She was devoted to Mrs Anderson?' Tobias stressed.

'Yes.' There was no expression in Campbell's face except sadness. 'It is natural enough. Mrs Anderson had apparently raised her as a daughter since she was twelve or thirteen. She would be an ungrateful creature not to have been. We respected it in her.'

'Of course,' Tobias agreed, nodding. 'Please continue.'

Reluctantly Campbell did so, describing the dinner that evening, the conversation over the table about Egypt, their each going about their separate pursuits afterwards.'

'And Mrs Gardiner did not dine with you?'

'No.'

'Tell us, Mr Campbell, did your sister say anything to you, that evening or earlier, about her feelings regarding the murder

315

of Treadwell, and the accusation against Mrs Gardiner?'

Rathbone rose to object, but he had no legal grounds, indeed no moral grounds either. He was obliged to sit down again in silence.

Campbell shook his head. 'If you are asking if I know what happened, or why, no, I do not. Verona was distressed about something. She was certainly not herself. Any of the servants will testify to that.'

Indeed they already had, although of course Campbell had not been in court at the time, since he had not yet appeared himself.

'I believe she had discovered something . . .' his voice grew thick, emotion all but choking him. 'It is my personal belief, although I know nothing to support it, that before she died, she knew who had killed Treadwell, and exactly why. I think that is why she returned alone to her room, in order to consider what she should do about it.' He closed his eyes. 'It was a fatal decision. I wish to God she had not made it . . .'

He had said very little really. He had brought out no new facts, and he had certainly not accused anyone, and yet his testimony was damning. Rathbone could see it in the jurors' faces.

There was no purpose in his questioning Campbell. There was nothing for him to say, nothing to elaborate, nothing to challenge. It was Friday evening. He had two days in which to create some kind of defence, and nothing whatever with which to do it – unless Monk found something. And there was no word from him.

When the court rose he considered pleading with Miriam one more time, and abandoned the idea. It would serve no purpose. Whatever the truth was, she had already convinced him that she would go to the gallows rather than tell it.

Instead he went out into the late September afternoon

and took a hansom straight to Primrose Hill. He did not expect his father to offer any answers; he went simply for the peace of the quiet garden in which to ease the wounds of a disastrous week, and prepare his strength for one to come, which promised to be even worse.

Chapter Eleven

❦

While Rathbone was sitting helplessly in the courtroom, Monk began his further investigations into the details of Treadwell's life. He had already asked exhaustively at the Stourbridges' house and generally in the area around Cleveland Square. No one had told him anything remotely helpful. Treadwell was tediously ordinary.

He began instead in Kentish Town where Treadwell had grown up. It was a long task and he held little hope of it proving successful. In time he began to fear that Miriam Gardiner was guilty as charged, and that poor Cleo Anderson had been drawn into it because of her love for the girl she had rescued. She had refused to recognise that beneath the charm and apparent vulnerability, Miriam had grown into a greedy and conniving woman who would not stop even at murder in order to get what she wanted. Love could be very blind. No mother wanted to see evil in her child, and the fact that Cleo had not borne Miriam would make no difference to her.

His earlier pity for Miriam hardened to anger when he thought of the grief it would bring to Cleo when she was faced with facts she could no longer deny to herself. Miriam may not have asked to be loved, or to be believed in but she had accepted it. It carried a moral responsibility, and she had failed it as badly as anyone could. The deception was worse than the violence.

He walked the streets of Kentish Town going from one public house to another, asking questions as discreetly as the desperately short time allowed. Twice he was too open, too hasty, and earned a sharp rebuff. He left and began again further along, more carefully.

By sundown he was exhausted, his feet hurt merely to the touch. He took an omnibus home. Monk would earn no further money in this case but he simply cared passionately to learn the truth. Lucius Stourbridge would have continued to pay him; indeed he had still implored Monk to help only a week ago. But Monk had refused to take anything further from him for something he was all but certain he could not accomplish. The young man had lost so much already, that to have given him hope he could not justify would be a cruelty for which he would despise himself.

Hester looked at his face as he came in, and did not ask what he had learned. Her tact was so uncharacteristic it told him more of his own disappointment, and how visible it was, than he would have admitted.

On the second day he gained considerably more knowledge. He came closer to Hampstead and discovered a public house where they knew Treadwell rather better. From there he was able to trace a man to whom Treadwell had lost at gambling. Since Treadwell was dead, the debt could not be collected.

'Someone ought to be responsible!' the man said angrily, his round eyes sharp and a little bloodshot. 'In't there no law? You shouldn't be able to get out of money you owe just by dyin'!'

Monk looked knowledgeable. 'Well, usually you would go to a man's heirs,' he said gravely. 'But I don't know if Treadwell had any . . . ?' He left it hanging as a question.

'Nah!' the man said in disgust. 'Answer to nob'dy, that one.'

'Have a drink?' Monk offered. He might be wasting his time, but he had no better avenue to follow.

'Ta. Don't mind if I do,' the man accepted. 'Reece.' He held out a hand after rubbing it on his trouser leg.

Monk took a moment to realise it was an introduction, then he grasped the hand and shook it. 'Monk,' he responded.

''Ow do?' Reece said cheerfully. 'I'll 'ave a pint o' mild, ta.'

When the pints had been ordered and bought, Monk pursued the conversation. 'Did he owe you a lot?'

'I'll say!' Reece took a long draught of his ale before he continued. 'Near ten pounds!'

Monk was startled. It was as much as a housemaid earned in six months!

'That choked yer, eh?' Reece observed with satisfaction. ''E played big, did Treadwell.'

'And lost big!' Monk agreed. 'He can't have lost like that often. Did he win as well?'

'Sometimes. Liked ter live 'igh on the 'og, 'e did. Wine, women and the 'orses. Must a won sometimes, I suppose. But where am I gonna get ten quid, you tell me that?'

'What I'd like to know is where Treadwell got it,' Monk said with feeling. 'He certainly didn't earn it as a coachman!'

'Wouldn't know,' Reece said with fading interest. He emptied his glass and looked at Monk hopefully.

Monk obliged.

'Coachman, were 'e?' Reece said thoughtfully. 'Well, I guess as 'e 'ad suffink on the side, then. Dunno wot.'

A very ugly thought came into Monk's mind, concerning Cleo Anderson's theft of medicines, especially morphine. Hester had said a considerable amount might have gone over a period of time. Maybe not all of it had ended in the homes of the old and ill. Anyone addicted to such a drug would pay a high price to obtain it. It would be only too easy to understand how Cleo could have sold it to pay Treadwell, or even have given it to him directly for him to sell. The idea gave him no pleasure, but he could not get rid of it.

He spent the rest of the day investigating Treadwell's off-duty hours, which seemed to have been quite liberal, and found he had a considerable taste for self-indulgence. But there appeared to be several hours once every two weeks or so which were unaccounted for, and he was driven to the conclusion that this time may have been used either for selling morphine, or for further blackmail of other victims.

The last thing Monk did, late in the evening, was to go and visit Cleo herself, telling the gaoler that he was Rathbone's clerk. He had no proof of such a position, but the gaoler had seen them together earlier, and accepted it. Or possibly his compassion for Cleo made him turn a blind eye. Monk did not care in the slightest what the reason was; he took advantage of it.

Cleo was surprised to see him, but there was no light of hope in her eyes. She looked haggard and exhausted. She was almost unrecognisable from the woman he had met only a couple of months ago. Her cheeks were hollow, her skin completely without colour, and she sat with her shoulders sagging under the plain dark stuff of her dress.

Monk was caught off guard by his emotions on seeing her. She stirred in him an anger and a sense of outrage at futility and injustice, more passionate than he had expected. If he failed in this he was going to carry the wound for a

322

very long time, perhaps always.

There was no time to waste in words of pity or encouragement, and he knew they would be wasted because they could have no meaning.

'Do you know if Treadwell was blackmailing anyone else apart from you?' he asked her, sitting down opposite her so he could speak softly and she could hear him.

'No. Why? Do you think they could've killed him?' There was almost hope in her voice, not quite. She did not dare.

Honesty forbade him to allow it. 'Enough possibility to raise a need to know how much you paid him, exactly,' he answered. 'I have a pretty good record of how much he spent over the last two or three months of his life. If you paid him all of it, then you must have been taking morphine to sell, as well as to give to patients.'

Her body stiffened, her eyes wide and angry. 'I didn't! And I never gave him any either!'

'We have to prove it,' he argued. 'Have you got any records of your pay from the hospital, of all the medicine you took, and the people to whom you gave it?'

'No – of course I haven't!'

'But you know all the patients you visited with medicine,' he insisted.

'Yes . . .'

'Then write them down for me. Here.' He offered her paper and pencil. 'Give me names and addresses, and what medicine you gave them and for how long.'

She stared at him for a moment, then obeyed, writing slowly and carefully.

Was this going to be worth anything, or was he simply finding a way of occupying time so he could delude himself he was working to save her? What could he achieve with lists? Who would listen, or care, regardless of what likelihood he could show? Proof was all the court would entertain. In their own minds they believed Cleo and Miriam guilty. They would have to be forced from that conviction, not merely shown that there was another, remote possibility.

Cleo finished the list. There were eighteen names on it.

'Thank you.' He took it and glanced at it. 'How much do you earn at the hospital?'

'Seven shillings a week.' She said it with some pride, as if for a nurse it were a good wage.

He winced. He knew a constable earned three times that.

'How long do you work?' The question was out before he thought.

'Twelve or fifteen hours a day,' she replied.

'And how much did you pay Treadwell?'

Her voice was tired, her shoulders slumped again. 'Five shillings a week.'

The rage inside him was ice cold, filling his body, sharpening his mind with a will to lash out, to hurt someone so this could be undone, so it would never happen again, not to Cleo and not to anyone. But he had no one to direct the anger towards. The only offender was dead already. Only the victim was still left to pay the price.

'He was spending a lot more than that,' he said quietly, his words coming between clenched teeth. 'I need to know where it came from.'

She shook her head. 'I don't know. He just came to me regularly and I paid him. He never mentioned anyone else. But he wouldn't . . .'

It was on the edge of Monk's tongue to ask her again if she had given Treadwell any morphine to sell, but he knew the answer would be the same. He rose to his feet and bade her goodbye, hating being able to make no promises, nor even speak any words of hope.

At the door he hesitated, wondering if he should ask her about Miriam, but what was there to say?

She looked up at him, waiting.

In the end he had to ask. 'Could it have been Miriam?'

'No,' she said immediately. 'She never did anything he could have made her pay for!'

'Not even to protect you?' he said quietly.

She sat perfectly still. It was transparent in her face that she did not know the answer to that – believe, possibly, even certainly – but not know.

Monk nodded. 'I understand.' He knocked for the gaoler to let him out.

He arrived home still turning the matter over and over in his mind.

'There was another source,' he said to Hester over the dinner table. 'But it could have been Miriam, which won't help at all.'

'And if it wasn't?' she asked. 'If we could show it was someone else? They'd have to consider it!'

'No they wouldn't,' he answered quietly, watching her face show her disappointment. 'Not unless we could bring them to court and prove that they were somewhere near the Heath that night, alone. We've got two days before Rathbone has to begin some defence.'

'What else have we?' her voice rose a little in desperation.

'Nothing,' he admitted.

'Then let's try! I can't bear to sit here not doing anything at all! What do we know?'

They worked until long after midnight, noting every piece of information Monk had gathered about Treadwell's comings and goings over the three months previous to his death. When it was written on paper it was easier to see what appeared to be gaps.

'We need to know exactly what his time off was,' Hester said, making further notes. 'I'm sure there would be someone in the Stourbridge household who could tell you.'

Monk thought it was probably a waste of time, but he did not argue. He had nothing else more useful to do. He might as well follow through with the entire exercise.

'Do you know how much medicine was taken?' he asked, then before she could deny it, 'or could you work it out if you wanted to?'

'No, but I expect Phillips could, if it would help. Do you think it really would?'

'Probably not, but what better have we?'

Neither of them answered with the obvious thing: acceptance that the charge was true. Perhaps it had not been with deliberate greed, or for the reasons Tobias was saying, but in fact, which was all that counted.

'I'll go tomorrow to the hospital and ask Phillips,' Hester said briskly, as if it mattered. 'And I'll go as well and find all the people on your list, and see what medicines they have. You see if you can account for that time of Treadwell's.' She stared at him very directly, defying him to tell her it was useless, or to give up heart. He knew from the very brittleness of it, the anger in her, that she was doing it blindly; against hope, not with it.

In the morning Monk left early to go out to Bayswater and get the precise times that Treadwell was off duty and see if he could find any indication of where else the coachman might have been, who could have paid him the huge difference between what Monk and Hester could account for, and what Treadwell had spent. He pursued it slowly and carefully, to the minutest detail, because he did not want to come to the end of it and have it proved to him what he already knew: that it would be of no use whatever in trying to save Cleo Anderson, or Miriam Gardiner either.

Hester went straight to the hospital. Fortunately even though it was a Saturday she knew Phillips would be there. Usually he took only Sundays off, and then quite often just the morning. Still she had to search for over half an hour before she found him, and then it was only after having asked three medical students, interrupting them in a long enthusiastic and detailed discussion of anatomy, which was their present preoccupation.

'Brilliant!' one of them was saying, his eyes wide. 'We're very fortunate to be here. My cousin is studying in Lincoln, and he says they have to wait weeks for a body to dissect, and all the diagrams in the world mean almost nothing compared with the real thing.'

'I know,' another agreed. 'And Thorpe is marvellous. His explanations are always so clear.'

'Probably the number of times he's done it,' the first retorted.

'Excuse me!' Hester said again sharply. 'Do you know where Mr Phillips is?'

'Phillips? Is he the one with red hair, bit of a stammer?'

'Phillips the apothecary!' She kept her temper with difficulty. 'I need to speak with him.'

The first young man frowned at her, looking at her more closely now. 'You shouldn't be looking for medicine; if one of the patients is—'

'I don't want medicines!' she snapped. 'I need to speak with Mr Phillips. Do you know where he is or not?'

The young man's face hardened. 'No, actually, I don't.'

One of the other young men relented, for whatever personal reason.

'He's down in the morgue,' he answered. 'The new assistant got taken a little faint. Gave him a bit of something to help. He's probably still there.'

'Thank you,' Hester said quickly. 'Thank you very much.' And she all but ran along the corridor, out of the side entrance and down the steps to the cold room below ground which served to keep the bodies of the dead until the undertaker should come to perform the formalities.

'Hello, Mrs Monk. You're looking a little peaked,' Phillips said cheerfully. 'What can I do for you?'

'I'm glad I found you.' She turned and regarded the young man, white-faced, who sat on the floor with his legs splayed out. 'Are you all right?' she asked him.

He nodded, embarrassed.

'Just got a scare,' Phillips said with a grin. 'One o' them corpses moved and young Jake 'ere near fainted away. Nobody told 'im corpses sometimes passes wind. Gases don't stop, son, just 'cos you're dead.'

Jake scrambled to his feet, running his hands through his hair and trying to look as if he were ready for duty again.

Hester looked at the tables. There were two bodies laid out under unbleached sheets.

'Not as many lately,' Phillips remarked, following her glance.

'Good!' she approved.

'No – not died here, brought in for the students,' he corrected. 'Old Thorpe's in a rare fury. Can't get 'em.'

'Where do they come from?'

'God knows! Resurrectionists!' he said with black humour.

Jake was staring at him, open-mouthed. He let out a sigh between his teeth.

'D'yer mean it?' he said hoarsely. 'Grave robbers, like?'

'No, of course I don't, you daft ha'porth!' Phillips said,

shaking his head. 'Get on with your work.' He turned to Hester. 'What is it, Mrs Monk?' All the light vanished from his face. 'Have you seen Cleo Anderson? Is there anything we can do for 'er, apart from hope for a miracle?'

'Work for one,' she said bleakly. She turned and led the way back up the stairs.

He followed close behind and when they were outside in the air he asked what she meant.

'Someone else was being blackmailed as well, we are almost sure,' she explained, stopping beside him. 'Treadwell spent a lot more money than Cleo gave him, or he earned . . .'

Hope lit in Phillips' face. 'You mean they could have killed him? How do we find out who it was?' He looked at her confidently as if he had every faith she would have an answer.

'I don't know. I'll settle at the moment just for proving he has to exist.' She looked at him very steadily. 'If you had to . . . no, if you wanted to, could you work out exactly how much medicine has gone missing in, say, the four months before Treadwell's death?'

'Perhaps . . . if I had a really good reason to,' he said guardedly. 'I wouldn't know that unless I understood the need.'

'Not knowing isn't going to help,' she told him miserably. 'Not charging her with theft won't matter if they hang her for murder.'

His face blanched as if she had slapped him, but he did not look away. 'What good can you do?' he asked very quietly. 'I really care about Cleo. She's worth ten of that pompous swine in his oak-panelled office!' He did not need to name Thorpe. She shared his feelings and he knew it. He was watching her for an answer, hoping.

'I don't really know – maybe not a great deal,' she admitted. 'But if I know how much is missing, and how much reached the patients she treated, if they are pretty well the same, then he got money from someone else.'

'Of course they're the same! What do you think she did? Give it to him to sell?' He was indignant, almost angry.

'If I were being blackmailed out of everything I earned except about two shillings a week, I'd be tempted to pay in kind,' she answered him.

He looked chastened. His lips thinned into a hard line. 'I'm glad somebody got that scheming sod,' he said harshly. 'I just wish we could prove it wasn't poor Cleo. Or come to that, anyone else he was doing the same thing to. How are we going to do that?' He looked at her expectantly.

'Tell me exactly how much medicine went over the few months before his death, as nearly as you can.'

'That won't tell us who the other person is – or people!'

'My husband is trying to find out where Treadwell went that might lead us to them.'

He looked at her narrowly. 'Is he any good at that?'

'Very good indeed. He used to be the best detective in the police force,' she said with pride.

'Oh? Who's the best now?'

'I haven't the slightest idea. He left.' Then in case Phillips should think him dishonest, she added, 'He resented some of the discipline. He can't abide pomposity either, especially when it is coupled with ignorance.'

Phillips grinned, then it vanished and he was totally serious again.

'I'll get you a list o' those things. I could tell you pretty exact, if it helps.'

'It'll help.'

She spent the rest of the day and into the early evening trudging from one house to the next with Monk's list of Cleo's patients, and Phillips' list of the missing medicines. She was accustomed to seeing people who were suffering illness or injury. It had been her profession for several years and she had seen the horror of the battlefield and the disease which had decimated the wounded afterwards. She had shared the exhaustion and the fear herself, and the cold and the hunger.

Nevertheless to go into these homes, which were too bare of comfort because everything had been sold to pay for food and warmth, to see the pain and too often the loneliness also, was more harrowing than she had expected. These men were older than the ones she had nursed in the Crimea; their wounds were not fresh. They had earned them in different battles, different wars, still there was so much that was the same it hurled her back those short four years and old emotions washed over her, almost to drowning.

Time and again she saw a dignity which made her have to swallow back tears as old men struggled to hide their poverty and force their bodies, disabled by age and injury, to rise and offer her some hospitality. She was walking in the footsteps of Cleo Anderson, trying to give some of the same comfort, and failing because she had not the means.

Rage burned inside her also. No one should have to beg for what they had more than earned.

She loathed asking for information about the medicine they had had. Nearly all of them knew that Cleo was being tried for her life. All Hester could do was tell the truth. Every last man was eager to give her any help he could, to open cupboards and show her powders, to give her day-by-day recounting of all they had had.

She would have given any price she could think of to be able to promise them it would save Cleo, but she could only offer hope, and little enough of that.

When she arrived home at quarter past ten, Monk was

beginning to worry about her. He was standing up, unable to relax in spite of his own weariness. She did notice that he had taken his boots off.

'Where have you been?' he demanded.

She walked straight to him and put her head on his shoulder. He closed his arms around her, holding her gently, laying his cheek to her brow. He did not need her to explain the emotion she felt; he saw it in her face and understood.

'It's wrong,' she said after a few minutes, still holding on to him. 'How can we do it? We turn to our bravest and best when we are in danger, we sacrifice so much – fathers and brothers, husbands and sons – and then a decade, a generation later we only want to forget! What's the matter with us?'

He did not bother to answer, to talk about guilt or debt, or the desire to be happy without remembering that others have purchased it at a terrible price – even resentment and simple blindness and failure of imagination. They had both said it all before.

'What did you find?' she said at last, straightening up and looking at him.

'I'm not sure,' he replied. 'Do you want a cup of tea?'

'Yes.' She went towards the kitchen, but he moved ahead of her.

'I'll bring it.' He smiled. 'I wasn't asking you to fetch one for me – even though I've probably walked as far as you have, and to as little purpose.'

She sat down and took off her boots as well. It was a particular luxury, something she would only do at home. And it was still very sweet to realise this was her home, she belonged here, and so did he.

When he returned with the tea and she had taken a few sips, she asked him again what he had learned.

'A lot of Treadwell's time is unaccounted for,' he replied,

trying his own tea and finding it a trifle too hot. 'He had a few unusual friends. One of his gambling partners was even an undertaker, and Treadwell did a few odd tasks for him.'

'Enough to earn him the kind of money we're looking for?' She did not know whether she wanted the answer to be yes or no.

'Not remotely,' he replied. 'Just driving a wagon, presumably because he was good with horses, and perhaps knew the roads. He probably did it as a favour because of their friendship. This young man seems to have given him entry to cockfights and dog races when he wouldn't have been allowed in otherwise. They even had a brothel or two in common.'

Hester shrugged. 'It doesn't get us any further, does it?' She tried to keep the disappointment out of her voice.

Monk frowned thoughtfully. 'I was wondering how Treadwell ever discovered about Cleo and the medicines in the first place.'

She was about to dismiss it as something that hardly mattered now, when she realised what he meant.

'Well, not from Miriam!' she said with conviction.

'From any of Cleo's patients?' he asked. 'How could Treadwell, coachman to Major Stourbridge in Bayswater, and gambler and womaniser in Kentish Town, come to know of thefts of morphine and other medicines from a hospital on Hampstead Heath?'

She stared at him steadily, a first, tiny stirring of excitement inside her. 'Because somewhere along the chain of events he crossed it! It has to be – but where?' She held up her fingers, ticking off each step. 'Patients fall ill and go to the hospital where Cleo gets to know of them because she works there as a nurse.'

'Which has nothing to do with Treadwell,' he answered.

'Unless one of them was related to him, or to someone he knew well.'

'They are all old, and live within walking distance of the hospital,' she pointed out. 'Most of them are alone, the lucky few with a son or daughter, or grandchild, like old John Robb.'

'Treadwell's family was all in Kentish Town,' Monk said. 'That much I ascertained. His father is dead and his mother remarried a man from Hoxton.'

'And none of them has anything to do with Miriam Gardiner,' she went on. 'So he didn't meet them driving her.' She held up the next finger. 'Cleo visits them in their homes and knows what they need. She steals it from the hospital. By the way, I'm sure the apothecary knew, but turned a blind eye. He's a good man, and very fond of her.' She smiled slightly. 'Very fond indeed. He regards her as something of a saint. I think she is the only person who really impresses Phillips. Fermin Thorpe certainly doesn't!' She recalled the scene in the morgue. 'He even teased the new young morgue attendant that Thorpe was buying his cadavers for the medical students from resurrectionists! Poor boy was horrified, until he realised Phillips was teasing him.'

'Resurrectionists?' Monk said slowly.

'Yes – grave robbers who dig up corpses and sell them to medical establishments for—'

'I know what resurrectionists are!' he said quickly, leaning forward, his eyes bright. 'Are you sure it was a joke?'

'Well, it's not very funny,' she agreed with a frown. 'But Phillips is like that – a bit – wry. I like him – actually I like him very much. He's one of the few people in the hospital I would trust...' Then suddenly she realised what he was thinking. 'You mean— Oh, William! You think he really was buying them from resurrectionists? He was the other person Treadwell was blackmailing! But how could Treadwell know that?'

'Not necessarily that he was blackmailing him,' he said, grasping her hand in his urgency. 'Treadwell was friendly with this undertaker! What simpler than to sell a few bodies? That could have been the extra driving he was doing: delivering corpses for Fermin Thorpe – at a very nice profit to himself!'

'Wonderful!' she breathed out with exquisite relief. It was only a chink of light in the darkness, but it was the very first one. 'At least it might be enough for Oliver to raise doubt.' She smiled with a twist. 'And even if he isn't guilty, I wouldn't mind seeing Thorpe thoroughly frightened and embarrassed – I wouldn't mind in the slightest!'

'I'm sure you wouldn't,' Monk agreed with a nod. 'Although we mustn't leap too quickly—'

'Why not? There's hardly time to waste . . .'

'I know. But Treadwell may not have blackmailed Thorpe. The money may all have come from selling the bodies.'

'Then let Thorpe prove it! That should be interesting to watch.'

His eyes widened very slightly. 'You really do loathe him, don't you?'

'I despise him,' she said fiercely. 'He puts his own vanity before relieving the pain of those who trust him to help them.' She made it almost a challenge, as if Monk had been defending him.

He smiled at her. 'I'm not trying to spare him anything. I just want to use it to the best effect. I don't know what that is yet, but we will only get one chance. I want to save my fire for the target that will do the most good for Cleo – or Miriam – not just the one that does most harm to Thorpe . . . or the one that gives us most satisfaction.'

'I see.' She did. She had been indulging in the luxury of anger and she recognised it. 'Yes, of course. Just don't leave it too long.'

'I won't,' he promised. 'Believe me – we will use it!'

On Sunday Monk returned to the undertaker to pursue the details of Treadwell's work for them, and find proof if indeed he had taken bodies to the North London Hospital, and been handsomely paid for it. If he were to use it, either in court, or to pressure Thorpe for any other reason, then he must have evidence that could not be denied or explained away.

Hester continued with her visits to the rest of Cleo's patients, just to conclude the list of medicines. She was uncertain if it would be any use, but she felt compelled to do it, and regardless of anything else, she wanted to go and see John Robb again. It was over a week since she had last been and she knew he would be almost out of morphine. He was failing, the pain growing worse, and there was little she could do to help him. She had some morphine left, again taken with Phillips' connivance, and she had bought a bottle of sherry herself. It was illogical to give it to him more than anyone else, but logic had no effect on her feelings.

She found him alone, slumped in his chair almost asleep, but he roused himself when he heard her footsteps. He looked paler than she had ever seen him before, and his eyes more deeply sunken. She had nursed too many dying men to delude herself he had long left now, and she could guess how it must tear Michael Robb to have to leave him alone.

She forced her voice to be cheerful, but she could not place the barrier between them of pretending that she could not see how ill he was.

'Hello,' she said quietly, sitting opposite him. 'I'm sorry I've been away so long. I've been trying to find some way of helping Cleo, and I think we may have succeeded.' She was aware as she spoke that if she embroidered the truth a little he would probably not live long enough to know.

He smiled and raised his head. 'That's the best news you could have brought me, girl. I worry about her. All the good she did, and now this has to happen. Wish I could do something to help – but I think maybe all I could do would make it worse.' He was watching her, waiting for her to reply.

'Don't worry, nobody will ask you,' she answered him. She was sure that the last thing the prosecution would do willingly would be to draw in the men like John Robb who would indeed confirm that Cleo had handed on the medicines, because they would show so very effectively why. The sympathies of every decent man in the jury would be with Cleo. Perhaps some of them had been in the army themselves, or had fathers or brothers or sons who had. Their outrage at what had happened to so many old soldiers would perhaps outweigh their sense of immediate justice against the killer of a blackmailing coachman. Tobias would not provoke that if he could help it.

Hester herself would be delighted if it came out into the public hearing, but only if it could be managed other than at Cleo's expense. So far she had thought of no way.

John Robb looked at her closely. 'But I was one she took those medicines for – wasn't I?'

'She took them for a lot of people,' Hester answered honestly. 'Eighteen of you altogether, but you were one of her favourites.' She smiled. 'Just as you're mine.'

He grinned, as if she were flirting with him. His pleasure was only too easy to see, in spite of the tragedy of the subject they were discussing. His eyes were misty. 'But some o' those medicines she took were for me, weren't they?' he pressed her.

'Yes. You and others.'

'And where are you getting them now, girl? I'd sooner go without than have you in trouble too.'

'I know you would, but there's no need to worry. The apothecary gave me these.' That was stretching the truth a little, but it hardly mattered. 'I'll make you a cup of tea and we'll sit together for a while. I brought a little sherry – not from the hospital, I got it myself.' She stood up as she said it. 'Don't need milk this time – we'll give it a bit of heart.'

'That'd be good,' he agreed. 'Then we'll talk a bit. You tell me some o' those stories about Florence Nightingale, and how she bested those generals and got her own way. You tell a good story, girl.'

'I'll do that,' she promised, going over to the corner which served as kitchen, pouring water into the kettle, then setting it on the hob. When it was boiled she made the tea, putting sherry fairly liberally into one mug, but leaving the morphine on the shelf so Michael would find it this evening. She returned with the tea, with the sherry in it for him, without for herself.

He picked up his mug and began to sip slowly. 'So tell me about how you outwitted those generals then, girl. Tell me the things you're doing better now because o' the war an' what you learned.'

She recounted to him all sorts of bits and pieces she could remember, tiny victories over bureaucracy, making it as funny as possible, definitely adding more colour than there had been at the time.

He drank the tea then set down the empty mug. 'Go on,' he prompted. 'I like the sound o' your voice, girl. Takes me back . . .'

She tried to think of other stories to tell, ones that had happy endings, and perhaps she rambled a bit, inventing here and there. Now and then he interrupted to ask a question. It was warm and comfortable in the afternoon sun and she was not surprised when she looked up and saw his eyes closed. It was just the sort of time to doze off. Certainly she was in no way offended. He was still smiling at the last little victory she had recounted, much added to in retrospect.

She stood up and went to make sure he was warm enough since the sunlight had moved around and his feet were in shadow. It was only then that she noticed how very still he was. There was no laboured breathing, no rasp of air in his damaged lungs.

There were tears already on her cheeks when she put her fingers to his neck and found no pulse. It was ridiculous. She should have been only glad for him, but she was unable to stop herself from sitting down and weeping, in wholehearted weariness, fear and from the loss of a friend she had come to love.

She had washed her face and was sitting in the chair, still opposite the old man, in the late afternoon when Michael Robb came home.

He walked straight in, not at first sensing anything different.

She stood up quickly, stepping between him and the old man.

Then he saw her face and realised she had been weeping. He went very pale.

'He's gone,' she said gently. 'I was here – talking to him. We were telling old stories, laughing a little. He just went to sleep.' She moved aside so he could see the old man's face, the shadow of a smile still on it, a great peace settled over him.

Michael kneeled down beside him, taking his hand. 'I should have been here!' he said hoarsely. 'I'm sorry! I'm so sorry . . .'

'If you had stayed here all the time, who could have earned the money for you both to live on?' she asked. 'He knew that – he was so proud of you. He would have felt terribly guilty if he'd thought you were taking time away from your work because of him.'

Michael bent forward, the tears spilling over his cheeks, his shoulders shaking.

She did not know whether to go to him, touch him, if it would comfort, or only intrude. Instinct told her to take him in her arms, he seemed so young and alone. Her mind told her to let him deal with his grief in private. Instinct won, and she sat on the floor and held him while he wept.

When he had passed through the first shock he stood up and went and washed his face in water from the jug, then boiled the kettle again. Without speaking to her he made more tea.

'Is that your sherry?' he asked.

'Yes. Take what you'd like.'

He poured it generously for both of them, and offered her one of the mugs. They did not sit down. There was only one vacant chair and neither wanted to take it.

'Thank you,' he said a little awkwardly. 'I know you did it for him, not for me, but I'm still grateful.' He stopped, wanting to say something and not knowing how to broach it.

She sipped the tea and waited.

'I'm sorry about Mrs Anderson,' he said abruptly.

'I know,' she assured him.

'She took all the medicines for the old and ill, didn't she . . .' It was not a question.

'Yes. I could prove that if I had to.'

'Including my grandfather . . .' That too was a statement.

'Yes.' She met his eyes without flinching. He looked vulnerable and desperately unhappy. 'She did it because she wanted to. She believed it was the right thing to do,' she went on.

'There's still morphine there now,' he said softly.

'Is there?'

'In the Lord's name – be careful, Mrs Monk!' There was real fear for her in his face, no censure.

She smiled. 'No need any more. Will you be all right?'

'Yes – I will. Thank you.'

She hesitated only a moment longer, then turned and went. Outside the last of the sun was on the footpath and the street was busy.

Chapter Twelve

❧

On Sunday evening Rathbone went to Fitzroy Street to see Monk. He could stand the uncertainty no longer, and he wanted to share his anxiety, and feel less alone in his sense of helplessness.

'Resurrectionists!' he said incredulously when Hester told him of their beliefs regarding Treadwell's supplementary income.

'Not exactly,' Monk corrected him. 'Actually the bodies were never buried, just taken straight from the undertaker's to the hospital.' He was sitting in the large chair beside the fire. The September evenings were drawing in. It was not yet cold, but the flames were comforting. Hester sat hunched forward, hugging herself, her face washed out of all colour. She had told him of John Robb's death quite simply, and without regret, knowing it to be a release from the bonds of a failing body, but he could see very clearly in her manner that she felt the loss profoundly.

'Saves effort,' Monk said, looking across at Rathbone. 'Why bury them and then have to go to the trouble and considerable risk of digging them up again if you can simply bury bricks in the first place?'

'And Treadwell carried them?' Rathbone wanted to assure himself he had understood. 'Are you certain?'

'Yes. If I had to I could call enough witnesses to leave no doubt.'

'And was he blackmailing Fermin Thorpe?'

Monk looked rueful. 'That I don't know. Certainly I've no proof, and I hate to admit it, but it seems unlikely. Why would he? He was making a very nice profit in the business. The last thing he would want would be to get Thorpe prosecuted.'

The truth of that was unarguable and Rathbone conceded it. 'Have we learned anything that could furnish a defence? I have nowhere even to begin . . .'

Hester stared at him miserably and shook her head.

'No,' Monk said wretchedly. 'We could probably get Thorpe to get rid of the charges of theft – at least to drop them – and I would dearly enjoy doing it, but it wouldn't help with the murder. We don't have anything but your skill.' He looked at Rathbone honestly, and there was a respect in his eyes which at any other time Rathbone would have found very sweet to savour. As it was, all he could think of was that he would have given most of what he possessed if he could have been sure he was worthy of it.

At seven o'clock on Monday morning Rathbone was at the door of Miriam's cell. A sullen wardress let him in. She had none of the regard or the pity for Miriam that the police gaoler had had for Cleo.

The door clanged shut behind him and Miriam looked up. She was a shadow of her former self. She looked physically bruised, as if her whole body hurt.

There was no time to mince words.

'I am going into battle without weapons,' he said simply. 'I accept that you would rather sacrifice your own life at the end of a rope than tell me who killed Treadwell and Verona Stourbridge – but are you quite sure you are willing to repay all Cleo Anderson has done for you by sacrificing hers also?'

Miriam looked as if she were going to faint. She had difficult finding her voice.

'I've told you, Sir Oliver, even if you knew, no one would believe you. I could tell you everything, and it would only do more harm. Don't you think I would do anything on earth to save Cleo, if I could? She is the dearest person in the world to me – except Lucius. And I know how much I owe her. You do not need to remind me as though I were unaware. If I could hang in her place I would! If you can bring that about I will be for ever in your debt. I will confess to killing Treadwell, if it will help.'

Looking into her wide eyes and ashen face he believed her. He had no doubt in his mind that she would die with dignity and a quiet heart if she could believe she had saved Cleo. That did not mean Cleo was innocent in fact, only that Miriam loved her, and perhaps that she believed the death sufficiently understandable in the light of Treadwell's own crimes.

'I will do what I can,' he said quietly. 'I am not sure if that is worth anything.'

She said nothing, but gave him a thin wraith of a smile.

The trial resumed in a half-empty court.

Rathbone was already in his seat when he saw Hester come in, push her way past the court usher with a swift word to which he was still replying as she left him and came to Rathbone's table.

'What is it?' he asked, looking at her pale, tense face. 'What's happened?'

'I went to Cleo this morning,' she whispered, leaning close

to him. 'She knows Miriam will hang, and there is nothing you can do unless the truth is told. She knows only a part of it, but she cannot bear to lose Miriam, whoever else it hurts – even if it is Lucius, and Miriam never forgives her.'

'What part?' Rathbone demanded. 'What truth does she know? For God's sake, Hester, tell me! I've got nothing!'

'Put Cleo on the witness stand. Ask her how she first met Miriam. She thinks it is something to do with that – something so terrible Miriam can't or won't remember it. But there's nothing to lose now . . .'

'Thank you . . .' Impulsively he leaned forward and kissed her on the cheek, not giving a damn that the judge and entire court were watching him.

Tobias gave a cough and a smile.

The judge banged his gavel.

Hester blushed fiercely, but with a smile returned to her seat.

'Are you ready to proceed, Sir Oliver?' the judge asked courteously.

'Yes, my lord, I am. I call Mrs Cleo Anderson.'

There was a rumour of interest around the gallery and several of the jurors shifted position, more from emotional discomfort than physical.

Cleo was escorted from the dock to the witness stand. She stood upright, but it was obviously with difficulty, and she did not look across at Miriam even once. In a soft, unsteady voice she swore to her name and where she lived, then waited with palpable anxiety for Rathbone to begin.

Rathbone hated what he was about to do, but it did not deter him.

'Mrs Anderson, how long have you lived in your present house on Green Man Hill?'

Quite plainly she understood the relevance of the question,

even though Tobias evidently did not, and his impatience was clear as he allowed his face to express exasperation.

'About thirty years,' Cleo replied.

'So you were living there when you first met Mrs Gardiner?' Rathbone asked.

'Yes.' It was little more than a whisper.

The judge leaned forward. 'Please speak up, Mrs Anderson. The jury needs to hear you.'

'I'm sorry, sir. Yes, I was living there.'

'How long ago was that?'

Tobias rose to his feet. 'This is old history, my lord. If it will be of any assistance to Sir Oliver, and to saving the Court's time and not prolonging what can only be painful, rather than merciful, the Crown concedes that Mrs Anderson took in Mrs Gardiner when she was little more than a child, and looked after her with devotion from that day forward. We do not contest it, nor require any evidence to that effect.'

'Thank you,' Rathbone said with elaborate graciousness. 'That was not my point. If you are as eager as you suggest not to waste the Court's time, then perhaps you would consider not interrupting me until there is some good reason for it?'

There was a titter of nervous laughter around the gallery, and distinct smiles from at least two of the jurors.

A flush of temper lit Tobias's face, but he masked it again almost immediately.

Rathbone turned back to Cleo.

'Mrs Anderson, would you please tell us the circumstances of that meeting?'

Cleo spoke with a great effort. It was painfully apparent that the memory was distressing to her and she recalled it only as an act of despair.

Rathbone had very little idea why he was asking her, only

that Hester had pressed him to, and he had no other weapon to use.

'It was a night in September, the twenty-second, I think. It was windy, but not cold.' She swallowed. Her throat was dry and she began to cough.

At the judge's request the usher brought her a glass of water, then she continued.

'Old Josh Wetherall, from two doors down, came beating on my door to say there was a young girl, a child, crying on the road, near in hysterics, he said, an' covered all over in blood. He was beside himself with distress, poor man, and hadn't an idea what to do to help.' She took a deep breath.

No one moved or interrupted her. Even Tobias was silent, although his face still reflected impatience.

'Of course I went to see what I could do,' Cleo continued. 'Anyone would, but being a nurse I suppose he thought I might know a bit more.'

'And the child?' Rathbone prompted.

Cleo's hands gripped the rail in front of her, as if she needed its strength to hold her up.

'Josh was right, she was in a terrible state . . .'

'Would you describe her for us?' Rathbone directed her, ignoring Tobias leaning forward to object. 'We need to see her as you saw her, Mrs Anderson.'

She stared at him imploringly, denial in her eyes, in her face, even in the angle of her body.

'We need to see her as you did, Mrs Anderson. Please believe me, it is important.' He was lying. He had no idea whether it meant anything or not, but at least the jury were listening, emotions caught at last.

Cleo was rigid, shaking. 'She was hysterical,' she said very quietly.

The judge leaned forward to hear, but he did not again request her to raise her voice.

No one in the body of the court moved or made the slightest sound.

Rathbone nodded, indicating she could continue.

'I've never seen anyone so frightened in my life,' Cleo said, not to Rathbone, or to the court, but as if she were speaking aloud what was indelibly within her. 'She was covered in blood, her eyes were staring but I'm not sure she saw anything at all. She staggered and bumped into things and for hour she was unable to speak. She just gasped and shuddered. I'd have felt better if she could have wept.'

Again she stopped and the silence lengthened, but no one moved. Even Tobias knew better than to intrude.

'How was she injured?' Rathbone asked finally.

Cleo seemed to recall her attention and looked at him as if she had just remembered he was there.

'How was she injured?' Rathbone repeated. 'You said she was covered in blood, and obviously she had sustained some terrible experience.'

Cleo looked embarrassed. 'We don't know how it happened, not really. For days she couldn't say anything that made sense, and the poor child was so terrified no one pressed her. She just lay curled over in my big bed, hugging herself and now and then weeping like her heart was broken, and she was so frightened of any man coming near her we didn't even like to send for a doctor.'

'But the injuries?' Rathbone asked again. 'What about the blood?'

Cleo stared beyond him. 'She was only wearing a big cotton nightgown. There was blood everywhere, right from her shoulders down. She was bruised and cut . . .'

'Yes?'

Cleo looked for the first time across at Miriam and there were tears on her face.

Desperately Miriam mouthed the word 'no'.

'Mrs Anderson!' Rathbone said sharply. 'Where did the blood come from? If you are really innocent, and if you believe Miriam Gardiner to be innocent, only the truth can save you. This is your last chance to tell it. After the verdict is in you will face nothing but the short days and nights in a cell, too short – and then the rope, and at last the judgement of God.'

Tobias rose to his feet.

Rathbone turned on him. 'Do you quarrel with the truth of that, Mr Tobias?' he demanded.

Tobias stared at him, his face set and angry.

'Mr Tobias?' the judge prompted.

'No, of course I don't,' Tobias conceded, sitting down again.

Rathbone turned back to Cleo. 'I repeat, Mrs Anderson, where did the blood come from? You are a nurse. You must have some rudimentary knowledge of anatomy. Do not tell us that you did nothing to help this blood-soaked, terrified child except give her a clean nightshirt!'

'Of course I helped her!' Cleo sobbed. 'The poor little mite had just given birth – and she was only a child herself. Stillborn, I reckoned it was.'

'Is that what she told you?'

'She was rambling. She hardly made any sense. In and out of her wits, she was. She got a terrible fever and we weren't sure we could even save her. Often enough women die of fever after giving birth, especially if it was a bad one. And she was too young – far too young, poor little thing.'

Rathbone was taking a wild guess now. So far this was all tragic, but it had nothing to do with the deaths of either Treadwell or Verona Stourbridge. Unless, of course, Treadwell had blackmailed Miriam over the child? But would Lucius care? Would such a tragedy be enough to stop him wanting to marry her? Or his family from allowing it?

Rathbone had done her no service yet. He had nothing to lose by pressing the story as far as it could go.

'You must have asked her what happened?' he said grimly. 'What did she say? If nothing else, the law would require some explanation. What about her own family? What did they do, Mrs Anderson, with this injured and hysterical child whose story made no sense to you?'

Cleo's face tightened and she looked at Rathbone more defiantly.

'I didn't tell the police. What was there to tell them? I asked her her name, of course, and if she had family who'd be looking for her. She said there was no one, and who was I to argue with that? She was one of eight, and her family'd placed her in service, in a good house.'

'And the child?' Rathbone had to ask. 'What manner of man gets a twelve-year-old girl with child? She would be twelve when it was conceived. Did he abandon her?'

Cleo's face was ashen. Rathbone did not dare look at Miriam. He could not even imagine what she must be enduring, having to sit in the dock and listen to this, and see the faces of the court, and the jury. He wondered if she would look at Harry or Lucius Stourbridge, or Aiden Campbell, who were sitting together in the front of the body of the court. Perhaps this was worse than anything she had yet endured. But if she were to survive, if Cleo were to survive, it was necessary.

'Mrs Anderson?'

'He never cared for her,' Cleo said quietly. 'She said he raped her, several times. That was how she got with child.'

One of the jurors gasped. Another clenched his fist and banged it short and hard on the rail in front of him. It must have hurt, but he was too outraged even to be conscious of it.

Lucius started to his feet, and then subsided again, helpless to know what to do.

'But the child was stillborn,' Rathbone said in the silence.

'I reckoned so,' Cleo agreed.

'And what was Miriam doing alone on the Heath in such a state?'

Cleo shook her head, as if to deny the truth, drive it away. Tobias was staring at her

As though she were aware of him she looked again at Rathbone imploringly. But it was for Miriam, not for herself. He was absolutely sure of that.

'What did she say?' he asked.

Cleo looked down. Her voice when she spoke was barely audible.

'That she had fled from the house with a woman, and that the woman had tried to protect her, and the woman had been murdered . . . out there on the Heath.'

Rathbone was stunned. His imagination had conjured many possibilities, but not this. It took him a moment to collect his wits. He did not mean to look at Miriam, but in spite of himself he did.

She was sitting white-faced with her eyes shut. She must have been aware that every man and woman in the room was staring at her, and her only hiding place was within herself. He saw pain in her face, almost beyond her power to bear – but no surprise. She had known what Cleo was going to say. That, more than anything else, made him believe it absolutely. Whether it had happened or not, whether there was any woman, whether it was the illusion of a tormented and hysterical girl in the delirium of fever, Miriam believed it to be the truth.

Rathbone looked at Hester and saw her wide-eyed

amazement also. She had known there was something – but not this.

He asked the question the whole court was waiting to hear answered.

'And was this woman's body found, Mrs Anderson?'

'No . . .'

'You did look?'

'Of course we did. We all looked. Every man in the street.'

'But you never found it?'

'No.'

'And Miriam couldn't take you to it? Again – I presume you asked her? It is hardly a matter you could let slip!'

She looked at him angrily. 'Of course we didn't let it slip! She said it was by an oak tree, but the Heath is full of oaks. When we couldn't find anything in a week of looking, we took it she was out of her wits, with all that had happened to her. People see all sorts of things when they've been ill, let alone the grief of having a dead child – and her only a child herself!' Her contempt for him rang through her words and he felt the sting of it even though he was doing what he must.

Tobias was sitting at his table shaking his head.

'So you assumed she had imagined at least that part of her experience – her nightmare, and you let it drop?' he pressed.

'Yes, of course we did. It took her months to get better, and when she was, we were all so glad of it we never mentioned it again. Why should we? Nobody else ever did. No one came looking for anybody. The police were asked if anyone was missing.'

'And what about Miriam? Did you tell the police you had found her? After all, she was only thirteen herself then.'

'Of course we told them. She wasn't missing from anywhere, and they were only too pleased that someone was looking after her.'

'And she remained with you?'

'Yes. She grew up a beautiful girl.' She said it with pride. Her love for Miriam was so plain in her face and her voice, no words could have spoken as clearly. 'When she was nineteen Mr Gardiner started courting her. Very slow, very gentle he was with her. We knew he was a good bit older than she was, but she didn't mind, and that was all that mattered. If he made her happy, that was all I cared.'

'And they were married?'

'Yes, a while later. And a very good husband he was to her too.'

'And then he died?'

'Yes. Very sad that was. Died young, even though he was older than her, of course. Took an attack and was gone in a matter of days. She missed him very badly.'

'Until she met Lucius Stourbridge?'

'Yes – but that was three years after.'

'But she had no children with Mr Gardiner?'

'No.' Her voice was torn. 'That was one blessing she wasn't given. Only the good Lord knows why. It happens, more often than you'd think.'

Tobias rose to his feet with exaggerated weariness.

'My lord, we have listened with great indulgence to this life story of Miriam Gardiner, and while we have every sympathy with her early experiences, whatever the truth of them may be, it all has no bearing whatever on the death of James Treadwell, or of Verona Stourbridge – except as it may, regrettably, have provided the wretched Treadwell with more fuel for his blackmailing schemes. If he knew of this first child of Mrs Gardiner's, perhaps he felt the Stourbridge family would be less willing to accept her – victim of rape, or whatever else it may have been.'

A look of distaste passed across the judge's face, but Tobias' point was unarguable and he knew it.

'Sir Oliver?' he said questioningly. 'It does seem that you have done more to advance Mr Tobias' case than your own. Have you further points to put to your client?'

Rathbone had no idea what to say. He was desperate.

'Yes, my lord, if you please.'

'Then proceed, but make it pertinent to the events we are here to try.'

'Yes, my lord.' He turned to Cleo. 'Did you believe that she had been raped, Mrs Anderson? Or do you perhaps think she was no better than she should be, and—'

'She was thirteen!' Cleo said furiously. 'Twelve when it happened! Of course I believed she had been raped! She was half out of her mind with terror!'

'Of whom? The man who raped her – then, nine months afterwards? Why?'

'Because he tried to kill her!' Cleo shouted.

Rathbone feigned surprise. 'She told you that?'

'Yes!'

'And what did you do about it? There was a man somewhere near the Heath who had raped this girl you took in and treated as your own, and then he subsequently tried to murder her – and you never found him? In God's name, why not?'

Cleo was shaking, gasping for breath, and Rathbone was afraid he had driven her too far.

'I believed she'd been raped, or seduced,' Cleo said in a whisper. 'But God forgive me, I thought the attack was all jumbled up in her mind, because of having a dead baby, poor little thing.'

'Until . . .?' Rathbone said urgently, raising his voice. 'Until she came running to you again, close to hysteria and terrified! And there was really a dead body on the Heath this time –

James Treadwell! Who was she running from, Mrs Anderson?'

The silence was total.

A juror coughed and it sounded like an explosion.

'Was it James Treadwell?' Rathbone threw it down like a challenge.

'No!'

'Then whom?'

Silence.

The judge leaned forward. 'If you wish us to believe you that it was not James Treadwell, Mrs Anderson, then you must tell us who it was.'

Cleo swallowed convulsively. 'Aiden Campbell.'

If she had set off a bomb it could not have had more effect.

Rathbone was momentarily paralysed.

There was a roar from the gallery.

The jurors turned to each other, exclaiming, gasping.

The judge banged his gavel and demanded order.

'My lord!' Rathbone raised his voice. 'May I ask for the luncheon adjournment so I can speak with my client?'

'You may,' the judge agreed and banged the gavel again. 'The court will reconvene at two o'clock.'

Rathbone left the courtroom in a daze and walked like a man half blind down to the room where Miriam Gardiner was permitted to speak with him.

She did not even turn her head when the door opened and he came in, the gaoler remaining on the outside.

'Was it Aiden Campbell you were running from?' he asked.

She said nothing, sitting motionless, head turned away.

'Why?' he persisted. 'What had he done to you?'

Silence.

'Was he the one who attacked you originally?' His voice was growing louder and more shrill in his desperation. 'For heaven's sake, answer me! How can I help you if you won't speak to me?' He leaned forward over the small table, but still she did not turn. 'You will hang!' he said deliberately.

'I know,' she answered at last.

'And Cleo Anderson!' he added.

'No – I will say I killed Treadwell too. I will swear it on the stand. They'll believe me, because they want to. None of them wants to condemn Cleo.'

It was true, and he knew it as well as she did.

'You'll say that on the stand?'

'Yes.'

'But it is not true!'

This time she turned and met his eyes fully. 'You don't know that, Sir Oliver. You don't know what happened. If I say it is so, will you contradict your own client? You must be a fool – it is what they want to hear. They will believe it.'

He stared back at her, momentarily beaten. He had the feeling that were there any heart left alive in her, she would have smiled at him. He knew that if he did not call her to testify, then she would ask the judge from the dock for permission to speak, and he would grant it. There was no argument to make.

He left, and had a miserable luncheon of bread which tasted to him like sawdust, and claret which could as well have been vinegar.

Rathbone had no choice but to call Aiden Campbell to the stand. If he had not, then most assuredly Tobias would have. At least this way he might retain a modicum of control.

The court was seething with anticipation. Word seemed to have spread during the luncheon adjournment, because now every seat was taken and the ushers had had to ban more people from crowding in.

357

The judge called them to order, and Rathbone rose to begin.

'I call Aiden Campbell, my lord.'

Campbell was white-faced but composed. He must have known that this was inevitable and he had had almost two hours to prepare himself. He stood now facing Rathbone, a tall, straight figure, tragically resembling both his dead sister and his nephew Lucius, who was sitting beside his father more like a ghost than a living being. Every now and again he stared up at Miriam, but never once had Rathbone seen Miriam return his look.

'Mr Campbell,' Rathbone began as soon as Campbell had been reminded that he was still under oath, 'an extraordinary charge has been laid against you by the last witness. Are you willing to respond to this—'

'I am!' Campbell interrupted in his eagerness to reply. 'I had hoped profoundly that this would never be necessary. Indeed, I have gone to some lengths to see that it would not, for the sake of my family, and out of a sense of decency, and the desire to bury old tragedies and allow them to remain unknown in the present, where they cannot hurt innocent parties.' He glanced at Lucius, and away again. His meaning was nakedly apparent.

'Mrs Anderson has sworn that Miriam Gardiner claimed it was you she was running away from when she fled the party at Cleveland Square. Is that true?' Rathbone asked.

Campbell looked distressed. 'Yes,' he said quietly. He shook his head a fraction. 'I cannot tell you how deeply I had hoped not to have to say this. I knew Miriam Gardiner – Miriam Speake as she was then, when she was twelve years old. She was a maid in my household when I lived near Hampstead.'

There was a rustle of movement and the startled sound of indrawn breath around the room.

Campbell looked across at Harry Stourbridge and Lucius. 'I'm sorry,' he said fervently. 'I cannot conceal this any longer. Miriam lived in my house for about eighteen months, or something like that. Of course she recognised me at the garden party, and must have been afraid that I would know her also, and tell you.' He was still speaking to Harry Stourbridge, as if this were a private matter between them.

'Obviously you did not tell them,' Rathbone observed, bringing Campbell's attention back to the business of the court. 'Why would it trouble her so much that she would flee in such a manner, as if terrified rather than merely embarrassed? Surely the Stourbridge family was already aware that she came from a different social background? Was this so terrible?'

Campbell sighed, and hesitated several moments before replying.

Rathbone waited.

There was barely a movement in the courtroom.

'Mr Campbell . . .' the judge prompted.

Campbell bit his lips. 'Yes, my lord. It pains me deeply to say this, but Miriam Speake was a loose woman. Even at the age of twelve she was without moral conscience.'

There was a gasp from Harry Stourbridge. Lucius half rose in his seat, but his legs seemed to collapse under him.

'I'm sorry!' Campbell said again. 'She was very pretty – very comely for one so young . . . and I find it repugnant to have to say so, but very experienced . . .'

Again there was a gasp from the gallery.

Several jurors were shaking their heads. A couple of them glanced towards the dock with grim disappointment. Rathbone knew absolutely that they believed every word. He himself looked up at Miriam and saw her bend her ashen face and cover it with her hands, as if she could not endure what she was hearing.

In calling Aiden Campbell, Rathbone had removed what ghost of a defence she had had. He felt as if he had impaled himself on his own sword. Everyone in the room was watching him, waiting for him to go on. Hester must be furious at this result, and pity him for his incompetence. The pity was worse.

Tobias was shaking his head in sympathy for a fellow counsel drowning in a storm of his own making.

Campbell was waiting. Rathbone must say something more. Nothing he could imagine would make it worse. At least he had nothing to lose now and therefore also nothing to fear.

'This is your opinion, Mr Campbell? And you believe that Mrs Gardiner, now a very respectable widow in her thirties, was so terrified that you would express this unfortunate view of her childhood and ruin the prospective happiness of your nephew—'

'Hardly unreasonable!' Tobias interrupted. 'What man would not tell his sister whom he loved that her only son was engaged to marry a maid no better than a whore?'

'But he didn't!' Rathbone exclaimed. 'He told no one! In fact you first heard him apologise to his brother-in-law this moment for saying it now!' He swung around. 'Why was that, Mr Campbell? If she was such a woman as you describe – should I say, such a child – why did you not warn your family rather than allow her to marry into it? If what you say is true . . .'

'It is true,' Campbell said gravely. 'The state she was in that Mrs Anderson described fits, regrettably, with what I know of her.' His hands gripped the rail of the witness box in front of him. He seemed to hold it as if to steady himself from shaking. He had difficulty finding his voice. 'She seduced one of my servants, a previously decent man, who fell into temptation too strong for him to resist. I considered dismissing him, but his work was excellent, and he was bitterly ashamed of his lapse from virtue. It would have ruined him at the start of his life.' He stopped for a moment.

Rathbone waited.

'I did not know at the time,' Campbell went on with obvious difficulty. 'But she was with child. She had it aborted.'

There was an outcry in the courtroom. A woman shrieked. There was a commotion as someone apparently collapsed.

The judge banged his gavel but it made little impression.

Miriam made as if to rise to her feet, but the gaolers on either side of her pulled her back.

Rathbone looked at the jury. To a man their faces were marked deeply with shock and utter and savage contempt.

The judge banged his gavel again. 'I will have order!' he said angrily. 'Otherwise the ushers will clear the court!'

Tobias looked across at Rathbone and shook his head.

When the noise subsided, and before Rathbone could speak, Campbell continued, 'That must be the reason that she was bleeding when Mrs Anderson found her wandering around on the Heath.' He shook his head as if to deny what he was about to say, somehow reduce the harshness of it. 'At first I didn't want to put her out either. She was so young. I thought – one mistake – and it had been a rough abortion – she was still . . .' He shrugged. Then he raised his head and looked at Rathbone. 'But she kept on, always tempting the men, flirting with them, setting one against the other. She enjoyed the power she had over them. I had no choice but to put her out.'

There was a murmur of sympathy around the court, and a rising tide of anger also. One or two men swore under their breath. Two jurors spoke to each other. They glanced up at the dock. The condemnation in their faces was unmistakable.

A journalist was scribbling furiously.

Tobias looked at Rathbone and smiled sympathetically, but without hiding his knowledge of his own victory. He asked no quarter for himself when he lost, and he gave none.

'I wish I had not had to say that,' Campbell was looking at Rathbone. 'I hesitated to tell Harry before because at first I was not even totally sure it was the same person. It seemed incredible, and of course she had aged a great deal in twenty-three years. I didn't want to think it was her . . . you understand that? I suppose I finally acknowledged that it had to be when I saw that she also recognised me.'

There was nothing for Rathbone to say, nothing left to ask. It was the last result he could have foreseen, and presumably Hester would feel as disillusioned and as empty as he did himself. He sat down utterly dejected.

Tobias rose and walked into the middle of the floor, swaggering a little. Beating Oliver Rathbone was a victory to be savoured, even when it had been ridiculously easy.

'Mr Campbell, there is very little left for me to ask. You have told us far more than we could have imagined.' He looked across at Rathbone. 'I think that goes for my learned friend as much as for me! However, I do wish to tidy up any details that there may be . . . in case Mrs Gardiner decides to take the stand herself, and make any charges against you, as suggested by Mrs Anderson – who may be as unaware of Mrs Gardiner's youthful exploits as were the rest of us.'

Campbell did not reply but waited for Tobias to continue.

'Mrs Gardiner fled when she realised that you had recognised her – at least that is your assumption?'

'Yes.'

'Did you follow her?'

'No, of course not. I had no reason to.'

'You remained at the party?'

'Not specifically at the party. I remained at Cleveland Square. I was very upset about the matter. I moved a little further off in the garden, to be alone and think what to do . . . and what to say when the rest of the family would inevitably discover that she had gone.'

'And what did you decide, Mr Campbell?'

'To say nothing,' Campbell answered. 'I knew this story would hurt them all profoundly. They were very fond of Miriam. Lucius was in love with her as only a young and idealistic man can be. I believe it was his first love . . .' He left the sentence hanging, allowing each man to remember his own first awakenings of passion, dreams, and perhaps loss.

'I see,' Tobias said softly. 'Only God can know whether that decision was the right one, but I can well understand why you made it. I am afraid I must press you further on just one issue.'

'Yes?'

'The coachman, James Treadwell. Why do you think she left with him?'

'He was the servant in the house she knew the best,' Campbell replied. 'I gather he had driven her from Hampstead a number of times. I shall not speculate that it was anything more than that . . .'

'Very charitable of you,' Tobias observed. 'Considering your knowledge of her previous behaviour with menservants!'

Campbell narrowed his lips but he did not answer.

'Tell me,' Tobias continued. 'How did this wretched coachman know of Mrs Anderson's stealing of hospital supplies?'

'I have no idea!' Campbell sounded surprised, then his face fell. He shook his head. 'No – I don't believe Miriam told him! She was conniving, manipulative, greedy – but no.

Unless it was by accident, not realising what he would do with the information . . .'

'Would it not be the perfect revenge?' Tobias asked smoothly. 'Her marriage to Lucius Stourbridge is now impossible, because she knows you will never allow it. Treadwell is ruining her friend and benefactress, to whom she must now return. In rage and defeat, and even desperation, she strikes out at him! What more natural?'

'I suppose so,' Campbell conceded.

Tobias turned to the judge. 'My lord, this is surely sufficient tragedy for one day. If it pleases the Court, I would like to suggest we may adjourn until tomorrow, when Sir Oliver may put forward any other evidence he feels may salvage his case. Personally, I have little more to add.'

The judge looked at Rathbone enquiringly, but his gavel was already in his hand.

Rathbone had no weapons and no will to fight any further.

'Certainly, my lord,' he said quietly. 'By all means.'

Rathbone had barely left the courtroom when he was approached by the usher.

He did not wish to speak to anyone. He was tasting the full bitterness of a defeat he knew he had brought upon himself. He dreaded facing Hester and seeing her disillusion.

'What is it?' he said brusquely.

'Sorry, Sir Oliver,' the usher apologised. 'Mrs Anderson asked if you would speak with her, sir. She said it was most important.'

The only thing worse than facing Hester was going to be telling Cleo Anderson that there was nothing more he could attempt on her behalf. He drew in his breath. It could not be evaded. If victory could be accepted and celebrated, then defeat must be dealt with with equal composure, and at the very least without cowardice or excuses.

'Of course,' he replied. 'Thank you, Morris.' He turned and was a dozen yards along the corridor when Hester caught up with him. He had no idea what to say to her. There was no comfort to offer, no next line of attack to suggest.

She fell into step with him and said nothing.

He glanced at her, then away again, grateful for her silence. He had not seen Monk, and assumed he was on some other business.

Cleo was waiting in the small room with the gaoler outside. She was standing facing them and she stepped forward as soon as Rathbone closed the door.

'He's lying,' she said, looking from one to the other of them.

He was embarrassed. It was futile to protest now, and he had not the emotional strength to struggle with her. It was over.

He shook his head. 'I'm sure you want to believe—'

'It has nothing to do with belief!' she said dismissively. 'I saw her then! She wasn't aborted. She'd gone full term.' She was angry now with his lack of understanding. 'I'm a nurse. I know the difference between a woman who's given birth and one who's lost her child or done away with it in the first few months. That child was born – dead or alive. The size of her – and she had milk, poor little thing.' She swallowed. 'How she wept for it . . .'

'So Campbell is lying!' Hester said, moving forward to Cleo. 'But why?'

'To hide what he did to her!' Cleo said furiously. 'He must have raped her, and when she was with child he threw her out!' She looked from Hester to Rathbone. 'Though he didn't even notice her condition! Who looks at housemaids, especially ones who are barely more than children themselves? Perhaps he'd already got tired of her – moved on to someone else? Or if he thought she'd had it aborted, and only then realised she hadn't! To avoid the scandal . . .'

'It wouldn't be much of a scandal,' Hester said sadly. 'If she were foolish enough to say it was his, he would simply deny it. No one would be likely to believe her . . . or frankly care that much even if they did. It isn't worth murdering anyone over.'

Cleo's face crumpled, but she refused to give in. 'What about the body?'

'Which body?' Rathbone was confused. 'The baby?'

'No – no, the woman!'

'What woman?'

'The woman Miriam saw murdered the night her baby was born! The woman on the Heath!'

Rathbone was still further confused. 'Who was she?'

Cleo shook her head. 'I don't know! Miriam said she had been murdered. She saw it – that was what she was running away from!'

'But who was the woman?'

'I don't know!'

'Was there ever a body found? What happened? Didn't the police ask?'

Cleo waved her hands in denial, her eyes desperate. 'No – no body was ever found. He must have hidden it.'

It was all pointless, completely futile. Rathbone felt a sense of despair drowning him as if he could hardly struggle for breath, almost a physical suffocation.

'You said yourself that she was hysterical.' He tried to sound reasonable, not patronising or offensive to a woman who must be facing the most bitter disillusion imaginable, and for which she would face disgrace she had not deserved, and a death he could not save her from. 'Don't you think the loss of her baby was what she was actually thinking of? Was it a girl?'

'I don't know. She didn't say.' Cleo looked as if she had caught his despair. 'She seemed so – so sure it was a woman . . . someone she cared for . . . who had helped her, even loved her . . . I . . .' She stopped, too weary, too hurt to go on.

'I'm sorry,' Rathbone said gently. 'You were right to tell me about the baby. If Campbell was lying, at least we may be able to make something of that. Even if we do no more than save Miriam's reputation, I am sure that will matter to her.' He was making wild promises, and talking nonsense. Would Miriam care about such a thing, when she faced death?

He banged on the door to be released again, and as soon as they were outside he turned to Hester.

But before he could begin to say how sorry he was, she spoke.

'If this woman really was killed, then her body must still be there . . .'

'Hester – she was delirious, probably weak from loss of blood and in a state of acute distress from delivering a dead child.'

'Maybe! But perhaps she really did see a woman murdered,' Hester insisted. 'If the body was never found, then it is out there on the Heath . . .'

'For twenty-two years!' he said incredulously. 'On Hampstead Heath! For heaven's sake . . .'

'Not in the open! Buried – hidden somewhere!'

'Well, if it's buried no one would find it now!'

'Perhaps it's not buried.' She refused to give up. 'Perhaps it's hidden somehow, concealed.'

'Hester . . .'

'I'm going to find Sergeant Robb and see if he will help me look.'

'You can't! After all this time there'll be nothing . . .'

'I've got to try! What if there really was a woman murdered? What if Miriam was telling the truth all the time?'

'She isn't!'

'But what if she was? She's your client, Oliver! You've got to give her the benefit of every doubt. You must assume that what she says is true until it is completely proved it can't be.'

'She was thirteen, she'd just given birth to a dead child, she was alone and hysterical . . .'

'I'm going to find Sergeant Robb. He'll help me look, whatever he believes, for Cleo's sake. He owes her a debt he can never repay, and he knows that.'

'And doubtless if he should forget, you will remind him!'

'Certainly!' she agreed. 'But he won't forget.'

'What about Monk?' he challenged her as she turned to leave.

'He's still busy trying to find out more about Treadwell and the corpses,' she said over her shoulder.

'Corpses! What corpses, Hester?'

But she had walked off, increasing her pace to a run, and short of chasing after her there was nothing he could do, except try to imagine how he was going to face the court tomorrow morning.

Michael Robb was sitting alone in the room where until recently his grandfather had spent his days. The big chair was still there, as if the old man might come back to it one day, and there was a startling emptiness without him.

'Mrs Monk!' Robb said with surprise. 'What is it? Is something wrong?'

'Everything is wrong,' she answered, remaining standing in spite of his invitation to sit. 'Cleo is going to be convicted unless we can find some sort of evidence that Miriam also is innocent, and our only chance of that is to find the body of the woman—?'

'What woman? Just a minute!' He held up his hand. 'What has happened in Court? I wasn't there.'

With words falling over each other she told him about calling Cleo to the stand and her story of how she had first met Miriam, and then Aiden Campbell's denial and explanation.

'We've got to find the woman that Miriam said was murdered!' she finished desperately. 'That would prove what she said was true! At least they would have to investigate it!'

'She's been out there for twenty-two years!' he protested. 'If she exists at all!'

'Can you think of anything better?' she demanded.

'No, but—'

'Then help me! We've got to go and look!'

He hesitated only a moment. She could see in his face that he considered it hopeless, but he was feeling lonely and guilty because Cleo had helped him in the way he valued the most, and he could do nothing for her. Silently he picked up his bull's-eye lantern and followed Hester out into the gathering dusk.

Side by side they walked towards Green Man Hill and the row of cottages where Cleo Anderson had lived until her arrest. They stopped outside, facing the Heath. It was now almost dark; only the heavy outlines of the trees showed black against the glimmer of the clear autumn sky.

'Where do you think we should start?' Robb asked.

She was grateful he had spoken of them as together, not relegating it to her idea in which he was merely obliging her.

She had been thinking about it as they had travelled in silence.

'It cannot have been very far,' she said, staring across the grass. 'Miriam was not in a state to run a distance. If the poor woman really was murdered, beaten to death as Miriam apparently said, then whoever did so would not have committed such an act close to the road.' She pushed away the thought, refusing to allow the pictures into her mind. 'Even if it was a single blow – and please God it was – it cannot have been silent. There must have been a quarrel, an accusation or something! Miriam was there, she saw it. She, at least, must have cried out – and then fled.'

He was staring at her, and in the light of the lantern she saw him nodding slowly, his face showing his revulsion at what she described.

'Whoever it was could not follow her,' she went on relentlessly. 'Because he was afraid of being caught. First he had to get rid of the body of the woman—'

'Mrs Monk . . . are you sure you believe this is possible?' he interrupted.

She was beginning to doubt it herself, but she refused to give up.

'Of course!' she said sharply. 'We are going to prove it! If you had just killed someone, and you knew a girl had seen you, and she had run away, perhaps screaming, how would you hide a body so quickly that if anyone heard and came to see, they would not find anything at all?'

His eyes widened. He opened his lips to argue, then began to think. He walked across the grass towards the first trees and stared around him.

'Well, I wouldn't have time to dig a grave,' he said slowly. 'The ground is hard and full of roots. And anyway, someone would very quickly notice disturbed earth.'

He walked a little further and she followed after him quickly.

Above them something swooped in the darkness on broad

wings. Involuntarily she gave a little shriek.

'It's only an owl!' he said reassuringly.

She swung around. 'Where did it go?'

'One of the trees,' he replied. He lifted the lantern and shining it around, lighting the trunks one after another. They looked pale grey against the darkness and the shadows seemed to move beyond them as the lantern waved.

She was acutely glad she was not alone. She imagined what Miriam must have felt like, her child lost, a woman she loved killed in front of her, and herself pursued and hunted, bleeding, terrified. No wonder she was all but out of her mind when Cleo found her.

'We've got to keep on looking!' she said fiercely. 'We must exhaust every possibility. If the body is here, we are going to find it!' She strode forward, hitching up her skirts not to fall over them. 'You said he wouldn't have buried it. He couldn't leave it in plain sight, or it would have been found. And it wasn't! So he hid it so successfully it never was found! Where?'

'In a tree,' he replied. 'It has to be. There's nowhere else!'

'Up a tree? But someone would find it, in time!' she protested. 'It would rot! It—'

'I know!' he said hastily, shaking his head as if to rid himself of the idea. He moved the lantern ahead of them, picking out undergrowth and more trees. A weasel ran across the path, its lean body bright in the beam for a moment, then it disappeared.

'Animals would get rid of it in time, wouldn't they?'

'In time, yes.'

'Well, it's been over twenty years! What would be left now? Bones? Teeth?'

'Hair,' he said. 'Perhaps clothes, jewellery, buttons. Boots, maybe.'

Hester shuddered.

He looked at her, shining the light a little below her face not to dazzle her.

'Are you all right, Mrs Monk?' he said gently. 'I can go on my own, if you like? I'll take you back, and then come back here again. I promise I will . . .'

She smiled at his earnestness. 'I know you would, but I am quite all right, thank you. Let's go forward.'

He hesitated for a moment, still uncertain, then as she did not waver, he shone the lantern ahead of them and started.

They walked together for forty or fifty yards, searching to left and right for any place that could be used for concealment. She found herself feeling more and more as if she were wasting her time and, more importantly, Robb's time as well. She had believed Miriam's story because she wanted to, for Cleo's sake, not because it was really credible.

'Sergeant Robb,' she began.

He turned round, the beam of light swinging across the two trees to their right. It caught for a moment on a tangle in the lower branches.

'What's that?' he said quickly.

'An old bird's nest,' she replied. 'Last year's, by the look of it.'

He played the light on it, then moved forward to look more closely.

'What?' she asked, with curiosity more than hope. 'Clever how they weave them, isn't it, especially since they haven't got any hands.'

He passed her the lantern. 'Hold this on to it, please. I want to take a closer look.'

'At a bird's nest?' But she did as he requested, and kept it steady.

With hands free it was easy enough for him to climb up until he was level with the nest and peer inside where it was caught in a fork in the branches, close to the trunk.

'What is it?' she called up.

He turned around, his face a shadowed mask in the upturned beam.

'Hair,' he answered her. 'Long hair, lots of it. The whole nest is lined with hair.' His voice was shaking. 'I'm going to look for a hollow tree. You just hold the light, and keep your eyes away.'

She felt a lurch inside. She had no longer believed it, and now here it was. They were almost there – in the next half-hour – more or less . . .

'Yes,' she said unsteadily. 'Yes, of course.'

Actually it took him only fifteen minutes to find the tree with the hollow core, blasted by some ancient lightning and now rotted. It was closer to the road than the nest, but the spread of branches hid the hole until it was deliberately sought. Perhaps twenty-two years ago it had been more obvious. The entire tree was hollow down the heart.

'It's in there,' Robb said huskily, climbing down again, the lantern tied to his belt. His legs were shaking when he reached the ground. 'It's only a skeleton but there's still cloth left . . .' He blinked, his face looked yellow grey in the beam. 'From the head, she was killed by one terrible blow . . . like Treadwell . . . and Mrs Stourbridge.'

Chapter Thirteen

Rathbone had slept little. A messenger had arrived at his rooms after midnight with a note from Hester:

Dear Oliver,
    We found the body. Seems to be a woman with grey hair. She was killed by a terrible blow to the head – just like the others. Am in the police station with Sergeant Robb. They do not know who she is. Will tell William, of course. I shall be in Court in the morning to testify. You MUST call me!
    Yours, Hester.

He had found it impossible to rest. An hour later he had made himself a hot drink and was pacing the study floor, trying to formulate a strategy for the next day. Eventually he went back to bed, and sank into a deep sleep, when it seemed immediately time to get up.

His head ached and his mouth was dry. His manservant brought him breakfast, but he ate only toast and drank a cup of tea, then left straight away for the courtroom. He was far too early and the time he had expected to use in preparing himself he wasted in pointless moving from one place to another, and in conversation from which he learned nothing.

Tobias was in excellent spirits. He passed Rathbone in the corridor and wished him well with a wry smile. He would have preferred more of a fight of it. Such an easy victory was of little savour.

The gallery was half empty again. The public had already made up their minds and the few present were here only to see justice done and taste a certain vengeance. The startling exceptions to this were Lucius and Harry Stourbridge who sat towards the front, side by side, and even at a distance, very obviously supporting each other in silent companionship of anguish.

The judge called the court to order.

'Have you any further witnesses, Sir Oliver?' he asked.

'Yes, my lord. I would like to call Hester Monk.'

Tobias looked across curiously.

The judge raised his eyebrows, but with no objection.

Rathbone smiled very slightly.

The usher called for Hester.

She took the stand, looking tired and pale-faced, but absolutely confident, and she very deliberately turned and looked up towards the dock and nodded to both Cleo and Miriam. Then she waited for Rathbone to begin.

Rathbone cleared his throat. 'Mrs Monk, were you in court yesterday when Mrs Anderson testified to the extraordinary story Miriam Gardiner told when she was first found bleeding and hysterical on Hampstead Heath twenty-two years ago?'

'Yes, I was.'

'Did you follow any course of action because of that?'

'Yes, I went to look for the body of the woman Miriam said she saw murdered.'

Tobias made a sound of derision, halfway between a cough and a snort.

The judge leaned forward enquiringly. 'Sir Oliver, is this really relevant at this stage?'

'Yes, my lord, most relevant,' Rathbone answered with satisfaction. At last there was warmth inside him, a sense that he could offer a battle. Assuredly he could startle the equanimity from Tobias' face.

'Then please make that apparent,' the judge directed.

'Yes, my lord. Mrs Monk, did you find a body?'

The court was silent, but not in anticipation. He barely had the juror's attention.

'Yes, Sir Oliver, I did . . .'

Tobias started forward, jerking upright from the seat where he had been all but sprawled.

There was a wave of sound and movement from the gallery, a hiss of indrawn breath.

The judge leaned across to Hester. 'Do I hear you correctly, madam? You say you found a body?'

'Yes, my lord. Of course I was not alone. I took Sergeant Michael Robb with me from the beginning. It was actually he who found it.'

'This is very serious indeed!' He frowned at her, his face pinched and earnest. 'Where is the body now and what can you tell me of it?'

'It is in the police morgue in Hampstead, my lord, and my knowledge of it is closely observed, but only as a nurse, not a doctor.'

'You are a nurse?' he was astounded.

'Yes, my lord. In the Crimea.'

'Good gracious.' He sat back. 'Sir Oliver, you had better proceed. But before you do so, I will have order in this court! The next man or woman to make an unwarranted noise will be removed! Continue.'

'Thank you, my lord.' Rathbone turned to Hester. 'Where did you find the body, Mrs Monk, precisely?'

'In a hollow tree on Hampstead Heath,' she replied. 'We started walking from Mrs Anderson's house on Green Man Hill, looking for the sort of place where a body might be concealed, assuming that Mrs Gardiner's story was true.'

'What led you to look in a hollow tree?'

There was total silence in the court. Not a soul moved.

'A bird's nest with a lot of human hair woven into it, caught in one of the lower branches of a tree near it,' Hester answered. 'We searched all around until we found the hollow one. Sergeant Robb climbed up and found the hole. Of course the area will have grown over a great deal in twenty years. It could have been easier to see, to get to then.'

'And the body?' Rathbone pursued. 'What can you tell us of it?'

She looked distressed; the memory was obviously painful. Her hands tightened on the railing and she took a deep breath before she began.

'There was only a skeleton. Her clothes had largely rotted away; only buttons were left of her dress, and the bones of her . . . undergarments. Her boots were badly damaged but there was still more than enough to be recognisable. All the buttons to them were whole and attached to what was left of the leather. They were unusual, and rather good.'

She stood motionless, steadying herself before she continued. 'To judge by what hair we found, she would have been a woman in her forties or fifties. She had a terrible hole in her skull, as if she had been beaten with some heavy object so hard it killed her.'

'Thank you,' Rathbone said quietly. 'You must be tired and extremely harrowed by the experience.

She nodded.

Rathbone turned to Tobias.

Tobias strode forward, shaking his head a little. When he spoke his voice was soft. He was far too wily to be less than courteous to her. She had the court's sympathy and he knew it.

'Mrs Monk, may I commend your courage and your single-minded dedication to seeking the truth. It is a very noble cause, and you appear to be tireless in it.' There was not a shred of sarcasm in him.

'Thank you,' she said guardedly.

'Tell me, Mrs Monk, was there anything on the body of this unfortunate woman to indicate who she was?'

'Not as far as I know. Sergeant Robb is trying to learn that now.'

'Using what? The remnants of cloth and leather that was still upon the bone?'

'You will have to ask him,' she replied.

'If he feels that this tragedy has any relevance to this present case, and therefore gives us that opportunity, then I shall!' Tobias agreed. 'But you seem to feel it has, or you would not now be telling me of it. Why is that, Mrs Monk, other than you desire to protect one of your colleagues?'

Spots of colour warmed Hester's cheeks. If she had ever imagined he would be gentle with her, she now knew better.

'Because we found her where Miriam Gardiner said she was murdered!' she replied a trifle tartly.

'Indeed?' Tobias raised his eyebrows. 'I gathered from Mrs Anderson that Mrs Gardiner – Miss Speake as she was then – was completely hysterical and incoherent. Indeed Mrs Anderson herself ceased to believe there was any woman, any murder, or any body to find!'

'Is that a question?' Hester asked him.

'No – no, it is an observation,' he said sharply. 'You found this gruesome relic somewhere on Hampstead Heath, in an unspecified tree. All we know is that it is within walking distance of Green Man Hill. Is there anything to indicate how long it had been there – except that it is obviously more than ten or eleven years? Could it have been twenty-five? Or, say, thirty? Or even fifty years, Mrs Monk?'

She stared back at him without flinching. 'I am not qualified to say, Mr Tobias. You will have to ask Sergeant Robb, or even the police surgeon. However, my husband is examining the boots and has an idea that they may be able to prove something. Buttons have a design, you know.'

'Your husband is an expert in buttons for ladies' boots?' he asked.

'He is an expert in direction of facts from the evidence,' she answered coolly. 'He will know whom to ask.'

'No doubt. And he may be willing to pursue ladies' boot buttons with tireless endeavour,' Tobias said sarcastically. 'But we have to deal with the evidence we have, and deduce from it reasonable conclusions. Is there anything in your knowledge, Mrs Monk, to prove that this unfortunate woman whose body you found, has anything to do with the murders of James Treadwell and of Mrs Verona Stourbridge?'

'Yes! You said Miriam Gardiner was talking nonsense because no body of a woman was ever found on Hampstead Heath such as she described. Well, now it has! She was not lying, nor was she out of her wits. There was a murder. Since she described it, it is the most reasonable thing to suppose that she witnessed it, exactly as she said.'

'There is the body of a woman,' Tobias corrected her. 'We do not know if it was murder, although I accept that it may very well have been. But we do not know who she was, what happened to her, and still less do we know when it happened.

Much as you would like to believe it is some support to the past virtue of Miriam Gardiner, Mrs Monk. And your charity does you credit, and indeed your loyalty, but it does not clear her of this charge.' He spread his hands in gesture of finality, smiled at the jury, and returned to his seat.

Rathbone stood up and looked at Hester.

'Mrs Monk, you were at this tree on the Heath and made this gruesome discovery; therefore you know the place, whereas we can only imagine. Tell us, is there any way whatever that this unfortunate woman could have sustained this appalling blow to her head, and then placed herself inside the tree?'

'No, of course not!' Her voice derided the idea.

'She was murdered and her body was afterwards hidden, and it happened long enough ago that the flesh has decomposed and most of the fabric of her clothes has rotted?' Rathbone made absolutely certain.

'Yes.'

'And she was killed by a violent blow to the head, in apparently exactly the same manner as James Treadwell and poor Mrs Stourbridge?'

'Yes.'

'Thank you, Mrs Monk.' He turned to the judge. 'I believe, my lord, that this evidence lends a great deal more credibility to Mrs Gardiner's original account, and that in the interest of justice we need to know who that woman was, and if her death is connected with those murders of which Mrs Gardiner and Mrs Anderson presently stand charged.'

The judge looked across at Tobias.

Tobias was already on his feet. 'Yes, my lord, of course. Mr Campbell has informed me that he is willing to testify again and explain all that he can, if it will assist the court. Indeed, since what has been said may leave in certain people's minds suspicion as to his own role, he wishes to have the opportunity to speak.'

'That would be most desirable,' the judge agreed. 'Please have Mr Campbell return to the stand.'

Aiden Campbell looked tired and strained as he climbed the steps again, but Rathbone, watching, could see no fear in him. He faced the court with sadness, but confidence, and his voice was quite steady when he answered Tobias' questions.

'No, I have no idea who the woman is, poor creature, nor how long she has been there. It would seem from the state of the body, and the clothes, that it was at least ten years.'

'Have you any idea how she came by her death, Mr Campbell?' Tobias pressed.

'None at all, except that from Mrs Monk's description of the wound, it sounds distressingly like those inflicted on Treadwell, and . . .' he hesitated, and this time his composure nearly cracked, '. . . upon my sister . . .'

'Please,' Tobias said gently. 'Allow yourself a few moments, Mr Campbell. Would you like a glass of water?'

'No – no thank you.' Campbell straightened up. 'I beg your pardon. I was going to say that this woman's death may be connected. Possibly she also was a nurse, and may have become aware of the thefts of medicine from the hospital. Perhaps she either threatened to tell the authorities, or maybe she tried her hand at blackmail . . .' He did not need to finish the sentence; his meaning was only too apparent.

'Just so.' Tobias inclined his head in thanks, turned to the jury with a little smile, then went back to his table.

There was silence in the gallery. Everyone was looking towards Rathbone, waiting to see what he would do now.

He glanced around, playing for time, hoping some shred of an idea would come to him and not look too transparently desperate. He saw Harry Stourbridge's face colourless and earnest, watching him with hope in his eyes. Lucius beside him looked like a ghost.

There was a stir as the outside doors opened and everyone craned to see who it was.

Monk came in. He nodded very slightly.

Rathbone turned to the front again. 'If there is time before the luncheon adjournment, my lord, I would like to call Mr William Monk. I believe he may have evidence as to the identity of the woman whose body was found last night.'

'Then indeed call him,' the judge said keenly. 'We should all like very much to hear what he has to say.'

Amid a buzz of excitement Monk climbed the steps to the stand and was sworn in. Every eye in the room was on him. Even Tobias sat forward in his seat, his face puckered with concern, his hands spread out on the table in front of him, broad and strong, fingers drumming silently.

Rathbone found his voice shaking a little. He was obliged to clear his throat before he began.

'Mr Monk, have you been engaged in trying to discover whatever information it is possible to find regarding the body of the woman from Hampstead Heath last night?'

'Since I was informed of it, at about one o'clock this morning,' Monk replied. And in fact he looked as if he had been up all night. His clothes were immaculate as always, but there was a dark shadow of beard on his cheeks and he was unquestionably tired.

'Have you learned anything?' Rathbone asked. Hearing his own heart beating so violently, he feared he must be shaking visibly.

'Yes. I took the buttons from the boots she was wearing, and a little of the leather of the soles, which were scarcely worn. Those particular buttons were individual, manufactured for only a short space of time. It is not absolute proof, but it seems extremely likely she was killed twenty-two years ago. Certainly it was not longer, and since the boots were almost new, it is unlikely to be less than that. If you call the police surgeon, he will tell you she was a woman of middle age, forty-five or fifty, of medium height and build, with long, grey hair. She had at some time in the past had a broken bone in one foot, which had healed completely. She was killed by a single, very powerful blow to her head, by someone facing her at the time, and right-handed. Oh . . . and she had perfect teeth – which is unusual in one of her age.'

There was tension in the court so palpable that when a man in the gallery sneezed the woman behind him let out a scream, then stifled it immediately.

Every juror in both rows stared at Monk as if unaware of anyone else in the room.

'Was that the same police surgeon who examined the bodies of Treadwell and Mrs Stourbridge?' Rathbone asked.

'Yes,' Monk answered.

'And was he of the opinion that the blows were inflicted by the same person?'

Tobias rose to his feet. 'My lord, Mr Monk has no medical expertise . . .'

'Indeed,' the judge agreed. 'We will not indulge in hearsay, Sir Oliver. If you wish to call this evidence, no doubt the police surgeon will make himself available. Nevertheless, I should very much like to know the answer to that myself.'

'I shall most certainly do so,' Rathbone agreed. Then, as the usher stood at his elbow: 'Excuse me, my lord.' He took the note handed to him and read it.

It could not have been a blackmailer of Cleo – she was not stealing medicines then. The apothecary can prove that. Call me to testify. Hester.

* * *

The court was waiting.

'My lord, may I recall Mrs Monk to the stand, in the question as to whether Mrs Anderson could have been blackmailed over the theft of medicines twenty-two years ago?'

'Can she give evidence on the subject?' the judge asked with surprise. 'Surely she was a child at the time?'

'She has access to the records of the hospital, my lord.'

'Then call her, but I may require to have the records themselves brought and put into evidence.'

'With respect, my lord, the court has accepted that medicines were stolen within the last few months without Mr Tobias having brought the records for the jury to read. Testimony has been sufficient for him in that.'

Tobias rose to his feet. 'My lord, Mrs Monk has shown herself an interested party. Her evidence is hardly unbiased!'

'I am sure the records can be obtained,' Rathbone said reluctantly. He would far rather Cleo's present thefts were left to testimony only, but there was little point in saving her from charges of stealing if she were convicted of murder.

'Thank you, my lord,' Tobias said with a smile.

'Nevertheless,' the judge added, 'we shall see what Mrs Monk has to say, Sir Oliver. Please call her.'

Hester took the stand and was reminded of her earlier oath to tell the truth, and only the truth. She had examined the apothecary's records as far back as thirty years, since before Cleo Anderson's time, and there was no discrepancy in medicines purchased and those accounted for as given to patients.

'So at the time of this unfortunate woman's death, there were no grounds for blackmailing Mrs Anderson, or anyone else, with regard to medicines at the hospital?' Rathbone confirmed.

'That is so,' she agreed.

Tobias stood up and walked towards her.

'Mrs Monk, you seem to be disposed to go to extraordinary lengths to prove Mrs Anderson not guilty, lengths quite above and beyond the call of any duty you are either invested with, or have taken upon yourself. I cannot but suspect you of embarking upon a crusade, either because you have a zeal to reform nursing and the view in which nurses are regarded – and I will call Mr Fermin Thorpe of the hospital in question to testify to your dedication to this – or, less flatteringly, a certain desire to draw attention to yourself, and fulfil your emotions, and perhaps occupy your time and your life, in the absence of children to care for.'

It was a tactical error. As soon as he had said it he was aware, but he did not know immediately how to retract it.

'On the contrary, Mr Tobias,' Hester said with a cold smile, 'I have merely testified as to facts. It is you who are searching to invest them with some emotional value because it appears you do not like to be proved mistaken, which I cannot understand, since we are all aware you prosecute or defend as you are engaged to, not as a personal vendetta against anyone. At least I believe that to be the case?' She allowed it to be a question.

There was a rustle of movement around the room, a ripple of nervous laughter.

Tobias blushed. 'Of course that is the case! But I am vigorous in it!'

'So am I!' she said tartly. 'And my emotions are no less honourable than your own, except that law is not my profession.' She allowed it to remain unfinished. They could draw their own conclusions as to whether she considered that to mark her inferiority in the matter, or the fact that she did not take money for it, and thus had a moral advantage.

'If you have no further questions, Mr Tobias,' the judge resumed command, 'I shall adjourn the court until such a time as this unfortunate woman is identified, then perhaps we shall also examine the hospital apothecary's records and be certain in the matter of what was stolen and when.' He banged his gavel sharply and with finality.

Monk left the court, without having heard Hester's second testimony. He went straight back to the Hampstead police station to find Sergeant Robb. It was imperative now that they learn who the dead woman had been. The only place to begin was with the assumption that Miriam had told the truth, and therefore she must have some connection with Aiden Campbell.

'But why is he lying?' Robb said doubtfully as they set out along the street in the hazy sunlight. 'Why? Let us even suppose that he seduced Miriam when she was his maid, or even raped her; it would hardly be the first time that had happened. Let us even say the woman on the Heath was a cook or housekeeper who knew about it; that'd be no reason to kill her!'

'Well, somebody killed her,' Monk said flatly, setting out across the busy street, disregarding the traffic and obliging a dray to pull up sharply. He was unaware of it and did not even signal his thanks to the driver who shouted at him his opinion of drunkards and lunatics in general, and Monk in particular.

Robb ran to catch up with him, raising a hand to the driver in acknowledgement.

'We've nowhere else to start,' Monk went on. 'Where did you say Campbell lived – exactly?'

Robb repeated the address. 'But he moved to Wiltshire less than a year after that. There won't necessarily be anyone there now who knows him, or anything that happened.'

'There might be,' Monk argued. 'Some servants will have left; others prefer to stay in the area and find new positions even stay in the house with whoever buys it. People belong to their neighbourhoods.'

'It's the far side of the Heath.' Robb was having to hurry to keep up. 'Do you want to take a hansom?'

'If one passes us,' Monk conceded, not slackening his pace 'If she wasn't part of the household, who could she be? How was she involved? Was she a servant, or a social acquaintance?'

'Well, there was nobody reported missing around that time, Robb replied. 'She wasn't local, or somebody'd have said.'

'So nobody missed her?' Monk swung around to face Robb and all but bumped into a gentleman coming briskly the othe way. 'Then she wasn't a neighbour or a local servant. This becomes very curious.'

They said no more until they reached the house where twenty-one years ago Aiden Campbell had lived. It had changed hands twice since then, but the girl who had been the scullery maid was now the housekeeper, and the mistress had no objection to Monk and Robb speaking with her; in fact she seemed quite eager to be of assistance.

'Yes, I was scullery maid then,' the housekeeper agreed 'Miriam was the tweeny. Only a bit of a girl, she was, poor little thing.'

'You liked her?' Monk said quickly.

'Yes – yes I did. We laughed together a lot, shared stories and dreams. Got with child, poor little soul, an' I never knew what happened to her then. Think it may 'ave been born dead for all that good care was took of 'er. Not surprising, I suppose Only twelve or so when she got like that.'

'Good care was taken of her?' Robb said with surprise.

'Oh yes. Had the midwife in,' she replied.

'How do you know she was a midwife?' Monk interrupted.

'She said so! She lived 'ere for a while, right before the birth. I do know that because I 'elped prepare 'er meals, an' took 'em up, on a tray, like.'

'You saw her?' Monk said eagerly.

'Yes. Why? I never saw 'er afterwards.'

Monk felt a stab of victory, and horror. 'What was she like? Think hard, Miss Parkinson, and please be as exact as you can. Height, hair, age!'

Her eyes widened. 'Why? She done something as she shouldn't?'

'No. Please – describe her!'

'Very ordinary, she was, but very pleasant-looking, an' all. Greyish sort of hair, although I don't reckon now as she was over about forty-five or so. Seemed old to me then, but I was only fifteen an' anything over thirty was old.'

'How tall?'

She thought for a moment. 'About same as me, ordinary, bit less.'

'Thank you, Miss Parkinson – thank you very much.'

'She all right, then?'

'No, I fear very much that she may be the woman whose body was found on the Heath.'

'Cor! Well, I'm real sorry.' She said it with feeling, and there was sadness in her face as well as her voice. 'Poor creature.'

Monk turned as they were about to leave. 'You didn't, by chance, ever happen to notice her boots, did you, Miss Parkinson?'

She was startled. 'Her boots?'

'Yes. The buttons.'

Memory sparked in her eyes. 'Yes! She had real smart buttons on them! Never seen no others like 'em. I saw when she was sitting down, her skirts was pulled sideways a bit Well I never! I'm real sorry to hear. Mebbe Mrs Dewar'll le me go to the funeral, since there won't be many others as' be there now.'

'Do you remember her name?' Monk said, almost holding his breath for her answer.

She screwed up her face in effort to take her mind back to the past. She did not need his urging to understand the importance of it.

'It began with a D,' she said after a moment or two. 'I' think of it.'

They waited in silence.

'Bailey!' she said triumphantly. 'Mrs Bailey. Sorry – thought it were a D, but Bailey it was.'

They thanked her again and left with a new energy of hope

'I'll tell Rathbone,' Monk said as soon as they were out in the street. 'You see if you can find her family. There can' have been so many midwives called Bailey twenty-two year ago. Someone'll know her. Start with the doctors and the hospital. Send messages to all the neighbouring areas. He may have brought her in from somewhere else. Probably did since no one in Hampstead reported her missing.'

Robb opened his mouth to protest, then changed his mind. It was not too much to do if it ended in proving Cleo Anderson innocent.

It was early afternoon of the following day when the cour reconvened. Rathbone called the police surgeon who gave expert confirmation of the testimony Hester had given regarding the death of the woman on the Heath. A cobbler swore to recognising the boot buttons, and produced a receipt showing that they had been purchased by one Flora Bailey some twenty-three years ago. Miss Parkinson came and described the woman she had seen, including the buttons.

The court accepted that the body was indeed that of Flora Bailey, and that she had met her death by a violent blow in a manner which could only have been murder.

Rathbone called Aiden Campbell once again. He was pale, his face set in lines of grief and anger. He met Rathbone's eyes defiantly.

'I was hoping profoundly not to have to say this,' his voice was hard. 'I did know Mrs Bailey. I had no idea that she was dead. I never required her services again. She was not, as my innocent scullery maid supposed, a midwife, but an abortionist.'

There was a gasp of horror and outrage around the court. People turned to one another with a hissing of breath.

Rathbone looked up at Miriam in the dock and saw the amazement in her face, and then the anger. He turned to Harry Stourbridge, sitting stiff and silent, and Lucius beside him, stunned almost beyond reaction.

'An abortionist?' Rathbone said slowly, very clearly.

'Yes,' Campbell confirmed. 'I regret to say so.'

Rathbone raised his eyebrows very slightly. 'You find abortion repugnant?'

'Of course I do! Doesn't every civilised person?'

'Of a healthy child, from a healthy mother, I imagine so,' Rathbone agreed. 'Then tell us, Mr Campbell, why you had the woman staying in your house – so that your scullery maid carried up her meals to her on a tray?'

Campbell hesitated, lifting his hands. 'If – if that was done, it was without my knowledge. The servants . . . perhaps they felt . . . I don't know . . . a pity . . .' He stopped. 'If that ever happened,' he added.

Tobias took his turn, briefly.

'Was that with your knowledge or approval, Mr Campbell?'

'Of course not!'

The court adjourned for luncheon.

The family of Flora Bailey arrived. Rathbone called her brother, a respected physician, as his first witness of the afternoon.

The gallery was packed. Word had spread like fire that something new was afoot.

'Dr Forbes,' Rathbone began, 'your sister spent time in the home of Mr Aiden Campbell, immediately before her disappearance. Were you aware of that?'

'No, sir, I was not. I knew she had a case she considered very important, but also highly confidential. The mother-to-be was very young, no more than a child herself, and whoever engaged her was most anxious that both she and the child should receive the very best attention. The child was much wanted, in spite of the circumstances. That is all she told me.'

Rathbone was startled. 'The child was wanted?'

'So my sister told me.'

'And was it born healthy?'

'I have no idea. I never heard from my sister again.'

'Thank you, Dr Forbes. May I say how sorry I am for the reason which brings you here.'

'Thank you,' Forbes said soberly.

'Dr Forbes, one last question. Did your sister have any feelings regarding the subject of abortion?'

'Very deep feelings,' Forbes answered. 'She was passionately opposed to it, regardless of the pity she felt for women who already had as many children as they could feed or care for or for those who were unmarried, or even who had been assaulted or otherwise abused. She could never bring herself to feel it acceptable. It was a matter of religious principle to her.'

'So she would not have performed an abortion herself?'

'Never!' Forbes' face was flushed, his emotion naked. 'If you doubt me, sir, I can name a dozen professional men who will say the same of her.'

'I do not doubt you, Dr Forbes, I simply wanted you to say it for the court to hear. Thank you for your patience. I have nothing further to ask.'

Tobias half rose to his feet, then sat down again. He glanced across at Rathbone, and for the first time there was misgiving in his face, even anxiety.

Again there was silence in the room. No one even noticed Harry Stourbridge stand up. It was not until he spoke that suddenly every eye turned to him.

'My lord,' he cleared his throat. 'I have listened to the evidence presented here from the beginning. I believe I now understand the truth. It is very terrible, but it must be told, or an unbearable injustice will be done. Two women will be hanged who are innocent of any wrong.'

The silence prickled like the coming of a storm.

'If you have information pertinent to this trial, then you should most certainly take the stand again, Major Stourbridge,' the judge agreed. 'Be advised that you are still under oath.'

'I am aware of it, my lord,' Stourbridge answered, and walked slowly from his seat, across the open space and up the steps of the witness box. He waited until the judge told him to proceed, then in a hoarse, broken voice, with desperate reluctance, he began.

'I come from a family of very considerable wealth, almost all of it in lands and property, with sufficient income to maintain them, and some extra to provide a more-than-comfortable living. However, it is all entailed, and has been so for generations. I inherited it from my father, and it will pass to my son.'

He stopped for a few seconds, as if regathering his strength. There was not a sound in the room. Everyone understood that here was man labouring under terrible emotions as he realised a truth that shattered his life.

'If I had not had a son,' he continued with difficulty, his voice trembling. 'The property would have passed to my younger brother.' Again he paused before gathering the strength to proceed. 'My wife found it extremely difficult to carry a child. Time and again she conceived, and then miscarried within the first few months. We had almost given up hope when she came to visit me in Egypt, while I was serving in the army there. It was a dangerous posting both because of the fighting, and the natural hazards of disease. I was anxious for her, but she was determined to come, at all costs.'

Now he was speaking, the words poured out. Every man and woman in the room was listening intently. No one moved even a hand.

'She stayed with me for over a month.' His voice cracked. 'She seemed to enjoy it. Then she returned by boat down the Nile to Alexandria. I have had much time to think over and over on what had happened, to try to understand why my wife was killed. She was a generous woman who never harmed anyone.' He looked confused, beaten. 'And why Miriam, whom we all cared for so much, should have wished her ill.

'I tried to recall what had been said at the dinner table. Verona had spoken of Egypt and her journey back down the Nile. Lucius asked her about a particular excursion, and she said she had wished to go, but had been unable because she had not been very well. She dismissed it as of no importance, only a quite usual complaint for her which had passed.'

His face was very white. He looked across at Lucius. 'I'm so sorry,' he said hoarsely. Then he faced forward again

'Yesterday evening I went and read her diary of the time, and found her reference to that day when she had written of the pain, and her distress, and then she had remembered Aiden's words of reassurance that it would all be well, if she kept her courage and told no one. And she had done exactly as he had said.' His voice dropped. 'Then at last I understood.'

Rathbone found himself hardly breathing, he was so intent upon Harry Stourbridge's white face and tight, aching voice.

'When she reached England again,' Stourbridge continued, 'she wrote and told me that during her stay with me she had become with child, and felt very well, and hoped that this time she would carry it until birth. I was overjoyed, for her even more than for myself.'

In the gallery a woman sobbed, her heart touched with pity, maybe with an empathy.

Rathbone glanced up at Miriam. She looked as if she had seen death face to face.

Harry Stourbridge did not look at her, or at Lucius, or at Aiden Campbell, but straight ahead of him into a vision of the past only he could see.

'In due time I heard that the child was delivered, a healthy boy, my son Lucius. I was the happiest man alive. Some short time after that I returned to duties in England, and saw him. He was beautiful, and so like my wife.' He could not continue. It took him several moments to regain even the barest mastery of his voice. When he spoke it was hoarse and little above a whisper.

'I loved him so much – I still do. The truth has no— has nothing to do with that. That will never change.' He took a deep breath and let it out in a choking sigh. 'But I now know that he is not my son, nor is he my wife's son . . .'

There was a shock wave around the room as if an earthquake had struck. Jurors sat paralysed. Even the judge seemed to grasp for his bench as if to hold himself steady.

Rathbone found his lips dry, his heart pounding. Harry Stourbridge looked across at Lucius. 'Forgive me,' he whispered. 'I have always loved you, and I always will.' He faced forward again, to attention. 'He is the baby my wife's brother, Aiden Campbell, begot by rape upon his twelve-year-old maid, Miriam Speake, so that I should have an heir, and his sister should not lose access to my fortune should I die in action, or from disease while abroad. She was always generous to him.'

There was a low rumble of fury around the room.

Aiden Campbell shot to his feet, but he found no words to deny what was written on every face.

Two ushers moved forward simultaneously to restrain him, should it become necessary.

Harry Stourbridge went on as if oblivious to them all. He could not leave his story unfinished. 'He murdered the midwife, so she would never tell, and he attempted to murder the mother also, but distraught, hysterical, she escaped. Perhaps she never knew if her baby lived or died – until at her own engagement party she saw Aiden wield a croquet mallet, swinging it high in jest, and memory returned to her, and with understanding so fearful she could only run from us all, and keep silence, even at the price of her life, rather than have anyone know, but above all Lucius himself, that he had fallen in love with his . . . own . . . mother.' He could no longer speak; in spite of all he could do, the tears spilled down his cheeks.

The noise in the court increased like the roar of a rising tide. A wave of pity and anger engulfed the room.

The ushers closed in on Aiden Campbell, perhaps to restrain him, perhaps even to protect him.

Rathbone felt dizzy. Dimly he saw Hester, and just beyond her shoulder, Monk, his face as shocked as hers.

He looked up at Miriam. Not for an instant now did he need to wonder if this was the truth. It was written in her eyes, her mouth, every angle of her body.

He turned back to Harry Stourbridge.

'Thank you,' he said quietly. 'No one here can presume to know what it must have cost you to say this. I don't know if Mr Tobias has any questions to ask you, but I have none.'

Tobias stood up, began to speak, and then stopped. He glanced at the jury, then back to the judge. 'I think, my lord, that in the interests of truth, some further detail is required. Terrible as this story is, there are . . .' he made a gesture of helplessness and left the rest unsaid.

Rathbone was still on his feet.

'I think now, my lord, that Mrs Gardiner has nothing left to protect. If I call her to the stand, she may be prepared to tell us the little we do not know.'

'By all means,' the judge agreed. 'If she is willing – and if she is able?' He turned to Stourbridge. 'Thank you sir, for your honesty. We need ask nothing further of you.'

Like a man walking through water, Harry Stourbridge went down the steps and stood for a moment in the middle of the floor. He looked up at the dock where Miriam had risen to her feet. There was a gentleness in his face which held the room in silence, a compassion and a gratitude that even in her anguish she could not have failed to recognise.

He waited while she came down, the gaoler standing aside as if he understood his duty was over.

Miriam stopped in front of Harry Stourbridge. Haltingly he reached out and touched her arm, so lightly she could barely have felt it. He smiled at her. She put her hand over his for an instant, then continued on her way to the steps of the witness stand, climbed up and turned to face Rathbone and the court.

'Mrs Gardiner,' Rathbone said quietly, 'I understand now why you preferred to face the rope for a crime you did not commit, rather than have Lucius Stourbridge learn the truth of his birth. But that is not now possible. Nor can Aiden Campbell any longer hide from his acts, or blame you for any part of them. I do not require you to relive a past which must be painful beyond our imagining, but justice necessitates that you tell the jury what you know of the deaths of James Treadwell and Verona Stourbridge.'

Miriam nodded very slightly, with just the barest acknowledgement, then in a quiet, drained voice she began.

'I ran from the croquet lawn. At first I did not care where I went, anywhere to be away from the house, alone – to try to realise what had happened, what it was I had remembered – if it could really be true. More than anything on earth, I did not want it to be.' She stopped for a moment.

'Of course – it was, but I did not fully accept it then. I ran to the stables and begged Treadwell to take me anywhere. I gave him my locket as payment. He was greedy, but not entirely a bad man. I asked him to drive me to Hampstead Heath. I didn't tell him why. I wanted to go back to where poor Mrs Bailey was killed, to remember what really happened – if the flash of recollection I had on the croquet lawn was even some kind of madness.'

Someone coughed and the noise made people start in the tingling silence.

'Aiden Campbell must have seen my recognition,' she went on. 'He also remembered, and perhaps knew where I would go. He followed us, and found us near the tree where Mrs Bailey's body was hidden. He had to kill Treadwell if he was going to kill me, or he'd have been blackmailed for the rest of his life. He struck Treadwell first. He caught him completely by surprise.

'I ran. I know the area better than he, because I lived near the Heath more recently, and for years. Perhaps desperation lent me speed. It was getting dark. I escaped him. After that I had no idea where to go or what to do. At last, in the morning, I went to Cleo Anderson . . . again. But this time I could not bear to tell even her what I knew.'

'And the death of Verona Stourbridge, after you were released back into the Stourbridges' custody?' Rathbone prompted her.

She looked at him. 'I couldn't tell anyone . . .'

'We understand. What do you know about Verona Stourbridge's death?'

'I believe she always thought Lucius was . . . an abandoned baby. She hid the truth from Major Stourbridge, but she had no knowledge of any crime, only her own deception, made from her despair that she would never bear a child for her husband. I know now that she knew it was Aiden's child, but not about me, or how he was concerned. She must have asked Aiden about it – and although he loved her, he could not afford to let her know the truth.' Her voice dropped. 'No matter how close they were, and they truly were, she might one day have told someone – she would have had to – to explain—' In spite of herself her eyes went to Lucius, sitting on the front benches, the tears running down his cheeks.

'I'm so sorry,' Miriam whispered. 'I'm so – so sorry . . .'

Rathbone turned to the judge.

'My lord, is it necessary to protract this any longer? May we adjourn for an hour or so, before we conclude? I have nothing further to ask, and I cannot believe Mr Tobias will pursue this any more.'

Tobias rose to his feet. 'I am quite willing, my lord. What

little remains can be dealt with after an adjournment. Major Stourbridge and his family have my deepest sympathy.'

'Very good.' The judge banged his gavel and after a moment's heavy stillness, people began to move.

Rathbone felt bruised, exhausted, as if he had made some great physical journey. He turned to Hester and Monk, who were coming towards him from the body of the court. Just behind them was a man with scruffy black hair and a beard that went in every direction. He was beaming with satisfaction, his eyes shining.

Hester smiled.

'You have achieved the impossible,' Monk said, holding out his hand to Rathbone.

Rathbone took it and held it hard for a few moments.

'We still have the matter of the medicines,' he warned.

'No, we don't!' Hester assured him. 'Mr Phillips here is the apothecary at the hospital. He has persuaded Fermin Thorpe that nothing is missing. It was all a matter of natural wastage, and a few rather careless entries in the books. No actual thefts at all. It was a mistake to have mentioned it.'

Rathbone was incredulous. 'How in heaven's name did you do that?' He regarded Phillips with interest, and a growing respect.

'Never enjoyed anything more,' Phillips said, grinning broadly. 'A little issue of one favour for another – resurrection, you might say!'

Monk looked at Hester narrowly.

She beamed back at him with complete innocence.

'Well done, Mr Phillips,' Rathbone said gratefully. 'I am much obliged.'

Headline hopes you have enjoyed THE TWISTED ROOT, and invites you to sample HALF MOON STREET, Anne Perry's compelling new novel in her Inspector Pitt series, now available from Headline . . .

Chapter One

The wraiths of mist curled up slowly from the grey and silver surface of the river, gleaming in the first light from the sun. To the right the arch of Lambeth Bridge rose dark against a pearly sky. Whatever barges followed the tide down towards the Port of London and the docks were still invisible in the dark and the September fog.

Superintendent Thomas Pitt stood on the stormy wet ledge of Horseferry Stairs and looked at the punt which nudged gently against the lowest step. It was moored now, but an hour and a half ago, when the constable had first seen it, it had not been. Not that a drifting boat was of any interest to the head of the Bow Street Police Station – it was what lay in it, grotesque, like some obscure parody of Millais's painting of Ophelia that captured his attention.

The constable averted his eyes, keeping them studiously on Pitt's face.

'Thought we should report it to you, sir.'

Pitt looked down at the body reclining in the punt, its wrists encased in manacles chained to the wooden sides, its ankles apart, chained also. The long green robes looked like a dress, but so torn and distorted it was impossible to tell its original shape. The knees were apart, the head thrown back, mimicking ecstasy. It was a feminine pose, but the body was unmistakably male. He had been in his mid-thirties, fair-haired, with good features and a well-trimmed moustache.

'I don't know why,' Pitt said quickly as the water slurped against the steps below him, perhaps the wash from some passing boat invisible in the coils of mist. 'This is not Bow Street area.'

The constable shifted uncomfortably. 'Scandal, Mr Pitt.' He still did not look at the boat or its occupant. 'Could get very nasty, sir. Best you're in at the beginning.'

Very carefully, so as not to slip on the river-wet stone, Pitt went further down. The melancholy sound of a foghorn drifted across the water, and from some unseen cargo barge a man's voice called out a warning. The answer was lost in the cloying vapour. Pitt looked again at the figure lying in the punt. It was impossible from this angle to see how he had died. There was no apparent wound, no weapon, and yet if he had died of a heart attack, or a seizure, then someone else had certainly had a grotesque part in leaving his corpse in such a way. Some family was going to begin a nightmare today. Perhaps life would never be quite the same for them again.

'I suppose you've sent for the surgeon?' Pitt asked.

'Yes, sir. Due any time now, I should think.' The constable swallowed and moved his feet, scraping his boots a little on the stone. 'Mr Pitt – sir.'

'Yes?' Pitt was still staring at the punt scraping its wooden prow on the steps and juggling a little with the wash of another boat.

'Weren't only the way 'e is that I called yer.'

Pitt caught something in the man's voice and swivelled to look up. 'Oh?'

'No, sir. I think as I might know 'oo 'e is, sir, which is goin' ter be very nasty, an' all.'

Pitt felt the river cold seep into him. 'Oh. Who do you think it is, Constable?'

'Sorry, sir. I think it might be a Monsewer Bonnard, 'oo was reported missing day afore yesterday, an' the French won't 'alf kick up a fuss if this is 'im.'

'The French?' Pitt said warily.

'Yes, sir. Missing from their embassy, 'e is.'

'And you think this is him?'

'Looks like it, Mr Pitt. Slender, fair 'air, good-lookin', small moustache, about five feet nine inches tall, an' a gent. Eccentric, by all accounts. Likes a bit of a party, theatricals an' the like.' His voice was heaving with incomprehension and disgust. 'Mixes with them aesthetes, as they calls 'emselves . . .'

Pitt was saved further comment by the clatter of hoofs and the rattle of wheels on the road above them, and a moment later the familiar figure of the police surgeon, top hat a trifle askew, came down the steps, bag in his hand. He looked beyond Pitt to the body in the punt, and his eyebrows rose.

'Another one of your scandals, Pitt?' he said drily. 'I don't envy you unravelling this one. Do you know who he is?' He let out a sigh as he reached the bottom step, standing precariously only a foot above the sucking water. 'Well, well. Didn't think there was much about human nature I didn't know, but I swear it's beyond me what some men will do to entertain themselves.' Very carefully he balanced his weight and moved over to stand in the punt. It rocked and pitched him forward, but he was ready for it. He kneeled down and started to examine the dead man.

Pitt found himself shivering, in spite of the fact that it was not really cold. He had sent for his assistant, Sergeant Tellman, but he had not yet arrived. Pitt looked back at the constable.

'Who found this, and what time?'

'I found it meself, sir. This is my beat along 'ere. I were goin' ter sit on the steps an' 'ave a bite to eat when I saw it. That were about 'alf-past five, sir. But o' course it could 'a bin there a lot longer, cause in the dark no one'd 'ave seen it.'

'But you saw it? Dark then, wasn't it?'

'More like 'eard it, bumpin', an' went ter see what it was. Shone me light on it, an' near 'ad a fit! I don't understand the gentry, an' that's a fact.'

'You think he's gentry?' Pitt was vaguely amused in spite of himself.

The constable screwed up his face. 'Where'd a working bloke get fancy clothes like that dress? It's velvet. An' you look at 'is 'ands. Never done a day's work wi' them.'

Pitt thought there was a strong element of prejudice in the constable's deductions, but it was good observation. He told him so.

'Thank you, sir,' the constable said with pleasure. He had aims of being a detective one day.

'You had better go to the French Embassy and fetch someone to see if they can identify him,' Pitt went on.

'Who – me, sir?' The constable was taken aback.

Pitt smiled at him. 'Yes. After all, you were the one alert enough to see the likeness. But you can wait and see what the surgeon says first.'

There were a few moments' silence, then the punt rocked a little, scraping against the stone. 'He was hit on the head with something very hard and rounded, like a truncheon,' the surgeon said distinctly. 'And I very much doubt it was an accident. He certainly didn't tie himself up like this.' He shook his head. 'God knows whether he put the clothes on, or someone else did. They're torn enough to indicate a struggle. Very difficult to do anything much with a dead body.'

Pitt had been expecting it, but it still came as a blow. Some part of him had been hoping it was an accident, which would be ugly and stupid, but not a crime. He also hoped profoundly it was not the missing French diplomat.

'You'd better see for yourself,' the surgeon offered. Pitt clambered inelegantly into the rocking punt and in the now clear, white light of sunrise, bent to examine the dead man carefully, detail by detail.

Cain His Brother

Anne Perry

Genevieve Stonefield's husband Angus has been missing for three days when she visits William Monk, a former police inspector turned private investigator. She is convinced Angus is dead, murdered by his twin brother Caleb. While her husband has long been a respected businessman, Caleb is a shadowy, dangerous figure living in the slums that border the Thames in Limehouse; the relationship between them, Monk is told, has often been violent, and Genevieve fears the worst.

Monk is not ready to assume a murder has taken place, let alone pinpoint a killer, though he quickly confirms that Angus has indeed vanished. But why did Caleb's woman Selina visit Angus's office the morning he disappeared? And why is Caleb so different from his impeccably behaved brother?

Without the authority or facilities of the police force behind him, Monk is thrown back on his own resources and the help of his friends, including his patroness Lady Callandra Daviot and nurse Hester Latterly, to bring one of the most bizarre and baffling cases he has ever encountered to its thrilling conclusion.

0 7472 4845 1

HEADLINE

The Demon Archer

Paul Doherty

The death of Lord Henry Fitzalan on the feast of St Matthew 1303 is a matter widely reported but little mourned. Infamous for his lecherous tendencies, his midnight trysts with a coven of witches and his boundless self-interest, he was a man of few friends. So when Hugh Corbett is asked to bring his murderer to justice it is not a matter of finding a suspect but of choosing between them.

Immediate suspicion falls on Lord Henry's chief verderer, Robert Verlian. His daughter had been the focus of Lord Henry's roving eye in the weeks before his death and he was not a man to take no for an answer. But the culprit could just as easily be Sir William, the dead man's younger brother. It is no secret that Sir William covets the Fitzalan estate – but would he kill to inherit it? The possibilities are endless, but the truth is more terrible than anyone could have imagined . . .

The best of its kind since the death of Ellis Peters' *Time Out*

Supremely evocative, scrupulously researched portrait . . . vivid, intricately crafted whodunnit' *Publishers Weekly*

Wholly excellent' *Prima*

0 7472 6074 5

HEADLINE

SNAKEHEA

Te..... years.
Twelve..... copies sold.
One ..... age superspy.

In the decade since it was first launched, the Alex Rider series has become a global phenomenon, setting the standard for a whole new genre of spy and action novels and inspiring countless new readers.

In these anniversary editions, Anthony Horowitz gives the reader exclusive behind-the-scenes access to the creation of the world of Alex Rider. Anthony says, "I'm so happy to see these new editions ... all eight of them. If you're only just discovering the world of Alex Rider, you've got a lot of catching up to do. Enjoy the ride!"

Anthony Horowitz is one of the most popular contemporary children's writers. Both The Power of Five and Alex Rider are number one bestselling series enjoyed by millions of readers worldwide.

When Anthony launched the Alex Rider series in 2000 he created a phenomenon in children's books, spurring a new trend of junior spy books and inspiring thousands of previously reluctant readers. Hailed as a reading hero, Anthony has also won many major awards, including the Bookseller Association/Nielsen Author of the Year Award, the Children's Book of the Year Award at the British Book Awards, and the Red House Children's Book Award. The first Alex Rider adventure, *Stormbreaker*, was made into a blockbuster movie in 2006.

Anthony's other titles for Walker Books include the Diamond Brothers mysteries; *Groosham Grange* and its sequel, *Return to Groosham Grange*; *The Devil and His Boy*; *Granny* and *The Switch*. His new collection of horror stories, *More Bloody Horowitz*, is coming soon. Anthony also writes extensively for TV, with programmes including *Foyle's War*, *Midsomer Murders*, *Poirot* and most recently *Collision*. He is married to television producer Jill Green and lives in London with his sons, Nicholas and Cassian, and their dog, Loony.

You can find out more about Anthony and his books at:

www.anthonyhorowitz.com

www.alexrider.com

www.powerof5.co.uk

Titles by Anthony Horowitz

SNAKEHEAD

ANTHONY HOROWITZ

WALKER
BOOKS

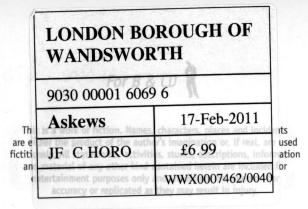

First published 2007 by Walker Books Ltd
87 Vauxhall Walk, London SE11 5HJ

First published in paperback 2008

6 8 10 9 7 5

Text © 2007 Anthony Horowitz
Coda © 2008 Anthony Horowitz
Afterword © 2010 Stormbreaker Productions Ltd
Cover design by Walker Books Ltd
Trademarks 2007 Alex Rider™,
Boy with Torch Logo™ © 2010 Stormbreaker Productions Ltd

The right of Anthony Horowitz to be identified as author
of this work has been asserted by him in accordance with
the Copyright, Designs and Patents Act 1988

This book has been typeset in Officina Sans

Printed and bound in Great Britain by Clays Ltd, St Ives plc

British Library Cataloguing in Publication Data:
a catalogue record for this book
is available from the British Library

ISBN 978-1-4063-1039-9 UK
ISBN 978-1-4063-2566-9 Aus/NZ

www.walker.co.uk
www.walkerbooks.com.au

CONTENTS

DOWN TO EARTH

Splashdown.

Alex Rider would never forget the moment of impact, the first shock as the parachute opened and the second – more jolting still – as the module that had carried him back from outer space crashed into the sea. Was it his imagination or was there steam rising up all around him? Maybe it was sea spray. It didn't matter. He was back. That was all he cared about. He had made it. He was still alive.

He was lying on his back, crammed into the tiny capsule with his knees tucked into his chest. Half closing his eyes, Alex experienced a moment of extraordinary stillness. He was motionless. His fists were clenched. He wasn't breathing. Already he found it impossible to believe that the events that had led to his journey into space had really taken place. He tried to imagine himself hurtling around the earth at seventeen and a half thousand miles an hour. It couldn't have happened. It had surely all been part of some incredible dream.

Slowly he forced himself to unwind. He lifted an arm; it rose normally. He could feel the muscle working. Just minutes before, he had been in zero gravity. But as he rested, trying to collect his thoughts, he realized that once again his body belonged to him.

Alex wasn't sure how long he was on his own, floating in the sea somewhere ... it could have been anywhere in the world. But when things happened, they happened very quickly. First, there was the hammering of helicopter blades. Then the whoop of a siren. He could see very little out of the window – just the rise and fall of the ocean – but suddenly there was a palm slamming against the glass. A scuba-diver. A few seconds later, the capsule was opened from outside. Fresh air came rushing in, and to Alex it smelled delicious. At the same time, a figure loomed over him, his body wrapped in neoprene, his eyes behind a mask.

"Are you OK?"

Alex could hardly make out the words, there was so much noise outside. Did the diver have an American accent?

"I'm fine," he managed to shout back. But it wasn't true. He was beginning to feel sick, and there was a shooting pain behind his eyes.

"Don't worry! We'll soon have you out of there..."

It took them a while. Alex had only been in space a short time but he'd never had any physical training for it, and now his muscles were turning against him, reluctant to start pulling their own weight. He had to be manhandled out of the capsule, into the blinding sun of a Pacific morning. Everything was chaotic. There was a helicopter overhead, the blades beating at the ocean and forming patterns that rippled and vibrated. Alex turned his head and saw – impossibly – an aircraft carrier as big as a mountain looming out of the water less than a quarter of a mile away. It was flying the Stars and Stripes. So he had been right about the diver. He must have landed somewhere off the coast of America.

There were two more divers in the water, bobbing up and down next to the capsule, and Alex could see a fourth man leaning out of the helicopter directly above him. He knew what was going to happen and he didn't resist. First a loop of cable was passed around his chest and connected. He felt it tighten under his arms, and then he was rising into the air, still in his Ark Angel uniform, dangling like a blue-suited puppet as he was winched up.

And already they knew. He had glimpsed it in the eyes of the diver who had spoken to him. The disbelief. These men – the helicopter, the aircraft carrier – had been rushed out to rendezvous with a module that had just re-entered the earth's atmosphere. And inside, they had found a boy. A fourteen-year-old had just plummeted a hundred miles from outer space. These men would be sworn to secrecy, of course. MI6 would see to that. They would never talk about what had happened. But nor would they forget it.

There was a medical officer waiting for him on board the USS *Kitty Hawk*, the ship that had been diverted to pick him up. His name was Josh Cook and he was forty years old, black with wire frame glasses and a pleasant, softly spoken manner. He helped Alex out of his tracksuit and stayed with him when Alex finally did throw up. It turned out that he'd dealt with astronauts before.

"They're all sick when they come down," he explained. "It goes with the territory. Or maybe I should say terra firma. You've certainly come down to earth. You'll be fine by tomorrow morning."

"Where am I?" Alex asked.

"You're about a hundred miles off the east coast of Australia. We were on a training exercise when we got a red alert that you were on your way down."

"So what happens now?"

"Now you have a shower and get some sleep. You're in luck. We've got a mattress made out of memory foam. It was actually developed by NASA. It'll give your muscles a chance to get used to being back in full gravity."

Alex had been given a private cabin in the medical department of the *Kitty Hawk* – in fact a fully equipped "hospital at sea" with sixty-five beds, an operating theatre, a pharmacy and everything else

12

that five and a half thousand sailors might need. The cabin wasn't huge, but he suspected that nobody else on the *Kitty Hawk* would have this much space. Cook went over to the corner and pulled back a plastic curtain to reveal a shower cubicle.

"You may find it difficult to walk," he explained. "You're going to be unsteady on your feet for at least twenty-four hours. If you like, I can wait until you've showered."

"I'll be OK," Alex said.

"All right." Cook smiled and opened the main door. But before he left, he looked back at Alex. "You know – every man and woman on this ship is talking about you," he said. "There are a whole pile of questions I'd like to ask you, but I'm under strict orders from the captain to keep my mouth shut. Even so, I want you to know that I've been at sea for a long, long time and I've never encountered anything like this. A kid in outer space!" He nodded. "I hope you have a good rest. There's a call button beside the bed if you need anything."

It took Alex ten minutes to get into the shower. He had completely lost his sense of balance, and the roll of the ship didn't help. He turned the temperature up as high as he could bear and stood under the steaming water, enjoying the rush of it over his shoulders and through his hair. Then he dried himself and got into bed. The memory foam was only a few centimetres thick but it seemed to mould itself to the shape of his body exactly.

He fell almost instantly into a deep but troubled sleep.

He didn't dream about the Ark Angel space station or his knife fight with Kaspar, the crazed eco-terrorist who had been determined to kill him even though it was clear that all was lost. Nor did he dream about Nikolei Drevin, the billionaire who had been behind it all.

But it did seem to him that, in the middle of his sleep, he heard the whisper of voices which he didn't recognize but which, somehow, he still knew. Old friends. Or old enemies. It didn't matter which, because he couldn't make out what they were saying; and anyway, a moment later they were swept away down the dark river of his sleep.

Perhaps it was a premonition.

Because three weeks before, seven men had met in a room in London to discuss an operation that would make them millions of pounds and would change the shape of the world. And although Alex had never met any of them, he certainly knew who they were.

Scorpia were back.

"DEATH IS NOT THE END"

It was the sort of building you could walk past without noticing: three storeys high, painted white, with perfectly trimmed ivy climbing up to the roof. It stood about halfway down Sloane Street in Belgravia, just round the corner from Harrods, and was one of the most expensive addresses in London. On one side there was a jewellery shop and on the other an Italian fashion boutique – but the customers who came here would no longer be needing either. A single step led up to a door painted black, and there was a window which contained an urn, a vase of fresh flowers and nothing else.

The name of the place was written in discreet gold letters:

Reed and Kelly
FUNERAL DIRECTORS
Death is not the End

At half past ten on a bright October morning, exactly three weeks before Alex landed in the Pacific Ocean, a black Lexus LS 430 four-door saloon drew up outside the front entrance. The car had been carefully chosen. It was a luxury model but there was nothing too special about it, nothing to attract attention. The arrival had also been exactly timed. In the past fifteen minutes, three other vehicles and a taxi had pulled up briefly, and their passengers, either singly or in pairs, had got out, crossed the pavement and entered the parlour. If anyone had been watching, they would have assumed that a large family had gathered to make the final arrangements for someone who had recently departed.

The last person to arrive was a powerfully built man with massive shoulders and a shaven head. There was something quite brutal about his face, with its small, squashed nose, thick lips and muddy brown eyes. But his clothes were immaculate. He was wearing a dark suit, a tailored silk shirt and a cashmere coat, unbuttoned. There was a heavy platinum ring on his fourth finger. He had been smoking a cigar, but as he stepped from the car he dropped it and ground it out with a brilliantly polished shoe. Without looking left or right, he crossed the pavement and entered the building. An old-fashioned bell on a spring jangled as the door opened and closed.

He found himself in a wood-panelled reception

room, where an elderly, grey-haired man sat with folded hands behind a narrow desk. He looked at the new arrival with a mixture of sympathy and politeness.

"Good morning," he said. "How can we be of service?"

"I have come about a death," the visitor replied.

"Someone close to you?"

"My brother. But I hadn't seen him for some years."

"You have my condolences."

The same words had already been spoken six times that morning. If even one syllable had been changed, the bald man would have turned round and left. But he knew now that the building was secure. The meeting that had been arranged just twenty-four hours earlier could go ahead.

The grey-haired man leant forward and pressed a button concealed under the desk. At once, a section of the wooden panelling clicked open to reveal a staircase leading up to the first floor.

Reed and Kelly was a real business. There once had been a Jonathan Reed and a Sebastian Kelly, and for more than fifty years they had arranged funerals and cremations until, at last, the time came to arrange their own. After that, the undertaker's had been purchased by a perfectly legitimate company, registered in Zurich, and it had continued to provide a first-class service for anyone who lived – or rather, *had* lived – in the area. But that was no longer the only purpose of the building in Sloane Street. It had also become the London headquarters of the international criminal organization that went by the name of Scorpia.

The name stood for sabotage, corruption, intelligence and assassination: its four main activities. The organization had been formed some twenty years before in Paris, its members being spies and assassins from different intelligence networks around the world who had decided to go into business for themselves. To begin with, there had been twelve of them. Then one had died of cancer and two had been murdered. The other nine had congratulated themselves on surviving so long with so few casualties.

But recently things had taken a turn for the worse. The oldest member had made the foolish and inexplicable decision to retire, which had, of course, led to his being murdered immediately. But his successor, a woman called Julia Rothman, had also been killed. That had been at the end of an operation – Invisible Sword – which had gone catastrophically wrong. In many ways this was the lowest point in Scorpia's history, and there were many who thought that the organization would never recover. After all, the agent who had beaten them, destroyed the operation and caused the death of Mrs Rothman had been fourteen years old.

However, Scorpia had not given in. They had

taken swift revenge on the boy and gone straight back to work. Invisible Sword was just one of many projects needing their attention, for they were in constant demand from governments, terrorist groups, big business ... in fact, anyone who could pay. And now they were active once again. They had come to this address in London to discuss a relatively small assignment but one that would net them ten million pounds, to be paid in uncut diamonds – easier to carry and harder to trace than banknotes.

The stairs led to a short corridor on the first floor with a single door at the end. One television camera had watched the bald man on his way up. A second followed him as he stepped onto a strange metal platform in front of the door and looked into a glass panel set in the wall. Behind the glass, there was a biometric scanner which took an instant image of the unique pattern of blood vessels on the retina in his eye and matched it against a computer at the reception desk below. Had an enemy agent tried to gain access to the room, he would have triggered a ten-thousand-volt electric charge through the metal floor plate, instantly incinerating him. But this was no enemy. The man's name was Zeljan Kurst and he had been with Scorpia from the beginning. The door slid open and he went in.

He found himself in a long, narrow room with three windows covered by blinds, and plain white walls with no decoration of any kind. There was a glass table surrounded by leather chairs and no sign of any pens, paper or printed documents. Nothing was ever written down at these meetings. Nor was anything recorded. There were six men waiting for him as he took his place at the head of the table. Following the disaster of Invisible Sword, there were now just seven of them left.

"Good morning, gentlemen," Kurst began. He spoke with a strange, mid European accent. The last word had sounded like "chintlemen". All the men at the table were equal partners but he was currently the acting head. A new chief executive was chosen as fresh projects arrived.

Nobody replied. These people were not friends. They had nothing to say to each other outside the work at hand.

"We have been given a most interesting and challenging assignment," Kurst went on. "I need hardly remind you that our reputation was quite seriously damaged by our last failure, and as well as providing us with a much-needed financial injection following the heavy losses we sustained on Invisible Sword, this project will suffice to put us back on the map. Our task is this. We are to assassinate eight extremely wealthy and influential people five weeks from now. They will all be together in one place, which provides us with the ideal opportunity. It has been left to us to decide on the method."

His eyes flickered around the table as he waited for a response. Zeljan Kurst had been the head of the police force in Yugoslavia during the 1980s and had been famous for his love of classical music – particularly Mozart – and extreme violence. It was said that he would interrogate prisoners with either an opera or a symphony playing in the background and that those who survived the ordeal would never be able to listen to that piece of music again. But he had guessed that one day his country would break up, and he had decided to quit before he was out of a job. And so he had changed sides. He had no family, no friends and nowhere he could call home. He needed work and he knew that Scorpia would make him extremely rich.

"You will have read in the newspapers," he continued, "that the G8 summit is taking place in Rome this November. This is a meeting of the eight most powerful heads of government, and as usual they will talk a great deal, have their photographs taken, consume a lot of expensive food and wine ... and do absolutely nothing. They are of no interest to us. They are, in effect, irrelevant.

"However, at the same time, another conference will be taking place on the other side of the world. It has been arranged in direct competition with the G8 summit, and you might say that the timing is something of a publicity stunt. Nonetheless, it has already attracted much more attention than G8. Indeed, the politicians have almost been forgotten.

21

Instead, the eyes of the world are on Reef Island, just off the coast of north-west Australia in the Timor Sea.

"The press have given this alternative summit a name: Reef Encounter. A group of eight people will be coming together, and their names will be known to you. One of them is a pop singer called Rob Goldman. He has apparently raised millions for charity with concerts all over the world. Another is a billionaire, considered by many to be the richest man on the planet. He created a huge property empire but is now giving his fortune away to developing countries. There is an ex-president of the United States. A famous Hollywood actress, Eve Taylor. She owns the island. And so on." Kurst didn't even try to keep the contempt out of his voice. "They are amateurs, do-gooders – but they are also powerful and popular, which makes them dangerous.

"Their aim, as they put it, is 'to make poverty history'. In order to achieve this, they have made certain demands, including the cancellation of world debt. They want millions of dollars to be sent to Africa to fight Aids and malaria. They have called for an end to fighting in the Middle East. It will come as no surprise to those of us in this room that there are many governments and businesses who do not agree with these aims. After all, it is not possible to give to the poor without taking from the rich; and anyway, poverty has its uses.

It keeps people in their place. It also helps to hold prices down.

"A representative from one of the G8 governments contacted us six weeks ago. He has decided that Reef Encounter should end the moment it begins – certainly before any of these meddlers can address the television cameras of the world – and that is our assignment. Disrupting the conference is not enough. All eight are to be killed. The fact that they will all be in one place at one time makes it easier for us. Not one of them must leave Reef Island alive."

One of the other men leant forward. His name was Levi Kroll. He was an Israeli, about fifty years old. Very little of his face could be seen. Most of it was covered by a beard and there was a patch over the eye which he had once, by accident, shot out. "It is a simple matter," he rasped. "I could go out this afternoon and hire an Apache helicopter gunship. Let us say two thousand rounds of 30mm cannon fire and a few Hellfire air-to-ground laser-guided missiles, and this conference would no longer exist."

"Unfortunately it isn't quite as straightforward as that," Kurst replied. "As I said in my opening remarks, this is a particularly challenging assignment because our client does not wish the Reef Island eight to become martyrs. If they were seen to be assassinated, it would only add weight to their cause. And so he has specified that the deaths must seem accidental. In fact, this is critical. There cannot be even the tiniest amount of doubt or suspicion."

There was a soft murmur around the table as the other members of Scorpia took this new information on board. To kill one person in a way that would arouse no suspicion was simple. But to do the same for eight people on a remote island that would doubtless have a tight security system – that was quite another matter.

"There are certain chemical nerve agents..." someone muttered. He was French, exquisitely dressed with a black silk handkerchief poking out of his top pocket. His voice was matter-of-fact.

"How about R5?" a man called Mikato suggested. He was Japanese, with a diamond set in one tooth and – it was rumoured – yakuza tattoos all over his body. "It's the virus we supplied to Herod Sayle. Perhaps we could feed it into the island's water supply."

Kurst shook his head. "Gentlemen, both of these methods would be effective but still might show up in the subsequent investigation. What we require is a natural disaster, but one that we control. We need to eliminate the entire island with everybody on it, but in such a way that no questions will ever be asked."

He paused, then turned to the man sitting opposite him at the end of the table. "Major Yu?" he asked. "Have you given the matter your consideration?"

"Absolutely."

Major Winston Yu was at least sixty years old and although he still had a full head of hair, it had turned completely white – unusual in a Chinese man. The hair looked artificial, cut in a schoolboy style with a straight fringe above the eyes and the whole thing perched on top of a head that was yellow and waxy and that had shrunk like an over-ripe fruit. He was the least impressive person in the room, with circular glasses, thin lips and hands that would have been small on a young boy. Everything about him was somehow delicate. He had been sitting very still at the table, as if afraid he might break. A walking stick with a silver scorpion entwined around the handle rested against his chair. He was wearing a white suit and pale grey gloves.

"I have spent a great deal of time working on this operation," he continued. He had a perfect English accent. "And I am happy to report that although, on the face of it, this seems to be a rather difficult business, we have been blessed with three very fortunate circumstances. First, this island, Reef Island, is in exactly the right place. Five weeks from now is exactly the right moment. And finally, the weapon that we require just happens to be here in England, less than thirty miles from where we are sitting."

"And what weapon is that?" the Frenchman demanded.

"It's a bomb. But a very special bomb – a proto-type. As far as I know, there is only one in existence. The British have given it a code name. They call it Royal Blue."

"Major Yu is absolutely right," Kurst cut in. "Royal Blue is currently in a highly secret weapons facility just outside London. That is why I chose to hold the meeting here today. The building has been under surveillance for the past month and a team is already waiting on standby. By the end of the week, the bomb will be in our possession. After that, Major Yu, I am placing this operation in your hands."

Major Yu nodded slowly.

"With respect, Mr Kurst." It was Levi Kroll speak-ing. His voice was ugly and there was very little respect in it. "I was under the impression that *I* would be in command of the next operation."

"I am afraid you will have to wait, Mr Kroll. Once Royal Blue is in our hands, it will be flown to Bangkok and then carried by sea to its final des-tination. This is a region of the world where you have no working experience. For Major Yu, however, it is another matter. Over the past two decades he has been active in Bangkok, Jakarta, Bali and Lombok. He also has a base in northern Australia. He controls a huge criminal network – his *shetou*, or snakehead. They will smuggle the weapon for us. Major Yu's snakehead is a formidable organization, and in this instance it is best suited to our needs."

The Israeli nodded briefly. "You are right. I apologize for my interruption."

"I accept your apology," Kurst replied, although he didn't. It occurred to him that one day Levi Kroll might have to go. The man spoke too often without thinking first. "Major?"

There was little left to be said. Winston Yu took off his glasses and polished them with his gloved fingers. His eyes were a strange, almost metallic grey with lids that folded in on themselves. "I will contact my people in Bangkok and Jakarta," he muttered. "I will warn them that the machine will soon be on its way. The delivery system has already been constructed close to Reef Island. As to this conference with its high ideals, you need have no worries. I am very happy to assure you that it will never take place."

At six o'clock in the evening, two days later, a blue Renault Megane turned off the M11 motorway, taking an exit marked SERVICE VEHICLES ONLY. There are many such exits in the British motorway system. Thousands of vehicles roar past them every hour and the drivers never give them a second glance. And indeed, the great majority are completely innocent, leading to works depots or police traffic control centres. But the motorway system has its secrets too. As the Megane made its way slowly forward and came to a shuddering halt in front of what looked like a single-storey office

27

compound, it was tracked by three television cameras and the security men inside went into immediate alert.

The building was in fact a laboratory and weapons research centre, belonging to the Ministry of Defence. Very few people knew of its existence and even fewer were allowed in or out. The car that had just arrived was unauthorized and the security men – recruited from the special forces – should have instantly raised the alarm. That was the protocol.

But the Renault Megane is one of the most inno-cent and ordinary of family cars, and this one had clearly been involved in a bad accident. The front windscreen had shattered. The bonnet was crum-pled and steam was rising from the grille. A man wearing a green anorak and a cap was in the driv-ing seat; there was a woman next to him with blood pouring down the side of her face. Worse than that, there were two small children in the back, and although the image on the screen was a little fuzzy, they seemed to be in a bad way. Neither of them was moving. The woman managed to get out of the car, but then she collapsed. Her husband sat where he was, as if dazed.

Two of the security men ran out to them. It was human nature. Here was a young family that needed help; and anyway, it wasn't that much of a security risk. The front door of the building swung shut behind them and would need a seven-digit code to reopen. Both men carried radio transmitters and 9mm Browning automatic pistols underneath their jackets. The Browning is an old weapon but a very reliable one, a favourite with the SAS.

The woman was still lying on the ground. The man who had been driving managed to open the door as the two guards approached.

"What happened?" one of them called out.

It was only now, when it was too late, that they began to realize that none of this added up. A car that had crashed on the motorway would have simply pulled onto the hard shoulder – if it had been able to drive at all. And how come it was only this one car, with these four people, that had been involved? Where were the other vehicles? Where were the police? But any last doubts were removed when the two security men reached the car. The two children on the back seat were dummies. With their cheap wigs and plastic smiles they were like something out of a nightmare.

The woman on the ground twisted round, a machine gun appearing in her hand. She shot the first of the security men in the chest. The second was moving quickly, reaching for his own weapon, taking up a combat stance. He never had a chance. The driver had been balancing a silenced Micro Uzi sub-machine gun on his lap. He tilted it and pulled the trigger. The gun barely whispered as it fired twenty rounds in less than a second. The guard was flung away.

The couple were already up and running towards the building. They couldn't get in yet, but they didn't need to. They made their way towards the back, where a silver box about two metres square had been attached to the brickwork. The man was carrying a toolkit which he had brought from the car. The woman stopped briefly and fired three times, taking out all the cameras. At that moment, an ambulance appeared, driving up from the motorway. It drew in behind the parked Megane.

The next phase of the mission took very little time. The facility was equipped with a standard CBR air filtration system – the letters stood for chemical, biological and radiological. It was designed to counter an enemy attack, but now the exact opposite was about to happen as the enemy turned the system against itself. The man took a miniaturized oxyacetylene torch out of his toolbox and used it to burn out the screws. This allowed him to unfasten a metal panel, revealing a complicated tangle of pipes and wires. From somewhere inside his anorak he produced a gas mask which he strapped over his face. He reached back into his toolbox and took out a metal vial, a few centimetres long, with a nozzle and a spike. He knew exactly what he was doing. Using the heel of his hand, he jammed the spike into one of the pipes. Finally he turned the nozzle.

The hiss was almost inaudible as a stream of potassium cyanide mixed with the air circulating inside the building. Meanwhile, four men dressed as paramedics but all wearing gas masks had approached the front entrance. One of them pressed a magnetized box no bigger than a cigarette packet against the lock. He stepped back. There was an explosion and the door swung open.

It was early evening and only half a dozen people were still working inside the facility. Most of them were technicians; one was the head of security. He had been trying to make an emergency call when the gas had hit him. He was lying on the floor, his face twisted in agony. The receiver was still in his hand.

Across the entrance hall, down a corridor and through a door marked RESTRICTED AREA: the four paramedics knew exactly where they were going. The bomb was in front of them. It looked remarkably old-fashioned, like something out of the Second World War: a huge metal cylinder, silver in colour, flat at one end, pointed at the other. Only a data screen built into the side and a series of digital controls brought it into the twenty-first century. It was strapped down on a power-assisted trolley and the whole thing would fit inside the ambulance with just inches to spare. But that, of course, was why the ambulance had been chosen.

They guided it back down the corridor and out through the front door. The ambulance was equipped with a ramp and the bomb rolled smoothly into the back, allowing room for the driver and one passenger in the front. The other three men and the woman climbed into the car. The dummies were left behind. The entire operation had taken eight and a half minutes. Thirty seconds less than planned.

An hour later, by the time the alarm had been raised in London and other parts of the country, everyone involved had disappeared. They had discarded the wigs, contact lenses and facial padding that had completely changed their appearance. The two vehicles had been incinerated.

And the weapon known as Royal Blue had already begun its journey east.

VISA PROBLEMS

"Alex Rider."

The blind man spoke the two words as if they had only just occurred to him. He let them roll over his tongue, tasting them like a fine wine. He was sitting in a soft leather armchair, the sort of furniture that would have been normal in an executive office but which was surprising in a plane, twenty-five thousand feet above Adelaide. The plane was a Gulfstream V executive jet which had been specially adapted for its current use, equipped with a kitchen and bathroom, a satellite link for worldwide communications, a forty-inch plasma TV connected to three twenty-four-hour news services and a bank of computers. There was even a basket for Garth, the blind man's guide dog.

The man's name was Ethan Brooke and he was the chief executive of the Covert Action Division of ASIS – the Australian Secret Intelligence Service. His department was inevitably known as CAD, but only by those who worked in it.

Very few others even knew it existed.

Brooke was a large man, in his mid fifties, with sand-coloured hair and ruddy, weather-beaten cheeks that suggested years spent outdoors. He had been a soldier, a lieutenant colonel with the commandos, until a landmine in East Timor had sent him first into hospital for three months and then into a new career in intelligence. He wore Armani sunglasses, tinted silver, rather than the traditional black glasses of a blind man, and his clothes were casual: jeans, a jacket and an open-necked shirt. A senior minister in the Australian defence department had once complained about the way Brooke dressed. That same minister was now carrying luggage in a three-star Sydney hotel.

Brooke was not alone. Sitting opposite him was a man almost half his age, slim, with short, fair hair. He was wearing a suit. Marc Damon had applied to join Australian intelligence the day after he had left university. He had done this by breaking into the headquarters of ASIS in Canberra and leaving his application on Brooke's desk. The two of them had now worked together for six years.

It was Damon who had produced the file – marked TOP SECRET: CAD EYES ONLY – that lay on the table between them. Although its contents had been translated into Braille, Brooke no longer had any need to refer to them. He had read the report once and had instantly memorized it. He now knew everything he needed about the boy called

Alex Rider. The only part that was missing from his consciousness was a true picture of the fourteen-year-old. There was a photograph attached to the cover, but as always he had been forced to rely on the official report:

PHYSICAL DESCRIPTION/ATTRIBUTES
Height: five feet four inches, still short for his age, but this adds to his operational value.
Weight: one hundred and twenty pounds.
Hair colour: fair.
Eyes: brown.
Physical condition: excellent, but may have been compromised by his recent injury (see *Scorpia* file).
Skills: has been learning karate since the age of six and has reached first *Kyu* grade (black belt). He is known to be fluent in two languages – French and Spanish – and is also proficient in German.
Weapons training: none.
Progress at school: has been slow, with negative feedback from many of his teachers. Spring and summer term reports from Brookland School are attached. However, it must be remembered that he has been absent from class for much of the past eight months.

PSYCHOLOGICAL PROFILE

AR was recruited by MI6 Special Operations in March of this year, aged fourteen years and two months. His father was John Rider – alias Hunter – who was killed in action. His mother died at the same time and he was brought up by his uncle, Ian Rider, also an active agent with MI6 before his death earlier this year.

It seems certain that the boy was physically and mentally prepared for intelligence work from the earliest age. Quite apart from the languages and martial arts, Ian Rider equipped him with many skills, including fencing, mountain climbing, white water rafting and scuba-diving.

And yet, despite his obvious aptitude for intelligence work (see below), AR has shown little enthusiasm for it. Like most teenagers, he is not a patriot and has no interest in politics. MI6 (SO) found it necessary to coerce him to work for them on at least two occasions.

He is popular at school – when he is there. Hobbies include football (Chelsea supporter), tennis, music and cinema. Evident interest in girls – see separate file on *Sabina Pleasure* and report by CIA operative Tamara Knight. Lives with American housekeeper, Jack Starbright (note: despite first name, Jack is female). No ambitions to follow his father and uncle into intelligence.

PAST ASSIGNMENTS – ACTIVE SERVICE
The British secret service refuses to admit that it has ever employed a juvenile, and so it has been difficult to draw together any concrete evidence of AR's record as an agent in the field. We believe, however, that he has worked for them on at least four occasions. He has also been seconded to the USA, where he has been employed by the CIA with equal success at least twice.

UK: See *Herod Sayle*: Sayle Enterprises, Cornwall; *Dr Hugo Grief*: Point Blanc Academy, France; *Damian Cray*: Cray Software Technology, Amsterdam; *Julia Rothman* (Scorpia executive): *Operation Invisible Sword*, London.

USA: FILES CLOSED. Possible links with *General Alexei Sarov*: Skeleton Key, Cuba; *Nikolei Drevin*: Flamingo Bay, Caribbean (termination of *Ark Angel* project).

Although it has so far proved impossible to confirm details, it would appear that in the space of one year AR has been involved in six major assignments, succeeding against impossible odds. He has survived assassination attempts by both Scorpia and the Chinese triads.

Current status: available.

Footnote: Last year the FBI attempted to recruit a teenage agent to combat drug syndicates operating out of Miami. The boy was killed almost immediately. The experiment has not been repeated.

Secret service files are the same the world over. They are written by people who live in a very black and white world and who, by and large, have no time for creative imagination – certainly not if it gets in the way of the facts. The various pages on Alex Rider had given Brooke a vague impression of the boy. They had certainly been enough to set his mind working. But he suspected that they left out as much as they revealed.

"He's in Australia," he murmured.

"Yes, sir." Damon nodded. "He dropped in on us from outer space."

Brooke smiled. "You know, if anyone else had told me that, I'd swear they were yanking my chain. He really went into space?"

"He was pulled out of the sea a hundred miles off the east coast. He was sitting in the re-entry module of a Soyuz-Fregat. Of course, the Americans aren't telling us anything. But it's probably no coincidence that according to NIWO, the Ark

Angel space station blew up at around the same time."

NIWO is the National Intelligence Watch Office. It employs around two thousand people who keep up a constant surveillance on everything happening in the world – and outside it.

"That was Drevin's big idea," Brooke muttered. "A space hotel."

"Yes, sir."

"I always had a feeling he was up to no good."

There was a moment of turbulence and the plane dipped down. The dog, in his basket, whined. He never had cared much for flying. But then they steadied and continued in their arc over the clouds, heading north-east to Sydney.

"You think we can use him?" Brooke demanded.

"Alex Rider doesn't like being used," Damon replied. "And from what I've read, there's no way he's going to volunteer. But it did occur to me that if we could find some sort of leverage, he'd be perfect for what we need. Put a kid into the pipeline and nobody's going to suspect a thing. It's exactly the same reason the Americans sent him to Skeleton Key – and it worked for them."

"Where is he now?"

"They're flying him over to Perth, sir. A bit of a hike but they wanted him somewhere safe and they've settled on SAS HQ at Swanbourne. He's going to need a couple of days to wind down."

Brooke fell silent. With his eyes permanently

covered, it was always difficult to work out what he was thinking; but Damon knew that he would be turning over all the possibilities, that he would come very quickly to a decision and stick by it. Maybe there was no way that ASIS could persuade this English kid to work for them. But if there was a single weakness, anything they could use to their advantage, his boss would find it.

A moment later, Brooke nodded. "We could pair him with Ash," he said.

And there it was. Simple but brilliant.

"Ash is in Singapore," Damon said.

"Operational?"

"A routine assignment."

"As of now he's reassigned. We'll put the two of them together and send them in. They'll make a perfect team."

Damon couldn't help smiling. Alex Rider would work with the agent they all called Ash. But there was just one problem.

"You think Ash will work with a teenager?" he asked.

"He will if this kid's as good as everyone says he is."

"He'll need proof."

This time it was Brooke's turn to smile. "Leave that to me."

The SAS compound at Swanbourne is a few miles south-west of Perth and has the appearance of a

40

low-rise holiday village, although perhaps one with more security than most. It stretches out next to the white sand and blue water of the Indian Ocean, sheltered from public view by a series of sand dunes. The buildings are clean, modern and unremarkable. But for the rise and fall of the barrier at the main gate, the military vehicles passing in and out, and the occasional sighting of men in khaki with sand-coloured berets, it would be hard to believe that this is the headquarters of Australia's toughest and most elite fighting force.

Alex Rider stood at the window of his room looking out over the main square with the indoor shooting range on one side and the gymnasium and fitness centre on the other. He wanted to go home and wondered how long they were going to keep him here. Certainly his stay on the *Kitty Hawk* had been short enough. He hadn't even had time to eat breakfast before he had been bundled into a Hawkeye jet, an oxygen mask strapped over his face, and then blasted off back into the sky. Nobody had even told him where they were taking him, but he had seen the name written in large letters on the airport terminal: PERTH. There had been a jeep parked on the runway, and the next thing he knew he was bouncing through the very ordinary-looking suburb of Swanbourne. The jeep drove into the SAS compound and stopped. A single soldier was waiting for him, his eyes shielded by sunglasses, his mouth a straight line that gave nothing away. Alex was shown into a comfortable room with a bed, a TV and a view of the sand dunes. The door was closed but it wasn't locked.

And here he was now. They had carried him the entire width of Australia. He wondered what would happen next.

There was a knock on the door. Alex opened it. A second soldier in green and ochre battle fatigues stood in front of him.

"Mr Rider?"

"I'm Alex."

"Colonel Abbott sends his compliments. He'd like to speak to you."

Alex followed the soldier across the compound. There was nobody else around. The sun was beating down on the empty parade ground. It was almost midday and the early Australian summer was already making itself felt. They reached a bungalow standing on its own near the edge of the complex. The soldier knocked and, without waiting for an answer, opened the door for Alex to go in.

A thin, businesslike man in his forties was sitting behind a desk, also wearing fatigues. He had been writing a report but he stood up as Alex came in.

"So you're Alex Rider!" The Australian accent came almost as a surprise. With his short, dark hair and craggy features, Abbott could have been mistaken for an Englishman. He reached out and shook Alex's hand firmly. "I'm Mike Abbott, and

I'm really pleased to meet you, Alex. I've heard a lot about you."

Alex looked surprised and Abbott laughed. "Six months ago, there was a rumour that the Brits were using a teenage agent. Of course, nobody believed it. But it seems they've been keeping you busy; and after you took out Damian Cray ... well, I'm afraid you can't blow up Air Force One in the middle of London without someone hearing about it. But don't worry! You're among friends."

Abbott gestured towards a chair and Alex sat down. "It's very kind of you, Colonel," he said. "But I really want to go home."

Abbott returned to his own chair. "I can understand that, Alex. And I really want to send you on your way. We just need to fix a couple of things."

"What things?"

"Well, you landed in Australia without a visa." Abbott held up his hands before Alex could interrupt. "I know that sounds ridiculous, but it has to be sorted out. As soon as I've got the green light, I'll book you on the first plane back to London."

"There's someone I want to call..."

"I suppose you're thinking about Jack Starbright. Your guardian." Abbott smiled and Alex wondered how he knew about her. "You're too late, Alex. She's been kept fully informed and she's already on her way. Her flight left Heathrow about an hour ago but it'll take her another twenty-five hours to arrive. The two of you will meet up in

Sydney. In the meantime, you're my guest here at Swanbourne and I want you to enjoy yourself. We're right on the beach, and it's the start of the Australian summer. So relax. I'll let you know as soon as there's any news about the visa."

Alex wanted to argue but decided against it. The colonel seemed friendly enough but there was something about him that made Alex think twice before speaking. You didn't rise up through the ranks of the SAS unless you were exceptionally tough – and there was certainly steel behind that smile.

"Anything else you want to know?"

"No thanks, Colonel."

The two of them shook hands.

"I've asked some of the boys to look after you," Abbott said. "They've been looking forward to meeting you. Just let me know if anyone gives you a hard time."

When Alex had been training with the SAS in the Brecon Beacons in Wales, a hard time was exactly what he had been given. But from the moment he left the bungalow, he saw that things were going to be different here. There were four young soldiers waiting for him and they all seemed to be easygoing and keen to introduce themselves. Maybe his reputation had gone ahead of him, but he could see right away that the Australian special forces were going to be the complete opposite of their British counterparts.

"It's great to meet you, Alex." The man who was speaking was about twenty-two and incredibly fit with a green T-shirt stretched tight over finely chiselled pectorals and bulging shoulders. "I'm Scooter. This is Texas, X-Ray and Sparks."

At first Alex thought they were using code names, but he quickly realized that they were just nicknames. All the other men were also in their early twenties and equally fit.

"We're just heading for lunch," Scooter went on. "You want to join us?"

"Thanks." Alex hadn't been given any breakfast and his stomach was empty.

They moved off as a pack. Nobody had even commented on his age. It was clearly no secret who he was. Alex began to feel a little more relaxed. Maybe a day or two here wouldn't be so bad.

From inside the bungalow, Colonel Mike Abbott watched them go. He had an uneasy feeling in his stomach. He was married with three children, and the eldest was only a few years younger than the boy he had just met. He had been impressed. After all he had been through, Alex had a sort of inner calm. Abbott didn't doubt that he could look after himself.

But even so...

He glanced again at the orders which he had received just a few hours ago. It was madness. What was being suggested was simply out of the question. Except that there was no question about it. He had been told exactly what he had to do.

And what if Alex was crippled? What if he was killed?

Not his problem.

The thought didn't comfort him one bit. In twenty years, Mike Abbott had never questioned his commanding officers, but it was with a sense of anger and disbelief that he picked up the telephone and began to issue the instructions for the night ahead.

NO PICNIC

Alex was worn out after all his travelling, and that afternoon he went back to his room and slept. When he was woken up – by the sound of knocking – the day was already drawing to a close. He went over to the door and opened it. The young soldier who had introduced himself as Scooter was standing there. Sparks was with him, holding a cool box.

"How are you doing?" Scooter asked. "We wondered if you'd like to come with us."

"Where are you going?"

"A picnic on the beach. We'll set up a barbecue. Have a few beers. Maybe swim." Scooter gestured at the compound behind him. There was nobody in sight. "There's a big exercise on tonight but we aren't part of it, and the colonel thought you might like to see a bit of the ocean before you leave."

The last three words caught Alex's attention. "I'm leaving?"

"Tomorrow morning. That's what I've heard. So how about it?"

"Sure." Alex had nothing else to do that evening. He didn't particularly want to watch TV on his own.

"Great. We'll pick you up in ten minutes."

The two men walked off, and it was only much later, when he was ten thousand miles away, that Alex would remember the moment and the way they had glanced at each other as if there was something that bothered them. But if he noticed it at the time, he didn't register it.

He went back into the room and pulled on his trainers. The SAS had provided him with some fresh clothes and he took a combat jacket out of the wardrobe. Scooter had talked about swimming but the sun was getting lower and Alex had already felt a cool breeze rolling in. He thought for a moment, then took a towel and a spare pair of boxers that would have to do instead of swimming trunks. Just as he was about to leave, he hesitated. Was this a good idea, heading off down the coast with a group of strangers almost ten years older than him? Suddenly he felt very alone and a long, long way from home. But Jack was on her way. Scooter had told him that he would be leaving the next day. He shook himself out of his mood and left the room, closing the door behind him.

Almost at once, a jeep drew up with Sparks driving and Scooter in the passenger seat. Texas and X-Ray were in the back with bags and cool boxes, blankets and a guitar piled up around them. They had left a narrow space for Alex. As he climbed in, he noticed that Texas was balancing an automatic pistol on his lap, testing the mechanism.

"You ever fired one of these?" Texas asked.

Alex shook his head.

"Well, now's your chance. When we get out there, I'll set up a few targets. See how you do."

Once again, Alex couldn't shake off a vague feeling that something was wrong; but then Sparks turned on the radio and, to a blast of music from some Australian band he had never heard of, they set off. It was going to be a beautiful evening. There were a few streaks of red in the sky but no clouds, and the sun – close to the horizon – was throwing long, stretched-out shadows across the ground. Scooter was slumped in his seat with one foot resting on the dashboard. X-Ray had his hand up, the wind streaming through his fingers. By the time they had passed through the barrier and hit the main road, Alex had relaxed. He only had one evening in Australia. He might as well enjoy it.

They followed the coast for about ten miles, then turned inland. To begin with they passed a number of suburban houses and shopping malls, but they soon left those behind; and by the time they had joined a four-lane motorway, they were driving through open countryside. None of them spoke. It was impossible in the open-top jeep with the wind rushing past. The music pounded out but any words were snatched away and lost.

After about twenty minutes, Scooter turned round and shouted, "You OK?"

Alex nodded. But secretly he was wondering how far they intended to travel and when they would arrive.

The journey lasted over an hour. They came off the motorway and took a road that cut through a wooded area. Then they turned onto a track, and suddenly they were bumping over a rough, uneven surface, eucalyptus and pine trees pressing in on both sides.

X-Ray had taken out a map. He leant forward and tapped Scooter on the shoulder. "Is this the right way?" he shouted.

"Sure!" Scooter shouted back without looking behind him.

"I think we've come too far!"

"Forget it, X-Ray. This is the right way..."

There was a barrier ahead of them, similar to the one at Swanbourne except that it was old and rusted. There was a sign next to it:

MILITARY ZONE
Absolutely no admittance.
Trespassers will be placed under
arrest and may be imprisoned.

Sparks slowed down and, without opening the door, Scooter leapt out of the jeep.

"Where are we?" Alex asked.

"You'll see," Sparks replied. "We come to a load of places around here. You'll like it."

"We've come too far," X-Ray insisted. "We should have turned off a mile back."

Scooter had opened the barrier – it obviously hadn't been locked – and the jeep rolled through. As it passed him, he leapt back into the passenger seat and at once Sparks stepped on the accelerator and they shot forward, bumping over roots and potholes.

It had become very dark. The last of the daylight had slipped away without Alex noticing, and suddenly the trees seemed very close, threatening to block the way ahead. The surface was getting worse and worse. Alex had to cling to the side as he was thrown around, the cool boxes lifting into the air and hanging there before crashing down again. Leaves and branches flickered briefly, a thousand black shadows caught in the headlights, before they whipped into the windscreen and disappeared behind. The track didn't seem to be going anywhere and Alex was having to fight back a sense of unease, wishing he hadn't come, when suddenly they burst through a clump of foliage and came to a shuddering halt, soft sand underneath the wheels. They had arrived.

Sparks turned off the engine and at once the gentler sounds of the evening surrounded them. Alex could hear the whisper of the breeze and the rhythmic breaking of the waves. They had come

51

to a beautiful place: a private beach with perfect white sand that curved round in a crescent, next to a black and silver sea. There was a full moon and a fantastic cluster of stars which seemed to go on for ever, stretching to the very ends of the southern hemisphere.

"Everybody out!" Scooter shouted. He kicked the door open and tumbled out onto the sand. "X-Ray, get me a beer. Texas, it's your turn to cook."

"I always cook!" Texas complained.

"Why do you think we invite you?"

"Here!" X-Ray had produced a can of Foster's. He threw it to Scooter, then turned to Alex. "You want a beer?"

"You got a Coke?" Alex asked.

"Sure!" X-Ray found a can and passed it over.

Meanwhile, Texas had begun to unload the jeep. Alex saw that the SAS men had brought sausages, burgers, steaks and chops – enough meat to feed a small army. But apart from a greasy, blackened steel grill, there was no sign of the promised barbecue.

Scooter must have read his mind. "We're going to build a bonfire, Alex," he said. "You can help collect wood."

Sparks had taken the guitar out of the back. He rested it on his knee and strummed a few chords. The music sounded faint, lost in the emptiness of the night.

"OK. Here's the plan," Scooter said. It seemed that he was the natural leader even if all four men were the same age and rank. "Alex and I will fetch firewood. Texas and X-Ray can start setting things up. Sparks – you keep playing." He took out a torch and threw it to Alex. "If you get lost, just listen out for the music," he said. "It'll guide you back to the beach."

"Right." Alex wasn't sure he would be able to hear the guitar once he was in the wood, but Scooter seemed to know what he was doing.

"Let's go," Scooter said.

He also had a torch, and flicked it on. The beam was powerful; even with the moonlight, it leapt ahead, cutting a path through the shadows. Alex did the same. The two of them moved away from the jeep, heading back up the track that had brought them here. The evening was warmer than Alex had expected. The breeze couldn't penetrate the trees. Everything was very still.

"You all right?" Scooter asked.

Alex nodded.

"We'll build a fire, get things cooking; then we can have a swim."

"Right."

They continued walking. It seemed to Alex that they had left the beach a long way behind them. He could still hear the music, but it was so distant that the notes seemed to have broken up and he couldn't make out any tune.

"See if you can find any dead wood. It burns better."

Alex trained his torch on the forest floor. There were broken branches everywhere and he wondered why they had come so far to collect them. But there was no point arguing. He reached down and gathered a few pieces together, then a few more. It didn't take him long to build up a pile; any more and it would be too heavy to carry. Clutching the wood to his chest, he straightened up and looked around for Scooter.

That was when he realized he was on his own.

"Scooter?"

There was no reply. Nor was there any sign of the SAS man's torch. Alex wasn't worried. It was likely Scooter had already collected his first bundle and was making his way back to the beach. Alex listened out for the sound of the guitar, but it had stopped. Now he felt the first prickle of doubt. He had been so busy collecting the branches that he had lost his sense of direction. He was in the middle of a wood, surrounded by blackness on all sides. Which way was the beach?

Ahead of him he saw a blink of white. A torch. Scooter. Alex called out his name a second time but there was no reply. It didn't matter. He had definitely seen a light, and, as if to reassure him, it flashed again. He headed towards it.

It was only when he had gone twenty or thirty paces that Alex realized he was nowhere near the beach; instead he had been drawn even further into the forest. It was almost as if it had been done on purpose. He was the moth and they had shown him the candle. But now the light had vanished. Even the moon had disappeared. Annoyed with himself, Alex dropped the wood. He could always pick more up later. All he wanted right now was to find his way back.

Ten more steps and abruptly the trees fell away. But he wasn't at the beach. Alex's torch showed him a wide, barren clearing with little hillocks of sand and grass. The forest circled all around him. There was no sign of Scooter or the flickering light that had led him here.

Now what?

Alex decided to go back the way he had come. He might be able to pick up his own footprints. The pile of wood he had dropped couldn't be too far away.

He was about to turn when something – some animal instinct – made him hesitate. About two seconds later, the whole world stopped.

He knew it was going to happen before it actually did. Alex had been in danger so many times that he had developed a sense, a sort of telepathy, that forewarned him. Animals have it – the awareness that makes their hackles rise and sends them running before there is any obvious reason to flee. Alex was throwing himself to the ground even before the missile fell, smashing the trees into matchsticks, scooping up a tonne of earth and hurling it into the sky, shattering the silence of the night and turning darkness into brilliant, blinding day.

The explosion was enormous. Alex had never felt anything like it. The very air had been transformed into a giant fist, a boxing glove that pounded into him, hot and violent; and for a moment he thought he must have broken a dozen bones. He couldn't hear; he couldn't see. The inside of his skull was boiling. Perhaps he was unconscious for a few seconds, because the next thing he knew, he was lying on the ground with his face pressed into a clump of grass and sand in his hair and eyes. His shirt was torn and there was a throbbing in his ears, but otherwise he seemed to be unhurt. How close had the missile fallen? Where had it come from? Even as Alex asked himself these two questions, a third, more unpleasant one, entered his mind. Were there going to be any more?

There was no time to work out what was going on. Alex spat out sand and dragged himself to his knees. At the same moment, something burst in the sky: a white flame that hung there, suspended high above the trees. Alex had tensed himself, expecting another blast, but he quickly recognized it for what it was: a Varey light, a lump of burning phosphorus, designed to illuminate the area for miles around. He was still kneeling. Almost too late he realized that he had turned himself into a target, a black cut-out against the brilliant, artificial glare.

He threw himself onto his stomach a second before a cascade of machine-gun bullets came fanning out of nowhere, pulverizing branches and ripping up the leaves. There was a second explosion, smaller than the first, this one starting at ground level and sending a column of flame shooting up. Alex covered his head with his hands. Earth and sand splattered all around him.

He was in a war zone. It was beyond anything he had ever experienced. But common sense told him that no war had broken out in Western Australia. This was a training exercise and somehow – insanely – he had stumbled into the heart of it.

He heard the blast of a whistle and two more explosions followed. The ground underneath him trembled and suddenly he found that he could no longer breathe. The air around him had been sucked away by the force of the blasts. More machine-gun fire. The entire area was being strafed. Alex glanced up, but even with the Varey light he knew there was no chance he would see anyone. Whoever was firing could be half a mile away. And if he stood up and tried to make himself seen, he would be cut in half before anyone realized their mistake.

And what about Scooter? What about X-Ray and the others? Had they brought him here on purpose? Alex couldn't believe that. What motive could they have to want him dead? He remembered what X-Ray had said in the jeep. *We've come too far. We should have turned off a mile back.* And when they'd invited him along, Scooter had said there was a big training exercise on that night. That was why they'd been free for a picnic on the beach. Some picnic! As insane as it seemed, the four SAS men must have driven to the very edge of the war zone. Alex had managed to stray away from the beach when he was collecting wood and had chosen the worst possible direction. This was the result – a mixture of bad luck and stupidity. But the two of them were going to get him blown apart.

A rhythmic pounding had begun, a mortar bombarding a target that had to be somewhere close by. As each shell detonated, Alex felt a stabbing pain behind his eyes. The power of the weapons was immense. If this was just a training exercise, he wondered what it must be like to get caught up in a real war.

It was time to go. With the mortar still firing, Alex scrambled to his feet and began to move, not sure which way he should go, knowing only that he couldn't remain here. Anyway, he had lost all sense of direction. There was the scream of something falling, and a great whump as it struck the ground somewhere over to Alex's left. That told him all he needed to know. He headed off to the right.

A crackle of machine-gun fire. Alex thought he heard someone shout, but when he looked round, there was no one there. That was the most unnerving thing, to be in the middle of a battle with not a single combatant visible. A tree had caught fire. The entire trunk was wrapped in flames and there were black and crimson shadows leaping all over the ground ahead. Just beyond, Alex caught sight of a wire fence. It wasn't much to aim for but at least it was man-made. Maybe it defined the perimeter of the war zone and he would be safer on the other side. Alex broke into a run. He could taste blood: he must have bitten his tongue when the first bomb went off. He felt bruised all over. He wondered if he might be hurt more than he actually knew.

He reached the fence. It was made of barbed wire and carried another sign: DANGER – KEEP OUT. Alex almost smiled. What danger could there possibly be on the other side that was worse than this? As if to answer the question, there were three more explosions less than a hundred metres behind him. Something hot struck Alex on the back of his neck. Without hesitating, he rolled under the fence, then stood up and continued running across the ground on the other side.

He was in a field. There was still no sign of the ocean. He was surrounded by trees on all sides. He slowed down and tried to take his bearings. His neck hurt. He had been burnt by whatever it was that had hit him. He wondered if Scooter and the others were looking for him. He would certainly have a few things to say to them – if he ever got out of here alive.

He continued. His right foot came down on something small and metallic. He heard – and felt – it click beneath his sole. He stopped. And at the same time, a voice came out of the darkness just behind him.

"Don't move. Don't even move a step..."

Out of the corner of his eye, Alex saw a figure roll under the fence. At first he thought it must be Scooter, but he hadn't recognized the voice and a few seconds later he saw that it was an older man with black curly hair and the beginnings of a rough beard, dressed in full military gear and carrying an assault rifle. The bombs and the shelling seemed to have faded into the distance. They must have been redirected at a target further away.

The man loomed up next to him, looking at Alex with disbelieving eyes. "Who the hell are you?" he asked. "How did you get here?"

"What am I standing on?" Alex demanded. Part of him knew the answer. He hadn't dared look down.

"The field is mined," the man replied briefly. He knelt. Alex felt his hand press gently against his trainer. Then the man straightened up. His eyes were dark brown and bleak. "You're standing on a mine," he said.

Alex was almost tempted to laugh. A sense of disbelief shivered through him and he swayed a little, as if he were about to faint.

"Stay exactly as you are!" the man shouted. "Stand up straight. Don't move from side to side.

If you release the pressure, you're going to kill both of us."

"Who are you?" Alex exclaimed. "What's going on here? Why is there a mine?"

"Didn't you see the sign?"

"It just said DANGER – KEEP OUT."

"What more did you need?" The man shook his head. "You shouldn't be anywhere near this place. How did you get here? What are you doing out here in the middle of the night?"

"I was brought here." Alex could feel a cold numbness creeping through his leg. It got worse the more he thought about what lay beneath his foot. "Can you help me?" he asked.

"Stay still." The man knelt down a second time. He had produced a torch, and he shone it on the ground. It seemed to take an age, but then he spoke again. "It's a butterfly," he said, and there was no emotion in his voice at all. "It's a Soviet PFM-1, a pressure-sensitive blast mine. You're standing on enough high explosive to take your leg off."

"What's it doing here?" Alex cried. He had to fight the instinct to lift his foot off the deadly thing. His entire body was screaming at him to run away.

"They train us!" the man rasped. "They use these things in Iraq and Indonesia. We have to know how to deal with them. How else are they going to do it?"

"But in the middle of a field?"

"You shouldn't be here! Who brought you?" The man straightened up. He was standing very close to Alex, his brown eyes boring into him. "I can't neutralize it," he muttered. "Even if I had the training, I couldn't risk it in the dark."

"So what do we do now?"

"I'm going to have to get help."

"Do you have a radio?"

"If I had a radio, I'd have already used it." The man laid a hand briefly on Alex's shoulder. "There's something else you need to know," he said. He was speaking softly; his mouth was next to Alex's ear. "These things have a delay mechanism ... a separate fuse which you'll have activated when you stepped on it."

"You mean it's going to blow up anyway?"

"In fifteen minutes."

"How long will it take you to find someone?"

"I'll move as quickly as I can. If you hear a click – you'll feel it under your foot – throw yourself flat on the ground. It's your only hope. Good luck."

"Wait..." Alex began.

But the man had already gone.

Alex stood there. He had lost any sense of feeling in his leg but his shoulder was burning and he was beginning to shiver quite violently as the shock set in. He forced himself to bring his body back under control, afraid that the slightest movement might trigger a hideous end to this ordeal. He could imagine the sudden flash, the pain, his leg separated from his body. And there was nothing he could do. His foot was glued to the device that was ticking away, even now, beneath him. He looked around. He noticed that the mine had been placed on top of a ridge, the ground sloping away steeply to a ditch at the bottom. Alex tried to work out the distances. If he threw himself sideways, could he reach the ditch before the mine exploded? And if the force of the blast was above him, would he perhaps escape the worst of it?

The bombing had stopped. Suddenly everything was very quiet. Once again Alex experienced the sense of being completely alone, standing like a scarecrow in the middle of an empty field. He wanted to call out but was afraid to, in case he accidentally shifted his body weight. How long had it been since the man had gone? Five minutes? Ten? And how accurate was the timer anyway? The mine could go off at any moment.

So did he wait? Or did he take his life into his own hands?

Alex made his decision.

He took a deep breath, tensing his body, trying to think of the muscles in his legs as coiled springs that would launch him to safety. His right foot was resting on the mine; the left was on flat ground. That was the one that would have to do most of the work. Alex had to force himself, knowing that he might be making the worst mistake of his life, that seconds from now he could be crippled, in agony.

Do it!

He jumped.

At the very last moment, he changed his mind but continued anyway, launching himself down the slope with all his strength. He thought he felt the mine shudder very slightly as his foot left it. But it hadn't exploded, at least not in the half-second that he had left the ground. Automatically he crossed his arms in front of his face, to protect himself from the fall – and the blast. The slope was rushing past him, a dark streak at the corner of his vision. Then he hit the ditch. Water, cold and muddy, splattered into his face. His shoulder hit something hard. Behind him, there was an explosion. The mine. Clumps of earth and grass rained down on him.

Then nothing. His face was underwater and he pulled his head back, spitting mud. A plume of smoke rose into the night sky. The fuse must have given him three seconds before it detonated the mine. He had taken those three seconds and they had saved him.

He got unsteadily to his feet. Water was dripping from his hair and down his face. His heart was pounding. He felt drained, exhausted. He lost his balance, put a hand out to steady himself and winced as he caught it on the barbed-wire fence. But at least he had found the way out. He rolled underneath and tried to work out which way to go. Seconds later, the question was answered for him. He heard the sound of an engine, saw two beams of light cutting through the trees. His own name was being called out. He hurried forward and found a track.

The four SAS men were in the jeep. This time X-Ray was driving. They were moving slowly through the wood, searching for him. Alex saw that they had left the cool boxes behind, but Sparks had remembered his guitar.

"Alex!"

X-Ray slammed on the brakes and Scooter leapt out of the passenger seat. He looked genuinely concerned, his face white in the glare of the headlamps.

"Are you OK? Jesus! We completely screwed up. We've got to get out of here. We shouldn't be any-where near this place."

"I told you—" X-Ray began.

"Not now!" Scooter snapped. He grabbed hold of Alex. "As soon as the bombs went off, I knew what had happened. I looked for you but we must have got separated. You look terrible, mate. Are you hurt?"

"No." Alex didn't trust himself to say any more.

"Get in. We'll get you home. I don't know what to say to you. We're complete idiots. We could have got you killed."

This time Alex took the front seat. Scooter climbed in the back with the others and they set off back down the track and out towards the main road. Alex still wasn't sure what had just happened

– how the SAS men had managed to get themselves into this mess. Nor did he care. He allowed the noise of the engine to drift away on the cool night air, and seconds later he was sound asleep.

ON THE ROCKS

Two days later, Alex had put his experiences at Swanbourne behind him. He was sitting outside a café in Sydney, the Opera House on one side, the great stretch of the Harbour Bridge on the other. It was the world's favourite picture postcard view and he had seen it many times. But now he was actually in it, eating vanilla and strawberry ice cream and watching as the Manly ferry came grinding into the quay, scattering the smaller craft. The sun was beating down and the sky was a dazzling blue. It was hard to believe that he was really here.

And he wasn't alone. Jack had joined him the day before, bleary-eyed with jet lag but awake and bursting with excitement the moment she saw him. It had taken her twenty-six hours to get here and Alex knew she would have been worrying all the way. Jack was meant to look after him. She hated it when he was away – and this time he had never been further. As soon as she'd arrived, she had made it clear that all she wanted was to get him on a plane and take him back to London. Yes, it was cold and drizzling there; the English winter had already arrived. Yes, they both deserved a holiday. But it was time to go home.

Jack was also eating ice cream, and although she was twenty-eight she suddenly looked younger with her untidy red hair, lopsided smile and her brightly coloured kangaroo T-shirt. More a big sister than a housekeeper. And above all a friend.

"I don't know why it's taking so long," she was saying. "It's ridiculous. By the time you get back, you'll have missed half the term."

"They said they'd have it this afternoon."

"They should have had it two days ago."

They were talking about Alex's visa. That morning, Jack had received a call at the hotel where they were staying. They had been given an address, a government office in Macquarie Street, just past the old parliament building. The visa would be ready at four o'clock. Alex could pick it up then.

"Could we stay here a couple more days?" Alex asked.

Jack looked at him curiously. "Don't you want to go home?"

"Yes." Alex paused. "I suppose so. But at the same time ... I'm not quite sure I'm ready to go back to school. I've been thinking about it. I'm worried I'm not going to be able to fit in."

"Of course you'll fit in, Alex. You've got lots of friends. They've all been missing you. Once you're back, you'll forget any of this stuff ever happened."

But Alex wasn't so sure. He and Jack had talked about it the evening before. After all he had been through, how could he go back to geography lessons and school lunches and being told off for running too fast down the corridor? The day MI6 had recruited him, they had built a wall between him and his past life and he wondered if there was now any way back.

"I've hardly been to school this year," he muttered. "I'm way behind."

"Maybe we can get Mr Grey to come in this Christmas," Jack suggested. Mr Grey was the teacher who had given Alex extra tuition during the summer. "You got on well with him, and he'd soon help you catch up."

"I don't know, Jack." Alex looked at the ice cream melting on his spoon. He wished he could explain how he felt. He didn't want to work for MI6 again. He was sure of that. But at the same time...

"It's half past three," Jack said. "We ought to get going."

They got up and made their way along the side of the Opera House and up into the Royal Botanic Gardens – the incredible park that seemed to contain the city rather than the other way round. Looking back at the harbour, the bustle of life below and the gleaming skyscrapers stretched out behind, Alex wondered how the Australians had managed to get it all so right. It was impossible not to love Sydney, and despite what Jack had said, he knew he wasn't yet ready to leave.

Together, the two of them made their way up past the Art Gallery of New South Wales and into Macquarie Street, where the parliament building stood, two storeys high, an elegant construction of pink and white that somehow reminded Alex of the ice cream he had just eaten. The address they had been given was just beyond, a modern glass block that was presumably filled with minor government offices. The receptionist already had visitor passes waiting for them and directed them to the fourth floor and a room at the end of a corridor.

"I don't know why they couldn't have just put you on a plane and sent you out of here," Jack grumbled as they left the lift. "It seems a lot of fuss about nothing."

There was a door ahead of them. They walked through without knocking and stopped dead in their tracks. There had obviously been some sort of mistake. Wherever they were, it certainly wasn't a visa office.

Two men were talking to each other in what looked like a library with antique furniture and a Persian rug on a highly polished wooden floor. Alex's immediate impression was that the room didn't belong to the building it was in. A golden Labrador lay curled up on a cushion in front of a fireplace. One of the men was behind a desk. He was the elder of the two, wearing a shirt and jacket and no tie. His eyes were concealed behind designer sunglasses. The other man was standing by the window with his arms folded. He was in his late twenties, thin and fair-haired, dressed in an expensive suit.

"Oh ... I'm sorry," Jack began.

"Not at all, Miss Starbright," the man behind the desk replied. "Please come in."

"We're looking for the visa office," Jack said.

"Sit down. I take it Alex is with you? The question may seem odd, but I'm blind."

"I'm here," Alex said.

"Who are you?" Jack asked. She and Alex had moved further into the room. The younger man came over and closed the door behind them.

"My name is Ethan Brooke. My colleague here is Marc Damon. Thank you very much for coming in, Miss Starbright. Do you mind if I call you Jack? Please – take a seat."

There were two leather chairs in front of the desk. Feeling increasingly uncomfortable, Jack and Alex sat down. The man called Damon walked across and took a third seat at the side. The dog's tail thumped twice against the wooden floor.

"I know you're in a hurry to get back to London," Brooke began. "But let me explain why the two of you are here. The fact of the matter is, we need a little help."

"You want our help?" Jack looked around her. Suddenly it all made sense. "You want Alex." She spoke the words heavily. She knew now who the men were – or at least what they represented. She had met their type before.

"We'd like to put a proposition to Alex," Brooke agreed.

"Forget it. He's not interested."

"Won't you at least listen to what we have to say?" Brooke spread his hands. He looked completely reasonable. He could have been a bank manager advising them on their mortgage, or a family lawyer about to read a will.

"We want the visa."

"You'll have it. As soon as I'm done."

Alex had said nothing. Jack looked at him, then turned to Brooke and Damon with anger in her eyes. "Why can't you people leave him alone?" she demanded.

"Because he's special. In fact, I'd say he's unique. And right now we need him, just for a week or two. But I promise you, Jack. If he's not interested, he can walk out of here. We can have him on a plane tonight. Just give me a minute to explain."

"Who are you?" Alex asked.

Brooke turned towards Damon. "We work for ASIS," the younger man replied. "The Australian Secret Intelligence Service."

"Special Operations?"

"Covert Action. The two are more or less the same. You could say we're the rough equivalent of the outfit Alan Blunt runs in London."

"I've read your file, Alex," Brooke added. "I have to say, I'm impressed."

"What do you want me for?" Alex demanded.

"I'll tell you."

Brooke folded his hands, and to Alex it seemed somehow inevitable, unsurprising even. It had happened to him six times before. Why not again?

"Have you ever heard the term 'snakehead', or *'shetou'*?" Brooke began. There was silence, so he went on. "All right, let me start by saying that the snakehead groups are without doubt the biggest and most dangerous criminal organizations in the world. Compared to them, the Mafia and the triads are amateurs. They have more influence – and they're doing more damage – than even al-Qaeda, but they're not interested in religion. They have no beliefs. All they want is money. That's the bottom line. They're gangsters, but on a huge scale.

"Have you ever bought an illegal DVD? The chances are that it was manufactured and distributed by a snakehead. And the profits they'll have made out of it will have gone straight into one of their other concerns, which you may not find so amusing. Maybe it's drugs or slaves or body parts. You need a new kidney or a heart? The snakeheads operate the biggest market in illegal organs, and they're not fussy about where they get them. Or weapons. There have been at least fifty wars around the world that have used weapons supplied by the snakeheads: shoulder-launched missiles,

AK-47s, that sort of thing. Where do you think terrorists go if they want a bomb or a gun or something nasty and biological that comes in a test tube? Think of it as an international supermarket, Alex. But everything it sells is bad.

"What else can you buy? You name it! Paintings stolen from museums. Diamonds mined illegally using slave labour. Ancient artefacts plundered from Iraq. Elephant tusks or tiger-skin rugs. A few years ago a hundred kids died in Haiti because someone had sold them cough medicine that happened to contain antifreeze. That was a snakehead – and I don't think it offered anyone their money back.

"But the biggest moneymaker for the snakeheads is people smuggling. You probably have no idea how many people there are being smuggled from one country to another all around the globe. These are some of the poorest families in the world, desperate to build themselves a new life in the West. Some of them are fleeing from hopelessness and starvation; others are threatened in their own countries with prison and torture." Brooke paused and looked directly at Alex, fixing him with his sightless eyes. "Half of them are under the age of eighteen," he said. "About five per cent are younger than you – and they're travelling on their own. The lucky ones get picked up by the authorities. What happens to the rest of them ... you don't want to know.

"People smuggling is a huge problem for Australia. We have illegal immigrants coming in from Iraq and Afghanistan. They come in boats from Bali, Flores, Lombok and Jakarta. My country used to welcome immigrants. We were all immigrants ourselves once. That's all changed now – and I have to say the way we treat these people leaves a lot to be desired. But what can we do? The answer is, we have to stop them coming. And to do that, we have to take on the snakeheads, face to face.

"There's one snakehead in particular. It operates throughout Indonesia, and it's more powerful and more dangerous than all the rest. As it happens, we know the name of the man in charge. Major Yu. But that's all we've managed to find out. We don't know what he looks like or where he lives. Twice now we've tried to infiltrate the organization. That is, we put agents inside, pretending to be customers."

"What happened to them?" Jack asked.

"They both died." It was Damon who had answered the question.

"And so now I suppose you're thinking about using Alex."

"We have no idea how our agents were discovered," Brooke went on. It was as if Jack hadn't spoken. "Somehow this man – Yu – seems to know everything we're doing. Either that or he's very careful. The trouble is, these gangs operate under a system known as *guanxi*. Basically, it means everyone knows everyone. They're like a family. And the fact is, a single agent coming in from outside and operating on his own is too obvious. We need to get inside the snakehead in a way that is completely original and also above suspicion."

"A man and a boy," Damon said.

"We have an agent in Bangkok now. We're going to set him up as a refugee from Afghanistan planning to be smuggled into Australia. He'll meet with the snakehead and gather names, faces, phone numbers, addresses – anything he can. But he won't be on his own. He'll be travelling with his son."

"We'll fly you to Bangkok," Damon continued, speaking directly to Alex. "You'll join our agent there and the two of you will be passed down the pipeline back here. And here's the deal. As soon as you're back on Australian soil, we'll send you first class, direct to England. You won't have to do anything, Alex. But you'll provide perfect cover for our man. He'll get the information we need and maybe we'll be able to break up Yu's network once and for all."

"Why Bangkok?" There were a hundred questions Alex could have asked. This was the first one that came to his mind.

"Bangkok is a major centre for the sale of false documents," Damon replied. "In fact, we'd very much like to know who supplies Yu's people with fake passports, export certificates and the rest of it. And now we have a chance. Our agent has been told to wait there until he is contacted. He'll be given the papers he needs and then he'll continue the journey south."

There was a brief silence.

Then Jack Starbright shook her head. "All right," she said. "We've listened to your proposition, Mr Brooke. Now you can listen to my answer. And it's no. Forget it! You said it yourself. These people are dangerous. Two of your spies have already been killed. There's no way I'm going to let Alex get mixed up in that."

"I'd have thought after all Alex has been through, he could make up his own mind," Brooke replied.

"He can make up his own mind. I'm just telling you what he's going to say. The answer's no!"

"There is one thing we haven't mentioned." Brooke rested his hands on the desk. His face gave nothing away but Damon knew what was about to come. His boss was the consummate poker player, only now preparing to show his hand. "I didn't tell you the name of our agent in Bangkok."

"And who is that?" Jack asked.

"You know him, I think. His name is Ash."

Jack sat back, unable to keep the shock out of her eyes. "Ash?" she faltered.

"That's right."

Alex had seen the effect the name had had on her. "Who's Ash?" he demanded.

"You don't know him?" Brooke was enjoying

himself now, though only Damon was aware of it. He turned to Jack. "Maybe you'd like to explain?"

"Ash was someone who knew your dad," Jack muttered.

"He was rather more than that," Brooke corrected her. "Ash was John Rider's closest friend. He was the best man at your parents' wedding, Alex. He's also your godfather."

"My..." Alex couldn't believe what he was hearing. He didn't even know he had a godfather.

"And for what it's worth, he was the last person to see your parents alive," Brooke went on. "He was with them, the morning they died. He was at the airport when they got on the plane for the South of France."

The plane had never arrived. There had been a bomb on board, placed there as an act of revenge by Scorpia. That much Alex knew.

Alex gazed at Jack. "Did you meet him?" He was feeling completely disorientated, as if the ground had just been stolen from under his feet. She looked exactly the same.

"I saw him a few times," she replied. "It was just after I started working for your uncle. Ash came to visit. He was checking up on you. After all, he was your godfather."

"How come you've never mentioned him?"

"He disappeared. You were still very young. He told me he was going away for good and I never saw him again."

"Ash was an agent with MI6," Brooke explained. "That was how he and your father met. They worked together as a team. Your dad even saved his life once – in Malta. You can ask him about that ... if you meet. I'd have thought the two of you would have a lot to talk about."

"How can you do this?" Jack whispered. She was looking at Brooke with utter contempt.

"Ash left MI6 a few months after your parents died, and emigrated here," Brooke continued. "He came with great references so we were happy to take him on at ASIS. He's been with us ever since. Right now he's in Bangkok, about to go undercover – like I said. But there's nobody better placed to pretend to be your father, Alex. I mean, he's almost that already. He'll look after you. And I think you'll find him interesting. What do you say?"

Alex said nothing. He had already made up his mind, but somehow he knew that Brooke wouldn't need to be told. He had figured that out for himself.

"I need time," he said, at length.

"Sure. Why don't you and Jack go and talk about it?" Brooke nodded and Damon produced a white card. He must have had it ready in his pocket from the very start. "Here's a number where you can reach me. We'll need to fly you into Bangkok tomorrow. So maybe you could call me this evening?"

"I know what you're thinking, but you can't possibly go," Jack said. "It's wrong."

Alex and Jack had wandered over to the Rocks, the little cluster of shops and cafés that nestled on the very edge of the harbour, right underneath the bridge. Jack had brought them here purposely. She wanted to mingle with the crowds somewhere bright and ordinary, a world apart from the hidden truths and half-lies of the Australian secret service.

"I think I have to," Alex replied.

And it was true. Earlier that afternoon, he had promised himself that he would never work for MI6 again. But this was different – and not just because it was the Australians that were asking him this time. It was Ash. Ash made all the difference, even though the two of them had never met and it was a name he had only just heard for the first time.

"Ash can tell me who I am," he said.

"Don't you know who you are?"

"Not really, Jack. I thought I knew. When Ian was alive, everything seemed so simple. But then, when I found out the truth about him, it all went wrong. All my life he was training me to be something I never wanted to be. But maybe he was right. Maybe it was what I was always meant to be."

"You think Ash can tell you?"

"I don't know." Alex squinted at Jack. The sunlight was streaming over her shoulders. "When did you meet him?" he asked.

"It was about a month after I started working for your uncle," she said. "At the time, it was just meant to be a vacation job, to support myself while

I was doing my studies. I didn't know anything about spies and I certainly didn't know I'd be sticking with you for ever!" She sighed. "You were about seven years old. Do you really not remember him?"

Alex shook his head.

"He was in London for a few weeks, staying in a hotel. But he came over to the house two or three times. Now I come to think of it, he never did talk to you very much. Maybe he felt awkward with kids. But I got to know him a bit."

"What was he like?"

Jack thought back. "I liked him," she admitted. "In fact, if you want the truth, I even went out with him a couple of times, though he was quite a lot older than me. He was very good-looking. And there was something dangerous about him. He told me he was a deep-sea diver. He was fun to have around."

"Is Ash his real name?"

"It's what he calls himself. A.S.H. are his initials – but he never told me what they stood for."

"And he's really my godfather?"

Jack nodded. "I've seen photos of him at your christening. And Ian knew him too. The two of them were friends. I never knew what he was doing in London but he was keen to check up on you. He wanted to be sure you were OK."

Alex drew a deep breath. "You don't know what it's like, not having parents," he began. "It's never bothered me, because I never knew them. I was so small when they died. But even so, I've often wondered about them. And it sometimes feels like there's a hole in my life, a sort of emptiness. I look back but there's nothing there. Maybe if I spend a bit of time with this man – even if I do have to dress up like an Afghan refugee – it'll fill something in for me."

"But, Alex..." Jack looked at him and he could see she was afraid. "You heard what Brooke said. This could be terribly dangerous. You've been lucky so far, but your luck can't last for ever. These people – the snakehead – they sound horrible. You shouldn't get involved."

"I have to, Jack. Ash worked with my dad. He saw my parents the day they died. I didn't know he existed until today, but now I do, I've got to meet him." Alex forced a smile. "My dad was a spy. My uncle was a spy. And now it turns out I've got a godfather who's a spy. You have to admit, it certainly runs in the family."

Jack rested her hands on Alex's shoulders. Behind them the sun was already setting, reflecting blood red in the water. The shops were beginning to empty. The bridge hung over them, casting a dark shadow.

"Is there anything I can say to stop you?" she asked.

"Yes." Alex looked her straight in the eye. "But please don't."

"All right." She nodded. "But I'll be worried sick about you. You know that. Just make sure you look after yourself. And tell Ash from me that I want you home by Christmas. And maybe this time, just for once, he'll remember to send a card."

Quickly she turned round and continued walking. Alex waited a minute, then followed.

Bangkok. The snakehead. Another mission. The truth was that Alex had always suspected it might happen – but even he hadn't thought it would come so soon.

CITY OF ANGELS?

Twenty-four hours later, Alex touched down at Suvarnabhumi International Airport in Bangkok. Even the name warned him that he had arrived at the gateway to a completely alien world. For all his travels, he had never been to the East. Now, following the nine-hour flight from Sydney, he was here – on his own. Jack had wanted to travel with him but he had decided against it. He'd found it easier to say goodbye to her at the hotel. He knew he needed time to prepare himself for what might lie ahead.

He had met once more with Brooke and Damon the night before. There hadn't been much more to say. Alex was booked into a room at the Peninsula Hotel in Bangkok. A driver would pick him up from the airport and take him there. Ash would meet him as soon as he'd arrived.

"You realize we'll have to disguise you," Brooke said. "You don't look anything like an Afghan."

"And I don't speak their language," Alex added.

"That's not a problem. You're a child and a refugee. No one will be expecting you to say anything."

The flight had seemed endless. ASIS had booked him into business class, but in a way that made him feel all the more alienated and alone. He watched a film, ate a meal and rested. But nobody spoke to him. He was in a strange, metal bubble, surrounded by strangers, being carried once again towards danger and possible death. Alex looked out of the window at the brilliant sunlight bouncing off a seemingly solid carpet of cloud and wondered. Was he making a mistake? He could board another plane at Bangkok and be back in London in twelve hours. But he had made his decision. This wasn't about ASIS or the snakehead.

He was the last person to see your parents alive.

Alex remembered what Brooke had told him. He was about to meet his father's best friend. His godfather. This wasn't just a flight from one country to another. It was a journey into his own past.

The 747 rumbled into its stall. The FASTEN YOUR SEAT BELT signs blinked off and the passengers stood up as one, scrabbling for the overhead lockers. Alex had one small suitcase and quickly passed through immigration and customs and out into the hot, sticky air of the arrivals hall. Suddenly he found himself in a crowd of jabbering, gesticulating people.

"Taxi! Taxi!"

"You want hotel?"

It felt strange emerging from business class into this. He was suddenly back in the noise and chaos of the real world. Down to earth in more senses than one.

And then he saw his name on a placard being held by a Thai man – black-haired, short, casually dressed like almost everyone around him. Alex went over to him.

"Are you Alex? Mr Ash sent me to collect you. I hope you had a good flight. The car is outside."

It was as they made their way out of the airport that Alex noticed the man with the poppy in his buttonhole. It was the poppy that first drew his attention. Of course, it was November. It would soon be Remembrance Day back in England. It was just strange to see any sign of it out here.

The man was wearing jeans and a leather jacket. He was European, in his twenties, with black hair cut short and dark, thoughtful eyes. He had very square features with high cheekbones and thin lips. The man had stopped dead in his tracks and seemed to be staring at something on the other side of the arrivals lounge. It took Alex a moment to realize that the man's attention was actually fixed on him. Did they know each other? He was just asking himself that question when a crowd of people moved between them, making for the exit. When the floor cleared again, the man had gone.

He must have imagined it. He was tired after the long flight. Maybe the man had simply been one of the other passengers on the plane. Alex followed the driver to the car park and a few minutes later they were on the wide, three-lane motorway that led into Bangkok – or, as the Thai people call it, Krung Thep. City of Angels.

Sitting in the back of the air-conditioned car, gazing out of the window, Alex wondered how it had got that name. He certainly wasn't impressed by his first sight of the city, a sprawl of ugly, old-fashioned skyscrapers, blocks of flats piled up on top of each other like discarded boxes, electricity pylons and satellite towers. They stopped at a pay toll where a woman sat in a cramped cubicle, her face hidden behind the white mask that protected her from the traffic fumes. Then they were off again. Alex saw a huge portrait of a man next to the road: black hair, glasses, open-necked shirt. It was painted on the entire side of a building, twenty storeys high, covering both the brickwork and the windows.

"That's our king," the driver explained.

Alex looked again at the portrait. What would it be like, he wondered, to work at a desk inside that office? To pound away at a computer for eight or nine hours a day but to look out at Bangkok through the eyes of a king.

They left the motorway, driving down a ramp into a dense, chaotic world of shrubs and food stalls, traffic jams and policemen at every intersection, their whistles screaming like dying birds. Alex saw tuk-tuks – motorized rickshaws – bicycles and buses that looked as if they had been welded together from a dozen different models. He felt a hollow feeling in his stomach. What was he letting himself in for? How was he going to adapt to a country that was, in every last detail, so different from his own?

Then the car turned a corner. They had entered the driveway of the Peninsula Hotel and Alex learnt something else about Bangkok. It was actually two cities: one very poor and one very rich, living side by side and yet with a great gulf between them. His journey had brought him from one to the other. Now he was passing through a beautifully tended tropical garden. As they drew up at the front entrance, half a dozen men in perfect white uniforms hurried forward to help – one to take the luggage, one to help Alex out, two more bowing to welcome him, two holding open the hotel doors.

The cold embrace of the hotel's air conditioning reached out to welcome him. Alex crossed a wide marble floor towards the reception area, piano music tinkling somewhere in the background, and was handed a garland of flowers by a smiling receptionist. Nobody seemed to have noticed that he was only fourteen. He was a guest; that was all that mattered. His key was already waiting for him. He was shown into a lift, itself the size of a small room. The doors slid shut. Only the pressure in his ears told him that they had begun the journey up.

His room was on the nineteenth floor.

Ten minutes later, he stood in front of a floor-to-ceiling window, looking at the view. His suitcase was on his bed. He had been shown the luxury bathroom, the widescreen TV, the well-stocked fridge and the complimentary basket of exotic fruit. Alex tried to shrug off the heavy fingers of jet lag. He knew he had little enough time to prepare himself for what lay ahead.

The city was spread out on the other side of a wide, brown river that curved and twisted as far as he could see. Skyscrapers towered in the far distance. Nearer by, there were hotels, temples, palaces with perfect lawns and – standing alongside them – shacks and slum houses and warehouses so dilapidated they looked as if they might fall over at any time. All manner of boats were making their way up and down the murky water. Some were modern, carrying coal and iron; some were ferries with strange, curving roofs, like floating pagodas. The nimblest were elongated, long and wafer thin with the driver leaning wearily over the tiller at the stern. The sun was setting, and the sky was huge and grey. It was like looking at a television screen with the colour control turned down.

The telephone rang. Alex went over and picked it up.

"Hello? Is that Alex?" It was a man's voice. Alex could make out a slight Australian accent.

"Yes," he replied.

"You arrived OK, then?"

"Yes, thanks."

"I'm in reception. You feel like a bit of dinner?"

Alex wasn't hungry but that didn't matter. Even though the man hadn't introduced himself, he knew who he was talking to. "I'll come straight down," he said.

He hadn't had time to shower or change after the flight. It would just have to wait. Alex left the room and took the lift back down. It stopped twice on the way, letting people in on the ninth and seventh floors. Alex stood silently in the corner. He was suddenly nervous, though he wasn't quite sure why. Finally they arrived. The lift doors opened.

Ash was standing in the reception area, dressed in a blue linen jacket, a white shirt and jeans. There were plenty of other people around but Alex recognized him instantly, and somehow he wasn't even surprised.

They had met before.

Ash was the soldier in the forest, the man who had told him he was standing on a mine.

"It was all a set-up, wasn't it?" Alex said. "The training exercise. The minefield. All of it."

"Yeah." Ash nodded. "I expect that must make you pretty annoyed."

"You could say that," Alex growled.

There was an eating area just outside the hotel,

softly lit, with the river in front and a long, narrow swimming pool to one side. The two of them were sitting at a table, facing each other. Ash had a Singha beer. He had ordered Alex a fruit cocktail: orange, pineapple and guava blended with crushed ice. It was almost dark now but Alex could still feel the heat of the evening pressing down on him. He realized it was going to take time to get used to the climate in Bangkok. The air was like syrup.

He looked again at his godfather, the man who had known him when he was a baby. Ash was leaning back with his legs stretched out, untroubled by the trick that had been played in the forest near Swanbourne. Out of uniform, with his shirt open and a silver chain glinting around his neck, he looked nothing like a soldier or a spy. He was more like a film star with his curly black hair, rough beard and suntanned skin. Physically he was slim – wiry was the word that sprang to Alex's mind. Fast-moving rather than particularly strong. He had brown eyes that were very dark and Alex guessed he could easily play the part of an Afghan. He certainly didn't look European.

There was something else about him that Alex found harder to place. A certain guarded quality in the eyes, a sense of tension. He might look relaxed but he never would be. He had been touched by something at some time and it would never let him go.

"So why did you do it?" Alex asked.

"It was a test, Alex. Why do you think?" Ash had a soft, lilting voice. The fourteen years he had spent in Australia had given him an accent but Alex could hear the English there too. "We weren't going to use a fourteen-year-old boy – not even you. Not unless we were damn sure you weren't going to panic at the first sign of danger."

"I didn't panic with Drevin. Or with Scorpia..."

"The snakeheads are different. You have no idea what sort of people we're up against. Didn't Brooke tell you? They've already killed two of our agents. The first one came home minus his head. They sent the second back in an envelope. They'd had him cremated to save us the trouble." Ash drank his beer and signalled to the waiter for another. "I had to see for myself that you were up to the job," he went on. "We created a situation that would have terrorized any normal kid. Then we watched how you got on with it."

"I could have been killed." Alex remembered how the first bomb had blown him off his feet.

"You weren't in any real danger. All the missiles were launched with pinpoint accuracy. We knew exactly where you were all the time."

"How?"

Ash smiled. "There was a beacon inside the heel of one of your trainers. Colonel Abbott arranged that while you were asleep. It sent out a signal to the nearest millimetre."

"What about the mine?"

"It had less explosive in it than you probably thought. And it was activated by remote control. I set it off a couple of seconds after you made that dive. You did pretty well, by the way."

"You were watching me all the time."

"Just put it behind you, Alex. It was a test. You passed. That's all that matters."

The waiter arrived with the second beer. Ash lit a cigarette – Alex was surprised to see that he smoked – and blew smoke out into the warm evening air.

"I can't believe we're finally meeting," he said. He examined Alex closely. "You look a hell of a lot like your dad."

"You were close to him."

"Yeah. We were close."

"And my mother."

"I don't want to talk about them, Alex." Ash shifted uncomfortably, then reached out and drank some of his second beer. "Do you mind? It was all a long time ago. My life's moved on since then."

"It's the only reason I'm here," Alex said.

There was a long silence. Then Ash smiled briefly. "How's that housekeeper of yours?" he asked. "Jack what's-her-name. Is she still with you?"

"Yes. She said hello."

"She was an attractive girl. I liked her. I'm glad she stuck by you."

"You didn't."

"Well ... I moved on." Ash paused. Then suddenly he leant forward. His face was deadly serious and Alex saw that this was a tough, cold-hearted man and that he was going to have to watch himself when they were together.

"All right. This is how we're going to play it," he began. "You're in this smart, luxury hotel because I wanted to ease you in. But tomorrow that all comes to an end. We're going to have breakfast and then we're going up to your room and you're going to become an Afghan boy, a refugee. We're going to change the way you look, the way you walk and even the way you smell. And then we're going out there..." He pointed across the river. "You enjoy your bed tonight, Alex, because where you sleep tomorrow night is going to be very different. And trust me. You're not going to like it."

He lifted the cigarette and inhaled. Grey smoke curled out of the corner of his mouth.

"We should make contact with the snakehead in the next few days," he went on. "I'll explain all that tomorrow. But this is what you've got to understand. You do nothing and you say nothing unless I tell you. You play dumb. And if I think the situation is getting out of hand, if I think you're in danger, you'll clear out. With no argument. Do you understand?"

"Yes." Alex was taken aback. This wasn't what he had expected. It wasn't what he'd flown five thousand miles to hear.

Ash softened. "But I'll make you this promise. We're going to be spending a lot of time together, and when I feel I know you better, when the time is right, I'll tell you everything you want to know. About your father. About what happened in Malta. About your mother and about you. The only thing I'll never talk to you about is the way they died. I was there and I saw it and I don't want to remember it. Is that OK with you?"

Alex nodded.

"Right. Then let's get some food in us. I forgot to mention – the stuff you'll be eating from now on may not be to your taste either. And you can tell me a bit about yourself. I'd like to know what school you go to and if you have a girlfriend, and things like that. Let's enjoy the evening. There may not be a lot of fun ahead."

Ash picked up his menu and Alex did the same. But before he could read it, a movement caught his eye. It was just chance really. The hotel had a private ferry that ran between the two banks of the river – a wide, spacious boat with antique chairs placed at intervals on a polished wooden floor. It had just arrived, and it was the roar of the engine going into reverse that had made Alex look up.

A man was just climbing aboard. Alex thought he recognized him, and his suspicion was confirmed when the man turned round and looked purposefully in his direction. The poppy had gone but it was the man from the airport. Alex was sure of it.

A coincidence? The man hurried on board, disappearing beneath the canopy as if anxious to get out of sight, and Alex knew that there was no chance about it. The man had spotted him in the arrivals lounge and followed him here.

Alex wondered if he should mention it to Ash. Almost at once he decided against it. It was impossible for the snakehead to know that he was here, and if he made a fuss, if Ash decided he had been compromised, he might be sent home before the mission had even begun. No. Much better to keep quiet. If he saw the man a third time, then he would speak out.

So Alex said nothing. He didn't even watch as the ferry began its crossing back to the other side. Nor did he hear the click of the camera with its special night scope and long-distance lens trained on him as his picture was taken, again and again, in the dwindling light.

FATHER AND SON

The next morning, Alex ate the best breakfast of his life. He had a feeling he was going to need it. The hotel offered a hot and cold buffet that included just about every cuisine – French, English, Thai, Vietnamese – with dishes ranging from eggs and bacon to stir-fried noodles. Ash joined him but spoke little. He seemed to be deep in thought, and Alex wondered if he was already having reservations about what lay ahead.

"You've had enough?" he asked as Alex finished his second croissant.

Alex nodded.

"Then let's go up to your room. Mrs Webber will be here soon. We'll wait for her there."

Alex had no idea who Mrs Webber was and it didn't seem that Ash wanted to tell him. The two of them went back up to the nineteenth floor. Ash hung the DO NOT DISTURB SIGN on the door and pointed Alex to a seat next to the window. He sat down opposite.

"OK," he began. "Let me tell you how this works. Two weeks ago, working with the Pakistani authorities, ASIS managed to pick up a father and a son heading into India on their way here. We interrogated them and discovered they'd paid the snakehead four thousand American dollars to smuggle them into Australia.

"Originally we were just going to send them back. But now we've decided to use them. The father's called Karim; the son is Abdul. Get used to the names, Alex, because from now on that's you and me. Karim and Abdul Hassan. We're taking their place, which means staying here in Bangkok. They were given an address and told to wait there until they were contacted by a man called Sukit."

"Who's he?"

"It took us a while to find out. But it turns out we're talking about a Mr Anan Sukit. He works for Major Yu. One of his lieutenants, you might say. Very high up. Very dangerous. It means we're one step down the pipeline, Alex. We're on our way."

"So we wait for him to get in touch."

"Exactly."

"What about the real Abdul?" Alex asked. He wondered how he could pretend to be someone he had never even met.

"You don't need to know much about him or his father. The two of them are Hazaras – a minority group within Afghanistan. The Hazaras have been persecuted for centuries. They get the worst education and the poorest jobs – in fact, most people think of them as hardly better than animals. *Kofr* – that's the word they use for them. It means 'infidel' and in Afghanistan it's the worst four-letter word you can call anyone."

"So where did they get their money?" Alex asked.

"They had a business in Mazar-e-Sharif which they managed to sell just before it was taken from them. They hid out in the Hindu Kush until they made contact with a local agent for the snakehead, paid the money and began their journey south."

"I don't suppose I look anything like an Afghan," Alex said. "What do these Hazara people look like?"

"Most of them are Asian – Mongol or Chinese. But not all. In fact, a lot of them managed to survive in Afghanistan precisely because they didn't look too Eastern. Anyway, you don't need to worry. Mrs Webber will take care of that."

"How about language?"

"You won't talk. Ever. You're going to pretend to be a simpleton. Just stare into the corner and keep your mouth shut. Try and look scared – as if I'm about to beat you. Maybe I will, from time to time. Just to make us look authentic."

Alex wasn't sure if Ash was being serious or not.

"I speak Dari," Ash went on. "That's the majority language in Afghanistan and it's the language the snakehead will use. I speak a few words of Hazaragi too, but we shouldn't need them. Just remember. Never open your mouth. If you do, you'll kill us both."

Ash stood up. While he had been talking, he had been grim – almost hostile. But now he turned to Alex with something close to desperation in his dark brown eyes. "Alex..." He paused, scratching at his beard. "Are you sure you want to do this? ASIS has got nothing to do with you. People smuggling and all the rest of it – you should be at school. Why don't you just go home?"

"It's a bit late now," Alex said. "I agreed. And I want you to tell me about my dad."

"Is that the main reason you agreed to this?"

"It's the only reason."

"I don't think I could forgive myself if anything happened to you. I'd be dead if it wasn't for your father. That's the truth of it." Ash looked away, as if trying to avoid the memory. "One day I'll tell you about it ... Malta, and what happened after Yassen Gregorovich had finished with me. But I'll tell you this right now. John wouldn't thank me for getting you into trouble. So if you'll take my advice, you'll call Brooke. Tell him you've changed your mind. And get out now."

"I'm staying," Alex said. "But thanks anyway."

In fact, what Ash had just said – the mention of Yassen Gregorovich – had only made Alex determined to learn more. Suddenly things were beginning to come together.

Alex knew that his father, John Rider, had pretended to be an enemy agent, working for Scorpia. When MI6 wanted him back, they had arranged for him to be "captured". That had been in Malta. It had all been a set-up. And Yassen Gregorovich had been there. Yassen was an international assassin and Alex had met him fourteen years later – first when he was working for Herod Sayle, a second time inside the evil empire of Damian Cray. Yassen was dead now but it seemed that he was still destined to be part of Alex's life. Ash had met him in Malta. And whatever had happened on that island was part of the story that Alex wanted to know.

"You're sure?" Ash asked him one last time.

"I'm sure," Alex said.

"Very well." Ash nodded gravely. "Then I'd better teach you this: *Ba'ad az ar tariki, roshani ast*. It's an old Afghan proverb, and there may come a time when you need to remember it. 'After every darkness, there is light.' I hope it will be true for you."

There was a knock at the door.

Ash went over and opened it and a short, rather dumpy woman walked in, carrying a suitcase. She could have been a retired matron or perhaps a very old-fashioned schoolteacher. She was wearing an olive-green two-piece suit and heavy stockings that only emphasized the fact that she had very shapeless legs. Her hair hung loose with no particular colour or style. Her face could have been made of putty. She was wearing no make-up. There was a single brooch – a silver daisy – pinned to her lapel.

"How are you doing, Ash?" She smiled as she came in and that, along with her broad Australian accent, seemed to bring her to life.

"Good to see you, Cloudy," Ash replied. He closed the door. "This is Mrs Webber, Alex," he explained. "She works for ASIS – a specialist in disguise. Her name is Chloe but we call her Cloudy. We think it suits her better. Cloudy Webber, meet Alex Rider."

The woman stumped over to Alex and examined him. "Hmm..." she muttered disapprovingly. "Mr Brooke must need his head examined if he thinks we're going to get away with this one. But I'll see what I can do." She heaved the suitcase onto the bed. "Let's have all those clothes off you, boy. T-shirt, boxers, the lot. The first thing we're going to start with is your skin."

"Wait a minute—" Alex began.

"For heaven's sake!" the woman exploded. "You think I'm going to see anything I haven't seen before?" She turned to Ash, who was watching. "It's the same for you, Ash. I don't know what you're grinning about. You may look a bit more like an Afghan than him, but I'm going to need all your clothes too."

She unzipped the suitcase and took out half a dozen plastic bottles filled with various dark liquids. Next came a hairbrush, a vanity bag and several tubes that might have contained toothpaste. The rest of the case was packed with clothes that looked – and smelled – as if they had come off a skip.

"The clothes are all from Oxfam," she explained. "Donated in England and picked up in the market in Mazar-e-Sharif. I'll give you two sets each, which is all you'll need: you'll wear them day and night. Ash, go and run a bath." She unscrewed one of the bottles. The smell – seaweed and white spirit – reached Alex even on the other side of the room. "Cold water!" she added sharply.

In the end she let Alex take a bath on his own. She had mixed two bottles of brown dye with half a bath of cold water. Alex was instructed to lie in it for ten minutes, submerging both his face and his hair. He was shivering by the time he was allowed out, and he didn't dare look in the mirror as he dried himself – but he noticed that the hotel towels now looked as if they'd been dragged through a sewer. He pulled on a pair of ragged, shapeless boxers and came out.

"That's better," Mrs Webber muttered. She noticed the raw scar just above his heart. It was where Alex had been shot and nearly killed by a sniper following his encounter with Scorpia. "That might be useful too," she added. "A lot of Afghan boys have got bullet wounds. Together, the two of you make quite a pair."

Alex didn't know what she meant. He glanced at Ash – and then he understood. Ash was just pulling on a loose, short-sleeved shirt and for a moment his chest and stomach were exposed. He too had a scar – but it was much worse than Alex's, a distinct line of white, dead skin that snaked across his belly and down below the waistline of his trousers. Ash turned away, buttoning up the shirt, but he was too late. Alex had seen the terrible injury. It was a stab wound. He was sure of that. He wondered who had been holding the knife.

"Come and sit down, Alex," Mrs Webber said. She had produced a tarpaulin which she had spread underneath a chair. "Let me deal with your hair."

Alex did as he was told and for the next few minutes he heard only the click of scissors and watched as uneven clumps of his hair tumbled to the floor. From the way she worked, he doubted that Mrs Webber had received her training in a London salon. A sheep-shearing farm was more likely. When she had finished cutting, she opened one of the tubes and smeared a thick, greasy ointment over his head. Finally she stepped back.

"He looks great," Ash said.

"The teeth still need work. They'd give him away in a minute."

There was another tube of paste for his teeth. She rubbed it in, using her finger. Lastly she produced two small plastic caps. They were both the size of a tooth but one was grey and one was black.

"I'm going to glue these in," Mrs Webber warned him.

Alex opened his mouth and allowed her to fix the fake teeth into place. He grimaced. His mouth no longer felt like his own.

"You'll notice them for a day or two but then you'll forget them," she said. She stepped back. "There! I'm all done. Why don't you get dressed and take a look at yourself?"

"Cloudy, you're damn good," Ash muttered.

Alex pulled on a faded red T-shirt and a pair of jeans – both of them dirty and full of holes. Then he went back into the bathroom and stood in front of the full-length mirror. He gasped. The boy he was looking at certainly wasn't him. He was olive-skinned with hair that was short, dark brown and matted in thick strands. Somehow the clothes made him look thinner than he really was. He opened his mouth and saw that two of his teeth seemed to have rotted and the rest were ugly and discoloured.

Mrs Webber came in behind him. "You won't need to worry about the skin colour for two weeks," she said. "Not unless you bath – and I don't think you'll be doing that. You'll have to check on the hair and teeth every five or six days. I'll make sure Ash has plenty of supplies."

"It's amazing," Ash said. He was standing at the door.

"I've got some trainers for you," Mrs Webber added. "You won't need socks. I doubt a refugee boy would wear any."

She went back into the bedroom and produced

a pair of trainers that were stained and torn. Alex tried to slip them on.

"They're too small," he said.

Mrs Webber frowned. "I can cut a hole for your toes."

"No. I can't wear them."

She scowled at him, but even she could see that the trainers were far too small. "All right." She nodded. "You can hang on to your own. Just give me a minute."

She dug around in the suitcase and produced a razor, some old paint and another bottle of some sort of chemical. Two minutes later, Alex's own trainers looked as if they'd been thrown away ten years before. As he slipped them on, she set to work on Ash. He too had completely changed. He didn't need to dye his skin, and his beard would have suited a Hazara tribesman. But his hair had to be hacked around and he needed new clothes as well. It was strange, but by the time she had finished, Alex and Ash really could have been father and son. Poverty had brought them closer together.

Mrs Webber packed all the clothes that Alex and Ash had been wearing into her suitcase. She zipped her bag shut and straightened up. She jabbed a finger in Ash's direction.

"You look after Alex," she commanded. "I've already had words with Mr Brooke. Sending a boy this age into the field: I don't think it's right. Just you make sure he comes back in one piece."

"I'll look after him," Ash promised.

"You'd better. Take care, Alex!"

And with that, she was gone.

Ash turned to Alex. "How are you feeling?"

"Grimy."

"It's going to get worse. Are you ready? It's time we left."

Alex moved towards the door.

"We'll take the service lift," Ash said. "And we'll find the back way out. If anyone sees us looking like this in the Peninsula Hotel, we'll be arrested."

The driver who had met Alex at the airport was waiting for them outside the hotel, and he took them over the river and then upstream towards Chinatown. Alex felt the air conditioning blowing cold against his skin and knew that it was a luxury he wasn't going to enjoy again for a while. The car dropped them off at a corner, and at once the heat, the grime and the noise of the city hit him. He was sweating before the door was even closed. Ash dragged a small battered case out of the boot and that was it. Suddenly they were on their own.

Bangkok's Chinatown was like nowhere Alex had ever been before. When he looked up, it seemed to have no sky – all the light had been blocked out by billboards, banners, electric cables and neon signs: TOM YUM KUNG RESTAURANT. THAI MASSAGE. SENG HONG DENTAL CLINIC (GREAT SMILE START HERE). The pavements were equally cluttered, every inch of them taken up by stalls spilling food and cheap clothes and electronics into the street. There were people everywhere, hundreds of them, weaving their way between the traffic, which seemed frozen in an endless, diesel-infested jam.

"This way," Ash muttered, keeping his voice low. From now on, whenever he spoke in English, he would make sure he wasn't overheard.

They pushed their way into the chaos, and in the next few minutes Alex passed vegetables that he had never seen before and meats he hoped he would never see again: hearts and lungs bubbling in green soup and brown intestines spilling out of their cauldrons as if trying to escape. Every scent on the planet seemed to be mixed together. Meat and fish and rubbish and sweat – every step brought another smell.

They walked for about ten minutes until they came to an opening between a restaurant – with a few plastic tables and a single glass counter displaying plastic replicas of the food it served – and a paint works. Here at last was an escape from the main road. A soiled, narrow alleyway led down between two blocks of flats piled up on top of one another as if thrown there at random. There was a miniature altar at the entrance, the incense adding another smell to Alex's collection. Further along, two cars had been parked next to a dozen crates of empty Pepsi bottles, a pile of old gas canisters and a row of tables and chairs. A Chinese woman was sitting cross-legged in the gutter, fixing ribbons to baskets of exotic fruit. Alex remembered the complimentary fruit basket in his hotel room. Maybe this was where it had come from.

"This is the place," Ash said.

It was the address that Karim Hassan and his son had been given by the snakehead. This was where they were expected to stay.

All the flats opened directly onto the alley and Alex could see straight in. There were no doors or curtains. In one front room, a Chinese man sat smoking at a table, dressed in shorts and glasses, his huge stomach bulging over his knees. In another, a whole family were eating lunch, crouching on the floor with chopsticks. They came to a room that looked derelict but was occupied. An old woman was standing beside a stove. Ash signalled to Alex to wait, then went over and spoke to her, relying on sign language as much as words and waving a sheet of paper in front of her face.

She understood and pointed to a staircase at the back. Ash grunted something in Dari and, pretending to understand, Alex hurried forward.

The stairs were made of cement with pools of murky water on at least half of them. Alex followed Ash to the third floor and a single door with no handle. Ash pushed it open. On the other side was a bare room with a metal bed, a spare mattress on the floor, a sink, a toilet and a grimy window. There was no carpet and no light. As Alex walked in, the biggest cockroach he had ever seen climbed over the side of the bed and scuttled across the wall.

"This is it?" Alex muttered.

"This is it," Ash said.

Outside in the alleyway, the man who had followed them all the way from the hotel made a note of the building. As he turned away he took out a mobile phone and dialled a number. By the time he had been connected he had disappeared into the crowd.

FIRST CONTACT

"Suppose they don't come," Alex said.

"They'll come."

"How much longer do you think we're going to have to wait?"

They had been living in Chinatown for nearly three days and Alex was feeling hot, frustrated ... and bored. Ash wouldn't let him have a newspaper or a book in English. There was always the chance that he might be caught reading it by someone entering the room. Nor was he able to see very much of Bangkok. There was no way of knowing when the snakehead might show up and they couldn't risk being out.

But Alex had been allowed to spend a couple of hours early each morning wandering on his own through the streets. It amused him that nobody treated him like a tourist – indeed, tourists stepped aside to avoid him. Mrs Webber had done her job well. He looked like a street urchin from somewhere far away, and after more than fifty hours without a shower or a bath – without even changing his clothes – he imagined he could be smelled long before he could be seen.

Slowly he managed to get to grips with the city, the way the shops and the houses, the pavements and the streets, all tumbled into each other, the clammy heat, the never-ending noise and movement. There seemed to be a surprise round every corner. A cripple with withered legs, scuttling past on his hands like a giant spider. A temple sprouting out of nowhere like an exotic flower. Bald-headed monks in their bright orange robes, moving in a crowd.

He also learnt a little more about Ash.

Ash slept badly. He had given Alex the bed and taken the mattress for himself, but sometimes in the night he would begin muttering and then jerk awake. He would clasp his hand to his stomach, and Alex knew that he was remembering the time he had been stabbed and that it was hurting him even now.

"Why did you become a spy?" Alex asked one morning.

"It seemed like a good idea at the time," Ash growled. He hated being asked questions and seldom gave straightforward answers. But that day he was in a better mood. "I was approached while I was in the army."

"By Alan Blunt?"

"No. He was there when I joined, but he wasn't

in the top spot. I was recruited a short while after your dad. I'll tell you why he joined, if you like."

"Why?"

"He was a patriot." Ash grimaced. "He really thought he had a duty to serve queen and country."

"Don't you?"

"I did ... once."

"So what happened? What made you change your mind?"

"It was a long time ago." Ash had a way of cutting off a conversation if he didn't want to say more. Alex had come to learn that when that happened, there was no point trying to go on. Ash could wrap silence around him like a coat. It was infuriating but he knew he would just have to wait. Ash would talk in his own time.

And then, on the fourth day, the snakehead came.

Alex had just got back with food from the local market when he heard the stamp of feet on the concrete steps. Ash threw him a look of warning and swung himself off the bed just as the door crashed open and one of the ugliest men Alex had ever seen walked into the room.

He was short, wearing a suit that looked as if it had shrunk in the wash to fit him. He was bald and unshaven so that both the top and bottom of his head were covered in a thin black stubble. On the other hand, he didn't seem to have any eyebrows – as if his skin were too thick and pock-marked to grow through. His mouth was impossibly wide, like an open wound, with as many gaps as teeth. Worst of all, he had no ears. Alex could see the discoloured lumps of flesh that remained. The rest had at some time been cut off.

This had to be Anan Sukit. There was a second man with him, dressed in a white T-shirt and jeans, carrying a camera – a clunky wooden box that could have come out of an antique shop. A third man followed. He looked similar to Ash – presumably an Afghan brought along to translate. Alex had quickly sat down in the corner. He glanced at the three men but tried not to show too much interest, as if he didn't want to be noticed himself.

Sukit snapped a few words at the translator, who then spoke to Ash. Ash replied in Dari and a three-way conversation began. As it continued, Alex noticed Sukit examining him. The snakehead lieutenant had tiny pupils which moved ceaselessly, darting left and right. The cameraman had started his work, and Alex sat still as several shots were taken of him. Then it was Ash's turn. He had already explained to Alex what sort of papers would be prepared. Passports, possibly with visas for Indonesia. A police arrest form for Ash. A hospital report showing that he had been injured during questioning. Perhaps an old membership card for the Communist Party. All these things would help them get refugee status once they arrived in Australia.

The photographer finished but the discussion went on. Alex became aware that something was wrong. Sukit nodded in his direction a couple of times; he seemed to be making some sort of demand. Ash was arguing, and he looked unhappy. Alex heard his name – Abdul – mentioned several times.

Then, suddenly, Anan Sukit walked over to him. He was sweating and his skin smelled of garlic. Without warning, he reached down and dragged Alex to his feet. Ash stood up and shouted something. Alex couldn't understand a word that was being said but he did what Ash had told him and stared with unfocused eyes as if he were a simpleton. Sukit slapped him, twice, on each side of his face. Alex cried out. It wasn't just the pain. It was the casual violence, the shock of what had happened. Ash let loose a torrent of words. He seemed to be pleading. Sukit spoke one last time. Ash nodded. Whatever had been demanded, he'd agreed. The three men turned and left the room.

Alex waited until he was sure they had gone. His cheeks were stinging. "I take it that was Anan Sukit?" he muttered.

"That was him."

"What happened to his ears?"

"A gang fight five years ago. Maybe I should have mentioned it to you before. Someone cut them off."

"He's lucky he doesn't need glasses." Alex

rubbed the side of his face with a grimy hand. "So what was all that about?" he asked.

"I don't know. I don't understand..." Ash was deep in thought. "They're getting the papers for us. They'll be ready this evening."

"That's good. But why did he hit me?"

"He made a demand. I refused. So he got angry – and he took it out on you. I'm sorry, Alex." Ash ran a hand through his curly dark hair. He looked shaken by what had just taken place. "I didn't want him to hurt you, but there was nothing I could do."

"What did he want?"

Ash sighed. "Sukit insisted that you collect the papers. Not me. He just wants you."

"Why?"

"He didn't say. He told me they'd pick you up at Patpong at seven o'clock this evening. You've got to be on your own. If you're not there, we can forget it. The deal's off."

Ash fell silent. He had lost control of the situation and he knew it.

Alex wasn't sure how to respond. His first encounter with the snakehead had been short and unpleasant. The question was, what did they want with him? Had they seen through his disguise? If he turned up at this place – Patpong – they could bundle him into a car and he might never be seen again.

"If they wanted to kill you, they could have

done it here and now," Ash said. It was as if he'd read Alex's thoughts. "They could have killed both of us."

"Do you think I should go?"

"I can't make that decision, Alex. That's up to you."

But if he didn't go, there would be no forged papers, no way for Ash to find out where they were being manufactured. Nor would the two of them be able to continue down the pipeline. The mission would be over before it had even begun. And Alex would have learnt nothing from Ash – nothing about his father, about Malta, about Yassen Gregorovich.

It was a risk. But it was one worth taking.

"I'll do it," Alex said.

Patpong showed Alex another side of Bangkok – and not one that he wanted to see. It was a tangle of bars and strip clubs where backpackers and businessmen gathered to drink the night away. Through the doorways he glimpsed half-naked dancers writhing in time to Western pop music. Fat men in floral shirts strolled past with Thai girlfriends. The neon lights flickered and the music pounded out, and the air was thick with the smell of alcohol and cheap perfume. It was the last place on earth that a fourteen-year-old English boy would want to find himself, and Alex was feeling distinctly uncomfortable, standing at the entrance to the main square. But he'd only been there a few minutes when a beaten-up black Citroën pulled over with two men inside. He recognized one of them. The man in the passenger seat had been carrying the camera and had taken the pictures of him and Ash.

So this was it. He had come to Thailand to investigate the snakehead and now he was delivering himself to them with no weapons, no gadgets – nothing to help him if things went wrong. Were they simply going to hand over the papers as promised? Somehow he doubted it. But it was too late for second thoughts. He climbed into the back of the car. The seat was plastic – and it was torn. Furry dice swung beneath the driver's mirror.

Nobody spoke to him – but then, of course, they didn't know his language. Ash had warned him not to say anything, no matter what happened. One word of English would mean an immediate death sentence for both of them. He would pretend he was simple, that he understood nothing at all. If things got out of hand, he would try to break away.

The Citroën joined the sluggish flow of traffic and suddenly they were surrounded by cars, lorries, buses and tuk-tuks. As always, everyone was hooting at everyone else. The heat of the evening only intensified the noise and the smell of exhaust fumes that hung thick in the air.

They drove for about thirty minutes. It was dark and Alex had no idea in which direction they were heading. He tried to pick out a few landmarks – a neon sign, a skyscraper with a strange gold dome on the roof, a hotel. Part of his job was to find out as much about the snakehead as he could, and the following day he might have to show Ash exactly where he'd been taken. The car turned off the main road and suddenly they were travelling down a narrow alleyway between two high walls. Alex was liking this less and less. He had the feeling that he was delivering himself into some sort of trap. Sukit had said he would hand over the papers but Alex didn't believe him. There had to be another reason for all this.

And then they broke out and he saw the river in front of him, the water black and empty but for a single rice barge making its way home. In the far distance, a tower block that he recognized caught his eye. It was the Peninsula Hotel, where he had spent his first night in Bangkok. It was less than half a mile upstream but it might as well have belonged to a different world. The car slowed down. They had come right to the river's edge. The driver turned off the engine and they got out.

The smell of sewage. That was what hit him first: thick, sweet and heavy. The surface of the water was covered with a layer of rotting vegetables and rubbish that rocked back and forth with the current like a living carpet. One of the men pushed him, hard, in the small of his back and Alex made his way over to a broken-down jetty where a boat was waiting to ferry them across, another hard-faced Thai man at the rudder. Alex climbed in. The other men followed.

They set off. The moon had risen, and out in the open everything was suddenly bright. Ahead of him Alex could see their destination. There was a long, three-storey building with a green painted sign advertising it to any passing river traffic: CHADA TRADING COMPANY. Alex didn't like the look of it one bit.

The building was on the very edge of the river, half falling into it, propped up on a series of concrete posts that held it about two metres above the water. It was made of wood and corrugated iron: a slanting, leaning assembly of roofs, verandas, balconies and walkways that looked as if it had been hammered together by a child. It seemed to have few doors and fewer windows. As they drew closer, Alex heard a sound: a low shouting that suddenly rose up like the noise of a crowd at a football match. It was coming from inside.

The boat arrived. A ladder led up to a landing platform and once again Alex felt a fist jabbing into his lower back. It seemed to be the only way these people knew how to communicate. He got unsteadily to his feet and grabbed the ladder. As he did so, he heard a splash and saw a streak of movement out of the corner of his eye. Something was living in the dark space underneath the building. There was another roar from inside and the chime of a bell. How had he got himself into this? Alex gritted his teeth and climbed up.

He went through a door and found himself in a narrow corridor that sloped down with doorways on each side. Naked bulbs dangled at intervals, throwing out a damp, yellow light. The whole place smelled of the river. Halfway down they stopped at one of the doors, which was thrown open to reveal a room that was like a cell, a couple of metres square with a tiny barred window, a bench and a table. There was a pair of brightly coloured shorts lying on the bench. Camera Man – Alex didn't know his name – picked up the shorts and spat out a sentence in Thai. This time the meaning was clear.

The door slammed shut. There was another roar from somewhere near by, the sound echoing outwards. Alex picked up the shorts. They were made of silk, recently laundered, but there were still dark spots embedded in the material. Old bloodstains. Alex clamped down the rising sense of fear. He looked at the window, but there was no way he was going to be able to climb out. He had no doubt the men were standing guard on the other side of the door. He heard the whine of a mosquito and slapped it against the side of his head. He began to undress.

Ten minutes later, they led him further along the corridor to a flight of steps that seemed to have collapsed in on itself like a house of cards. Alex was now wearing the shorts and nothing else.

They started high on his body, above the waist, and came down to his knees. They were the kind worn for a boxing or wrestling match. Which of them was it going to be? Or was he being led towards something worse than either?

He could hear music playing. The crackle of a loudspeaker and a stream of words, amplified, all in Thai. Laughter. The soft babble of many people talking. At last he emerged into a scene that was like nothing he had ever experienced before – and something he would never forget.

It was an arena, circular in shape with dozens of narrow pillars holding up the ceiling, a raised boxing ring in the middle and wooden seating slanting up around the sides. It was lit by neon strips that dangled on chains and there were twenty or thirty fans turning slowly, trying to redistribute the hot, sticky air. Thai music was blaring out of speakers and, bizarrely, there were old television sets facing outwards, each one showing a different programme.

The ring itself was surrounded by a wire fence which had been built to keep either the players in or the audience out. There must have been about four hundred people in the room, chattering excitedly among themselves as they swapped bright yellow slips of paper. Alex had read somewhere that betting was illegal in Thailand but he recognized at once what was going on here. He had arrived just at the end of a fight. A young man was being dragged feet first across the ring, his arms splayed out, his shoulders painting a red streak along the canvas as he was hauled away. And the members of the audience who had bet on his opponent were collecting their winnings.

Alex was at the very back of the arena. As he arrived, another man – dressed like him in shorts – was led down to the ring, his entire body taut with fear. Seeing him, the audience laughed and applauded. More yellow betting slips changed hands. Someone put a hand on Alex's shoulder and pushed him down onto a plastic seat. There was a crack in the floor and he caught a glimpse of silver, the river water lapping at the concrete posts underneath. He was sweating and the mosquitoes had picked up his scent. He could hear them right inside his ear. His skin crawled as he was bitten again and again.

The new challenger had passed through the audience and reached the wire fence. Someone had placed a string of flowers around his neck, and he looked as if he were about to be sacrificed. It occurred to Alex that in a sense he was. Two burly Thai men led him through an opening in the fence and helped him climb into the ring. They forced him to bow to the audience. Then, in the far corner, the champion appeared.

He wasn't big – but he emanated power and speed. Alex could see every single muscle on his body. They were locked together like metal plates and he didn't have a single spare ounce of fat.

His hair, very black, was cut short. His eyes were black too. He had a boy's face, completely smooth, but Alex guessed he was in his mid twenties. His name – Sunthorn – was written in white letters on his shorts. He bowed to the audience and danced on his feet, raising his fists to acknowledge their applause.

The challenger awaited his fate. The flower garland had been removed and the other men had left the ring. The music stopped. A bell rang.

At once Alex understood what he was seeing. He had been expecting the worst and this was it. Muay Thai, also known as the science of eight limbs, one of the most aggressive and dangerous martial arts in the world. Alex had learnt karate but he knew that it was a world apart from Muay Thai, which permitted strikes by the fists, elbows, knees and feet with no fewer than twenty-four targets – from the top of the head to the rear calf – on your opponent. And this was a dirty, illegal version. Neither of the fighters had hand wraps, shin pads or abdomen protectors. The fight would continue until one of them was carried out unconscious – or worse.

Alex watched the first round with a mixture of fascination and horror, knowing that he was going to be next. The fight had begun with both men weaving around, weighing up each other's weaknesses. Sunthorn had struck out a few times, first with a right side elbow attack, then twisting his body round in a fast knee strike. But the challenger was faster than he looked, dodging both blows and even trying a counter-kick, slicing his left foot into the air and missing Sunthorn's neck by centimetres, a move that sparked a roar of excitement from the crowd.

But then, at the end of the first round, he made his fatal mistake. He had allowed his guard to drop, as if waiting for the bell. Suddenly Sunthorn lashed out, a rear leg push kick that slammed into the other man's chest, winding him and almost throwing him off his feet. It was only the chime of the bell a second later that saved him. He staggered into the corner, where someone forced a bottle of water between his lips and flannelled down his face. But he was barely conscious. The next round wouldn't last long.

In the brief interval, more music blasted out of the speakers and the televisions flickered back on. Yellow slips were exchanged and Alex noticed people gesturing wildly, angrily tapping their watches. He was feeling sick. He realized now that the spectators weren't betting on who was going to win the fight. With Sunthorn in the ring, there could be no doubt of that. They were betting on how long a fighter could last against him.

The bell rang for the next round, and as expected it was all over very quickly. The challenger moved forward as if he knew he was walking to his execution. Sunthorn examined him with a cruel smile then finished the fight in the most vicious way he could: a kick to the stomach followed by a second, much harder kick straight into the face. A great flower of blood erupted into the ring. The audience howled. The challenger crashed down on his back and lay still. Sunthorn danced around him, waving his fists in triumph. The cleaners climbed into the ring to clear away the mess.

And now it was Alex's turn.

He was suddenly aware of a man leaning over him – a weird, stretched-out face like a reflection in a fairground mirror. It was Anan Sukit. The snakehead lieutenant spoke to him first in Thai, then in another language. Once again, Alex smelled the stale scent of garlic. Sukit paused. Alex stared straight ahead, as if he hadn't even heard what had just been said. Sukit leant forward. He said something in bad French. Then he repeated it in English.

"You fight, or I kill you."

Alex had to force himself to pretend that he hadn't understood. The man couldn't possibly have known who he was or where he came from. He was simply saying the same thing in as many languages as possible. And finally he used the most effective language of all, grabbing Alex by the hair and pulling him out of his seat and then propelling him down the aisle towards the ring.

As he walked down between the audience, Alex felt himself being examined and evaluated on every side. Once again the yellow markers were being handed out, and he could imagine the bets being placed. Fifteen seconds ... twenty seconds – it was obvious that this foreign boy wouldn't last long. His heart was pounding – he could actually see the movement in his naked chest. Why had he been chosen for this? Why not Ash? He could only assume that these people got a sick satisfaction out of ringing the changes. During the course of the evening, they had seen a number of men beaten up. Now they were going to watch the same thing happen to a teenager.

He passed through the opening in the fence. The two seconds were waiting for him, grinning and offering to help him up into the ring. One of them was carrying a garland of flowers to put around his neck. Alex had already made up his mind about that. As their hands reached towards him, he struck out at them, drawing laughter and jeers from the crowd. But he wasn't going to be touched by them and nor was he going to parade in their flowers. He pulled himself into the ring just as two cleaners climbed out, lowering themselves between the ropes. They took with them the bloody rags that they had used to clean the canvas floor.

Sunthorn was waiting in the opposite corner.

It was only now that he was closer that Alex could see the arrogance and the cruelty of the man he was about to face. Sunthorn had probably been training all his life and knew that this next fight was going to be over as soon as it began. But he didn't care. Presumably he was being paid and would cheerfully maim Alex, provided he got his cheque. Already he was smiling, showing cracked lips and uneven teeth. His nose had been broken at some time and it had set badly. He might have had the body of a world-class athlete but he had the face of a freak.

A plastic bottle of water was forced between Alex's lips and he drank. It was horribly warm in the arena and that would only sap his strength. He wondered how Sunthorn had managed to continue for so long. Perhaps he was given some sort of drug. The military music was blasting out all around him. The fans were turning. Alex clung to the rope, trying to work out some sort of strategy. Would it be easier just to take a dive the moment the fight began? If he allowed himself to be knocked out in the opening seconds, at least it would be over. But there was a risk in that too. It would all depend how hard Sunthorn hit him. He didn't want to wake up with a broken neck.

The music stopped. The bell rang. The spectators fell silent. It was too late to work out any plan. The first round had begun.

Alex took a couple of steps forward. He could feel the eyes of the crowd boring into him, waiting for him to go down. Sunthorn looked completely relaxed. He had taken up the standard stance with his body weight poised on his front foot – the basic defence in almost every martial art – but he barely looked interested. It occurred to Alex that if he had any chance at all in this fight, it would be in the opening seconds. Nobody in the arena could possibly know that he was a first grade *Dan* – a black belt in karate. The fight was completely unfair. Sunthorn had the advantages of size, weight and experience. But Alex had the advantage of surprise.

He decided to use it. He continued forward and, at the last second, when he knew he was close enough, he suddenly twisted round and lashed out with all his strength. He had used the back kick, one of the most powerful blows in karate, and if he had made contact he would have taken his opponent out then and there. But to his dismay his foot hit only empty air. Sunthorn had reacted with fantastic speed, springing back and twisting so that the kick missed his abdomen by a centimetre.

The audience gasped, then chattered with new excitement. Alex tried a front jab but this time Sunthorn was ready. He blocked the attack with his right arm, then followed through with a counter-kick that slammed into Alex's side, propelling him back against the ropes. Alex was bruised and winded. Red spots danced in front of his eyes. If Sunthorn hit him a second time, it would be over. Alex rested with the ropes against his shoulders and waited for the end.

It didn't come. Sunthorn was smiling again, enjoying himself. The foreign boy hadn't been the easy kill that everyone expected and he knew he could enjoy himself here. The audience wanted blood but they wanted drama too. He could play with the boy for a while, weaken him before the final blow that would put him in hospital. He reached out with his hand, bending his fingers as if to say "Come on!" The crowd roared their approval. Even the gamblers who had already lost and were tearing up their yellow slips wanted to see more.

Alex drew a deep breath and straightened up. There was a red mark where Sunthorn's foot had caught him, just above the waist. The man had a sole that could have been made of the toughest leather and leg muscles like steel rods. How could Ash have got him into this? But Alex knew it wasn't his godfather's fault. He should have listened to Jack when he was in Sydney. Right now he could have been safely back at school.

For the next couple of minutes, the two of them circled each other, throwing a few feints, but neither landing a real punch. Alex tried to keep his distance while he recovered his breath. How long did each round last? He had seen that there were intervals and he desperately needed a few seconds on his own, unthreatened: time to think. The sweat was dripping off him. He wiped his eyes, and that was when Sunthorn attacked, a whirl of jabbing elbows, knees and fists, any one of which could have knocked Alex down.

In the next thirty seconds, Alex used every defence technique he had ever been taught, but he knew that in truth he was simply relying on his instincts, dodging and weaving as the arena seemed to spin around him, the audience shouting, the fans turning and the sluggish heat weighing down on him from all sides. A right hook caught him on the side of the face and his whole head jerked round, a spasm of pain travelling down his neck and spine. Sunthorn followed through with a side knee to the ribs. Alex doubled up, unable to help himself. He hit the canvas just as the bell rang for the end of the first round.

There was applause and cheering. The music blared out. Sunthorn leapt back, grinning and waving, enjoying the fight. Alex felt he had no strength left. He was aware of the two men acting as his seconds shouting at him, gesturing for him to return to his corner. Somehow he forced himself to his feet. His nose was bleeding. He could taste the blood as it trickled into his mouth.

He wasn't going to last another round: that much was obvious. All the odds were against him. But he had come to a decision. Sunthorn was older, taller, heavier and more experienced than he was, and there was only one way Alex was going to beat him.

He was just going to have to cheat.

ONCE BITTEN...

One of the men who had been chosen to look after Alex while he was fighting wiped away the blood with a wet sponge. The other helped him drink. Alex felt the cold water trickle down the sides of his face and over his shoulders. Both men were grinning at him, muttering words of encouragement as if he could understand a single word they were saying. They had probably done exactly the same during the previous fight – and Alex had seen the result. Well, he wasn't going to let that happen to him. These people were in for a surprise.

He felt the water bottle being forced one last time between his lips and sucked in as much as he could. A moment later, a bell rang and the bottle was whisked away. The interval music stopped. There were shouts from different parts of the audience. Glancing to one side, Alex saw Anan Sukit striding down to take a place in the front row. Presumably he wanted a closer view of the final knockout.

Alex moved forward cautiously, fists raised, weight evenly distributed on the balls of his feet. Sunthorn was waiting for him. That was good. The one thing Alex had most feared was a fast, direct attack. That wouldn't leave him time for what he had in mind. But Alex had shown his true colours in the first round. Sunthorn knew that he had trained in at least one martial art and he was planning his moves carefully. Alex had come close to knocking him out; Sunthorn wasn't going to give him a second chance.

In the end Sunthorn went for a straight clinch, the wrestling grip that, in Muay Thai, is also known as the standard tie-up. Suddenly they were face to face, their feet almost touching. Sunthorn had locked his hands behind Alex's head and he was sneering, utterly confident. With his extra height, he had the complete advantage. He could throw Alex off balance or finish him with an explosive strike from his knee. The audience saw that the last seconds of the fight had arrived and roared their approval.

It was exactly what Alex wanted. It was exactly what he had been inviting. Before Sunthorn could make his move, he acted. What nobody knew – not Sunthorn, nor the seconds nor the audience – was that Alex's mouth was still full of water and had been since the round began. Now he spat it out, straight into Sunthorn's face.

Sunthorn reacted instinctively, jerking his head

back in surprise and loosening his grip. For a second, he was blinded. Alex acted instantly, striking out with a savage uppercut that sent his fist crashing into his opponent's jaw. But that wasn't enough. He wouldn't get a second chance: he had to finish this now. Alex swung round, putting all his strength into a single powerhouse kick, his bare foot landing square in the man's solar plexus.

Even Sunthorn's advanced muscle structure wasn't up to such a blow. Alex heard the breath explode from his lips. All the colour left his face. For a moment, he stood there, hands hanging limply beneath him. The crowd had fallen silent, as if in shock. Then Sunthorn collapsed onto his knees and finally slammed face down, unconscious, on the canvas.

The entire arena erupted with cries of anger and outrage. The audience had seen what had happened – and they couldn't believe it. The foreign boy had been brought here to entertain them but he had cheated them instead. They had lost money. And their champion – Sunthorn – had been humiliated.

It was only now, hearing the shouting all around him, that Alex realized he had put himself in fresh danger. If he had played his part as expected, he might have been carried out on his back with a broken nose – or worse. But presumably there would have been a consolation prize. He would have been driven home with the false documents that Ash had sent him here to collect. There was no longer any chance of that. He had offended the snakehead, taken out their prize fighter. Somehow he doubted that they were going to thank him and give him a gold cup.

He stepped over the unconscious body and made as if to climb out of the ring. But he saw at once that he was right. Anan Sukit was back on his feet, his face dark with fury, his eyes ablaze. He had pulled a gun out of an inside pocket of his suit. Unbelieving, Alex watched as he brought it round and aimed. Sukit was going to shoot him, right there, in front of all these people – a punishment for the trick that had just been played. And there was nothing Alex could do, nowhere to hide. He watched as the cold eye of the muzzle focused on his head.

Then all the lights went out.

The darkness was absolute. It seemed to fold in from all sides, like a collapsing box. Sukit had chosen that moment to fire. Alex saw two bursts of orange flame and heard the shots. But he was already moving. The bullets had been aimed at his head but he had dropped down onto the canvas and was rolling away, searching for the ropes on the other side of the ring. He found them. Reaching up with one hand, he swung himself through, then down into the ringside area below.

The spectators had reacted to the blackout with silence, but the sound of the two shots had provoked instant panic. They were suddenly blind and someone had a gun! Alex heard screams, the clatter of seats being pushed to the ground. Someone ran into him, then tumbled back. There were more cries of protest. Alex crouched where he was, waiting for his eyes to get used to the dark.

At least that happened quickly. As Alex had approached the building from the river, he had seen how dilapidated it was; and although there were few windows, the roof and the walls were full of cracks. The moon was still shining and the light was spilling in everywhere, not enough to distinguish faces but Alex was in no mood to make new friends. All he wanted was the way out and he could see it, straight in front of him, up a flight of concrete steps.

He got to his feet and ran, immediately crashing into the wire fence that surrounded the ring. Where was the opening? Desperately he felt his way along, using his palms against the wire. He found the gap and stumbled through, forcing himself on towards the raked seating which climbed steeply up to the door where he'd come in. There was a third shot and a man standing next to him twisted round and fell. Sukit had spotted him, which was hardly surprising. Alex's bare shoulders and brightly coloured shorts made him a target even in the dark. He scrambled on, fighting his way through the crowd. His skin was slippery, covered in sweat, and at least that made it difficult for anyone to grab hold of him. A Thai man stepped in front of him, muttering something in his own language. Alex raised a hand, driving the heel straight into his face. The man grunted and fell backwards. The knife he had been holding clattered to the floor. Now Alex understood the rules. He was to be captured and killed. That seemed to be the price of winning the fight.

Alex was unarmed. He was half naked. And members of the snakehead were all around him. He knew that only speed and the darkness were on his side. He had to find his way out of this building in the next few minutes. And that meant retrieving his own clothes first. He reached the door – and it was then that the lights flashed back on.

Sukit saw him at once. He pointed with a stubby finger and shouted. Alex saw half a dozen young men running towards him, all of them black-haired, dressed in black shirts. They were coming at him from both sides. Sukit fired. The bullet hit a pillar and ricocheted into one of the television sets. The glass shattered and there was a crackle of electricity. Alex saw a tongue of flame and wondered if the whole place might catch light. That would help him. But the walls were too damp. The river was everywhere, even in the air he was breathing.

He hurled himself through the doorway and down the wooden staircase on the other side, almost losing his balance on the crazy fairground steps. A splinter buried itself in his toe. Alex ignored the pain. He was back in the corridor.

Which way had they led him? Left or right? He had less than a second to make a decision and the wrong choice might kill him.

He went right. That way, the corridor sloped upwards and he remembered that, coming in, he had gone down. Behind him he heard a burst of gunfire: not one gun but several. That was strange. He was out of sight now, so who were they firing at? The dull yellow light bulbs flickered overhead. It seemed that war had broken out in the arena. Was it possible...? Alex wondered if Ash could have somehow followed him here. Certainly there seemed to be someone on his side.

He found the room where he had undressed and ran in, swinging the door shut behind him. His clothes were where he'd left them, and gratefully he pulled them on. At least he looked normal again – and he needed the trainers if he was going to run over any more wooden floors. When he was dressed, he went back to the door and slowly opened it. Sweat trickled down his face. His hair was drenched. But there didn't seem to be anyone outside.

The end of the corridor and the exit to the jetty were about twenty metres away. But as he made his way towards the open air, Alex heard the roar of an engine, and knew that a boat had just pulled in. He guessed what was going to happen next. Luckily he was outside one of the other rooms. He threw himself inside just as the main door crashed open and the new arrivals began to make their way down the corridor. There were two of them. They were both carrying old-fashioned, Russian-made RPK-74 light machine guns. The barrels had been modified to make them shorter. As Alex crouched in the shadows, he heard them move towards him. They were searching the changing rooms, one by one. In less than a minute they would be here.

Alex looked around him. This room was almost identical to the one he had left, with no cupboards, nowhere to hide and a single window, securely barred. But there was one difference. Part of the floor had rotted away; he could just make out the water churning underneath. Could he fit through? There was a crash as the door of the room next to his was thrown open. He heard one of the men call out in Thai. They would be here in a few seconds. Alex didn't like to think what he might be getting himself into. The water was a long way down and the current might suck him beneath the surface. But if he stayed here, he would die anyway. He went over to the hole, took a deep breath, and dropped through it.

He fell into darkness, and just had time to put a hand over his nose before he hit the river. The water was warm and sluggish, covered by a layer of filth and rotting vegetation. The stink was almost unendurable. It was like plunging into the oldest, dirtiest bath in the world. As Alex broke back through the surface, he could feel the liquid, like oil, running down his cheeks and over his lips. Some sort of slime was clinging to his face. He tore it off, forcing himself not to swallow.

He was out of the arena but he still hadn't escaped. He could hear voices above him. It was almost impossible to see anything. He was underneath the building, treading water, surrounded by the concrete pillars that held the place up. In the distance he could just make out the shape of the boat that must have brought the two men with machine guns. It was alongside the jetty, its engines still running. There was the stamp of footsteps and he looked up as two flickering shadows passed above his head. They belonged to men running along the veranda outside the arena. Sukit must have given the order to surround the place. Presumably they were still searching it inch by inch.

And then something climbed onto his shoulder.

It was only now that he remembered the movement he had seen when he had arrived: something living in the water and the shadows beneath the building. Alex reached out and grabbed one of the pillars, steadying himself. Then, very slowly, he turned his head.

It was a rat, heavy and bloated, over thirty centimetres long, with vicious yellow teeth and eyes the colour of blood. Its tail, curling round behind Alex's neck, added another twenty-five centimetres to its length and it was clinging to his shirt with little claws, scrabbling feverishly at the material. And it wasn't alone. As Alex froze in utter horror, two more rats appeared, then a fourth. Soon the water was swarming with them. Another one climbed onto the side of his face, scratching the skin as it pulled itself on top of his head. Alex wanted to scream – but it was the one thing he couldn't do. There were armed men standing above him, only a few metres away. If he so much as splashed too loudly, it would all be over.

Were the rats going to bite him? That was the terrible thought. Was he going to be eaten alive? He felt something nudge his shirt. One of the creatures had dived underwater and was trying to dig its way inside. He could feel its nose and claws burrowing against the soft flesh of his stomach. With a feeling of nausea, he reached down and gently pushed it away. If he was too rough the rat would bite him, and once the others got a scent of his blood...

He stopped himself. Better not even to imagine.

His only hope was to do nothing. Let the rats decide that he was just another bit of pollution that had been dumped in the river. He tried to send his thoughts out to the pack. I'm not edible. You wouldn't like me.

The rat that had climbed onto his head was now nestling in his hair. Alex winced as it pulled out a few strands and began to chew on them, checking out the taste. The first rat, the one that had started all this, was still on his shoulder. Without moving, Alex glanced down and saw a pointed nose twitching right beside his jugular. Behind it he could make out two eyes, gleaming with excitement, fascinated by the rapid pulsing – in exact time with Alex's heart. All it had to do was bite through the flesh, find the vein. Alex was certain it was about to strike.

He was saved by an explosion, a fireball that erupted in the very centre of the building, reflecting down into the water. At once, all the rats took fright, leaping off him and disappearing behind the pillars. What the hell was going on? Had he perhaps wandered into some war between two rival snakeheads? That didn't matter now. He had to move before the rats came back. Alex launched himself away from the pillar and swam through the muck, trying to keep his face out of the water.

The arena was on fire. He could hear voices yelling and saw the flicker of red. A piece of blazing wood tumbled out of nowhere and fell, hissing and spitting, into the river. Alex glanced upwards. The building had been rickety to begin with. He didn't want it collapsing now – not when he was underneath. The jetty was straight ahead of him. Even if there were men standing on guard, Alex doubted he would be noticed. With all that was going on inside, nobody would be looking down into the water. Anyway, he didn't care any more. He'd had enough of this. It was time to go.

He reached the side of the boat, a sheer metal wall rising up into fresh air and freedom. There was a net hanging over the side and Alex grabbed it gratefully. Somehow he found the last reserves of strength he needed to climb up. The boat was one of the old river ferries, with a red roof to show that it crossed continually from one side to the other. There was one man on board – presumably the driver – a Thai wearing jeans and a jacket but no shirt. He was leaning against the side, watching the fire with a look of astonishment.

The wooden building was crackling loudly. Flames had caught hold of the roof and the back wall and were leaping up into the night sky. The wood was splintering, pieces of it splashing down. Alex didn't even try to be quiet. He hauled himself over the rail on the other side of the ferry, behind the driver. The man didn't turn round. Alex ran across the deck and grabbed him by his collar and belt. He was lucky. The man weighed very little. Alex heaved him up over the rail and into the river. Then, still dripping wet, water running into his eyes, he went over to the controls and slammed the throttle down as far as it would go.

This was going to be his way out of here. Once he was downriver, nobody would be able to find him.

The engines roared and the propellers thrashed at the water, turning it white. The boat surged forward. Alex grinned. But a second later, he was almost thrown off his feet as the boat seemed to slam into a brick wall. Still gripping the steering wheel, he turned round and saw, to his dismay, that the boat had been moored to one of the pillars supporting the building. The propellers were churning up the water. If the rats were anywhere near, they would be chopped to pieces. But the boat wasn't going anywhere. A length of rope almost as thick as Alex's arm stretched between the stern and the pillar.

And he didn't have time to untie it. Alex eased the throttle back, afraid the engines would explode, and the rope sagged. Then somebody shouted something, and with a heavy heart he saw Anan Sukit appear on the walkway outside the arena, anger stretching his mouth even further across his hideous face. He had seen Alex. He still had his gun. Once again he took aim. He was about twenty metres away but he had a clear shot.

Alex did the only thing he could. Once again he slammed down the throttle, and suddenly it seemed to him that everything happened at once.

There were three shots. But Alex wasn't hit. And it wasn't Sukit who had fired. The snakehead lieutenant seemed to throw his own gun into the river, as if he no longer had any use for it. Then he followed it in, pitching head first into the water. He had been shot from behind, the bullets hitting him between the shoulders. Alex thought he saw a shadowy figure standing in a doorway, but before he could make out who it was, the boat surged forward again. And this time it took the pillar with it, ripping it out from beneath the burning building.

Alex felt himself propelled into the middle of the river incredibly fast. He risked a last look back and saw the arena consumed by fire, sparks dancing above it. In the distance he could hear fire engines. But they weren't going to be needed. He had torn out a vital part of the structure. Even as he watched, the entire building slumped to its knees, as if in surrender, then slid off the bank and into the river. All of it went. The water rushed in through the rotting wood, eager at last to reclaim it. Alex heard screams coming from inside. Another burst of gunfire. And then the Chada Trading Company had disappeared as if it had never existed. Only the green sign remained, floating on the surface, surrounded by other pieces of splintered wood and debris. The flames sat briefly on the river before extinguishing themselves. Dozens of shadowy figures thrashed and shouted in the water, trying to reach dry land.

Alex dragged at the steering wheel and brought the ferry under control. It was incredible, but he really was the only person on board. So which way now? North would take him to familiar territory. He could see the Peninsula Hotel in the far distance. He wondered what he must look like. Bruised, scratched, soaked, in rags – he didn't think they'd be too happy to let him check in.

And anyway, there was still Ash, presumably waiting for him in Chinatown. Alex steered the ferry towards the next public jetty. They would have to do without the forged papers. He just hoped Ash would understand.

WAT HO

Major Winston Yu selected an egg and cress sandwich and held it delicately between his gloved fingers. He was at the Ritz Hotel in London, which – even if they did allow too many tourists into the main rooms – was still his favourite hotel in the world. And tea was definitely his favourite meal. He loved the little sandwiches, cut in perfect triangles, with a scone served with jam and cream to follow. It was all so very English. Even the bone china teapot and cup had been made by Wedgwood, the Staffordshire family firm established in 1759.

He sipped his tea and dabbed his lips with a serviette. The news from Bangkok, he had to admit, was not good. But he wasn't going to let that spoil his tea. His mother had always told him that every cloud has a silver lining and he was looking for one now. It was true that it wouldn't be easy to replace Anan Sukit. But on the other hand, every organization – even a snakehead – needs a change of personnel from time to time. It keeps people on their toes. There were plenty of young lieutenants who deserved promotion. Yu would make a choice in due course.

Much less welcome was the man sitting opposite him. It was very rare for two members of Scorpia to be seen together in public, but Zeljan Kurst had telephoned him and insisted on a meeting. Major Yu had suggested the Ritz, but now he felt it had been a mistake. The big Yugoslavian with his bald head and wrestler's shoulders couldn't have looked more out of place. And he was drinking mineral water! Who drank mineral water at five o'clock in the afternoon?

"Why didn't you report to us about the boy?" Kurst asked.

"I didn't think it was relevant," Yu replied.

"Not relevant?"

"This is my operation. I have everything under control."

"That's not what I've heard."

It didn't surprise Yu that the executive board had already learnt about the destruction of the Chada Trading Company offices and the death of Sukit. They were always watching one another's backs, doubtless working out where to place the knives. It was sad that criminals weren't the same any more. No one trusted anyone.

"We're still not sure what has just happened," Yu said. It might be teatime in England but it was midnight in Bangkok. "It's not even clear the boy was responsible."

"This is Alex Rider," Kurst snapped. "We underestimated him once before and it was an expensive mistake. Why haven't you killed him already?"

"For obvious reasons." Yu's hand hovered over another sandwich but he changed his mind. He had rather lost his appetite. "I was aware of Alex Rider's presence in Bangkok the moment he landed," he continued. "I knew they were coming – a boy and a man – even before they arrived."

"Who told you?"

"That's my secret and I intend to keep it that way. I could have arranged to have the Rider child gunned down at Suvarnabhumi Airport. It would have been simple. But that would have told ASIS I was aware of their plans. They already suspect I have inside information. This would have confirmed it."

"So what do you intend to do?"

"I want to play with him. The fight at the arena was just the beginning, and there's no real harm done. The place was falling down anyway. But if you ask me, the situation is quite amusing. Here's the famous Alex Rider, dressed up as an Afghan refugee. He thinks he's so clever. But I have him in the palm of my hand and I can crush him at any time."

"That was what Julia Rothman thought."

"He's a child, Mr Kurst. A very clever child, but a child all the same. I think you're overreacting."

Something deadly flickered in Kurst's eyes and Yu made a mental note not to eat anything more. He wouldn't put it past Scorpia to slip a radioactive pellet into an egg and cress sandwich. After all, they had done it before.

"We will be monitoring the situation," Kurst said at length. "And I'm warning you, Major Yu, if we feel that things are getting out of hand, you will be replaced."

He got up and left.

Yu stayed where he was, thinking about what had just been said. He suspected that Levi Kroll was behind this. The Israeli had been playing power games ever since Max Grendel had retired. He had also volunteered for the Reef Island business. He would be itching to move in if Yu failed.

He was not going to fail. Royal Blue had been thoroughly tested by Yu's operatives in Bangkok. The detonation system had been adapted. And in less than two days' time it would set off on the next leg of its journey. All according to plan. But Yu decided to take out a little insurance. He and he alone would set off the bomb. He was the one who would take the credit for the worldwide destruction that would follow.

So how to stop Kroll from seizing control?

It was very simple. A little technological tinkering and nobody would be able to replace him. Yu smiled to himself and called for the bill.

* * *

"I should never have let you go," Ash exclaimed. "I can't believe I let them do that to you."

It was one o'clock in the morning in Bangkok and Alex and Ash were in their room on the third floor.

Alex had abandoned the ferry downriver on the other side of an ugly, modern bridge. From there he'd had to find his way across the city on foot, dripping wet, without money and relying only on his sense of direction. He had stopped twice to ask for directions from a monk and from a stallholder closing up for the night. They spoke little English but were able to understand enough to point him in the right direction. Even so, it had been well after midnight by the time he had reached China-town. Ash had been pacing the room like a lion in a cage, sick with worry, and had grabbed hold of Alex when he finally arrived. He had listened to the story with disbelief.

"I shouldn't have let you go," he said again.

"You weren't to know."

"I've heard about these fights. The snakeheads hold them all the time. Anyone who crosses them can end up in the ring. People get crippled – or killed."

"I was lucky."

"You were smart, Alex." Ash looked at him approvingly, as if seeing him in a new light. "You say someone was there, shooting. They attacked the building. Did you see who they were?"

"I got a glimpse of someone. But I'm sorry, Ash. It was dark and it was all happening too quickly."

"Were they Thai or European?"

"I didn't see."

Alex was sitting on the bed, wrapped in a blanket. Ash had laid his clothes out to dry – not that there was much chance of that. The night itself was damp, on the edge of a tropical storm. He had also brought Alex a bowl of chicken broth from the restaurant at the end of the alley. Alex needed it. He hadn't eaten since late that afternoon. He was starving and exhausted.

Ash examined him. "I remember the first time I met your father," he said suddenly. The change of subject took Alex by surprise. "I'd been sent out on a routine operation in Prague. I was just back-up. He was in charge – for the first time, I think. He was about the same age as me." He took out a cigarette and rolled it between his fingers. "Anyway, everything that could go wrong did go wrong. A building blown to smithereens. Three ex-KGB agents dead in the street. The Czech police crawling all over us. And he was just like you are now."

"What do you mean?"

"I mean you take after him," Ash explained. "John always had the luck of the devil. He'd walk into trouble and somehow he'd get out of it in one piece. And then he'd sit there – the same as you – as if nothing had happened. Untouched by it."

"His luck ran out in the end," Alex said.

"Everyone's luck runs out in the end," Ash replied and turned away, a haunted look in his eyes.

They didn't talk much more after that. Alex finished his soup and fell asleep almost immediately. The last thing he remembered was Ash, hunched over a cigarette, the red tip winking at him in the darkness as if sharing a secret.

Despite everything, Alex woke early the next morning. There were a couple of fat cockroaches crawling up the wall right next to him, but by now he had got used to them. They didn't bite or sting; they were just ugly. He ignored them and got out of bed. Ash had already been out, taking Alex's wet clothes to a laundry to be spin-dried. He dressed quickly and the two of them went out for a bowl of jok, the rice porridge which many of the stalls served for breakfast.

They ate in silence, squatting on two wooden crates at the edge of the road, the traffic rumbling past. It had rained in the night and there were huge puddles everywhere, which somehow slowed the city down even more. Once again Ash had slept badly, and there were dark rings under his eyes. His wound was hurting him. He did his best not to show it, but Alex noticed him wince as he sat down and he looked more ragged and drawn out than ever.

"I'm going to have to cross the river," Ash said at last.

"The Chada Trading Company?" Alex shrugged. "You won't find very much of it left."

"I was thinking the same thing about our assignment." Ash threw down his spoon. "I'm not blaming you for what happened last night," he said. "But it may well be that our friends in the snakehead have no further interest in smuggling us into Australia. One of their main lieutenants is dead. And it has to be said, you took out a large chunk of their operation."

"I didn't set fire to the building!" Alex protested.

"No. But you pulled it into the river."

"That put the fire out."

Ash half smiled. "Fair point. But I need to find out how things stand."

"Can I come?"

"Absolutely not, Alex. I think that's a bad idea. You go back to the room – and watch out for yourself. It's always possible they'll send someone round to settle the score. I'll be back as soon as I can."

He walked off. Alex thought back over what he'd just said. Was Ash angry with him? It was difficult to read his moods, as if a life in the secret service had put any display of emotion under wraps. But Alex could see that things hadn't quite gone as expected. His job was to infiltrate the snakehead, not start a war with it. And the fake papers that were so important to Ash might well be sitting on the bottom of the river – and the rest of the Chada Trading Company with them.

Alex got to his feet and began to walk slowly along the street, barely glancing at the brightly coloured silks that every shop in this area seemed to sell. Thai high streets certainly weren't like English ones. In England things were spread out. Here you had whole clusters of shops all selling the same thing: whole streets of silk, whole streets of ceramics. He wondered how people chose where to go.

He wished Ash had let him go with him. The truth was, he didn't want to spend any more time on his own and he'd had enough of Bangkok. As for his hopes that meeting Ash would tell him anything about himself, so far all he had been given was a few glimpses of the past. He was beginning to wonder if his godfather would ever open up enough to say anything meaningful at all.

Alex was just approaching the top of the alleyway when he realized that the entrance was being watched.

Ash had warned him to keep his eyes open, and perhaps it was thanks to him that Alex spotted the man on the other side of the road, half hidden behind a vegetable stall. He didn't need to look twice. The man had changed his clothes. Gone were the red poppy and the leather jacket. But Alex was absolutely certain. This was the same square, hard-edged face that he had already seen at the airport and then again at the Peninsula Hotel. Now he was here. He must have been trailing Alex for days.

The man had disguised himself as a tourist, complete with camera and baseball cap, but his attention was fixed on the building where Alex and Ash were staying. Perhaps he was waiting for them to come out. Once again Alex had the feeling that he knew the man from somewhere. But where? In which country? Could this be one of his old enemies catching up with him? He examined the cold dark eyes beneath the fringe of black hair. A soldier? Alex was just about to make the connection when the man turned and began to walk away. He must have decided that there was no one at home. Alex made a snap decision. To hell with what Ash had told him. He was going to follow.

The man had set off down Yaowarat Road, one of the busiest streets in Chinatown with huge signs carrying Chinese characters high into the air. Alex was confident he wouldn't be seen. As ever, the pavement was cluttered with stalls, and if the man glanced back he could find somewhere to hide in an instant. The real danger was that Alex might lose him. Despite the early hour, the crowds were already out – they formed a constantly shifting barrier between the two of them – and the man could disappear all too easily into a dozen entrances. There were shops selling gold and spices. Cafés and restaurants. Arcades and tiny alleys. The trick was to stay close enough not to lose him but far enough away not to be seen.

But the man didn't suspect anything. His pace

hadn't changed. He took a right turn, then a left, and suddenly they were out of Chinatown and heading into the Old City, the very heart of Bangkok, where every street seemed to contain a temple or a shrine. The pavements were emptier here and Alex had to be more careful, dropping further back and hovering close to doorways or parked cars in case he had to duck out of sight.

They had been walking for about ten minutes when the man turned off, passing through the entrance to a large temple complex. The gateway itself was decorated with silver and mother-of-pearl and opened onto a courtyard filled with shrines and statues: a fantastic, richly decorated world where myth and religion collided in a cloud of incense and a blaze of gold and brilliantly coloured mosaic.

The Thai word for a Buddhist monastery or temple is *wat*. There are thirty thousand of them scattered across the country, hundreds in Bangkok alone. There was a sign outside this one, giving its name in Thai and – helpfully – in English. It was called Wat Ho.

Alex only had a few moments to take in his surroundings: the ornamental ponds, and the Bodhi trees which grow in every wat because they once gave shelter to the Buddha. He glanced at the golden figures, half woman half lion, that guarded the main temple, the delicate slanting roofs and the mondops – incredible, intricate towers with hundreds of tiny figures that must have taken years to carve by hand. A group of monks walked past. Everywhere there were people kneeling in prayer. He had never been anywhere so peaceful.

The man he was following had disappeared behind a bell tower. Alex was suddenly afraid that he was going to lose him, at the same time wondering what it was that had brought him here. Could he have been mistaken? Could the man be a tourist after all? He hurried round the corner and stopped. The man had gone. A crowd of Thai were kneeling at a shrine. A couple of backpackers were having their photograph taken in front of one of the terraces. Alex was angry with himself. He had been too slow. The entire journey had been a waste of time.

He took a step forward and froze as a shadow fell across him and a hand pressed something hard into his back.

"Don't turn round," a voice commanded, speaking in English.

Alex stood where he was, a sick feeling in his stomach. This was exactly what Ash had warned him against. The snakehead had sent someone after him and he had allowed himself to be led straight into a trap. But why here, in a Thai temple? And how did the man know he spoke English?

"Walk across the courtyard. There's a red door on the other side of the shrine. Do you see it?"

Alex nodded. The man had a Liverpudlian

accent. It sounded weird in the context of a Bangkok temple.

"We're going through the door. I'll give you more instructions on the other side. Don't try anything."

Another jab with the gun. Alex didn't need any further prompting. He walked away from the bell tower, skirting round the Thai people lost in their prayers. Briefly he considered starting a fight, out here, while there were still witnesses. But it would do him no good. The man could shoot him in the back and disappear before anyone realized what had happened. The moment would come ... but not yet.

The red door was set in the wall of a cloister, somewhere for the monks to walk in silent contemplation. It was surrounded by images of the Ramakien, the great story of gods and demons known to every child in Thailand. Gods or demons? He had little doubt to which group this man belonged.

As he approached, the door clicked open automatically. There had to be a surveillance camera somewhere but, looking around, Alex couldn't see it. There was a modern corridor on the other side, with bare brick walls slanting down towards a second door. This one opened too. All the sounds of the wat had faded away behind him. He felt as if he were being swallowed up.

Alex wasn't going to let that happen. He timed his move very carefully. The second doorway was

159

narrow, leading into a square-shaped hall that could have been the reception area of a solicitor's office or a smart private bank. The walls were covered in wooden panels. There was an antique table with a lamp, a fan turning overhead. And, more bizarre than anything, on the opposite wall, a picture of Queen Elizabeth II. As Alex made his way in he hesitated, allowing the man to catch up, then suddenly punched backwards with his elbow and brought his fist swinging round.

It was a move he had been taught when he was training with the SAS in the Brecon Beacons in Wales. The elbow jab winds your man; the fist carries the gun aside, giving you time to spin round and kick out with all your strength. Never try it in the open because you'll end up getting shot. It only works in a confined space.

But not this time. The man seemed to have been expecting the manoeuvre. He had simply stepped aside the moment Alex began his move. Alex's first strike didn't make contact with anything, and before he could even begin to turn he felt the cold farewell of the gun pressed against the side of his head.

"Nice try, Cub," the man said. "But much too slow."

And that was when Alex knew.

"Fox!" he exclaimed.

The gun didn't matter any more. Alex turned to face the man – who was now grinning at him like an old friend. Which, in a sense, he was. The two of them had actually met in the Brecon Beacons. There had been four men in the unit to which Alex had been assigned: Wolf, Eagle, Snake and Fox. None of them had been allowed to use their real names. While he was with them, Alex was Cub. And now that he thought about it, there had been one with a Liverpudlian accent. It seemed incredible that the two of them should have met up again in Bangkok, but there could be no doubt about it. Fox was standing in front of him now.

"You were at the airport," Alex said. "I saw you, wearing a poppy."

"Yes. I should have taken that off. But I'd just flown in from London."

"And you were at the Peninsula Hotel."

Fox nodded. "I couldn't believe it was you when I first saw you, so I followed you to be sure. I've been keeping an eye on you ever since, Alex. Lucky for you..."

"Last night." Alex's head swam. "Was that you at the arena? You set the place on fire!"

"I followed you over to Patpong and I was there when those men picked you up. Then I followed you down to the Chada Trading Company. It wasn't easy, I can tell you. And it took me ages to weasel my way in. When I arrived you were already in the ring. I thought you were going to be beaten to a pulp. But I'd seen where the main fuses were, so I nipped back and turned out all the lights. Then I came looking for you. Things got a bit dodgy when the lights came back on; I had to shoot a few of the opposition and chuck a couple of grenades. The last time I saw you, you were in a ferry, trying to get away. It might have helped if you'd untied it first."

"You shot Anan Sukit."

"Was that his name? Well, he was trying to shoot you. It was the very least I could do."

"So what is this place?" Alex looked around him. "What are you doing in Bangkok? And what's your real name? You can't go on expecting me to call you Fox."

"My real name's Ben Daniels. You're Alex Rider. Of course, I know that now."

"You've left the SAS?"

"I got seconded to MI6 Special Operations. And since you ask, that's where you are now. This is what you might call the Bangkok office of the Royal & General Bank."

The words were hardly out of his mouth when a door opened on the other side of the hallway and a woman walked out. Alex caught it at once – the faint smell of peppermint.

"Alex Rider!" Mrs Jones exclaimed. "I have to say, you're the last person I expected to see. Come into my office immediately. I want to know – why aren't you at school?"

ARMED AND DANGEROUS

The last time Alex had seen Mrs Jones, she had been visiting him in a north London hospital. Then she had seemed unsure of herself, regretful, blaming herself for the security lapse that had left Alex close to death on the pavement outside the MI6 offices in Liverpool Street. She had also been at her most human.

Now she was much more like the woman he had first met, dressed severely in a slate-coloured jacket and dress with a single necklace that could have been silver or steel. Her hair was still cut short, and her face – with those night-black eyes – was utterly serious. Mrs Jones was not attractive, but then she did not try to be. In a way, her looks exactly suited her work as deputy head of MI6 Special Operations, one of the most secretive departments of the British secret service. They gave nothing away.

Once again she was sucking a peppermint. Alex wondered if she had given up smoking at some point. Or was the habit also related to her job?

When Mrs Jones spoke, people sometimes died. It wouldn't surprise him if she felt the need to sweeten her breath.

The two of them were sitting in an office on the first floor of the building that stood directly behind Wat Ho. It was a very ordinary room with a wooden table and three leather chairs. Two large, square windows looked out over the temple courtyard. Alex knew that all this could be deceptive. The glass was probably bulletproof. There would be hidden cameras and microphones, and how many agents were there, mingling among the orange-robed monks? When it came to MI6, nothing was ever quite what it seemed.

Ben Daniels, the man he had known as Fox, was also there. He was younger than Alex had first thought, no more than twenty-two or twenty-three, laid-back and thoughtful. He was sitting next to Alex. The two of them were opposite Mrs Jones, who had taken her place behind the table.

Alex had told her his story, from the time he had splashed down off the Australian coast to his recruitment by ASIS, his meeting with Ash in Bangkok and his first encounter with the snakehead. He noticed that she reacted uncomfortably at the mention of Ash. But then, of course, she must have known him. She had been at MI6 when his father was undercover with Scorpia. She might even have been involved in the operation in Malta that had brought him safely home.

"Well, Ethan Brooke certainly has a nerve," she remarked when he had finished. "Recruiting you without so much as a by-your-leave! He could have talked to us first."

"I don't work for you," Alex said.

"I know you don't, Alex. But that's not the point. At the very least you're a British citizen, and if a foreign agency is going to use you, it ought to ask." She softened slightly. "For that matter, what ever prompted you to go back into the field? I thought you'd had enough of all this."

"I wanted to meet Ash," Alex said. Another thought occurred to him. "Why did you never tell me about him?" he asked.

"Why should I have?" Mrs Jones replied. "I haven't seen him for years."

"But he worked for you."

"He worked for Special Operations at the same time as me. In fact, I had very little to do with him. I met him once or twice. That's all."

"Do you know what happened in Malta?"

Mrs Jones hesitated. "You'd have to ask Alan Blunt," she said. "That was his operation. You know it was all a set-up. John – your father – was pretending to work for Scorpia and we had to get him back. We set up a fake ambush in a place called Mdina, but it went wrong and Ash was nearly killed. After that he was confined to desk duty, and not long after your parents died he left the service. That's all I can tell you."

"Where is Mr Blunt?"

"He's in London."

"So why are you here?"

Mrs Jones looked at Alex curiously. "You've changed," she said. "You've grown up a lot. I suppose we're to thank for that. You know, Alex, we weren't going to use you again. Alan and I had agreed: after what happened with Scorpia, that was going to be the end of it. But the next thing we learn, you're in America, up to your neck in it with the CIA. I ought to congratulate you, by the way. That business with the Ark Angel space station was quite remarkable."

"Thank you."

"And now ASIS! You certainly get around." Mrs Jones reached forward and flipped open a file lying on the table in front of her. "It's strange that we should have run into you this way," she went on. "But it may be less of a coincidence than you think. Major Yu. Does that name mean anything to you?"

"He's in charge of the snakehead." Ethan Brooke had told Alex the name when he was in Sydney.

"Well, to answer your question, we're investigating him. That's why I'm here. That's why Daniels is here too." Mrs Jones tapped the file with her index finger. "How much did ASIS tell you about Major Yu?"

Alex shrugged. He felt uncomfortable suddenly, caught in the middle of two rival intelligence agencies. "Not very much," he admitted. "They don't seem to know a lot about him. That's part of my job..."

"Well, maybe I can help you." Mrs Jones paused. "We've been interested in Major Winston Yu for some time, although we haven't managed to find out too much about him ourselves. We know he had a Chinese mother. His father is unknown. He was brought up in poverty in Hong Kong – his mother worked in a hotel – but cut forward eight years and you find him being privately educated in England. He went to Harrow School, for heaven's sake! How his mother managed to afford the fees is another question.

"He was an average student. We have copies of his reports. On the other hand, he seems to have fitted in quite well, which is surprising, considering his background. There was a question mark over a rather nasty incident that took place at the end of his second term – a boy killed in a car accident – but nothing was ever proved. He was also very good at sport, a triple house blood, whatever that means.

"He left with reasonable A levels and read politics at London University. Gained a second-class degree. After that he went into the army. Trained at Sandhurst and did much better there. He seems to have taken to the army life and achieved the highest score in military, practical and academic studies, for which he received the Queen's Medal.

He joined one of our country's most distinguished regiments – the Household Cavalry – and did three tours in Northern Ireland.

"Unfortunately he developed a bone condition which brought an end to his army career. But he was snapped up by intelligence, and for a time he worked for MI6 – not Special Operations. He was fairly low-grade, gathering and processing information, that sort of thing. Well, eventually he must have had enough of it, because one day he disappeared. We know he has been active in Thailand and Australia, but there's no record of his activities; and it's only recently that we've been able to identify him as the leader of one of the most powerful snakeheads in the region."

Mrs Jones paused. When she looked up again, her eyes were bleak. "This may put you off, Alex. It may even persuade you to go home – and believe me, I wouldn't blame you. According to our sources, Major Yu may have contacts with Scorpia. It's even possible that he's on the executive board."

Scorpia. Alex had hoped he would never hear that name again. And Mrs Jones was right. If Ethan Brooke had given him that information, he might have thought twice about the whole thing. He wondered if the head of ASIS Covert Action had known. Almost certainly. But he'd needed Alex so he'd decided to keep it under his hat.

"You still haven't told me why you're interested in him," Alex said.

"That's top secret." Mrs Jones gestured with one hand. "But I'll tell you. Apart from anything else, it may well be that you're in a position to help us – assuming that's something you'd even consider. Anyway, I'll explain and you can make up your own mind.

"Have you ever heard of the daisy cutter?"

Alex thought for a moment. "It's a bomb." He remembered talking about it once at school, during history. "The Americans used it in Vietnam."

"They've also used it in Afghanistan," Mrs Jones said. "The daisy cutter, also known as BLU-82B or the Blue Boy, is the largest conventional bomb in existence. It's the size of a car – and I mean a five-seater. Each bomb contains twelve and a half thousand pounds of ammonium nitrate, aluminium powder and polystyrene, and it's powerful enough to destroy an entire building, easily. In fact, it'll probably take out a whole street."

"The Americans used it because it's terrifying," Daniels muttered. He was speaking for the first time. "It may not compare to a nuclear bomb, but there's nothing on earth like it. The shock wave that it releases is unbelievable. You have no idea how much damage it can do."

"They used it in Vietnam to clear landing sites for helicopters," Mrs Jones went on. "Drop one on the jungle and you have no jungle for half a mile around. They called it the daisy cutter because that was the pattern the explosion made. It was used in Afghanistan to scare the Taliban, to show them what they were up against."

"What's this got to do with Major Yu?" Alex asked. He was also wondering, with a sense of growing unease, what it might have to do with him.

"For the last few years, the British government has been developing a second generation of daisy cutters," Mrs Jones explained. "Scientists have managed to create a similar type of bomb, except it's a little smaller and it's more powerful, with an even greater shock wave. They gave it a code name, Royal Blue, and they built a prototype at a secret laboratory just outside London." She took out a peppermint and twisted off the wrapper with a single movement of her thumb and forefinger. "Four weeks ago the prototype was stolen. Eight of our people were killed. Three of them were security guards; the rest were technicians. It was a very professional operation: perfectly timed, ruthlessly executed." She slid the peppermint between her lips.

"And you think Major Yu...?"

"These things aren't easy to transport, Alex. They need to be carried in a Hercules MC-130 transport plane. We lost sight of the bomb, but two days later a C-130 took off with a flight plan that brought it to Bangkok via Albania and Tajikistan. We were able to identify the pilot; his name was Feng. He in turn had been employed by a criminal based here in Bangkok, a man called Anan Sukit—"

"—and he works for the snakehead!" Alex finished the sentence.

"He *worked* for the snakehead," Mrs Jones remarked sourly. "Until Daniels put three bullets into him."

It was all beginning to make sense. MI6 Special Operations were chasing a missing bomb which had led them to the snakehead. Alex was investigating the snakehead and that had led him to MI6. It was as if they had met in the middle.

"We were planning to put Daniels into the snakehead," Mrs Jones said. "We'd arranged a cover story for him. He was a rich European who'd flown out from London, hoping to put together a big drug deal. Of course, everything changed the moment he spotted you. As soon as we realized you were here, we decided to keep an eye on you and find out what you were up to. I have to say, we were very surprised when you changed your appearance." She ran an eye over Alex. "If we hadn't seen you at the airport, we wouldn't have recognized you."

"I like the teeth," Daniels muttered.

"So what now?" Alex asked. "You said you wanted me to help you."

"You and Ash have already penetrated the snakehead. You've also shaken things up a bit – no surprises there. Maybe you can find Royal Blue for us."

"It shouldn't be too hard to spot," Daniels said.

"It's bloody huge. And if it goes bang you'll hear it ten miles away."

Alex considered. Getting involved with MI6 again was the last thing he wanted; but, in a way, what Mrs Jones had told him changed nothing. He was still working for ASIS. And if he did come across a bomb the size of a family car, there would be no harm in reporting it.

"What do they want it for?" he asked.

"That's what most worries us," Mrs Jones replied. "We've got no idea. Obviously they must be planning something big – but not that big. A nuclear bomb would be about a thousand times more powerful."

"So they're not out to destroy a whole city," Daniels added.

"But if this is a Scorpia operation, you can be pretty sure it's serious and large-scale. These people aren't bank robbers – you know that better than anyone. I have to admit, we're in the dark. Anything you can find out will be helpful to us."

Once again Alex fell silent. But he had made up his mind. "I'll have to tell Ash," he said.

Mrs Jones nodded. "I don't see any harm in that. And in return, we can help you. You and Daniels already know each other. There's no point trying to put him in undercover now. But he can continue to watch over you."

Ben smiled. "I'd be happy to do that," he said.

"We can give you something to contact him

at any time. Have ASIS provided you with any equipment?"

Alex shook his head.

Mrs Jones sighed. "That's the trouble with the Australians. They rush into everything without a second thought. Well, we can give you what you need."

"Gadgets?" Alex's eyes lit up.

"You've got an old friend here; I think you ought to meet."

Smithers was down the corridor in a room that was a cross between a library, an office and a workshop. He was sitting at a desk, surrounded by bits of machinery – like a destructive child on Christmas Day. There was a half-dismantled alarm clock, a laptop computer with its insides spilling out, a video camera divided into about fifty different pieces and a whole tangle of wires and circuits. Smithers himself was wearing sandals, baggy shorts and a bright yellow short-sleeved shirt. Alex wondered how he could possibly carry so much weight around in this heat. But he looked perfectly composed, sitting with his great stomach stretching out towards his knees and two very plump, pink legs tucked away below. He was fanning himself with a Chinese fan decorated with two interweaving dragons.

"Alex? Is that you?" he exclaimed as Alex came into the room. "My dear chap! You don't look like yourself at all. Don't tell me! You must have spent some time with Cloudy Webber."

"Do you know her?" Alex asked.

"We're old friends. The last time we met was at a party in Athens. We were both in disguise, as it happened, and we chatted for half an hour before we recognized each other." He smiled. "But I can't believe you're back again. So much has happened since I last saw you. That was in America. Did my Stingo mosquito lotion come in useful?"

Now it was Alex's turn to smile. The liquid that Smithers had invented attracted insects instead of repelling them and it had been very useful indeed, helping him to get past a checkpoint on Flamingo Bay. "It was great, thanks," he said. "What are you doing here?"

"Mrs Jones asked me to think up a few gadgets for our agents out here in the East," Smithers replied. He lifted the fan. "This is one of them. It's very simple but I rather like it. You see, it looks like an ordinary fan but actually there are very thin plates of galvanized steel hidden under the silk. And when you bring them together" – he folded the fan, then brought it smashing down onto the desk and the wood shattered – "it becomes a useful weapon. I call it—"

"—the fan club?" Alex suggested.

Smithers laughed. "You're getting used to my little ways," he said. "Anyway, I've had all sorts of ideas since I came to Bangkok." He rifled around the surface of the desk and finally found a packet with a dozen sticks of incense. "Everyone burns incense out here," he explained. "It comes in jasmine and musk and it's rather lovely – but my incense has no smell at all."

"So what's the point?"

"After thirty seconds it will make a whole room of people throw up. It's quite the most disgusting gadget I've ever invented, and I have to say we had no fun at all testing it. But it's still quite useful, I think."

He unfolded a sheaf of drawings. "I'm also working on one of these local three-wheeled taxis. They call them tuk-tuks, but this one has got a missile launcher built into the front headlight and a machine gun directly controlled by the handlebars, so I suppose you could say it's an attack-tuk."

"What's this?" Alex asked. He picked up a small bronze Buddha sitting in the lotus position. With its round stomach and bald head, it reminded him a little of Smithers.

"Oh, do be careful with that!" Smithers exclaimed. "That's my Buddha hand grenade. Twist the head twice and throw it, and anyone within ten metres can say their prayers."

He took it back and placed it carefully in a drawer.

"Mrs Jones said you're taking on a snakehead," he continued, and suddenly he was serious. "You be careful, Alex. I know you've done tremendously well in the past, but these people are extremely nasty."

"I know." Alex thought back to his first meeting with Anan Sukit and the fight in the riverside arena. He didn't need to be told.

"There are all sorts of things I'd love to equip you with," Smithers said. "But as I understand it, you're working undercover as an Afghan refugee. Which means you won't be carrying very much. Is that right?"

Alex nodded. He was disappointed. Smithers had once given him a Game Boy jammed with special devices, and he would have felt more confident having something like that with him now.

Smithers opened an old cigar box. The first object he took out was a watch, a cheap fairground thing on a plastic strap. He handed it to Alex.

Alex looked at the time. According to the watch, it was half past six. He shook it. "This doesn't work," he said.

"We have to think about the psychology," Smithers explained. "A poor Afghan refugee wouldn't own many possessions, but he would be very proud of the few he did have – even a broken watch. But this watch will work when it matters. There's a powerful transmitter and a battery inside. If you get into trouble, set the hands to eleven o'clock and it will send out a signal which will repeat every ten minutes until it runs out of power. We'll be able to pick you up anywhere on the globe."

Smithers rummaged around in the box again and took out three coins. Alex recognized them. They were Thai currency: one baht, five baht and ten baht, worth about twenty-five pence in total.

"I don't think anyone would worry about a few local coins," he said, "and these are rather fun. They're actually miniature explosives. Let me show you how you detonate them."

He produced a half-empty packet of chewing gum. At least, that was what it looked like. But then he turned it round in his podgy fingers and slid open a secret panel. There were three tiny switches on the other side, marked with the figures 1, 5 and 10.

"This is how it works," he explained. "The coins are magnetic so you can stick them to a metal surface when you want to use them. They won't be activated until you flick the appropriate switch – just make sure you get the right value. The coins will blow open a lock or even smash a hole in a wall. Think of them as miniature landmines. And do try not to spend them!"

"Thanks, Mr Smithers."

"And finally, I've got something that might come in very useful if you find yourself off the beaten track." Smithers pulled open a drawer in the desk and took out an old belt with a heavy silver buckle. "You can slip it into your jeans. There's a particularly sharp knife hidden inside the buckle. It's made out of toughened plastic and is rather cunningly designed so it won't show up on X-ray machines if you go through an airport. And if you slice open the belt, you'll find matches, medicine, water-purifying tablets and knockout pills that are guaranteed to work on eleven different varieties of snake. I developed it for use in the jungle, and although you're not heading that way, you never know." He handed it across. "It's a shame, really. I'd love to give you the trousers that go with it. The legs are highly inflammable."

"Exploding jeans?" Alex asked.

"Flares," Smithers replied. He reached out and shook Alex's hand. "Good luck, old bean. And one last word of advice." He leant forward as if afraid of being overheard. "I wouldn't trust these Australians if I were you. They're not a bad lot. But they are a bit rough, if you know what I mean. They don't play by the rules. Just keep your wits around you." He tapped the side of his nose. "And call for help the moment you need us. That Ben Daniels is a good chap. He won't let you down."

Alex gathered up his few weapons. As he left, he heard Smithers humming behind him. The song was that old Australian favourite, "Waltzing Matilda". Alex wondered what Smithers had meant by his warning. Did he really know something that Alex didn't or was he just being mischievous?

Ben Daniels was waiting outside.

"Are you ready, Cub?" he asked.

"Armed and dangerous," Alex replied.

The two of them left together.

THE SILENT STREETS

Ash was already in the room when Alex got back. At first he was angry.

"Where the hell have you been, Alex?" he growled. "I was worried about you. I told you to wait for me here." Then his eyes narrowed. He glanced down at Alex's waist. "That's a nice belt. Where did you get it?"

Alex was impressed. His godfather had spent nearly half his life as a spy, and of course he had been trained to notice every detail. Despite everything that had happened in the last twenty-four hours, Ash had immediately picked up on this one tiny change in Alex's appearance.

"It was given to me," Alex said.

"Who by?"

"I met some old friends..."

Quickly Alex described what had happened: how he had seen Ben Daniels in the crowd, followed him to Wat Ho and found himself in the MI6 stronghold. Mrs Jones had given him permission to tell Ash about Royal Blue and he mentioned the possible link between Major Yu and Scorpia. Ash's eyes grew dark when he heard the name.

"Nobody told me they were involved," he muttered. "I don't like this, Alex. And nor will Ethan Brooke. You and I are meant to be gathering information. Nothing more, nothing less. Now it's getting messy."

"That's not my fault, Ash."

"Maybe I should go to this temple, have a word with Mrs Jones." Ash thought for a moment, then shook his head. "No. There's no use arguing with her. Go on..."

Alex went on with his story. It seemed he was now working for not one but two secret services. He supposed Ash had a point. The mission had already been bent out of shape, and suddenly there was a ticking bomb at the heart of it. Why did Scorpia need Royal Blue? If Scorpia were involved, it was bound to be something messy – they wouldn't care how many people died. But why this bomb? Why not any other?

Alex tried to put it out of his head. He finished by describing how once again Smithers had equipped him.

"So Smithers is still with MI6!" Ash smiled briefly. "He's quite a character. And he supplied the belt? What does it do – besides keeping your trousers up?"

"I haven't had a chance to examine it yet," Alex admitted. "But there's a knife in the buckle. And there's stuff hidden inside. Some sort of jungle survival kit."

"Who said you were heading into the jungle?"

Alex shrugged.

Ash shook his head. "I'm not sure you should have it."

"Why not?"

"Because it may not fit in with your cover. It didn't come from Afghanistan like everything else you're wearing. If we get into any more trouble, it could be noticed."

"Forget it, Ash. I'm keeping it. But if you like, I'll make sure it's out of sight." Alex untucked his shirt and let it hang over the belt.

"What about the watch? Did Smithers give you that too?"

"Yes." Alex wasn't surprised that Ash had also noticed the watch. He held out his wrist. "In case you're wondering, the hands don't move. It's got a transmitter in it. I can contact MI6."

"Why would you want to do that?"

"I might need help."

"If you need help, you can call me."

"I don't have your number, Ash."

Ash scowled. "I'm not sure ASIS would be too happy about any of this."

Alex held his ground. "That's too bad," he said.

Ash could see that Alex was in no mood for an argument. "All right," he said. "Maybe it's for the best. I won't have to worry about you so much if

I know you've got back-up. But don't contact MI6 without telling me, OK? Promise me that. I don't work for them any more and when all is said and done, I've got my reputation to consider."

Alex nodded. He had decided not to mention the three exploding coins and the detonators concealed in the chewing gum packet. Ash might try to take those too. He changed the subject. "How did you get on?" he asked. "Did you go to the river?"

Ash lit a cigarette. It still surprised Alex that a man who looked after himself so carefully in every other respect chose to smoke. "It's all good news," he said. "I found the arena where you were taken – or what was left of it – and spoke to a guy called Shaw. You may remember him. He was the one who took the photographs. Richard Shaw. Or Rick to his friends."

"What was he doing there?"

"There were dozens of them, salvaging what they could out of the wreckage. Papers, computer disks, that sort of thing. Our late friend Mr Sukit had his offices there, and there was plenty of stuff they wouldn't want the police to find."

"What did Shaw say?"

"I got him to take me to Sukit's deputy. Another charming guy. Looked like he'd been in a street fight – face all over the place. He obviously had a lot on his mind, but I persuaded him to send us on the next step of our journey. After all, we'd paid the money. And you'd done what they wanted. You'd taken part in their fight, even if you had humiliated their champion."

"What about the fire and all the rest of it?"

"Nothing to do with you. They think the Chada Trading Company was hit by a rival gang. The long and the short of it is that they're happy to get us out of the way. We leave for Jakarta tonight."

"Jakarta?"

"We're moving further down the pipeline, Alex. They're smuggling us into Australia via Indonesia. I don't know how, but it'll almost certainly involve some sort of ship. Jakarta's only about forty-eight hours by sea from Darwin. Maybe it'll be a fishing boat, or possibly something bigger. We'll find out soon enough."

"How do we get to Jakarta?"

"We fly just like anyone else." Ash produced a folder containing two plane tickets, passports, visas and a letter of credit written on smart paper with the name UNWIN TOYS printed across the top. "We're being met at Jakarta Soekarno-Hatta International Airport," he went on. "I'm now a sales manager for Unwin Toys. Flying in to look at their new range and bringing my son with me."

"Unwin Toys ... I've heard of them."

The name had seemed familiar the moment he saw it. Now Alex remembered. He had seen their products all over London, often on market stalls or bargain basements on Oxford Street. They specialized in radio-controlled cars, building kits and water pistols – always made out of brightly coloured plastic, manufactured in the Far East and guaranteed to fall apart a few days after they were opened. Unwin Toys wasn't a great name but it was a well-known one, and he found it hard to believe that it could be tied in with the snakehead.

It was as if Ash knew what was in his mind. "Think about it, Alex," he said. "A big company like Unwin Toys would be a perfect cover for a smuggling operation. They're moving goods all over the world, and the fact that they're for little kids – it's the last place you'd think of looking."

Alex nodded. He could imagine it. A crate full of plastic trucks, each one loaded with a stash of heroin or cocaine. Water pistols that were actually the real thing. Teddy bears with God knows what inside. All sorts of unpleasant secrets could hide behind such an innocent facade.

"We're making real progress," Ash said. "But we still have to be careful. The more we know, the more dangerous we become to the snakehead." He thought for a moment. "What you said just now, about calling me. You're right. I want you to remember a phone number. Write it on your hand."

"What phone number?"

"If anything happens, if we get separated, call the number before you contact anyone else. It's my mobile. But the number's special, Alex. It was given to me by ASIS. You can call from anywhere in the world and you'll be put through instantly. It will cost you nothing. The numbers will override any security system in any telephone network so you can reach me any time, anywhere. What do you say?"

Alex nodded. "Fine."

Ash gave him the number. There were eleven digits but otherwise it was like no phone number Alex had ever heard before. He wrote them on the back of his hand. The numbers would soon fade, but by then he would have memorized them.

"What now?" he asked.

"We rest. Then we get a taxi to the airport. It's going to be a long night."

Alex realized the moment had come. They might not be able to speak to each other in Jakarta or on the way to Australia – certainly not in English – and very soon after that, the whole business would be over. Once they had arrived in Darwin, Alex wouldn't be needed any more.

"All right, Ash," he said. "You promised you'd tell me about my mum and dad. You were the best man at their wedding and they made you my godfather. And you were there when they died. I want to know all about them because, for me, it's like they didn't exist. I want to know where I came from, that's all ... and what they thought about me." He paused. "And I want to know what happened in Malta. You said that Yassen Gregorovich was there. Was he the one who gave you that scar? How did that happen? Was my dad to blame?"

There was a long silence. Then Ash nodded slowly. He stubbed out his cigarette.

"All right," he said. "On the plane."

They were thirty thousand feet above the Gulf of Thailand, heading south on the short flight to Jakarta. The plane was only half full. Alex and Ash had a whole row to themselves, right at the back. Ash had smartened himself up a little with a white shirt and a cheap tie. He was, after all, meant to be a sales manager. But Alex hadn't changed. He was grubby and a little ragged, still wearing the clothes he had been given in Bangkok. Perhaps that was why the two of them had been seated on their own. In front of them the other passengers were dozing in the strange half-light of the cabin. Outside, the sun had set. The plane hung in the darkness.

Ash hadn't spoken while they took off and climbed into the sky. He had accepted two minia-ture whisky bottles from the stewardess but he was still sitting in silence, his dark eyes darker than ever, fixed on the ice in his glass as it slowly melted. He looked even more exhausted than usual. Alex had noticed him swallow two tablets with his drink. It had taken him a while to realize that Ash was in constant pain. He was beginning to wonder if his godfather really was going to tell him what he wanted to know.

And then, without warning, Ash began to speak.

"I met your dad on my first assignment for

Special Operations. He joined just before me, but he was completely different. Everyone knew John Rider. Top of his class. Golden boy. On the fast track to the top." There was no rancour in Ash's voice. There was no emotion at all. "He couldn't have been more than twenty-six. Recruited out of the Paras. Before that he'd been at Oxford University. A first-class degree in politics and economics. And did I mention that he was also a brilliant athlete? Rowed for Oxford – and won. A good tennis player too. And now he was in Prague, in charge of his first operation, and I was a nobody sent along to learn the ropes.

"Well, as it turned out, the whole thing was a shambles. It wasn't John's fault. Sometimes it just happens that way. But afterwards, at the debriefing, I met him properly for the first time, and you know what I liked most about him? It was how calm he was. We had three agents dead – not ours, thank God. The Czech police were going crazy. And the Museum of East European Folk Art and Antiquities had burnt down. Actually, it wasn't really a museum, but that's another story. Your dad wasn't much older than me and he wasn't even worried. He didn't shout at anyone. He never lost his temper. He just got on with it.

"After that we became friends. I'm not sure how it happened. We lived near each other – he had a flat in an old warehouse in Blackfriars, set back from the river. We started playing squash together.

In the end we must have played about a hundred games, and you know what? I won at least a couple of them. Sometimes we met for a drink. John liked black velvet: champagne and Guinness. He was away a lot, of course, and he wasn't allowed to tell me what he'd been doing. Even though we were in the same service, I didn't have clearance. But you heard things, and I looked in on him a couple of times when he was in hospital. That was how I met your mother."

"She was a nurse."

"That's right. Helen Beckett. That was her maiden name. She was very attractive. Same colour hair as you. And maybe the same eyes. I actually asked her out, if you want to know. She turned me down very sweetly. She was already going out with your dad. She knew him from Oxford; they'd met when she was studying medicine."

"Did she know then what my dad did?"

"I don't know how much he told her, but of course she knew something. When you're treating someone with two broken ribs and a bullet wound, you don't imagine they fell over playing golf. But it didn't bother her. The next thing I knew, she had moved in with him and we weren't playing squash quite so often."

"Did you ever get married, Ash?" Alex asked.

Ash shook his head. "Never met the right girl, although I had fun with quite a few wrong ones. I'm actually quite glad, Alex. I'll tell you why.

"You can't afford to get scared in our business. Fear's the one thing that will kill you faster than anything, and although it's true to say that all agents are fearless, generally what that means is that they're not afraid for themselves. All that changes when you get married, and it's even worse when you have kids. Alan Blunt didn't want your dad to marry. He knew that in the end he'd be losing his best man."

"He knew my mother?"

"He had her investigated." Alex looked shocked and Ash smiled. "It was standard procedure. He had to be sure she wasn't a security risk."

So somewhere inside MI6 Special Operations there was a file on his mother. Alex made a mental note of it. Maybe one day it would be something he would dig out.

"I was quite surprised when John asked me to be his best man," Ash went on. "I mean, he was such a hotshot and nobody had even noticed I existed. But he didn't really have much choice. His brother, Ian, was away on an assignment ... and there's something else you might as well know. Spies don't have many friends. It goes with the territory. John was still in touch with one or two people from university – he'd told them he was working for an insurance company – but friendship doesn't really work when you have to lie all the time."

Alex knew that was true. It was the same for him at school. Everyone at Brookland had been told he had been struck down by a series of illnesses in the past eight months. He'd been back at school a bit and he'd even joined a school trip to Venice. But he'd felt like an outsider. Somehow his friends knew that something wasn't adding up, and the knowledge had soured their relationship.

"Did he have any other family?" he asked.

"Apart from his brother?" Ash shook his head. "There was no family that I knew of. The wedding was at a registry office in London. There were only half a dozen people there."

Alex felt a twinge of sadness. He would have liked his mother to have had a white wedding in a country church with a big party in a marquee and speeches and dancing and too much to drink. After all, he already knew that her happiness wasn't going to last long. But he understood that he was getting a glimpse of a secret agent's life. Friendless, secretive and a little empty.

The plane trembled briefly in the air, and further down the aisle one of the call lights blinked on. Outside the window, the sky was very black.

"Tell me more about my mother," Alex said.

"I can't, Alex," Ash replied. He twisted in his seat and Alex noticed a flicker of pain in his eyes. The tablets hadn't kicked in yet. "I mean, she liked to read. She went to the cinema a lot – she preferred foreign films if she had a choice. She never bought expensive clothes but she still looked good." Ash sighed. "I didn't know her that well.

And she didn't really trust me, if you want the truth. Maybe she blamed me. I was part of the world that put John in danger. She loved your dad; she hated what he did. And she was smart enough to know that she couldn't talk him out of it."

Ash opened the second miniature and poured the contents into his plastic glass.

"Helen found out she was expecting you when John was in the middle of his toughest assignment," Ash continued. "The timing couldn't have been worse. But a new organization had come to the attention of MI6. I don't need to tell you its name. I guess you know more about Scorpia than I do. Anyway, there it was: an international network of ex-spies and assassins. People who'd gone into business for themselves.

"At first they were useful. You have to remember that MI6 actually welcomed them at the beginning. If you wanted information about what the CIA were up to or how the Iranians were getting on with their nuclear programme, Scorpia would sell it to you. If you wanted to do something outside the law with no way of having it traced back to you, there they were! That was the whole point about them. They were loyal to no one. They were only interested in money. And they were bloody good at their job. Until you came along, Alex, they had never really failed.

"But MI6 became worried about them. They could see that Scorpia were getting out of control, particularly when a couple of their own agents were murdered in Madrid. All around the world, intelligence agencies are regulated, which is to say they play by the rules – at least, to a certain extent. But not Scorpia. They were growing bigger and more powerful, and at the same time they were becoming more ruthless. They didn't care how many people they killed so long as they got their cheque.

"So Alan Blunt – who'd just become the chief executive of MI6 Special Operations – decided to put your father into Scorpia. The idea was to place him inside the organization, to get them to recruit him. Once he was there, he'd find out everything he could about them. Who was on the executive board? Who was paying them? Who were their connections within the intelligence agencies? That sort of thing. But to do that, MI6 had to put your dad into deep cover. That meant faking everything about him."

"I know about this," Alex interrupted. "They pretended he'd been in jail."

"They actually sent him to jail for a time. They had to be thorough. There were newspaper stories about him. Everyone turned against him. It looked like he lost all his money and he had to sell the flat. He and Helen moved to some dump in Bermondsey. It was very hard on her."

"But she must have known the truth."

"I can't tell you that. Maybe your dad told her. Maybe he didn't."

Alex couldn't believe that. Somehow he was sure his mother would have known. "He was recruited by Scorpia," he said.

"That's right. They sent him to their training facility on the island of Malagosto, just a few miles from Venice."

The name made Alex shiver. He had been sent there himself when Scorpia had tried to recruit him.

"As far as Scorpia were concerned, John Rider was a gift," Ash said. "He was a brilliant operator. He had an excellent track record inside British intelligence. And he was desperate. He was also a very good-looking man, by the way. One of the board members at Scorpia took a fancy to him."

"Julia Rothman." Alex had met her too. She had talked about his father over dinner in Positano.

"The very same. She quickly saw John's potential, and soon he was a senior training officer with special responsibility for some of Scorpia's younger recruits. And she gave him a code name. He was called Hunter."

"How do you know all this?" Alex asked.

"That's a good question." Ash smiled. "Because, finally, someone had noticed I existed. Alan Blunt sent me out to shadow John in the field. I was his back-up. My job was to stay close but not too close, to be there if he needed to make contact. And that's how I came to be there when it all ended."

"In Malta."

"Yeah. In Malta."

"What happened?"

"Your dad was coming in. He'd had enough of Scorpia *and* MI6. You had just been born. John wanted a normal life; and anyway, he'd achieved what he'd set out to do. Thanks to him, we knew a great deal about the structure of command within Scorpia. We had the names of most of their agents. We knew who was paying them and how much.

"The job now was to bring him home without arousing suspicion. We knew Julia Rothman would kill him if she found out he was a spy. The plan was to get him back to England and then let him disappear. A new home. A new identity. The whole works... He'd start a new life in France with you and your mum. I should have mentioned that he spoke fluent French, by the way. If things had gone the way they'd planned, you'd be speaking French now. You'd be in a *lycée* in Marseilles or somewhere and you wouldn't know anything about all this.

"Well, it was right at this time that Scorpia unwittingly provided an opportunity for us to get John out. There was a man called Caxero. He was a petty criminal: a drug dealer, a money launderer ... that sort of thing. But he must have rubbed someone up the wrong way, because someone had paid Scorpia to hit him. Your dad was sent to do the job.

"Caxero lived in Mdina in the middle of Malta. It's an old citadel, completely surrounded by walls.

Caxero's home town has another name too. It is so quiet and full of shadows, even in the winter, that the locals call it the Silent City. And MI6 realized it was the perfect place for the ambush that would bring John home.

"Your dad wasn't sent there alone. He was accompanied by a young assassin, one of the best who ever came out of Malagosto. I understand you met him. His name was Yassen Gregorovich."

Alex shivered again. He couldn't help himself. They were certainly digging deep into his past tonight.

He remembered the slim, fair-haired Russian with the ice-cold eyes. Alex had met Yassen on his first mission. Yassen could have killed him then but had chosen not to. And then they had met a second time in the South of France. It had been Yassen who had led him into the nightmare world of Damian Cray. Alex thought back to the last moments they had been together. Once again Yassen had refused to kill him, and this time it had cost him his own life.

"What can you tell me about Yassen?" he asked.

"An interesting young man," Ash replied, but there was a sudden coldness in his voice. "He was born in a place called Estrov. You won't have heard of it, but it was certainly of interest to us. The Russians had a secret facility there – biochemical warfare – but one day the whole place blew up. Hundreds were killed – and Yassen's father was one of them. His mother was injured, and died six months later.

"The Russians tried to hush the whole thing up. They didn't want to admit anything had happened, and even now we don't know the whole truth. But one thing was certain. By the end of the year, Yassen was totally alone. He was just fourteen years old, Alex. The same age as you are now."

"How did Scorpia find him?"

"He found them. He crossed the whole of Russia on his own, with no money and no food. He worked in Moscow for a while, living on the street and running errands for the local mafiya. We still don't know how he managed to find his way to Scorpia, but all of a sudden he turned up at Malagosto. Curiously, your dad was in charge of his training for a time. He told me the boy was a natural. It's funny, isn't it? In a way, the two of you and Yassen had a lot in common." Ash turned to Alex and he seemed suddenly ghost-like in the artificial light of the plane. A strange look came into his eyes. "John had a soft spot for Yassen," he said. "He really liked him. What do you make of that? The spy and the assassin. A bit of an odd couple, I'd say..."

And fifteen years after his father had saved his life, Yassen had sacrificed himself for Alex, repaying the debt of an old friendship. But Alex didn't tell Ash that. For some reason, he wanted to keep it to himself.

"This was the deal in Malta," Ash said. Suddenly

he sounded tired, as if he wanted to get this over with. "Caxero was a man of habit – and that's dangerous if you're in crime. He liked to have a black coffee and a cognac every night at a little café in the square opposite St Paul's Cathedral in Mdina. That was where they were going to kill him. John let me know when the hit was arranged. It was going to be at eleven o'clock at night on 11 February. We'd be there waiting. We'd wait until they'd killed Caxero – he was a nasty piece of work and we decided we might as well let Scorpia get him out of the way – and then we'd move in and grab John. But we'd let Yassen escape. He'd report back to Scorpia. He'd tell them that their man had been captured.

"It had to look good. I was in charge of the operation. This was the first time I had been given command. I had nine men, and even though John was our target we were all carrying live ammunition – not blanks. Yassen might have been able to tell the difference. He was that smart. We were all wearing concealed body armour. John wouldn't be aiming at us when we moved in but Yassen would. And we already knew he was a crack shot.

"I'd put a couple of my people in place that morning. The cathedral had these two bell towers – one on either side – and I put a man in each. I remember it also had two clocks. One of them was five minutes slow. I thought it was strange, the faces showing different times. Anyway, the men in the towers had night-vision glasses and radios. They could see the whole town from up there. They'd make sure that nothing went wrong."

Ash paused.

"Everything went wrong, Alex. Everything."

"Tell me."

Ash sipped his whisky. All the ice had melted.

"We arrived at Mdina just after half past ten. It was a beautiful night. This was February, before the tourist season had started. There was a sliver of a crescent moon and a sky full of stars. As we came in through the south gate, it was like stepping back a thousand years in time. The roads in Mdina are narrow and the walls are high. And all the bricks are different shapes and sizes. You can almost imagine them being laid, one by one.

"The whole place felt deserted. The shutters were closed on the houses and the only light seemed to come from the wrought-iron lamps hanging over the corners. As we made our way up the Triq Villegaignon – the main street – a horse-drawn carriage crossed in front of us. They use them to ferry tourists, but this one was on its way home. I can still hear the echo of the horse's hooves and the rattle of the wheels on the cobbles.

"I got a whisper in my earpiece from one of the lookouts in the towers. Caxero was in his usual place, drinking his coffee and smoking a cigar. No sign of anyone else. It was a quarter to eleven.

"We crept forward, past an old chapel on one

side of the road, a crumbling palazzo on the other. All the shops and restaurants were closed. I had seven men with me; we were all dressed in black. We'd spent half the day studying the map of Mdina and I signalled them to spread out. We were going to surround the square, ready to move in.

"Ten to eleven. I could see the time on the cathedral clock. And there was Caxero. He was a short, round man in a suit. He had a fancy moustache and he was holding his coffee cup with his little finger pointing into the air. There were a couple of cars parked in the square next to some cannons and a waiter standing in the doorway of the café. Otherwise, nothing.

"But then, suddenly, they were there, John Rider and Yassen Gregorovich – or Hunter and Cossack. Those were the names they used. They were five minutes early ... or so I thought. That was my first mistake."

"The clocks..."

"The cathedral clocks. Yes. One was right and one was wrong, and in all the tension I'd been looking at the one that was five minutes slow. As for Yassen, it was like some trick in a film. One minute he wasn't there, the next he was, with John next to him. It was a ninja technique – how to move and stay invisible – and the irony was, it was probably your dad who'd taught him.

"I don't think Caxero saw them coming. They walked straight up to him and he was still holding his coffee cup in that stupid way. He looked up just as a complete stranger shot him in the heart. Yassen didn't do it quickly. I remember thinking that I'd never seen anyone so relaxed.

"I was worried that my men wouldn't be in place yet, that not all the exits from the square would be covered. But in a way that didn't matter. Don't forget we wanted Yassen to escape. That was part of the plan.

"I stepped out of my hiding place. Yassen saw me and all hell broke loose.

"Yassen fired at me. Two of his bullets missed but I felt the third slam into my chest. It was like being hit by a sledgehammer, and if I hadn't been wearing an armour-plated vest, I'd have been killed. As it was, I was blown off my feet. I went smashing down into the cobbles, almost dislocating my shoulder. But I didn't hang around, Alex. I got straight back up again. That was my second mistake. I'll come to that later.

"Anyway, suddenly everyone was firing at once. The waiter turned round and dived for cover. About half a second later, the plate-glass window of the café shattered. It came down like a shower of ice. The men high up in the cathedral were using rifles. The others were entering the square from different sides. Your dad and Yassen had separated – as I knew they would. It was standard procedure. Staying together would have just made it easier for us to catch both of them. For a moment, I thought everything was going to work out all right after all.

"It didn't.

"Three of my men grabbed hold of John. They'd cornered him and it really did look as if there was nothing he could do. They made him throw down his weapon and lie flat on the ground. That left three others to go after Yassen. Of course, they'd let him get away. But it would still be close. That was the plan.

"Yassen Gregorovich had plans of his own. He was halfway across the square, making for one of the side streets. But then suddenly he stopped, turned round and fired three times. The gun had a silencer; it hardly made any sound. And this time he wasn't aiming for the chest. His bullets hit one of my men between the eyes, one in the side of the neck and one in the throat. Two of them died instantly. The third went down and didn't move.

"There was still one agent left. His name was Travis and I'd chosen him personally. He was on the far side of the square and I saw him hesitate. He didn't know what to do. After all, I'd given him orders not to shoot Yassen. Well, he should have disobeyed me. The situation was out of control. Enough people had already died that night. He should have shot Yassen or got the hell out of there, but he did neither. He just stood there and Yassen gunned him down too. A bullet in the leg to bring him down and then another in the head to finish him off. The square was littered with bodies.

And this whole thing was meant to be bloodless!"

Ash fell silent.

Alex noticed he had finished his whisky. "Do you want another drink, Ash?" he asked.

Ash shook his head. Then he went on.

"Yassen had gone. We had John. So, in a way, we'd succeeded. Maybe I should have left it at that. But I couldn't. This was my first solo operation and Yassen Gregorovich had wiped out almost half my task force. I went after him.

"I don't know what I was thinking. Part of me knew that I couldn't kill him. But nor could I just let him go. I pulled off my body armour; it had a quick release and I couldn't run with it on. Then I started across the square and towards the northern wall. I heard someone shout after me – it might even have been John. But I didn't care. I turned a corner. I remember the pink stone and a balcony like something in an opera house. I couldn't see anyone. I thought Yassen must have got away.

"And then, without any warning, he stepped out in front of me.

"He'd waited! A whole town crowded with MI6 agents and he just stood there like he owned the place and none of us could touch him. I ran straight into him. I couldn't stop myself. His hand moved so fast that I didn't see it. I felt it smash into the nerve points in my wrist. I lost my gun; it went spinning away into the darkness. At the same time, his gun pressed against my neck.

"He was ten years younger than me. A Russian kid who'd got sucked into all this because his parents had died in an accident. And he'd beaten me. He'd taken out nearly half my team. I was going to be next.

"Who are you?

"MI6.

"There was no point lying. We wanted Scorpia to know.

"How did you know we would be here?

"I didn't answer that. He pushed harder with the gun, hurting me. But that didn't matter. It would all be over soon anyway.

"You should have stayed at home.

"And then he turned and ran.

"To this day, I don't know why he didn't shoot me. Maybe his gun had jammed. Or perhaps it was simpler than that. He'd killed Caxero, Travis and three more of my men: maybe he'd run out of ammunition. I watched him disappear down the next alleyway and that was when I realized he'd had a knife as well as a gun. The hilt was sticking out of my stomach. I didn't feel anything. But looking down... There was so much blood. It was pouring out of me. It was everywhere."

Ash stopped. The soft scream of the plane's engines rose in pitch for a moment. Alex wondered if they were coming into Jakarta.

"The pain came later," Ash said. "You have no idea how bad it was. I should have died that night.

Maybe I would have, but your dad had come after me. He'd feared the worst – and he'd put his own life at risk, because if Yassen had seen him, he would have known that the whole thing was a set-up. By then I was on the ground. I was slipping away fast. And I was cold. I've never felt so cold.

"Your father didn't take the knife out. He knew that would kill me straight away. He put pressure on the wound and kept it there until the ambulance came. I was airlifted to Valletta, where I stayed on critical for a week. I'd lost five pints of blood. In the end I came through, but … you've seen the scar. I'm missing about half my stomach. There wasn't anything they could do about that. There are about a hundred things I'm not meant to eat because there's nowhere for them to go. And I have to take pills … a lot of pills. But I'm alive. I suppose I should be grateful for that."

There was a long silence.

"Scorpia got my dad in the end," Alex said.

"Yeah. A couple of months later. Just after you were christened, Alex. It was almost the last time I saw your dad – and if it makes you feel any better, I'd never seen him look happier than when he was holding you that day. He and your mother. It was like you made them real people again. You brought them out of the shadows."

"You went with them to the airport. They were on their way to France. You said they were going to Marseilles."

"That's right. They had to leave you behind. You had an ear infection, so you couldn't fly. Otherwise you'd have been with them."

"You were there when the bomb went off on their plane."

Ash looked away. "I said I wouldn't talk about that and I meant it. Somehow Scorpia found out they'd been tricked and they took revenge. That's all I know."

"What happened to you, Ash? Why did you leave MI6?"

"I'll tell you that, Alex, and then that's the end of it. I think I've lived up to my side of the bargain."

Ash crumpled his plastic glass and shoved the broken pieces into the compartment in front of him.

"I didn't come out of the Malta operation too well if you want the truth," he said. "I was on sick leave for six weeks and the day I returned to Liverpool Street, Alan Blunt called me into his office. He then gave me a bollocking for everything that had gone wrong.

"First of all, there was the thing with the time. The wrong clock. But it turned out that the most stupid mistake I'd made was to stand up after Yassen had shot me. You see, that had told him we were all wearing body armour, and that was the reason why he'd shot Travis and the others in the head. It was all my fault – at least, according to Blunt."

"That wasn't fair," Alex muttered.

"You know what, mate? I thought more or less the same thing. And then, chasing after Yassen when the whole point was to let him get away. That was the final nail in my coffin. Blunt didn't fire me. But I was demoted. He made it clear that I wouldn't be heading up any more operations. It didn't matter that I'd almost been killed. In a way, that just made it worse. A nice guy, Mr Blunt. All heart!"

Ash shook his head.

"It was soon afterwards that your parents died together on that plane, and after that my heart sort of went out of it. I told you when we were in Bangkok: it was your dad who was the patriot, serving his country. Maybe I felt like that for a time, but by the end I'd had enough. I did a few more months' desk duty, but then I handed in my resignation and headed down under. ASIS were keen to have me. And I wanted to start again.

"I saw you a few times, Alex. I looked in on you to see that you were OK. After all, I was your godfather. But by then Ian had started adoption proceedings. I had a drink with him the night before I left England and he told me he was going to look after you. It was obvious you didn't need me. In fact, if truth be told, you were probably better off without me. I hadn't been much help, had I!"

"You shouldn't blame yourself," Alex said. "I don't."

"Anyway, I saw you again. I was in London, working with the Australian embassy. You were still at primary school – and Jack was looking after you."

"You went out with her."

"A couple of times. We had a laugh together." Ash glanced briefly at Alex as if searching for something. "I couldn't believe it when I heard that MI6 had recruited you," he muttered. "Alan Blunt certainly is a cold-hearted son of a bitch. And then, when you wound up in Australia! But I still wish you hadn't come on this mission, Alex. I don't want you to get hurt."

"A bit late now, Ash."

The lights in the cabin came back on, and the stewardesses began to move up the aisle. At the same time, Alex felt his stomach lurch as they began to come down.

They had arrived in Jakarta, the next step on their journey. The end of the pipeline was in sight.

UNWIN TOYS

Sometimes Alex wondered whether all the airports in the world had been designed by the same architect: someone with a love of shops and corridors, plate-glass windows and potted plants. Here he was at Soekarno-Hatta, the international airport of Jakarta, but it might just as well have been Perth or Bangkok. The floors might be more polished and the ceilings higher, and every other shop seemed to be selling rattan furniture or the colourful printed cloth known as batik. But otherwise he could have been right back where he started.

They came through passport control quickly. The official in his glass-fronted booth barely glanced at the forged documents before stamping them, and without a word being spoken they were in. Nor did they have to wait at baggage claim. They had just one suitcase between them and Ash had carried it on and off the plane.

Alex was tired. It was as if the events of the last five days in Bangkok had finally caught up with him and all he wanted to do was sleep – although somehow he doubted he would be spending the night in a comfortable bed. Most of all, he wanted time on his own to reflect on what Ash had told him. He had learnt more about his past in the last hour than he had in his entire life, but there were still questions he wanted to ask. Had his father blamed Ash for the mistakes that had been made in Mdina? Why had he been with them at the airport? And what had he seen that he was so unwilling to talk about?

They passed into the arrivals lounge, and once again they were surrounded by a crowd of touts and taxi drivers. This time there were two men waiting for them, both Indonesian, slim and athletic in jeans and short-sleeved shirts. One of them was holding a placard that read KARIM HASSAN. Alex stared at it for a few seconds before the name registered, and he was annoyed with himself. He had completely forgotten that it was the name under which Ash was travelling. Ash was Karim; he was Abdul. It didn't matter how tired he was. A mistake like that could get them both killed.

Ash went over to them and introduced himself using a mixture of Dari and sign language. The two men didn't even try to be friendly. They simply turned and walked away, expecting Ash and Alex to follow.

It was ten o'clock, and outside, away from the artificial climate of the air conditioning, the heat was thick and unwelcoming. Nobody spoke as they crossed the main concourse to the kerbside, where a dirty, white van was parked with a third man in the driving seat. The van had double doors at the back with no windows. Alex glanced nervously at Ash. He felt as if he were about to be swallowed up, and he remembered the last time he had got into a car with members of the snakehead. But Ash didn't look worried. Alex followed him in.

The doors slammed shut. The two men got in the front with the driver and they moved off. Alex and Ash sat on a metal bench that had been welded to the floor. Their only view was out of the front windscreen, and that was so filthy Alex wondered how the driver could see where they were going. The van was at least ten years old and had no suspension at all. Alex felt every bump, every pothole. And there were plenty of both.

The airport was about twelve miles from the city, connected by a motorway that was clogged with traffic even at this time of the night. Squinting over the driver's shoulder, Alex barely saw anything until, at last, Jakarta came into sight. It reminded him at first of Bangkok, but as they drew closer he saw that it was uglier and somehow less sure of itself, still struggling to escape from the sprawling shanty town it had once been.

The traffic was horrible. They were carried into Jakarta on a concrete flyover, and suddenly there were cars and motorbikes above them and below them as well as on both sides. Skyscrapers – bulky rather than beautiful – rose up ahead, a thousand light bulbs burning uselessly in offices that were surely empty, colouring the night sky yellow and grey. There were brightly coloured food stalls – *warungs* – along the pavements, but nobody seemed to be eating. The crowds were drifting home like sleepwalkers, pushing their way through the noise and the dirt and the heat.

They turned off the flyover, leaving the main sprawl of the city as quickly as they had entered it. Suddenly the van was rumbling over a dirt track, splashing through puddles and weaving around loose bricks and rubble. There were no street lamps, no signs, no illumination from a moon that had been blocked out by cloud. Alex saw only what the headlights showed him. This was some sort of sub-urb, a slum area with narrow streets, houses with tin roofs and corrugated iron patches, walls held up by wooden scaffolding. Strange spiky shrubs and stunted palm trees grew at the side of the road. There was no pavement. Somewhere a dog barked. But nowhere was there any sign of life.

They came to gates that seemed to have been cobbled together from pieces of driftwood. Two words – in Indonesian – had been scrawled across them in red paint. As they approached, the driver pressed a remote control in the van and the gates opened, allowing them into a large, square compound with warehouses and offices, lit by a couple of arc lamps and fenced in on all sides. The van stopped. They had arrived.

There didn't seem to be anyone else there. The doors of the van were flung open and the two men led Alex and Ash into one of the warehouses. Alex saw crates stacked high, some of them open, spilling out straw and plastic toys. There was a pile of scooters, tangled together, and a Wendy house lying on its side. A furry monkey was slumped with its legs apart, foam hanging out of a gash in its stomach, staring at them with empty glass eyes. Alex hoped it wasn't an omen. He had never seen a collection of toys that looked less fun. From the state of them – dusty and dilapidated – they could have been here for years.

Two thin mattresses spread out on the floor told him the worst. This was where they were supposed to sleep. There was no sign of any toilet or anywhere to wash. Ash turned to the men and signalled, cupping his hands to his mouth. He was thirsty. The men shrugged and walked out.

It was to be the longest nine hours of Alex's life. He had no sheets or blankets and the mattress did almost nothing to protect him from the stone floor underneath. He was sweating. His clothes were digging into him. The whole of Jakarta was in the grip of a storm that refused to break and the air seemed to be nine parts water. Worst of all were the mosquitoes. They found him almost immediately and refused to leave him alone. There was no point slapping at his face, and after a while Alex stopped bothering. The mosquitoes didn't seem to care. The only escape would be sleep, but sleep refused to come.

Ash couldn't talk to him. There was always a chance there might be microphones in the room. Anyway, he was used to this. To Alex's annoyance, his godfather was asleep almost at once, leaving him on his own to suffer through every minute of the night.

But at last the morning came. Alex must have drifted into some sort of half-sleep because the next thing he knew, Ash was shaking him and grey daylight was seeping in through the windows and the open door. Someone had brought them two glasses of sweet tea and a basket of bread rolls. Alex would have preferred eggs and bacon but decided it was probably better not to complain. Squatting on his mattress, he began to eat.

What was going on? Alex realized that the false passports they had been given in Bangkok had been enough to get them into Indonesia, but Australia, with far stricter border controls, would prove more difficult. Here on the island of Java was about as near as they could get to Australian soil, and the last part of their journey would be across the sea – a passage of approximately forty-eight hours, Ash had said. The place they were in now was connected to Unwin Toys – a storage depot and office complex, from what Alex had seen

213

the night before. They were going to have to wait here until their boat was ready. And what sort of boat would that be? He would find out in good time.

Shortly after nine o'clock, one of the two men who had met them at the airport came for them and led them out of the warehouse where they had slept. The morning light was thick and gloomy but at least it allowed Alex to take better stock of his surroundings. Unwin Toys reminded him of an old-fashioned prisoner-of-war camp, something out of a Second World War film. The buildings were made of wood and seemed to have been bashed together in a hurry, using whatever was at hand. Rickety staircases led up to the first floor. The main square was cracked and uneven with weeds sprouting out of the concrete. It was hard to imagine that a brightly coloured toy wrapped up under a Christmas tree in England might have begun its life here.

By now there were a dozen or so men and women in the complex. Some of them were office staff, sitting behind windows and tapping away at computers. A truck had arrived and there were people unloading it, passing cardboard boxes from hand to hand. Two guards stood by the gates. They seemed to be unarmed, but, noticing the wire fence surrounding them, the arc lamps and the security cameras, Alex suspected they were carry-ing guns. This was a secret world. It wanted to keep its distance from the city outside.

He looked up. The clouds were thick, an ugly shade of grey. He couldn't see the sun but he could feel it, pressing down on them. Surely it would rain soon. The entire atmosphere was like a balloon filled with water. At any second it could burst.

It was time to go. The white van was there with its engine running. The back doors were open. Somebody called out to them. Ash took a step forward.

Alex would remember the moment later. It was like a flash photograph – a few seconds caught in time when everything was normal and everyone in the picture was still unaware of the approaching danger. He heard a vehicle coming towards the main gates. It occurred to him that it was being driven far too fast, that it would surely have to slow down so that the gates could be opened. Then the realization came that the car wasn't going to slow down, that the driver didn't need open gates to enter.

Without any further warning the gates of the complex were smashed to pieces, one flying open, the other hanging drunkenly off its hinges as first one then a second huge Jeep Cherokee burst through. Each vehicle carried five men, who came tumbling out almost before the Jeeps had stopped. They were all armed with CZ-Scorpion sub-machine guns or AK-47 assault rifles. Some also carried knives. They were dressed in combat outfits and most of them wore red berets, but they didn't look like soldiers. Their hair was too long and they hadn't shaved. Nobody seemed to be in charge. As they spread out across the square, waving their weapons from side to side and screaming out orders, Alex was convinced that he had stepped into the middle of an armed robbery and that he was about to witness a shoot-out between different Jakarta gangs.

Ash had stopped dead. He turned to Alex and muttered a single word. "Kopassus." It meant nothing to Alex. So, making sure that nobody could hear him, Ash added in English, "Indonesian SAS."

He was right.

Kopassus was an abbreviation of Komando Pasukan Khusus, one of the most ruthless fighting forces in the world. It consists of five different groups specializing in sabotage, infiltration, direct action, intelligence and counter-terrorism. The men who had just broken into the compound came from Group 4, a counter-intelligence group based in the south of Jakarta with special responsibility for smuggling operations in and out of the city. It might have been luck that had brought them here, or it could have been the result of a tip-off. But either way, the result would be the same. They were under arrest, and even if they were able to talk their way out of jail – Ash would only have to prove that he worked for ASIS – their work would be over. They would have destroyed their cover. They would never find out how the snakehead had

216

planned to get them into Australia. And, Alex reflected bitterly, he would never catch up with the stolen weapon that Mrs Jones was looking for – Royal Blue. He would have failed twice.

But there was nothing he could do. The Kopassus soldiers had taken up positions across the square so that every angle was covered and nobody could move without being seen. They were still shouting in Indonesian. It didn't really matter what they were saying. Their aim was to confuse and intimidate the opposition, and they seemed to have succeeded. The civilians inside the compound were standing helplessly. Some of them had raised their arms. Kopassus was in control.

They were made to line up. Alex found himself between Ash and one of the men who had met them at the airport. They were covered by at least half a dozen guns. At the same time, three of the soldiers were searching inside the offices and ware-houses, making sure nobody was hiding. One of the toy workers had decided to do exactly that. Alex heard a scream, then the smash of breaking glass as the unfortunate man was hurled, head first, through a window. He came crashing into the courtyard, blood streaming from his face. Another of the soldiers lashed out with a foot and the man howled, then staggered to his feet and limped over to join the line.

One last man had climbed out of the Jeep. This was presumably the commanding officer. He was unusually tall for an Indonesian with a long, slender neck and black hair down to his shoulders; Alex heard one of the soldiers refer to him as *kolonel*. Slowly he made his way along the line, shouting out instructions. Alex guessed he was asking for ID.

One after another the toy workers produced scraps of paper, driving licences or work permits, the man who had been thrown out of the window holding his up with shaking hands. The colonel didn't seem interested in any of them. Then he reached Ash. Alex tried not to look as Ash took out the fake passport he had been given in Bangkok. He was afraid his eyes might give something away. He glanced down as the colonel opened the passport and held it up to the light. On the edge of his vision, he saw the colonel hesitate. Then suddenly the man struck out, hitting Ash on both sides of the face with the offending document and screaming at him in Indonesian. Two soldiers appeared from nowhere, pinning Ash's arms behind his back and forcing him to his knees. The barrel of a sub-machine gun was pressed into his neck. The colonel handed the passport to one of his subordinates. For a moment, he examined Ash's face, gazing into his eyes as if his true identity might be found there. Then he moved on.

He stopped in front of Alex.

Alex looked up. He was scared and he didn't care if it showed. Maybe the man would decide that he was just a kid and leave him alone. But the colonel didn't care how old he was. He smelled blood. Something like a smile spread across his face and he rapped out a sentence in Indonesian, holding out a hand for Alex's ID. Alex froze. He didn't have his own passport. That was in Ash's pocket. But even if he was able to produce it, the colonel would know it was fake. Should he tell the man who he was? Just a few words in English would do the trick. End the danger.

End the mission too.

It began to rain.

No. It wasn't quite like that. In London rain has a beginning, a few drops that send people scattering for cover and allow time for umbrellas to rise. In Jakarta, there was no warning. The rain fell as if a dam had burst. In an instant it was flooding down, warm and solid, an ocean of rain that spluttered out of the drainpipes, hammered against the roofs and turned the earth to mud.

And with the flood came a brief moment of confusion. Up until then, Kopassus had been in complete control of the complex, working to a plan that allowed the soldiers to cover every inch of ground. The sudden downpour changed things. Alex didn't even see where the gunfire began. But someone must have decided that they had too much to lose and that the rain would give them enough cover to risk shooting their way out. There were half a dozen shots from somewhere near the warehouse where Alex had slept. They came from a single gun, fired carefully, at precise intervals.

The Kopassus men reacted instantly, diving for cover, returning fire even as they went. The sound of their sub-machine guns was deafening. They didn't seem to care where they were aiming. Alex saw an entire wall ripped apart, the wooden planks shredded. A man who had been standing near the warehouse was blown off his feet by the first volley. Alex had seen him just minutes before, sweeping the yard.

But the Kopassus soldiers were falling too. At least three guns were now being fired at them. As Alex turned, searching for cover, the soldier whose gun had been pressed against Ash's neck fell back, a mushroom of blood erupting from his shoulder. Immediately a second man stepped into his place, firing in the direction from which the bullets had come, the nozzle of his sub-machine gun flashing white behind the rain.

The colonel had pulled out a pistol, a Swiss-made SIG-Sauer P226 and one of the ugliest 9mm weapons on the market. Alex saw him take aim at Ash. His intention was clear. He had been about to arrest a man and that had provoked a firestorm – at least, that was what he thought. Well, whoever the man was, the colonel wasn't going to let him get away. Rough justice. He would execute him here and now and bring an end to all this.

Alex couldn't let it happen. With a cry he hurled

himself sideways, his shoulder slamming into the colonel's stomach. The gun went off, the bullet firing into the air. Carried by Alex's velocity, the two of them came crashing down into a puddle. The colonel tried to bring the gun round to aim at Alex. Alex caught hold of his wrist and slammed it down, smashing the back of his hand against the concrete. The colonel cried out. Rain was driving into Alex's face, blinding him. He forced the colonel's hand up and down a second time. The fingers opened and the gun fell free.

Part of him knew that this was all wrong. He was on the same side as Kopassus, both of them fighting the snakehead, the true enemy. But there was no time to explain. Alex saw a soldier throw something – a round, black object about the size of a cricket ball – through the deluge. He knew at once what it was, even before the explosion that tore open the side of a warehouse, smashed three windows and blew a hole in the roof. A tongue of flame leapt up, only to be driven back by the rain.

More gunfire. The man who had thrown the grenade cried out and reeled backwards, clutching his shoulder. The white van was moving. Alex heard the engine rev, then saw the van begin a clumsy three-point turn. Ash grabbed hold of his arm. His hair was matted; water was streaming down his face.

"We have to go!" he shouted. With the noise of the rain and the shooting, there was no chance of his being overheard.

The colonel lunged sideways, trying to reach the gun. Ash kicked it away, then brought a fist crashing down into the man's head.

"Ash—" Alex began.

"Later!"

The van had completed its first turn. It was being brought round to face the shattered gates. Ash started forward and Alex followed. They caught up with the van just as it began to pick up speed. The driver wasn't waiting for them. Ash reached out and wrenched open the back doors. There was a burst of machine-gun fire and Alex cried out as a line of bullet holes stitched themselves across the side of the van, right in front of him.

"Go!" Ash shouted.

Alex threw himself through the doors into the back of the van. A second later, Ash followed, landing on top of him. The driver didn't seem to notice them. All he cared about was getting away. One of the wing mirrors exploded, the glass shattering and the metal casing tearing free. The engine screamed as the driver pressed his foot on the accelerator. They leapt forward. There was an explosion, so close that Alex felt the flames scorch the side of his face. But then they were away, shooting out through the gates and into the street beyond.

The van skidded all over the road. It slammed into a wall and one side crumpled, sparks flickering as metal and brickwork collided. Alex glanced back. One of the van's doors had been blown off and he saw two soldiers – they looked like ghosts – kneeling in the gateway, firing at them. Bullets, burning white, sliced through the rain. But they were already out of range. The van hurtled up the track they had come down the night before; by now it was little more than a brown river of mud and debris. Alex looked back again, expecting Kopassus to be following. But the rain was falling so hard that the warehouse complex had already disappeared; if the two Jeep Cherokees were after them, it was impossible to tell.

The driver was the same man who had brought them from the airport. He was clutching the steering wheel as if his life depended on it. He looked in the mirror and caught sight of his two unwanted passengers. At once he let loose a torrent of Indonesian. But he didn't slow down or stop. Alex was relieved. It didn't matter where they were heading. All that mattered was that they hadn't been left behind.

"What was that about?" he demanded. His mouth was right next to Ash's ear and he was confident that the driver wouldn't be able to hear what he said or what language he was speaking.

"I don't know." For once, Ash had lost his composure. He was lying on his side, trying to catch his breath. "It was routine ... bad luck. Or maybe someone hadn't paid. It happens all the time in Jakarta."

"Where are we going?"

Ash looked out of the back. It was hard to see anything in the half-light and swirling water of the storm, but he must have recognized something. "This is Kota. The old city. We're heading north."

"Is that good?"

"The port is in the north."

They had joined the morning traffic, and now they were forced to slow down, falling in behind a line of cars and buses. All the food stalls had disappeared beneath a sea of plastic sheeting and the people were crowded in doorways or squatting under umbrellas, waiting for the storm to pass.

The driver turned round and shouted something. Even if it had been in English, Alex doubted that he would have been able to hear.

"He's taking us to the boat," Ash explained.

"You speak Indonesian?"

Ash nodded. "Enough to understand."

The van emerged from a side street and cut across a main road. Alex saw a taxi swerve to avoid them, its horn blaring. Behind them an old house loomed out of the rain. It reminded him of something he might have seen in Amsterdam, but then the whole city had belonged to the Dutch once, a far outpost of their East India Company. They crossed a square. It was lined with cobblestones and, lying in the back of the van, Alex felt every one of them. A crowd of cyclists swerved to avoid them, crashing into each other and tumbling over in a tangle of chains and obscenities. A man pushing a food stall threw himself out of the way with seconds to spare.

Then they were on another main road. There was more traffic here – an endless procession of lorries, each one piled up with goods that were concealed beneath garish plastic tarpaulins. The lorries looked overloaded, as if they might collapse at any time under the weight.

Finally, just ahead, the buildings parted and Alex saw fences, cranes and ships looming high above them. There were warehouses, guard posts and offices made of corrugated iron, huge gantries and great stretches of empty concrete with more lorries and vans making their way back and forth. It was almost impossible to see anything through the endless rain, but this was the port. It had to be. There was a security barrier straight ahead of them, and beyond that a stack of containers behind a barbed-wire fence. The van slowed down and stopped. The driver turned round and explained something in a torrent of Indonesian. Then he was gone.

"Ash—" Alex began.

"This is Tanjung Priok Docks," Ash cut in. "They must be taking us on a container ship." He pointed. "You see those fenced-off areas? They're EPZs: export processing zones. Stuff comes into Jakarta. It gets assembled there and then it's shipped out again. That's our way out of here. Once we're in an EPZ, we'll be safe."

"How do we get in there?" Alex had seen the barriers ahead of them. There were guards on duty, even in the driving rain.

"We pay." Ash grimaced. "This is Indonesia! The docks are run by the military; but the military are in the pay of the Indonesian mafia. Small beer compared to the snakeheads, but still in control around here. You can do anything, so long as you pay." Ash got to one knee and peered out of the window. There was nobody in sight. He glanced at Alex. "Thank you for what you did back there."

"I didn't do anything, Ash."

"The colonel was about to shoot me. You stopped him." Ash shrugged. "That's Kopassus for you. Kill the wrong guy and send flowers to the funeral. Really charming."

"What happens when we get to Australia?"

"Then it's over. I get a pat on the back from Ethan Brooke. You go home."

"Will we see each other again?"

Ash looked away. Like Alex he was completely drenched, his clothes dripping and forming a pool around him. The two of them both looked like shipwrecks. "Who knows?" he growled. "I haven't been much of a godfather, have I? Maybe I should have sent you a Bible or something."

But before Alex could respond, the driver returned and this time he wasn't alone. There were three men with him, their faces hidden under the hoods of their plastic anoraks. They were all talking at once, jabbing their fingers at Alex and Ash, gesticulating wildly. Slowly their meaning became clear, and Alex felt a chasm open up beneath him. They wanted Alex to go with them. But Ash was to stay behind.

The two of them were being separated.

He wanted to cry out, to argue – but even one word would be fatal and he forced himself to keep his mouth shut. He tried to resist, pulling away from the hands that grabbed at him. It was useless. As he was bundled out of the van, he took one last look at Ash. His godfather was watching him almost sadly, as if he had guessed that something bad was going to happen and knew that he was powerless to stop it now that it had.

Alex was half dragged onto the road. Ahead of him a gate had swung open, and he was marched through with a man on each side of him and one ahead. A security guard appeared briefly but the men shouted at him and he quickly turned away.

It was hard to see anything in the driving rain. There was a quayside ahead of them, and a ship, bigger than any Alex had ever seen, the equivalent of about three football pitches in length. The ship had a central section where the crew worked and lived. Alex could see the bridge with four or five huge windows and giant windscreen wipers swinging back and forth, fighting against the rain. The ship had a name, printed in English along the bow: *Liberian Star*. It was being loaded with containers, the rectangular boxes dangling from the huge spreader which loomed over them like some sort of monster in a science-fiction film. A man in a cabin was controlling the cables and pulleys, lowering each box into place with incredible precision.

They entered the EPZ where the next lorryloads of containers were waiting their turn, each one painted a different colour, some displaying the names of the companies that owned them. Alex saw a yellow box sitting on one of the lorries and knew that it was his destination. The name was painted in black: UNWIN TOYS. He looked back, hoping against hope that Ash would be following him after all. But they were alone. Why had the two of them been separated like this? It made no sense. After all, they were supposed to be father and son. He just hoped that Ash would be in a second container and that somehow they would meet up again when they arrived in Darwin. He turned his hand over. The phone number that Ash had given him had almost vanished, reduced to an inky blur by the constant rain. Fortunately Alex had committed it to memory – or at least he hoped so. He would know for sure soon enough – if he ever found a phone.

They reached the yellow container and Alex saw at once that it was locked. More than that, there was a steel pin connected to the door. He guessed its purpose. All containers had to be checked by customs officials both going on and coming off a ship. Obviously they couldn't be opened on their journey, or anything – guns, drugs, people – could be added. The steel pin would have a code number which would already have been checked; it would be checked a second time when they arrived in Australia. If the pin had been tampered with or broken, the entire container would be impounded and examined.

So how was he expected to get in? Alex could see that this was how he was going to travel. Presumably it was too dangerous for him to have a cabin on board the ship; and anyway, as far as the snakehead was concerned, this was all he was: cargo, to be dumped along with all the other merchandise. The man who had been leading the way turned and put a hand on his shoulder, urging him to get down. Alex realized that he was expected to clamber underneath the lorry, between the wheels.

A moment later, he saw why. The container had a secret entrance, a trapdoor that was open, hanging down. He could climb in without touching the main door or the pin that secured it, and once the container was in place, part of a tower with dozens more on top and below, there would be no way that anyone could examine it. The whole thing was simple and effective, and part of him even admired the snakehead. It was certainly a huge business, operating in at least three countries. Ethan Brooke had been right. These people were much more than simple criminals.

He started to crawl under the lorry. Immediately he felt claustrophobic. It wasn't just the weight of the container pressing down on him. He could see that the trapdoor would be locked from the outside. There was a single, solid bolt that slid across. Once that happened, he would be trapped. If the ship sank or if they simply decided to drop the whole thing overboard, he would drown in his own oversized metal coffin. He hesitated and at once the man jabbed him between the shoulders, urging him forward.

Alex turned, pretending to be scared, pleading with his eyes to be reunited with Ash. But how could he make himself understood when he couldn't utter a single word? One of the other men thrust something into his hands: a plastic bag with two bottles of water and a loaf of bread. Supplies for the long journey ahead. The first man pushed him again and shouted.

Alex couldn't delay any longer. He crawled over to the trapdoor. The men gestured and he pulled himself up. But as he went, he stumbled. One of his hands caught hold of the sliding bolt and he steadied himself.

That was his last sight of Indonesia. Mud, dripping rain and the undercarriage of a lorry. He pulled himself into the container and seconds later the trapdoor slammed shut behind him. He heard the bolt slide across with a loud clang. Now there was no way out.

It was only as he straightened up that he realized he could see. There was light inside the container. He looked around. A crowd of anxious faces stared at him.

It seemed he wasn't going to make this part of the journey alone.

THE LIBERIAN STAR

In fact, there were twenty people inside the container, huddled together in the half-light thrown by a single battery-operated lamp. Alex knew at once that they were refugees. He could tell from their faces: not just foreign but afraid, far removed from their own world. Most of them were men, but there were also women and children, a couple of them as young as seven or eight. Alex remembered what Ethan Brooke had told him about illegal immigrants when he was in Sydney. *Half of them are under the age of eighteen.* Well, here was the proof. There were whole families locked together in this metal box, hoping and praying that they would arrive safely in Australia. But they were powerless and they knew it, utterly dependent on the good will of the snakehead. No wonder they looked nervous.

A gaunt, grey-haired man, wearing a loose, brightly coloured shirt and baggy trousers, made his way forward. Alex guessed he was in his sixties. He might once have been a farmer; his hands were coarse and his face had been burnt dry by the sun. He muttered a few words to Alex. He could have been speaking any language – Dari, Hazaragi, Kurdish or Arabic – it would have made no difference. Alex knew that without Ash he was exposed. He had no way of communicating and nobody to hide behind. What would these people do if they discovered that he was an impostor? He hoped he wouldn't have to find out.

The man realized that Alex hadn't understood him. He tapped his chest and spoke a single word. "Salem." That was presumably his name.

He waited for Alex to reply; and when none came he gestured to a woman, who came forward and tried a second language. Alex turned away and sat in a corner. Let them think he was shy or unfriendly. He didn't care. He wasn't here to make friends.

Alex drew his legs up towards him and buried his face against his knees. He needed to think. Why had he been separated from Ash? Had the snakehead somehow found out that the two of them were working for ASIS? All in all, he doubted it. If the snakehead even suspected who they were, they would have dragged them out together and shot them. There had to be another reason for the last-minute decision at the harbour, but try as he might Alex couldn't work out what it was.

There was a sudden jolt. The whole container shook and one of the children began to cry. The other refugees drew closer together and stared around them as if they could somehow see through the flat metal walls. Alex knew what had happened. One of the huge machines – the spreaders – had picked them up, lifting them off the lorry and loading them onto the *Liberian Star*. Right now they could be fifty metres above the quay, dangling on four thin wires. Nobody moved, afraid of upsetting the balance. Alex thought he heard the hum of machinery somewhere above his head. There was a second jolt, and the electric lamp flickered. And that was a horrible thought. Suppose it went out! Could they endure the entire voyage in pitch darkness? The container was swaying very slightly. Somebody shouted, a long way away. They began the journey down.

Alex hadn't been able to see very much of the *Liberian Star* in the rain and the confusion of their arrival, but he had taken in the great metal boxes piled on top of one another with seemingly no space in between. Where would they end up? On top, in the middle or buried somewhere deep in the hold? Once again he had to fight back a sense of claustrophobia. There were no holes drilled in the walls. The only air would come in through the cracks around the door and the secret trapdoor. The container had already reminded Alex of a coffin. Now he felt as if he and the twenty other occupants were about to be buried alive.

They came to a halt. Something clanged against

the outer wall. Two of the children whimpered and Salem went over to them, putting his arms round their shoulders and holding them close. Alex took a deep breath. There could be no going back now – that much was certain. They were on board.

And what next? Ash had said it would take them forty-eight hours to reach northern Australia, and by the time they had waited to be unloaded it could be as much as three or four days. Alex wasn't sure he could bear to sit in here all that time, locked up with these strangers. The two bottles of water and the bread that he had been given at the last moment were all he had. Presumably the other refugees had brought their own supplies. There was a chemical toilet in the far corner, but Alex knew that conditions inside the container would soon become disgusting. For the first time, he understood how desperate these people must be to make such a journey.

For his own part, he knew he couldn't just sit here. He was worried about Ash – and he was going to learn nothing about the snakehead locked up in the dark. Of course, there was always the watch that Smithers had given him. But despite everything, there was no real reason to send out a distress signal. There was still a chance that Ash was somewhere on board the *Liberian Star*. Alex was just going to have to find him.

He had made up his mind. There was nothing he could do until the ship had left Jakarta, but once they were at sea, there was every possibility that the container would be unguarded. Why bother when there was no chance of escape? Alex closed his eyes and tried to sleep. He needed to gather his strength. He wasn't going to use the watch but there was another gadget Smithers had given him. Alex had already slipped it into position. When the time was right, he would use it to break out.

He waited until he guessed they were at least half-way into their journey before he made his move.

Over twenty-four hours had passed, night blending into day with no difference between the two inside this blank, airless box. The smell was getting worse and worse. At least no one had been sea-sick, but the chemical toilet was barely adequate for so many people. Nobody was talking. What was there to say? The crossing had become a sort of living death.

Alex had caught up on some of the sleep he'd missed in Jakarta, although he'd had bad dreams ... Ash, Thai boxing, sardines! Now he'd had enough.

He dug into his pocket and took out the packet of chewing gum, then slid open the panel in the side. He had to hold it against the light to see properly, but there were the three numbers: 1, 5 and 10, each with its own switch.

The five-baht coin was already in position. When Alex had climbed into the container he had pretended to stumble, and as he reached out to steady himself he had slipped it behind the sliding bolt. So long as none of the snakehead members had seen it, it would still be there, magnetically held in place underneath him. Now was the time to find out. He would just have to hope that the noise of the engines and the sea swell would cover any sound made by the explosion.

He went over to the trapdoor and knelt beside it. He couldn't hear anything outside, but that was hardly surprising. The other refugees were looking at him, wondering what he was doing. There was no point waiting any longer. Alex pressed the switch marked 5.

There was a sharp crack under the trapdoor and a wisp of acrid smoke rose up inside the container. One of the women began to gabble at Alex but he ignored her. He pressed down with one hand and to his relief the trapdoor fell open, forming a small chute that angled out into darkness. The bolt had snapped in half. There was just enough room for Alex to slither out – but into what? It was always possible that he would find himself in the very depths of the hold, hemmed in on all sides, with nowhere else to go.

He had caused a minor panic inside the container. Everyone was talking at once, at least half a dozen languages fighting with one another all around him. Salem came over to him and tugged at his shirt, pleading with him not to do whatever it was he had planned. He looked bewildered. Who was this boy, travelling on his own, who dared to antagonize the snakehead by attempting to leave without permission? And how had he done it? They had heard the bolt shatter but that was all. It seemed to have happened by magic.

Alex looked Salem in the eye and pressed a finger against his lips. He was pleading with the old man to be silent and not to let the others give him away. It was the most he could hope for. These people were here to make a journey. He was nothing to do with them. With a bit of luck, none of them would try to follow him out or, worse still, tell the ship's crew what had happened. But if he waited any longer, one of them might try to stop him. It was time to go.

Still not sure what he was letting himself in for, Alex slid through the trapdoor head first, easing himself into the black square that had opened up below. It was much cooler outside. He had been sharing the same air with twenty people for an entire day and night and he had been unaware how stifling it had become. It was noisier too. He could hear the hum of the ship's engines, the grinding of machinery in constant motion.

But at least there was a way out. Alex found himself in what was effectively a long, flat tunnel. The containers were piled up on top of him and he could sense their huge weight pressing down. But there was a crawl space about half a metre high between the floor above him and the ceiling of the container below. He could see the daylight bleeding in – a narrow strip like a crack in a brick wall. Using his knees and elbows, he pushed himself towards it. It was a painful process, Alex constantly scraping his legs and banging his shoulders on the rusty metal above and below him.

At last he reached the edge, only to find himself high above the deck, caught three storeys up a tower of containers with no obvious way to climb down. Alex could see the ocean rushing past on the other side of the ship. There was no sign of land. For a moment, he was tempted to crawl back inside. He had nowhere to run. He would be safer with Salem and the others.

And was there really any chance of finding Ash? The *Liberian Star* was huge. It probably held more than a thousand containers. Ash could be stuck in any one of them, locked up with his own crowd of refugees. Alex felt helpless. But going back would be admitting defeat. Ever since he had first encountered the snakehead in Bangkok, he had allowed them to push him around. He'd had enough. It was time to fight back.

He had come out at one of the long sides of the container, and there was a sheer drop to the deck below. There was no way down so he crawled all the way along the edge and round to the front. Here he had more luck. The container doors were fastened with long steel rods that formed a climbing frame, and there were the metal security pins and padlocks that would provide perfect footholds. Alex knew he had to move quickly. It was still light – he guessed it must be late afternoon – and he would be seen by anyone who happened to appear on deck. On the other hand, he would have to be careful. If he slipped, there was a long way to fall.

Holding on to one of the rods, he began the journey down, trying to ignore the sea spray that whipped into his back and made every surface slippery. His worst fear was that a crew member would come out, and despite the danger he forced himself to move faster, finally dropping the last few metres and crashing down onto the deck, anxious to get himself out of sight. Nobody had seen him. He looked back up, checking the position of the container in case he needed to return. There was the name, UNWIN TOYS, in great black letters. Alex thought about the secret it concealed. He had to admit that he had never come across a criminal organization – or a crime – quite like this.

He looked around him. It was only now, crouching in the open air, that he realized quite how enormous the *Liberian Star* actually was. It measured at least three hundred metres in length and it must have been about forty metres across. The containers were piled up like metal office blocks, surrounded by decks, gantries and ladders that allowed the crew to scurry around in what little space was left. Alex was at the stern of the ship, where the huge anchor chains disappeared into a cavity below. In front of him the bridge rose up, the eyes and brain of the entire ship. Behind him the water boiled, churned up by the propellers below. He guessed they must be travelling at about thirty-five knots – forty miles per hour.

He had already accepted the fact that he had no hope at all of finding Ash. But now that he was out, he decided to explore. They could only be about twenty-four hours from Darwin. If he could survive that long without being seen, he might be able to get off the ship there and find a telephone. The number that Ash had given him was still just visible on the back of his hand. All he wanted to do was make contact. Assuming, of course, that Ash was still able to take his call.

In the next couple of hours, Alex explored a large part of the ship. He quickly realized that despite its great size, it was almost entirely made up of containers and the layout was actually very simple, with two decks running all the way from fore to aft and only a limited area for the crew to live and work in. The crew seemed surprisingly small. Only once did he spot a couple of crewmen – Filipinos in blue overalls, leaning against a handrail, smoking cigarettes. Alex slipped behind a ventilation shaft and waited until they left. That was something else to his advantage in this strange, entirely metal world. There were a thousand places to hide.

It was more dangerous inside, where the clean, brightly lit passageways were lined with dozens of doors, any one of which could open at any time. Alex was looking for the food store – he was hungry – but just as he came upon it, another crewman appeared and he had to duck down the nearest stairway. The stairs led to a cargo hold. As he waited for the man to disappear, Alex heard voices. They were speaking in English. Intrigued, he continued down.

He came to a platform perched on the edge of an area that was like an oversized metal cube with sheer walls rising to the deck above. A single container had been stored here. It was also marked UNWIN TOYS and was locked with the same security pin as the others. Four men were standing in a semicircle, deep in conversation. One of them was obviously in charge. He was standing with his back to Alex, and from his position high above, all Alex could make out was a thin, rather frail-looking body and strange white hair. The man was leaning on a walking stick. He was wearing grey gloves.

Alex assumed they were going to unlock the container, but what happened next took him completely by surprise. One of the men lifted something that looked like a television remote control and pressed a button. At once one side of the container opened electronically, the sections separating like lift doors. There was a click and then the floor of the container slid forward, bringing the contents out where they could be examined.

Alex knew at once what he was looking at. There could be no mistaking it.

Royal Blue.

That was the name Mrs Jones had given it. She had told him it was the most powerful non-nuclear weapon on the planet. Alex's first impression was that the bomb was so bomb-shaped it was almost like a cartoon. In the great emptiness of the hold it looked small, but he guessed that it was about the size of a car, just as Mrs Jones had said. He wondered what it was doing out here – and where were they taking it? Australia? Was Major Yu planning to set it off there?

Right now it was surrounded by a bank of machinery, and as soon as the container had clicked into position two of the men set to work, connecting it all up. There was some sort of scanner – it looked like an office photocopier – and a laptop. A third man was explaining something. He was black with a pock-marked face, very white teeth and cheap plastic spectacles that were too heavy for his face. He was wearing a short-sleeved shirt with half a dozen pens in the breast pocket. Alex edged forward to hear what he was saying.

"...we had to modify the bomb to change the method of detonation." The man had an accent that Alex couldn't quite place – French, perhaps. "It would normally explode one metre above the ground. But this one will be required to explode one kilometre below it. So we have made the necessary adaptations."

"A radio signal?" the white-haired man asked.

"Yes, sir." The black man indicated a piece of equipment. "This is how you communicate with the bomb. The timing is crucial. I estimate that Royal Blue will only be able to function at that depth for around twenty minutes. You must send the signal during that time."

"I want to be the one who sends the signal," the white-haired man said. He spoke perfect English, like an old-fashioned newsreader.

"Of course, sir. I received your email from London. And as you can see, I've arranged a fairly simple device. It allows you to scan your fingerprints into the system. From that moment on, you will have sole control."

"That's absolutely top-hole. Thank you, Mr Varga."

The white-haired man pulled off one of his gloves, revealing a hand that was small and withered; it could have belonged to a dead person. Alex watched as he placed it against the scanner. Varga pressed a few buttons on the laptop. A green bar of light appeared underneath the hand, travelling across the palm. It only took a couple of seconds and then it was over.

One of the other men was overweight, with thinning ginger hair. He was about fifty years old, dressed in trousers and a white shirt with blue and gold bands on the shoulders. The white-haired man now turned to him.

"You can put Royal Blue back into the container, Captain de Wynter," he said. "It'll be unloaded the moment we arrive at East Arm."

"Yes, Major."

"And one other thing—"

But the white-haired man – the major – never finished the sentence. There was a scream from a siren, so loud that Alex was almost knocked off the platform and had to cover his ears to protect himself from the noise. It was an alarm signal. The fourth man, who had so far said nothing, swung round revealing a machine gun – a lightweight Belgian M249 – hanging at his waist. Captain de Wynter pulled out a mobile phone and speed-dialled.

The siren stopped. The captain listened for a few seconds, then reported what he had heard, speaking in a low voice. Half deafened, Alex couldn't hear a word he said.

The white-haired man shook his head angrily. "Who is he? Where did he come from?"

"They are holding him on the deck," de Wynter replied.

"I want to see him for myself," the major exclaimed. "Come with me!"

The four of them made for a door set in the side of the hold. A moment later, they were gone, and to his astonishment Alex found himself alone with the bomb. It seemed a heaven-sent opportunity and, without even hesitating, he clambered down the staircase and went over to the container.

And there it was right in front of him. MI6 were searching for Royal Blue all over Thailand but he had found it in the middle of the Indian Ocean. He had found Winston Yu at the same time – for that was surely who the white-haired man must be. After all, he had just heard the captain call him Major. But why were they both here? What did the major want with the bomb? Alex wished he had heard more.

He ran his eyes over it. Close up, it struck him as one of the ugliest things he had ever seen – blunt and heavy, built only to kill and destroy. For a fleeting moment, he wondered if he could detonate it. That would put an end to Yu's plans, whatever they were. But Alex had no wish to die; and anyway, there were at least twenty refugees, some of them children, concealed on the ship. They'd be killed too.

Perhaps he could disarm it. But there was no point. Yu or the man called Varga would soon see what he had done and simply reverse it. Could he use another of the exploding coins? No – even if they could penetrate the thick shell of Royal Blue, what then? Anything he damaged, Yu could easily replace.

He had to do something. The four men might be back at any time. He glanced at the laptop and that was when he saw the instruction, printed in capital letters, on the screen.

> PLACE HAND ON SCREEN

The laptop was still connected to the scanner. Alex could see the outline of a human hand, positioned exactly to read the user's fingertips. Acting on impulse, he placed his own hand on the glass surface. There was a click and the green light rolled underneath his palm. On the laptop, the readout changed.

> FINGERPRINT PROFILE ACCEPTED
> ADD FURTHER AUTHORIZATION? Y/N

Alex reached out and pressed the Y. The screen returned to its first message.

> PLACE HAND ON SCREEN

So that was interesting. He had given himself the power to override the system if he ever happened to come across it again – and with a bit of luck neither Major Yu nor Mr Varga would notice.

There was nothing more he could do. Alex made his way back to the staircase and went up, intending to find somewhere to hide. He would wait until he got to Darwin. Then he would contact Mrs Jones and tell her about her precious bomb.

If she asked him nicely, he could even defuse it for her.

He reached the deck. Major Yu had arrived there ahead of him – Alex could hear his voice although he couldn't make out any of the words. Quickly he climbed a ladder that led to a narrow passageway dividing two of the container towers. There was no chance of anyone spotting him here. Feeling bolder, he made his way to the end and found himself looking down on the foredeck, where a single communications mast rose up amid a tangle of winches and cables.

What he saw there chilled him.

He had thought the siren was a useful diversion, perhaps announcing some problem in the engine room. It had got Major Yu and his men out of the way at exactly the right moment. But now he realized that it hadn't been good news at all. In fact, it could hardly have been worse.

The old man from the container – Salem – had decided to follow Alex out. He must have squeezed through the trapdoor and found his way onto the deck. But there his luck had run out. A couple of the crew had discovered him. They were holding him now with his hands pinned behind his back, while Major Yu questioned him. Captain de Wynter and Varga were watching. Salem was having difficulty making himself understood. He had been beaten. One of his eyes was swollen half shut, and there was blood trickling from a cut on his cheek.

He finished speaking, a gabble of words swept away by the wind. It wasn't cold out on the deck but Alex found himself shivering. Major Yu still had his back to him. Alex watched as he carefully removed one of his gloves and reached into his jacket pocket. He took out a small pistol. Without hesitating, without even pausing to aim, he shot the old man between the eyes. The single report of the bullet was like the crack of wood. Salem died on his feet, still held up by the two crewmen. Yu nodded and the men tilted him backwards, tipping his lifeless body over the rails. Alex saw it fall into the water and disappear.

Then Major Yu spoke again, and somehow his words carried up as if amplified.

"There is a child on this ship," he exclaimed. "He has escaped from the container; I don't know how. He must be found immediately and brought to me. Do not kill him unless absolutely necessary."

Alex was on his own, unarmed, on a ship many hundreds of miles from dry land. He had nowhere to run. There were going to be thirty men looking for him and he had no doubt that they would all be armed. They would start at one end and sweep all the way to the other. And when they found him, he knew exactly what to expect.

He backed away and set about finding somewhere to hide.

HIDE-AND-SEEK

The captain of the *Liberian Star* was not normally a nervous man, but right now he was sweating. Standing in front of the stateroom door, he tried to compose himself, mopping his forehead and tucking his cap under his arm. He was aware that he might have only a few minutes to live.

Hermann de Wynter was Dutch, unmarried, out of shape and saving up for a retirement somewhere in the sun. He had been working for the snakehead for eleven years, transporting containers all over the world. Never once had he asked what was inside. He knew that in this game the wrong question could prove fatal. So could failure. And now it was his duty to tell Major Yu that he had failed.

He took a deep breath and knocked on the door of the stateroom that Yu occupied on the main deck.

"Come!"

The single word sounded cheerful enough, but de Wynter had been present the day before. Yu had smiled as he killed the Afghan refugee.

He opened the door. The room was well appointed with a thick carpet, modern English furniture and soft lighting. Yu was sitting at his desk, drinking a cup of tea. There was also a plate of shortbread, which de Wynter knew was organic and came from Highgrove, the estate belonging to the Prince of Wales.

"Good day, Captain." Yu motioned for him to come in. "What news do you have for me?"

De Wynter had to force the words into his mouth. "I am very sorry to have to report, Major Yu, that we have been unable to find the boy."

Yu looked surprised. "You've been searching for nearly eighteen hours."

"Yes, sir. None of the crew have slept. We've spent the whole night searching the ship from top to bottom. Frankly, it's incredible that we have found no trace of him. We've used motion detectors and sonic intensifiers. Nothing! Some of the men think the child must have slipped overboard. Of course, we still haven't given up..."

His voice trailed off. There was nothing more to say and he knew that making too many excuses would annoy Major Yu all the more. De Wynter stood there, waiting for whatever might come. He had once seen Yu shoot a man simply for being late with his tea. He just hoped his own end would be as quick.

But to his amazement, Major Yu smiled pleasantly. "The boy certainly is trouble," he admitted.

"I must say, I'm not at all surprised that he's managed to give you the slip. He's quite a character."

De Wynter blinked. "You know him?" he asked.

"Oh yes. Our paths have crossed once before."

"But I thought..." De Wynter frowned. "He's just a refugee! A street urchin from Afghanistan."

"Not at all, Captain. That's what he'd like us to believe. But the truth is, he's unique. His name is Alex Rider. He works for British intelligence. He's what you might call a teenage spy."

De Wynter sat down. This was in itself remarkable. After all, Major Yu hadn't offered him a seat.

"Forgive me, sir," he began. "But are you saying that the British managed to smuggle a spy on board? A child...?"

"Exactly."

"And you knew?"

"I know everything, Captain de Wynter."

"But ... why?" De Wynter had completely forgotten his earlier fear. Somewhere in the back of his mind it occurred to him that he had never spoken to Major Yu so familiarly, or for such a length of time.

"It amused me," Yu replied. "This boy is rather full of himself. He travelled to Jakarta and disguised himself as a refugee. His mission was to infiltrate my snakehead. But all along I knew who he was and I was simply choosing the moment when I would bring his young life to a fitting end. I have friends who wanted me to do it sooner rather than later. But the timing was my choice."

Yu poured himself some more tea. He picked up a shortbread biscuit, holding it between his gloved fingers, and dipped it into the cup.

"My intention was to allow him to travel as far as Darwin," he continued. "I was going to deal with him then. Unfortunately the old man was unable to tell me how he managed to break out of the container, and it's certainly an unwelcome surprise. But I am still confident that you will be able to locate him eventually. After all, we have plenty of time."

The Dutchman felt his mouth go dry. "I'm afraid not, sir," he muttered. "In fact, it may already be too late."

Major Yu's eyebrows rose behind the round wire frames. "Why is that?"

"Look out of the window, sir. We've arrived at Darwin. They've already sent out a couple of tugs to tow us in."

"Surely we can delay docking for a few more hours."

"No, sir. If we do that, we could be stuck here for a week." De Wynter ran a hand over his jaw. "The Australian ports run like clockwork," he explained. "Everything has to be very precise. We have an allocated time for arrival and it's a small window. If we miss it, another ship will take our place."

Yu considered. Something very close to anxiety appeared in his shrunken, schoolboy face. This was exactly what Zeljan Kurst had warned him about in London. Like it or not, Alex Rider had taken on Scorpia once before and beaten them. Yu had thought it impossible that such a thing could happen a second time. And yet the boy did seem to have the luck of the devil. How had he managed to get out of the container? It was a shame nobody had been able to understand the old man before he had died.

"Even if we dock, the boy cannot possibly leave the ship," de Wynter said. "There is only one exit – the main gangway – and that will be guarded at all times. He can jump into the sea but I will have men on lookout. We can cover every angle with rifles. We'll pick him off in the water. A single shot. No one will hear anything. We'll only be in Darwin for a few hours. Our next port is Rio de Janeiro. We'll have three weeks to flush him out."

Major Yu nodded slowly. Even as de Wynter had been speaking, he had made up his mind. In truth he had little choice. Royal Blue had to be disembarked immediately in order to continue its journey. He couldn't wait. But there was something that Alex Rider didn't know. Whatever happened, all the cards were in Yu's hand.

"Very well, Captain," he muttered. "We'll tie up at Darwin. But if the boy does slip through your fingers a second time, I suggest you kill yourself." He snapped a biscuit in half. "It will spare me the trouble and it will, I assure you, cause you a great deal less pain."

*　*　*

Alex Rider had heard everything that Major Yu had said.

The man who sat on the executive board of Scorpia and who was in charge of the most powerful snakehead in South East Asia would have been horrified to know that Alex was hiding in perhaps the most obvious place in the world. Under his own bed.

Alex had known what he was up against. The moment he had seen the refugee killed on the deck and had heard Yu give the order for the crew to hunt him down, he had realized he needed to find somewhere on the ship where nobody would even dream of looking. It was true there were hundreds of hiding places – ventilation shafts, the crawl spaces between the containers, cabins, cable housings and storage units. But none of these would be good enough, not with the entire crew searching for him non-stop through the night.

No ... it had to be somewhere completely unthinkable – and the idea had come to him almost at once. Where was the last place he would go? It had to be the captain's cabin, or better still Major Yu's own quarters. The crew almost certainly weren't allowed in either. It wouldn't even occur to them to look inside.

He'd only had a few minutes' head start. As the crew members organized themselves and the various listening devices were handed out, Alex was racing. The layout of the ship was fairly easy to understand. He had seen much of it already. The engine room and the crew's cabins were somewhere down below. Yu, the captain and the senior officers – anyone important – would surely be housed above sea level, somewhere in the central block.

Breathless, imagining the crewmen fanning out behind him, Alex stumbled on a door that led to one of the spotlessly clean, brightly lit corridors that he had explored. He was on the right track. The first door he came to after that opened into a conference room full of charts and computers. Next came a living space with a bar and TV. He heard the clatter of saucepans and ducked back as a man wearing a chef's hat suddenly crossed the corridor and disappeared into a room opposite. A moment later, he emerged again and went back the way he had come, carrying a box of canned food.

Alex hurried forward. The chef had clearly entered some sort of larder and Alex wasted a few seconds pulling out a bottle of water for himself. He was going to need it. Continuing down the corridor, he passed a laundry, a games room, a miniature hospital, and finally a lift. There were six floors on the *Liberian Star*. Alex noticed the numbers as he ran past.

He came upon Yu's stateroom at the very end of the corridor. It wasn't locked – but there wasn't a man on board the *Liberian Star* who would have dared enter even if the door had been open and Yu miles away. Alex slipped inside. He saw a desk with a number of files and documents spread across the surface and wished he had time to examine them. But he didn't dare touch anything. Moving even one page a fraction of an inch might give him away.

He looked around him, taking in the pictures on the walls – scenes of the English countryside with, in one image, a traditional hunt setting out across what might be Salisbury Plain. A sophisticated stereo system and a plasma TV. A leather sofa. This was where Yu worked and relaxed when he was on board.

The bedroom was next door. Here was another bizarre touch: Yu slept in an antique four-poster bed. But Alex knew at once that it was perfect for his needs. There was a silk valance that trailed down to the floor and, lifting it up, he saw a space half a metre high that would conceal him perfectly. It reminded him of being seven years old again, playing hide-and-seek with Jack on Christmas Eve. But this wasn't the same. This time he was on a container ship in the middle of the Indian Ocean, surrounded by people who wouldn't think twice about killing him.

Same game. Different rules.

Alex took a swig of the water he had stolen and slid under the bed, easing the silk valance back into position. Very little light bled through. He prepared himself, trying to find a comfortable position. He knew he wouldn't be able to move a muscle once Yu entered the room.

He was suddenly struck by the craziness of his plan. Could he really stay here all night? How stupid would he look if Yu found him! He was briefly tempted to crawl out and find somewhere else. But it was already too late. The search would have begun and he couldn't risk starting again.

In fact, it was several hours before Yu came in. Alex heard the outer door open and close again. Footsteps. Then music. Yu had turned on the stereo system. His taste was classical: Elgar's *Pomp and Circumstance*, the music they played at the Albert Hall in London every summer. He listened to the piece while he ate his dinner. Alex heard one of the stewards deliver it to him and caught a faint scent of roast meat. The smell made him hungry. He sipped a little more water, glumly reflecting that it was all he had to last the night.

Later Yu turned on the television. Somehow he had managed to tune into the BBC, and Alex heard the late night news.

"The pop singer Rob Goldman was in Sydney this week, before the conference taking place on Reef Island, which has been nicknamed Reef Encounter and which has been scheduled to take place at exactly the same time as the G8 summit in Rome.

"Goldman played to a packed-out Sydney Opera House and told an enthusiastic crowd that peace and an end to world poverty were possible – but that they would have to be achieved by people, not politicians.

"Speaking from 10 Downing Street, the British prime minister said he wished Sir Rob every success but insisted that the real work would be done in Rome. It's a view not many people seem to share..."

Much later, Major Yu went to bed. Alex barely breathed as he came into the bedroom. Lying in the semi-darkness with muscles that were already aching, he heard the major undress and wash in the adjoining bathroom. And then came the inevitable moment: the creak of wood and shifting metal springs as Yu climbed into bed, just inches above the boy he was so determined to find. Fortunately he didn't read before going to sleep. Alex heard the click of a light switch and the last glimmer of light was extinguished. Then everything was silent.

For Alex, the night was yet another long, dreary ordeal. He was fairly sure that Major Yu was asleep but he couldn't be certain, and he didn't dare sleep himself in case the sound of his breathing or an accidental movement gave him away. All he could do was wait, listening to the hum of the engines and feeling the pitch of the ship as they drew ever closer to Australia. At least that was one consolation. Every second that he remained undiscovered brought him a little closer to safety.

But how was he to get off the *Liberian Star*? One exit – guarded. The decks watched. Alex didn't like the idea of diving overboard and swimming, even assuming he could manage it without being crushed or drowned. And there would be a dozen or more men waiting to take a potshot at him. Well, he would just have to worry about that when the time came.

The ship ploughed on through the darkness; the minutes dragged slowly past. At last the first streak of light crept across the floor, pushing away the shadows of the night.

Yu woke up, washed, dressed and took his breakfast in the stateroom. That was the worst part for Alex. He had barely moved for ten hours and all his bones were aching. Still Yu refused to leave. He was working at his desk. Alex heard the rustle of pages turning and, briefly, the rattle of computer keys. And then the steward brought tea and shortbread, and soon after that de Wynter arrived with the news of his failure.

So Major Yu knew who he was – and had known from the start! Alex tucked that information away, hoping he would be able to make sense of it later. For now, all that mattered was that his plan had worked and the long hours of discomfort had been worth it. They were docking at Darwin. Surely, any minute now, Yu would go out on deck to see dry land.

But it was another two hours before Yu left. Alex

waited until he was quite sure that he was alone, then rolled out from under the bed. He glanced into the stateroom. Yu had gone but he had left some of the biscuits and Alex wolfed them down. He tried to ease some feeling back into his muscles. He had to prepare himself. He knew that he had one chance to get away. They would set off to sea again in just a few hours' time, and if he was still on board he would be finished.

He went over to the window. The *Liberian Star* had already berthed at the section of the Port of Darwin known as the East Arm Wharf. To his dismay, Alex realized that they were still a very long way from land. The East Arm was an artificial, cement causeway stretching far out into the ocean with the usual array of gantries, cranes and spreaders waiting to receive the ships. It was a different world from the docks at Jakarta. Quite apart from the blinding Australian sun, everything seemed very clean and ordered. There were two long rows of parked cars, and beyond them a neat, modern warehouse and some gas tanks – all of them painted white.

A van drove by, heading up the quay. Two men walked past in fluorescent jackets and hard hats. Even assuming Alex could get off the ship, he still wouldn't be safe. It was at least a mile to the mainland and presumably there would be security barriers at the far end. Yu wouldn't dare gun him down in plain sight. That was one consolation. But however Alex looked at it, this wasn't going to be as easy as he had hoped.

Even so, he couldn't wait any longer.

Alex crept over to the door and opened it an inch at a time. The corridor was empty, lit by the same hard light that made it impossible to tell if it was night or day. He had already worked out a strategy based on what he had overheard in the stateroom. Everyone was waiting for him to break out. That meant their attention would be fixed on the main deck and the gangplank. So the rest of the ship was his. Right now he needed a diversion. He set out to create one.

He hurried past the lift and found a staircase leading down. He could hear a deep throbbing coming from below and guessed that he was heading the right way – to the engine room. He came upon it quite suddenly, a strangely old-fashioned tangle of brass valves and silver pipes and pistons, all connected to one another in a steel framework like an exhibition in an industrial museum. The air was hot down here; there was no natural light. The machinery seemed to stretch on for a mile and Alex could imagine that a ship the size of the *Liberian Star* would need every inch of it.

The control room was raised slightly above the engines, separated from them by three thick glass observation windows and reached by a short flight of metal stairs. Alex crept up on his hands and feet and found himself looking at a much more modern room with rows of gauges and dials, TV screens, computers and intricate switchboards. A single man sat in a high-backed chair, tapping at a keyboard. He looked half asleep. He certainly wasn't expecting trouble down here.

Alex saw what he was looking for: a metal cabinet about fifteen metres high with thick pipes leading in and out and a warning sign:

AIR SUPPLY
DANGER: DO NOT CUT OFF

He didn't know what needed the air or what would happen if it didn't get it, but the bright red letters were irresistible. He was going to find out.

He reached into his pocket and took out the one-baht coin that Smithers had given him. Using it would leave him with only the ten-baht coin. With a bit of luck, he wouldn't be needing it. Alex watched the man in the chair for a minute, then slipped into the control room and placed the coin against the pipe just where it entered the cabinet. The man didn't look up. The coin clicked into place, activating the charge inside. Alex tiptoed out again.

He found the chewing gum packet, slid the side open and pressed the switch marked 1. The bang was very loud and, to his surprise and relief, highly destructive. The explosion not only tore open the pipe, it wrecked the electrical circuits inside the cabinet. There was a series of brilliant sparks, and something like white steam gushed out into the control room. The man leapt up. Another alarm had gone off and red lights were flashing all around him. Alex didn't wait to see what would happen next. He was already on his way out.

Down the stairs, past the engines and back up again. This time he took the lift, guessing that in an emergency the crew would be more likely to use the stairs. He pressed the button for the sixth floor and the lift slid smoothly up.

He knew where he was heading. He had seen the bridge when he was being loaded into the container at Jakarta, and had noticed that it had its own deck, a sort of balcony with a railing and a view over the entire ship. This was going to be his way off the *Liberian Star*. For – once again – Yu's guns might be pointing everywhere else, but surely they wouldn't be pointing here.

The lift reached the sixth floor and the doors slid open. To Alex's dismay, he found himself facing a squat Chinese crewman. The man was even more shocked than Alex and reacted clumsily, scrabbling for the gun that was tucked into the waistband of his trousers. That was a mistake. Alex didn't give him time to draw it, lashing out with his foot, aiming straight between the man's legs. It wasn't so much a karate strike, more an old-fashioned kick in the groin, but it did the trick. The man gurgled and collapsed, dropping the gun. Alex scooped it up and continued on his way. Now he was armed.

Alarms were going off everywhere and Alex wondered what damage he had done with the second coin. Good old Smithers! He was the one person in MI6 who had never let him down.

The corridor led directly to the bridge. Alex passed through an archway, climbed three steps and found himself in a narrow, curving room, surprisingly empty, with large windows overlooking the decks, the containers and, to one side, the port.

There were two men on duty, sitting in what could have been dentist's chairs in front of a bank of television screens. One was a second officer that Alex hadn't seen before. The other was Captain de Wynter. He was on the telephone, talking in a voice that sounded strained and hoarse with disbelief.

"It's the reefers," he was saying. "We're going to have to shut them all down. The whole ship could go up in flames..."

The reefers were refrigerated containers. There were three hundred of them on the *Liberian Star*, storing meat, vegetables and chemicals that needed to be transported at low temperatures. The containers themselves needed constant cooling and Alex had smashed the pipes that provided exactly that. At the very least, he was going to cause Major Yu tens of thousands of pounds' worth of losses as the contents deteriorated. He might even have set the whole ship on fire.

The second officer saw Alex first. He muttered

something in Dutch and de Wynter looked round, the phone still in his hand.

Alex raised the gun. "Put it down," he said.

De Wynter went pale. He lowered the phone.

What did he do now? Alex realized that he had made it this far without any real plan at all. "I want you to get me off this ship," he said.

De Wynter shook his head. "That's not possible." He was afraid of the gun, but he was even more afraid of Major Yu.

Alex glanced at the phone. Presumably it could be connected to Darwin. "Call the police," he said. "I want you to bring them here."

"I cannot do that either," de Wynter replied. He looked a little sad. "There is no way I will help you, child. And there is nowhere for you to go. You might as well give yourself up."

Alex looked briefly out of the window. One of the containers bound for Australia was already being lifted off the ship, dangling on wires beneath a metal frame so huge that in comparison it seemed no bigger than a matchbox. The spreader was controlled by a man in a glass-fronted cabin, high up in the air. The container rose up. In a few seconds it would swing across and down to the piles that were already mounting on the quayside.

Alex judged the distance and the timing. Yes – he could do it. He had arrived at the bridge at exactly the right moment. He pointed the gun directly at de Wynter. "Get out of here," he snapped.

The captain stayed where he was. He didn't believe Alex had the nerve to pull the trigger.

"I said – get out!" Alex swung his hand and fired at a radar screen right next to the chair where de Wynter was sitting.

The sound of the gunshot was deafening inside the confined space. The screen shattered, fragments of glass scattering over the work surface. Alex smiled to himself. That was another piece of expensive equipment on the *Liberian Star* that was going to need replacing.

De Wynter didn't need telling again. He got up and hurried away from the bridge, following the second officer, who was already clambering down the stairs. Alex waited until they had gone. He knew they would call for help and come back with half a dozen armed men, but he didn't care. He had seen his way out. With a bit of luck he would be gone long before they arrived.

A glass door led onto the outer walkway. Alex opened it and found himself about twenty metres above the nearest container, far enough to break his neck if he fell. The sea was another thirty metres below that. Diving into the water was out of the question. He could see Yu's men on the main deck, waiting for him to try. But he was too high. They wouldn't need to shoot him. The impact would kill him first.

The container he had seen being lifted was now nearly above him, moving closer all the time as it travelled over the deck. Alex climbed onto the railing in front of him and tensed himself. The container loomed over him. He jumped – not down, but up, his arms stretching out. For a moment, he was suspended in space and he wondered if he was going to make it. He grimaced, trying not to imagine the crushing pain, his legs smashing into the deck, if he fell. But then his hands caught hold of the lashings beneath the container and he was being carried outwards, his legs dangling in the air, his neck and shoulder muscles screaming. The man operating the spreader couldn't see him. He was like an insect, clinging to the underbelly of the container. And Yu's men hadn't noticed him either. They were following orders, their eyes fixed on the deck and the sea below.

Alex had thought the container was moving quickly when he was on the bridge. Now that he was desperately holding on, it seemed to take for ever to reach the quay and he was certain that at any moment one of Yu's men would glance up and see him. But he was already over the side of the ship and now he saw another danger. Drop too early and he would break a leg. Leave it too late and he risked being crushed as the container was set down.

And then someone saw him.

He heard a yell of alarm. It was a docker on the wharf. He probably wasn't working for Yu but that didn't matter – as far as Alex was concerned he was just as much of a threat. Alex couldn't wait any longer. He let go with both hands and fell through the air for what seemed like an eternity. He had been hanging over a container with a tarpaulin cover. The tarpaulin provided a soft landing – even if the wind was knocked out of him as his back slammed into it. He didn't stop to recover his breath but rolled over and climbed down the side.

As he ran down the quay, dodging behind containers, Alex tried to work out a strategy. The next few minutes were going to be vital. If he was captured by the port authorities, there was always a chance that he might be handed back to Major Yu. Or if he was locked up, Yu would know where to find him. Either way, Alex knew what the result would be. He would end up dead. He had to stay out of sight until he had reached the mainland itself. So long as he was on East Arm Wharf, he would never be safe.

But luck was on his side. As he came round the corner of the last container tower, a pick-up truck drew up in front of him, the back filled with old cartons and empty petrol cans. The driver rolled down the window and yelled something at another dock worker. The man replied and the two of them laughed. By the time the truck rumbled forward again, Alex was in the back, lying on his stomach, concealed among the cartons.

The truck followed a railway line, curving round on the edge of the water, and stopped at a barrier as

Alex had expected. But the security guards knew the driver and waved him through. The truck picked up speed. Alex lay there, feeling the warm Australian breeze on his shoulders as they drove away.

He had done it! He had achieved everything that Ethan Brooke and ASIS had demanded. He had been smuggled illegally into Australia, and on the way he had uncovered much of Major Yu's network: the Chada Trading Company in Bangkok, Unwin Toys, the *Liberian Star*. For that matter, he had also located Royal Blue for Mrs Jones. If he could just reach Darwin in one piece and contact Ash, his mission would be over and he could finally go home. All he had to do was find a phone.

Twenty minutes later, the truck stopped. The engine cut out and Alex heard the driver's door open and shut. Cautiously he looked out. The port was out of sight. They had parked outside a café, a brightly coloured wooden shack beside an empty road. It was called Jake's and it had a hand-painted sign that read: THE BEST PIES IN DARWIN. Alex was desperate for food. He had barely eaten anything for two days. But it was what he saw next to the café that mattered more to him right now. It was a public telephone.

He waited until the driver had disappeared into the building, then climbed out and ran over to the phone. Apart from the last coin that Smithers had given him he had no money, but according to Ash he wouldn't need any to make a call. Now, what was the number? For a horrible moment, the separate digits danced in his head, refusing to come together. He forced himself to concentrate: 795... No ... 759... Somehow the full number took shape. He punched it in and waited.

He'd got it right. The numbers were able to override the system and Alex heard the connection being made. The phone rang three times before it was answered.

"Yes?"

Alex felt a wave of relief. It was Ash's voice. "Ash, it's me. Alex."

"Alex ... thank God! Where are you?"

"I'm in Darwin, I think. Or somewhere near it. There's a café called Jake's. About twenty minutes from the port."

"Stay where you are. I'm coming to get you."

"Are you here too? How did you get here?"

A pause, then Ash replied, "I'll tell you when I see you. Just watch out for yourself. I'll be with you as soon as I can."

He hung up, and it was only in the silence that followed that Alex realized something was wrong. It had definitely been Ash on the phone but he hadn't sounded himself. His voice had been strained and there had been something in that last pause. It was almost as if he had been waiting to be told what to say.

Alex made a decision. He had contacted Ash first as he had promised. But that might not be enough.

He twisted his wrist and looked at the watch that Smithers had given him, then deliberately moved the hands to eleven o'clock. According to Smithers, the watch would send out a signal every ten minutes. Ash might not be happy about it but Alex didn't care. He wasn't going to take any more chances. He just wanted to know that MI6 were on their way.

After that he waited for Ash to arrive. Alex couldn't think what else to do. He was exhausted after three nights with almost no proper sleep and weak from lack of food. He crept round the side of the café and sat in the shade, keeping himself out of sight. It was likely that Major Yu's men were still looking for him, and apart from the knife concealed in his belt he had no way of defending himself. He had left the gun behind on the bridge. He wished he had it with him now.

Ten minutes later, the door of the café opened and the driver who had brought him here came out, carrying a brown paper bag. He got into the pickup truck and drove off again, leaving a plume of dust behind him.

More time passed. There were flies buzzing around Alex's face but he ignored them. The café seemed to be in the middle of nowhere, surrounded by scrubland and on the edge of a road with little traffic. The sun was beginning to dip down to the horizon and Alex had to struggle not to doze off. But then he saw a car heading towards him, a black four-by-four with tinted windows. It pulled in outside the café. Ash got out.

But he wasn't alone. He hadn't been driving. His hands were chained in front of him. His black hair was in disarray and his shirt was torn; a streak of blood ran down the side of his face. He looked dazed. He hadn't seen Alex yet.

Major Yu got out of the back of the car. He was wearing a white suit with a lavender shirt buttoned at the neck. He moved slowly, supporting himself on his walking stick. As always his hands were gloved. At the same time, the driver and another man got out. They were taking no chances. The three of them surrounded Ash. Yu took out the pistol he had used to kill the old man on the *Liberian Star*. He held it against Ash's head.

"Alex Rider!" he called out in a thin voice filled with hate. "You have three seconds to show yourself. Otherwise you will see your godfather's brains all over the tarmac. I am counting now!"

Alex realized he wasn't breathing. They had Ash! What was he to do? Give himself up and they would both be killed. But could he forgive himself if he turned and ran?

"One..."

He regretted now that he hadn't used the phone to call ASIS, the police, anyone. He had known something was wrong. How could he have been so stupid?

"Two..."

He had no choice. Even if he tried to run, they would catch him. There were three of them. They had a car. He was in the middle of nowhere.

He stood up, showing himself.

Major Yu lowered the gun and Alex began to walk forward, worn out and defeated. Ash must have been on the *Liberian Star* all the time, a prisoner like him. He seemed to be in pain. His eyes were empty.

"I'm sorry, Alex," he rasped.

"Well, here you are at last," Major Yu said. "I have to say, you've caused me a great deal of time and inconvenience."

"Go to hell," Alex snarled.

"Yes, my dear Alex," Yu replied. "That's exactly where I'm taking you."

Yu raised the hand with the walking stick, then swung it with all his strength. This was the last thing that Alex remembered – a silver scorpion glinting brilliantly as it swooped towards him out of the Australian sun. He didn't even feel it as it smashed into the side of his head.

"Pick him up!" Yu commanded.

He turned his back on the unconscious boy and climbed back into the car.

MADE IN BRITAIN

There was a vase of roses on the table. Alex smelled them first ... sweet and slightly cloying. Then he opened his eyes and allowed them to come into focus. The roses were bright pink, a dozen of them arranged in a porcelain vase with a lace mat underneath. Alex felt sick. The side of his head was throbbing and he could feel the broken skin where the walking stick had hit him. There was a sour taste in his mouth. It was dark outside and he wondered how long he had been here.

And where was he? Looking around at the antique furniture, the grandfather clock, the heavy curtains and the stone fireplace with two sculpted lions, he would have said he was back home in Britain – although he knew that wasn't possible. He was lying on a bed in what could have been a country hotel. A door to one side opened into an en suite bathroom. There were bottles of Molton Brown shampoo and bubble bath beside the washbasin.

Alex rolled off the bed and staggered into the

bathroom. He splashed water on his face and examined himself in the mirror. He looked terrible. Quite apart from the dark hair and skin colour and the two fake teeth, his eyes were bloodshot, there was a huge bruise next to his eye and generally he looked as if he had been dumped here by a rubbish truck. On an impulse, he reached into his mouth and pulled the two plastic caps off his teeth. Major Yu knew perfectly well who – and what – he was. There was no need for any further pretence.

He ran himself a bath, and while the tub was filling he went back into the bedroom. The main door was locked, of course. The window looked out onto a perfect lawn with – bizarrely – a set of croquet hoops arranged in neat lines. Beyond, in the moonlight, he could see a rocky outcrop, a jetty and the sea. He turned back. Someone had left him a snack: smoked salmon sandwiches, a glass of milk, a plate of McVitie's Jaffa Cakes. He ate the lot greedily. Then he stripped off and got into the bath. He didn't know what was going to happen next – and he didn't like to think – but whatever it was, he might as well be clean.

He felt a lot better after half an hour in the hot, scented water, and although he hadn't been able to get off all the make-up Mrs Webber had given him, at least some of his own colour had returned. There were fresh clothes in the wardrobe: a Vivienne Westwood shirt and Paul Smith jeans and underwear – both London-based designers. He still had his old clothes, but the belt Smithers had given him had been removed. Alex wondered about that. Had Major Yu discovered the knife in the buckle or the jungle supplies hidden inside the leather itself? He was sorry he hadn't had the chance to use it. Maybe there would have been something inside that could have helped him now.

Luckily nobody had searched the pockets of his jeans – or if they had, they had missed the ten-baht coin and the chewing gum packet with the secret detonators. The watch was also untouched, the hands fixed at eleven o'clock, and that gave Alex a sense of reassurance. The eleventh hour indeed. Major Yu might think he held all the cards but the watch would still be transmitting, and even now MI6 Special Operations had to be closing in.

Alex got dressed in the new clothes and sat down in a comfortable armchair. He had even been supplied with some books to read: Biggles, the Famous Five and Just William. They weren't quite to his taste but he supposed he should appreciate the thought.

A few minutes later, there was a rattle of a key turning in the lock and the door opened. A maid wearing a black dress and a white apron came in. She looked Indonesian.

"Major Yu would like to invite you to dinner," she said.

"That's very kind of him," Alex replied. He closed

Biggles Investigates. "I don't suppose there's any chance of our eating out?"

"He's in the dining room," the maid replied.

Alex followed her out of the room and down a wood-panelled corridor with oil paintings on the walls. They were all scenes of the English country-side. Briefly he thought of overpowering the maid and making another bid for freedom, but he decided against it. There was a part of him that reacted against the idea of attacking a young woman; and anyway, he had no doubt that – following the events on the *Liberian Star* – Yu would be taking no chances. Security here would be tight.

They reached a grand staircase that swept down to a hall with a suit of armour standing beside a second, monumental fireplace. More English land-scape paintings everywhere. Alex had to remind himself that he was still in Australia. The house didn't fit here. It felt as if it had been imported brick by brick, and he was reminded for a moment of Nikolei Drevin, who had transported his own fourteenth-century castle from Scotland to Oxford-shire. It was strange how very bad men felt a need to live somewhere not just spectacular but slightly insane.

The maid held back and gestured Alex through a door and into a long dining room with floor-to-ceiling windows looking out over the sea. The room was carpeted, and had a table and a dozen chairs suitable for a medieval banquet. The paintings in this room were modern: a portrait by David Hockney and a wheel of colour by Damien Hirst. Alex had seen similar works in galleries in London and knew that they had to be worth millions. Only one end of the table had been laid. Major Yu was sitting there, waiting for him, the walking stick leaning against his chair.

"Ah, there you are, Alex," he said in a pleasant voice, as if they were old friends meeting up for the weekend. "Please come and sit down."

As he walked forward, Alex examined the snake-head boss properly for the first time, taking in the round, shrunken head, the wire frame glasses, the white hair that sat so oddly with the Chinese features. Yu was wearing a striped blazer with a white open-necked shirt. There was a silk handkerchief poking out of his top pocket. His gloved hands were crossed in front of him.

"How are you feeling?" Yu asked.

"My head hurts," Alex replied.

"Yes. I'm afraid I must apologize. I really don't know what came over me, hitting you like that. But the truth is, I was angry. You did a lot of damage on the *Liberian Star* and made it necessary for me to kill Captain de Wynter, which I didn't really want to do."

Alex filed the information away. So de Wynter was dead. He had paid the price for failing a second time.

"Even so, it was unforgivable of me. My mother

used to say that you can lose money, you can lose at cards but you should never lose your temper. Can I offer you some apple juice? It comes from High House Fruit Farm in Suffolk and it's quite delicious."

"Thank you," Alex said. He didn't know what was going on here but he decided he might as well play along with this madman. He held out his glass and Yu poured. As he did so, the Indonesian maid came in with the dinner: roast beef and Yorkshire pudding. Alex helped himself. He noticed that Yu ate very little and held his knife and fork as if they were surgical implements.

"I'm very glad to have this opportunity to meet you," Major Yu began. "Ever since you destroyed our operation, Invisible Sword, and caused the death of poor Mrs Rothman, I've been wondering what sort of boy you were..."

So Mrs Jones had been right. Major Yu was indeed part of Scorpia. Alex understood with a sense of dread that it gave Yu another reason to want to kill him – to settle an old score.

"It's just a shame that we have so little time together," Yu went on.

Alex didn't like the sound of that. "I have a question," he said.

"Please go ahead."

"Where is Ash? What have you done with him?"

"Let's not talk about Ash." Yu gave him a thin smile. "You don't have to worry about him. You'll never see him again. How is the beef, by the way?"

"A little bloody for my taste."

Yu sighed. "It's organic. From Yorkshire."

"Where else?" Alex was getting a bit fed up with all this. He toyed with his knife, wondering if he had the speed and the determination to stick it into the man's heart. It might be five or ten minutes before the maid came back. Enough time to find a way out of here...

Yu must have seen the idea forming in Alex's eyes. "Please don't try anything foolish," he remarked. "There is a pistol in my right-hand jacket pocket and, as the Americans would say, I am very quick on the draw. I could shoot you dead before you had even left your chair, and that would spoil a perfectly pleasant meal. So come now, Alex. I want to know all about you. Where were you born?"

Alex shrugged. "West London."

"Your parents were both English?"

"I don't want to talk about them." Alex looked around him. Suddenly the paintings, the furniture, the clothes, even the food, made sense. "You seem to like England, Major Yu," he remarked.

"I admire it greatly. If I may say so, Alex, I have enjoyed having you as my adversary because you are British. It is also one of the reasons I have invited you to dine with me now."

"But what about Invisible Sword? You tried to kill every schoolchild in London."

"That was business, and I really was very unhappy about it. You might also like to know, by the way, that I voted against sending a sniper to kill you. It seemed so crude. Some more apple juice?"

"No, thank you."

"So where do you go to school?"

Alex shook his head. He'd had enough of this game. "I don't want to talk about myself," he said. "And certainly not to you. I want to see Ash. And I want to go home."

"Neither of which is possible."

Major Yu was drinking wine. Alex noticed even that was English. He remembered Ian Rider once describing English wine as unnatural, undesirable and undrinkable. But Yu sipped it with obvious enthusiasm.

"I love England, as a matter of fact," he said. "Since you won't talk about yourself, perhaps you will permit me to tell you a little about me. My life has been remarkable. Maybe one day someone will write a book about me..."

"I've never much cared for horror stories," Alex said.

Yu smiled again – but his eyes were cold. "I like to think of myself as a genius," he began. "Of course, you might remark that I have never invented anything or written a novel or painted a great painting, and despite what I've just said, it is unlikely that I will become a household name. But different people are talented in different ways, and I think I have achieved a certain greatness in crime, Alex. And it's not surprising that my life story is a remarkable one. How could someone like me have anything other?"

He coughed, dabbed his lips and began again.

"I was born in Hong Kong. Although you wouldn't believe it to look at me now, I began with nothing. My cot was a cardboard box filled with straw. My mother was Chinese. She lived in a single room in a slum and worked as a chambermaid at the famous Victoria Hotel. Sometimes she would smuggle home soaps and shampoos for me. It was the only luxury I ever knew.

"My father was a guest there, a businessman from Tunbridge Wells, in Kent. She never told me his name. The two of them began an affair, and I have to say that she fell hopelessly in love with him. He used to talk to her about the place where he lived, this country called Great Britain. He promised her that as soon as he had enough money, he would take her with him and he would turn her into an English lady with a thatched cottage and a garden and a bulldog. For my mother, who had nothing, it was like an impossible dream.

"I'm sure you have no attachment to your country, being young; but the truth is, it's a remarkable place. At one time, this tiny island had an empire that stretched all around the world. You have to remember that when I was born, you even owned Hong Kong. Think how many inventors and explorers, artists and writers, soldiers and statesmen, have come out of Britain. William Shakespeare! Charles

Dickens! The computer was a British invention – as was the World Wide Web. It's sad that much of your country's greatness has been squandered by politicians in recent years. But I still have faith. One day Britain will once again lead the world.

"Anyway, my mother's affair came to an unhappy end. I suppose it was inevitable. As soon as he found out that she was pregnant, the businessman abandoned her and she never saw him again. Nor did he ever pay a penny towards my upkeep. He simply disappeared.

"But my mother never lost sight of her dream. If anything, it became more intense. She was determined that I should grow up with full recognition of my English blood. She named me Winston, of course, after the great wartime leader Winston Churchill. The first clothes I wore had been made in Britain. As the years went on, she became more and more fanatical. One day she decided that I should be educated at a British public school – even though it was obviously quite impossible when she was earning only a few pounds an hour changing beds and cleaning toilets. But nonetheless, when I was six years old, she left her job and began to look for other ways to make money.

"It took her just two years – a tribute, I think, to her single-mindedness and courage. And that was how I found myself at a prep school in Tunbridge Wells itself, and later at Harrow, dressed in that smart blue jacket with the marvellous straw hat. All the boys wore them. On Sundays we dressed in cut-off tailcoats – bum freezers we used to call them. It's Winston Churchill's old school, and I found it hard to believe I was there. I mean, I could actually imagine I might be sitting at his desk or reading a book that had once belonged to him. It was thrilling, and my mother was so proud of me! I did sometimes wonder how she could possibly afford it all, but it wasn't until the end of my second term that I found out – and I must say it came as a bit of a surprise.

"This is what happened..."

He poured himself some more wine, swirled it round the glass and drank.

"You might imagine that I was bullied at Harrow," he said. "After all, this was back in the fifties and there weren't many half-Chinese boys there, particularly with a single parent. But by and large everyone was very kind to me. However, there was one boy, a chap by the name of Max Odey. He had a brother called Felix, and I must say I liked both of them. Max was a pleasant enough chap, very good with money. Anyway, I don't quite know what I did to upset him but he made a lot of rather hurtful remarks and for a couple of terms, thanks to him, life was very uncomfortable. But then my mother heard about it and I'm afraid she dealt with him very severely. A hit-and-run and they never found the driver. But I knew who it was and I was horrified. It was a side of my mother I had never seen before. And that was when I discovered the truth.

"It turned out that when I was just six years old, she had managed to track down one of the main snakeheads operating in Hong Kong and had volunteered her services as a paid assassin. I know it sounds remarkable, but I suppose that being abandoned so cruelly had changed her. She no longer had any respect for life. And the fact was, she was extremely good at her new job. She was very small and Chinese, so nobody ever suspected her; and she was utterly without mercy – because mercy, of course, wouldn't pay the school fees. And that was how she was supporting me at Harrow! Every time a bill arrived at the start of a new term, she would have to go out and kill someone. It's strange to think that fifteen men died to make my education possible – sixteen, in fact, when I decided to take up horse-riding.

"After she'd finished with Max, I never had any more trouble. Even the teachers went out of their way to be pleasant to me. I was made head boy in my last term, although between you and me I was the second choice."

"What happened to the first choice?"

"He fell off a roof. From Harrow I went to London University, where I studied politics, and after that I joined the army. I was sent to Sandhurst, and I will never forget the day of my passing out parade, when I received a medal from

286

the Queen. I'm afraid it was all too much for my mother. A few weeks later, she died quite suddenly. A massive heart attack, they said. I was shaken to the core because I loved her very much – and here's something you might like to know. I bribed one of the gardeners and had her ashes scattered in the grounds of Buckingham Palace ... in the roses. I knew it was something she would have appreciated."

Major Yu had finally finished eating and the maid suddenly appeared to clear the dishes. Alex wondered how she had known when to arrive. Pudding was a rhubarb crumble served with cream. At the same time, the maid brought in a cheese-board: Cheddar, Stilton and Red Leicester. All English, of course.

"There is not much more to tell," Yu continued. "I served with distinction in Northern Ireland and was given a letter of commendation. I was as happy in the army as I had been at Harrow – happier, in fact, as I had discovered that I rather enjoyed killing people, particularly foreigners. I rose to the rank of major, and it was then that the great tragedy of my life occurred. I was diagnosed with a quite serious illness, a rare form of osteoporosis known as brittle bone disease. The name tells you everything you need to know. What it meant was that my bones had become very fragile. In recent years the condition has got considerably worse. As you can see, I need a stick to walk. I am forced to wear gloves to protect my hands. It is as if my entire skeleton is made of glass and the slightest blow could cause a terrible injury."

"You must be all broken up about that," Alex remarked.

"I shall ignore your lame attempts at humour," Yu remarked. "Soon you will have cause to regret them."

He poured himself another glass of wine.

"I was forced to leave active service but that was not the end of my career. I still had an excellent mind and I was recommended for a job in intelligence – in MI6. That's quite a coincidence, don't you think? In other circumstances, you and I could have been working together. Unfortunately it didn't quite work out that way.

"You see, at first I thought it was all going to be very exciting. I imagined myself as quite the young James Bond. But I was never invited to be part of Special Operations like you, Alex. I never met Alan Blunt or Mrs Jones. I was sent to the communications centre at Cheltenham. A desk job! Can you imagine someone like me, slaving away from nine to five in a boring little office, surrounded by secretaries and coffee machines? It was miserable. And all the while I knew that my disease was getting worse and that it was only a matter of time before I would be thrown out onto the scrap heap.

"And so I decided to look out for myself. Despite everything, a lot of the information that passed my way at Cheltenham was highly sensitive and confidential. And of course there was a market for stuff like that. So, very carefully, I began to steal secrets from British intelligence – and guess where I took them! I went to the very snakehead which had employed my mother when she was in Hong Kong. They were delighted to have me – like mother, like son.

"In the end I had to resign from MI6. The snakehead were paying me a fortune and they were offering me all sorts of career opportunities. Very quickly, I rose up the ladder until – by the early eighties – I had become number two in what was now the most powerful criminal organization in South East Asia."

"And I suppose number one fell off a roof," Alex said.

"As a matter of fact, he drowned ... but you seem to have got the general idea." Yu smiled. "Anyway, it was about this time that I heard rumours of a new organization that was being formed by people who were, in their own way, quite similar to me. I decided to diversify, and using my snakehead connections I managed to contact them; and eventually we met up in Paris to finalize details. That, of course, was the birth of Scorpia, and I was one of the founding members."

"So what are you doing now? Why do you need Royal Blue?"

Major Yu had been helping himself to cheese.

He froze with a piece of Cheddar on the end of his knife. "You saw the bomb?" he asked.

Alex said nothing. There was no point denying it.

"You really are a very capable young man, Alex. I see now that we were quite unwise to underestimate you last time." Major Yu dropped the cheese onto his plate and reached for a biscuit. "I'm going to tell you what the bomb is for because it will amuse me," he went on. "But then I'm afraid you must be on your way." He looked at his watch. "We've chatted for quite long enough."

"Where am I going, Major Yu?"

"We'll get to that in a minute. Cheese?"

"Do you have any Brie?"

"Personally, I find French cheese disgusting." He ate silently for a moment. "There is an island in the Timor Sea, not very far from the north-west coast of Australia. Its name is Reef Island. You may have heard of it."

Alex remembered the news report he had heard on board the *Liberian Star*. A conference was to take place there in a few days' time. The alternative to the G8 summit. A meeting of famous people who were trying to make the world a better place.

"Scorpia have been given the job of destroying the island and the eight so-called celebrities who will be on it," Yu went on. He sounded pleased with himself. Alex imagined one of the problems of being a criminal was that you could never tell anyone about your crimes. "But what makes the task particularly interesting is that we have to make it look like an accident."

"So you're going to blow them up," Alex said.

"No, no, no, Alex. That wouldn't work at all. We have to be much more subtle. Let me explain." He swallowed a piece of cheese and dabbed his lips with his napkin. "As it happens, Reef Island is located in what is known as a subduction zone. Perhaps you've studied that in geography. What it means is that, under the sea, a few hundred miles north of the island, there are two tectonic plates pushing against each other with a fault line between them.

"Among its many business interests, the Chada Trading Company is involved in deep-sea oil exploration and leases an oil platform in the Timor Sea. In the last couple of months, I have arranged for a shaft to be driven into the seabed precisely over the fault line. This was quite a feat of engineering, Alex. We used the same reverse circulation system that was developed to build the ventilation shafts for the Hong Kong underground railway. And I'm delighted to say that it was designed by Seacore, a British company – once again, one step ahead of the world.

"Normally the pipe running down from the rig would be no more than thirteen centimetres in diameter by the time it hit the oilfield. However, our shaft will have ample room for Royal Blue. We will place the bomb one kilometre below the surface of the seabed. I will then travel to the oil platform and personally detonate it."

But what was the point? Alex went through what he had just been told and suddenly he understood. He knew exactly what the result would be. Not just an explosion. Something much, much worse.

He couldn't keep the horror out of his voice. "You're going to cause a wave," he said. "A huge wave..."

"Go on, Alex." Yu couldn't keep the glee out of his voice.

"A tsunami..." Alex whispered the word.

He could see it clearly. That was what had happened on 26 December 2004. An earthquake underneath the sea. A tsunami that had hit first Sumatra, and even reached the coast of Somalia. More than two hundred thousand people had died.

"Exactly. The bomb will have the effect of lubricating the fault line." Yu rested one hand on top of the other. "This will force one of the plates to rise." He lifted the upper hand a few centimetres. "The result will be a deep water wave, just one metre high. You wouldn't think it could do much harm. But as it approaches the coastline, where the seabed begins to rise, the front will slow down and the rest of the water will pile up behind. By the time it hits Reef Island, a thirty-metre wall of water will have formed, travelling at about five hundred and fifty miles an hour – the speed of a jumbo jet. One cubic metre of water weighs about one tonne, Alex. Imagine hundreds of cubic metres rushing in. There will be no warning. The island will be destroyed. It is low-lying; there will be nowhere to hide. Every building will be smashed. Every single person on the island will be killed."

"But the tsunami won't stop there!" Alex exclaimed. "What will happen to it after that?"

"That's a very intelligent observation. No. The tsunami will unleash the same amount of energy as several thousand nuclear weapons. It will continue on its way until it hits Australia. We'll be all right up here in Darwin, but I'm afraid a very large section of the western coast will disappear. Everything from Derby to Carnarvon. Fortunately there's nowhere very important or even attractive in that part of the country. Broome, Port Hedland ... few people have even heard of these places. And they're not exactly overpopulated. I wouldn't expect more than about ten or twenty thousand people to die."

"But I don't understand." Alex could feel his chest tightening. "You're going to do all this just to kill eight people?"

"Perhaps you didn't hear what I said. Their deaths have to look accidental. Our job is to make the world forget that this stupid conference was ever organized. And so we will provide a natural disaster on a massive scale. Who will care about the extinction of eight people when the number of deaths rises into the thousands? Who will remember a little island when an entire continent has been hit?"

"But they'll know it was you! They'll know it was all started with a bomb."

"That would be true if we used a nuclear bomb. There is an international network of seismographs: the Poseidon satellite in outer space, the Pacific Tsunami Warning Center, and so on. But the blast made by Royal Blue won't register. It will be lost as the tectonic plates shift and the devastation begins."

Alex tried to make sense of what he was hearing. He had been sent to uncover a smuggling operation, and somehow, instead, he had stumbled into this terrible nightmare – another attempt by Scorpia to change the world. He had to stop himself glancing at his watch. Hours had passed since he had set the hands to eleven o'clock. Surely MI6 were on their way.

"I expect you're wondering whether such a relatively small bomb will really be able to cause such havoc," Major Yu continued. "Well, there is one other thing you need to know. As luck would have it, in four days' time a rather special event is taking place. I'm afraid I don't know the astronomical term for it, but what we're talking about is the alignment of the sun, the earth and the moon. And the moon is going to be particularly close. At midnight, in fact, it will be as close as it ever is.

"As a result, there will be a particularly strong gravitational pull on the earth's surface. I'm sorry,

Alex. I'm beginning to sound like a schoolteacher. Let me put it more simply. The sun will be pulling one way; the moon will be pulling the other. And for just one hour, from the moment of midnight, the tectonic plates will be at their most volatile. A single explosion on the stroke of midnight will be more than enough to begin the process I have described. Royal Blue is the perfect weapon for our needs. Undetectable. Invisible. And above all, British. I'm very proud of that."

Yu fell silent, and in that moment Alex heard the drone of a plane. He looked out of the window and saw that a series of floodlights had been turned on. There was a seaplane circling, a tiny two-seater with floats instead of wheels. It could land on the water right outside the house and tie up on the jetty that Alex had seen from his room. He knew it had come for him.

"Where are you taking me?" he demanded.

"Ah, yes. Now we come to the rub." Major Yu sat back and suddenly the gun was in his hand, pointing at Alex. He had certainly moved quickly; Alex hadn't even seen him draw it. "The easiest and perhaps the most sensible thing would be to shoot you now," he said. "In half an hour you could be at the bottom of the ocean and neither Mrs Jones nor Mr Ethan Brooke would ever know what had happened to you.

"But I'm not going to do that. Why? Two reasons. The first is that I really don't want to get blood on the carpet. You may have noticed that it's an Axminster – from the town of Axminster in Devon. The second is more personal. You owe me a great deal of money, Alex. You have to pay for the damage you caused on the *Liberian Star*. And there is still the rather more considerable debt that you owe to Scorpia following the collapse of Invisible Sword. The truth is, although you may not realize it, right now you are worth a great deal to me alive.

"How much were you told about my snakehead? People smuggling, weapons, drugs – these are all part of my organization. But I have another highly profitable business based a couple of hundred miles from here in a facility hidden in the heart of the Australian jungle. This facility deals in the sale of human organs."

Alex said nothing. No words would come.

"Do you know how hard it is to find a kidney donor, even if you are rich and live in the West?" Yu pointed the gun at Alex's stomach. "I will be able to sell your kidney for one hundred thousand pounds. And the operation won't even kill you. You will live through it; and after that we'll be able to come back, perhaps, for your eyes." The gun rose up to the level of Alex's head. "Your eyes will sell for twenty thousand pounds each, leaving you blind but otherwise in good health." The gun dropped again. "You can live without your pancreas. It will make me a further fifty thousand pounds. While you are recovering from each operation, I will drain off your blood and your plasma. They will be kept frozen and sold at five hundred pounds a pint.

"And finally, of course, there is your heart. The heart of a young, healthy boy could fetch up to a million. Do you see, Alex? Shooting you does me no good at all. But keeping you alive is good for business; and you might even get some satisfaction in knowing, when you do eventually die, that you have restored the health of quite a few people around the world."

Alex swore. He spat out every foul word he knew. But Major Yu was no longer listening. The door to the dining room had opened again but this time it wasn't the maid who came in. Two men. Indonesian, like the maid. Alex hadn't seen them before. One of them placed a hand on his shoulder but Alex shrugged it off and stood up on his own. He wasn't going to let them drag him out of here.

"We'll fly you out tomorrow morning," Major Yu said. He glanced briefly at the two men. "Make sure he's locked up. Don't let him out of your sight." One last look at Alex. "Would you like an After Eight before you leave?"

Alex said nothing. Major Yu signalled. The two men took him away.

SPARE PARTS

The plane was a two-seater Piper PA-18-150 Super Cub with a top speed of just one hundred and thirty miles an hour – but Alex had already been told that they wouldn't be travelling very far. He was sitting behind the pilot in the cramped cockpit with the buzz of the propeller wiping out any chance of conversation. Not that Alex had anything to talk about. His wrists and ankles were shackled. The seat belt had been fastened in such a way that he couldn't reach the release buckle.

He wondered briefly about the balding, red-necked man in front of him – paid to carry a boy to an unspeakable death. Was he married? Did he have children of his own? Alex considered trying to bribe him. ASIS might pay twenty thousand dollars or more for his safe return. But he never even got a chance. The pilot only glanced at him once, revealing black sunglasses and a blank face, then put on headphones. Alex guessed he would have been chosen carefully. Major Yu wasn't going to make any more mistakes.

But his worst mistake had already been made. He had left the watch on Alex's wrist: the same watch that was even now – surely – sending out a distress signal to MI6. It had to be. Inside him Alex knew that without this one hope, if he didn't believe that despite everything he still had the advantage, he would be paralysed with fear. Major Yu's plan for him was the most evil thing he had ever heard – turning him from a human being into a bag of spare parts. Ash had certainly been right about the snakehead, and maybe Alex should have listened to his warnings. These people were death itself.

And yet...

Alex had been locked up at Yu's house through-out the night and for much of the morning. It was now almost midday. How long had it been since he had begun sending the signal? Sixteen hours at the very least. Maybe longer. MI6 would have received the signal in Bangkok; it would take them time to reach Australia. Surely they would be tracking him even now, watching him every inch of the way as he moved eastwards.

But Alex had to force himself to ignore the little voice in his ear that told him they should have been here by now. Perhaps they had decided not to bother. After all, he had called them once be-fore when he had been a prisoner in Point Blanc Academy. That time, the panic button had been concealed in a CD player. He had pressed it and they had done nothing. Was it happening again?

No. Don't go there. They would come.

He had no idea where they were heading, and the pilot's body was effectively blocking out the compass and any of the other controls which might have given him a clue. He had assumed at first that they would stick to the coast. After all, the plane had no wheels; it had to land on water. But for the last hour, they had been flying inland and only the position of the sun gave him any idea of the direction. He looked out of the window, past the blur of the propeller. The landscape was flat and rocky, covered in scrub. A brilliant blue river snaked down like a great crack in the surface of the world. Wherever this was, it was huge and empty. There was no sign of any roads. No houses. Nothing.

He tried to make out more of the pilot's features but the man's eyes were fixed on the controls as if he were making a deliberate effort to ignore his passenger. He pulled on the joystick and Alex leant to one side as the plane dipped. Now he saw a canopy of green ... a band of rainforest. Yu had spoken of the Australian jungle. Was this what he had meant?

The plane dipped down. Alex had been in rainforests before and recognized the extraordinary chaos of leaves and vines, a thousand different shades and sizes, each one of them endlessly fighting for a place in the sun. Surely there would be nowhere for them to land here? But then they flew over the edge of the canopy, and Alex saw a clearing and a river that swelled suddenly into a lake with a cluster of buildings around the edge and a jetty reaching out to welcome them.

"We're landing," the pilot said – for no obvious reason. It was the first time he had spoken throughout the flight.

Alex felt his stomach shrink, and his ears popped as they circled round and began their descent. The sound of the engine rose as they neared the surface of the water. They touched down, sending spray in two directions. An osprey, frightened by the sudden arrival, leapt out of the undergrowth in a panic of beating wings. The pilot brought the plane round and they headed smoothly towards the jetty.

Two Aboriginal men had come out. They were both muscular, unsmiling, dressed in dirty jeans and string vests. One of them had a rifle slung over his bare shoulder. The pilot cut the engine and opened the door. He had unhooked a paddle from the side wall of the cockpit and used it to steer the plane the last few metres. The two men helped tie it to the jetty. One of them opened the door and released Alex from his seat. Nobody spoke. That was perhaps more unnerving than anything else.

Alex took a look around him. The compound was clean and well ordered with neat flower beds and lawns that had recently been mown. All the buildings were made of wood, painted white, with low roofs stretching out over long verandas. There were four houses, square and compact, with open shutters and fans turning within; each of them had a balcony on the first floor with views down to the lake. One of the buildings was an office and administration centre connected to a metal radio tower with two satellite dishes. There was a water tower and an electric generator with a fence running round it, topped with razor wire.

The last building was the hospital itself, long and narrow with a row of windows covered in mosquito nets and a red cross painted on the front door. This was where Alex would be sent when the time came ... not once but again and again, until there was nothing of him left. The thought made him shiver despite the damp heat of the afternoon and he turned his head away.

At first sight, there didn't seem to be too much security – but then Alex noticed a second fence, this one on the edge of the compound and about ten metres high. It was painted green to blend in with the forest beyond. There were no boats moored to the jetty and no sign of any boathouse, so an escape downriver would be impossible too – unless he swam. And what would be the point of breaking out of here? He had seen from the plane. He was in the middle of the outback with nowhere to go.

The two guards had each clamped hold of an arm and now they led him towards the administrative building. As they reached the door a young woman appeared, dressed as a nurse. She was short, plump and blonde. She had put on bright red lipstick, which seemed strangely at odds with her starched white uniform. One of her stockings was laddered.

"You must be Alex," she said. "I'm Nurse Hicks. But you can call me Charleen."

Alex had never heard such a broad Australian accent. And what the woman was saying was simply crazy. She was welcoming him as if he might actually be glad to be here.

"Come straight in," she continued. Then she noticed the cuffs. "Oh, for heaven's sake!" she exclaimed in a voice full of indignation. "You know we don't need those here, Jacko. Will you please remove them?"

One of the men produced a key and freed Alex's hands and feet. The nurse tut-tutted at them, then opened the door and led Alex down a corridor that was clean and simple with rush matting and white-washed walls. Fans were turning overhead and there was music playing somewhere, a Mozart opera.

"The doc will see you now," the nurse said cheerfully, as if Alex had booked an appointment weeks ago.

There was another door at the far end and they went through. Alex found himself in a sunny, sparsely furnished room – little more than a desk and two chairs. There was a screen to one side, a small fridge and a trolley with some bottles, a stethoscope and two scalpels. The window was open with a view of the jetty.

A man was sitting behind the desk, dressed not in a white coat but jeans and a brightly coloured open-necked shirt with the sleeves rolled up. He was in his forties, with thick blond hair and a craggy, weather-beaten face. He didn't look like a doctor. He hadn't shaved for a couple of days and his hands were grubby. There was a glass of beer on his desk and an ashtray filled with butts.

"Good day, Alex." He also spoke with an Australian accent. "Take a seat!"

It wasn't an invitation. It was a command.

"I'm Bill Tanner. We're going to be seeing a lot of each other over the next few weeks, so I might as well get a few things clear from the start. Fancy a beer?"

"No," Alex replied.

"You'd better drink something anyway," the nurse said. "You don't want to get dehydrated." She went over to the fridge and produced a bottle of mineral water. Alex didn't touch it. He had already decided he wasn't going to play these people's game.

"How was the flight?" Tanner asked.

Alex didn't answer.

The doctor shrugged. "You're feeling sore. That's OK. I'd be pretty sore if I were in your shoes. But maybe you should have thought about the consequences before you took on the snakehead."

He leant forward and Alex knew, with a sense of revulsion, that he'd had this conversation many times before. Alex wasn't the first person to be brought unwillingly to this secret hospital. Others had sat right where he was sitting now.

"Let me tell you how this works," Dr Tanner began. "You're going to die. I'm sorry to have to tell you that, but you might as well get used to it. We all have to die sometime, although for you it's probably a little sooner than expected. But you have to look on the upside. You're going to be well looked after. We have a really qualified team here and it's in our interests to keep you going as long as possible. You're going to have a lot of surgery, Alex. There are some bad days ahead. But you'll come through ... I know you will. We'll help you to the finishing line."

Alex glanced briefly at the trolley, measuring the distance between himself and the scalpels. He thought about making a grab for one of them, using it as a weapon. But that wouldn't help him. Better to take it with him, to find a use for it later. He realized that the doctor was waiting for him to reply. He answered with a single, ugly swear word. Tanner just smiled.

"Your language is a little ripe, son," he said. "But that's no worries. I've heard it all before." He gestured out of the window. "Now, you're probably wondering how you can escape from here. You've seen the fence and you're thinking you can climb over it. Or maybe you've looked at the river and decided you can try swimming. It all looks pretty easy, doesn't it! No TV cameras. Just the seven of us in the compound. Me, four nurses, Jacko and Quombi. Not much security – that's what you're thinking.

"Well, I'm sorry to tell you, mate, but you're wrong. You go out at night and you'll have to reckon with Jacko's pit bull. His name is Spike and he's a nasty piece of work. He'll rip you apart as soon as look at you. As for the fence, it's electrified. Touch it and it'll take you a week to wake up. And you're not getting anywhere near the generator – not unless you know how to bite your way through razor wire – so you can forget about tampering with the current.

"And even if you did manage to get out, it wouldn't do you much good. We're on the edge of the Kakadu National Park – two thousand million years old and as bad as the world was when it began. The start of Arnhem Land is about a mile from here, but that's a mile of tropical rainforest and you'd never find your way through. Assuming a death adder or a king brown didn't get you, there are spiders, wasps, stinging nettles, biting ants and – waiting for you on the other side – saltwater crocodiles." He jerked a thumb. "There are a hundred ways to die out there and all of them are more painful than anything we've got lined up for you here.

306

"That leaves the river. Looks pretty tempting, doesn't it! Well, there are no boats here. No canoes or kayaks or rafts or anything else you can get your hands on. We even keep the coffins locked up after one guy tried to bust out in one of those. You remember that, Charleen?"

The nurse laughed. "He was using the lid as a paddle."

"But he didn't get very far, Alex, and nor would you. Because this is the pre-monsoon season, what the Aboriginals call Gunumeleng. The water's swollen and fast-moving. About ten minutes downriver you'll hit the first rapids, and after that it just gets worse and worse. You try to swim, you'll be cut to pieces on the rocks. You'll almost certainly drown first. And waiting for you a mile downstream are the Bora Falls. A fifty-metre drop with a tonne of water crashing down every minute. So do you get what I'm saying? You're stuck here, mate, and that's that."

Alex said nothing but he was storing away everything Tanner was telling him. It was just possible that the doctor was giving away more than he realized. Outside, he heard a sudden whirring. The engine of the Piper had started again. He glanced out and saw the seaplane moving away from the jetty, preparing to take off.

"We're not going to lock you up, Alex," Tanner went on. "The grub's good and if you want a beer, just help yourself. There's no TV but you can listen to the radio, and I think we've got a few books. The point I'm trying to make is that, right now, you're here as our guest. Soon you'll be here as our patient. And after we've begun work, you won't be going anywhere. But until then, I want you to take it easy."

"We have to watch your blood pressure," the nurse muttered.

"That's right. And now, if you don't mind, I'd like you to roll up a sleeve so I can take a blood sample. It doesn't matter which arm. I also want a urine sample. It looks to me like you're pretty fit but I need to get it all down on the computer."

Alex didn't move.

"It's your choice, son," Tanner said. "You co-operate or you don't cooperate. But if you want to play hardball, I'll have to call Jacko and Quombi in. They'll rough you up a little and then they'll tie you down and I'll get what I want anyway. You don't want that, do you? Make it easy on yourself..."

Alex knew there was no point refusing. Although it made him sick, he allowed Tanner and the nurse to give him a thorough examination. They checked his reflexes, probed his eyes, ears and mouth, weighed and measured him and took the various samples. At last they let him go.

"You've looked after yourself, Alex," Tanner said. "For a Pom, you're in great shape." He was obviously pleased. "Your blood type is A positive," he added. "That's going to be an easy match."

It was as he was putting his clothes back on that he did it. Tanner was typing something into his computer; the nurse was looking over his shoulder. Alex was pulling on his trainers, leaning against the trolley as if to support himself. He allowed one hand to cover a scalpel, then slid it sideways and dropped it into his trouser pocket. He would have to walk very carefully or he'd give himself a nasty cut. He just hoped nobody would notice what he had done.

The nurse looked up and saw that he was dressed. "I'll take you to your room," she volunteered. "You should rest. We'll bring you supper in about an hour."

The sun had almost set. The sky was a deep grey with a streak of red like a fresh wound above the horizon. It had begun to rain, fat drops of water bursting one at a time on the ground.

"There's going to be another storm," the nurse said. "I'd tuck up and have an early night if I were you. And remember – stay indoors. The dog's trained not to come into the buildings. I mean, this *is* a medical facility. But take one step outside and he'll go for you – and we don't want you losing too much of that blood of yours, do we! Not at five hundred pounds a pint!"

She left Alex alone in a small room on the ground floor. It had a bed, a table and a single fan rotating in the centre of the ceiling; in one corner, there was a heavy silver filing cabinet. Alex opened it but there was nothing inside. A second door led into a small shower room, which also contained a toilet and a sink. Alex slid the scalpel out of his pocket and hid it inside the hanging roll of toilet paper. He didn't know if he would have any use for it, but at least it made him feel better having taken it. Maybe these people weren't quite as clever as they thought.

He went back into the bedroom. A single window looked down to the lake. With the Piper Super Cub gone, somehow Alex felt more abandoned than ever.

He sat down on the bed and tried to collect his thoughts. Only the day before, he had been in Darwin, congratulating himself on what he had achieved, thinking that his mission was over. And now this! How could he have been so stupid? He wondered what was happening to Ash. He still didn't understand why the two of them had been separated. If Yu knew that Ash was working for ASIS, why hadn't he sent him here too? Alex was filled with a longing to see his godfather again. It made everything even worse, being here alone.

About an hour later, the door opened and a second nurse came in, carrying a tray. She was dark-haired and slim and would have been pretty except that she had a rash over the lower part of her face. She was younger than Charleen but equally welcoming.

"I'm Isabel," she said. "I'm going to be looking after you. I've got a room just past the stairs, halfway down the corridor, so if you need anything just yell."

She set the tray down. Alex's dinner consisted of steak and chips, fruit salad and a glass of milk, but the sight of the food sickened him. He knew they were only building him up for what lay ahead.

He noticed two pills in a plastic cup. "What are these?" he asked.

"Just something to help you sleep," Isabel replied. "Some of our patients have difficulty nodding off, especially the first couple of nights. And it's important you get your rest." She paused at the door. "You're the youngest we've ever had," she said, as if Alex wanted to know. "Leave the tray outside the door. I'll collect it later."

Alex picked at the food. He wasn't hungry but he knew he had to keep his strength up. Outside, the rain fell more heavily. It was the same tropical rain that he had experienced in Jakarta. He could hear it hammering on the veranda roof and splashing into ever-widening puddles. There was a flicker of lightning and for a couple of seconds he saw the rainforest, black and impenetrable. It seemed to have moved closer, as if it were trying to swallow him up.

Later, somehow, he slept. He didn't take off any of his clothes. He couldn't bear to. He simply lay down on the bed and closed his eyes.

When he opened them again, the first light of the morning was already slanting in. His clothes felt damp. His muscles ached. He lifted his wrist and examined the watch. The hands were still set at eleven o'clock.

Almost thirty-six hours had passed since he had called for help. He listened to the world outside. The harsh cry of some sort of bird. The rustle of the grasshoppers. The last drip of the water as it fell from the branches. There was nobody out there. MI6 still hadn't arrived, and Alex couldn't fool himself any longer.

Something had gone wrong. The watch wasn't working.

They were never going to come.

DEAD OF NIGHT

The following afternoon, the silence of the rain-forest was punctured by the drone of the engine. The Piper Super Cub had returned.

By now Alex had fallen into a strange mood and one that he could barely understand. It was almost as if he had accepted his fate and could no longer find the strength or even the desire to escape it. He had met the two other women working at the hospital: Nurse Swaine and Nurse Wilcox, who had proudly told him that she would be his anaesthetist. Nobody had been unkind to him. In a way, that was what made it all so nightmarish. They were always checking that he had food and water. Would he like something to read? Would he like to listen to some music? Soon the very sound of their voices made his skin crawl. He couldn't break free of the feeling that they owned him and always would.

But he hadn't given up completely. He was still searching for a way out of this hideous trap. The river was impossible. There were no boats; nothing that would pass as a boat. He had followed the fence all the way round. There were no gaps, no convenient overhanging branches. He had considered blowing a hole in it. He still had one of the three coins that Smithers had given him. But the fence was connected to an electrical circuit. The guards would know instantly what he had done, and without a map, a compass or a machete, Alex doubted he would be able to find a way through the rainforest.

He thought about sending a radio message. He had seen the radio room in the administration building, and it was neither locked nor guarded. He soon realized why. The radio transmitter was connected to a numeric keypad: you had to punch in a code to activate it. Major Yu really had thought of everything.

Alex watched as the plane hit the surface of the lake and began a slow, lazy turn towards the jetty. He had been expecting it. Dr Tanner had told him it would be coming the night before.

"It's your first customer, Alex," he had said cheerfully. "A man called R. V. Weinberg. You may have heard of him."

As usual, Alex said nothing.

"He's a reality TV producer from Miami. Very successful. But he's contracted a serious eye disease and he needs two transplants. So it looks as if we'll be starting with your eyes. We'll operate first thing tomorrow morning."

Alex examined the American from a distance as he was helped out of the plane. Dr Tanner had warned him not to approach or try to speak to the "customer". It was one of the house rules. But, looking at him, Alex found himself filled with more hatred than he had ever felt for any human being.

Weinberg was overweight in a soft, flabby way. He had curling grey hair and a face that could have been made of putty, with sagging cheeks and jowls. He was a millionaire yet he dressed shabbily, his gut pressing against his Lacoste shirt. But it wasn't just his appearance that disgusted Alex. It was his selfishness, his complete lack of heart. Tomorrow Alex would be blind. This man would take his sight without thinking about it, simply because it was what he wanted and he had the money to pay for it. Major Yu, Dr Tanner and the nurses were evil in their own way. But Weinberg, the successful businessman from Miami, made him physically sick.

Alex waited until the man had disappeared into the house that had been prepared for him, then walked down to the edge of the lake. So this was it. He had just one night to make his escape. After that it really would be impossible.

But the anger that Alex felt had broken through his sense of hopelessness. It had come like a slap in the face and suddenly he was ready to fight back. These people thought he was helpless. They thought they'd covered everything. But they hadn't noticed the missing scalpel. And there was something even more important that they'd overlooked – despite the fact that it was sitting there right in front of them.

The plane.

The pilot had climbed out, dragging a kitbag with him. It looked as if he was going to stay until Weinberg was ready to leave. Alex had no doubt that the Piper would be incapacitated, the engine closed down and the keys locked away. And Dr Tanner would be fairly certain that no fourteen-year-old boy knew how to fly.

But that was his mistake: to leave the plane, and everything inside it, moored to the jetty.

Alex examined it, working out the angles, thinking about what lay ahead.

He might have found the way out.

They sent Alex to bed at half past eight and Nurse Isabel came into the room once he was tucked up. She was carrying two sleeping pills and a little cardboard cup of water.

"I don't want to sleep," Alex said.

"I know, dear," Isabel replied. "But Dr Tanner says you've got to get your rest." She held out the pills. "It's going to be a big day for you tomorrow," she went on. "You need your sleep."

Alex hesitated, then took the pills. He threw them into his mouth and swallowed the water.

The nurse smiled at him. "It won't be too bad,"

she said. "You'll see." She put a hand to her mouth. "Or rather, you won't..."

They checked Alex's room an hour later and again at eleven. Both times they saw him lying, utterly still, in bed. Dr Tanner was surprised. He had been expecting Alex to try something. After all, Major Yu had warned him to take extreme care with this particular boy, and tonight was his last chance. But it sometimes happened that way. It seemed that – despite his reputation – Alex had accepted the hopelessness of his situation and had chosen to find a brief escape in sleep.

Even so, Dr Tanner was a cautious man. Before he went to bed himself, he called the two guards, Quombi and Jacko, into his office.

"I want the two of you outside the boy's room all night," he ordered.

The two men looked at each other in dismay.

"That's crazy, boss," Jacko said. "The kid's asleep. He's been asleep for hours."

"He can still wake up."

"So he wakes up! Where's he going to go?"

Tanner rubbed his eyes. He liked to get a good night's sleep before he operated and he was in no mood for a lengthy debate. "I've got my orders from Major Yu," he snapped. "You want to argue with *him*?" He thought for a moment, then nodded. "All right. Let's do it this way. Jacko, you take the first shift until four o'clock. Quombi, you take over then. And make sure that dog stays outside the

317

whole time too. I want to be sure that no one goes anywhere tonight. OK?"

The two men nodded.

"Good. I'll see you tomorrow..."

At half past three that night, Jacko was sitting on the veranda outside Alex's room, flicking through a magazine he had read fifty times before. He was in a bad mood. He had passed Alex's window at least a dozen times, listening out for the faintest sound. There'd been nothing. It seemed to Jacko that everyone had got themselves into a complete panic about this kid. What was so special about him? He was just one of the many who had passed through the hospital. Some had screamed and cried; some had tried to buy their way out. All of them had ended up the same way.

The last thirty minutes of his guard duty ticked by. He stood up and stretched. A few metres away, lying on the grass, Spike cocked an ear and growled.

"It's all right, dog," Jacko said. "I'm going to bed. Quombi will be here soon."

He belched, stretched a second time and walked off into the darkness.

Ten minutes later, Quombi took his place. He was the younger of the two men and had spent almost a third of his life in jail until Dr Tanner had found him and brought him here. He liked his work at the hospital, and enjoyed taunting the patients as they got weaker and weaker. But he was in a bad mood right now. He needed his sleep. And he didn't get paid overtime for working through the night.

As he reached the building, his eye was caught by something glinting in the grass, just in front of the door. Some sort of foreign coin. Quombi didn't even wonder how it had got there. Money was money. He walked straight over and bent down to pick it up.

He was faintly aware of something falling out of the sky but he didn't look up quickly enough to see it. The silver filing cabinet could have crushed him but he was lucky. One corner struck him a glancing blow on the side of the head. Even so, it was enough to knock him out instantly. Fortunately the cabinet made little sound as it thudded onto the soft grass. Quombi fell like an axed tree. The dog got up and whined. It knew that something was wrong but it had never been trained for this. It went over and sniffed at the motionless figure, then sat on its hind legs and scratched.

On the first-floor balcony, Alex Rider looked down at his handiwork with grim satisfaction.

He had never been asleep. He had palmed the pills and swallowed only water and had been waiting quietly ever since. He had got up several times in the night, waiting for Jacko to leave, and had heard the words he had spoken to the dog. That was when he had got dressed and set to work.

Carrying the heavy filing cabinet up one flight

of stairs had almost been beyond him, and it was probably only desperation that had lent him strength as he clutched it in both arms and balanced it on his knee. The worst part had been making sure the metal frame never banged against the walls or the wooden steps. Nurse Isabel had a room on the ground floor, halfway down the corridor, and the slightest sound might wake her. He had dragged the cabinet into the room over the front door, and with one last effort had somehow managed to heave it up onto the balcony rail, balancing it there while he fumbled in his pocket.

He had only just been in time. Quombi had made his appearance a few seconds after Alex had dropped the ten-baht coin that Smithers had given him onto the lawn as bait. From that moment, the trap had been set.

And it had worked. Jacko was in bed. From the sound of it, Nurse Isabel hadn't woken up. Quombi was unconscious. With a bit of luck, he might even have fractured his skull. And the dog hadn't spoilt it all by barking.

The dog was next.

Alex crept back downstairs and went over to the main door. As he appeared, Spike began to growl, its hackles rising and its ugly brown eyes glaring out of the darkness. But – like Dr Tanner – Nurse Hicks had told him more than she should have. She had said that the dog was trained not to come into the buildings. The animal was clearly lethal. Even for a pit bull it was ugly. But it wouldn't harm him as long as he didn't step outside.

"Nice dog," Alex muttered.

He stretched out his hand. He was holding the piece of steak that he had been given on the first night. It had been kind of Dr Tanner to warn him that there was a dog. Cut into the meat were the six sleeping pills that he had been given over the last three days. The question was – would the dog take the bait? It didn't move, so Alex threw the meat onto the grass, close to the sprawled-out body of the guard. The animal ran over to it, its stubby tail wagging. It looked down, sniffed and scooped up the meat greedily, swallowing it without even chewing.

Just as Alex had hoped.

It took ten minutes for the pills to take effect. Alex watched as the dog grew more and more lumpen, until finally it collapsed onto one side and lay still, apart from the rise and fall of its stomach. At last things seemed to be going his way. Even so, he stepped outside cautiously, expecting either the dog or Quombi to wake up at any time. But he had no need to worry. He scooped up the coin – it was lying a few centimetres from the edge of the filing cabinet – and hurried into the night.

There was a soft echo of thunder that trembled through the air like a drum rolling down a hill. It wasn't raining yet but there was going to be another storm. Good. That was exactly what Alex wanted. He checked left and right. The compound was kept permanently lit by a series of arc lamps. The rest of the hospital staff, the pilot and the American television producer would all be fast asleep. Alex hesitated for just a few seconds, thinking how wonderful it would be if MI6 – perhaps Ben Daniels and a platoon of SAS men – chose this moment to make their appearance. But he knew that wasn't going to happen. It was all down to him.

He hurried towards the jetty. If only he had learnt how to fly! He might have been able to get the Piper started up, and in minutes he would have been out of here, on his way to freedom. But at fourteen, and despite all the other skills his uncle had taught him, he had been too young for flying lessons. Never mind. The plane was still going to be useful to him – for that was Dr Tanner's big mistake. The security at the hospital had been thoroughly checked – *but only when the Piper had been away*. Right now it was back; and even though he couldn't fly it, the seaplane was still going to help him escape.

Alex reached the jetty without being seen and crouched in the shadow of the plane, which was sitting on its two floats, rocking gently in the water. There was another rumble of thunder, louder this time, and a few drops of water splashed on his shoulders. The storm was going to break very soon. Alex examined the Piper Super Cub. There were two metal struts on each side, supporting the weight of the cockpit and fuselage. They tapered to a point where they were bolted into the long, fibreglass floats. Just as he remembered.

Alex reached into his pocket and took out the ten-baht coin again. It was the last one Smithers had given him, and it occurred to him that, if this went according to plan, all three would have saved his life. He placed it against the larger of the metal struts and looked up at the sky. There were few stars tonight, the clouds swirling overhead. Behind them the lightning flickered, white and mauve. Alex had the chewing gum packet in his hand. He waited for the thunder and pressed the switch at exactly the right moment.

There was a flash and a small explosion. Even without the storm it might not have been heard. But the coin had done its job. One of the struts had been ripped apart; the other had come free from the float. The Piper sagged in the water. Alex lay down on the jetty and pressed his feet against the float, pushing with all his strength. Slowly the float moved away from the main body of the plane. Alex pushed harder and the float came free. The plane sagged uselessly in the water. Moving more quickly now, Alex grabbed hold of the float and dragged it to the shore.

What he had was something almost exactly the same shape and size as a kayak or a canoe. He had even managed to blow a hole in the top which would allow his legs to fit inside. Admittedly the float had no foot braces, no thigh hooks and no support for his lower back. The hull was too flat. That would make it stable in the water but with such a wide footprint it would be hard to control. It was also much too heavy. Most modern kayaks are made of Kevlar or graphite cloth, glued together and strengthened with resin. The float from the Piper would be as nimble as a London bus. But at least it would carry him. It would just have to do.

Alex had gone kayaking three times in his life. Twice with his uncle, Ian Rider, in Norway and Canada; and once in Wales with Brookland School when he was doing his Duke of Edinburgh's Award. He'd had some experience of rapids – the pillows and eddies, the holes and the pourovers that made the journey such a white-knuckle ride. But the truth was, he was no expert. Far from it. All he could remember of his last trip was speed, screams and exploding water. He had been thirteen at the time and had thought himself lucky to come out alive.

The scalpel was back in his pocket, wrapped in toilet paper to prevent the blade cutting him. Now he took it out and unwrapped it, glad that he'd decided to take it from Dr Tanner's office. Being careful not to slip and slice open the palm of his hand, he cut away the jagged edges of the hole, trying to make a smooth line. He knew that the journey ahead was going to be tough; he didn't want his stomach and hips to be cut to pieces. The blade was small but very sharp. Soon the float was ready, and he left it on the shoreline.

Now he needed a paddle.

That was the easy part. For all his smug jokes about coffin lids, Dr Tanner had overlooked the obvious. The Piper Super Cub itself carried a paddle as part of its safety equipment. Alex had noticed it when he had flown in, clipped to the side wall of the cockpit. The pilot had used it to steer the plane ashore.

Alex went back to the edge of the lake, where the plane seemed to have tilted even further below the surface of the water. Eventually it would sink. He found a piece of the broken strut and twisted it free. Now he had a makeshift crowbar. He waited for another roll of thunder, then used it to smash a window. Opening the passenger door from the inside, he reached in and took the paddle.

Alex was tempted to get under way at once, but he made himself wait. If the rapids were as bad as Tanner had described, he couldn't possibly risk hitting them in the dark. He needed the first light of dawn. It was raining harder now, and Alex was soaked through. But in a way he was glad. The rain would provide him with cover if anyone chanced to look outside. While he was on the wide section of the lake he would be exposed. It would take him about five minutes of hard paddling to reach the cover of the rainforest.

He needed a diversion, and it suddenly occurred to him that the Piper could provide it. Once again he worked out the various possibilities. He had at least another hour until he would have enough light to take on the river. He might as well put the time to good use. And he wanted to leave his mark on Dr Tanner, R. V. Weinberg and this entire set-up.

Alex smiled grimly. These people were poison but they'd been in control for too long.

Now it was time to bite back.

WHITE WATER

Alex went back to the plane and, rummaging around in the hold, soon found what he was looking for: two empty jerrycans which might have been used to carry water or fuel. He needed a length of rubber tubing and tore it out of the engine itself. It didn't matter: this plane wasn't going anywhere. He opened the cap under the wing and put one end of the rubber tube into the fuel tank and the other into his mouth and sucked, reeling back, gagging as the acrid taste of aviation fuel cut into his throat. Nothing happened. He forced himself to try again and this time it worked. He had created a vacuum and the liquid was flowing out. He dragged over the jerrycans and filled them both.

By the time he had finished, the cans were almost too heavy to lift. Gritting his teeth, he set off across the lawn, heading back to the hospital. He knew he was taking a risk but he didn't care. He wondered how many other people had been brought here, poor refugees who had set out in hope of a better life but who had never arrived. He wanted to wipe this place off the face of the earth. Someone should have done it years ago.

The biggest risk of all was creeping into Dr Tanner's office. The first thin cracks of light were appearing in the sky and one of the nurses might wake up at any time. But he found what he was looking for in a drawer of the doctor's desk. A cigarette lighter. Tanner should have known that smoking could be harmful to his health. It was certainly going to prove expensive.

Moving faster but still being careful not to make any sound, Alex splashed the fuel over the side of the hospital, the veranda, the porch. It sat on top of the rainwater, not mixing with it. He saw it in the puddles, a strange mauve colour that almost seemed to glow. When he had just half a can left, he went back to the lake, leaving a trail of fuel behind him. He threw the empty can into the water, then climbed into his makeshift kayak, resting the paddle across his legs.

He was almost ready.

The paddle was too short and the kayak hopelessly unbalanced. It should have been trimmed out, the bow and the stern holding the same position in the water, but unfortunately the hole he had made wasn't central. He tried to shift his weight. At once he found himself wavering helplessly and thought he was going to capsize, but at the last minute he managed to right himself. He tried again more cautiously, and this time he succeeded. The float sat evenly on the surface. He dropped a shoulder. The fibreglass dug into his back but the kayak tilted slightly. He had it under control.

He took a deep breath and pushed off.

At the last minute, he flicked the lighter on. The tiny flame leapt up, battling against the falling rain. Alex touched it against the grass and at once the fire took hold, rushing up towards the hospital, which was now clearly visible in the rapidly breaking day. Alex didn't wait to see it arrive. He was already paddling, leaning forward and driving with his shoulders to give each stroke more power. He wobbled a couple of times as he got used to the weight, but the float was living up to its name. It was carrying him away.

Behind him, the line of flames reached the hospital.

The result was more spectacular than Alex could have hoped for. The rainwater had spread the aviation fuel everywhere, and although the wood was wet on the surface, years of Australian sunshine had baked it dry inside. Alex heard the soft explosion as the fire caught hold and felt the heat on his shoulders. He glanced back and saw that the entire building had become a fireball. The rain was actually steaming as it hit the roof and there was an epic struggle going on between the falling water and the rising flames.

Nobody had come outside yet, but a moment later Jacko was there, shocked out of his sleep and unable to take in what was happening. He was followed by Dr Tanner. By now, it wasn't just the hospital that was on fire. The administrative centre and one of the houses had also caught alight. The whole compound was being torn apart. Suddenly the American, R. V. Weinberg, appeared, dressed ridiculously in striped pyjamas, his trouser legs on fire. Alex smiled grimly as he hopped about, screaming, in the rain. It wasn't just his eyes that were going to need medical treatment.

Tanner looked around him and saw Quombi lying motionless on the grass, next to the great bulk of the filing cabinet. He understood at once.

"The boy!" he shouted. "Find the boy!"

Weinberg had thrown himself into a puddle and lay there whimpering. The rest of them ignored him, scattering around the complex searching for Alex. But even if they had thought to look out at the lake, they would have been too late. Alex was already out of sight, behind the curtain of rain.

There was a deafening crack and the generator shuddered to a halt with a series of sparks and a plume of black smoke. Unable to contend with the joint attack of water and fire, the electricity had failed. Tanner howled.

"Sir – the plane!" Jacko had noticed the Piper resting lopsidedly on its single float.

With the rain streaming down his face, Tanner gazed at it and pieced together what had happened. Now he knew where Alex had gone. He scanned the river, searching for him, but the smoke, the rain and the half-light had blotted out the world. The kid couldn't have gone far, though. It wasn't over yet.

Dr Tanner dragged his mobile phone out of his pocket and began to dial.

Alex heard the first rapids before he saw them. The lake wasn't a lake at all – it was simply a widening of the river. There was probably a word for it, but it had been a long time since he had sat in a geography lesson. At the far end, it became narrower again, the banks closing in like a letter V, and Alex could feel the current driving him on. He hardly had any need to paddle. At the same time, the rainforest pressed in on both sides, the trees towering above him, the foliage squeezing out the very air. And there was a sound which he remembered well. It was distant and elemental and immediately filled him with dread. Rushing water, somewhere round the corner, daring him to come on.

He dipped the paddle into the water, testing his makeshift kayak, knowing that he would have to be able to twist and turn, reacting to whatever the river threw at him with split-second timing. He could see already that he wasn't going to be able to stop. The current was too strong and the banks too steep. The nearest trees simply disappeared into the water, their roots trailing down with ugly-looking rocks behind. But at least he was putting distance between himself and the compound – or what was left of it. And Dr Tanner had already told him that there were no boats. The Piper was a wreck. Smoke was still rising from the hospital – he could see it over the line of the trees. There was no way that anyone would be able to follow him.

He turned the corner and came to the first section of rapids. The sight reminded him that he wasn't safe yet. The worst still lay before him, and he might only have exchanged one death for another.

Ahead of him the river dipped steeply downwards, hemmed in by massive boulders and tree trunks on both sides. A series of jagged ledges had created a sort of natural staircase. If he landed where the water was too shallow, the kayak would be snapped in half – and Alex with it. White water was frothing and foaming, thousands of gallons thundering down from one level to the next. To make matters worse, the whole stretch was dotted with boils, areas where the water was rushing to the surface as if it were being heated in a saucepan. Hit one of those and he would lose all control, and then he'd be completely at the mercy of the river.

The thing is, Alex, you're never really in control, whatever you may think. Just keep paddling and never fight the current, because the current will always win.

The words of his uncle, spoken what seemed like a lifetime ago, came to his mind. Alex wished he could grasp some comfort from them. He felt like a loose button in a washing machine. His fate was out of his hands. Gritting his teeth, he tightened his hold on the paddle and charged forward.

Nothing quite made sense after that. He was fighting, thrown left and right, blind. Water was shooting past him, smashing into his face, pounding him from above. He dug down, using a forward sweep to turn the float, missing a black boulder with vicious razor-sharp edges by a matter of centimetres. The green canopy spun around him. The trees had all blurred into one another. He couldn't hear. His ears were full of water and when he opened his mouth, gasping for air, water rushed down his throat. Two more sweep strokes, dodging the rocks, then a terrible crash as the kayak slammed into one of the shelves. Mercifully it stayed in one piece. A huge blanket of water fell on him and he went under. He was drowning.

But then suddenly, somehow, he was through. He felt battered and exhausted, as if he had just been in hand-to-hand combat with the river, which in a sense he had. His stomach and back were on fire where the broken edges had cut into him. Alex slid a hand under the sodden rag that was his shirt and felt the damage. When he took it out, his fingers were bloody. Behind him the white water leapt and hurled itself against the rocks, displaying its fury that the kayak had got through.

Alex knew he wouldn't be able to take much more. It was only desperation – and pure luck – that had brought him this far. From the moment he had entered the white water, he had lost all sense of his centre of gravity, which really meant that he had lost everything. He might as well have been a piece of driftwood being swept no matter where. It wasn't just that the kayak was the wrong shape. It wasn't a kayak at all. It was a float ripped off a seaplane, and if Alex had decided, after all, to steal a coffin for the journey, he doubted he would have had any less control.

He tried to remember what Dr Tanner had told him about the river. After the first rapids, it got worse. And then, a mile downstream, came something called the Bora Falls. Alex didn't like the sound of that. He would have to find somewhere to come ashore and take his chances in the rainforest. He had already covered a fair amount of ground. With a bit of luck he might even have reached the edge of the flood plain on the other side. There had to be some civilization somewhere in the area: a ranger, a flying doctor, somebody! Somehow he would find them.

But there was still nowhere to land. The banks climbed steeply, rocks forming an almost unbroken barrier. When he looked up, the tops of the trees seemed a long way away. As wet as he was, Alex wasn't cold. The rainforest throbbed with its own muddy heat. He was moving swiftly, still being swept along by the current. He was listening out for the next stretch of rapids – but that wasn't what he heard. Instead it was the last thing he had expected.

A helicopter.

If he had still been in the rapids he wouldn't have been able to hear the chatter of the blades, but right now he was in one of the straits where the water was fast-moving but silent. Even so, he had to look up to make sure he wasn't imagining it. Somehow it seemed unlikely, early in the morning, in the middle of an Australian rainforest. But there it was. It was still a small speck, some distance behind, but drawing nearer with every second.

Alex's first thought was that MI6 had finally arrived, almost when it was too late. He looked back a second time and felt his hopes shrivel and die. There was something mean and sinister about the helicopter, the way it was zeroing in on him like an insect about to sting. If MI6 were coming, they would have been here days ago. No. This was something else. And it wasn't on his side.

The helicopter was a Bell UH-1D, a "Huey", one of the most famous flying machines in the world ever since the Americans had sent hundreds of them to Vietnam back in the sixties. Alex recognized the long, slim fuselage with the extended tail. The cargo door was open and there was a man sitting with his legs hanging out and some sort of weapon on his lap. It had to be nothing more than bad luck. Dr Tanner couldn't have summoned up support in the few minutes that Alex had been gone. The helicopter must have been on its way anyway, perhaps dropping off supplies, and Tanner had simply redirected it after him.

Alex had nowhere to hide. He was in the middle of the river and he wasn't moving fast enough to get away. At least the helicopter didn't seem to be equipped with door guns, rocket launchers or anti-tank missiles. And the man only had a rifle. That was good too. If it had been a machine gun, Alex would have had no chance at all. But even so, a half-decent marksman would be able to pick him off with no trouble. Suddenly Alex's back and shoulders felt horribly exposed. He could almost feel the first bullet slamming into them.

He lowered his head towards the water, changing his centre of gravity and tilting the float onto its side. His left shoulder was touching the water now as he lanced forward, pounding down with the paddle, heading for the nearest bank. It was a stroke known as the low brace and Alex hoped that as well as giving him extra momentum through the water, it would also present less of a target to the sniper up above.

Something snapped against the surface centimetres from his head, and a microsecond later he heard the discharge of the rifle. The bullet had reached him faster than its sound. Alex jerked upright again. Water dripped off the side of his face. But he had reached his destination: a clump of trees hanging over the river, forming a green tunnel for him to go through. At least he would be out of sight for about fifty metres.

The next stretch of white water was about fifty metres in front of him, directly ahead. The rapids had been his enemy, but now, in a strange way, they had become his friend. The churning water, the spinning current and the waves tossing him from side to side would make him more difficult to hit. But could he reach them? The helicopter was directly above. The leaves and branches were thrashing around madly, tearing themselves apart. The downdraught was beating at the river and the howl of the Huey's engine was shattering the very air.

Alex emerged from the tunnel and dug down, using all the strength of his upper body and shoulders to propel himself forward. There were two more shots. One of them hit the kayak and Alex found himself staring at a hole right in front of him. It had been fired at an angle, boring through the fibreglass and exiting just above the waterline. It must have missed his leg with barely a centimetre to spare.

Left and then right, two more power strokes and he was into the rapids. He hadn't had time to pick a line – or form any strategy for surviving the next section. And this stretch was even worse than the first one, with faster water, a bigger slope, rocks that seemed purpose-built to impale him or tear him in half.

Even the sniper seemed to hesitate, letting the river do its work for him.

When in doubt, keep paddling. That had been another of Ian Rider's instructions and Alex did just that, swinging the paddle automatically, first one side, then the other, battling his way through. The helicopter had disappeared. The spray had wiped it out. Surely that meant they couldn't see him. There was an ear-splitting bang but it wasn't the rifle. The nose of the kayak had slammed into a rock, jerking Alex round in a crazy circle so that for the next few seconds he found himself travelling down the river backwards. He jammed the paddle in, using the current to turn. His arms were almost torn off by the strain but the float came round, then shot forward. All the water in the world fell on him. But then it was over. He was through.

Ahead of him the river was wider, and this time the vegetation was set further back, providing no cover. The kayak was being carried at speed. In fact, the river seemed to be moving faster and faster. Why? But Alex had no time to find an answer. He glanced up and saw the sniper taking aim. He was so close that Alex could make out the stubble on his chin, the finger closing on the trigger.

There was only one thing he could do, one last trick he could play. It might easily kill him but Alex was fighting back and he wasn't just going to sit there and let this anonymous man gun him down. The sniper fired. Alex felt the bullet crease the side of his neck, just above his shoulder. He wanted to scream. It was as if someone had drawn a kitchen knife across his flesh. But at that exact moment, he took a deep breath, threw himself sideways, jerked up a knee and turned the kayak upside down.

He wanted the sniper and the helicopter pilot to think that they had got him. From the air, all they would be able to see was the upturned hull of the kayak. Alex was dangling beneath, his face and shoulders buffeted by the current, the paddle gripped tightly in his hands. He was still travelling at speed. If he hit a rock, he would be killed. It was as simple as that. But it was either that or a bullet from above.

The next minute was the longest of Alex's life. He could feel himself moving but he could see nothing. When he tried to look, everything was a swirl of dark grey and the water beat against his eyes. He could hear strange echoes of the river and, far away, the helicopter hovering in the air. His legs were trapped, locked above his head inside the kayak. His heart was pounding. His lungs were beginning to demand fresh air.

But he had to stay underwater. How long would

the helicopter follow him before the sniper decided that his work was done? His chest was getting tighter. There were bubbles escaping from his mouth and ears, precious oxygen leaking out of him. He had no idea how long he had been submerged. He felt the kayak hit something, sending a shudder down his spine. This was madness. He was drowning. If he waited much longer, he wouldn't have the strength to flip himself back up.

At last, at the very end of his endurance, on the edge of a blackout, he acted. The move was called the hip snap. Alex curled his face into his body and pushed with the paddle. At the same time, he rolled his hips, forcing the kayak to turn.

Everything happened at once. His head and shoulders cleared the surface, water streaming down his face. Daylight burst all around him. The float swayed, then righted itself. Gasping, dazed, Alex found himself in the middle of the river, moving faster than ever.

And he was alone. The helicopter had gone. He could see it looping away towards the column of black smoke still rising from the hospital compound. So it had worked. They thought he was dead.

Alex looked ahead of him. And saw that he was.

Now he understood why they had left him. It wouldn't have mattered if he was still alive underneath the kayak, because what lay in front of him would kill him anyway.

He had reached the Bora Falls.

A straight line that marked the end of the world. The river was rushing over it, hundreds and thousands of gallons. There was a white cloud, a mist hanging over the abyss. And beyond that – nothing. He could hear the water thundering down endlessly and knew that there could be no going back. There was no power on earth that could stop him now.

Alex Rider opened his mouth and yelled as he was swept helplessly over the edge.

BATTERIES NOT INCLUDED

For a long-drawn-out second, he hung in space with the roar of the Bora Falls in his ears, the spray in his eyes and the certainty that he couldn't possibly survive. The water was like some huge, living thing, rushing and exploding over the side of the rock face. And there would be no safe landing. Looking down, Alex saw a boiling cauldron, fifty metres below, waiting to receive him.

There was no time to think, no time to do anything but react instinctively, half remembering lessons taught long ago. Somehow he had to lessen the impact when he hit the surface below. Be aggressive! Don't let the waterfall just take you. At the very last moment, before he fell, Alex tensed himself, took a deep breath and then pulled hard with a single, powerful stroke.

The world tilted.

The roar in his ears was deafening. He was blind. His head was being hammered. He was only aware of his hands gripping the paddle, the wrists locked, his muscles seizing up.

Lean forward. You don't want to fight the water – you have to go with it. The higher the drop, the more angle you'll need when you hit the bottom. And – he remembered when it was almost too late – turn your head to one side or the impact will smash every bone in your face.

He was falling. Half in the water, half in the air. Faster and faster.

Try to aim for the white. That's where there's the most air in the water and the air will cushion your fall. Don't shout. You have to hold that breath.

How much further could it be? And how deep was the basin? God – he would be smashed to pieces if he hit a rock. Too late to worry about that now. The spray was stinging his eyes. He closed them. Why watch his own death?

The kayak hit the cauldron nose first and was instantly sucked inside, dragging Alex with it. He felt his legs and stomach take the full force of the impact before the water overwhelmed him. It was pounding down on his shoulders, crushing him. His head was thrown back and he felt the whiplash on his neck. The paddle was torn free. And then he was floundering, scrabbling desperately with his hands, trying to free himself from the kayak, which was dragging him into the depths below. His elbow struck a rock, almost breaking the bone. The shock made him release his breath and he knew he had only seconds to reach the surface. But his legs were trapped. He couldn't pull them free. The kayak was sinking, taking him with it. Using all his strength, he twisted his lower body and somehow his hips cleared the edge of the float. He pulled. First one leg, then the other. He was swallowing water. He no longer knew which way was up and which was down. His feet were free. He lashed out once and then again. The water was spinning him, throwing him violently from side to side. He couldn't take any more. One last try...

...and his head and shoulders burst up into the air. He was already far downstream. The Bora Falls were behind him, impossibly high. There was no sign of the float. It must have been smashed to pieces. But as Alex sucked in fresh air, he knew that he had done everything right and that by a miracle he had survived. He had taken on the falls and he had beaten them.

The current had slowed down. Alex's arms and legs were completely limp. All his strength had gone, and the best he could manage was to keep himself afloat, tilting his head back so that his mouth stayed in the air. He felt as if he had swallowed a gallon of water and vaguely wondered about cholera, yellow fever or whatever else this tropical river might contain. ASIS hadn't bothered giving him any injections before he flew to Bangkok. Well, he'd have to worry about that later. Complain to them when the time came...

He had never felt so exhausted. The water had

become a cushion and he almost wanted to lie back and go to sleep. How far had he travelled? Dr Tanner had said that the falls were a mile from the compound, but he felt he had gone twice that distance. No sign of the helicopter. That was a good thing. They thought he was dead. So they'd leave him alone.

Sometime later, he found himself lying on a riverbank made up of shingle and sand. He had been washed up without even noticing and must have nodded off, because the sun was now much higher in the sky. He allowed the warmth to creep into him. As far as he could tell, none of his limbs were broken. His neck and back were badly bruised and hurting – his spine had taken the full force of the impact – and there were cuts and scratches all over his torso, hips and legs. But he knew he had got off lightly. The chances of his surviving the waterfall had been tiny, but to have done so without a major injury was a miracle. He remembered what Ash had told him about his father. *The luck of the devil*. Well, that was something Alex seemed to have inherited.

Ash.

Reef Island.

The tsunami heading for Western Australia.

Alex had been so worried about himself that he had lost sight of the bigger picture. How long did he have before Major Yu set off the bomb that would have such a devastating effect on the earth's tectonic plates? Was he already too late? Alex forced himself into a sitting position, trying to get life back into his battered frame as he warmed himself in the sun. At the same time, he worked it out. Yu had spoken of four days. At midnight on the fourth day the earth was going to be in the grip of some sort of gravitational pull and the fault line deep down below the seabed would be at its most vulnerable.

Four days. Alex had spent three of them as a prisoner. So it was going to happen tonight! Right now it couldn't be much later than ten o'clock in the morning. So Alex had just over twelve hours to prevent a terrible catastrophe, the murder of eight people on Reef Island and the deaths of thousands more in Australia.

And that was when the complete hopelessness of his situation hit him. It was true he had managed to escape from the horrific death Major Yu had planned for him. But where was he? Looking around him, Alex saw that he had left the rainforest behind. He was on the edge of a flood plain with mountains in the far distance, perhaps fifty miles away. He was surrounded by stubby, dwarf-like trees that he couldn't name, a few boulders and some termite mounds. There was a sweet smell – something like mouldering wood – in the air. And that was all. If nowhere had a middle, this was it.

There was nothing he could do. Nobody was going to operate on him, but he would die anyway

– from either starvation or disease. Assuming, of course, that a saltwater crocodile didn't get him first. Alex wiped a grimy hand across his face. It seemed to him that from the moment this mission had begun, nothing had gone right. He had never been in control. He cast his mind back to the office in Sydney and Ethan Brooke outlining what he would have to do. He would be there to provide cover, that was all. It would be easy. Instead of which, he had been thrown into the worst two weeks of his life. God! He should have listened to Jack!

He looked again at the mountains. It would take him a day to reach them at the very least. Too long. And why should he assume anyone lived there? He hadn't seen any roads or houses from the plane. If only he could get in touch with MI6. He glanced at his wrist. Miraculously, despite the battering it had taken, the watch was still in one piece. The question was – why hadn't it worked? Smithers had built it for him personally. The watch *had* to be sending out a signal. So what possible reason could MI6 have to ignore it? Alex remembered his meeting with Mrs Jones and Ben Daniels – Fox as he had once been known. He couldn't believe that the SAS man would let him down. So what had gone wrong?

He took the watch off and examined it. Although it looked cheap and tacky, something he might have got in a street market in Afghanistan, the watch would have been built to last. The strap must have been strong to survive the journey over the Bora Falls, and Alex guessed the case was waterproof. The hands were still showing eleven o'clock. He turned the watch over. There was a groove running all the way round the underside: the back screwed off. He pressed his thumb against it and twisted, and the case opened with surprising ease.

The watch contained some complicated microcircuitry which Smithers must have designed and installed. It was completely dry. There was no evidence of any water seeping in. The whole thing was powered by a battery that should have been sitting in a circular compartment, right in the middle.

But there was no battery. The compartment was empty.

So there was his answer. That was the reason why his signal hadn't been heard. There had been no signal. But how could it have happened? Smithers had always been on his side. It was completely unlike him to forget something so basic. Alex fought back a wave of fury. His whole life snatched away from him simply because of a missing battery!

And how would he find a replacement? Somehow he doubted he was going to discover a Boots in the middle of the outback. For a moment, Alex was tempted to fling the watch into the river. He never wanted to see the bloody thing again.

For a long time he didn't move. He let the sun beat down on him, drying out his clothes. A fly buzzed around his head and he swatted it away.

He found himself playing back everything that had happened to him: the waterfall, the flight through the rapids, the moment he had set the hospital ablaze. Had it really all been for nothing? And before that, his dinner with Major Yu, the chase on the *Liberian Star*, the discovery of Royal Blue, the sudden appearance of Kopassus, the toy warehouse in Jakarta.

No battery!

He remembered his time in Bangkok and what Ash had told him about his parents. That was the only reason he had agreed to all this, to learn something about himself. Had it been worth it? Probably not. The truth was, Ash had disappointed him. His godfather. Alex had hoped he would become a friend, but despite all the time they had spent together, he had never really got to know him. Ash was too much of a mystery – and from the very start he had set out to trick Alex, with that business in the forest near Swanbourne.

He remembered his first sight of Ash, dressed as a soldier and carrying an assault rifle, looming out of the darkness as Alex stood on a fake mine in the middle of a fake barrage. How could they have done that to him?

You weren't in any real danger. We knew exactly where you were all the time.

That was what Ash had told him that night at the Peninsula Hotel, sitting out by the swimming pool. Alex remembered it now.

And how had they known?

There was a beacon inside the heel of one of your trainers.

His trainers.

Alex looked down at them. All the colour had faded and they were ragged, full of holes. Was it possible, what he was thinking? He had been given the trainers when he was on the aircraft carrier that had picked him up when he landed in the Pacific. The beacon had been added by Colonel Abbott when he was staying with the SAS in Swanbourne.

He was wearing the same trainers now.

He had been given a complete change of clothes by Cloudy Webber when she had dressed him as an Afghan – but the shoes hadn't fitted him so she had allowed him to keep his own. He hadn't changed again until his dinner with Major Yu. He had worn the English designer shirt and jeans until he had arrived at the hospital, where there had been fresh clothes in his room. But neither Major Yu nor Dr Tanner had provided him with new footwear. So the beacon that had been planted in Swanbourne had to be on him still. It wouldn't be working. It had been designed for short-range use.

But it might be battery operated.

Alex fought back the surge of excitement. He was too afraid of being disappointed. He leant down and pulled the trainers off so that he could examine them. Ash had told him the beacon was inside one of the heels. Alex turned the shoes over.

The soles were made of rubber and he couldn't see any openings or anything that looked like a secret compartment. He pulled out the insoles. And that was when he found it. It was in the left shoe, directly over the heel: a flap that had been cut into the fabric and then sealed.

It took Alex ten minutes to prise it open, using his fingers, his teeth and a sharp stone from the riverbank. As he worked, he knew that this might all be for nothing. The battery had been there for two weeks. It might be dead. It surely wouldn't fit the transmitter in the watch anyway. But the chances of finding a battery in the Australian outback had been zero to begin with.

He pulled open the flap and there it was – the little pack of circuitry that had been designed to save his life during the bombardment in the forest. And there was the power source too: a straight-forward lithium battery, about twice the size of the one that should have been in the watch. Alex eased it out and held it in the palm of his hand as if it were a nugget of pure gold. All he had to do was connect it. He had no screwdriver, no conductor, no metal contacts, nothing. Easy!

In the end he snapped two spikes off a nearby shrub and used them as miniature tweezers to prise out some of the wires from inside the heel. It seemed to take for ever, and as the sun climbed higher he felt the sweat trickling down his forehead, but he didn't stop to rest. Painstakingly he unstitched the inside of the radio beacon and then broke off two lengths of wire, each one barely more than a centimetre long. Did the battery still have any life? He rubbed the wires against it, and to his delight he was rewarded by a tiny spark. So now all he had to do was connect the battery to the watch, using a couple of pebbles to keep everything in place.

There was nothing more he could do. He set the battery next to the watch with the wires touching, feeding precious electricity into the transmitter, and balanced the entire thing on a rock. After that he went and lay down in the shade of a tree. Either the transmitter was working now or it wasn't. He would find out soon enough.

A few minutes later, he was sound asleep.

ATTACK FORCE

Alex was woken by the sound of a helicopter. For a moment, he was filled with dread, fearing the Bell UH-1D had returned. If that were the case, he would let them take him. He simply didn't have any more reserves of energy. He had nothing left with which to fight back. But squinting into the sun he saw at once that this was a bigger helicopter with two sets of rotors: a Chinook. And there was a figure already leaning out of the door.

Dark eyes. Short black hair. A hand raised in greeting. It was Ben Daniels.

Alex clambered to his feet as the Chinook landed on a patch of scrubland a short distance away. He went over to it, taking care where he put his bare feet. It would be just his luck to step on a death adder now! Ben climbed out and stared at him. Then, before Alex could stop him, he grabbed hold of him and pulled him into a crushing embrace.

"So here you are!" he exclaimed, shouting over the noise of the rotors. "I've been so worried about you!" He let Alex go. "What the hell are you doing out here? Where have you been?"

"It's a long story," Alex said.

"Has it got anything to do with the smoke coming from upriver?" Ben jerked a thumb. "We saw it as we flew in."

"That used to be a hospital." Alex couldn't hide his relief that things were finally going his way. "I'm really glad to see you..."

"Mrs Jones has been going frantic. We knew you'd flown to Jakarta, but we lost you after that. She's got people all over Indonesia but she sent me to Darwin in case you made it across. I've been waiting there for three days, hoping you'd get in touch. You look terrible! Like something the cat dragged in."

"That's how I feel." Alex stopped. "What time is it, Ben?" he asked.

Ben was obviously surprised by the question. He looked at his watch. "It's ten past one. Why do you ask?"

"We have to get moving. We've got less than twelve hours."

"Until what?"

"I'll tell you on the way..."

Alex was feeling better than he had in a long time. He was warm and dry and fed, and the dangers of the last few days had slipped away behind him. He was lying on a comfortable bunk in a military compound just outside Darwin, which was where Ben Daniels had brought him earlier that day. He was wearing combats, the only clothes Ben had been able to find for him. For the last few hours, he had been left on his own.

He could see a certain amount of activity taking place outside the window. Soldiers crossing the parade ground, jeeps speeding in and out of the main gate. The helicopter was still sitting where it had landed. Half an hour ago a truck had pulled up and Alex had watched as refuelling began. He wondered if it was significant. Maybe something was happening at last.

Despite everything, he couldn't relax completely. It was half past six and very soon the sun would be setting; at the same time, the earth and the moon would be moving into the alignment that Major Yu had been waiting for. At midnight Royal Blue would be lowered beneath the seabed and detonated. The devastation would begin.

And what were MI6 and ASIS doing to prevent it?

Alex had explained everything, not just to Ben but to a whole posse of Australian army officers. His story was incredible, almost beyond belief, but the strange thing was that not one person in the room had doubted him. This was, after all, the boy who had dropped in from outer space. Alex supposed that where he was concerned, anything was now considered possible. One of the men was a munitions

355

expert and he had quickly confirmed what Major Yu had said. It would be possible to manufacture an artificial tsunami. At midnight the fault line would be in the grip of enormous gravitational pressure. Even a relatively small explosion would be enough to trigger a global catastrophe, and Yu had all the power of Royal Blue at his command.

Of course, in one sense Scorpia's mission had already failed. Thanks to Alex the intelligence agencies knew what they were planning, and even if everyone on Reef Island were killed in a freak wave, nobody would now think it was an accident. Alex assumed that the island would be evacuated anyway, just to be on the safe side. There was no longer any need for Major Yu to press the button. If he was sensible, he'd already be looking for somewhere to hide.

There was a knock on the door. Alex straightened up as Ben Daniels entered. He was looking grim.

"They want you," he said.

"Who?"

"The cavalry's just arrived. They're in the mess..."

Alex walked across the compound with Daniels, wondering what had gone wrong. But at least he was still being included. MI6 had always treated him as a spy one minute, a schoolboy the next, dumping him whenever it suited them. The mess was a low, wooden building running the full length of the square. With Daniels right behind him, Alex opened the door and went in.

Most of the officers he had spoken to earlier that day were still there, poring over maps and sea charts that had been spread out over the dining tables. They had been joined by two men that Alex recognized at once. This was the cavalry that Ben had referred to. Ethan Brooke was sitting at a table, Marc Damon standing just behind him. Presumably they had been flown up from Sydney. Garth – the guide dog – saw Alex come in and thumped his tail. At least someone was pleased to see him.

"Alex!" The blind man had become aware of his presence. "How are you doing?"

"I'm OK." Alex wasn't sure he was too happy to see the head of ASIS Covert Action. Ethan Brooke had manipulated him as cold-bloodedly as Alan Blunt would have done in London. It seemed to him that all these people were the same.

"I know what you've been through. I can't believe the way things played out. But you did a fantastic job."

"Major Yu knew about me all the time," Alex said. Even as he spoke the words, he knew they were true. The fight in Bangkok had been designed to cripple him. And on the *Liberian Star*, Alex had overheard Yu boasting to the captain. He had known Alex's identity before he entered the container. He had simply been playing with him for his own amusement.

"Yes. We have a security leak and it's worse than we thought." Brooke glanced in the direction of his deputy, who looked away, as if he didn't want to make any comment.

"What's happened to Ash?" Alex asked.

"We don't know. We only know what you told us." Brooke fell silent and Alex could see he was preparing himself for what he had to say.

"So what are you going to do?" Alex asked.

"We have a problem, Alex," Brooke explained. "Here's the situation ... I'll give it to you straight. The first thing is, the Reef Island conference is still going ahead."

Alex was shocked. "Why?"

"We told them they were in danger. Obviously we couldn't give them all the details, but we suggested in the strongest possible terms that they pack their bags and get out of there. They refused. They said that if they left, they'd look like cowards. Tomorrow's their main press conference, and how's it going to look if they've all skulked away overnight? We're still arguing with them, but in a way, I suppose they've got a point. Scorpia want them out of the picture. If they simply disappear, they'll be doing the job for them."

Alex took this in. It was bad news – but Reef Encounter was only part of the picture. After the tsunami hit the island, it would continue on its way towards Western Australia.

"Have you found Major Yu?" he asked.

"Yes." Brooke smiled briefly. "He told you he would be on an oil platform in the Timor Sea, and we've gone through all the records, including the latest satellite images. There's an oil rig licensed to the Chada Trading Company of Bangkok. It's a semi-submersible platform moored in twelve hundred metres of water a few hundred miles north of Reef Island."

"Right over the fault line," Damon muttered. It was the first time he had spoken since Alex came into the room. "It's called Dragon Nine."

"So that's it," Alex said. It seemed obvious to him. "You bomb it. Blow it out of the water. Kill Major Yu and everyone who works for him."

"I wish it was as easy as that," Brooke replied. "But first of all, Dragon Nine is just outside Australian waters. It's in Indonesian territory. If we send a strike against it, it'll be like declaring war. We can't even send one man in a boat without written authority, and that could take days. Officially, we're stuck..."

"Why can't you ask the Indonesians for help?"

"They don't trust us. By the time we've persuaded them we're telling the truth, it'll be too late."

"So you're just going to sit back and let him get on with it?" Alex couldn't believe what he was hearing.

"Obviously not. Why do you think we're here?"

Ben Daniels took a step forward. "Why don't you tell Scorpia that you know what they're up to?" he asked. "You said it just now. The plan only works if we all think the tsunami was caused naturally. If we tell them they've failed, maybe they'll back off."

"We've already thought of that," Damon replied. "But Dragon Nine has shut down. It's observing radio silence. And even if we did find a way to contact Major Yu, he might go ahead anyway. Why not? He's obviously mad. And if the bomb's already in place..."

"So what is the answer, Mr Brooke?" one of the other officers asked.

"A small British and Australian task force. Un-authorized and illegal." Brooke turned to Alex. "I've already spoken to your Mrs Jones and she's agreed. We have very little time but I've assembled some of our best people. They're kitting up right now. You and Daniels go with them. We parachute you onto the oil rig. You find Royal Blue and deactivate it. Meanwhile, my people kill Major Yu. If you can locate the whereabouts of Ash, so much the better – but he's not a priority. What do you say?"

Alex was too shocked to say anything, but next to him, Ben Daniels shook his head. "I'm happy to go," he said. "But you can't be serious, asking Alex. He's only a kid, if you hadn't noticed. And I'd have said he's already done enough."

Some of the Australian officers nodded in agree-ment, but Brooke wasn't having any of it. "We can't do it without Alex," he said simply.

And Alex knew he was right. He had already told them what he had done on board the *Liberian Star*. "I scanned my fingerprints into Royal Blue," he said. "I'm the only one who can deactivate it." He sighed. It had seemed like a good idea at the time.

"I'll expect you to look after him, Mr Daniels," Brooke continued. "But we don't have a lot of time to argue about this. It's already seven o'clock and you've got a long flight ahead of you." He turned to Alex. "So, Alex. What do you say?"

Two men and a woman were watching the sun set on Reef Island.

The island was only a quarter of a mile long but it was strikingly beautiful with white beaches, deep green palm trees and a turquoise sea ... all the colours somehow too vivid to be quite real. Limestone cliffs covered in vegetation rose up on the north side of the island, with mangroves below. Here sea eagles circled and monkeys chattered in the trees. But on the southern side, everything was calm and flat. There was a wooden table and a bench on the sand. But no deckchairs, no sun umbrellas, no Coke bottles or anything that might suggest that, just over the horizon, the twenty-first century was ticking on.

There was only one building on Reef Island, a long, wooden house with a thatched roof, partly on stilts. There were no generators; the only electricity was supplied by wind or water power. A large organic garden provided all the food. The owner of the house ate fish but not meat. A few cows, grazing in a field, were milked twice a day.

361

There were chickens to lay eggs. An elderly goat, wandering free, was no use at all, but it had been there so long that nobody had the heart to ask it to leave.

In the last few days, the island had been invaded by a press corps, which had established itself in a series of tent-like structures behind the house. The journalists had brought their own generators. And meat. And alcohol. And everything else they would need for the press conference the next day. They were enjoying themselves. It was nice to be able to report a story that people actually wanted to hear. And the weather during the last few days had been perfect.

The woman on the beach was the actress – Eve Taylor – who owned the island. She had made quite a lot of bad films and one or two good ones and she didn't really care which were which. They all paid the same. One of the men was an American multimillionaire – a billionaire, in fact, although in recent years he had given much of his wealth away. The other man was the pop singer Rob Goldman, who had just arrived following his tour of Australia.

"ASIS are still insisting we should leave," Goldman was saying. "They say we could all be killed."

"Have they explained the nature of the threat?" the billionaire asked.

"No. But they sounded serious."

"Of course they did." The actress let sand run through her fingers. "They want us to go. This is a trick. They're just trying to scare us."

"I don't think so, Eve," Goldman said.

Eve Taylor gazed at the horizon. "We're safe," she said. "Look how beautiful it is. Look at the sea! That's part of the reason we're here. To protect all this for the next generation. I don't care if there's a danger. I'm not going to run away." She turned to the billionaire. "Crispin?"

The man shook his head. "I'm with you," he said. "I never ran away from anything in my life and I'm not starting now."

Three hundred miles further south, in the towns of Derby, Broome and Port Hedland, thousands of people were watching the same sunset. Some of them were on their way home from work. Some were tucking children into bed. In pubs, in cars, on the beaches, wherever ... they were simply edging towards the end of another day.

And none of them knew that in a few hours' time, the bomb known as Royal Blue would begin to inch its way down the pipe which would carry it to the seabed and below. That the earth and the moon were moving, inexorably, into an alignment with the sun which wouldn't happen again for another century. And that a madman was waiting to press the button which would unleash chaos on the world.

Five hours until midnight.

And in an army camp south of Darwin, Alex Rider gave his answer and the final preparations began.

DRAGON NINE

Ethan Brooke had hand-picked ten soldiers from the Australian SAS for his assault team and at least some of them needed no introduction. As Alex joined them in the hangar that was going to be used as a briefing room, he saw Scooter, Texas, X-Ray and Sparks waiting for him, and suddenly he was back where this had all begun, in the forest near Swanbourne. He wasn't sure if he should be glad or annoyed to meet up with them again.

Scooter was equally uncomfortable. "I'm really sorry about that trick we pulled on you, Alex," he said. "We all felt bad about it. But we had our orders."

"Colonel Abbott asked us to pass on a message," Texas added. "No hard feelings. And if you ever come back to Swanbourne, we'll throw you a proper Aussie barbecue."

"With no hand grenades," Alex muttered.

"You got it."

Alex looked at the other soldiers. None of them

seemed to be older than twenty-four or twenty-five, meaning there was an age gap of just ten years between him and them. Maybe that was why all of them had accepted him. Like Alex, they had changed into night combat gear. A couple of them carried balaclavas. The rest had painted their hands and faces black.

The hangar was vast and empty. A blackboard had been placed in the middle in front of two rows of metal benches. Alex sat down next to Ben. The others took their places, Scooter facing them. Once again he seemed to be in charge. Scooter was looking tired. He seemed to have grown a lot older since Alex had last seen him – or maybe it was just that he knew how much was at stake.

"We haven't got a lot of time," he began. "But nor do we have much of a plan ... so this won't take long.

"We're parachuting in from about eight thousand feet. I know a boat would have been easier and less conspicuous, but by the time we got there it would all be over. Anyway, it's always possible our friend Major Yu has radar."

He turned to the blackboard. Someone had taped up what could have been an engineer's drawing of two oil platforms – one square, the other triangular, joined together by a narrow bridge. Each of the platforms had three cranes and one had a helicopter pad, represented by an H in a circle. Scooter picked up a stick which he used as a pointer.

"All right – listen up!" He tapped the plan. "This is what we *think* Dragon Nine looks like. We don't *know*, because we don't have any pictures and we haven't had time to take any. All I can tell you for certain is that it's a semi-submersible platform, which means that basically the whole thing floats on the surface of the water, connected to the seabed by a dozen steel tethers. In case you're wondering, each one is about two kilometres long."

"What happens if they break?" someone asked.

"Nothing much. The whole thing will float away, like a ship without an anchor. At least that's something we don't have to worry about." He pointed again. "This is the processing platform on the left. Dragon Nine isn't in production so the whole area will be quiet – and that's where we're going to start. We'll land on the helipad, this H here..."

Now Scooter turned his attention to the square-shaped rig.

"This is the drilling platform," he continued. "Once we've assembled and checked that everyone's there, we'll make our way across the bridge, heading for the main derrick – this metal tower over the well hole. And that's where we're going to find Royal Blue. Our friend Major Yu will be using some sort of system – maybe guide wires – to lower it down to the seabed."

"So let's blow it up," X-Ray growled.

"It's our first target," Scooter agreed. "The power unit will be our second. But we can't take anything for granted. Despite what Yu told Alex, he could just as easily be using a submarine to take the bomb down. That's why Alex is here. Our job is to find the control room and get him there. He can deactivate Royal Blue but no one else can – so if he gets shot we might as well pack up and go home. You hear what I'm saying? I want you to watch his back. And his front and his sides."

Alex glanced down. He understood what Scooter was saying and why he had to say it, but he still didn't like being singled out in this way.

"I'm afraid this mission isn't as easy as it seems," Scooter added, although Alex wouldn't have said it looked simple to begin with. "We've no idea where the control room is. There are five different levels, two separate platforms. Yu could be on either. You've got to think of Dragon Nine as two metal cities. They've got their own storage depots, dormitories, messes and recreation rooms, as well as fuel tanks, desalination units, pump rooms, engineering blocks and all the rest of it. Somehow we have to navigate our way through all that until we find what we're looking for. Then we have to deal with Royal Blue. And when we start, it's possible that we're going to be spread out all over the place. We're lucky there's not too much breeze, and no moon. Just try not to fall into the sea."

He paused. Eleven silent faces watched him from the two rows of benches. Alex could feel the clock already ticking. He wanted to be out and away.

"So what do we have on our side?" Scooter asked. "Well, first there's the element of surprise. Major Yu thinks Alex is dead, so he'll have no idea we're on our way. And there's the question of timing." He looked at his watch. "Yu can't detonate the bomb whenever he likes. He's got to wait until midnight. That's when the sun, moon and earth are going to be in the right position. It's nine o'clock now, and we're only two hours from drop-off. That means we'll have one hour to find Yu before he can throw the switch. And there's something else we know, thanks to Alex. The bomb can only remain at that depth of one kilometre below the seabed for twenty minutes. So it's not there yet. And if all goes well, it never will be."

He looked around. "Any questions?"

There were none.

"We've got to move quickly and quietly," he concluded. "Take out as many of Yu's people as we can before they know we're there. Leave the guns and grenades for as long as possible. Use your knives. And find the control room! That's what this is all about."

He put down the pointer.

"Let's go."

Everyone stood up. Ben had Alex's parachute – black silk, for a night drop. He'd packed it himself before the briefing and now he helped Alex put it on, pulling the straps tight across his chest and around his thighs.

"It's probably a bit too late to ask you this," he muttered. "But have you ever parachuted before?"

"Only once," Alex admitted. That had been nearly eight months ago. He had landed on the roof of the Science Museum in London. But he decided not to go into all that right now.

"Well, don't worry if you miss the target," Ben said. "The sea's warm. Conditions are perfect. And with a bit of luck, there won't be too many sharks."

The Australian SAS men were already moving. Ben strapped on his own parachute and the two of them followed the others out of the hangar. There was a helicopter waiting for them on the tarmac – the same one that had picked Alex up in the jungle. The Chinook CH-47 was the ideal machine for this night's work. Often used to ferry troops or supplies, its wide rear exit was also perfect for parachute drops. It would fly them to the target at one hundred and ninety miles an hour and at an altitude no higher than eight and a half thousand feet. That wouldn't leave long to deploy the chute.

Ben must have been reading his thoughts. "We're using static line," he said. The static line deployment system meant that they wouldn't have to pull a ripcord. The parachutes would open automatically.

Alex nodded. His mouth was suddenly too dry to speak.

They climbed in the back. In the jungle Alex had used a door just behind the cockpit, but this time the whole rear section of the Chinook had been opened, forming a ramp big enough to take a jeep. Alex looked in. The pilot and the co-pilot were already in their seats. There was a third man, a flight engineer, checking a 7.62mm M60 general-purpose machine gun which must have been bolted on at some point during the day. Alex hoped it wouldn't be needed.

The twelve of them took their places. Two long rows of seats faced each other on either side of the fuselage. Although they were made of canvas stretched over metal, they reminded Alex a little of dining-room chairs. Normally the Chinook carries thirty-three men, so at least there was plenty of room. Alex sat next to Ben. It was clear that every-one expected them to stick together – although how they would manage that parachuting out into the night was something they hadn't discussed. Scooter leant over and clipped Alex's ripcord to a silver rail running all the way to the cockpit. The pilot pressed a switch and slowly the rear door closed. A red light flashed on, the helicopter lurched off the ground, and moments later they were on their way.

It was dark and there was nothing to see out of the windows, which were too small anyway to pro-vide much of a view. Alex could only tell their height from the feeling in his stomach and the pressure in his ears. The SAS men were sitting silently, some of them checking their weapons – machine guns, pistols with silencers attached and a wide variety of vicious-looking combat knives. Next to him, Ben Daniels had nodded off to sleep. Alex guessed he'd be well practised at taking a catnap whenever he needed it, conserving his strength.

But Alex couldn't sleep. He was in a Chinook helicopter with the Australian SAS, on his way to attack an oil rig and defuse a bomb before it caused a tsunami. And as usual he was the only one who hadn't been given a gun. How had he managed to get himself into this? For a moment, he remembered walking with Jack around the Rocks in Sydney. It seemed a long, long time ago. How could he have allowed it all to happen?

The helicopter droned on through the night. Below them the Timor Sea was black and still. They were rapidly approaching Indonesian airspace.

The light turned orange.

Smoothly, a centimetre at a time, the great door at the back of the helicopter dropped open, revealing the black rush of the night outside. Although it was true there was no moon, the sea seemed to be shining as if with some natural phosphorescence – Alex could see it glinting far below.

He hadn't even thought about the parachute jump until now, but as the reality hit him, his stomach lurched. The simple truth was that he wasn't some sort of daredevil who enjoyed the prospect of hurling himself eight thousand feet from a helicopter in the dark. Right now he would have given anything to be back in London with Jack. Well, all he had to do was survive the next hour. One way or another, in just sixty minutes this would all be over.

The door had gone down as far as it could and clicked into position. It was jutting out of the back of the helicopter. A short walk into nothing.

"I'll be watching you," Ben shouted. With the roar of the wind, only Alex heard. "Don't worry! I'll stick close..."

"Thanks!" Alex shouted back the single word.

Then the light went green.

No time to think. Because of his position, Alex was going to be the first out. Maybe they had planned it that way. He didn't hesitate. If he stopped to think what he was doing, he might lose his resolve. Three steps, trailing the cord from his parachute behind him. Suddenly the blades were right over his head, thrashing the air. He felt a hand on his shoulder. Ben.

He jumped.

There was a moment of complete disorientation – he remembered it from the last time – when he couldn't quite believe what he'd done and had no idea what would happen next. He was falling so fast that he couldn't breathe. He was completely out of control. Then the parachute opened. He felt the jolt as his descent slowed. And then the peace. He was floating, dangling underneath an invisible silk canopy, black against the black night sky.

He looked down and saw the oil rig. He could only make out its vague shape – two geometric islands with a narrow corridor in between. There were about twenty lights, flickering and still tiny on the twin platforms. By joining them together in his imagination, Alex was able to draw a mental image of Dragon Nine.

He twisted round and saw the helicopter, already far away, and beneath it the eleven black flowers that were the other parachutes. It seemed to him that the Chinook was surprisingly quiet. If he could barely hear it at this altitude, perhaps Major Yu would have heard nothing below. Just as Scooter had promised, there was no wind. The sea was utterly flat. Alex didn't need to steer himself. He seemed to be heading in exactly the right direction. He could make out the white H in the middle of the helipad. H for happy landing ... at least, that was what he hoped.

There are three stages to a parachute descent. The raw fear of the jump itself. The sense of calm once the chute has opened. And the panic as the ground rushes up. Alex reached the third stage all too soon, and that was when he realized he had drifted off course after all. Maybe he had been overconfident. Maybe some sea breeze had caught him unawares. But suddenly he found himself with nothing but water below him. He was drifting away from the triangular processing platform. Urgently Alex tugged the two cords at his shoulders, trying to change direction. He was plunging towards the sea. He couldn't let that happen. The splash might give the others away. Worse than that, he might drown.

Alex jerked and writhed helplessly, but at the last minute another breeze caught him and carried him over the lip of the drilling platform and onto one of the decks. He had been doubly lucky. The deck was wide enough to allow him to land safely, dropping to one knee and folding in his parachute in a single movement. And the area was like a metallic courtyard, enclosed on all sides. With a bit of luck he would be completely out of sight. No worries there. He had landed on a bumpy, uneven surface, close to some sort of electrical generator. The noise of the machinery would have covered the crash of his feet as they made contact with the metal surface.

Five seconds later, a figure dropped out of the sky and landed just a few metres away. It was Ben Daniels. Unlike Alex, he had chosen the deck with pinpoint accuracy. He gathered in his chute and gave Alex the thumbs up. Alex twisted round. As far as he could see, all the other SAS men had landed on the processing platform. He looked up. The helicopter had already gone but presumably it would be near by, in case it was needed.

Alex realized that his own inexperience had spoilt Scooter's plan. The whole idea had been to stick together; it was vital that Alex should be protected at all times. Now he and Ben were cut off on the drilling platform. The SAS men would have to make their way across the bridge to find him. And if Yu's control room was on the other side, they would have to take Alex all the way back again.

Not good.

He looked around him. He was standing on a row of pipes. The whole deck was covered with them, cut into lengths of about three metres. A huge metal trough rose up out of the ground, slanting towards the tower that housed the well head. Presumably the pipes would be dragged up and somehow assembled in a straight line before they were lowered all the way to the seabed and beyond. On the other side, a metal wall rose up, like the side of a fortress. There were windows on the third or fourth floor but they were so covered in dirt and grease that surely nobody would be able to see through them. One of the cranes stretched out over the water, its arm silhouetted against the stars and the night sky.

Ben Daniels had taken off his parachute. He scuttled over to Alex, keeping low. He must have already come to the same conclusion as Alex, but he had decided what to do.

"We won't wait," he whispered. "We'll start looking over here. We don't have a lot of time."

Alex didn't have a watch. He looked at Ben's. It was ten past eleven. He wondered how so much time could have passed so quickly.

The two of them set off together, making their way across the pipes, trying to find the entrance into the well head. Dragon Nine was bigger than Alex had expected, and every inch was crammed with pipes and cables, cog wheels, chains, dials and valves. The oil rig was a living thing, throbbing and humming as different machines carried power or coolant to the various outlets. It was a hard, unpleasant environment. Every surface had a permanent coating of mud, oil, grease and puddles of salt water. Alex could feel his trainers sticking to the floor as he walked.

But Yu didn't seem to have posted any guards. Scooter had been right about that. With Alex supposedly dead, why should he have been expecting any trouble, miles from anywhere, in the middle of the Timor Sea? Together they eased their way round corners and between ventilation towers, immediately lost in the great tangle that had been designed to pump oil from the seabed, more than a thousand metres below. Ben was carrying a miniature torch which he kept cupped in his left hand, allowing only a trickle of light to escape. His right hand held an automatic pistol, a Walther PPK with a Brausch silencer attached.

Scooter and the other SAS men had dropped out of sight. Alex could imagine them moving towards him on the other side of the water. In the far distance he thought he heard a sound: a soft thud, the clatter of metal against metal, a stifled cry cut off very quickly. Maybe there were guards after all. If so, one of them might be wishing that he had been a little bit more alert.

Ben was opening doors, peering in through windows. There was still no sign of life on the drilling platform. They climbed a flight of steps that brought them to a metal walkway on the very edge, high over the sea. Alex looked down, and that was when he saw it. The oil rig was actually balancing on four huge legs, like an oversized metal table. One of the legs had a ladder which ran all the way down to the surface of the water and disappeared beneath it. Next to the ladder and tucked away almost underneath the drilling platform was an executive yacht, the sort of thing that would have looked more at home in a private marina in the South of France. The boat was about forty-five feet in length, sleek and white, with several sun decks and a bow that was clearly designed for speed. Alex tapped Ben on the shoulder and pointed. Ben nodded.

It had to belong to Major Yu. It was surely there to provide him with a fast escape, which meant that he had to be close by. If Alex had known the make of the yacht, there would have been no doubt in his mind at all. It was a Sealine F42-5 flybridge motorboat with a unique extending cockpit system. It had been designed and manufactured in Britain.

Ben signalled the way forward. More than ever,

Alex wished that Scooter and the others were with them. They were following a narrow gantry that led to a door set in a circular building, jutting out over the corner of the rig with curved windows that provided views in three directions.

The control room. It had to be.

They crept towards it. Alex didn't know what Ben had in mind. Maybe he was going to wait for the rest of the squadron to catch up. That would have been the sensible thing to do.

But in the end he was never given a choice. Without warning, a spotlight swept through the air, searing its way across the drilling platform. A second later, a machine gun began firing, bullets ricocheting crazily off the railings, slamming into the walls and sparking as they flew off the metal walkways. A siren began to wail, and at the same time Alex heard answering fire from the other side of the bridge. The silence of the night had been shattered. There was an explosion, a ball of flame erupting into the night like a brilliant flower. More shooting. Ben twisted and fired twice. Alex didn't even see his target but there was a cry and a man fell out of the sky, slammed into a gantry and bounced off it into the sea.

"This way!" Ben shouted. He had already started forward and Alex went after him, knowing that Yu would be expecting them now but that there could be no going back. Yu's men would be taking up positions all over the oil rig. They had the advantage.

There were a dozen ladders they could climb, and decks high above from where they could pick off the invaders one by one. He and Ben would be safer inside. The door was ahead of them, leading into the circular room. Ben reached it and crouched down.

"Stay back!" he commanded.

Alex saw him count to three.

Ben slammed the door open and went in firing. Despite what he had been told, and even though he wasn't carrying a weapon himself, Alex followed. And that was how he saw what happened in the next few seconds, even though it would be a lot longer before he took it all in.

There were two men in the control room, surrounded by computer screens, radio transmitters and the equipment that Alex had seen on the *Liberian Star*. One of them was Major Winston Yu. He was holding the pistol which he had just used to gun down Ben Daniels. Ben was lying on the floor in a spreading pool of his own blood. The Walther PPK had dropped out of his hand and lay pointing towards Alex. There was another man lying face down a short distance away, and Alex realized that Ben must have shot him as he came in. Major Yu himself was unhurt. He was staring at Alex in astonishment and disbelief.

Somehow he managed to recover. "Well, this is a surprise," he said.

Alex didn't move. He was less than three metres

away from Yu. He had nowhere to go. Yu could shoot him at any time.

"Come in and close the door," Yu ordered.

Alex did as he was told. Outside, the battle was still going on – but it was happening on the other platform. Too far away. The heavy door clicked shut.

"I knew you hadn't drowned in the river," Yu said. "Something told me. And when we couldn't find your body..." He shook his head. "I have to say, Alex, you're very hard to kill."

Alex didn't reply. Out of the corner of his eye he could see Ben's pistol lying on the floor, and part of him wondered if he could dive down and grab it. But he would never be able to bring it round and fire it in time. He was too easy a target.

"You're finished, Major Yu," Alex said. "And you've failed. ASIS know what you're trying to do. Reef Island has been evacuated. There's no point setting off a tsunami. Everyone will know it was you."

Yu considered his words carefully. Part of what Alex had said was a lie – the Reef Island conference was still taking place – but there was no way Yu could know that. Alex was here. He had brought the SAS with him. The facts spoke for themselves.

Eventually Yu sighed. "You're probably right," he said. "But I think we'll go ahead anyway. After all, it's taken meticulous planning and I'd like to make my mark on the world."

"But you'll kill thousands – for no reason."

"What reason can you give me to spare them?" Yu shook his head. "World chaos does have its uses, Alex. This was never just about Reef Island. The reconstruction of the Australian coastline will cost billions, and I have commercial interests all over South East Asia. The Chada Trading Company has shares in many building firms who will be first in line for the new contracts. Unwin Toys will offer gifts to the many hundreds of new orphans – paid for, of course, by the Australian government. There are all sorts of other interests too. A snakehead thrives on misfortune and unhappiness. For us it just means new business."

He glanced at one of the television screens. Alex saw a white line running straight from the top to the bottom. There was a blinking red square attached to it, moving slowly downwards.

"Royal Blue," Yu said. "In six or seven minutes it will reach the seabed and enter the shaft that I told you about. The shaft continues a further one kilometre down. At midnight exactly the bomb will detonate and my work will be done. By then I will be a long way away, and you will be no more than a fading memory."

Yu raised the gun. The single black eye searched for him.

"Goodbye, Alex."

But then there was a movement, and the man who had been shot by Ben Daniels groaned and dragged himself into a sitting position.

Major Yu was delighted. "How very fortunate," he exclaimed, lowering the weapon. "Before you die, let me introduce you to one of my most trusted and effective colleagues. Although, on second thoughts, I believe you've already met."

The man looked up.

It was Ash.

He had been shot twice in the chest and the life was seeping out of him. Alex could see it in the dark eyes which were filled with pain and remorse and something which was less definable but which might have been shame.

"I'm sorry, Alex," Ash gasped. He had to pause to catch his breath. "I didn't want you to know."

"I'm not sure Alex is surprised," Yu remarked.

Alex shook his head. "I guessed."

"May I ask how?"

This time there was no point in ignoring the question. Yu had been about to shoot him anyway. The longer Alex could keep him talking, the more chance there was that the SAS might finally arrive. Alex could still hear the alarm but there was less shooting and it seemed to be further away. Had the SAS been overpowered or were they already in command and on their way? He glanced at the television screen. The little red square was continuing its journey down.

"Everything went wrong from the start," he said, talking directly to Major Yu. "Ethan Brooke had already lost two agents. Somehow the snakehead knew everything he planned. They knew about me too. Why else was I chosen for that fight in Bangkok? At first it didn't make any sense. But then, when I was in the arena, Anan Sukit said something to me. He said he'd kill me if I didn't take part, and he said it first in French, then in English. Why? If he'd really believed I was an Afghan boy, he'd have known I wouldn't speak either.

"I wondered about that. But it got worse. Ash gave me an emergency telephone number. I called it and it led me straight to you."

Ash opened his mouth to speak but Alex cut in.

"I know," he said. He looked briefly at the dying man. "You made it look good with the fake blood, as if you'd been taken prisoner like me. But then I lost two of the gadgets Smithers had given me and that was when I knew it had to be you.

"I told you about the watch and the belt. Somehow the battery went missing out of the watch. I suppose you must have removed it when I was asleep, that night in Jakarta. As for the belt, Major Yu took that when I was in his house. But I'd never told you about the coins. Smithers had also given me three coins with explosive charges, and they stayed in my pocket. If I'd told you, I guess they would have gone too."

He stopped.

"When did you start working for Scorpia, Ash?" he asked.

Ash glanced at Major Yu.

"Tell him – but be quick," Yu snapped. "I don't think we have very much time."

"It was after Mdina." Ash's voice was weak. His face was grey and he could no longer move from the waist down. One hand was on his chest; the other lay palm upward on the floor. "You can't understand, Alex. I was so badly hurt. Yassen..." He coughed and blood speckled his lip. "I had given everything to the service. My life. My health. I wasn't even thirty and I was crippled. I was never going to sleep properly, never eat properly. From that day on it was just pills and pain.

"And what was my reward? Blunt humiliated me. I was demoted, taken out of the field. He told me..." Ash swallowed painfully. With every word he was finding it harder to go on. "He told me what I already knew," he rasped. "I was second-rate. Never as good ... as your dad."

He had almost come to the end of his strength. His shoulders slumped and for a moment Alex thought he had gone. Blood was all around him now. A steady flow trickled from his mouth.

Major Yu was enjoying himself. "Why don't you tell him the rest, Ash?" he crowed.

"No!" Ash straightened his head. "Please..."

"I already know," Alex said. He turned to Ash one last time. He could hardly bear to look at him. "You killed my parents, didn't you? The bomb on the aeroplane. You put it there."

Ash couldn't answer. His hand tightened on

his chest. He had only seconds left.

"We had to test him," Major Yu explained. "When he came over to us, we had to make sure he was telling us the truth. After all, we had just been tricked by one British intelligence agent – your father. So we set him a very simple task, one that would prove to us with no doubt that he was ready to switch sides."

"I didn't want to..." It wasn't Ash's voice. It was just a whisper.

"He didn't want to, but he did. For the money. He put the bomb on the plane and he detonated it with his own hand. Rather more successful than his mission in Mdina. And the start of a long association with us."

"Alex..."

Ash tried to look up. His head fell forward. He died.

Major Yu prodded him with his foot. "Well, as they say, Ash to ashes and dust to dust," he remarked. "I'm glad you heard that from him, Alex. You can take it with you to the grave."

He raised the gun once again and pointed it at Alex.

There was an explosion, loud and near. The entire room shook, and dust and metal filings came showering down from the roof. Alex heard a shearing of metal as the crane overhead broke in half and came crashing down. The shock sent Major Yu reeling back. His arm banged against one of the work surfaces and the gun went off, the bullet smashing harmlessly into a wall. Major Yu was shouting in agony and Alex realized that the impact of the blow had shattered the brittle bone in his arm. The gun now lay on the ground.

Deafened, half dazed, Alex threw himself onto Ben's gun, snatched it in both hands and pulled the trigger over and over again until it clicked uselessly. It was the first time he had fired in anger and with the deliberate intention to kill. But he had missed. The room was full of smoke, and even in his pain Yu had been quick-thinking enough to use it as a screen, crouching down, clutching his broken arm. He had lost his gun. He knew that he had run out of time. The SAS were here. Alex Rider would have to wait until another day.

There was a trapdoor set in the floor with the ladder Alex had spotted earlier leading down underneath. Somehow, using his one good arm, Yu pulled it open and clambered down, dropping into the boat below. But the fall was too much for his bones. Howling with agony, barely able to crawl, Yu groped his way over to the controls. He used a knife to cut through the mooring rope. A second later, he was speeding away.

Meanwhile Alex had staggered over to the controls. On the TV, the little square representing Royal Blue was about two centimetres above the seabed but edging closer all the time. There was the scanner, wired into the computer. Alex slammed his palm onto the glass panel and let out a sigh of relief as a line of text appeared on the computer screen.

> AUTHORIZATION ACCEPTED

There was a pause, then a second line scrolled across.

> OVERRIDE MASTER COMMANDS? Y/N

Alex hit the Y key just as the door crashed open and about half a dozen SAS men burst in, covering every angle with their weapons. Scooter was at the front, Texas and X-Ray right behind him. It looked as if Sparks, the young soldier who had once played a guitar on an Australian beach, hadn't made it.

Scooter saw Alex. "Where's Yu?" he demanded.

"Gone." Alex's attention was fixed on the screen. A menu had come up. He ran his eye down the list of options, looking for the one that said DISARM or DEACTIVATE. But it wasn't there. Instead his eyes settled on the last command.

> DETONATE

"Over here!" It was Texas. He had found Ben Daniels and was already kneeling beside him, tearing open his shirt to examine his wound. One of the other soldiers rushed over with a medical kit.

Alex slid the mouse, highlighting the last command. He looked at the television screen. Royal Blue was still above the seabed but was gradually closing in. He remembered what he had heard. The bomb had to travel one kilometre down into the earth's crust before it was in place. A digital clock read 23:47:05:00, the microseconds flickering and changing too fast for his eye to follow. The bomb still had thirteen more minutes until it was in position. The sun, moon and earth were not quite ready yet.

Could Alex destroy the bomb without accidentally causing a tsunami?

In desperation he turned to the SAS leader, who seemed to understand the stakes almost at once.

"Do it," he said.

Alex double-clicked on the command.

One thousand and fifty metres below Dragon Nine but one hundred and fifty metres above the seabed, the bomb exploded. Alex felt the entire oil rig shudder violently, and the floor veered crazily beneath his feet as five of the steel tethers along with the drill pipe itself were torn apart.

And half a mile away, speeding through the water in his Sealine yacht, Major Yu heard the explosion and knew, with an overwhelming sense of bitterness and defeat, that even his last hopes had been destroyed. Somehow Royal Blue had been detonated too early. There would be no tsunami.

He sat, hunched up in front of the steering wheel, moaning quietly to himself. He had failed.

He didn't even feel the shock wave from the explosion until it hit him, but this of course was the main purpose of Royal Blue, to flatten any-thing for miles around. The pulse smashed into the boat, destroying the electrics, snuffing out the lights, ripping every fitting apart. Major Yu's bone structure wasn't strong enough to withstand it. Every single bone in his body fractured at the same time. For about two seconds, he remained vaguely human. Then his body, with no frame to support it, crumpled in on itself: a bag of skin full of broken pieces. The boat veered round, a quarter of a mil-lion pounds' worth of British engineering with no one to steer it. Zigzagging crazily, it disappeared into the night.

Back on Dragon Nine, Yu's remaining men were being rounded up. The SAS had lost two men dead with three more injured. Ben Daniels was still alive. He'd been given a shot of morphine and there was an oxygen mask strapped to his face.

Scooter had finally noticed the other body lying in the control room.

"Who was that?" he asked.

Alex took one last look at his godfather.

"It was nobody," he said.

DINNER FOR THREE

"It's very good to see you, Alex. How are you getting on at school?"

It seemed a very long time since Alex had last found himself in this room, the office on the sixteenth floor of the building in Liverpool Street which called itself the Royal & General Bank but which in fact housed the Special Operations division of MI6. Alan Blunt, its chief executive, was sitting opposite him, his desk as neat and as empty as ever: a couple of folders, some papers awaiting his signature, a single pen, solid silver, resting at an angle. Everything in its place. Alex knew that Blunt liked it that way.

Blunt didn't seem to have changed at all. Even the suit was the same, and if there was a little more grey in his hair, who would notice when the man had been entirely grey to begin with? But Blunt was not the sort of person to grow old and wrinkled, to wear baggy jumpers, play golf and spend more time with his grandchildren. His job, the world he inhabited, had somehow pinned him down. He was, Alex decided, a twenty-first-century fossil.

It was the last week of November and suddenly the temperature had dropped, as if in response to the Christmas decorations which were going up all around. There had even been a few scatterings of snow. There wasn't enough to settle but it had added a certain chill to the air. Walking to the office, Alex had passed a Salvation Army band playing "Good King Wenceslas". The players had been huddled together as if for comfort and even their music had been cold and mournful – as well as slightly out of tune.

He couldn't hear the music in the office. The windows would doubtless have been double- or triple-glazed to stop any sound coming in or – more importantly – leaking out. He focused his attention on the man sitting opposite him and wondered how he should answer the question. Blunt would know already, of course. He probably had access to Alex's school reports before they were even printed.

Alex had just completed his first week back at Brookland School. Blunt would know that too. Alex had no doubt that he had been under twenty-four-hour surveillance from the moment his Qantas flight had touched down at Heathrow Airport and he had been hurried out through the VIP channel to the waiting car outside. The last time he had taken on Scorpia he had been shot, and MI6 certainly weren't going to let that happen again. He thought he had seen his tail once: a youngish man standing on a street corner, seemingly waiting for a taxi. When he had looked for him a second later, the man had disappeared. Maybe it was; maybe it wasn't. Blunt's field agents knew how to live in the shadows.

And so, finally, he was back at school.

For most kids of his age, it meant coursework and homework, lessons that dragged on too long and terrible food. For Alex it was all that and something more. He had been nervous, walking back into Brookland on a chilly Monday morning. It had seemed a long time since he had seen the familiar buildings: the bright red brickwork and the long stretches of plate glass. Miss Bedfordshire, the school secretary who had always had a soft spot for him, had been waiting in reception.

"Alex Rider!" she had exclaimed. "What has it been this time?"

"Glandular fever, Miss Bedfordshire."

Alex's illnesses had become almost legendary over the past year. Part of him wondered if Miss Bedfordshire really believed in them or if she was just playing along.

"You're going to have to drop back a whole year if you're not careful," she remarked.

"I'm very careful, Miss Bedfordshire."

"I'm sure you are."

In Sydney Alex had been worried that he wouldn't fit in, but from the very first moment he arrived it was almost as if he hadn't been away. Everyone was pleased to see him, and he wasn't as far behind as he had feared. He would have extra tuition in the Christmas holidays, and with a bit of luck he would be at the same level as everyone else by the start of next term. Surrounded by his friends and swept along by the day's routine – the ringing bells, the slamming doors and desks – Alex realized that he wasn't just back at school. He was back in normal life.

But he had been expecting Alan Blunt to make contact, and sure enough he had got the call on his mobile. Blunt had asked Alex to come to a meeting on Friday afternoon. Alex had noticed the one small difference. Blunt had asked. He hadn't demanded.

So here he was with his backpack full of books for the weekend's homework: a particularly vicious maths paper and *Animal Farm* by George Orwell. A British writer, he reflected. Major Yu would surely have loved it. Alex was wearing his school uniform – dark blue jacket, grey trousers and purposely crooked tie. Jack had bought him a scarf when she was on holiday in Washington and it was hanging loosely around his neck. Apart from this, he felt comfortable looking the same as everyone else.

"There are a few things you might like to know," Blunt said. "Starting with a message from Ethan Brooke. He asked me to pass on his thanks and his good wishes. He said that if you ever decide to emigrate to Australia, he'll be happy to arrange a permanent visa."

"That's very kind of him."

"Well, you did a remarkable job, Alex. Quite apart from tracking down our missing weapon, you've more or less destroyed the snakehead. The Chada Trading Company has gone out of business, as has Unwin Toys."

"Did you realize it was an anagram?" Mrs Jones asked. She was sitting in a chair next to the desk, one leg crossed over the other, looking very relaxed. Alex got the sense that she was glad to see him. "Unwin Toys. Winston Yu. That was the vanity of the man – he named it after himself."

"Have you found him?" Alex asked. He had last seen Yu climbing down the ladder towards the motor launch and didn't know if he'd got away.

"Oh yes. We found what was left of him. Not a pleasant sight." Blunt folded his hands in front of him. "Yu dealt with quite a lot of his own people before ASIS could reach them," he went on. "I think you know that he killed the captain of the *Liberian Star*: de Wynter. After your escape from the hospital, Dr Tanner committed suicide, possibly following orders from Yu. ASIS did manage to pick up the rest of the staff, though. Two guards – one of them with a fractured skull – and a handful of nurses. They also arrested a man called Varga."

The name meant nothing to Alex.

"He was a technician," Mrs Jones reminded him.

"He helped adapt Royal Blue to work underground. He also organized the detonation procedure."

Now Alex recalled the man he had glimpsed on the *Liberian Star*, setting up the scanner for Major Yu.

"He was a fairly low-level Scorpia operative," Blunt added. "From Haiti, I understand. He's being questioned and may provide some useful information."

"How is Ben?"

"He's still in hospital in Darwin," Mrs Jones said. "He was lucky. The bullets didn't do any serious damage and the doctors say he'll be out by Christmas."

"We'll look after him," Blunt added.

"Better than you looked after Ash." Alex looked Blunt straight in the eye.

"Yes." Blunt shifted uncomfortably. "I wanted you to know, Alex, that we had no idea about Ash's association with Scorpia. Even now I find it hard to believe that he had any involvement with ... what happened to your parents."

"I'm so sorry, Alex," Mrs Jones cut in. "I understand how you must be feeling."

"Do you think Ethan Brooke knew?" Alex asked. It was something he had been thinking about on the long flight home. "He knew someone was a traitor. Someone had been feeding the snakehead information all along. He put me together with Ash. Was that what he really wanted? To flush him out?"

"It's quite possible," Blunt said, and Alex was surprised. The head of MI6 wasn't normally so honest. "Brooke is a very devious man."

"It's what makes him so good at his job," Mrs Jones remarked.

It was five o'clock. Outside, it was already dark. Alan Blunt went over to the window and shooed away some pigeons. Then he lowered the blind.

"There are only a couple of things to add," he said as he took his seat again. "Most important of all, we want you to know that you're safe. Scorpia aren't going to have another crack at you." He blinked twice. "Not like last time."

"We've been in contact with them," Mrs Jones explained. "We've made it clear that if anything happens to you, we'll let the whole world know that they have been beaten – for a second time – by a fourteen-year-old boy. It would make them a laughing stock and destroy what little reputation they have left."

"Scorpia may be finished anyway," Blunt said. "But they've got the message. We'll keep an eye on you just to be on the safe side, but I don't think you need have any concern."

"And what was the other thing?" Alex asked.

"Only that we hope you found what you were looking for." It was Mrs Jones who had answered.

"I found some of it," Alex said.

"Your father was a very good man," Blunt muttered. "I've told you that before. You obviously take after him, Alex. And maybe, when you leave school, you'll think again about intelligence work. We need people like you, and it's not a bad career."

Alex stood up. "I'll show myself out," he said.

He took the tube back to Sloane Square and then a bus along the King's Road to his house. He had told Jack he would be late home from school. The two of them would have supper together when he arrived, and then he would start his homework. He was seeing his friend Tom Harris tomorrow. Chelsea were playing at home to Arsenal and somehow Tom had managed to scrounge two tickets. Otherwise, he had no plans for the weekend.

Jack Starbright was waiting for him in the kitchen, putting the final touches to a salad. Alex helped himself to a glass of apple juice and hoisted himself onto one of the bar stools by the counter. He liked to talk to Jack while she cooked.

"How did you get on?" she asked.

"It was fine," Alex said. He reached out and stole a piece of tomato. "Alan Blunt offered me a job."

"I'll kill you if you take it."

"Don't worry. I let him know I wasn't interested."

Jack knew everything that had happened to Alex since she had left him in Sydney, including Ash's final moments on Dragon Nine. He had told her his story the moment he got home, and when he had finished she had turned away and sat for a long minute in silence. When she had finally turned back again, there had been tears in her eyes.

"I'm sorry," Alex had said. "I know you liked him."

"That's not what's upsetting me, Alex," she had replied.

"Then what?"

"It's this world. MI6. What it did to him, to your parents. I suppose I'm scared about what it'll do to you."

"I think I've finished with it, Jack."

"That's what you said last time, Alex. But the question is – has it finished with you?"

Now Alex glanced at the table. He noticed that it was set for three. "Who's coming for supper?" he asked.

"I forgot to tell you." Jack smiled. "We have a surprise guest."

"Who?"

"You'll find out when they get here." She had barely spoken the words when the doorbell rang. "That's good timing," she went on. "Why don't you answer it?"

Alex noticed something strange in her eyes. It wasn't like Jack to have secrets from him. He was still holding the piece of tomato. He tossed it back into the salad, swung himself down and went out into the hall.

He could just make out a figure behind the mottled glass panels of the front door. Whoever it was had activated the automatic light in the porch.

Alex threw open the door and stopped in surprise.

A young, dark-haired and very attractive girl was standing there. The car that had dropped her off was just moving away. Alex was so stunned that it took him a moment to recognize her. Even then, he didn't believe who it was.

"Sabina!" he exclaimed.

The last time he had seen Sabina Pleasure, the two of them had been under Richmond Bridge beside the Thames, and she had told him she was leaving for America. He had been convinced that he would never see her again.

That had only been a few months ago, but she looked completely different. She had to be almost sixteen now. Her hair had grown longer and her shape had changed. She looked wonderful in tight-fitting DKNY jeans and a soft cashmere jersey.

"Hi, Alex." She stayed where she was, as if a little wary of him.

"What are you doing here?"

"Aren't you pleased to see me?"

"Of course I am. But..." Alex's voice trailed off.

Sabina smiled. "That was my dad in the car. We're visiting for Christmas. He's over here writing a story for the paper. Something about some sort of weird Church. He got me out of school early and we're going to stay over here until the new year."

"In London?"

"Where else?"

"Is your mum here too?"

"Yeah. We're renting a flat in Notting Hill."

The two of them stared at each other. There were so many things Alex wanted to say. He didn't know where to begin.

"Are you two going to come inside?" Jack called from the kitchen. "Or would you like me to serve dinner in the street?"

There was a moment of awkwardness. Alex realized that he hadn't even invited Sabina in. Worse than that, he was actually blocking the way. He moved to one side to let her pass. She smiled a little nervously and stepped inside. But the doorway was narrow, and as she came in he felt her briefly against him. Her hair brushed his cheek and he smelled the perfume she was wearing. At that moment, he realized how glad he was to see her. It was as if everything was beginning all over again.

Now she was in the hall and he was the one outside.

"Sabina..." he began.

"Alex," she said, "I'm freezing. Why don't you shut the door?"

Alex smiled and closed the door and the two of them went in.

What follows is an extra chapter which I wrote as a bonus for anyone who's had to wait until now to buy the paperback. It gives you a final glimpse of Ash and provides the answer to a question many of you have asked since the hardback version of *Snakehead* was published. But to save you having to buy a second copy, you can download the chapter at www.alexrider.com/snakehead.

AH

CODA

The airport belonged to another age, a time when air travel was an adventure, when planes still had propellers and had to stop at strange-sounding places to refuel on their way across the world. There was just one runway, a narrow strip of silver-grey concrete cutting through grass that had been perfectly mown. The single terminal was a white building with a curving entrance and a terrace where people could watch the planes take off. It could have been the clubhouse of an expensive golf course.

The airport had no name. Although it was only an hour outside London, there were no road signs pointing to it. Indeed, it seemed to have done its best to lose itself in a maze of country lanes that looped and twisted through thick woodland. The local residents – and the nearest house was more than a mile away – believed it was a private flying club, used by millionaires with their own planes. For a brief time, it had been.

It had been bought by the British secret service back in the seventies, and now it was used for flights that nobody talked about. People who weren't meant to be in the country arrived here on planes that didn't exist. There was no passport control, because very few of the travellers carried passports – and if they did, they would probably be fake. A white control tower stood at the far end of the runway. It managed not just the incoming and outgoing flights but all the surrounding airspace. When planes were ready to take off here, Heathrow and Gatwick just had to wait.

At nine thirty on a cold morning at the end of April, a blue Rover Vitesse was making its way towards this secret airport. The sound of the V8 engine was almost inaudible as it cruised through a virtual tunnel of leaves. The start of the month had been warm and sunny, but there had been a cold snap the night before, and the result was a layer of fog floating over the ground, deadening everything and turning the world a ghostly white.

A man and a woman were sitting in the back.

The driver had no idea who they were. His name was Enderby and he was a low-level MI6 operative trained for certain duties – the first of which was never to ask questions. He had picked them up at a London hotel at six o'clock exactly, loaded a single suitcase into the boot and brought them here.

And yet, glancing in the rear-view mirror, Enderby couldn't stop himself wondering about his passengers. He guessed they were husband and wife. There was something about their body language that said as much, even though neither of them had uttered a word throughout the journey. The man was in his thirties, well built with close-cropped fair hair and dark, tired eyes. He was wearing a suit with an open-necked shirt. What would you think he was, seeing him in the street? Something in the City, perhaps. Private security. Ex-army. This was a man who knew how to look after himself. He had the relaxed confidence of someone who is very dangerous.

The woman sitting next to him was unhappy – Enderby had noticed that from the moment she had stepped reluctantly into the car. He could see it now in her eyes. They were nice eyes: blue, very bright. But they were troubled. All in all, she was very attractive. A couple of years younger than the man, maybe an actress or a dancer. She was wearing a jacket and grey trousers and – yes, there it was – a wedding ring on her finger.

Enderby was right. The two people in the back of his car were called John and Helen Rider. They had been married for four years. They were here because they were leaving the country – perhaps permanently. They had been apart for a long time, but that was all over now. Their new life together was about to begin.

They had almost arrived. Enderby had driven this route many times and recognized the elm tree with the nesting box hanging from one of its branches. The airport was half a mile away. However, he was completely unaware of the advanced high-resolution camera with its 25mm varifocal lens concealed inside the nesting box. And he would have been surprised to learn that even now his face was being examined on a television screen inside the control tower. It was actually the third hidden camera they had passed in the last five minutes.

The car broke out of the wood and crossed a cattle grid set in the road. If the driver had been identified as an enemy agent, the grid would have rotated and shredded the tyres. The airport lay ahead; a plane was waiting on the runway. It was an old twin-engine Avro Anson C19 that might have been rolled out of a museum. Once used by the RAF for coastal patrol, the Anson hadn't been seen in regular service for twenty years. Certainly it suited the airport. They were both relics of the past.

A slim, dark-haired man stepped out of the terminal building, supporting himself on a heavy walking stick. He had been sent to supervise the departure. Enderby recognized him with surprise. He had visited the man a couple of times recently in hospital and had worked with him in the past. His name was Anthony Howell. His middle name was Sean.

People called him Ash.

The car slowed down and stopped. The man got out, went round and opened the door for the woman. The two of them moved forward to meet Ash.

"John. Helen." Ash smiled at them but he had recently been in too much pain. It still showed.

"How are you, Ash?" John Rider asked.

"I'm OK."

That obviously wasn't true. Ash was feverish, sweating. His hand was gripping the walking stick so tightly that the knuckles were white.

"You look terrible."

"Yeah." Ash didn't disagree. "They sent me to say goodbye. Are you ready? I'll get your case loaded on board."

He limped past them, over to the car. Enderby unlocked the boot and took out the suitcase.

"He's not very talkative," Helen muttered.

"He's hurt." John glanced at his wife. "Are you OK?"

"I don't like leaving Alex."

"I know that. Nor do I. But we didn't have any choice. You heard what the doctor said."

Alex Rider was three months old. Just a few days before, he had developed an ear infection which meant that he couldn't fly. Helen had left him with a cheerful Irishwoman, Maud Kelly, a maternity nurse who had been with them since the birth. Helen's first instinct had been to stay with her infant son. But she also needed to be with her husband. The two of them had been apart for too long.

"Maud will come out with him next week," John Rider said.

"His new home." Helen smiled, but a little sadly. "It's strange to think he'll grow up speaking French."

"With a dad who's a fisherman."

"Better a fisherman than a spy."

Secret agents don't often retire. Some are killed in action; some leave the field and end up behind a desk, providing support for the men and women who have taken their place. Even when they leave the service, they are still watched – just in case they decide to sell their secrets or go into business for themselves.

John Rider was different. He had recently completed a long and brutal assignment which had culminated in a shoot-out on the island of Malta, followed by his faked death on Albert Bridge in London. During that time, he had inflicted serious damage on the criminal organization known as Scorpia. If Scorpia discovered that he was still alive, they would make him a primary target. MI6 knew that. They understood that his usefulness was effectively over. They had decided to let him go.

Ash came back over to them. He had a mobile phone in his hand. "The control tower just called," he said. "You're all set for take-off."

"Why don't you come and stay with us, Ash?" Helen suggested. "You could fly down with Alex. A week in the sun would do you good."

Ash tried to smile but something prevented him. "That's kind of you, Helen. Maybe..."

"Well, keep in touch." John Rider was examining the other man with a certain unease. The two of them had worked together, but they had also been friends for many years.

"Good luck." Ash seemed in a hurry to get away.

They shook hands. Then Ash leant forward and kissed Helen once on the cheek, but so lightly that she barely felt his lips. The husband and wife began to walk towards the plane.

"What's wrong with him?" Helen asked as soon as they were out of earshot. "I know he's hurt. But he seems so ... distant."

"He's being axed." John spoke the words casually. "He screwed up in Malta and he knows it. Blunt wants him out."

"What will happen to him?"

"An office job somewhere. A junior outpost."

"Does he blame you?"

"I don't know, Helen. To be honest, I don't really care. It's not my business any more."

They had reached the plane. The pilot saw them through the cockpit window and raised a hand in greeting. His name was Robert Fleming and he had flown with the RAF in the Falklands War. Killing Argentine soldiers, some of them just kids, had

408

changed his mind about active service; and after that he had allowed himself to be recruited by MI6. Now he flew all over the world for them. The co-pilot was a man called Blakeway. Both of them were married. There was no cabin crew.

Standing on the terrace outside the terminal, Ash watched John and Helen Rider climb the metal staircase that led up to the plane. John stood aside to let Helen go first, gently taking her arm as she reached the top step. They entered the aircraft and pulled the door shut from inside. A couple of ground crew in white overalls wheeled the steps away. The first of the Anson's two propellers began to turn.

Ash thought he was going to faint. The pain in his stomach was worse than ever. It was as if the Russian assassin Yassen Gregorovich had somehow managed to stab him a second time and was twisting the knife even now. The plane's engines had both started up but he could barely hear the sound. The sky, the grass, the airport, the Anson ... nothing connected any more. He could feel beads of sweat on his forehead. They were ice-cold.

Could he really do this?

Was he going to go through with it?

He had been released from hospital after six weeks of treatment that had included being given eleven pints of blood. The doctors had told him what he already knew. He would never be the same again. Not completely. There had been too much damage. And the pain would always be with him. He would need a barrage of drugs to keep it at bay.

And had they been grateful, the people he worked for, the ones who had caused this to happen to him? He still remembered his meeting with Alan Blunt. The head of MI6 Special Operations had given him precisely five minutes: his injuries were his own fault. He had totally mishandled the operation in Mdina. He had disobeyed orders. He was being taken off active duty with immediate effect.

Blunt hadn't even asked how he was feeling.

Ash had known what he was going to do even before he left Blunt's office. For a moment, the pain was forgotten; he felt only anger and disbelief. How could they treat him like this? No. It was obvious now. They had *always* treated him like this. Nothing had changed. He had been overlooked and underrated from the start.

But he had numbers. He had contacts. He didn't care what he had to do. He would show MI6 that they were wrong about him. They had made a mistake they were going to regret.

He made the call as soon as he was in the street, away from the eavesdropping devices that were scattered all over Special Ops HQ. After that, things happened very quickly. That same evening, he met a man in a south London pub. The next day, he was interviewed at length by two blank-faced men in an abandoned warehouse behind the old meat market at Smithfield in Clerkenwell. Patiently he repeated everything he had said the night before.

The next call came two days later. Ash was given twenty minutes to get across London to the Ritz Hotel and a suite on the second floor. He arrived in exactly the specified time, knowing that he had almost certainly been followed the whole way and that it had been arranged like this to prevent him communicating with anyone else. There was to be no chance of a trap.

After he had been thoroughly searched by the two men he had met before, he was shown into the suite. A woman was waiting for him, sitting on her own in an armchair, her perfectly manicured fingers curving round a flute of champagne. She was strikingly beautiful with shoulder-length black hair and glittering, cruel eyes. She was wearing a designer dress, a whisper of red silk; diamond earrings; and a single large diamond at her throat.

Ash tried not to show any emotion. But he knew the woman. He had never met her but he had seen her file. It was hard to believe that he was actually in the same room as her.

Julia Rothman.

According to the file, she was the daughter of Welsh nationalists, who had married – and murdered – an elderly property developer for his wealth. She was on the executive board of Scorpia. Indeed, she was one of its founding members.

"You want to join us," she said, and he heard a hint of Welsh in her voice. She seemed amused.

"Yes."

"What makes you think we'd be interested in you?"

"If you weren't interested in me, you wouldn't be here."

That made her smile. "How do I know we can trust you?"

"Mrs Rothman..." Ash wondered if he should have used her name. He spoke slowly. He knew he would only have this one chance. "I've spent four years with MI6. They've given me nothing. Now I've finished with them – or perhaps I should say they've finished with me. But you probably know that already. Scorpia always did have a reputation for being well informed. How do you know you can trust me? Only time will give you an answer to that. But I can be useful to you. A double agent. Think about it. You want someone inside Special Operations. That can be me."

Julia Rothman sipped her champagne but her eyes never left Ash. "This could be a trick," she said.

"Then let me prove myself."

"Of course. Anyone who joins Scorpia has to prove themselves to our complete satisfaction, Mr Howell. But I warn you: the test might not be an easy one."

"I'm ready for anything."

"Would you kill for us?"

Ash shrugged. "I've killed before."

"Before it was duty. For queen and country. This time it would be murder."

"I've already explained: I want to join Scorpia. I don't care what I have to do."

"We'll see." She set the glass down, then produced a white envelope. She slid it towards him.

"There is a name inside this envelope," she said. "It is the name of a man who has done us a great deal of harm. Killing him will prove beyond all doubt that you mean what you say. But a warning. Once you open that envelope, you will have committed yourself. You cannot change your mind. If you try to do so, you will be dead before you leave this hotel."

"I understand." Ash was uneasy. He picked up the envelope and held it in front of him.

"We will provide the manner of his death," Mrs Rothman went on, "but you will be the one who pulls the trigger. And when he is dead, you will be paid one hundred thousand pounds. It will be the first payment of many. Over the years, if you stay true to us, Scorpia will make you very rich."

"Thank you." Suddenly Ash's mouth was dry. The envelope was still balanced on his fingertips.

"So are you going to open it?"

He made his decision. He ripped the envelope open with his thumb. And there was the name in front of him. Black letters on white paper.

JOHN RIDER

Julia Rothman looked at him quizzically.

So they knew. That was his first thought. The elaborate trick that had been played on Albert Bridge hadn't worked – or if it had, there had somehow been a leak. They had learnt that John Rider was still alive. And as for this test, they knew exactly what they were doing. Ash would have been happy to kill anybody in the world. He would have killed Blunt or anyone else in MI6. But Scorpia had gone one better.

They were asking him to kill his best friend.

"John Rider..." His mouth had gone dry. "But he's—"

"Don't tell us that he's dead, Mr Howell. We know he is not."

"But why...?"

"You said you didn't care what you did. This is your assignment. If you want to prove yourself to us, this is what you have to do."

But could he do it? He asked himself again now, watching the ancient plane as it completed the final checks before take-off. The propellers were buzzing loudly; the whole fuselage was vibrating. And it wasn't just John. It was Helen Rider too. He had once loved her – or thought he had. She had rejected him. But John had always stood by him. No. That wasn't true. Blunt had axed him and John had done nothing to help.

The plane jerked forward and began to rumble down the runway, picking up speed.

The bomb was on board. Ash had no idea how Scorpia had got it there, or even how they had found out about the flight in the first place. Such details didn't matter. The fact was that it was there, and the cruelty of it was that Scorpia could easily have detonated it without his help. The bomb could have had a timer. They could have transmitted the signal themselves. But they had turned this into the ultimate test. If he did this, there would be no going back. He would be theirs for life.

We will provide the manner of his death, but you will be the one who pulls the trigger.

He couldn't do it. They were his closest friends. He was the godfather of their child.

He had to do it. John and Helen were dead anyway. And Scorpia would kill him if he failed.

The plane was halfway down the runway. Slowly it rose into the air.

Ash took out his mobile phone and pressed a three-digit number, followed by SEND.

The explosion was huge, much bigger than he had expected. For a moment, the plane disappeared completely, replaced by a scarlet fireball that hovered fifteen metres above the runway. There were no wings, no propellers, no wheels. Only flames. And then, like some hideous firework, broken pieces of glass and metal burst out of the inferno, bouncing off the tarmac and slamming into the lawn.

The plane had gone. There was nothing left of it. The people inside would have died instantly.

Already alarms were sounding. Enderby and half a dozen men were running towards the wreckage, coming from every direction – as if there was anything they could do. Black smoke billowed into the sky.

Ash turned away and walked back inside. He was sure that Scorpia would be watching. They would know that he had done it. He had passed the test. He took a deep breath and tasted smoke and burning aviation fuel.

A new life. But how was he going to enjoy it when he was empty inside? Too late. He had made his choice.

Slowly he made his way down the stairs and out onto the runway, limping towards the flames that for him would never die.

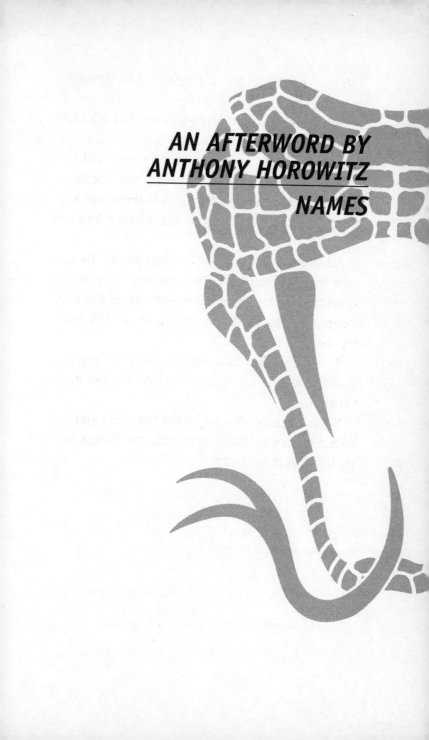

*AN AFTERWORD BY
ANTHONY HOROWITZ*
NAMES

I spend an awful lot of time thinking up names ... both for the books and for the characters who inhabit them.

Titles, of course, are extremely important. They have to be short, strong, memorable and relevant to the story. They have to be something that my publishers can illustrate. When I announce a new Alex Rider book, it's the first thing that everyone wants to know. In a way, the title is there to sell the book. It's a quick promise of what is to come.

And yet sometimes the titles take me months to get right (and even then I can't be sure that I've cracked it). This book was easy. As soon as I learned that there were gangs in Asia known as snakeheads, there was no need to look any further.

But the one that followed it – *Crocodile Tears* as it eventually became – was a nightmare. This was a story to be set in Scotland, London and Kenya, which involved an international charity and GM crops. I initially wanted to call the book *Endurance*

Point, which, in my imagination, could have been the name of the valley where the deadly crops are grown, but I didn't get a lot of enthusiasm in schools that I visited and anyway I had already used the word "point" both in *Point Blanc* and *Christmas at Gunpoint*, an Alex Rider short story which appears in *The Mission Files*. (In that story, Gunpoint turns out to be a ski resort in America.) Then I tried *Dark Harvest*, which seemed quite powerful and certainly described the poisonous wheat field. But everyone said it sounded too much like a horror story. At different times the book was *Wolf Moon*, *First Aid* (the name of the charity), *Poison Dawn* and *No Spy Like Alex*.

The strange thing is that the actual title had come to me quite quickly and seemed perfect. Crocodile tears are fake or hypocritical tears and Desmond McCain, the villain in the book, certainly sheds plenty of them. They also connected with the Kenyan setting ... if you've read the story, you'll know that crocodiles are very much involved. So what was the problem? Sadly, very few people knew what the title meant. Language is changing all the time and it seems that the phrase – "crocodile tears" has slipped out of use. Well, hopefully by now it's back in business because that was the title I went with. I had to add the definition on the first page.

My favourite title of all the Alex books is probably *Skeleton Key* because those two words say so many different things. A skeleton makes you think of death. A skeleton key is something a burglar or a spy might use to break into a house. A key is also a type of island (I was thinking of Key West in Florida) and much of the story takes plays on Cayo Esqueleto, near Cuba.

For the same reason, I'm also quite fond of *Point Blanc* – which has a double meaning. You shoot someone point blank. And I invented a mountain in the French alps called "White Point". But if I'm going to be completely honest, I got it slightly wrong. If there really were a mountain with that name, apparently it would be called Pointe Blanche. It also worries me that very few English readers would set out to buy a book with a French title ... and I wonder how many sales I've lost because of that!

Stormbreaker, the name of the first Alex book, is a strong title, I think. I needed to work out what a brand new, highly advanced computer might be called, and I thought about the electricity that powered it and the codes that went into it (spies break codes). The book was very nearly called *Stormchaser*. Just a few weeks before it was to be printed, we discovered that another well-known writer had come up with the same name. It was a near miss. I'm not sure what would have happened if two books with identical titles had appeared at around the same time.

Character names are equally important. Often, the

first thing you know about someone that you meet in a book is their name – and it very much helps the opinion you form of them. This is something that my great hero, Charles Dickens, recognized in his books. When he called a teacher Gradgrind, you knew you wouldn't want to be in his class. Or what about Uriah Heep? Someone to avoid, surely!

Alex Rider's name is probably the most important decision I ever made. Would you, for example, enjoy the books as much if I had decided to call him Maurice Thwaite? As a matter of fact, naming Alex was quite easy. The son of a friend of mine came to lunch just as I had started writing *Stormbreaker* (or *Stormchaser*). His name was Alex, he was thirteen, spoke fluent French (he had a French dad) and was learning Tae kwondo. I wouldn't say I modelled Alex on him, but I certainly stole his name. As for Rider, it's a solid, action name. And, by coincidence, it's also the name of one of my favourite characters in the James Bond novels. Honeychile Ryder is the beautiful fishing girl who rescues Bond in *Dr No*.

A lot of the names in Alex Rider have secret meanings and I'm going to finish this afterword by sharing some of them with you. Names can really help a writer. They can act a bit like a pedestal. That is, they put someone or something into my mind which then helps me build the character.

This won't be a complete list – I don't have the space – but it'll give you an idea of how I work:

ALAN BLUNT

The head of MI6 was always going to be an important character because I knew he'd appear in all the Alex Rider books. I named him Blunt after one of the most famous spies in British history. Sir Anthony Blunt was a traitor, an art historian who looked after the King's pictures and secretly worked for the Russians. My own spymaster is a bit cold and untrustworthy and I think the name with its dark history suits him.

MRS JONES

She is, of course, Blunt's deputy and curiously she is named after my agent – Anthony Jones – who handles all my contracts and business deals. I'm not quite sure what made me think of him. I always liked the idea that she had no Christian name, at least in the first four books. Then, in *Scorpia*, we discover that she is called Tulip. No wonder she never uses it!

JACK STARBRIGHT

Alex's loyal friend and housekeeper was originally named after a girl called Jacks who worked at my publishers. I have no idea how I came up with Starbright. Maybe I'd been having too many coffees. I'm afraid this is my least favourite name of all my characters.

DEREK SMITHERS

I've discussed Smithers in the afterword of *Eagle Strike*. The original Smithers is a minor character in Ian Fleming's *Goldfinger* but I liked the name because it was so old-fashioned.

JOHN CRAWLEY

He's another MI6 agent who turns up from time to time. I'm not entirely sure where his name came from but when we were making the film of *Stormbreaker* we were told we weren't allowed to use it. Does this mean that there's a real John Crawley, who really is a spy, somewhere in the world? If so, his cover has been well and truly blown.

YASSEN GREGOROVICH

The assassin who turns up in two of the books and who changes Alex's life, was inspired by a children's book illustrator whom I met in Sweden. I often "borrow" the names of people I meet and the moment he told me his name I knew that I had found my perfect cold-blooded killer. I've never found out if Mr Gregorovich is pleased or annoyed to be a character in my books.

SABINA PLEASURE

A friend of Alex's who appears in three of the books, Sabina has a slightly absurd name (rather like the nurse who looks after Alex in *Ark Angel*, Diana Meacher, and the American agent, Tamara Knight). This is a nod at Ian Fleming, the Bond author, who gave his girlfriends suggestive names such as Plenty O'Toole and Pussy Galore! In *Point Blanc*, I gave the girl that Alex saves the name Fiona Friend, but I'm afraid nobody got it. I was thinking of the television programme *Who Wants to be a Millionaire* and the three choices: fifty-fifty, ask the audience or...

HEROD SAYLE

The bad guy in *Stormbreaker* was inspired by a famous businessman called Mohamed al Fayed. Not that I think that Mr al Fayed is an evil man, although he's certainly larger-than-life and has often been mocked in the British press. Like him, Herod is an outsider, somebody who feels he has been badly treated by the establishment. His name is taken from Harrods Department Store, which is owned by al Fayed. Every Christmas, there's a Herod Sayle.

ALEXEI SAROV

The general who wants to bring back communism in *Skeleton Key* was originally called Skeletov. That was how I got the name of the book. Although he's in many ways the most sympathetic villain, I wanted a name with a hint of death. But Skeletov was more than a hint. It was a dollop. And then I remembered some terrorists who had attacked the Japanese train system with a poison called Sarin and the right name fell into place.

DAMIAN CRAY

I found it quite difficult coming up with a believable name for the mad pop singer who combats Alex in *Eagle Strike*. His surname is taken from the Kray brothers, two vicious criminals who terrorized London back in the sixties. His first name was an echo of Damon Albarn, the lead singer of a group called Blur.

JULIA ROTHMAN

My only female villain, so far, was partly inspired by the Welsh actress, Catherine Zeta-Jones. I wanted her to have a name that was both attractive and yet somehow deadly and I came up with the idea of naming her after a cigarette.

DESMOND McCAIN

The villain of *Crocodile Tears* is an ex-politician who has been sent to jail for fraud and who has seemingly converted to Christianity and now runs an international charity. I chose the first name, Desmond, thinking of Desmond Tutu, the South African cleric and anti-apartheid campaigner who is a bit of a hero of mine. I originally called him Desmond Cain, again thinking of the Bible – Cain, the first murderer. But this seemed a bit obvious so I changed it to McCain and had him found, as a baby, wrapped in a used bag of McCain Oven Chips.

SCORPIA

This is the deadly organization that Julia works for. It stands for Sabotage, Corruption, Intelligence and Assassination, but it got its name in quite a different way. I was at the end of *Eagle Strike*. Yassen was dying on the President's plane and told Alex to go to Venice to search for ... what? I couldn't think of a name and I was in a hurry. I was late delivering the book. As it happened, there was an opera – Puccini's *Tosca* – playing on my iPod. It was the moment when the villain makes his grand entrance and he is called Scarpia. In an instant, Scarpia became Scorpia and I had my next book.

TOM HARRIS & JAMES HALE

Alex's closest friends come from two different sources. Tom is named after an old friend of mine from my university days. But James demonstrates another way you can get into an Alex Rider book: the charity auction. His father paid a very generous sum of money and James's appearance in *Crocodile Tears* was the prize. I was hugely relieved that he had such a simple name. It could have been Polish with seventeen syllables!

There are two more books in the Alex Rider series and I'm still looking for names. Often, when I do book signings, I come across an interesting name in the queue and I always make a note of it. Then, months later, I'll rummage around in my name box and pull it out. Zeljan Kurst, the exotic-sounding gangster who takes over Scorpia, was actually a boy who came to get a book signed. Kolo, the guard who tries to drown Alex in *Ark Angel*, was a perfectly pleasant boy I met in a school in Belgium.

So do watch out if you come to get a book signed. You never know where you might end up.

Anthony Horowitz
January 2010

ACKNOWLEDGEMENTS

As with all the Alex Rider books, I've tried to make *Snakehead* as accurate as possible – and I wouldn't have been able to do this without the generous help of people all around the world. So it seems only polite to mention them here.

Dr Michael Foale at NASA spoke to me at length for a second time, and the opening chapter is largely based on his own experiences returning from outer space. The mechanism by which Major Yu attempts to bring chaos to the world was suggested to me by Professor Bill McGuire at University College London; he also came up with the planetary alignment that makes it feasible.

Panos Avramopoulos at CMA CGM Shipping (UK) Ltd kindly arranged for me to visit a container ship, and Captain Jenkinson allowed me on board. A few weeks later, Andy Simpson of Global SantaFe and Rupert Hunt from Shell gave up a whole day of their time to show me round an oil rig near Aberdeen. Neither of these visits would have been possible without Jill Hughes, to whom I am eternally grateful.

I spent a week in Bangkok, where I was looked after by the author Stephen Leather, who took me to all sorts of locations, many of which I wasn't allowed to mention in the book! He also accompanied me to the Thai kick-boxing fight which is the basis of Chapters 8 and 9. I also want to thank Justin Ractliffe, who showed me round Perth and Sydney during a lengthy book tour.

Joshua King, Alfie Faber, Max Packman-Walder and Emma Charatan all read the manuscript and gave me great notes and advice. Not for the first time, my son Cassian suggested some major changes.

Finally, my assistant Cat Taylor organized everything and then organized it again when I changed my mind. Justin Somper continues to be the guiding light behind much of Alex's success. And my very lovely editor, Jane Winterbotham, spent hours trawling through some of the most complex notes ever to come out of a publishing house to ensure that all the dates and times make sense.

AH